D1606212

THE
BOOK OF
LUKE

DON MEDLEY

Published by RĀ Publishing Company

1207 17th Avenue South, Suite 303
Nashville, TN 37212

385 B Highland Colony Parkway, Suite 501
Ridgeland, MS 39157

www.ra-publishing.com

©2003 Don W. Medley
Cover and Interior Design: George Otvos for EGO Design
Author Photograph: Robinson Photography
Editors: Jim Beatty & Andrew Ackers
Production Manager: Anna McFarland

First Printing, November 2003
ISBN 0-9706983-5-6
Library of Congress Cataloging-in-Publication Data has been applied for.
Printed in Canada on acid-free paper

10 9 8 7 6 5 4 3 2 1

THE
BOOK OF
LUKE

RĀ Publishing

Nashville   Jackson

CHAPTER ONE

Luke Daniels stood up from behind his desk and stretched. It had been a long day, finishing up a long week, and he was tired. Almost five o'clock and there was still another client to see. Days like this made him wonder why he had ever gone to law school.

Liz, his secretary, would already have her desk cleared and be ready to walk out the door. She was good about staying with him after five o'clock when there was something he needed, but not on Fridays. Recently divorced, Friday nights usually meant 'out on the town' for her.

"You have anything else for me today?" Liz buzzed him. "I've finished all the dictation and the mail's ready to go. I thought I might get it to the post office before five o'clock."

Luke knew that meant her day was officially over. He wished he could talk her into staying. "Is Ms. Weeks here yet?"

"Who?"

He looked up to see Liz standing at the door to his office.

"Susan Weeks. She called this morning wanting to see me. I tried to set up something next week but she insisted on today. Five o'clock was the best I could do. If I had known what a day this was going to be I wouldn't have agreed. She went on about how she needed some advice on a matter before this weekend. Anyway, she said she'd be here by five."

"Well, she's not here and I need to go."

"Okay, go ahead. I'll hang around here for a while and if she doesn't make it soon then I'm out of here, too. If she misses the best lawyer in town, then it's her loss."

"Yeah, right," Liz chuckled. "Good luck with Ms. Weeks. I'll see you Monday." She was out the door.

Luke walked into the hallway where he propped the foyer door open so he could hear his new client when she came in. The receptionist he shared with the other lawyer in the building was already gathering up her things to bolt as well.

"Hey, Jenny, you ready to go? Are we the last ones?"

"Yeah. Tommy's playing golf this afternoon and Pam left about three o'clock. Look, are you sure you don't need me to stick around?"

"No, go ahead. I'll be fine." Luke didn't imagine Jenny really wanted to stay. He was hoping that this Ms. Weeks would come on so he could get out of there, too. He didn't have any particular plans for the weekend but was ready to be away from the office for a couple of days. A car pulled up to the front door."

"There's my ride, Luke. I'll see you Monday."

Luke moved to the door and stepped outside. The street and sidewalk were filled with people headed home from work. He looked up and down the way hoping to catch the eye of someone looking for his office. He had no idea what this woman looked like. There were plenty of familiar faces out there and some unfamiliar ones, but none were headed to his door. He went back inside and sat down to wait for his prospective client. He wished he had been able to find out more from her before committing to an appointment. It seemed that she had spoken quite a bit when she was on the phone but now he couldn't remember anything specific. He did remember a pleasant voice. Maybe this would be a pleasant meeting. Right now, that meant getting it over quickly. He picked up a magazine and began to flip the pages as he waited.

Susan Weeks was actually an attractive twenty-six year old, a petite 5'6" with an absolutely perfect body, well proportioned from top to bottom. She had a beautiful thick mane of black hair that swept back from her face and fell to her shoulders. Bad hair days were not something she ever had to worry about. No matter what the time of day or the type of weather, a quick brush-through and she was ready.

In undergraduate school the other girls were all envious of her 'no maintenance' hair. It was also what caught the attention of the photographer who first influenced her to model, although her other features were equally as attractive. Susan's face was a photographer's dream with well-defined features and unblemished skin. She rarely took a bad picture. She had a way of smiling into the camera that would disarm anyone that looked through the lens or at the final work. She could model anything. No matter what the item of clothing, she made it look good. This included bathing suits, especially bikinis.

At first she hadn't been comfortable posing with so little on, but then she rationalized that she did wear bathing suits to the beach. After all, the pictures were just for some local commercials and it was a big help paying for college.

Her part time modeling enabled her to finish her degree and go right on to graduate school. College days filled with more fun than attention to a degree found her at the end of four years without enough direction to get her a diploma in anything more specific than business administration. Her advisor had been able to pull that together out of a hodge-podge of courses. That same advisor planted the seed of going on to graduate school in marketing. He reasoned she was already familiar with many of the principles through her experience in modeling and commercials. The money she made from her part time work would be enough to pay to continue school. With an MBA in marketing she would be able to command a much better position than with the nondescript business degree.

It was the right decision. She loved the coursework and excelled with a straight 4.0. It had also been the right decision as far as the job market, securing her offers from several major banks. Hibernia National had practically begged her to come with them but she just didn't like the idea of living in New Orleans. Bank of Florida had also made an attractive offer. In the end she decided to stay in Mississippi and go with Guaranty National in Jackson. They were the only ones who agreed to let her continue modeling. She enjoyed the work and didn't want to give it up so when they said they would not oppose it, she jumped at the chance. They made it work to their advantage, too. In exchange, she agreed to do commercials for them with no compensation above her regular salary.

The arrangement was a success. Her boss at Guaranty, Mr. Hayes, had not been too keen on the idea at first; but when he saw what a good worker she was, he mellowed. He was a great guy, and because he knew he could count on her to always stay on top of her work, he never complained about her being out of the office on modeling assignments.

After two years in that arrangement he came to her with what he called a sad announcement. His higher-ups needed someone to head up the marketing division for the southern portion of the state and, they wanted him to pick the best man for the job. To his own disdain, the best man for the job was Susan Weeks.

The salary boost was nice but it also involved a move from the Jackson office to Hampton. She discussed the move at length with Mr. Hayes, her parents, friends and anybody else she could get an ear from. It was a big decision.

While Jackson was not New York or LA, it was still a big city compared to Hampton and she had always thought that when she moved up in her career, it would be to a larger place. However, since the salary and responsibilities were much better, it was off to Hampton.

That was a year ago, and what a year it had been. This thriving Southern community was an amazing mix of society, politics and, as she was slowly learning, corruption. A year ago she couldn't have dreamed of the predicament she now found herself in. She was angry at herself for being so stupid, hurt that people she trusted could be so uncaring, and at a loss as to what steps she should take to correct the situation.

And that was why she made the appointment with Luke Daniels. She glanced at her watch and winced. Five o'clock. She was at least ten minutes from downtown and with it being Friday, there was a chance he wouldn't wait. He had not seemed eager to make the appointment when she talked with him that morning. After fumbling around for his number, she punched it into her phone.

Luke had made it through the latest issues of Sports Illustrated and Field and Stream when the phone rang. It startled him out of a good story about trout fishing in Arkansas which is where he wished he was at that moment. He pulled himself out of a great picture, got up from the chair and ambled over to the front desk phone. "Hello, this is Luke Daniels."

"Mr. Daniels, this is Susan Weeks. I'm so glad I caught you."

"Yes, Ms. Weeks. I was expecting you at five o'clock." Luke allowed more gruffness in his voice than he meant.

"I'm sorry, Mr. Daniels, but I had to go out of town this afternoon unexpectedly. There was a ribbon cutting for the new vault door at our branch in Collins and the bank felt I just had to be there."

Luke suppressed a chuckle that came on partly at the idea of having a ribbon cutting for a new vault door, and partly at her exasperation at having to attend such a function.

She went on "I hope I haven't put you out by being late."

"Oh, no. I was just catching up on some reading." Yeah, right, some reading. He was sure she wouldn't have guessed he meant Field and Stream. He wanted to be curt with her for keeping him waiting on a Friday afternoon, but such a gentle, easy voice floated through the phone that he found it hard to muster up the brusqueness he had wanted.

"Where are you now?"

"I'm out on the highway about ten minutes or so from downtown."

Ten minutes or so from downtown meant fifteen or twenty to get to his office. This appointment could keep him here well over an hour. She must have felt his displeasure through the phone because she quickly jumped in.

"I know it's getting late, but I would really appreciate it if we could get together. Would you consider meeting me somewhere for a cup of coffee or maybe a drink?"

Hmm. He had to ponder this one. Normally, he would not meet a client, especially a new client outside the office unless there was a very good reason. He was so ready to get out of the office however, that he thought that was reason enough. When he hesitated she went on.

"Are you familiar with the Magnolia Bar and Grill on Hyde Park? What do you say we meet there in ten minutes? We'll decide if it's coffee or a drink when we get there."

Luke couldn't think of any reason right at the moment why he should say no so he responded with a "Sure, that'll be fine."

"Great. I'll be there in ten minutes."

Luke hung up the phone and immediately realized he had no idea what this woman looked like, although she had a remarkable voice over the phone. He had heard about some of those '900' numbers where women with beautiful, sexy voices would turn out to be any-thing but. Oh well, he'd worry about it when he got there.

He threw the magazine in his hand onto one of the tables in the foyer and locked the front door. Back in his office there were two files on his desk that he wanted Liz to work on first thing Monday. He picked up the files, flipped off the light and stepped out to Liz's desk. As he laid the files on her desk, he caught his reflection in the hallway mirror and paused momentarily.

Luke was in good shape. His six foot frame was kept lean by his unfailing devotion to running. A handsome man, he maintained a fair sense of male ego, though he noticed that his starched white button-down shirt looked like he had been sleeping in it. He had a fresh one in the bathroom closet and thought it would be appropriate to clean up some before heading out to meet Ms. Weeks. With clean shirt, hair brushed and a little splash of cologne he was out the back door to his car.

His car was a Cadillac XLR convertible. Not a brand new one but a used model that he bought from a client. Roy Bryant had made him a deal he couldn't refuse. Luke had settled a case for Roy some time ago and one of the first things Roy did was go out and buy the car, with a lot of other expensive items. In less than a year's time Roy was realizing that the $600,000 settlement would not last forever and so decided to try to undue some of his wild spending spree. He came to Luke for help and offered to sell him his car.

It was silver with a matching top. When Luke saw it he first thought it too rich looking for him. Roy was ready to get rid of it and convinced him that if Luke didn't buy it some-body else would get a great deal. Luke was about ready to treat himself to something special anyway, so a deal was struck and Luke became the owner of a Cadillac.

The solo practice of law is not always a vocation that allows one to live extravagantly. As the saying went, it was either feast or famine. The times of feast had to be stretched out to cover the lean times of famine. And buying a Cadillac was a bit extravagant. It was a used Cadillac, Luke told himself, but it didn't look it. And he was damn proud of the car. Other young lawyers his age looked at him with envy. He was single and doing well and he had the car to prove it.

As he stepped into the street, another car pulled up and rolled down the window. It was Robby Wells.

"How's it going, Luke."

Robby and his partner, Leon Harris, owned the firm of Harris and Wells. Luke worked for them for five years before going out on his own. Robby told Luke that he would regret leaving them and always enjoyed the lack of any signs of success in his former employee's life during those first years. Now that Luke was driving a Cadillac, some of Robby's smugness had disappeared. As he stood there in the street chatting, Luke was glad he had on a fresh shirt and the new Armani tie. The shirt was a brilliant white and he knew it had to hurt Well's eyes to look up at him.

"Fine, Rob. You okay?

"Yes, yes. Things must be looking up for you, Luke. I like the new car."

"Oh, that! It's not new. Just picked up a good deal, that's all. How are things at your office?"

"You know how it is. There's good and there's bad. Busy, though. We just put on a new kid who graduated in August, just passed the bar exam a few weeks ago. Green as a gourd and doesn't know a damn thing about law. I wonder what they're teaching them at law school."

Luke laughed. He knew that while most law school graduates took a while to get their feet wet and learn the tricks of the trade, he also knew from experience that Rob Wells thought nobody really knew anything about practicing law but himself. He stood there looking down at his old boss, thinking how glad he was that he didn't still work for him. His earlier fatigue slipped away as he stood there and suddenly remembered his appointment.

"Look, Rob, I've gotta run. I'm meeting a client and I'm late already. See you around." He knew that Wells would be impressed with his leaving the office after five o'clock on a Friday to meet a client. Thank you, Ms. Weeks, for being late today.

Luke strode up to the Cadillac, punched the electronic lock and swung the door open. He could feel Wells' eyes still on him. As he crawled into the front seat, he waved goodbye to his old employer and shut the door behind him. He saw Wells drive on. Yesss! A rewarding moment after a long day.

And now on to Ms. Weeks. As he pulled out of the parking lot, the misty rain in the air left the streets wet and slippery. The clouds made the hour seem later than five thirty. He arrived at the Magnolia in short time, parked his car and headed inside.

The Magnolia was located in an older, two-story, bungalow-style house built in the 1930's. Its original owner, John Stetelman, had been a real estate developer and the house had been built in one of his first city projects. Most of the houses were now businesses with only a few remaining residences.

There was a dress shop next door owned and operated by the wife of another attorney in town. Next to that was an insurance office. Across that street was Robert Lott's CPA practice. On down the street was a furniture store owned by the Wilkinson family.

The main entrance to the restaurant was on the side of the building. Luke stepped up and pulled open the door. Inside he was met by a flurry of voices chattering away along with the tinkling of glass and china.

The Magnolia made perfect use of the original character of the old home. Walls had been taken out from the first structure so that the whole downstairs was used for a restaurant with the kitchen in the back. Just a few steps from the door, a curved staircase swept up to the second floor bar. The receptionist looked up from the podium and smiled.

"Good evening, sir. My name is Kelly. May I help you?"

She was in her early twenties and gorgeous. Luke was constantly amazed at how the place always kept such pretty young girls working the front door.

"Yes, Kelly, I'm meeting someone here but I don't know what she looks like." Luke managed to get this somewhat awkward statement out as he scanned the room. He rebuked himself for not having asked for a description.

"Well, it's still kind of early yet. We don't have that many people seated in the restaurant. Perhaps you'd like to look around upstairs in the bar. There's quite a few people up there."

"Okay, that's fine. If she should come in her name is Susan Weeks and she should be looking for me. I'm Luke Daniels." Never missing the opportunity, Luke pulled a card from his pocket and handed it to the young lady.

"Sure, Mr. Daniels, I'll watch out for her."

Luke headed up the stairs and at the top looked around the room. It was almost full.

Luke wondered how these people got here so soon after five o'clock. He was usually at the office until this time and later. A closer look told him that many of these people had already been there for a while. Of course it was Friday, but still…

The room was filled with mostly professional types. There were a lot of button-down shirts with the necks loosened and ties pulled down. He noticed a few lawyers and waved. There were bankers, insurance brokers he knew and the general mix of downtown business specimens. He didn't see a single woman anywhere that looked like she was looking for someone.

He decided to move on over to the bar and get a better look. As he worked his way there, he waved to several other folks he knew. There was Buddy Blakely, the city councilman, Dave Tolbert, a county supervisor, and there at the bar was Sally, Sally Gray. She had been formerly known as Mrs. Luke Daniels.

"Hello, Sally."

She turned around in the swivel bar stool and looked up at him with a start.

"Oh, hi, Luke." The hesitation in her voice almost made it quiver. Her eyes darted around not knowing where to settle and unable to look him in the eye. To anyone else, there would appear nothing out of the ordinary, but Luke knew how uncomfortable the encounter made her. The confrontation was only in her mind, but the uneasiness was evident to Luke. Her apprehension at what he might say or do seeped from her, filling the air around them.

Luke held back the urge to smile, even though he couldn't help but enjoy the moment. There had been only a few of these chance encounters in the two years since their divorce. It was amazing to him that in a town the size of Hampton they did not run into each other more often.

Sally had new friends now and he didn't keep up with them. He had heard that she was a regular with the happy hour crowd that roamed the few bars in town. It was not surprising that he didn't run into her in that scene because hanging out in bars was not something that had ever appealed to Luke. He ran out with a few friends every once in a while for a drink but it was rare. Usually ten minutes after arriving, he was bored.

"You're looking good, Luke. I like that tie." Sally always said he could pick the best ties.

"Thanks. I bought it down in New Orleans. It's an Armani." Luke cringed at himself for mentioning the designer's name. He hated pretentiousness and felt that the remark had put him right into the snob big league.

"I hear you have a new car, too. You must be doing well."

She heard? He loved it that she still kept up with him. "Nah, not a new car, it's second hand." He was almost blushing but soaking it all up. His ego needed to have her acknowledge his success after the way she had left him.

She was Sally Gray and her best friend was Leon Harris's younger sister. They were both twenty-five when they met and a relationship blossomed immediately. They waited because Luke wanted to be sure. They dated for almost three years before finally getting married.

Not long after getting married there had been problems. Sally was not happy with the pace of his associate's position at Harris and Wells. Then, two years after their marriage, he started talking about leaving the firm and going out on his own. Sally freaked. Suddenly, she loved the stability of the firm. He couldn't make it on his own. There was too much competition in the town. For Luke, there was too much about Harris and Wells he didn't like. They were well-connected and could get things done, but the manner in which they did so turned him off. So, after five years with them he left, and the problems between him and Sally multiplied.

He did alright on his own but things were tight. There was not enough money for very many extras. For three years after he went solo, he and Sally fought constantly. Then they were divorced. It happened almost overnight. After three years of dating and five years of marriage - boom - they were divorced in sixty days.

Her leaving freed him. He had been constantly fighting at work to keep his law practice afloat and then at home the constant fighting with Sally. He felt certain that the unending stress of their relationship had caused her miscarriage. They both received the news of her pregnancy with apprehension. Each could see in the other's eyes the struggle to appear happy. But two months later he came home from work and she was standing in the kitchen. With almost no emotion she told him she had lost the baby. It had happened that morning. She went to the doctor and he confirmed it. She had come home in the afternoon and rested. During that time she made her decision. She didn't want to do this anymore. Her bags were packed. They were already in the car and she was leaving.

The divorce said irreconcilable differences. Luke remembered looking at that term as if for the first time when he sat in the judge's chambers with Sally. To him, the only difference she couldn't reconcile was the balance in his checkbook. He had not been able to keep her in the style which she thought she deserved. He always wondered about the miscarriage. Was that the reason she left? Or was it the lean times his practice was having. He would probably never know for sure.

"So, what are you doing out tonight?" she asked without any real interest.

"I'm supposed to be meeting a client here. Just thought I'd look around for a bit. I don't see her though." Luke didn't want to end up in any longwinded conversation with his ex-wife and was fairly certain that she didn't either. Although his new status, meaning money, might have made him attractive to her again, the feeling was not mutual.

As he looked at Sally sitting there on her bar stool he wondered what he had ever seen in her. She seemed almost sad, sitting there at happy hour. Sally was over thirty now and her dress was still that of a college girl, or even teenager. Luke said goodbye and removed himself from the situation.

His immediate thought was to get back downstairs and get a table and wait on Susan Weeks. Before he could do that Judge Dickerson was standing up to shake his hand. Luke went through the niceties and then quickly got himself headed down the stairs.

The young lady working the door was not at her post at the moment and Luke considered leaving and worrying about Susan Weeks later. He could tell that in the short time he was upstairs several tables had filled in the restaurant. He stood around for a few moments until a waiter stopped him.

"Can I help you, sir?

"I'm supposed to be meeting someone here and she was not upstairs. The young lady at the door, Kelly, was going to watch out for anyone asking for me."

"I'm not sure where she is at the moment. There is a woman by herself at a table in the other room. Would you like for me to check for you?"

"Yes, if you would. Thank you."

The waiter withdrew around the corner. Kelly reappeared and saw Luke standing there.

"I'm sorry Mr. Daniels but no one has come in asking for you. I guess your party was not upstairs?"

"No, she wasn't. But the waiter said a woman was sitting at a table by herself and he's checking."

The waiter came back and said "Mr. Daniels, there's a Ms. Weeks already at a table waiting for you."

Kelly gave Luke a sheepish grin as he walked by. Luke shrugged and walked on.

As he stepped into the next room, a woman stood up from her table and stuck out her hand.

"Mr. Daniels? Hi, I'm Susan Weeks."

Luke stretched out his hand as he looked back at a woman who was stunningly beautiful and too much for him to take in all at once. His first thought was how well put together she was. She wasn't tall, even somewhat petite. She had dark hair. Was it black or just dark brown? Whatever the exact color it framed her face perfectly and rested on her shoulders in a distinctly natural way. Her face radiated an undeniable beauty. The lights in the restaurant were not good but it was as if she had her own inner glow. Her whole countenance was radiant with that same glow emanating from every part of her being. Luke realized that he must be staring and tried to think of some bit of conversation to use as a distraction.

"I looked for you upstairs, but you weren't there," Luke blurted out. What an idiot. Of course, she wasn't there. Go ahead, Luke. Impress her with the words of the great barrister, the master of his profession.

Susan responded politely, "When I arrived, there was no one at the desk to ask. So I stood at the front door for a few moments not knowing if I should go upstairs. I decided to look around first for you down here. A waiter put me at this table. I decided it was as good a place to wait as any." She smiled warmly as she completed her own tale.

Her smile seemed to somehow be there all the time; she just seemed to recharge it at will. Luke tried to collect himself even though he was still a bit overwhelmed. Susan Weeks was wearing a brown-and-black hound's tooth check in a trench-coat style, double-breasted with a wide belt. On anyone else, the dress might have meant nothing, but on her it imparted a sense of professional style that was fashionable yet understated.

The neckline formed a deep 'V' which stopped just in the perfect spot to reveal the right amount of an absolutely perfect bosom. A small piece of black lace showed at the bottom of the 'V' and Luke thought it had probably been put there to look slightly out of place, giving just the right effect. He suddenly realized again that he was staring and looked back up into the eyes of Susan Weeks. He blushed as she looked back at him knowing where his eyes had just been fixed. She smiled again without any embarrassment or annoyance and Luke smiled back.

"Will this be alright?"

"Yes, sure," Luke replied. They seated themselves with the waiter helping Susan Weeks with her chair. The waiter excused himself explaining he would be back shortly.

"I can't tell you how much I appreciate your meeting me on such short notice. I'm sorry I made it so late. I didn't know when I talked to you that I had to go to a ribbon cutting." The smile faded slightly for just a moment.

"Ah, yes, the new vault door, was it?" Luke regained his composure somewhat and chuckled. "That sounds like an exciting afternoon, Ms. Weeks."

"Please call me Susan."

"Alright, Susan. What is it you do for the bank? And which bank is it, by the way?"

"Guaranty National. I'm in charge of marketing and public relations for the southern district. If that sounds exciting, it's not. I organize events like the ribbon cutting this afternoon. Usually, I have someone else to go but today I was the lucky one. Have you been to Collins?"

"Yes, I handle some cases there."

"Well, the branch is small. Ribbon cuttings are not my usual responsibility, but anything for a little publicity. The local newspaper was there and took pictures. The employees were excited…"

As she went on about her afternoon at the ribbon cutting, Luke listened more to her voice than the words. It was having an intoxicating effect on him. The smile that rested so naturally on her face carried through in her voice so that the listener felt continuously exhilarated. Luke was slowly being carried away by the sound.

There was also something else. Her perfume mingled with a natural scent produced a wonderful fragrance. The combination of her manner, the sound of her voice and her fragrance were wafting across him in a delicious way until another sound broke the mood.

"Would you folks care to look at a menu?" came suddenly from the waiter.

Susan looked across at Luke with inquisitive eyes as if he were supposed to respond for her. He abruptly remembered that they were here for coffee or a drink and she was waiting for his lead. Luke wasn't sure what he wanted at this point. What he really wanted was for her to go on talking and for him to listen.

"What'll you have, Susan?" he responded almost lamely.

"I think that I could go for a glass of wine, if that's alright. How about you?"

"That's sounds great." Earlier he had thought that at best he would have a cup of coffee and get the meeting over with. Now his fatigue dissipated in the presence of this lovely creature and he was now only interested in finding out more about Susan Weeks. "How about two, please?"

"Certainly, sir. Would you care to look at our wine list? Our house wines are very good." Luke read from a handsomely designed placard in the center of the table.

"Two glasses of your house merlot would be great."

"Coming right up." The waiter made a slight notation on his pad and left their table.

"I'm glad you opted for the wine. It's been a hectic week and I need to relax a little. You're really easy to talk to."

Luke laughed. Mostly because he could not have told her a word of what she had been talking to him about. Whatever it had been she had conveyed it beautifully.

"I'm surprised we haven't met before." Susan started again. "My work puts me in a lot of social settings and I've met many of the attorneys in town."

She didn't add that she would not want any of them to represent her. Hampton had quite a few lawyers for a city its size, but none she met had impressed her. One of the girls in the office used Luke in a divorce and had only good things to say about him, which was why Susan had called. Now she was certainly glad she had. He was not like any of the lawyers she knew.

Her first impression was that he was very professional. He was a little haughty, like most lawyers, but somehow different. She was drawn to him immediately when they met. He was definitely handsome. His face was young but there was a fleck of gray sprinkled through the sides of his dark hair. She had never seen such vivid, deep blue eyes and was enjoying having them in front of her, looking at her.

Susan was used to being looked at. With cameras and agents and advertising types, she was always being scrutinized. But this was different. His eyes had a gentle quality that made the gaze not a stare but something else. There was a sensitiveness that was disarming. Watch it, Susan, she reminded herself. You don't need to trust anyone, especially right now. Not too quickly anyway. She had checked him out with some other people and she had no indication from anyone that he was anything but honorable. In fact, most had spoken very highly of Luke Daniels. But, she knew that she needed to make her own final appraisal.

He had apparently made a good name for himself over the past handful of years and was recognized as quite a capable attorney. She had run his name through their computers and came up with nothing. He didn't do business with her bank, which was not a sin. She would have liked to have been able to get some more information on him, but to have done further research would have aroused suspicion. She was not really supposed to be able to do what she had done, anyway.

Right now, she was not worried about it. Her instincts told her that this was someone she could trust and that's just what she needed.

"Tommy Chipman is in the same building with you, isn't he?" a question for which she already knew the answer.

"Yes he is. You know Tommy?"

"Only through the bank. He does a lot of title work. I don't have much to do with that end of the business, but I've met him there. He delivered a title opinion to the bank and Bob Fowler introduced us. He's very charming," she added. Tommy was one of the professional males that visited the bank and eyed the young girls. Tommy was attractive, tall and had sandy brown hair. He seemed nice enough, but she was never quite sure.

"He's okay. I've never thought much about his being charming. His father-in-law owned a big portion of that little bank you were at today before it merged with Guaranty National. The majority of his practice is bank related and mostly from his father-in-law, Willis Becker. Tommy practices law a lot on the golf course."

"I take it you don't approve."

"I wouldn't say that. Maybe jealous a little of his having his livelihood just handed to him. Tommy's never had to struggle."

"And you have?" she asked as delicately as she could.

"You might say that. I practiced with a firm for a few years right out of law school. They threw me all the trash they didn't want to handle for five years and then I decided it was time to do something else. I left them, set up my own office and never looked back. It was rough there for a while but things have started looking up. Yeah, I struggled for a while. I'm not really jealous of Tommy. I like where I am right now."

Luke smiled to himself. He definitely liked where he was right this moment, sitting across from such a captivating young woman. The waiter arrived with their wine and set the glasses in front of them with a flourish.

"Would you like to look at a menu?"

"No thank you, this is fine," Susan replied.

The waiter left and another voice came from another direction.

"Ah, Ms. Weeks, how are you?" A distinguished looking man who appeared to be in his fifties stepped up to the table. Susan offered her hand to him without getting up.

"Hello, Dr. Bautista. It's nice to see you. Luke, this is Dr. Raul Bautista from the Marketing Department at the University of Southern Mississippi. Dr. Bautista, Luke Daniels."

Luke stood and pleasantries were exchanged. Dr. Bautista's wife was behind him and after everyone shook hands, Luke learned that Dr. Bautista was Susan Weeks' advisor in the doctoral program she was enrolled in at the University of Southern Mississippi in Hattiesburg. She had begun in the summer and would finish her course work next spring at which time she would have to complete her dissertation on an as yet undetermined topic.

After the Bautistas left, Luke looked back at Susan and asked with a smile, "So, you're going to be Dr. Weeks?"

"It hasn't happened yet. But I decided, why not? The bank's paying for it so I might as well take advantage of the opportunity. It's been a little hectic working it around my modeling jobs, but I like to stay busy."

"Modeling jobs?" Luke looked at her incredulously. "How does that fit into the banking business?"

Susan laughed out loud at the look on Luke's face.

"It must sound a little crazy when you get the bits and pieces like this. I've been modeling since my undergraduate days. It's fun, something I enjoy doing and so I've kept it up. You might call it moonlighting. The bank doesn't completely approve but as long as I do my job they don't complain. And I do my job very well, I might add. At least they think so.

Let me back up a little. When I was at Millsap College, I did some modeling for a local department store in Jackson. They liked my work and kept me on after I got my bachelor's degree. I decided to go straight on to graduate school and get my masters so I kept up the modeling to pay for it. The modeling jobs just kept coming. The more I did, the more I was offered. I turned down quite a few then just because I didn't have the extra time.

Anyway, after getting my MBA in marketing, I went to work for Guaranty National. I had other offers but chose Guaranty because they agreed to let me continue modeling. Then they offered me the job here. I didn't want to move to Hampton but they made me an offer I couldn't refuse, so here I am.

I never intended to go back to school but it just happened. Getting enrolled in the doctoral program was easy because the bank promoted it. Dr. Bautista is on the board of directors for the bank and I've worked with him in my position as director of marketing for this area. He convinced me that the Ph.D. would give me an advantage over my associates. I think he sensed that I was not really thrilled about being in Hampton and had my sights set on a bigger picture."

"And do you?" Luke asked.

"Right now, I'm just planning to get the degree and see what happens. I've even considered modeling full time. Some others have tried to convince me that it is the route I should take. But I don't know. Some things about the modeling business bother me." Her face clouded. For the first time since Luke met her the smile had completely left her face. In its wake Luke saw a brief glimmer of a frightened little girl. He wondered just what age she was and was about to ask when her face quickly brightened.

"After all, I'm still young. I feel like I'm doing pretty well for my age." The question must have been on Luke's face because she responded, "I'm twenty-six. Does that surprise you?"

"No. Well, yes. I was guessing that you were somewhere between eighteen and thirty-five."

"Thirty-five!"

"No, please, it's a compliment. You're beautiful and could be any age. You have the look of youth, but you're also very cultured and confer a sense of experience."

"Well, I'm twenty-six. Would you like to see my driver's license?"

Luke picked up the wine glass he had hardly touched. "Here's to twenty-six!"

She laughed and touched her glass to his. It was the most relaxed she had been in days. Or weeks. This man had put her at ease and didn't even know it. Or did he? Perhaps that was part of his charm. He handled everything with such composure that it made her feel safe, something that had become foreign to her.

Susan watched him. He reminded her somehow of her father. He was tall like her dad. And lean. He looked to be in good shape. She wondered how old he was. He had to be in his early thirties. He was a good looking man, but it was not just his looks. His overall appearance was one that exuded self-assurance. Confidence. Even the way he had walked into the room. He didn't know her when he walked up but he seemed completely in control. Whatever it was, she found it appealing. She liked this man.

She remembered that she hadn't come here to meet a man. She was meeting Luke Daniels because he was a lawyer and she needed some good sound advice to help her with the situation she had found herself in. Now that she was here she wasn't sure just how to approach it. She was certain that talking to a lawyer was the thing to do, but now she wasn't sure how to get to the subject. What should she say? 'Mr. Daniels, I'm being blackmailed. Someone has nude photos and is using them against me.' What would he say? What advice would he have for her? Perhaps she should have gone to the police instead. Could she trust this man to be totally confidential?

She didn't go to the police because she was afraid of being ridiculed. She knew that as soon as she talked to them it would make it a public case and the news could leak out. Probably the whole police department would get a good laugh over it. They would pursue the case fiercely, she was sure. Not to help her, but to help their own careers. The prosecution in such a case would make headline news, and make heroes of the defenders of justice at the Hampton Police Department. The District Attorney would be outraged and get on the news every chance he could to decry the disgrace to the good citizens of Hampton and all of Bedford County. And where would all this leave Susan Weeks? Probably without a job.

If the bank found out that their head of marketing had nude photos floating around it would be a disaster. She would be let go immediately. Not fired. They would be too discreet for that. They would suggest that it would be best for her to find other employment. How could she refuse? That was what worried her the most. She knew this wasn't the only job in the world, but to leave this way would be disastrous for her career. What bank would want her? And what would happen to her doctoral studies?

There was just too much riding on her life and career to let it all fall apart now. Damn, why hadn't she been more careful? What was she going to do? This was the right step. Maybe

Luke Daniels could help her.

Luke decided to pick up the conversation which had become idle for several moments. "How long have you been in Hampton?"

"Oh, about a year, now," she responded quickly. Not knowing how she was going to make herself talk about her dilemma, Susan was glad for the lighter conversation. Maybe if she just relaxed a bit more, things would work out.

"Where are you living?" Luke asked innocently.

"Out in Willow Oaks. I have a house. It's not mine. It belongs to Jennifer Holt. Well, really her father. You may know him. Bud Holt?" she inquired.

"Bud? Sure, I know him," Luke responded with a snicker.

"Why do you say it like that? Sounds like you don't think much of him." She watched Luke closely, wondering what he knew about Mr. Holt.

"Let's just say we have a different approach to the practice of law. That is, what's legal and what's not." Luke added. He didn't want to say too much because she roomed with the man's daughter, but Luke had never thought too highly of Bud Holt.

"Do you think he is dishonest? He's not involved in anything illegal, is he?" Luke's tone had piqued her curiosity.

"Oh, no. Not that I'm aware of. Mr. Holt is too smart to be involved in anything illegal himself. Let's just say he plays fast and loose with the legal system."

Luke quickly checked himself. "Look, I shouldn't be saying anything of this sort. I don't know that the man's ever been anything but purely honest. He has a certain reputation, but that's really just idle gossip that I don't like to be a party to so, please, forget I said anything. Jennifer is a very nice girl. I know her myself. She's younger than I but we've met on several occasions."

The waiter appeared again. "Would you like a refill?"

Luke was glad for the interruption and answered for them.

"Yes, we would. Same thing again, please."

The waiter left and Luke smiled back at Susan.

"How is Jennifer? Doesn't she work at Guaranty National, also?"

"Yes, that's where we met. She was one of the first people I met when I came down here to interview. She was executive assistant to Ken Wildmon, the president of the bank. No one could have been any nicer to me than she was. Of course, so was Mr. Wildmon. There are a lot of wonderful people there. That was one of the reasons I found it easy to make the decision to come here from Jackson."

They talked on for a while playing the consummate Southern game of 'Say, do you know so-and-so.' Luke soon found that in the twelve short months Susan had been in town she had met nearly everyone but him. She talked about some of the old families of Hampton as if they were her good friends. She also knew a lot of lawyers. Luke wondered why he wasn't one of them.

He couldn't deny that he was attracted to this woman. As he sat here talking with her he was not thinking at all of representing her in a legal capacity. Why hadn't he met her before? 'Luke, you're working too hard,' he admonished himself.

It was true. Since his divorce from Sally he was not interested in having a social life. Almost all of his waking hours were spent at work. About the only outlet he allowed himself was his running. Too much work, though. That was going to have to change. Maybe Susan Weeks was just the diversion he needed.

There was only one problem. She had called him about a legal matter. Luke had some very strict rules about not mixing his business and personal lives. By agreeing to meet a client outside his office, especially a new one, he had already violated one of his rules. And, now he was having a drink with his new client. He was a little irritated with himself for getting into this situation. He had set stringent standards for himself and he kept them. Until now.

Why had she called on a Friday? Why was he worried when he was enjoying himself so? He knew because that was the reason you set standards in the first place. You apply them when your better judgment was affected by stress, fatigue or some other ailment. Well, he was here now enjoying himself. He'd just have to deal with it.

Susan was also having a good time. Her recent anxieties had her so pent up that she was always a bundle of nerves. The glass of wine had her relaxed and it was wonderful. At least she thought it was the wine. Or was it Luke Daniels? She had a great feeling about it all. She just knew he was someone who would have the answers. She felt so good about it that she was going to put the issues aside for the time being and just enjoy the moment.

Luke pushed his chair back and stood up.

"Hello, Judge Dahl. Mrs. Dahl. How are you this evening?" Luke sounded genuinely glad to see them.

"Fine, Luke. How are things with you?" They shook hands.

Mrs. Dahl put her hand up to Luke's arm and patted him. "How's my favorite attorney?" she beamed.

"Doing great, Mrs. Dahl. Your husband hasn't taken a bite out of me in over a month now. Of course, I haven't had a case before him either."

"Let's just see that the next time you are before me you have the right file with you, Luke," Judge Dahl retorted with half a smile.

"Judge, is it my fault the secretary put the wrong label on it?" Luke laughed.

"Yea, that's right, blame it on the secretary. It hasn't been that long since I practiced. I know your tricks. Wait 'till I see Liz and let her know you're faulting her for your own short-comings." Judge Dahl was looking at Susan when Luke realized that he had not introduced her.

"And who are you?" Judge Dahl started.

"Susan Weeks." Susan offered her hand to them.

"Keep an eye on this one, young lady, he's not to be trusted," the Judge exclaimed with a grin. They excused themselves and moved on to be seated at a table. Luke noticed that it was one where Mrs. Dahl had a good view of the two of them.

Luke liked Mrs. Dahl but she was known to be the biggest gossip in town, which was not very becoming for a judge's wife. She often knew too much that should have been kept confidential by her husband. He was sure that her tongue would be wagging as soon as she could get to a phone. Not really a problem, he thought. Who wouldn't want to be seen with this woman? They could talk all they wanted.

He turned back to Susan but before he could say anything, she was waiving at someone across the room.

"I'm sorry," she said, "this will only take a moment. She works at the bank. I tried to reach her all day and couldn't." Susan stood and made her way in the direction she had waved.

Luke's eyes followed her across the room. He tried not to stare but couldn't help it. She floated between the tables like a lioness with her hair streaming behind like a dark mane. She was also in excellent shape. He could see her taut body moving slightly under the dress. Her legs were covered in dark hose that led down to black heels. Even her ankles were pretty. Sexy. She was beautiful from head to toe, Luke thought. She was wearing a thin diamond bracelet on her wrist which he had not noticed before. He had noticed that she was not wearing a wedding ring.

She sat down gracefully at the edge of a chair at her friend's table, perched like an elegant Siamese cat. As Luke watched her from afar he was overcome by her exquisite manner.

Her friend was a red head about Susan's age and there was a man at their table. Luke didn't know him and didn't care. He could hardly take his eyes off Susan. She soon stood and started back toward their table.

He noticed the diamond bracelet again. It sparkled elegantly as she walked. She was also wearing a gold chain with a diamond pendant that also captured light from the period sconces along the restaurant's perimeter. As she approached he stood to get her chair. This time he noticed the bit of black lace scantily peeking out from her dress neckline.

"I'm sorry, Luke. I guess this was not the best place to meet. We keep getting interrupted." She smiled across the table.

"Yes, it reminds me of why I have a certain rule."

"What is that?"

"I make it a rule not to meet clients outside the office; especially new clients." He immediately wondered if he sounded too harsh.

"Why did you then?"

"You caught me at a weak moment. It was Friday afternoon and I wanted to get out of the office. We probably should have done this Monday. But you sounded so urgent this morning on the phone. Is it still that crucial?" Luke really didn't want to talk business with her right now but the question came out naturally. As soon as he saw her face he wished he could take the question back.

She frowned. The smile that glowed on her face was gone. It was like a cloud on a spring day drifting across the sun. But even the frown seemed to shine back.

"Maybe we could find a better place to talk," she offered. "It didn't occur to me that this place would be so busy and we'd get so many interruptions. What do you think?"

Luke was fine with anything that kept them together longer. Right now he didn't want any of it to stop.

"Sure. We could even get something to eat. Let me pay the bill and we'll decide on our way out."

"No way on the tab. I'm supposed to be hiring you, remember?" she said with a laugh. "Please, let me get it."

She reached down and touched his hand on the table. He could feel a light flowing into him from her touch.

Luke looked closely into her dark emerald eyes and felt himself stir. She was looking back at him directly and for a brief moment there was a bond, a link of some kind. Susan's eyes flickered and he read something. It was a plea for help. A resolve. 'I know you can help me,' she was saying without uttering a sound. She moved her hand away and picked up her purse. She pulled out some money and laid it on the table.

"That should do it. Are you ready?" She said it this time with her determined and beautiful smile.

Across the room, Judge Dahl appeared not to notice as his wife craned her neck to get a better view of Luke Daniels and the woman with him.

"Are we having fish tonight, dear?" he asked with only slight irritation in his voice. Even though he feigned displeasure, Judge Dahl knew only too well that his wife's gossipy nature was a big part of his political success. She knew everything about everybody and was expert in understanding the politics of the three-county area which was his district. She knew before he did if there was someone who had been offended by the Judge or his actions and would get to work immediately to assuage the aggrieved, diminishing the problem.

"What's that, Judge?" She liked calling him Judge when he got that out-of-sorts voice with her. It seemed to put everything in perspective.

"I said, are we having fish tonight?" This time he asked without the irritation. "One of the specials is blackened red fish. You know how good they do it here."

"Yes," she responded, but had not looked at the menu because she was trying to make sure that she took in everything about Luke and Susan. "Haven't we met that young lady with Luke before? I think she was at the reception for Bob Walker when he became president of Guaranty National."

"I don't remember. She's pretty enough, though. I should." The Judge liked to think of himself as having an eye for pretty girls. "What about the fish?"

Mrs. Dahl's eyes followed Luke and Susan as they got up from the table and left the restaurant. When they were gone she turned back to the menu and said to the Judge, "Yes, the blackened red fish sounds fine to me. You know how good they do it here."

Luke and Susan made their way outside to a cool night and a gentle refreshing breeze. The earlier rain had left the air with a clean uncorrupted scent that one could almost taste. The fragrance of pine trees filled the air with the squeaky clean odor of evergreen and the leaves on the nearby magnolia trees glistened from the fresh bath.

Luke felt good as they stood for a moment outside the restaurant. He didn't know why exactly, except for having such a beautiful woman at his side.

"So what should we do?" Susan asked first.

Luke thought for a moment and realized that any place they went in Hampton would be filled with people they both knew, which made for little privacy. Luke also thought of asking her to his house but quickly dismissed the idea when she spoke.

"We could get some sandwiches and take them to my place. Jennifer is gone for the weekend and no one will bother us."

As soon as she said it Susan wished she hadn't. What would he think? They had just met and she was inviting him to her home. She only wanted to be alone with him so they could talk.

Susan stopped herself. The real reason was that she just wanted to be alone with him. She was in trouble. From the first moment he sat down at her table, Susan felt herself drawn to Luke Daniels. There was a steadfastness that led her to feel if he just put his arm around her that everything in the world would be alright. What must he be thinking right now? Surely, he was taken aback by her offer. She had shocked herself by asking.

"Okay," Luke said. "Should I follow you in my car?"

They looked at each other, both of them surprised at what was happening. When she suggested that they go to her house, it was perfectly natural to Luke. It should have surprised him but it didn't. He wanted to say yes, so he did.

Susan was even more perplexed by his response. He had just been telling her inside the restaurant about his rule of not meeting clients outside of the office. And suddenly he was saying yes to come back to her house. 'Stop questioning, Susan, and stop worrying. Relax.' And she did.

What was happening was okay for now. They were going to her house so they could sit and talk without interruption. They were both grown adults. Professionals. There was absolutely nothing wrong. In fact, it made sense.

"Why don't we stop at Robby's and get some po-boys to take with us," Luke proposed. "Come on. I'll walk you to your car."

They moved through the parking lot and suddenly Susan exclaimed, "Oh, no!"

"What?"

"That's my car," she said pointing, "I left the lights on."

The disappointment in her voice turned to laughter quickly.

"I was in a hurry when I got here and it was raining slightly. I had the lights on and when I got out of the car, I must have forgotten to turn them off. I hope it cranks."

It didn't. The engine gave a slight moan and that was it. And, in the spot where she parked there was no way to get in to the battery to jump it off.

Luke, suddenly feeling the eternal optimist, said positively, "Susan, it's not a problem. You can ride with me for now and tomorrow morning when the parking lot is empty we'll find a way to get over here and take care of it."

She looked back at him with the rush of earlier thoughts. Dependable. Reliable. Trustworthy. All the things she needed in her life right now, rolled up in one package. And, a law degree to boot. Without any further hesitation, she grabbed her purse and keys, locked the car door and headed off to Luke's car.

They reached his car and Luke guided her to the passenger's side and opened the door. The car suited him. Sleek and sporty, just like Luke, she thought with a grin. As he walked around to his side she felt again that this man knew what he was doing and would be able to resolve her situation appropriately. Luke got in, picked up his car phone and dialed a number. They placed a call to Robby's, put in an order and then drove away.

CHAPTER TWO

Willow Oaks was a fairly new subdivision with cute names for streets that twisted around like a labyrinth. The sack of po-boys sat warm between them as Susan guided Luke through the maze where Dogwood Cove connected to Willow Bend, running into Oak Manor Drive. Finally, Susan pointed to a house with 313 Birch Place on the mailbox. Luke pulled into the driveway and let out a low whistle.

The lot was covered with trees so thick that at first the house was only barely visible. The drive way split with one way to the front door and the other around back to the garage. She explained that since the garage door opener was in her car they would have to go to the front door.

Luke was glad because he wanted to pull up to the front. The house was not enormous but had a look of grandeur about it. He thought it was stucco but she explained it was only an exterior finish that looked like stucco. There were two columns supporting a small portico at the entrance. The front door was solid wood with side panels of glass. The light in the portico came from a copper fixture that had a classic green patina to it. Susan pulled out her keys and opened the front door.

They stepped inside to a marbled floor with what looked like pink leather on the walls. Luke thought it most unusual but striking above the pink-hued marble. A large modern silver and blown glass fixture hung from the vaulted ceiling.

Susan moved on from the foyer and turned on a lamp ahead of them. Luke could see straight from the foyer across another room to a wall filled with windows. The foyer opened into the living area, or great room, as Susan explained, that had a ceiling that was about twenty feet high. The back wall of the room was all glass. The top of the room went up to a cupola, although it wasn't exactly rounded, but had windows on all sides. She flipped on the outside lights, which gave fuller illumination to the room.

In contrast to the extravagance of the structure, the furnishings were modest. A chintz covered sofa was backed up to the table with the lamp Susan had turned on. There were two chairs and an ottoman in the room but no other furniture. Actually, there wasn't the need for anything else. A TV simply placed on dark stained shelves with a stereo and a fireplace completed the interior setting.

It was the right place for the most regal Susan Weeks to live in, Luke thought. He also found it interesting for her to have found such a house so suitable to her own subdued elegance.

"Let's get those sandwiches out," she started with Luke following her into the kitchen.

"What would you like to drink?" She opened the refrigerator door and continued, "Are you up for another glass of wine. Jennifer has a bottle here that I know she wants us to open." She looked back at Luke with the same magnificent sparkle in her eyes.

She had the bottle out and was digging through a drawer for a corkscrew which she handed to Luke before he had a chance to answer. It was Chablis that he knew would do well with their po-boys. They both had picked soft shell crab and confessed that it was their favorite. Luke dutifully opened the bottle of wine and knew instantly that it was a good one. The cork was evenly moist and the wine had the right subtle aroma. Susan handed him two glasses and he poured a taste for both of them. She was surprised by the act. Most men she knew would have poured a taste for themselves and then tried to impress her with their knowledge.

He tasted his and then asked "What do you think? Will it do?"

She tasted hers and said, "Yes, this will do just fine."

They sat down at the table and pulled out the food. As they ate Susan talked about the house. Jennifer's father purchased it when he and her mother were separated and headed for divorce. There was a reconciliation and the house sat empty for a while until Jennifer moved in. Last year when Susan accepted the job, Jennifer was looking for a roommate because she didn't like living in the house alone. It worked out splendidly. The house had bedrooms at either end with the living area in the middle. They hardly saw each other.

With the food finished they took their glasses and bottle of wine and went to the sofa. Susan moved over to the stereo and started looking through discs.

"The stereo is also Jennifer's but a lot of the discs are mine. Anything in particular you'd like to hear?"

"No, it's dealer's choice," Luke responded with a smile. She could put on anything she wanted and he was sure it would be perfect.

She chose Sade. The clear tones of her sensual voice instantly filled the room. Susan returned to the sofa and read Luke's expression. "I take it you approve."

"One of my favorites," Luke said with a grin. He looked over at Susan as she got comfortable on the sofa. As she straightened her pillow, he began to think about how the evening had begun and how they had wound up here on her sofa with a bottle of wine. Was this a business meeting? He was certain that the Internal Revenue Service wouldn't approve. At some point in the evening the nature of their meeting had shifted. He just wasn't sure when or where it had happened, and he was not really sure that he cared.

They talked about music, the design of the house, the all-glass wall that let them see out into the woodsy backyard, and they talked about themselves. Luke even told her about his divorce.

At some point their hands touched and neither of them moved away. After a while, Luke picked up her hand and kissed the back of it. Susan smiled and placed her hand over his and gave it a gentle squeeze. As she did, she pulled herself closer to him and he put his arm around her as she leaned her head on his shoulder. They sat for a while saying nothing.

The music finished and Susan got up to put on something else. She found Billie Holliday. When she returned to the sofa, she went right to the spot she had left and nestled herself next to him. She smiled as she thought how comfortable it was and looked up directly at Luke. Their lips met and he kissed her. She kissed him back. It was gentle and tender and lasted for a long time. His tongue caressed the outline of her lips and she placed her hand alongside his cheek. He kissed along her cheek and around her ear and down her neck. Only then did he pull back to look at her again.

He combed his fingers through her hair and it felt so incredible. His hands massaged the back of her neck and then he kissed her again. Susan couldn't believe how much she wanted to give herself to this man. She wanted the moments of his sweet caressing to last forever, for his touch to never leave her. He moved both his arms around her and hugged her to him. She returned the embrace. She wanted to never let go, to remain in his arms and be safe.

As she placed her head on his chest and rubbed her hand down his side she could feel the ripple of muscle under his shirt. She wanted to feel his bare skin. She tugged the shirt out and ran her hand underneath. He shuddered.

Luke felt that he was beyond reason and control. He didn't want this to stop. It wasn't just sex. He knew it was crazy, but he felt that he was in love with the woman. He crushed her hair to his face and breathed in her scent. Her hand under his shirt was sending waves of sensation across his body. He wanted to hold her against him completely. He wanted her completely. Their lips met again and it was dizzying. As they kissed the fervor grew until they were both breathless.

She pulled back from him and stood up. "Will you come with me to the bedroom?"

He stood up with her and took her face in his hands and kissed her again. He wanted to make love to her but couldn't bear to have his lips away from her. They kissed for a long time standing illuminated by the outdoor light, embracing again. They swayed to the music until she pulled his hand to her lips and kissed it and then led him toward her bed. As they moved down the hall they could still hear the voice of Billie Holliday singing faintly from the other room.

Luke lay in the bed with his eyes fixed on the ceiling. He was still reeling from the events of the evening and how he had wound up in this woman's bed. After an hour or more of passionate love-making like he had never experienced before, they rested.

It started off slowly, tenderly, sensitively and had grown to a frenzy of lust; of desire so potent that the intensity of it had spooked him. A spot on his shoulder still smarted where her teeth clenched on his skin during their intimacy. They had given themselves to each other with such complete and reckless abandon that it was as if they had been transformed from the bed into another dimension. During the throes of their passion, Luke felt that nothing else existed other than their two bodies bound together in rapture.

Now his arm was wrapped around her and the touch of her skin was like purest silk. Her head was just below his chin and the smell of her hair filled his nostrils. The marvelous aroma like an amorous pheromone began to penetrate his head. It was intoxicating, making him again want to throw all caution and reason to the wind.

He had pretty much done that all evening. Since first coming into contact with Susan he had compromised himself. If not his principles, then certainly the standards he had set-standards that he maintained in his life that were guides with which to make decisions at times when reason left off or circumstances led astray.

Luke tried to run back over the events that had occurred since he was last at the office. 'Never meet a client outside the office.' This was not one of the Canons of Ethics which lawyers were to be guided by but merely a rule Luke had established. It kept the setting business-like and made it easier for him to keep things in perspective. At his office, surrounded by his lawyerly trappings he was able to approach situations in a legal fashion and look at them impassively and detached.

This was good for the clients, too. They received a straight-forward opinion from Luke about the merits of their case, good or bad. There were exceptions to this rule: Established clients often had instances arise that called for Luke to meet with them outside the office, in a setting that met the needs of a particular situation. But, never a new client. He always made them come to his office. 'Keep it professional,' he constantly told himself. It was the best way to avoid any misunderstanding; any misconception about intentions. At the office he was the lawyer and they were the client. The way it should be. And where was he now?

Early on in the evening he had bent that first rule. He was ready to get out of the office when she called. She had made it so easy to accept her suggestion. He had pushed his rule aside and off he had gone to meet his new client.

And then wine. That was her suggestion, too. So easy. At one point in the evening he had lost track entirely of the lawyer-client relationship and something else had taken its place. What was it? He wanted to say he loved this woman but he knew that the thought was ridiculous. Luke was too much of a realist to go for that love at first sight jazz, but something drew him to her. Something about her. With all her sophistication, there was a vulnerable quality that had made him want to put his arms around her and hold her forever. To protect her. To tell her that everything was going to be alright.

What a fool. He didn't even know what there was that she needed to be protected from. What exposure she might have. He was angry with himself. If they had met at his office that would have been the first thing they would have talked about. Remember who the lawyer is and who the client is. That was a laugh now. They had talked about everything but her legal situation. Was it a crisis? She certainly made it sound urgent that morning on the phone, but then tonight she had not been at all eager to get to the subject. The whole situation confused him.

Luke was angry with himself for being in this predicament. What must she think of him? Winding up in bed with a new client on their first meeting was not the image he wanted to project. Would she be able to trust him now as an attorney and counselor-at-law? He wanted her to. He wanted to be able to take whatever was wrong in her life and make it right. To be her hero. Her knight in shining armor.

His head was spinning. The leftover effect of the wine and the nagging uncertainty over the whole situation was making him uncomfortable. He was wide awake. Luke decided the best thing for him to do was to get himself up and away for a while. He wasn't sure what he should tell Susan but he needed to let his head clear.

"Susan, are you awake?" There was no sound. He slipped his arm from around her and sat up on the edge of the bed. He sat there for a few moments trying to get his bearings in the darkened room. He slipped on his clothes and turned back to the bed. She lay crumpled in the sheet and again Luke was overcome with the feeling of her vulnerability. She looked like an innocent child as she lay there hugging the pillow.

Outside the clouds broke and moonlight shone through the window, casting a glow all around the bed. He didn't want to leave. He reached down again and kissed her on the cheek. Her smile was still there. She was as stunning in the moonlight as anything he had ever seen and he couldn't believe what feelings were moving through him. He would leave her asleep and call her first thing in the morning. They could talk then and perhaps get this all on the right course. Whatever it was supposed to be.

Luke walked out of the bedroom and made his way down the hall toward the front door. It was dark and before reaching the door he collided with a statue that banged his toe and slammed into the wall making a horrific noise. He was sure that would have awakened Susan.

He let himself out the front door and went straight to his car. The moon was still peeking through the mix of clouds that covered the night sky. He walked around to the driver's side, opened the door and crawled behind the wheel. When he shut the door, he sat for a moment in the silence thinking. The clock on the dash said 12:17 a.m. It was just after midnight. Part of him wanted to go straight back inside, wake her up and tell her how he felt. Or, just be with her and not say a word. It was a compelling urge that nearly pulled him out of the car, but he had to get away for now. They could talk it all out in the morning. Both their heads would be clear in the light of day.

Susan lay in the bed with her head buried in the pillow. Although she fought them back, tears filled her eyes. How could she have been so stupid? She called this man for legal advice and wound up in bed with him. What must he think! She was so ashamed of herself. How would she ever explain to him that this was not her?

She couldn't believe it herself. She needed to talk to him and now he was gone. Why hadn't she said something before he had left? 'Luke, don't go.' She thought it sounded so needy. But she was needy. She needed the help of this man. The earlier feelings of refuge and shelter were replaced with emptiness and longing. It had seemed so right.

Susan tried to imagine what Luke must be thinking. How easy she had been. What was she going to do? Tomorrow would be here and she would have to see Mr. Lambert and she didn't know what to tell him. Earlier she had been sure that Luke had the answer to her situation and would clearly and candidly explain to her what she had to do. Now she was on her own again. And she didn't have an answer.

Right now she was filled with shame and humiliation. She wished she could talk to Luke and explain. This was not her. Something had happened that drew her to him and made her drop all her reserve. Normally, she would have held herself at a distance on a first date. Most of the guys she went out with bored her to death in the first hour, especially those lecherous types at the bank that tried to treat her as if her job depended on their conquest. How she loathed them.

But Luke was different. From the moment they had met something had started building between them that had culminated in bed. That was real. She wasn't mistaken about it. And he had kissed her as he left. Such an affectionate kiss. He touched his lips to her cheek as gentle as a child. Half-asleep at the time, she knew its touch. It carried an essence of devotion in its tenderness. Something wonderful had happened and she was sure of it. She didn't know why he had left but he would be back. He had to. She wouldn't survive without him. Susan rolled over in bed, pulled the covers up about her and gazed out the window at the shadows from the moon.

The front door rattled sending a noise all through the house. Susan raised herself from dozing and sat up. It must be Luke, she thought. He's come back. She climbed out of bed and grabbed for her robe that lay in a chair. She pulled the sleeves on as she left the bedroom. One arm was still not in as she called out, "Luke, I'm coming. Give me a minute." She wanted to run down the hall to him but decided she had displayed enough eagerness for one evening.

As she reached for the front door, her feelings getting the better of her, she exclaimed, "I'm so glad your back!" In response the door was pushed open and a gloved hand struck her in the face. She stumbled back in the foyer stunned and tripped over something on the floor. As she looked up another blow hit her across the cheek. Her head hit the floor and she bounced into the wall.

She tried instantly to get up and run. He grabbed her leg and she kicked at him with her other foot and struck him in the face. He drew back from the blow and she wrenched herself loose and scrambled down the hallway. Panic had taken hold of her completely. She could feel him right behind her as she jumped toward her bedroom door. She tried to slam it behind her but he was there almost immediately. Somehow, with strength she didn't know she had, she got the door shut and locked. He pounded away on the outside trying to force it open. With adrenaline pumping her body forward she reached the phone and dialed 911. It rang.

As it rang the door burst open shattering the facing, sending bits of wood flying into the room. Susan could see the outline of the face as he stepped across the short distance to her and grabbed her arm and wrenched the phone away. She beat at him with her other arm as he laid the phone down. He pushed her and she fell back on the bed clawing at him. He took another swing at her head and landed it right to the temple, leaving her dazed and disoriented. Her arms flailed about her trying to get him off her but his strength overcame her. As he continued to beat her she called Luke's name, wishing he could hear her.

At first she thought this man wanted to rape her but he made no effort. He was strong and much bigger than she was but he was moving carefully and methodically as if he had something else planned. She fought at him and managed to break away and she slipped off the other side of the bed.

He caught her robe that now hung loosely on her nude body and yanked it back and she let it slide off her arms. The motion threw her off balance and she slipped on the floor. As she came down her head hit the corner of a table by the window with such force that she was numbed. Feeling seemed to leave her legs first and then her arms. The room began to spin and suddenly her head felt like it was removed from her body. The blackout came on her slowly after that. She felt herself slipping away as if she were falling into a cavern. Slowly, slowly, slowly she drifted into a deep hole of consciousness until everything finally stopped.

"This is 911. What is your emergency?" Cindy Yates, the dispatch operator at the Hampton Police Department, answered the 911 call just in time to hear a click. As she listened the phone went dead and the dial tone came on. She looked up at her screen and saw the information from the call. She dialed the number and waited. After four rings, an answering machine came on.

"Hi, this is Jennifer. We're not home now, but please leave us a message after the beep." The words came across the phone line from the recording.

"This is the 911 Operator. We were trying to check on your call," Cindy said to the machine. There was no reply. She hung up the phone and noted the address on the computer screen which reflected further information from the call. The screen listed the time, date and phone number of the call along with the house address and the name of the person associated with the phone number. This was the enhanced version of 911 that Hampton had recently accessed. Before, the caller had to identify themselves and give all the information to the operator. Only the phone number was displayed. With the new system all the information was available simultaneously on a screen right in front of Cindy.

She debated for a moment. The screen showed the phone was listed to Jennifer Holt with an address in one of the newer subdivisions of Hampton. Cindy switched to a different screen and checked to see what patrolman she had in that area.

"Hampton to 108," she recited into her radio using the officer's badge number.

"Go ahead, Hampton. This is 108." It was Patrolman Garriga.

"I have a 911 call from a residence at 313 Birch Place. When the call came in there was no one on the line and when I called back I got an answering machine. Can you check it out for me?"

"No problem Hampton. I'm about ten minutes away. Did you dispatch Mobile Medic?" Garriga asked.

"They're next on my list. Thanks 108." Cindy switched off the radio and placed her next call to the Mobile Medic office. When they answered she explained the situation and found out they had one vehicle out on a call and the other one down for repairs. She advised that she had an officer on the way and they agreed to get back in touch as soon as she heard from the officer.

Cindy put the phone down and almost immediately got another 911 call. This time it was a man phoning from his car about debris in the road. Then another call came in, which she handled routinely, and then another and another until she forgot about 313 Birch Place.

Officer Garriga made it to 313 Birch Place in little over ten minutes. He flipped on his spot light and shined it into the trees covering the wooded lot. They were so thick he couldn't see a thing. He noted the number on the mail box and pulled into the driveway and up to the front door. He used the spotlight again to light up along the edge of the house and saw nothing unusual.

He got out of his car, went up to the front door and rang the bell. As he looked through the side windows he could see right through the house to windows in the back. Lights shone out in the back yard. When no one came to the door after a second ring Garriga started around the house with his flashlight. At the garage window he saw spaces for two cars that were both empty. He walked on into the backyard which was lit up by lights along the eave of the house. He put his hands up to the glass windows and looked inside. Nothing.

Garriga continued on around the house and finally concluded there was no one at home. The call must have been a fluke. He got back to his car and radioed the station.

"108 to Hampton."

"Go ahead 108." This time it wasn't Cindy but another dispatcher.

"I'm at 313 Birch Place." He filled her in on all the checks he had made and then concluded, "There are no cars in the garage and it looks like no one's home. No sign of any disturbance at all. I can check further if you want but it doesn't look like anything to me."

"Standby while I check with the shift captain." The radio was silent for a few moments and then she was back. "He says don't worry about it, 108. We'll chalk this one up to that crazy equipment. Probably had something to do with the rain we had earlier."

"Ten-four," he chuckled. Crazy equipment was right. Garriga didn't understand any of that computer stuff they had back there in dispatch and didn't care to learn. He put his radio mike down and drove away from the call.

Inside the house, Susan's body lay where she had fallen. She had drawn her last breath only moments ago. The blows she took from the attack had hurt her but the blow from the table as she had slipped and fell were hard. Hard enough to render her unconscious and hard enough to give her a concussion.

After striking the table her head hit the floor in the exact same spot contributing to the damage and causing internal bleeding. It only took a few minutes for the bleeding to spread throughout her head. Parts of her brain began to shut down and in a moment her breathing stopped. Susan's beautiful nude body lay lifeless on the floor in the bedroom of the house where just a short while ago she had known such joy, such peace, such contentment with a man named Luke Daniels.

CHAPTER THREE

Luke awoke early on Saturday morning. He needed to speak with Susan. The night before he had almost called her several times to let her know where he was. He hadn't. He was afraid he might say something stupid like he loved her. He did. He was sure of it. And that surprised him. His divorce left scars that he felt would keep him from falling in love for a long time. People told him they would slowly fade but he knew otherwise. Now, after one night with this woman he was definitely in love again. Madly in love. Crazy in love. It was impossible, but he was certain of it.

He wished he hadn't left her last night. This morning he was not sure why he had. Last night he was confused. The clarity of the morning was still obscured by the wine, the fatigue, the abruptness of it all. And fear. If he was honest with himself he had to admit that he was afraid of another relationship. But when he had gazed into Susan's eyes there was no other relationship. There was nothing else to think about but the future. There was only a marvelous future with the sensational Susan Weeks. A future he wanted to get started on right away.

He picked up the phone to dial her number. He didn't know her number, of course. They had just met last night. That reminded him how ridiculous this all was. His mind was planning a life with a girl and he didn't even know her phone number. Without slowing down, he dug into the night stand for his local phone book. There was no listing. Damn, Luke thought, how could he get her number? And then he remembered her roommate. He flipped through to look for Jennifer Holt and dialed immediately.

"Hi, this is Jennifer. We're not home now, but please leave us a message after the beep". The beep sounded. It stunned Luke. He was expecting to hear that glorious voice on the other end and not a machine. He didn't want to talk to a machine; he wanted to talk to Susan. With nothing to say, he hung up.

Luke sat by the phone and wondered why Susan hadn't answered. His mind raced with all sorts of notions. He cursed under his breath for having left her the night before while his mind considered the possibilities before him. Why hadn't she answered? The first thought that came to him was that she was humiliated that he had left and now never wanted to speak to him or see him again. Or, his intense feelings were his alone and she was not really interested in seeing him again, anyway. Still not good.

Maybe she wasn't awake. Maybe. Luke looked at the clock and realized it was only six thirty a.m., the time when he usually took his morning run. Most people slept in on Saturday and that was what Susan was doing. He needed to put in his six miles and when he got back she would be up.

Within minutes he was dressed and ready to go. Outside, he started the routine. He always preceded his run with five minutes of stretching and then did the six miles in about forty-five minutes, walking it out for five more. That would put him back in the house in less than an hour. Susan would be awake by then and they could talk with clear heads. He wanted to run to her house and wake her but decided to stick to his routine. He completed the warm-up and headed down the street.

Luke's muscles slowly relaxed as he fell into the rhythm of the run. He let his mind go and take in the scenery. It was October in Hampton and, while the area didn't have much in the way of autumn, there were already decorations of the season on many of the houses. It was also Halloween.

There were witches, ghosts and the like flying from trees and porches along the street. Some of the houses had beautiful wreaths on the doors with gold, orange and black frills. Many had yards filled with brilliantly colored leaves exemplifying the efforts of the residents. The streets would be lined with kids that night and the air filled with trick-or-treat, the trees with rolls of toilet paper. At Webster Avenue, Luke made his usual turn and cut through the school yard. His feet slashed across windblown piles of leaves from the huge pecan trees. At the back side of the playground he hopped the fence and struck out along Palmetto Drive. As he passed the halfway mark at the school his legs started moving him along faster and faster. The run cleared his head and he was anxious to get back to his house. Whatever help Susan needed he would straighten out. He would handle it himself. He needed to get back to the house and get hold of Susan. He had to tell her how he felt on a personal level. He would handle the professional but his personal, private intimate feelings for her were so strong it was overpowering and had to be dealt with first. The night before he was not sure whether it was love or lust that filled him. Today, he was sure.

The thought frightened him. Luke was embarrassed about his behavior the night before, bolting out on her like that. She was probably angry with him and had every right to be. He had to get to her soon and explain. A smile came over him as he thought of that lovely face. How would it look with anger? Luke couldn't imagine it being anything but magnificent. He tried to envision the black eyebrows knit together, sparks flying from her green eyes, luscious lips set firmly together. The image stirred him and he leaped to his porch as the house came in sight. He practically ripped off the door as he bounded into the house and grabbed the phone.

Luke quickly dialed her number and after the same three rings the answer machine responded again. This time he was concerned. Maybe she really was angry. Maybe his middle-of-the-night departure had upset her so that she was dismissing him and this was her way of doing it. When the beep came, he started to say something but when he opened his mouth no words came out, so he hung up again.

Luther Lambert sat in the front room of his house finishing his morning coffee and reading the paper. There was not much to the Saturday edition of the Hampton News, so he also read the Jackson paper. Finishing up the last section he folded it on the floor beside him and gazed out the window. The morning sun was tipping over the houses across the street and into his window. It always bothered him that his house faced east. Sitting in the morning sun required that he come up to the formal living room or go out on the front porch. For thirty years in this house he complained that he was going to sell it and get another with the kitchen and breakfast area toward the day's first light.

Luther was not a happy man. Never quite comfortable. The chair he sat in this morning was not quite big enough for his hulking, six-foot-two inch frame. He was fifty-five years old and more than fifty-five pounds overweight. He needed to do something about it but could never get away from all the other demands in his life to concentrate the right things to correct his corpulence.

He was a bull of a man, in appearance and in character. He had a thin, pointy nose that looked out of place until he was angered and then it flared wide making his breathing sound like a snort. This he kept in check most of the time. Years of running over people to accomplish his own ends allowed his unprincipled maneuvers to operate facilely while maintaining a picture of innocence.

Today, as he surveyed the scene, Luke Daniels came jogging down the block. He already knew that Luke Daniels was with Susan Weeks the night before. Little that went on in the town escaped Luther Lambert. He wondered about their companionship. They were both single. Was it a date? He was curious about what brought them together.

His earlier conversation with Jerry Mason was brief. Jerry assured him that Susan Weeks would not talk. That was a relief. He couldn't stand the idea of that little bitch screwing up his arrangement. Things were going too smoothly. The studio, DeWeese Advertising, was doing well and he didn't want to lose it. Not right now, anyway. He had plans for it.

Jim DeWeese had been an advertising genius from his first days of college. His professors saw in him natural ability that pegged him for greatness in the advertising world. Others saw it as well, and he landed a job right out of college with a Los Angeles agency and went straight to the top. In just a few years he and another of the firm's whiz kids left the company and started their own firm. However, the fast life of Los Angeles took its toll on him.

Along with many of his high paying clients, he dabbled in drugs, particularly cocaine. So, as fast as he went up, he came down. He came down hard. Three years into his venture, the cocaine was eating up his creativity and his money. The partner with whom he shared the agency also shared the addiction. They fought bitterly on a regular basis.

Almost overnight the business crumbled down around them. With creditors at their door and business nearly gone, DeWeese packed up his few belongings and moved back to his hometown of Hampton.

Moving in with his parents he shook the cocaine habit. Almost. He still had the desire.

But most of the time he avoided it. His health began to return. With his mother's cooking he gained back weight, leaving behind the gaunt look of the Los Angeles life. His blonde hair was beginning to thin, but he had worked out and put himself into much better health. Slowly he was back to his old self. His creative genius, only slightly tarnished, began to surface. With the help of an old friend of his dad's, he opened DeWeese Advertising.

That old friend was Luther Lambert. Luther was a very successful lawyer. He was an old codger who fought his way up from the dark side of the tracks in Hampton. Lambert was also an only child raised by a mother whose marriage vows were always uncertain. He never knew his father. He had her story memorized about how his father had been killed in an auto accident coming back to Mississippi from Texas, but that was all he knew. There was nothing about his family. His mother merely left it that her husband had no family. Luther's birth certificate simply said Henry Lambert of Houston, Texas. Whenever he tried to get more out of his mother, she brushed him off and changed the subject. He always swore to himself that he would someday find out about his dad and his family, but he never did. His mother had been dead for ten years and he no longer had the interest or the inclination to know. He had money now. Hell, he was rich. He had crossed the line into millionaire status years ago and by Bedford County standards that was real wealth.

Luther stood up and moved the lace curtains apart with his stocky hand. He watched as Daniels continued on down the street and out of sight. He was curious about what Luke and Susan Weeks had been up to the night before. The last thing he needed right now was that young bastard screwing around in his business.

Luke was smart, and a good lawyer. From his perch of thirty years of law practice in this town it was easy to get an overview of the young lawyers. He could almost tell when they rode into town which ones would make it and which ones wouldn't. His first impression of Daniels was that he had what it took.

Within a few months of Luke's arriving on the legal landscape in Hampton, Lambert had the opportunity to observe Daniels in the courtroom. Lambert watched him maneuver himself through a maze riddled with traps that the experienced opposing counsel had set, beaming with delight as his prey drove deeper and deeper into the ambush.

But it didn't happen. Luke guided himself right out of the situation keeping the best interest of his client shielded with a solid knowledge of the law. Lambert was impressed.

As Lambert watched Luke disappear down the street, he recalled having heard about his recent successes. At Momma Doris' all the talk recently had been about Luke's settlement of a major case. Momma Doris' was a small restaurant where many of the lawyers downtown gathered in the morning to drink coffee and gossip. The rumor was that he had settled a case for a multiple six-figure sum. Some said it was over five hundred thousand and others said five million. Whatever the amount, it was substantial for Hampton, Mississippi. Less than a year ago, Luke had a jury verdict on an insurance malpractice and bad faith case that awarded his client $350,000 in punitive damages over a fire loss. Those two in one year definitely set the boy up as a contender, Lambert thought. Lambert also remembered seeing Luke recently driving a new Cadillac. And last night he was with Susan Weeks. What was that all about? Was the reason libido or legal? He would have to get the low down on that one right away.

Lambert decided to get to his office and contact his investigator, Jerry Mason, to do a little poking around. Daniels might know things that wouldn't be beneficial for Lambert's immediate interests. He certainly didn't want an ambitious young attorney gumming up the works. Not now while he had everyone so well-oiled. That wouldn't do.

With his hand to his chin, Lambert tapped a finger against his lips a few times as he pondered the situation. After a moment he turned from the window and headed back to the bedroom to get ready to go to the office.

From the bedroom, he could see into the open door of the huge closet where his wife was getting dressed. She looked up as he rustled around.

"What can I get you for breakfast, honey?" she asked cheerfully.

"Can't this morning. I've got to get down to the office to see some folks." He glanced at the clock by the bed. It was almost seven-thirty a.m. He threw his robe on the bed and hurried into the shower.

Eloise Lambert came out of the closet and sighed. After thirty years of marriage to this man, she no longer let his absence from the house bother her. He was at the office almost every Saturday and often on Sundays. Or at least that's what he told her. She chose not to doubt him. She understood that it took hard work and a lot of it to earn the kind of money they had. And, she enjoyed the money. She hung up his robe and went to the kitchen to prepare her own breakfast, alone.

At the office, Lambert went immediately to the phone and dialed the number to Mason's pager. He barely got the phone down before his line was ringing. He picked it up knowing it would be Mason.

"Jerry, that you?"

"Yeah, boss, what's up?" Jerry Mason liked referring to Lambert as Boss. It suited them both. Lambert enjoyed the image the term portrayed and Mason fancied himself sidekick to the rich old man. The two egos complimented one another.

Lambert craved the compliment. In his own mind he viewed himself as the boss. Boss Hawg. The great Southern master ruling the plantation. Lambert's plantation was the earthy political terrain of the city of Hampton, Bedford County and the surrounding area. In his own mind, Lambert was Big Daddy. His strategic use of money made it so in other minds too. When Lambert predicted something, it came true because he put enough funding behind it that failure was not an option. He was smart, with the political shrewdness of Attila the Hun.

"We need to talk and not over the phone. How soon can you get down to my office?"

It was a question delivered as a command.

Jerry looked over at his wife. She was bending over at the oven getting biscuits out for their breakfast. He knew she would be furious but he couldn't refuse Lambert so he said, "I'll be right there."

Doris heard his last statement and stood up with the pan of biscuits nestled between two pot holders.

"You'll be right where? You're not going anywhere until we eat," she said only half jokingly. The baby was still asleep and she was looking forward to a nice leisurely breakfast with her husband in the quiet and solitude before their two year old was awake.

Jerry looked at her sheepishly. He didn't want to leave. Her robe was only loosely tied, exposing bosom and leg that beckoned. He wanted to forget the biscuits and take her back to the bedroom or maybe right there on the kitchen table. His appetite was growing just looking at her standing there with tousled head. But he couldn't refuse Lambert. Jerry made the biggest part of his income from cases Lambert got him. Doris didn't understand these things.

"Sorry, girl, duty calls," he stated with an air of importance. Noticing the look in her eyes, he continued, "You know I've been working on something big for the man. I've got to keep the momentum going and he's waiting on me."

Doris slammed the pan of biscuits down on the counter and pulled her robe tighter around her. Jerry winced at her action, realizing that her appetite, too, was for more than breakfast. He grabbed a biscuit and headed out the back door.

"I'll make it up to you, babe, I promise," he said over his shoulder as he closed the door. Through the window, he could see the scowl on her face. God, how he hated to leave right now. But you just didn't keep a man like Lambert waiting.

The coffee pot was just finishing when Lambert heard a knock at the back door of his office. There was a small kitchen in the back of the building that served as a meeting room for Lambert's many conferences. He loved meeting with people in this informal setting. With the coffee pot nearby, he could sit around the kitchen table with certain clients, chew tobacco, spit and drink coffee. In the evening hours it served as a bar with the basics: bourbon, scotch and gin. The big man liked to make his guests feel at home here.

At the same time, it was his own turf. He was a master at lulling others into a false sense of security, drawing them into his confidence as if they were the most important thing in the world to him. They rarely were. His mind only worked on what would profit him. Not always money, but always to his advantage in one way or another.

Lambert let Jerry in. Jerry was barely thirty and looked even younger. His thick brown hair was always parted and combed perfectly, never a hair out of place. Bushy brown eyebrows made a straight line over eyes the same color as his hair. He had a square face and a square body that gave him a dense look. His dark complexion and nearly six foot frame made him almost attractive if it wasn't for the doltish look he presented. His hair and complexion shined but it was not enough to cover the dull in his eyes. They grabbed coffee and gabbed about the weather and other vacuity until Lambert stood up to replenish his cup.

"So, how is work going on the DeWeese case," Lambert asked almost casually.

Jerry loved it. Lambert was an expert at asking about something without really asking about it. The question concerned Jerry's meeting with Susan Weeks. But instead of going right to the point, Lambert had to play the game. Lambert had him keeping an eye on DeWeese and the agency Lambert's money had set up. It was how Luther had originally found out about the pictures.

"Great. Everything is coming together fine. We should be able to have everyone in the right negotiating posture." Jerry was afraid of saying too much. The way Lambert kept himself above the fray worried Jerry at times. There had been other situations where he had handled something when Lambert blew up at him for going too strong. Lambert put things in such a way that there was no mistaking exactly what was to be done. But later, Lambert acted as if he didn't know why Jerry had done something the way he did. Jerry always wondered just how Lambert would handle it if things blew up. He didn't have to wonder much. He suspected that the wily old lawyer would protect himself and Jerry would have to do the same. For that reason, Jerry had taken to holding back on telling Lambert everything. It was best if some things were left unsaid. He had learned that much from Lambert.

The smug response angered Lambert. "Right negotiating posture." Jerry's attitude worried Lambert sometimes. But he couldn't do everything himself. He looked down at Jerry over his glasses.

"I saw Luke Daniels out jogging this morning. You said he was with this Weeks girl last night." It was a question Mason had already answered.

"Yeah, they met at the Magnolia around six and then went back out to her place." Jerry knew Lambert wanted more, but he enjoyed having something Lambert wanted, so he usually dragged it out.

"How long were they together?" Lambert was irritated with Mason.

"He went home around midnight. They were at her house for several hours. No one else was there and there where no lights on for a long time. I think they were doing the hokey-pokey," Mason smiled at his own witticism. Lambert was getting more irritated by the minute.

"Hell, Jerry, just tell me what you know." Lambert demanded.

"I don't really know any more," Jerry responded sullenly. The fierceness of Lambert's tone stunned Jerry. Jerry would say no more. He had been bullied by this man before, but not this morning.

Lambert plopped down in his chair and looked at Mason across the table. Lambert wiped his hand across the lower part of his face and decided to let it be for now. This was a delicate situation that needed to be handled with a cool head. He still didn't know if Daniels learned anything from Susan Weeks, but for now he would wait.

There was a noise at the back door which startled them. Keys jangled and the door opened. Lambert was on his feet only to see Arlita Johnson standing there with a new mop in her hand.

"Oh, Mr. Lambert, I didn't know you was here. I can come back later. You know I likes to do my big cleaning when no one is around. But I can come back; I can come back." Lambert always made Arlita nervous.

Arlita came every night to clean the office. The light stuff, anyway: emptying trash, ash trays, vacuuming, cleaning up any messes left by the white folk. She did her serious cleaning over the weekend when she had more time and no one was around. She didn't like being in the office when there were people in the building. She always felt like she was in the way.

"No, no, Arlita, you come right on. We were just finishing up. Besides, you won't bother us a bit. You go ahead. This place needs a good cleaning."

She tried to escape but Lambert would have it no other way. Arlita came on in, grabbed a few trash bags out of the closet and went straight up to the front of the building. She could busy herself up there and maybe they would leave. She got the vacuum cleaner out and went right to work.

Lambert set his coffee cup in the sink, saw Jerry out the back and headed to his desk to make a few phone calls. He could hear the vacuum running up front and was sure Arlita couldn't hear what he was saying. He finished quickly and as he was about to leave, caught his reflection in the mirror hanging outside the door. The sports shirt bulged around the sleeves from large arms that used to be muscle. The close-cropped hair needed a trim. His jowly face was red from the tension of Jerry, making him look more puffy than normal. Maybe after taking care of a little business he'd get out and get some fresh air on the golf course.

Jerry Mason left in a foul mood. He thought about going back to Doris but was sure she was no longer in a tender mood. He decided to drop by his old stomping grounds, the police department, and see what was cooking. Jerry worked for the Hampton PD for five years before becoming a private investigator. He had started off in patrol, worked there for four years and was then transferred to the detective division where he worked until he struck out on his own. His ego always got a boost when he dropped by and today would be a good day for a boost.

Things were often quiet on Saturday mornings. The administrative personnel at the department were not around and the detective division would be relaxed. Unless, of course, Friday night had been active. Then things jumped.

Jerry pulled his Chevy around to the back of the station to let himself in through the coded locked door. He punched in the same old code, 19-05-24, and smiled at the inside joke of those numbers. They corresponded with the letters of the alphabet: s-e-x. This was a domain where macho was in full swing. Hampton had no female officers. There were a few women in administration or with city court but they were only secretarial types. All the commissioned policemen were just that - men. And that's the way they liked it. That way they could carry on about their sexual prowess, berate their wives, chew tobacco, burp, fart, and generally do other manly things without females around to get in the way. Male domination was the unspoken philosophy of this department from top to bottom.

This morning things were slow. There were three detectives in with whom Jerry had worked. Dick Limox was at his desk, Jimmy Crowley and Tom Feder were standing at the coffee pot. There were donuts on the table.

"Hey, guys, what's up?" Jerry sailed into the room.

"Jerry, my man, you're out early," Jimmy started off. "How about a donut?"

The lone biscuit he had snatched at the house was fading and the donuts looked good. Why is it police always have donuts, Jerry mused. Right now he was glad they did.

"How about that coffee? Can you spare another cup?"

"You got it, bud." Tom called everybody bud. He pulled out one of the Styrofoam cups and filled it up for Jerry. "How do you take it?"

"Hot and black, just like I like my women," came the response from Jerry. The old joke never failed as snickers went around the room.

"I'll bet Doris doesn't appreciate that little quirk," Dick said with a grin. Dick and Doris were distant cousins. Some familial relation Jerry never could keep straight. Dick had attended Pearl River Community College never earning the associate's degree. He was in his thirties now and still taking college courses. The perpetual student, he would take one at the community college and then one at University of Southern Mississippi in Hattiesburg. Jerry thought he should surely have a degree by now. No one knew how many hours he had or whether he passed or failed the courses. Dick didn't talk much about it other than to always be sure his higher ups knew he was working on his degree. That was how he made sergeant; he was working on a degree. The guy gave new meaning to the term continuing education.

Jerry, set up with the coffee and donuts, pulled up a chair at Dick's desk.

"This desk looks like a man at work, brother. What y'all got going on?" Jerry said with his good old boy drawl.

"I've got cases here I don't know what to do with. You know how it is, Jerry. We're loaded down to the gills and can't work on what we got for new stuff coming in." Dick's tone indicated exasperation as he swiped his hand through the wiry hair that stuck out on top of his head.

They talked on for the better part of the morning about anything, everything and nothing until it was time for lunch. Jimmy had left on a call at some point, and Tom was waiting on his girlfriend, so Jerry and Dick headed out for a burger. DiBetto's was only a few blocks away, the best greasy cheeseburger in town.

"Wanna take my car?" Jerry offered.

"No, I got to get out on a case as soon as we finish. Better take my own. I'll see you there," Dick replied as he popped open the door on his unmarked Buick. Jerry got in his car and they drove off to DiBetto's.

The afternoon sky filled with dark clouds that began to rumble and roar. Before long the sun was blocked out and by five o'clock Hampton was in a downpour. The rain fell in sheets that frustrated all activity. Trick-or-treaters had long since gone scurrying for cover. Luke stood on his front porch watching a few teenagers in costumes dancing in the deluge, their faces runny with the makeup of a former masquerade that gave a macabre appearance to their frolicking. He dumped the last of the candy in one sack, went inside and shut the door behind him. The rain brought a chill to the house that made him shiver. He wished he could get a fire going to throw off the damp but there was no wood in the house.

He wished he had Susan there to share a fire with him but he hadn't reached her all day. One more time he picked up the phone and dialed her number. The same recording played again that he had heard countless times earlier after which the beep sounded with him saying nothing. He could not talk to the machine. At first he was sure he would get her later and then he was so unsettled by not reaching her that he had nothing to say and now he would just hold the phone with a temporary lapse in reason. Earlier he was certain when he talked with her everything would be fine. Now he didn't know what to think. So he did nothing. Nothing but mope around his house and listen to the rain.

The rain beat a rhythm that drove his mood into deeper and deeper gloom. Twenty-four hours ago exactly, he noticed as he glanced at the clock on the stove, he had laid eyes on Susan Weeks for the first time. His disposition changed then, too, but in the other direction. From first sitting down at the table he was thrilled by her company. Each moment that passed with her escalated the pleasure, like he was on a ride at the fair that only had good parts, making him glad he had used his ticket. Now the best part of the ride was over. He was descending, falling into despair because he wasn't with her. Where was she? Damn it, didn't she know he wanted her, wanted to talk to her?

How could she? He left in the middle of the night like a thief, a criminal. A swindler who snatched her love in the midst of passion and desire and then stole away into the dark. All day long he berated himself for his behavior. It was so unlike him. Luke Daniels, who prided himself on his genuineness of spirit and straightforward feelings. Solid like a rock.

Luke couldn't get over his behaving without any sense of propriety. He deserved it if she never spoke to him again. Looking back, he couldn't believe he had been such a fool as to get up and leave her side. Clearly now, he saw that he should have stayed and held on to her forever. 'Susan, please forgive me,' he said aloud for no one but himself to hear. 'I need a second chance.'

The rain in Hampton did not extend to the beautiful Mississippi Gulf Coast where Jennifer Holt was spending her Halloween. She and four of her college sorority sisters were together for the first time in almost a year. The five of them had been inseparable in college and maintained a steadfast sisterhood since graduation three years ago. Barbie Blair lived in Hattiesburg and the other three, Janie Desporte, Sarah Longcoy, and Shelly Osbourne, lived on the coast. It was Janie's idea that they get together for Halloween. Grand Casino was having a costume party and on the Gulf Coast, where Mardi Gras was a staple of the social scene, everyone loved to get dressed up. Janie convinced them all that last year's party was one they shouldn't have missed. And poor Barbie was separated from her husband of only one year. She needed some perking up and Janie was sure this would be just the thing.

It didn't take much convincing for Jennifer. Her social life in Hampton had reached rock bottom. Those jokers at the bank who constantly tried to hit on her thought a good time was getting her out for a drink and telling her how their wives didn't understand them. She was sick of them and sick of Hampton. She jumped at the chance to get out of town, if only for the weekend.

She and Barbie were staying with Janie who had a condo on the beach. Well, almost. You didn't really get on the beach here in Mississippi. But at certain spots along Highway 90 the beach was right across the street. The place was nice. Janie's family had money and her mother helped her fix it up magnificently. The living room was all white: walls, carpet, drapes, and leather sofa. It was a daring choice that Jennifer would never have gone for herself but was crazy about as soon as she saw it. The dining table was two white elaborate pedestals with a glass top. Everywhere you looked was white but with a diversity of textures and treatments that gave the room total elegance.

It suited Janie. She herself was elegance personified. Not the snooty rich bitch kind, but someone from whom affluence and grandeur exuded out of the very pores of her radiant and flawless skin. Janie always made them feel welcome in her ivory haven on the beach. Even Barbie was livening up as they toasted each other with champagne. Janie always said it was hard not to have a good time when you were drinking champagne. And she was right.

As they waited on the other girls to arrive, Jennifer thought about the evening. They were first going to stop by a party that some friends of Janie's parents were giving but her mind was racing ahead to the costume gala at Grand Casino.

"Janie, how long do you think we'll be at the Bertucci's party?"

"Oh, not long. We just need to stop in and say hi. You know how mother is. She's got to see us in our costumes," Janie said with a sparkle. She did sparkle. Her costume tonight was also all white. "Snowy Pocahontas," she called herself. It was a soft, supple leather top and skirt adorned with all sorts of white beads, crystal jewels that sparkled like diamonds and white feathers. There was also a head dress that fit her head like a cap with a mask, all in white leather and feathers. She looked astonishing. Her dark complexion glowed under the white dressing.

"How do I look? Ya'll like it."

"Janie, you're too much," Barbie remarked.

"Me? Have you looked in the mirror?" Janie shot back with a laugh.

Barbie was a real life nurse and tonight she had taken her profession to the height of eroticism. She had on a nurse's uniform that had been altered for the occasion to fit her like a glove. The top button strained to keep itself in place from the pressure of her ample bosom. The push up bra gave her a look that would make Dolly Parton blush. The skirt had been taken up to about six inches above her knee and barely covered her butt. Underneath the skirt which you could see through the thin material was a white garter belt that stretched down her legs to white stockings with a seam down the back and a shimmering glisten down her long legs into the highest spike heels Jennifer had ever seen. Her hair was pulled up in a sexy pile with a white pencil stuck in it and, around her neck, to finish the effect, was a stethoscope.

"Girlfriend, you are going to knock 'em dead. You're going to have guys falling out at your feet just to get in your hospital," Janie said with a cackle as they convulsed with laughter. "And get a load of Miss Jennifer."

Jennifer was dressed in red silk. There was no tail but there was no mistaking the intent: she-devil. A red mask was painted on her face across the eyes with red streaks that stretched into her blonde hair. The hair swooped up into a sophisticated French twist with a tiara on top that gave her an aristocratic air. The sleeveless dress dipped in the back to a shocking level that would not let her hide the fact that she was wearing nothing underneath, even if she had wanted to. She had on a rhinestone choker and an exquisite pair of rhinestone earrings. Matching red high heels, long red gloves and a red feather boa finished off the outfit.

The door bell rang. It was Sarah and Shea. They came in amid more peals of laughter over the wild costumes. Janie immediately started herding them all to the door with Jennifer's help, and they were off.

Jennifer awoke Sunday morning with a slight hangover. She had downed quite a few drinks the night before, and, oh, what a night they had. These were some great friends that she dearly cherished. She wished she had pressed harder for Susan to come down with her. Susan would fit right in. Maybe next time. She looked over at the clock. It was almost ten and they were supposed to meet up for champagne brunch at the Isle of Capri Casino. Janie stuck her head around the corner.

"There's coffee in the kitchen if you're ready."

"Sounds great. And, how about some aspirin?"

"I think I can handle that."

An hour later they were off for another day. Sarah had called and some guys were joining them. Brunch was going to be wonderful. Jennifer reminded herself and then Barbie that they had to drive back today. It was only about an hour to Hampton but she wanted to be home before dark. She made a mental note to be ready to leave at five o'clock.

CHAPTER FOUR

⚖

Jennifer Holt arrived back in Hampton Sunday evening just as the sun dropped to the horizon. There was still light out as she pulled into the driveway at home in Willow Oaks. Dusk was upon her as she followed the way into the garage. The door went up to reveal two empty spaces. She wondered where Susan might be as she pulled her luggage out of the trunk and made it to the door.

The door was unlocked as usual since the garage door always locked down into place. The inside door opened to a small room that was all doors hiding a closet, the heating, a pantry, a small bathroom, and the door to her bedroom. She dropped her bags and walked on to the kitchen straight ahead. The table in the breakfast room was messy, crumbs scattered over it, she noticed. It was unlike Susan to leave a mess; she was usually neater than Jennifer.

A cold front had followed the rain into south Mississippi and the house was chilly. There was the feeling that no heat had been on all day. Jennifer walked into the den to the thermostat to get some heat going. There were no lights on in the house but all the backyard floods were on. They must have been on all night, she thought, and fine with her. They often left the outsides on all night for security. It made them both feel better.

There were two wine glasses sitting on the coffee table. What had Susan been up to, she mused. The stereo was still on. Jennifer grinned and turned to go back to her bedroom when something caught her eye. The lion sculpture overturned, broken and lying in the middle of the front foyer. It usually sat by the end of the wall that led down the hall to Susan's bedroom at the other end of the house. Jennifer stopped for a moment in place. She took a few steps toward the foyer and noticed several gashes in the wood floor with chips off the lion. Suddenly her mouth went dry and she was holding her breath.

This is silly she thought as she shook off the momentary panic that had gripped her. She called out Susan's name and there was no answer. Almost without thinking she started down the hall that led to Susan's bedroom. She refused to let herself be frightened yet the whole time she was trembling, pulse racing.

Before she got to the bedroom door she could see the splintered wood of the facing shattered into pieces that lay about on the floor. Inside she saw the bed left a mess with covers on the floor and pillows askew. Jennifer wanted to turn and run but her body would not cooperate. She knew she should get out of there and fast but she didn't turn. Slowly she moved closer to Susan's room. Without thinking, without breathing she reached the doorway and looked around the room. Everything seemed to be in place except for the messed up door and the bed.

The bed was a complete wreck. Sheets were loose around the edges, the comforter off to one side and one pillow was on the floor. Suddenly she saw the foot and part of the leg. Inside her head a voice was screaming, 'Run, Jenn, run!' but she couldn't. She stepped through the doorway to the foot of the bed and then on over to the side. It was there that she saw Susan Weeks' nude body, her head laying in a puddle of blood.

Every muscle in Jennifer tightened as she convulsed. The voices came back again, run, Jennifer, run. But she couldn't. She couldn't breathe, she couldn't move, she couldn't speak. Fear immobilized her. Her head sent out the message to back up, back up. She backed into the dresser, leaning against it in terror. Her hands gripped the edge and suddenly pushed against it, moving her body forward. She darted through the door and down the hall, picking up speed. She checked herself at the front door, the quickest way out of the house, yanked it open and flung herself out.

She was running now down the drive. Away. Away from the house was her only thought. All her energy focused on movement away from the house. She couldn't even scream. She couldn't even stop. When she saw the car, it was barely moving. It stopped but she didn't. She slammed into the front fender, rolled over the hood and fell in the street on the other side. The driver immediately jumped out and knelt down beside her.

"Help us, help us, help us," she said in a whisper before she closed her eyes and lost consciousness entirely.

Fire rescue responded in less than four minutes to the scene of the accident and Mobile Medic was there shortly afterwards. Another car down the street saw what had happened and dialed 911 who dispatched help immediately. A Hampton patrol unit pulled up next.

The medical team checked her over and found no serious injuries - no broken bones and cervical spine manipulation was okay. However, she had a pretty large scrape on her forehead.

"She's in shock." It was one of the paramedics who finally spoke up, tucking the blanket around her.

From the depths of her subconscious Jennifer could sense all the activity around. She didn't know where she was or what was going on. She must be dreaming, she thought. Somebody was outside and something was going on out there. She felt a push from within to get up and see about it. She had to rouse herself and go see what was happening. There were a lot of people talking. Faintly she heard a dog barking in the distance. She was cold. She needed to get up anyway and turn on some heat. She shivered.

"Hey, this is not good. We're losing her fast. Let's get some vital signs. Eyes are fixed and dilated." He put the stethoscope to her chest. "Heart beat's weak and irregular."

"Blood pressure 70 over 40. She's barely with us, guys. We've got to do something fast."

Jennifer was fighting inside to get up. She wanted to see what the commotion was all about. And, there was something else, too that she had to tell them. Tell them what? She knew she had to wake up but couldn't. Maybe she should pinch herself awake.

The medic prepared an IV to start getting fluids into her system. He pulled her sweater up and stuck the catheter into her arm.

"Oww!" Jennifer jerked her arm and her eyes fluttered and opened. She looked right into the face of the paramedic with fear in her eyes. She tried to get up but he wouldn't let her.

"Hold on there, young lady, you're going to be alright. But you need to be still."

"Help Susan"

"Don't try to talk right now. Just lie still." He used his most soothing tone. "

"No, I'm alright. You've got to help Susan." She felt so weak her voice was barely more than a whisper. She tried to tell him louder, "You've got to help Susan."

"What is your name?" was the response she received.

"Jennifer Holt. I live right there." She tried to point. "My room mate is in there and she's hurt."

The paramedic called the policeman who stood over her listening. She felt stronger now, but they would not let her sit up. In bits and pieces she finally was able to relate what she found when she arrived home. Astounded by her story, the patrolman went to his car radio and requested backup. He walked on up to the house where he found the front door open. He stepped inside warily and flipped on his flashlight. The house was dark. He set one foot down in front of the other slowly as he proceeded down the hall anxious about what he was going to find. His radio squawked and he jumped. The girl said her roommate was in the end bedroom. He noticed the splintered facing on the door and then his flashlight caught the bare leg and followed it up to the head. It was not a pretty sight.

Stepping back quickly, he went down the hall, out the front door to the fresh air and took several deep breaths before getting on the radio to dispatch. He confirmed his earlier call and asked that a detective be sent out.

Detective Sergeant Dick Limox was off duty and had just finished his work-out at the gym when he heard the call over the police radio in his car about a Signal 25, the department code for a death. Every police department around the country had a signal code for use on the airwaves which designated various offenses. The codes avoided announcing over the radio what they were dealing with. Police scanners were not limited to police and so the code numbers were used to give them a language of their own without telling the world what they were doing. They covered everything from a Signal 1 for an auto accident to a Signal 18 for out to get a cup of coffee. These were used in conjunction with the 10 codes such a 10-4 for affirmative and 10-20 for your location or 10-37 which meant you were out to eat.

The call Sergeant Limox heard was 10-99 on a signal 25 which meant that the officer needed emergency assistance on a death and gave the address as 313 Birch Place. He knew instinctively that this was one he needed to be in on. Promotions came to people who had the high profile cases and a death in the Willow Oaks area would be a good one. Nice houses and people with money. Probably a murder and if he were first on the scene it would be his case even if he were off duty. A cop was never really off duty. Whenever he was in his car he was 10-8 meaning in service. He picked up the radio to notify dispatch he would be in route.

"63 to Hampton."

"Go ahead, 63."

"I'm responding to that Signal 25 on Birch."

"10-4."

He was only a short distance from Willow Oaks and was tempted to put on his blue light. The call had been for emergency assistance, but instead he just broke all traffic rules without the light. The thrill was already pumping inside him. A death. Possible murder. The bad guys against the coppers. He pushed the pedal down hard, accelerating on the street toward the entrance to the subdivision. Within minutes he was at the scene.

Walking up the drive the patrolman briefed him on what he saw in the house. Realizing now that the girl must have been dead for some time, the Patrolman shook off his earlier fear and led Limox down the hall to the bedroom.

As soon as he saw the splintered door and the disheveled bed, he mentally established a probable murder. Foul play had been unleashed in this room and he sensed it wouldn't be a pretty sight. Immediately he was staring down at a nude body - a fine nude body, he thought, after positioning himself closer to the corpse. The face was obscured by the girl's long black hair matted together in what had once been a pool of blood around the head but was now nearly dry.

"Looks to me like about two days ago," Limox said flatly, with the tone of a seasoned detective, as if murder was a regular occurrence in this quiet Southern town. Of course there were murders, but rarely of this type. What the Hampton police department usually found were two drunks killing one another. Or dopers. This had the feel of something different. Yeah, real different, Limox thought. This just might be different enough to move him into the next lieutenant spot that opened up.

"We need to get Dunnigan out here right away," he said aloud. He pulled his radio off his hip and put the call through. Dunnigan was also a detective, not yet a sergeant, and their chief crime scene investigator. All the detectives did crime scenes but Dunnigan had developed a special affinity to all the detail work this would require. With Dunnigan on his way, Limox walked around the house taking in details. Force in the form of a big strong foot had kicked the bedroom door in. He noticed the lion in the foyer and the scuff marks, the two wine glasses on the table in front of the sofa. Probably good finger prints. There wasn't much else so he went down to the street to talk with the roommate and see what she knew.

The conversation with Jennifer Holt revealed nothing more than her coming home a short while ago and finding her friend. Jennifer was a good looking girl and Limox thought he saw her noticing the definition in his arm muscles, showing prominently from his recent workout. The talk concluded when Dunnagin arrived. They went to the house and the detectives started the process of collecting evidence. The coroner was called, as was the District Attorney. Before long the house was filled with people working on the case.

The District Attorney for Bedford County was William Porter Gafford. Billy Gafford finished law school and went directly to work as an assistant DA in the Hampton office. He worked in that capacity under Luther Lambert for several years until Luther was defeated by Jack Raybern in a bitter, nasty, mud-slinging election that cast a pall over the whole county because of its viciousness. Raybern accused Lambert of having New Orleans Mafia connections and of using the position to line his own pockets. The allegations were partly truth and partly fiction. No one ever knows for sure about the Mafia but there was no question about the personal gain Lambert had reaped from the office.

Lambert tried in vain to paint Raybern as an alcoholic do-nothing that would give free rein to the criminal element in Hampton. He even spread stories about Raybern having tried marijuana in college. Nothing would take root. There were stories about Lambert making large donations to certain churches in order to get the pastor and then the congregation behind him, but it didn't work. In the end, the bitterly fought-for votes turned up in Raybern's favor and Lambert was out.

Lambert conceded graciously, saying he was anxious to get back into the private practice of law and to his many business interests in Hampton and elsewhere. He went so far as to say he had even considered not running to begin with, which was a lie. He had fought hard to keep the office and the power and prestige that went with it. Those were the things he hated to lose most of all and secretly he vowed that he would get them back, one way or another.

Raybern only held the office for one term. He made the mistake of keeping on the assistant D.A., Billy Gafford. Billy practically worshiped at the feet of Lambert and wanted to follow him to private practice. But, Lambert didn't offer him a position. Something about how he would need some time to get re-established and generate business. The truth was Lambert thought Billy a little slow and not that good a lawyer. The only reason he was worth keeping around was that he did what he was told. So after the election Lambert devised a different plan for Billy.

In the forty-five days before Raybern took office, Lambert convinced Billy that he should stay where he was. He explained that the experience he would gain from working under two different prosecutors would make him the better lawyer and possible candidate later on. Lambert was a master of persuasion, filling the young attorney's head with sights of future glory.

Billy was not hard to convince. With little in the way of options he began to suck up to Jack Raybern, who, out of imprudent sympathy, let him stay on.

Lambert was positively tickled at his own insidious dealings. On the surface he made a big show of letting bygones be bygones, when all the time he was plotting ruthlessly for the future. Over the next few years he groomed Billy as his own personal minion. Billy became addicted to the attention and little favors Lambert showered on him and his family, all done so discreetly that no one else knew a thing. Nothing. Until the election four years later when Lambert financed Billy in his own campaign for District Attorney.

Raybern chose not to run for another term. Certain things leaked out about him that were less than favorable; things collected by Billy and channeled to Lambert. Packages of items began arriving in the mail: pictures of Raybern's car at a motel in Jackson, pictures of a Puerto Rican woman leaving his house. Without any explanation other than his interest in his private practice, Raybern chose not to run. Several others jumped into the race at the last minute, but with Lambert's money and connections, the election went to William Porter Gafford.

Billy idolized Lambert for helping him develop his political career. He tried to mimic him in every way, even wearing his hair short in the same Lambert style. Billy was nearly the same height as Lambert but twenty years younger, prompting many to start calling him Luther, Jr. Billy, dense as he was, thought it was a compliment.

That was eleven years ago. Billy had been out of law school now for nearly twenty years and had never done anything else but prosecute criminals. He was good, but it was hard to do anything for twenty years and not be halfway good. After a while all the cases were the same: the same offenses and the same faces. Only the names changed, and even they didn't change that often. In this day and age of revolving door prisons Billy Gafford found himself prosecuting the same people over and over again. Druggies that did their time came right back and did the same things over again. Petty thieves that went to prison and learned how to be serious thieves came back and got caught again and went back to prison. Billy was bored with it all.

However, at this point he couldn't leave. If he would stay in the state's employ just five more years he could take his retirement and go in with a firm. Hopefully, Luther Lambert's. Luther's son was in with him now. There was another lawyer working there but he was not a serious contender. They never were. Over the years Lambert always kept a string of two or three young lawyers working for him mainly as attendants to his whims. They practiced law as Luther Lambert told them to do. They would stick around until they tired of his tyrannical oppression and then escape. Most struck out on their own, hanging out a shingle and hoping for the best. Few went to other firms because most of the other firms didn't want to have anything to do with any lawyer that had been associated with Lambert.

Billy knew he would be different. Lambert never promised anything, but it was sort of unspoken that in a few more years Billy would come on down to the firm and it would be Lambert and Gafford, Attorneys-at-Law. Or Lambert, Gafford and Lambert, now that young Wilson Lambert was in with his dad. That wouldn't be asking too much. After all, look at the experience Billy had earned. Yes, that had a nice sound to it. Lambert, Gafford and Lambert, Attorneys-at-Law.

Billy was lost in these thoughts at his home on Sunday evening. His wife and three kids were at church and he was enjoying the solitude when the phone rang. He roused himself up from his chair and, on the phone, listened to the police department describe the murder. The house where it happened belonged to Bud Holt, an attorney in Hampton. Billy decided he'd better get out there and take a look at the scene. He didn't want that bozo Limox screwing things up for him later on. And besides, the news media would be there and it never hurt to be able to crow to them.

On Monday morning the Hampton News carried the story of the murder front page. There was a picture of the covered body being carried out of the house on a stretcher and another of the D.A. with a statement saying how shocked he was at the brutal slaying of a beautiful girl. There was an explanation from the roommate about what she found when she came home with a biography on Susan Weeks, also secured from Jennifer, both employed by Guaranty National Bank. There was no comment from the bank.

All the talk that morning downtown at Momma Doris's was about the murder. Several of the lawyers knew her and so there were several descriptions about what a looker she was, along with several other theories on the motive for the murder. The paper quoted the coroner and the crime scene investigator as placing the death at some time around midnight. The District Attorney had also stated that it might also be a rape murder. He promised a more detailed report to the press when the autopsy was completed.

Word had already spread among the downtown crowd that Susan Weeks had been with Luke Daniels on Friday night and speculation was rampant. There is no worse group of people for fanning rumors and hearsay than a handful of lawyers. They were riotous with the sensationalism of the news and the fact that the name of one of their own was somehow linked to the tragedy spiced it up even more. Several people saw Luke and Susan together at the Magnolia Friday night and had seen them leaving together. Everybody there had a little something to throw into the melting pot of stories.

"That Susan was one fine looking little lady. Kind of a bitch, though. I went out with her a couple of times a while back. Looked good, but in the beginning she was cold as ice." It was James Germany. He had never gone out with Susan. He had tried but she resisted in her congenial way. She never really said no, she just never said yes, either. Now no one was the wiser so he crowed about his virility.

"The paper said she was working on a Ph.D. I'll bet she made big bucks with the bank," commented Van Weitz.

On-and-on the comments went, which was the normal morning fare at Momma's. The gang had fodder to work on for some time with this one and probably just keep the stories going.

Luke Daniels was oblivious to it all Monday morning. Didn't even look at the paper as he usually did over breakfast. Didn't even eat breakfast. Hadn't run since Saturday morning. He worked himself into a state of depression over being unable to talk to Susan. He tried to put it out of his mind. Then he tried to convince himself it didn't matter. He'd made a wrong decision in leaving her and he was sorry. He thought she would understand if he could just talk to her, but, hey, he hadn't been able to, so that was that.

On the way into the office the thought came to him that she would have to be at work today. He could catch her there. Yesss! She might not take his call but if she didn't he would just walk over to her office and she would have to see him or he would make a scene. He had before. He could be very insistent when he wanted to be. Of course, Susan probably could be also. He sensed a strong will in that girl. She might make a scene and have him thrown out.

Luke arrived at his office without any lightening of his mood. His despondency hung around his neck like a sign saying "No Entry." When he walked through the front door, Jenny took one look at him and was immediately taken aback by his attitude. He didn't say anything as he breezed by her into his office. She wasn't sure what to think. Liz had brought the paper to work with her and they already talked about it. They both knew he had an appointment with this very girl, Susan Weeks, Friday afternoon. But both of them left before she showed. She buzzed Liz.

Liz didn't answer but instead stuck her head through the hall door.

"Did he say anything?" Liz asked.

"Not a word. And he looks awful. Did you see him?"

"No, I was away from my desk when he came in. I'm going in now."

Liz stepped through the hall and into the doorway to Luke's office. He did look kind of rough. Like a bad weekend.

"Well?" she asked.

"Well what?" Luke came back rudely.

"How was your appointment Friday?"

"What appointment? What are you talking about?" Luke was not in the mood to play games and wished she'd get to the point.

"When I left Friday, you had another appointment. A Ms. Weeks was coming in, some kind of urgent matter she had to talk with you about?" Liz nudged at his memory.

"Oh, yeah, Susan Weeks, I saw her. What's the big deal?"

"Nothing, Luke. God, what's wrong with you this morning. I was just wondering if you might have any idea what might have happened to her." She overlooked his brusque manner more than she really wanted to.

Her last statement caught his attention.

"What do you mean, what happened to her?"

"Haven't you seen the papers?" She stepped out to her desk and came back with the front page. She laid the paper down in front of him.

"She's dead, Luke."

The words caught him so unaware that he thought he was going to black out. He looked at the picture in the paper. Saw the front door he left from. Saw the hand sticking out from the covered stretcher. His eyes picked out the word in the headline. "Murder."

Tunnel vision enveloped him and everything turned black. As if from down a long tube, he could see the article, but only one word stood out to him. Murder. He tried to read some of the text but could only focus on the one word. Murder. He could hear Liz talking to him but couldn't make out what she was saying. Murder. His mind raced back over the time since Friday night wondering where Susan had been and now how to find out. Murder. Slowly he started making out some of the words on the paper in front of him. Friday night. Midnight. My god, he thought, I was there at midnight.

Liz stopped in mid-sentence and looked at Luke. He was ashen, like he had seen a ghost. His lips were pale and his eyes seemed glazed over.

"Luke, are you alright?" she asked softly. "Luke?"

"I was there."

"You were where? Are you sure you're alright?" He didn't look alright. He appeared dazed. Unsure, like he didn't know where he was.

"I was there."

"Where?" she asked again.

"At the house," he said barely audibly.

"Who's house?" she asked. "This house?" she asked again. "When?" She sat down in the chair across from his desk.

"At midnight. I left after midnight," Luke was remembering the clock in his car as he drove out the driveway from Susan's house.

Liz was unnerved by his statement. What had he just said? He was at Susan Weeks house after midnight. The paper said she was murdered sometime after midnight.

"What did you say, again, Luke?" She was hoping she had misunderstood him but knew that she had not.

"I was there with Susan Friday night. I left after midnight."

They stared across the desk at each other, neither one of them speaking. Liz was afraid to say anything. She didn't know what Luke was saying to her. She didn't want to hear more.

Luke didn't want to think more. He had thought and thought all weekend about what could have happened to Susan and now this. For two days now he had chastised himself for leaving her. All day Saturday and Sunday he had argued with himself about why she wasn't taking his calls; why she wouldn't pick up the phone; how he wanted to talk to her and explain. But he could never explain. She was dead.

His eyes went back to the article, picking up more of the details. She had died sometime between midnight and four a.m. Found by her roommate Sunday evening. D.A. was investigating as a possible rape murder. My god, he thought, what must have happened? Did some one break in after he left? The article said no visible signs of a break in. He looked back over at Liz, still sitting across the desk. She stared back at him.

Liz didn't know what to think. He was her boss. She had worked for him for how long now, six years. In six years, you'd think you'd know someone. Was he capable of murder? No way.

Was he? What had he said to her there at first? He was there after midnight. What was he doing there after midnight? Liz didn't have her down in the appointment book, but she remembered him telling her it was for five o'clock. He was waiting for her when Liz left on Friday and that was just before five o'clock. Liz didn't know if she should ask any more questions or not. But she couldn't help herself.

"Luke, did you see Susan Weeks in here Friday?" she asked what she thought was a safe question.

"Yes, I mean, no. I didn't see her in here. I did see her, though." He related to Liz how Susan had called and was running late and asked if they could meet somewhere besides his office and maybe get a cup of coffee or something. He went on about how they met at the Magnolia and that it was crowded and they had left and gotten something to eat. He didn't mention that they had two glasses of wine.

"Every place we thought about was crowded. You know how it is on a Friday night in this town. So we got po-boys from Robby's and took them to her house. We talked for a long time and I left there after midnight."

He didn't tell her they drank a whole bottle of wine at Susan's and he didn't tell her they slept together. "Somebody must have broken in on her after I left."

Liz was in overload. It was too early in the morning for her to be taking this all in. She looked back across the desk at Luke and all she could say was, "I need another cup of coffee."

"Yeah, me, too," Luke said. "Will you bring me one?"

Luke never asked Liz to fix his coffee. He never considered it her job to run and fetch for him. It was not something that was a big deal to Liz but something that Luke just had not asked of her. He treated her as a professional legal secretary. But right now he couldn't get up if he tried.

"Well, what did he say?" Jenny wanted to know as Liz poured the coffee.

"Don't ask," was all Liz responded.

This was a law office. Clients came in all the time. All of the communications were confidential. A lot of things Liz told her about and some things she didn't. There were occasions when Jenny suspected some sordid detail in one of the cases handled here that she wanted to gossip with Liz about. And on some of those occasions Liz would admonish her that this was not one to discuss with the simple "Don't ask." This time it was different. Something in her tone had been disturbing, distressful. There was more there than the two simple words. It was a 'Don't intrude on this right now.'

Liz merely picked up the two coffees and headed back to Luke's office. Jenny stood there surprised. Why was Liz so abrupt? The phone started ringing and Jenny had to hurry back out front to her desk to catch it.

Luke was unable to focus on anything. His mind flipped back to Friday night and how easily he and Susan had fallen in together. He recalled how precious she was sitting in his arms on the sofa with the music playing. And, later in the bed. Like two sensual, lustful beasts, they had romped and gamboled across her bed sharing their new found love. While he held Susan next to him it was as if no other woman in the world existed. Yes, he had let himself be carried away with the moment but it was more than that. Much more. In that brief time he had known a love that others only dreamed about. He was certain the fulfillment they shared was a rare jewel. Now he could see that. But now she was gone. And he could never share it with her again. Never tell her about the feelings that filled him to overflowing. Never. Tears welled up in his eyes, a mere flicker of his anguish. He would never be able to hold her again. He would never be able to tell her why he left. It seemed so trifling now. Although he had been worried about his precious ethics, they were meaningless to his ravaged heart. This woman that rekindled love, devotion, desire in him was now no more.

Liz walked back into the office and stopped in mid-stride when she looked at Luke. She'd never seen him like this. She thought she knew him pretty well, but now there was something she didn't recognize. His face was cheerless, his eyes glazed.

"Luke, are you alright?" She knew he was not but didn't know what else to ask.

He looked around to her, finally resting his eyes on Liz's face. His mind was still on having left Susan alone Friday night. Over and over his mind was asking 'Why did you leave her, why, why? What must I have been thinking,' he said half-aloud.

The statement shook Liz down to her toes. Luke was acting weird and she didn't like it. There was a woman dead. Murdered. And her boss was with her the night she was murdered. She didn't like him acting strange like this. She wanted to tell him to straighten up and act right. She didn't really know what to say exactly. She sipped on her coffee and looked at him and asked the same stupid question to which she already knew the answer.

"Luke, are you alright?" She was hoping he would get a hold of himself and start making sense.

He didn't answer. This was giving her the creeps. She stood up from the chair she had taken and left him alone.

At her desk, the phone rang immediately. It was Jenny.

"Liz, Nita just called me and said Mr. Robinson came in from Momma Doris' with the craziest story. He said all the talk up there this morning was about this dead girl and how Luke was out with her Friday night. They were seen together drinking at the Mag."

Liz didn't say anything.

"Liz, did you hear me. That's that girl Luke had an appointment with and they left here and went out. Several people said they were real cozy at the Mag. Can you believe it? Luke taking that girl out like that." Jenny was about to get carried away with gossip.

"They were never here," Liz told her. "She called here after we left and Luke met her at the Magnolia."

"Oh, come on, Liz. Luke met a client outside the office? You know how he is about that. He never does that." Jenny's tone was incredulous.

"I know, I know. But that's what he told me." Liz didn't want to say any more.

"Well, what did she want?" Jenny asked unabashedly.

"He didn't tell me that," Liz replied with a forlorn quality in her voice. There was a lot he didn't tell her that she wondered about. What did the girl want? And, why did Luke meet her away from the office? Jenny was right. He always made a big deal out of that, saying it was best to keep things professional and meet here in the office. Something made this time different, apparently, Liz thought. Her mind wanted to ramble on, but she didn't want it to. She shook it off and said to Jenny, "Look, I don't have time for this. I've got work to do." And with that she hung up the phone and tried to busy herself with the files on her desk.

A few blocks away at the Bedford County Courthouse in the Office of the District Attorney, Billy Gafford sat with Dick Limox talking about the murder of Susan Weeks. The autopsy was not complete yet but the coroner had ruled death from unnatural causes, specifically massive head trauma and severe internal bleeding caused by several brutal blows to the head and face.

The investigators found traces of semen on the girl's leg indicating sexual assault. The DA and the detective were sitting here now trying to come up with their version of just what happened. One thing was clear. What ever had happened in that bedroom on Friday night had been fierce and barbaric. The poor girl's body held injuries from one end to the other. From the friction injury to her vagina she must have been raped numerous times over a several hour period. There were scratch marks on her body where the attacker had almost drawn blood. Skin fragments were found under her fingernails, obviously from her attempts to fight the rapist off. There were fingerprints on all four bed posts. And one really good shoe print from where the bedroom door was kicked in. Police personnel were still on the scene looking for other evidence. What they had was already on its way to the State Crime Lab in Jackson for testing.

"Dick, we're going to have to stay on this one heavy, such a high profile case. I guess you've seen this morning's paper."

"Yeah," Limox replied. He thanked his lucky stars for catching this call on the radio and being the first one on the scene.

"What about the roommate. Do you think she's telling all she knows?" Gafford asked.

"She was pretty shaken up when I got there. I don't believe she's holding anything back.

Weeks just got the wrong character after her. We should know more when we get an evidence report back from Jackson. It was rape. There's no doubt in my mind about that."

"Have you been able to pick up anything on the street?"

"I'm going to work on that today. The victim worked at Guaranty National. I'm checking that out when I leave here."

"Okay, Dick. Keep me posted."

Luther Lambert rushed through the front door of his office with the newspaper under his arm. He sped past the receptionist without even a nod and went straight to his desk. He read the article again and cursed under his breath. Susan Weeks was dead. His mind sifted through the meeting with Jerry Mason on Saturday as anger seethed. Lambert didn't want the girl dead. This could get nasty. He didn't know what happened and feared the worst.

"You've seen the paper?"

Lambert looked up to see his son, Wilson, standing at the door.

"I'll bet you don't know the rest of the story." Young Wilson always loved to be the first to tell his dad something. The older Lambert prided himself on knowing everything in Hampton almost before it happened. Wilson got a sense of elation out of finding out something before the old man. It happened rarely and when it did Wilson milked it for all it was worth, reveling in the feeling of self-importance.

"What is it, Wilson? I haven't got time for your silly games this morning." Lambert looked back at his son with loathing. He didn't have time to be feeding the little twit's ego at a time like this. "Goddammit, son, if you've got something to say, say it. What is it?"

Lambert's harsh tone deflated Wilson's thrill of bringing news to his father. He constantly craved the man's approval and rarely received it.

"I was up at Momma Doris's earlier and guess what the rumor mill was turning out?" Wilson remarked, his cockiness brought down several notches.

"What?" was the only reply Lambert could utter. He was using all his strength to keep from reaching up and throttling his only son.

"It seems that Mr. Luke Daniels was out Friday night with the young lady whose demise you are reading about on the front page of the Hampton News," Wilson said with a snicker, a little of the superior air seeping back into his voice. "They were out drinking at the Magnolia Bar & Grill and several people saw them leaving together. No one saw her alive after that."

Wilson was on a roll now. He realized his father did not know about this and Wilson delighted in the elder's attention.

"Who saw them?" Lambert asked.

"Judge Dahl for one. Oh yeah, and his wife. They talked to them. And a couple of other attorneys, too.

Lambert's brain was clicking. Right off the bat, it whirred around the obvious. Did Daniels kill the girl?

"It wouldn't surprise me if he did it," Wilson said, reading his father's thoughts. "You remember that deposition I had with him. He practically tried to attack me then. I'm sure with a little alcohol in him he could have done a number on this poor girl. She was a looker, too. I've met her several times over at the bank. What a body on her!" Wilson uttered a low whistle. He was rolling now, filling in Big Daddy on all the latest gossip and like everyone else adding his own private embellishment.

Luther Lambert's mind was off and running. He had to find out some more of the details of the situation from someone a little more reliable than Wilson. Luther knew how much his son liked to get carried away with gossip. Worse than an old woman. He listened to Wilson ramble on for a few more moments and then maneuvered him out of his office and down the hall. Luther was immediately back to his desk and on the phone.

His first call was to Jim DeWeese. He wasn't at the studio and a call to his house got a groggy response.

"Hello," DeWeese mumbled into the phone. He was back in town late after a weekend in New Orleans. He had arrived suddenly in New Orleans early Saturday morning, still drunk and quite out of it from the night before. The Quarter had been wild for Halloween and Sunday was still so good he decided he couldn't tear himself away. It was after three when he got in bed.

"Jim, are you awake?" The bastard should have been up and at work hours ago, Lambert thought. You couldn't run a successful business if you slept 'till nine o'clock, and this was Lambert's money he was trifling with. "Have you seen the paper?"

"No," DeWeese hated these early morning calls from Luther. Especially after the weekend he had just survived. The man thought just because he put up some money for the studio he had a right to tell Jim what to do. And Jim DeWeese didn't want any man telling him what to do. Well, almost any man, he thought with a sly grin.

"Susan Weeks is dead,"

"What?" He responded still unsure what to think.

"Weeks is dead. It's in the paper. Rape or murder or something. She's dead."

"Who? Why? What happened?" DeWeese was wishing he wouldn't get an answer to these questions but they just came out.

"All I know's what's in the paper. Read it and call me back. I'm at the office." Lambert set the phone down hard and the bang ricocheted through DeWeese's head like a .22 cartridge.

He jerked away from the phone a little too fast and for a minute thought he was going to pass out. He couldn't pass out. He had to get that paper and find out about Susan.

This was too important to go unnoticed. Susan Weeks was actually dead. The cold floor went unnoticed as he grabbed his robe and went to the front door for the paper. There it was.

A wave of remorse alloyed with relief swept through him as he looked at the headlines. Susan Weeks was dead.

DeWeese stumbled back inside and plopped down on the couch. He read the article again as if more words could come out. He tried to envision Susan as they had found her. The paper said her nude body was on the floor of her bedroom.

He knew that nude body too well. He had photographed it. Had lusted after it. Had tried to get next to it. But he couldn't. She considered him an old man. Him, old at thirty-nine. He would've shown her a thing or two.

Aside from the perfect body, face and everything, she could look into a camera in a way that gave life to a picture. Worth more than a thousand words, her image replicated on film was alive in its vibrancy. She made you want to leap into the picture just to be with her. Every man that looked at her likeness felt privileged to be holding her in his hands. Every woman wanted to capture whatever that quality was for herself.

Yet, Susan was oblivious to it all. She was career-oriented in a different direction. She focused on getting herself educated. The modeling was no more than a hobby. DeWeese never understood why. She could have been making a fortune looking into a camera and he told her that regularly. She merely smiled that hypnotizing smile and said she had other things she wanted to do. To her, modeling was a diversion, something to do in her spare time that just so happened to make her money. His grand portraits of how she could be living the high life in Hollywood went in one ear and out the other with hardly a momentary consideration. She knew what she was doing and where she was headed and Los Angeles was not it.

DeWeese's illusions of taking her back to California with him as agent slowly faded. He got nowhere with her on the subject and decided to make the most of what he had with her. He used her whenever he wanted to make the big sell. Having her for the model on any project got the pockets open, especially if his company contact was a man. They took whatever package he put together just so they could have a chance to be near her. And, they all wanted to be in on the shoot. It became an unspoken joke between him and Susan.

She played it to the hilt and would flirt innocently or shamelessly. She looked like a goddess but she could also convince you that she was a goddess that was only yours; that nothing else in this world was as important to her as you were at that moment.

Susan took direction easily, following his guidance in their sessions. Many of these would last into the night when it would be only the two of them in the studio. DeWeese loved having her all to himself then, like she was his. After a long shoot she would get silly and start to clown. In her jesting, she would play roles, being the shy virgin or the sultry vamp. As their work relationship grew she became bolder with her acting. One such time led to her baring more and more until she was completely nude.

DeWeese was ecstatic. He shot frame-after-frame with her soaking up the adoration of the camera. She cavorted around the studio in positions that almost made him blush. She blossomed with erotic pleasure, touching herself tenderly, and then screaming in passion, always cognizant of his flashing lens. When it ended he was exhausted and so was she. It was as if they had made frenzied love. He had it all on film.

DeWeese sat back and closed his eyes, trying to force himself to think. He had to get his head straight before talking with Lambert. The thought of that conversation made him shudder. He knew with a certainty that Lambert would be ranting and raving like a wild man. Lambert had a way of making everything that happened someone else's fault.

DeWeese didn't know what to say to Lambert, but he was glad he had decided to be out of town for the rest of the weekend. If this deal with his pictures of her got out, well, he was fortunate he was seen in New Orleans on Saturday and Sunday. With that thought a cold chill came over him. The temperature in the room affirmed that November had arrived and winter was just around the corner. But it wasn't the weather that brought on this chill. DeWeese thought about his weekend. There were plenty of people in New Orleans that knew where he was. But what would it cost him to use that alibi? Would he be exonerated or condemned?

DeWeese thought again that he was going to be sick. He waited for the nausea to pass. It moved through him slowly like a viscous solution of evil that emptied from every cell of his body. He lay there on the couch trying to regulate his breathing and grab hold of himself. It was finally gone and he stood up and staggered back through the house toward the shower. He turned on the hot water and let its steam envelop him as the burning flow eased the pain in his head. The lines of water beat into his blonde hair and streamed down his lean body, still in good shape for almost forty. He thought about his weekend and the story of Susan and how he happened to be at this point in time. He was a good looking man and he could have been good for Susan. But she wouldn't listen to him. She wouldn't listen to anybody.

At Guaranty National Bank a somber spirit hung in the air like a vapor of grief. Everyone there liked Susan Weeks. Well, almost everyone. The men liked her because they couldn't help themselves. They all, without exception, thought she was strikingly beautiful. More than a few had hit on her, all of whom she resisted. She made it her policy not to go out with anyone at work and several of them resented her for that. The bank housed a notorious lair of promiscuity. Responsible married men of the bank treated the bevy of bank girls as their own private harem, to pick and choose from at will. Many of the girls felt powerless to resist the advances.

The political incorrectness of sexual harassment had not reached this domain. They all read about it in the papers; but when it came down to one man and one woman and the job, the oft-repeated response was a simple demure smile. Jennifer Holt's new job at the bank came as a result of an amorous liaison gone awry. Her relationship with Wildmon burned hot for only a short while before she realized his ego was the only thing that would benefit from the passion. She was foolish for letting herself get involved, but it happened and then after only a short while it seemed only crazy. She got nothing out of it and she could see his eye moving on to someone else. She was old news. He began to check out another conquest.

But not with Susan Weeks. Susan said no, politely, and then went about her job in such an adept and competent manner that they were hard pressed to make an issue of it. And, hey, they thought, there was always the possibility the girl would change her mind if they played their cards right. So Susan benefited from her refusal to stoop to the level of so many of her cohorts.

Many of the women resented this. They all liked Susan because it was too hard to dislike her. They envied her beauty, her style and her abilities. They disliked the freedom she seemed to have with so many of the bank's men and several of the worst meddlers had, on occasion, allowed themselves to stretch the truth of a story to the disadvantage of Susan's reputation. The work she did with DeWeese Advertising fed the rumormongers' craving for lascivious fare. They had seen the bathing suit ads that left little to the imagination. Many of them also knew of the rumors surrounding DeWeese and his trials and tribulations in California, including his antics in New Orleans. Those artsy types always skirted on the edge. What really happened on their business trips to Los Angeles and Florida? They loved to ruminate exotic schemes of carnal intrigue. At the bank, there was always enough smoke to help them concoct a fire.

Now Susan was dead. The sudden horror of the incident left some humiliated by their envy. She deserved not one bit of their malice for a generous and forgiving spirit filled her life with reverence for all that she encountered. Now contrition hovered over their conversations. They shooed any sense of envy away with indignation over the heinous crime of her murder. Vindication for this poor sweet girl was on everyone's lips. Stories from Momma Doris's made their way up Oak Street and the few blocks to the bank. Susan Weeks was last seen alive with Luke Daniels.

Jennifer Holt was not at the bank. In the office where she worked, several of her coworkers gathered near her desk discussing the tragedy. Cynthia Puckett, the supervisor, had talked with her earlier and recognized how obviously shaken Jennifer still was. Cynthia told her to go ahead and take a few days off to rest. If something urgent came up Cynthia would call her.

Cynthia waited outside Mr. Wildmon's office while he was on the phone, ready to fill him in on the situation. Up until only three months ago Jennifer was Wildmon's executive secretary. She moved into loan closings because she wanted to learn different aspects of the banking business. That's what Jennifer told her. Cynthia suspected some sort of riff with Mr. Wildmon but nothing was ever mentioned. They were still very cordial with each other whenever Wildmon came to the mortgage loan department but Cynthia was certain she detected a note of, Cynthia just couldn't say. Never more than just a fleeting sense of ill-ease she thought she picked up from Jennifer. Cynthia never allowed herself much time to think about it. It was not her job to keep up with the myriad of emotional mind games that went on at the bank. She had all she could do to keep herself on the right track and Jennifer seemed perfectly capable of taking care of herself.

But so did Susan Weeks and she was dead. Cynthia had been as shocked as everyone else when she picked up the morning paper. She had known Susan well. Susan's work in the marketing department brought her into contact with Cynthia as head of mortgage loans. What she read in the papers sickened her. Susan was such a wonderful girl and the paper's depiction of the rape-murder gave Cynthia horrible visions of how the poor girl must have died. The rumors going around the bank that she was with Luke Daniels Friday night were just incredible. Could he have killed Susan? The question seemed to be on everyone's mind and many were not hesitant to verbalize the opinion.

"Cynthia, come on in, please," she heard Mr. Wildmon say as he hung up the phone.

She walked into his office and selected one of the plush green wing chairs that sat in front of his desk. Green was Mr. Wildmon's favorite color. The color of money, he was fond of saying. The whole office had a richness about it that said, unmistakably, that this man liked money. The large desk was a dark walnut, almost black. There was hardwood on the floor stained the same near black of the desk.

On top of that was an oriental rug in differing shades of green lanced with beige and blue. The wall behind the desk was paneled in tones that matched the rug. On the window to the right there were wide-slated wooden blinds with green brocaded drapes that always made Cynthia think of Scarlet O'Hara tearing them down to make herself a new dress. Two potted palms sat in enormous brass planters in front of the drapes. The walls were covered in an elegant cream color on textured wall paper. A black and brass fan hung from the ceiling with an exquisite light fixture attached. The fan turned gently even now, despite the cool temperatures brought by the changing season. This was the room for the man that controlled the money that did anything in Hampton.

"Cynthia, I can hardly bring myself to even speak about this horrible tragedy," Ken Wildmon started off. "Susan Weeks dead, and Jennifer finding her like that. I don't know what to say. I am outraged at this whole affair."

"I feel the same way, Mr. Wildmon. Susan was such a wonderful girl. It's hard to believe it's true." Cynthia's eyes filled with tears as she thought about Susan again, the many times they had worked together. "I talked to Jennifer earlier. She's at her parents' house. I told her to take a few days and give me a call."

"Yes, yes, by all means. Is she alright?" Wildmon sat forward in his chair slightly.

"Yes, she says she's fine. The doctors told her to just rest up and she'll be good as new. The bump on her head is sore, a mild concussion, but nothing to worry about, they say."

"What's the word on the murder? Do the police have anything?" he asked naturally.

She filled him in with what she knew. How the bank was all abuzz with the talk of Susan being out with the lawyer, Luke Daniels, on Friday night and how no one had seen her alive after they left the Magnolia. The police were holding any clues they had tightly.

The phone rang at the secretary desk and since no one was there, Wildmon picked it up.

"Yes, yes, I see. All right, why don't you bring him up to the third floor lobby and I'll meet you there." He hung up the phone and turned back to Cynthia.

"There's an Officer Limox downstairs from the Hampton Police Department. He's here to question us about Susan Weeks." Wildmon said with a hint of sarcasm. "I don't know what he thinks he'll find here. The murderer is certainly not in this bank."

He stood up and almost as an afterthought spoke again to Cynthia. "Let's get together again after this officer does his poking around. I need to get with the marketing department; the people that worked with Susan. This is going to be a nightmare for the bank." With that he walked out of the office and Cynthia followed.

Wildmon and Cynthia stepped out of the reception area of his office into the lobby of the third floor. As if on cue the elevator doors opened. One of the many beauties of the bank was there with the officer. Wildmon stuck out his hand with a calculating sense of propriety and unmistakable air of confidence, then waiting until the officer was at arms length to continue.

"Officer, I'm Ken Wildmon, President of the bank."

"Detective Sergeant Dick Limox," was the reply as they shook hands, the firmness from each of them speaking volumes about their respective positions. The dedicated law enforcement officer on a case of deadly seriousness had the firm handshake that came from the ritual bravado of a cop. Wildmon's came from a mixture of aplomb and arrogance that said as plainly as if it had been spoken 'I have nothing to hide.'

"I'm so sorry we have to meet under these circumstances. Everyone here in the bank is absolutely grief-stricken. This is a terrible tragedy. Terrible. Certainly we want to help you in any way we can. Tell me, what do you need us to do?"

Limox explained that he would need to talk with a few co-workers of the deceased. Cynthia went off to make the arrangements while Wildmon guided Limox back to his reception area. Wildmon left for a moment to talk on the phone privately and then came back and sat down in a chair across from the detective.

"I've arranged for our vice-president, Mr. Robert Fowler, to assist you. He'll stay with you and help you with anything you need. All you have to do is ask. As I said, we are all disturbed by this tragedy and want to do everything we can to assist you. I've read the paper but, tell me, do you have any idea at all what might have happened? Who could have done this to such a fine young lady?"

"Right now we're collecting information. I'm hoping to learn something from some of Miss Weeks' friends here at the bank that would give us some leads." Limox was enjoying this personal attention from Mr. Ken Wildmon. Never hurt to make friends. It might come in handy when he and the missus decided to buy a house.

The door opened and in walked a tall, slender man in his late thirties, Limox surmised. He was a good looking man with perfectly groomed hair and fine chiseled features. Limox observed the athletic build of the man with thick shoulders and a thin waist, attesting to time spent in the gym. The suit he wore probably cost $500.00, Limox thought. He would have been shocked to know it actually cost $1,200.00.

Wildmon introduced Limox to J. Robert Fowler whom everyone called Bob. Fowler smiled as he shook hands, flashing a perfect set of brilliantly white teeth. The deep, rich tone of his skin suggested to the detective that golf or tennis maintained that healthy glow. Or, maybe just a tanning bed. Limox knew the Fowler family went way back with the bank but was not sure if this was one of the immediate family. That question was soon answered.

"This bank was started by my grandfather, Sergeant. He would be rolling over in his grave to know something like this had happened to one of his employees. I'm at your disposal for anything you need. The sooner the murderer is put behind bars, the better for all of us," Fowler said smoothly.

Cynthia stuck her head in the door announcing she had a conference room ready on the second floor and could have whoever sent up when they were ready.

"Cynthia, why don't you take Captain Limox on down and Bob will be there in a minute," Wildmon said. "I have a few things demanding immediate attention and Bob and I have to confer."

She led Limox into the hall before he could even half-heartedly protest that it was only Sergeant Limox, not Captain. When the door closed Wildmon gave Fowler a look and they went into Wildmon's personal office and closed the door.

"I wish we would have had a chance to talk before that imbecile got here. What do you think, Bob?" with more deference than he gave to any other vice-president. The title notwithstanding, Ken Wildmon knew that J. Robert Fowler's interest in this bank was much stouter than his position belied.

"Let's hope he can find something that will help identify the murderer. From what I hear, that shouldn't be too hard for even them. It's all over the place that she was with Luke Daniels Friday night. You'd think they would be starting there."

"You'd think. I don't believe they know that, yet. From my short conversation with him, they're just collecting evidence blindly. Starting from scratch, basically."

"It won't take him long once he talks to a few of the girls from marketing. And if the idiot hasn't got sense enough to get it out of them himself, I'll make sure that he does." Fowler said with a smirk. "I'd better get down there. I'm going to sit in the interviews with him so I'll know what's happening."

They stood up and walked out to the lobby. Fowler skipped the elevator and put his hand on the door to the stairwell as he turned back to Wildmon.

"What's with the worried look, Ken? There's nothing for us to be concerned about. Is there?" Fowler looked at him askance.

"No, no, not really. I'm just worried about the bank's image, that's all. This happened to an employee and the roommate was also an employee. It doesn't make for good press.

Every time the damn news media mentions it, they're going to mention the bank as well." Wildmon cast a sideways glance at Fowler.

"You've got a point," Fowler acknowledged, wondering at the same time if that was the only reason for the distress he picked up in Wildmon. Ken was such a master at only presenting the image he wanted you to see. "Look, I'd better get on down there. You know where I'll be."

Wildmon stood by the stairwell door for a while after it slammed behind Fowler. He didn't trust that cocky little prick any more than he did a rattlesnake. But he was the best one to keep an eye on this investigation for the bank. And Ken would keep an eye on him.

Bob Fowler arrived at the luxurious conference room on the second floor as Limox was going in with his first interview. The room had not changed much since the building was built in the 1920's. Many of the furnishings were new but the designer had maintained the earlier style. The leather chairs were worn and comfortable. The room had only been used for board meetings through the years which had not been held here in quite some time.

Bob walked right in behind Limox and placed himself in one of the high back chairs at the mahogany table. Limox looked at him uncomfortably, but said nothing. Fowler introduced the young lady to Limox as Kelly Brown. She was the receptionist in marketing and public relations and knew Susan quite well. Susan came to this department from their main office in Jackson and, in a year's time, had made friends with almost everyone. Yes, Susan was a wonderful person. No, she couldn't think of anyone who would want to kill her or why someone might.

After giving them his most concerned look for some time, Fowler's eyes moved around the room. He remembered having a conversation with Susan at this very table. If these walls could talk, he imagined there would be quite a lot this old detective would have to write on his pad. Fowler wondered just what Limox was writing since it didn't appear to him that Kelly had anything of importance to add to this investigation. Fowler did notice the fine outline of her body in the slim-cut dress she was wearing. Yes, he had noticed this young lady before. Maybe he should talk with her later, a little more on the investigation.

A smile curled up on the edges of his lips. Limox had caught several facial changes on Fowler out of the corner of his eye. He also caught Kelly casting her eyes in the direction of Fowler. Did the vice-president make her uncomfortable? As the interview grew to a close, Limox thanked her for her time and gave her his card for her to call him if she thought of anything that might be of help. She left with the instruction to have Cynthia send in the next person.

"Mr. Fowler, I appreciate your help, but I think it would be best if I talked with these people alone," he said, trying to sound official.

"I'm sorry, but that's out of the question," Fowler stated emphatically. "Captain Limox, this is a very sensitive matter for this bank, as I'm sure you can understand. If anything is discovered from one of our employees, we need to know about it immediately. The possibility for damage to the sense of trust our customers have with the bank is paramount here." Fowler's life of means and affluence endowed him with the sense that he should not be challenged. His position at the bank as vice-president and the son of one of the wealthiest stockholders allowed him to rarely hear anyone say no.

"It's Sergeant Limox. I do understand, Mr. Fowler, but I'm conducting a murder investigation and I need to know that these people feel free to talk openly with me. I can't do that with you sitting here breathing down their neck." Limox's anger flared, unthinkingly, and he quickly added, "Look, I'm just trying to do my job, Mr. Fowler."

"I know that. And, I'm trying to do mine. Part of that job is protecting the bank's interest in every way possible. So you see, I have to be here."

"I will not be able to conduct a proper investigation with you sitting in. If you are not willing to let me speak with them alone, then I can do it elsewhere. Or if you like, I could get a court order. I'm sure if I explain to the Judge that the bank was impeding my investigation…" Limox seriously doubted he could get Judge Jones to issue a court order against the bank. They were bank employees and expected to work. He could talk with them after work at their homes or even at the station, but not as easily as this. It was a bluff, but one that could work.

Fowler tried to quickly change his tactics. He didn't want this moron getting in a huff. "Look, Sergeant Limox, the bank wants this cleared up as soon as possible. Surely, you can see that. We want to help you do your job in any way we can. I'll tell you what, can we make a deal here? You go ahead with your questioning, but if anything comes out that you see is going to look bad for the bank, promise me you'll let me know in advance so we can take some steps to lessen the impact."

"What do you think is going to come out, Mr. Fowler," Limox asked, thinking he might be on to something. He kept thinking about the expressions he'd observed on Fowler. What did the bank have to cover up?

"Good god, man, the head of our marketing department's been murdered and one of our loan officers was her roommate who found her. That's bad enough right there. I don't for a second think this has anything to do with the bank, but still, the way it looks. You can see that."

Limox nodded. He hadn't really thought about it that way. "All right," he conceded. "If anything turns up involving the bank, you'll know before anyone else. Okay?"

"Thank you, Sergeant Limox," Fowler responded with a broad grin. "I can see why they have you on this case. You have a good understanding of the total picture. Thank you. Thank you very much."

"Do you have a card? I can give you a call if anything comes up. Maybe even your home or cell number?" Limox asked, thinking he had made a friend in the banking world that might be a good chip for him to cash in later.

"Yes, yes, of course."

Fowler handed him a business card, thanked Limox again and excused himself. He quickly went to his office which was also on this floor two doors down from the conference room. From behind his desk he fiddled with a few dials and switches until he got the monitor adjusted precisely the way he wanted it. This panel controlled the closed-circuit system in his office as well as in the conference room. He could now hear, see and record on video the interviews and no one would have to know.

The system had been installed to document meetings and conferences for accuracy purposes. It would now serve the bank's interest in a different way. Fowler's father would want to know every detail about the police interviewing bank personnel. Their money built this bank long before it was Guaranty National. The buy-out left them with a considerable amount of stock which had to be tended. Bob Fowler would be stepping into Wildmon's position as president soon and he was not going to let this incident cast a shadow over his future prospects.

Poor Susan. She was a strong-willed one, for sure. Never let anyone get next to her. Fowler had tried for a year. She never knew he was the one that planted the seed that brought her to this position. They had met when she worked in Jackson. From the first moment he looked at her he was smitten. He thought about the line from a movie, "You had me from hello." He wondered how many people thought that of Susan. She was so beautiful. And, she had seemed attracted to him. The way she looked at him. But then she played hard to get.

In the year she was at the bank, she was always too busy for him. She kept putting people in their path to a relationship. There was always something. But he had waited patiently. She wasn't the only girl in the bank he had thought. There were others that were glad to give themselves to the future president; the one who could make or break their careers. He could also break Susan's. She had finally realized that. But maybe she realized it just a little too late.

He had a file in his desk drawer with every advertisement she had ever modeled. And, some pictures that had not made it into ads. He always showed interest in her portfolio. He sat there thinking about some of those pictures. That face, the hair, her skin. The forbidden fruit he had wanted for so long. His mind wandered while Limox droned on with boring questions being recorded from the monitor atop his credenza.

Luke ordered lunch in at the office: a plate lunch from Momma Doris. Liz got one, too, and they sat at the table in the break room watching the local news. The lead story was the murder of Susan Weeks. They reported almost identically what had been in the paper with the final note that the police had not listed any suspect. The two of them watched in silence until Luke flipped the channel to CNN. He finally commented on one of the stories and they talked idly about pending cases they had.

Luke spent the rest of the afternoon in his office over files, dictating on various matters. He was having a time concentrating and not accomplishing much at all. Close to four o'clock, Jenny buzzed his office announcing that a Mr. Jeff Woodall was here to see him. At first Luke thought he forgot an appointment.

"Jenny, I don't have anything down. Who is he?" Luke asked.

"He says he's with the Hampton News. He said he didn't have an appointment." She held on waiting for Luke to give some response.

"Tell him to have a seat. I'll step out there in a minute to see what he wants."

When Luke stepped into the lobby, the newspaper man was sitting down with nothing but a pad in his hand. He had on jeans and scruffy tennis shoes and a loose fitting flannel shirt. Luke walked over to him and offered his hand.

"Mr. Woodall? I'm Luke Daniels." The man was really only a boy, probably a student.

"Hi, Mr. Daniels. I'm with the Hampton News. I was wondering if I could talk with you about the murder of Susan Weeks."

Luke felt his body stiffen involuntarily. He was taken aback by the effect of the question and his mind quickly raced across a field of reasons as to why the man was here.

"And why would you want to talk with me?" Luke asked uneasily.

"I understand you were with Ms. Weeks Friday night and may have been the last one to see her alive."

Luke looked at the boy cautiously, not sure what he should say. That fact was bound to come out. They were at the Magnolia, for heaven's sakes. They had even run into Judge Dahl and numerous other people. Thoughts raced across Luke's mind like a video on fast forward. He remembered all the people they had seen Friday night, and everyone that had seen them leaving together.

"Is that true, Mr. Daniels? Mr. Daniels?" the boy repeated when Luke did not answer. They were standing in front of the reception desk, neither of them moving from when they shook hands. "Mr. Daniels, do you deny you were with the deceased Friday night?"

Luke still stood motionless, not uttering a word, unable to grab hold of anything from the blur of images in his head. "No, no, I was with her Friday night. But why are you here talking with me about this."

"I'm just following up on the story. Our word is that several people saw you leave with her Friday night from the Magnolia about seven o'clock. Is that true?"

"I really don't remember what time we left," and he didn't. When he left the Magnolia Friday night he was so mesmerized by Susan Weeks he barely knew what planet he was on.

"I don't see what that's got to do with anything." But he did. He knew why he was being questioned and he knew it would happen again.

"Where did you go when you left the Magnolia?" the kid continued pursuing his story.

"We got something to eat," Luke said without offering anything further.

"And what did you do after that?" Jeff went on stubbornly.

"Look, I don't have time for this. I've got work to do. I'm sorry but you're going to have to leave. I have nothing else to say." He was certainly not going to tell this little pipsqueak about his night with Susan.

The reporter was young but determined and knew he was getting some stuff his boss would love. This could be better than what you read in the tabloids. Jeff stood his ground and popped another question.

"What restaurant did you eat at? Do you recall what time it was when you left the restaurant?"

"No. I said I didn't have time for this and you are going to have to leave." And with that Luke grabbed the boy's arm and tried to move him toward the door, only a few feet away. But the boy didn't move. Instead, he jerked his arm free of Luke's grip and fired off another question.

"Mr. Daniels, what time did you last see Susan Weeks?"

Without answering, Luke grabbed his arm again, this time with more determination and a shove toward the door. In his wrenching to get free, Jeff stumbled over the chair behind him which knocked against the table sending the lamp to the floor. He didn't fall because Luke had a grip on his arm.

"One more question, Mr. Daniels, Was she alive when you saw her last?"

The question hit Luke like a blast of fire hurled from a torch. It enraged him like nothing ever had before.

"Why, you little sonofabitch, how dare you imply such a thing. Get out of my office." In his frenzy, Luke grabbed the pad from the surprised boy's hand and threw it across the room. With one arm he slammed the boy against the door with such force that it rattled through the building. Luke yanked the door open and pushed him out into the street, where he fell on the curb. Luke wanted to follow him out and jump on him with all his might for even suggesting that he may have harmed Susan. Instead, he stared at him from the doorway.

Jeff's pants were torn at the knee from his fall and a button was ripped on his shirt. A trickle of blood oozed at his mouth where his face hit the door facing. He looked back at Luke in the doorway and had never been so scared in all his twenty-one years. A few people up the street stopped in their tracks and stared at him. He wanted to go back in and get his notepad, but backed across the street and headed around the block to his car.

Luke slammed the front door and turned around. Jenny was still at her desk, white as a ghost. Luke had forgotten she was even there. She had witnessed the entire incident. At the door to the main hallway, stood Liz and Tommy Chipman. All of them stood there expressionless, no one knowing what to say.

"Damned smartass reporter," Luke was the first to speak, not directing it to anyone in particular. When no one else spoke, he said excuse me and walked out of the room, leaving them all there in silence.

In his office, Luke couldn't sit, couldn't stand, couldn't do anything. He wanted to scream, wanted to kick something. He didn't know what to do. He grabbed his coat off the hook behind the door and walked out. They were all still standing in the lobby. He walked right past them to the front door and turned back before he went out.

"I'm getting out of here. I'll see you all tomorrow."

CHAPTER FIVE

In the days that followed, Hampton was alive with rumors surrounding the death of Susan Weeks. Gossips flocked to the stories like bees making honey. There were few that didn't involve Luke Daniels. From that first Monday morning when the paper carried the news on its front page, the report of the deceased being last seen with Luke Daniels gave fuel to the fire that carried speculation to unheard of extremes.

Luke's run in with the reporter didn't help matters at all. The day after Luke threw the upstart out of his office, the headlines read like a tabloid. "ATTORNEY DENIES MURDER" was on the front page with a picture of Luke that made him look like a thug. Another article followed up with "LAWYER HAS LAST SUPPER WITH VICTIM." Neither of the articles had much in the way of substance and basically recited the same facts over and over again. They didn't even mention the fracas between Luke and the Woodall boy, which was odd because William Rogers, President, Publisher and former owner of the Hampton News, rarely missed an opportunity to make money. He loved sensationalism but, on this occasion, nothing went in about Woodall's being roughed up at the hands of Luke Daniels.

That didn't stop it from being thrown into the public grinder of sordid stories. Each day Momma Doris' was full of people trading stories about the murder. 'Did you know such and such?' 'Have you heard so and so?' Luke made it a point to avoid Momma's these days. He had gone up a few times shortly after the story broke, but found it unpleasant after a while. If he ate with friends, there were stares and whispers from other tables. If he walked in alone, folks he knew would pretend not to see him so as to avoid feeling constrained to ask him to join them.

Luke knew they were all talking about him and he tried to not let it bother him. He went on with his work each day, continuing to do well. If anything, his practice seemed to be thriving. He settled several small cases and even signed up some new clients. His status as an up-and-coming successful attorney was only slightly tarnished by the circulation of accounts of his association with a deceased bank employee.

One thing that helped, Luke thought, was his conversation with District Attorney Billy Gafford. Luke handled a fair amount of criminal cases and had a good working relationship with Billy. In fact, he considered them friends. In the midst of the swirling insinuations being tossed about by the prattle of vicious, meddlesome busybodies, Luke decided he should confront the situation head on. After all, it was not his style to tuck his tail and hide. Luke had nothing to hide.

Early one morning in the middle of November, Luke had the Lannie Gristel file on his desk with the intention of checking on some discovery that was due from the DA's office. The informal motion for discovery was filed and their answer past due. Instead of sending another letter, he called the DA under the guise of asking if he could come and pick up what was due him on the case.

When the secretary, Wanda Walker, told him Gafford was on the phone, he asked if he was going to be in for a while. Wanda replied that he should be in all day, so Luke grabbed his file on the Gristel case and headed to Gafford's office.

He arrived with the man still on the phone. Luke chuckled to himself that it was the same with everybody. The practice of law was done ten percent in the court room, twenty percent in the books, and the rest on the telephone. He recalled many work days where he would not lay the phone down, going from one call to another the entire day.

Luke chatted with Wanda until she noticed Gafford got off the phone and Wanda went back to let him know Luke was there. She returned shortly asking Luke to come on back. He strolled in to Billy's office and Wanda closed the door behind her as she left.

"Luke, my boy, it's good to see you. How've you been?" Billy said with a broad smile, rising from his chair for the greeting and shaking Luke's hand vigorously.

"Doing great, Billy, can't complain at all." Their conversation went on about the upcoming holidays, hunting season, Billy's plans for next year. It was an election year. It would be Gafford's fourth term. Not unheard of in Mississippi, but it surely gave him pause.

"I wonder sometimes if it's what I really want to do. You know, Luke, I've had this position for a while."

"Yeah, but you're good at it, Billy. You do the people of Bedford County a fine job. You're fair and honest. Things not always found in our politicians." Never hurt to blow a little smoke, Luke thought.

"Well, I never like to think of myself as a politician, but, rather a country lawyer trying to see that justice is done." Billy paused for a thoughtful moment, and gazed off at the wall behind Luke. A look that anyone who had ever tried a case with the man knew only too well. He was good with a jury. No doubt about it. They loved him and his do-gooder rallies for truth, justice and the American way. He was a good politician.

"At any rate, whatever you decide to do, you know I'll be behind you 100 percent. I can't think of a soul in this county that could make a better prosecutor than you, Billy."

"I appreciate that, Luke, I really do. But, hell, you didn't come up here to talk about me. What can I do for you?"

Luke pulled out the Gristel file and they talked about it for a few moments. Billy assured him the discovery would be forthcoming, that he could get it today in fact. He buzzed Wanda on the intercom and asked her to make a copy of the material they had on the case.

"There's something else, Billy. You've heard the rumors about me and Susan Weeks."

Gafford wondered if Luke was going to get around to that. He could have easily called up the secretary himself and asked for the Gristel discovery material and she would have gotten it for him. He had heard the rumors; had discussed some of them on more than one occasion. He looked Daniels over carefully trying to get a feel for where he was coming from. In his many years of dealing with criminals he had developed a sixth sense about who was guilty and who was not. Right now he needed to apply that sense to the man sitting in front of him.

"Hell, Luke, you know I stay away from that stuff. If I listened to half the rumors that went on in this town, I'd be too busy to do my job. I try to stick to facts."

"I just wanted you to know that if you ever want to talk about it, I'll be glad to sit down and go over everything that happened. It's nothing at all like some of the stories that have gotten back to me, and I'm sure I don't hear the juicy ones."

"I appreciate your honesty, Luke. You've always dealt straight up with me and I don't expect that to change now just because a few people with nothing better to do than flap their jaws want to go meddling in something they ought to leave alone. If I feel like I need anything from you, I'll talk to you straight up about it. Fair enough?"

"Sounds good to me. I appreciate it, Billy."

Luke stood up and offered his hand to the man across the desk. They shook hands again and Billy came around the desk to see Luke out. When the door closed, Billy stood wondering how and when he and Luke would confront this issue again.

Luke felt good after leaving the DA's office. The persistent tension brought on by the rash of vicious rumors was affecting Luke in subtle ways. That tension relaxed somewhat as he walked down the street headed back to his office. He thought back over his conversation with Gafford, remembering his words about not paying attention to gossip. Billy had been the brunt of Hampton's rumor mill a while back, but had survived. There was talk he had a unique way of working out probation for certain individuals, but nothing ever came of it. That recollection made Luke glad Billy was still District Attorney. Luke could trust him to go on the facts and not on idle small talk. Feeling reassured, Luke picked up the pace and shortly popped through the front door to his office.

Liz immediately noticed a change in Luke's mood. The scowl was not as pronounced. His eyes seemed brighter. She knew something had occurred when he asked her to lunch. They had a great working relationship, were even friends, but rarely went out together, for lunch or anything else.

"You buying?" was her response.

"Sure, why not. Where you want to go?" Luke was even chipper.

"Hey, momma taught me to never look a gift horse in the mouth. Let's go, and you pick the place."

November in Hampton was usually the first month you could do without air conditioning. The temperature was in the comfortable sixty-five degree range and they drove leisurely with the windows down and the music playing. It was the most relaxed Liz had seen her boss in weeks. He didn't mention where he had gone or what had happened and she didn't ask. She was just glad for the relief.

Luke pulled up to McKenzie's Deli, a place known for their fabulous daily specials. They went inside and after looking over the menu both ordered the stuffed eggplant, a house specialty. They talked about the food, the place and the weather. Never once did they talk about the murder of Susan Weeks.

Tommy Chipman got to talk about the murder more than he wanted to. No matter where he went, people thought they should talk about the investigation and the involvement of his law partner. Tommy regularly reminded them that he and Luke were not partners. They shared office space. There was a big difference. Rarely did the two of them work on a case together. They were in the same building and had the same receptionist but everything else was separate. They had separate secretaries, separate equipment, separate filing cabinets and separate lives. Right about now, Tommy wished they had separate buildings.

He was sick of hearing the gossip, the rumors, the vicious, nasty cruelty slung about by people who considered themselves honorable. At first, he was as shocked by learning of Luke's association with the Weeks girl as anyone else. Luke was a top notch attorney that took his work and his profession seriously. Tommy couldn't imagine him being involved in anything so offensive. So gruesome. They had not talked about it. Several times Tommy wanted to go to Luke and tell him all the things people were saying. But he didn't. He had not been able to bring himself to confront Luke with the subject.

That afternoon Tommy was in the courthouse checking records on a house sale for the bank. The county courthouse was always teeming with lawyers and today was no exception. Tommy could hardly get his title work done for people coming up to him with their latest chronicle of the Susan Weeks murder saga. James Germany sauntered over in Tommy's direction, making Tommy wish he could disappear. Germany's tie was dirty and his shirt and pants rumpled. His beefy frame and disheveled appearance gave him a slovenly look that annoyed Tommy. How could he be a decent lawyer if he didn't take care of himself any better than that?

Germany made small talk for a few moments and, even though Tommy tried to appear too busy, finally asked about Luke, relishing the opportunity to talk smut about a fellow attorney.

"Tommy, what's going on down at your office?"

"What do you mean?" Tommy asked, knowing full well where James was headed. He continued to work on his records check without looking up, hoping the cold shoulder treatment would work, but it didn't.

"You know, with your partner," Germany said with his best come-on-good-buddy routine.

"I don't have a partner," was Tommy's reply, still not looking up. But Germany was not to be put off so easily.

"You know what I mean," practically begging him to throw some juicy, inside tidbit.

"You mean Luke."

"Yeah, sounds to me like the boy's bit off more than he can chew," Germany said, grinning salaciously. "You know I used to go out with Susan. Quite a number. I'll bet ole Luke didn't know how to charm her like I did. She got him all worked up and then said no. And then he said yes a little too strongly. Don't get me wrong. I can understand. Hell, I don't know what I would have done if she had turned me down. That little bitch was a wild woman in bed, though, I'll tell you that."

Tommy allowed himself to throw a glance of disgust in Germany's direction. He wanted to throw up. Everyone at the bank knew Germany had tried to get Susan to go out with him, but she wouldn't have anything to do with him. And now he was standing there claiming they had a torrid love affair. Germany, you're disgusting, Tommy wanted to say but, rather, said nothing in hopes that if he kept quiet, Germany would go away. He didn't.

"But now I'll tell you what I just heard if you promise not to repeat it. They're saying now that Luke had gotten involved in drugs and that…"

"James, I don't know anything about that and don't have the time or the inclination to stand here talking about it. I've got to get this title work over to the bank. I'll see you later."

He exited the courthouse by the back door and made it to his car without seeing anyone else. What a relief! He wished he had never even gone to the records room. He should have played golf today. Tommy was an avid golfer, playing at least three times a week, sometimes four, if he could get in two on the weekend. He wished he was there today. November was a good month for golf in Hampton. Leaves were turning, the temperature was cool and there was usually great sunshine. Maybe he could still get in nine holes.

He drove over to the bank to give them a report of his findings with the promise that his written opinion would be ready before noon tomorrow. He rushed to get in the front door before it closed at four o'clock. Once inside he ran into Robert Fowler, headed for the elevator.

"Tommy, my good man, how are you?"

Like Robert, Tommy had family connections to his bank. His father-in-law was majority owner of a bank in a town near Hampton and sold his interest to the bigger operation of Guaranty National. They first met in law school. Robert was in the MBA-JD program earning a Masters degree in banking and finance and a Juris Doctorate at the same time. Tommy didn't have the Masters but felt just as accomplished with his law degree. Both of them could have retired at the early age of thirty if they had chosen. They were wealthy, outright millionaires, from the money their families bestowed upon them.

Robert's position as vice president and Tommy's private practice with three-quarters of his business from the bank made them both naturally attentive to the best interests of Guaranty

National. The two friends had not seen each other in a couple of weeks and exchanged greetings warmly, Tommy inviting Robert to come join him on the golf course. They reached the elevator and rode up together. As the doors closed, Fowler wasted no time in going straight to the subject Tommy hated to come up the most.

"I hear you witnessed the altercation between Daniels and that reporter. Was it as bad as they say? Did Luke bust him up pretty good?" Fowler inquired shamelessly.

"Oh, it wasn't that bad." Tommy was torn in this situation between his long standing friendship with Fowler and his current business arrangement with Luke.

"Rumor has it the reporter wound up with a busted lip and a black eye. What happened down there?"

"I was in my office and heard shouting out front. I walked out in time to see Luke body slam the guy into the wall and then physically pitch him into the street." Tommy wished he had been somewhere else that day.

"Sounds like our old pal Luke got pretty hot under the collar. What did the reporter say?"

"Jenny said he asked Luke if Susan was alive when he last saw her. That's what set him off."

Fowler thought back over the interviews with Sergeant Limox. He asked all the bank employees about who Susan was dating. No one mentioned Luke Daniels. Yet, it was common knowledge that the two of them were together the night she was killed.

"What does he say about being out with her that Friday night?"

"Rob, to tell you the truth, I haven't even talked to him about it. I wanted to that day after the quarrel with the reporter, but Luke stormed out of the office right afterwards. Since then I just haven't found the right time. I need to have a few questions answered if the two of us are going to continue to be in that building together."

Tommy thought he knew why he had not talked with Luke. He was afraid of what Luke might say. Luke appeared to have a chip on his shoulder lately and Tommy wasn't interested in being the one to knock it off or to be there when it fell off.

"You need to talk to him," Fowler encouraged. "I don't have to tell you what a delicate situation this is for the bank. I'm hopeful they'll find the killer soon and put this thing to rest. The police have been here questioning people that worked with Susan and it's putting a strain on everyone. I'm worried how this will look up in Jackson. And, how it will sit with our customers. I'm doing everything I can to minimize the situation. If you hear anything I should know, you'll give me a call won't you?"

Tommy knew what that meant. Fowler wanted him to talk with Luke and report back. In any other situation, Tommy would have been offended. But the bank's welfare was his welfare. Not to mention the value of his family's stock. Banking in Mississippi was a competitive, cutthroat business. He would talk with Luke and do it soon.

Luke finished the day with a sanguine heart. The mood of the earlier talk with the

District Attorney and the pleasant lunch with his secretary continued the rest of the afternoon. Shortly after five o'clock he left the office, went home and got dressed for a run.

His route took him through streets where dry leaves played tunes with the wind as they struggled to hold on for one more day. Cars whipped by him and made small wind storms that swept up those leaves that had already fallen from the towering branches overhead. Birds flew low to the ground without song as if too busy with preparations for the approaching winter to waste any energy on melody. The sun lay low in the sky casting long shadows from the huge branches that covered the street stretched out before Luke.

He chose a different route today and in a short while found himself passing by the home of Judge Jones. He saw the Judge in the back yard working on an old lawnmower with his son and, in an instant, made a loop around the block and came up the alley to the back of the house.

"Must be time to buy a new one, Judge," Luke proclaimed as he dropped his pace to a walk.

"Hello, Luke. You might be right. Casey, here, won't argue with you." The boy's real name was Wendell Garmon Jones, IV. Since little league days he had been an outstanding hitter and thus the tag "Casey" Jones. The boy and his father loved it. Judge Jones was crazy about his star baseball player. A senior in high school now, young Casey was last year's state all-American and could lead his team to a state championship this spring.

Judge Wendel Garmon Jones, III, was not an athlete. He was the epitome of his father who had been judge before him for Bedford County. And, his grandfather before that. The same flaming red hair carried over from generation-to-generation like a judicial crown. They were all small of stature, standing only five-feet-eight but with booming husky voices that bellowed from the bench sending waves of terror through anyone that might draw their ire. The coarseness of the current Judge Jones' voice was intensified by his constant smoking. Rarely did anyone see Judge Jones that he did not have something. Cigarettes, cigar, pipe - his lungs would probably have made a coal miner's look healthy.

The red hair did not carry over to Jones the fourth. Casey had dark brown hair and was almost a head taller than his father.

As Luke stood there with them in the back yard, the sun dove below the horizon leaving them in the twilight of late autumn. Much to Luke's satisfaction, Casey excused himself to go study for tomorrow's chemistry exam, and Luke and the Judge were left alone.

"Judge, I know you've been hearing the rumors going around this town lately," Luke paused for some response.

"You mean about that young girl killed back in October? As much as I try to keep myself removed from spurious insinuations and wicked rumormongers, I am still forced to hear more than I want."

Luke did his best to stifle a laugh. Everyone in the town, in the state, just about, knew Judge Jones and knew if anybody liked to gossip it was him. The state Supreme Court had publicly admonished him on more than one occasion for his less than judicious behavior in carrying on about matters before him. He had been known to get himself involved in things that would eventually wind up in his court, a clear and direct conflict of interest, where he saw no conflict whatever.

"Yes, I've heard some of the talk. They tell me you knew this girl. My wife says you were out with her the night she was killed. I don't know what to say, Luke. You're an upstanding member of the bar and should be on your way to becoming a wealthy man, what with some of the settlement papers I've signed in the last year. By the way, I like that new car you're driving."

Luke blushed. He hadn't realized that even the Judge kept up with his personal life.

"Whatever you've heard, Judge, you should remember that there's two sides to every story. I don't know why people can't mind their own business, but I know I don't like bearing the brunt of all the innuendos. And, there's not much I can do to stop it. My concern is my clients. What I want to know from you, Judge, is whether the rumors are going to affect how you deal with me and my clients in the courtroom?" Luke asked pointedly.

"Why, Luke, I am wounded that you would even ask such a question. Surely, you know me better than that. I believe in the concept that all men are innocent until proven guilty and I would never let such weak evidence as hearsay from a bunch of blood thirsty hounds influence me. There's no place for it in my courtroom and no place for it in my life."

Suddenly, there was a tension in the air. They were standing in total darkness, save for the light from a street lamp that filtered through the bare tree limbs. With the setting sun, a chill crept into the night that hung around them like an eerie phantom. These two had experienced moments before in the courtroom where they goaded each other into near rage, but never outside the courtroom. Luke's heart was racing, still elevated from the run and now beating even more furiously. And, he didn't know why. He quickly searched for words that would give some relief to whatever had reared up between them.

"Judge, I respect you for that. And I never presumed anything other from you. You've always treated me honorably and I hope we can continue that relationship. My career is important to me. After all, I have to make a living," Luke said with a grin.

As soon as Luke arose, the air cleared. In his running shorts and T-shirt, he suddenly realized that it was cold, said good-by to the Judge and trotted off down the street.

By the time Thanksgiving arrived, the Weeks murder dropped into second rate news. No suspect was officially identified. An occasional item in the paper reported that the investigation was still underway. People in Hampton soon tired of an old subject and moved on to another topic for their trivial babbling. They busied themselves with preparation for the holidays, travel plans and shopping.

The end of the year was rapidly approaching. December came with colder weather and the downtown crowd busied themselves with finishing out their year. Lawyers scrambled to close out cases and collect fees in all areas of their practice. The plaintiffs' lawyers tried to use the season as a time to get generous settlements for their clients. Defense attorneys liked the idea of getting cases closed in order to call on the deep pockets of their insurance clients to pay up before Christmas. Everybody was in a good mood. 'Tis the season.

Even the criminal docket was packed tight, with cases on top of cases that could never reasonably be tried. Judge Jones allowed it because he understood the bar. Lawyers set their criminal cases for trial in December for several reasons. For the most part, they all knew their clients were guilty. But they couldn't admit that to the prosecutor. With the docket so heavy, the District Attorney couldn't possibly try all the cases so the prospect of a good plea bargain was eminent. And, the District Attorney, that valiant protector of the people of the State of Mississippi, was much more lenient as refrains of good will to all men filled the air.

Defendants hated the prospect of going to jail anytime. But at Christmas time they, too, were especially eager to forego their multitudinous rights guaranteed under the constitution and cop a plea so as to be home for Christmas.

For some of these same reasons, the public defender found himself busy, swept up in the December flurry to clear cases off the docket. The public defender in Hampton was Danny Holliwall. He was paid not by the case but by salary for the year. He resented watching the other lawyers jockey for position with the District Attorney, knowing they were taking plea negotiations back to their client that would be used to flush money out of the client's pocket and into the lawyer's. He resented watching guys he had been in school with prosper while he still drove the same old Plymouth he'd had since law school.

His idealism, protecting the rights of the wrongly accused, had tarnished in the face of realism that was one more guilty black kid after another. He hardly saw anything but black faces standing in front of him with the same story over and over. He could almost quote their lines for them. He rarely listened any more. He let his mind wander to the golf course while they recanted their story and then told them they could go to trial and get ten years or they could enter a plea and get three years. Those were the options.

With very few exceptions that was the situation in every case he handled in his function as public defender. It was a part time position that took almost all his time. It paid $29,000 a year. For that money he went to the DA's office, wrote down what their recommendation was and went back to his client with the pronouncement. Rarely did he listen to much talk about guilt or innocence. He didn't have time for that. They could accept the plea or go to trial.

The choice left the defendant was between going to trial and getting the maximum from Judge Jones when the jury found you guilty or taking the one to three offered by the public defender. They knew that he didn't care about them, their case, or their lives. No argument they put forth phased him and for that reason they often took his recommendation, not because they were guilty but because they had no money to hire another lawyer and it was unequivocally clear that going to trial with this one would be suicide. And so, Danny

Holliwall also contributed to clearing the criminal docket for Judge Jones in December in Hampton, Bedford County, Mississippi.

It was not a perfect system but one that had worked for many years. Docket call, the utter waste of time that began this process, started at nine o'clock a.m. on the first Monday of December. Judge Jones flowed into the courtroom, took his seat at the bench and struck his gavel precisely at nine. The bailiff, upon seeing the Judge, jumped up.

"All rise," he bellowed to the outer reaches of the entire courthouse. The feisty Judge Jones was already in place and banging his gavel before the last spectator lifted from his seat.

"Hear ye, hear ye, hear ye, this the December term of the Circuit Court for the County of Bedford, is now in session, the Honorable Wendell Garmon Jones, the Third, presiding. God bless the State of Mississippi and this hallowed proceeding.

"Ladies and Gentlemen of Hampton County, members of the bar and those of you present in the gallery, we welcome you to opening day of the term. Before we begin, I'm going to ask Attorney Ben Cannon if he would open with prayer."

Another sign of Judge Jones' political savvy, he defied the United States Supreme Court openly with his prayers at the beginning of each term. His defiance earned him little more than harsh words from the State Supreme Court. But from the voters of Hampton and Bedford County, it earned him a solid constituency that believed he was more concerned about the moral fiber of his country than about a bunch of liberal federal judges. The truth of the matter was he was more concerned about the votes this action got him than anything else. When asked about the Supreme Court's position on the constitutional issue of separation of church and state he would retort mischievously that those guys don't vote. And he was right. They didn't vote in Bedford County and there was very little else they could do to Judge Jones.

The Mississippi Supreme Court lambasted his practice on more than one occasion. It was listed in every appeal brief that went up as a point of reversible error. In their opinions, the court would rant and rave about the Judge's proclivity to mix prayer into the legal system and then in the end would fail to find that it was reversible error. After all, they too had to be re-elected in Mississippi.

"Cause Number 19,432. State of Mississippi vs. Reginald Foxworthy. Is this case ready for trial?"

And so began the long and arduous task of the calling of the docket. It consisted of Judge Jones going through the huge docket book page-by-page calling out the number and the name of the case. It was a display of power for Judge Jones. He loved sitting at the bench knowing he had every member of the bar in his courtroom. From the great to the not so great, if you had a case on his docket then you had to attend docket call.

Luke walked in as the first case was being called with all eyes turning to him as a hush fell upon the group. Since Susan's death, he had not been in a group of lawyers, or a group of any other sort. He avoided groups lately and wanted to avoid this one but was afraid that his absence would be noted and provide even more grist for the rumor mill.

"Mr. Daniels, docket call begins at nine a.m. In the future I'd appreciate it if you would show me the courtesy of arriving on time." Judge Jones broke through the suppressed uneasiness and then continued with his show.

"Cause Number 19,773, State of Mississippi vs. Willie Terrell."

"Your Honor, if you would show that case continued. I'm expecting some discovery from the District Attorney and should have an announcement at the next term of court," Luke said self-assuredly.

"Mr. Daniels, according to the docket, the discovery time on this case is well past due. I'm inclined to set it for trial during this month."

Luke knew the case was old but didn't want it set for trial. He needed to let the case cool for as long as possible and was delaying with everything he had. Willie Terrell was a black man with a lawn care service in Hampton. He cut Luke's yard. He also cut another man in a fight at the Tip Top lounge about a year ago in an argument over a woman. According to Willie, it was purely self defense and everyone knew it. Apparently, everyone except the DA. Luke was hoping to get it reduced to simple assault, a misdemeanor, and was biding his time until he could get the DA in the right frame of mind.

"Mr. District Attorney, what do you say about this case?" Judge looked over in the direction of Billy Gafford and waited for an answer. Gafford checked his docket and answered without looking at Luke.

"We're ready for trial, your honor."

Luke was surprised. He had not expected Gafford to make such an announcement, and this angered him. Luke had asked for some show of evidence against his client but had as of yet not seen any. He didn't want to push the case right now. He expected the DA didn't have much, but then in these situations you could never be sure. He was tempted to go ahead and get a trial date but instead tried to punt.

"Your honor, I believe if Mr. Gafford would check his records, he would see that I filed a discovery request which is still pending. If we could get that straightened out then I would be ready to set a date."

"Very well, you two confer and get back to me at the conclusion of the docket." Without much of a pause Judge Jones continued on to the next case.

Luke was relieved. He knew that being passed to the foot of the docket was as good as a continuance to the next term, because at the conclusion of docket call everyone was so sick and tired of hearing cases called, they just wanted to bolt, lawyers, the DA and the Judge. Luke made a note to get his client in and talk to him. The guy had paid Luke zero up to this point and about all he would ever get out of him was his yard mowed. He definitely didn't want to end up in a trial.

Judge Jones finished the last case, closed the book with a flourish and bounded from the bench, hardly giving the court bailiff a chance to say his "all rise." Before leaving the bench he gave Billy Gafford a see-me-in-my-chambers look and, in short order, Billy came into the secreted office.

"How many of these are going to trial, Billy," the Judge started off.

"Hard to say, Judge. We'll probably have that last minute scramble where we get pleas right when it's time for trial." Billy knew the Judge was well aware of the December dance they always did, but the court's calendar was discussed as if it were the first time.

"Well, I don't want my schedule tied up with a lot of bull that's not worth a tinker's damn. You hear me. I've got some civil cases that may have to be tried and I don't want any of these petty criminal matters getting in the way of that." Judge Jones delivered this edict with his usual bluster. Billy felt there was some hidden agenda in Jones' attitude that he was masking. He'd have to look at the civil docket and see what the Judge was all riled up about.

"What's the latest on the murder of that bank girl? Do they have any suspects?" Jones asked, knowing where all the gossip pointed, despite his election to be a fair and impartial jurist.

"The lab reports confirm that she was raped. There was a shoe print on the door to the bedroom that came back as a size ten and a half. It's a shoe called the Nike Air something or other. Limox has checked around and found it's one of the most popular shoes on the market and the most popular size. His guess is there were between three and four thousand sold in this area alone. There were fingerprints on the wine glasses. No match on those yet." Gafford hesitated. He was moving onto shaky ground. He knew it was against all rules to be discussing any of this with the Judge but he also knew Judge Jones wanted to hear all the details. It was an all too familiar position for him. Gafford knew he won the majority of his cases by getting the Judge on his side before they went into the courtroom. He didn't pretend to be an outstanding trial lawyer. He won his cases because neither the Judge nor the jury wanted to go soft on crime.

Judge Jones listened to it all quietly. He wondered how much Gafford knew about Luke Daniels' relationship with the victim. He usually said very little in these sessions with his District Attorney. It was not a good idea for him to get too involved in the prosecutor's case, but, hell, if he didn't, Gafford was so dumb he would mess around and lose the damn case. And that didn't look good at election time. When people thought of the court they thought of the judge and the prosecutor together and would vote the same way. It couldn't be helped.

"The news media has slacked off a bit about the case, but that's just because it's Christmas," Gafford continued. "I'm sure when news is slow after the first of the year they'll be on me and the police to find the killer. Maybe somethin' will turn up before then."

"Let's hope so," Jones said sarcastically. "You know we've got an election coming up next summer. We don't want anyone getting ideas about trying to use this case against us." Jones was trying to make it as plain as he could for his less than astute prosecutor.

"Yeah, I hear you." Gafford may not be the brightest lawyer in the world, but he got the picture on this. Find somebody.

Jim DeWeese waited in the lobby of Luther Lambert's office. He had a briefcase with him that had inside it a folder which held the pictures he had taken of Susan Weeks. When he talked with Lambert previously, the man had yelled and screamed at him about where the pictures were and what would happen if someone found them. DeWeese was not a lawyer but he knew enough to understand that it would not be healthy for anyone else to see the pictures, anyone in Hampton that is. He was certain that in some markets in Hollywood the pictures would bring a small fortune. The stills alone could be sold for a tidy sum.

But there was more than photographs. He had three video cameras set up that had started rolling when he flipped a switch. Susan never even knew. They caught some fantastic footage as well. DeWeese never told Lambert about the videos. He regretted Lambert's finding out about the pictures, because Lambert always seemed to pop up unexpectedly before DeWeese could cover himself. He sat there in Lambert's office now, waiting, the pictures and the negatives beside him. In their meeting after the girl's murder, Luther had demanded that the pictures be destroyed. DeWeese had not been able to make himself do it. He had put it off and put it off until, when Lambert asked him about it again, his face gave him away. There was another explosion from Lambert and the demand that he bring them to the office at once. DeWeese drug his feet for a while, but Lambert would not rest until he had his hands on them.

Now DeWeese sat in Lambert's office with the pictures and the negatives in his briefcase. As he waited, Wilson came through the front door and they visited briefly. Wilson looked very much like his father. The same dirty blonde hair, same lanky body that always seemed too big for the clothes on it. Wilson was not as big as his father, more like a smaller version that never grew as much because it was always in the shadow of the bigger man.

"Wilson, I haven't seen you in a while. What have you been up to?" DeWeese put on his best phony face of interest.

Wilson was returning from court, he explained, implying some big case. That much of him was his father, also. They were always involved in the most important of matters. Nothing but the very highest of legal exertion. DeWeese grew tired of it quickly. There was no question about their status. DeWeese just wished he didn't have to hear it all the time.

"And how is that pretty little wife of yours?" DeWeese asked, again feigning interest. Wilson did have a pretty little wife. Rita Clay Lambert was a former beauty queen that had lived for a time in California. Her family was good friends with DeWeese's and he heard about her from his mother. She would have loved him marrying someone like Rita. He often wondered how she wound up with a jerk like Wilson Lambert. Wilson was nothing but for his daddy's money. He strutted and preened and for the most part was laughed at behind his back when he tried to act like the power mogul, just like he was doing now; always so self-important. A client of Wilson's came in the front door and, to DeWeese's relief, the lesser Lambert excused himself to take the client back to his office.

DeWeese paced the floor and was ready to ask how much longer he was going to have to wait when the receptionist put down her phone and told him Mr. Lambert would see him now. Finally, DeWeese thought. Another of Luther's little power plays. He loved to get people down to his office and then make them wait, as if he was so full of important matters that he was doing you a favor by seeing you. Hell, Luther was the one who called him down here. Disgruntled, he yanked his brief case up from the floor and headed back to Lambert's office.

The trail back to Luther's office was filled with shoddy file cabinets and raggedy carpet. This place had needed a remodeling job since he had come back to Hampton, DeWeese thought. He never understood why a man of Lambert's means allowed his workplace to be kept in such a state of disrepair. There was cheap paneling on the walls and pictures that looked liked they were bought somewhere along the side of the road. He passed by Wilson's office where the door was open. His office had been the most recently redone. It was newer than everything else in the firm but looked out of place. All done in very chic, modish decor that already seemed dated. Little embellishments sitting around the room gave it a prissy air, just like Wilson.

"Jim, good to see you. I'm sorry you had to wait but the damn phone. You know how it is. They won't leave me alone." Luther was standing in his doorway to greet DeWeese with hand extended. They shook hands and Luther almost jerked him into the office and shut the door.

"You're looking a little peaked, my boy," Lambert started off. DeWeese hated the condescending tone Lambert used so arrogantly. He regretted having ever allowed himself to become involved with this man but was now uncertain how to deftly extricate himself.

He did not want his business to fail. He had to make it. It may be his only chance. Yet, he often wondered if suffering in the clutches of this intolerable control freak was too great a price to pay for anything. The feeling was especially severe when he had to subject himself to these obsequious little meetings where Lambert filled the room with his ego like a monstrous deity demanding veneration. DeWeese did not toady well.

"All this hard work, Luther. You know, I've got to protect our investment," he said with a chuckle. The groveling was coming a bit easier today. "It takes a lot of work to maintain a business such as this. You know, you can't count on anyone to see something the way you do, so you wind up doing it all yourself. I'm sure you find that here in your office. Of course, you have Wilson. That makes it easier on you." DeWeese could not help himself with the double-intended remark.

"I've been there, son, believe me. You don't think I got where I am sitting on my duff." Luther grinned at DeWeese and leaned back in his chair. "There's been a lot of hard work within these walls." Lambert wanted to get down to business and after a few more moments of cajoling slid into his real agenda.

"So, did you bring me something to look at?" Luther asked absently. The master was plying his specialty. To the casual observer, he might have been asking about most anything, work, finances, the latest market report. The directness was understood only by the person in front of him. Get'em out boy and let's get this over with. Luther's hulking frame hunched over his desk with eyes flickering

DeWeese opened the case, pulled out a sheath and his long, thin fingers handed it over the desk without saying a word. He wore a suit today since he was here in the lawyer's office. Pin-striped with a rich blue shirt and loud tie that he had bought in New Orleans. He wanted to make the statement of successful advertising executive. The film he developed himself was there with nothing on the folder to suggest the contents. He looked at Lambert as he eagerly flipped it open and pulled out the contents which DeWeese could hardly bring himself to view. They brought back too many memories.

Why hadn't she gone away with him? They could be living the high life in LA right now. He could have said goodbye to Luther, to Hampton and he and Susan could have been on top of the world. But, no, she had to say no. Damn her.

Lambert looked like a devilish adolescent sneaking his first look at Playboy. He held the photographs of the naked beauty in his hands, slowly going through them with salacious intensity. DeWeese knew what was in his mind. Partly. In a way, it was a shame she was gone.

"It's too bad the poor girl had to go and get herself killed," Lambert mumbled in an odd tone. DeWeese watched him closely. The old lawyer was practiced in the art of deceit, of covering his thoughts. But there was something there. Lambert had expressed his laments earlier over the loss. We could have really used her was the way he had put it, DeWeese recalled. They had agreed that she could have been the goose that laid a golden egg for DeWeese Advertising, and Jim had verbalized the thought. He remembered Lambert grinning like a Cheshire cat and adding that, yes, we could have really used her.

DeWeese was familiar with all the local rumors about what happened the night she died. Now they were being shaded with some other reflections that he couldn't quite fix in his mind. The tone Lambert used. Was that it? Did he know something else about the murder? DeWeese knew he was tight with the DA. Had Luther learned something that was not public knowledge? For some reason, a sense of uneasiness came over him. The room suddenly felt enclosed and smothering. He heard the furnace kick on down the hall and hot air from the duct blew down and across his face with a sickly, defiled staleness that made his lips feel parched. Something flashed in his mind of his decline in California where cocaine controlled his life. Lambert said something that he didn't catch.

"What's that?" He asked.

"I said I think it's best these don't get out. It might give someone the wrong impression, what with the murder investigation and all." Lambert stared straight into DeWeese, filling him with near panic. "I'm going to put them away where no one can get to them. If anything should ever come up, I can claim confidentiality as an attorney."

"But I thought you wanted them destroyed…" DeWeese trailed off not sure of Lambert's intent. What was on that table also represented evidence that could point to just a handful of people who really knew.

"Don't you worry about it. These are the only ones, right?"

DeWeese nodded.

Lambert slid his chair over and opened two doors on the credenza behind his desk, revealing a safe hidden behind some books.

"I'm the only one with the combination to this. No one even knows this safe exists except my secretary, and she won't know they're here. They'll be in here, just in case."

With Lambert's last words the rush of anxiety overwhelmed DeWeese again and he wanted out of this room. Just in case of what? How much did Lambert know about DeWeese and Susan? She and DeWeese had spent a lot of time together: on the road, in the studio. DeWeese realized the intimacy between them. Almost physical. And then the breakup. And, the blackmail. Did Lambert know? Just what did he know?

"Okay, that's fine. Well, look, I've got some people at the studio so I need to get going." And without waiting for a response, he stood up and left the office.

Outside in the air, DeWeese breathed in deeply, trying to let the flush of discomfort pass from him. What had happened in there? He wondered if it was some strange flashback from his not-so-far-removed drug habit. He walked slowly to his car and quickly got it going down the street with the window open letting the fresh air wash across his ashen face. He thought for a while he might have to see a doctor. As he drove it faded away and he felt better. But the memory invaded his mind like a demon. And he couldn't forget the blackouts. He hoped he never felt like that again. He hoped it was not something that drugs had done to him permanently, some disability that hard living in California had set in him, to forever haunt some nook and cranny of his head, lurking with lecherous intent and then not knowing what he had done. He hoped it wasn't that. And, he usually kept himself in check.

It didn't occur to him that it might be something else. That it could have been something Lambert said. What had he said, really? He was sure Lambert explained that he wanted the pictures destroyed. But then he decided to keep them. What for? What else could Lambert want to do with those pictures? Surely, he wouldn't try to use them in any way again. How could he? And what was that remark about confidentiality? Did Lambert think he had something to do with Susan's death? DeWeese shuddered again and thought that he would be sick.

Or maybe it was the fact that he had lied to Lambert. He did have another set of the pictures. And another set of negatives. All securely tucked away in a safety deposit box at Guaranty National Bank. But what good were they to him? He had Susan's signature on enough releases. He could use them. But for what? If they came out now, would it somehow give him a motive for killing her? DeWeese was scared. He wished he had someone to talk to about this mess. He needed a lawyer, but he couldn't talk to anyone here in Hampton. What could he do?

CHAPTER SIX

Rita Clay Lambert was the wife of Wilson Hughes Lambert, Attorney-at-law. She was a beautiful woman, two-time former beauty queen: Miss Hampton one year and Miss University from Ole Miss another year. And almost Miss Mississippi. She finished as first alternate in both of those tries and vowed the second time that she had enough. No more beauty pageants.

She never loved her husband. She had only gone out with him on a whim. He was good looking and witty and flashy and she was bored with her life in Hampton. But she was never seriously interested. After several months of dating him exclusively only because there was nothing else to do in Hampton, she began to see how much power and control the father wielded over the son and decided she wanted no part of it. But Wilson begged her not to break up with him. He pledged his undying love and devotion. And then he proposed marriage.

Even though she said no, the paper carried an announcement of the engagement and a party was planned. They were running her life and she felt completely helpless. She was furious and immediately headed to Wilson's office to tell him so. When she arrived he was not there but his father was. He could tell she was angry and put on his most consoling, paternal character. He convinced her to come on back to his office. At first he talked about what a good life she and Wilson could have. But, I don't love him was her response. But you'll grow together was his counter. I can't marry him was her final word.

Then the benevolent persona transformed and she saw another man before her. He pulled an envelope from the safe in his office and handed it across to her. She knew without looking what it was. She sat there and began to cry.

Rita went to college with high hopes. She wanted to be Miss Mississippi. In February of her sophomore year she was in the Miss Hampton pageant and won. At the state pageant, she was everybody's favorite. But she only won first alternate. Everyone reassured her that it was her first time, that many girls were in the pageant three or four times and that she should try again. Her spirits lifted and she set her sights on next year.

Next year came and her sorority promoted her strongly in the Miss University pageant at Ole Miss. She won. Her talent was strong, her body was in great shape, the auburn haired beauty was at the top of her game. She was constantly flattered with remarks that she was surely the next Miss Mississippi. The state pageant came and she was ready. But when it was over, she was again only first alternate.

This time the well-wisher's words of maybe next year fell on unreceptive ears. She knew she had enough. She had done her best and if that was not good enough, well… She was through with it, that's all she knew.

Shortly after the state pageant she got engaged and her fiancé went off to medical school in Jackson. She didn't need that beauty queen stuff. She would finish her degree and they would get married next June. One weekend, she drove to Jackson to surprise him on a Friday night and found him in bed with one of his fellow students. She was devastated. She drove on to Hampton that night and never went back to Ole Miss.

A sorority sister worked for the William Morris Agency in Los Angeles, so one day Rita arrived on her doorstep. She got a job, but the pay was terrible by California standards. Everything was so expensive.

She met a photographer who was mesmerized by her beauty. After the slap in the face from her medical student's infidelity and the wounded ego from the beauty pageant, her positive mental attitude needed a boost. She soaked up the photographer's praises and before she knew it she had moved from modeling pictures to nudity. When a small part in a movie turned out to require more than just nudity she freaked and ran out of the shooting. She packed her bags and caught the first flight home.

And then Luther Lambert wound up with the pictures. How could he have gotten them, she wondered as she sat in front of him, tears slowly dropping down her lovely face.

He didn't want to expose her, he explained. He went on about how it would hurt her family. He would never do that he said. As long as she didn't hurt his family. His son. Blackmail, plain and simple.

And this is how she began a life with Wilson. They got married, a fabulous wedding, with his father taking care of everything, of course. And now they had two children. But she had never loved her husband. He was spineless, letting his father dictate every detail of his life. She goaded him about it continually. Some of their worst arguments were about his father. His comeback was always about how she loved the money that came from his working with his father. And that was usually how their bouts ended.

It was not about money. And it was about money. There was no doubt in her mind that Wilson would never be able to make it on his own as a lawyer. His success was because he was his father's son. It was about money because money made her life bearable. There were times when she forgot that her father-in-law had the pictures. And there were times when she forgot that she didn't love her husband. But they were rare. The sparkle that once emitted from her was gone. She was still a very attractive woman with a good body. There were a few extra pounds on the five-foot-four frame and there was a streak or two of gray in the auburn hair that she never worried about covering up. But her former radiance clouded from the strain that living a life of pretense imposed.

Rita lived a comfortable life. She had a nice house, compliments of the father. A nice car, also compliments of the father. A maid, again compliments of the father. He thought he owned everything and everybody. She felt sorry for poor Arlita, the maid. Her life was as controlled by Luther Lambert as was Rita's. Arlita cleaned the law office, she cleaned at home for Eloise Lambert and she cleaned here at the home of Rita and Wilson.

She was here today. The children were in school and Rita busied herself as Arlita went about the regular cleaning. About the same age, Arlita had five children to Rita's two, worked two part time jobs that were almost full-time and took college courses, too. The woman amazed Rita. Whenever she began to feel sorry for herself she would take a good look at the life Arlita lived and start to feel not so bad.

Rita was busy getting ready for a party. The annual bar Christmas party was to be held the following Saturday night at their house. It was not a party she was looking forward to but, once again, their house, her house, had been offered by Luther. She knew it was him. The annual affair was given by the Bar Auxiliary, of which she was a member, but before they had even asked, Luther suggested it to Wilson who sprung it on Rita. She didn't really mind because putting on a function such as this was a bright spot in her life. It was one more thing to keep her from thinking about the misery of her personal life. She had plenty of help. Luther saw to that. And the Auxiliary wives did, too. Several of them would arrive shortly to start putting the finishing touches on the decorations. Outside, the sound of a car in the drive way drew her to the window, where she saw Wilson's mother getting out with a box of decorations.

"Need any help?" Rita called out from the back door.

"Yes, please, I've got two more boxes in the trunk." Eloise Lambert was a wonderful woman who treated Rita like her own daughter. Wilson was an only child and Eloise often confided in Rita that she had always wished for another child, a girl, so she would have a daughter to do things with. As she put it, the minute Wilson was born he was lost to her as his father groomed him to be the heir apparent to the Lambert legacy.

"Oooh wee, Miz Eloise, these are some fine things you brought. You jest always get the prettiest stuff." Arlita joined them with her mouth agape at the beautiful trimmings and ornaments. Soon several more ladies arrived with boxes of decorations and in no time the house was beginning to look a lot like Christmas.

The Bar Auxiliary Christmas Party posed a little problem for Luke. He always went and he wanted to go this year. But he didn't want to go alone. That meant he needed to get a date. And that was the problem. Where was he going to find a date? Recent events had worked on him to such an extent that while he was not a hermit he was also not in big demand on the Hampton social scene. He was not very interested in a social life, preferring to spend his days and much of the night working, his only outlet being his habitual devotion to running. That kept him sane, but it did not provide much of an opportunity for a date.

There was a race coming up Saturday in Gulfport and he decided that would be a nice release for the week's pent up anxieties. It was barely an hour's drive and the getaway would do him good.

On Saturday, he arrived in Gulfport in plenty of time to warm up before the race. He felt great and was ready for the run when the starting gun sounded. The course was smooth and flat with a view of the beach. He relaxed completely as he breathed in the fresh salt air. His pace was good and as he progressed down the 5 kilometer distance he realized that he was having one of his best times ever. This spurred him on even more and when the finish line was in sight he poured it on and burned under the timer. When the results were tallied he finished second in his age division, good enough to get him a trophy. He was thrilled. With all the goings on in his life he needed a little something good. Placing gave him a boost while he hung around and chatted with the other racers. A guy he knew from law school was there and as they talked a group formed. One of the racers was a female who appeared to be unattached. As time went by she and Luke found themselves alongside one another and in short order the whole group was headed off to get breakfast.

Luke's new acquaintance was an interesting lady. Her name was Christy Weidmann and she worked for an advertising agency. Originally from New Orleans, she came to Biloxi when she started with the agency four years ago. Twenty-nine years old, she had a runner's lean taut body with long straight blonde hair. She displayed a more than passing interest in Luke and he returned the attention. They finished their breakfast and withdrew to the parking lot, saying their goodbyes and readying to leave. Luke walked Christy to her car where they lingered. Without warning, Luke heard himself inviting Christy to attend the Christmas party with him.

"It's in Hampton at the home of Wilson Lambert. It should be quite an event. The Lamberts are known for overdoing it when it comes to parties. What do you think? Could you join me? We could drive back to the coast afterwards or you could stay in Hampton."

"Why don't we go back to my apartment and let me call my cousin and see what she's up to this evening. Maybe I could spend the night with her."

She liked this guy but didn't want to wind up out of town with someone she hardly knew and no place to stay. They left the restaurant with Luke following her in his car. She drove a sporty yellow Chrysler LeBaron with a white convertible top and white interior. At her apartment she left Luke in the living room with the stereo while she went into the bedroom to call her cousin. She was back shortly with a smile.

"Shelly says to come on, she'd loved to have me," Christy offered pleasantly. "I can't leave until later this afternoon, though. Why don't you give me your number and I'll call you when I get there."

"Sounds great." Luke was beaming. His first thought was to give her a business card but they were in the car. He scribbled his home number on a pad. She walked him out to his car and in saying goodbye offered him her hand which he took but then leaned over and gave her a gentle kiss on the cheek.

"This'll be fun," he declared as he pulled the door shut on the Cadillac. As he navigated from the parking lot, she chased after him.

"Luke, wait. What'll I wear to this thing?"

He looked at her standing there in her runner's shorts and T-shirt and wanted to say she should just wear that. Her well-toned legs still carried a good tan. He thought for a minute before answering.

"There'll be all sorts of outfits there. Pretty dressy though, I imagine. I'll be wearing a suit. With legs like yours, let me suggest something short," he said with a grin.

"Something short. Boy, you're a real help. Alright, I'll see you tonight."

The drive back to Hampton was great for Luke. The weather was one of those typical south Mississippi days where it was hard to know for sure if it was winter or fall. The air was cool but the sun shone down brightly, pretending that there weren't just fifteen shopping days left until Christmas. Luke had done very little in getting ready for the season. There were no decorations up at his house. The girls at the office had put up a few things and had talked about getting a tree. Maybe he should do that today.

He got to his house, showered and then set out to get a tree for his house and the office. There was a place out in the country that cut live trees and he found his way there shortly. Picking out two trees he had them cut and ready to go before he realized he had no way to get them back to town. The owners of the tree farm didn't blink before coming up with a plan. In no time, the convertible top was down and he had two huge trees sticking out the Caddy.

Driving back into town Luke got some funny looks but friendly smiles acknowledging his effort for the season. He took both trees back to his house, arriving in time to see his yard man finishing up.

"Willie, you're just the man I need to see. Come help me with these trees."

"Mr. Luke, you beat all I ever seen. Who else would use a Cadillac to haul a Christmas tree?" Willie laughed.

They got the trees unloaded with Willie giving Luke orders about the proper way to do the job. They needed to soak, Willie explained. Luke fetched some large buckets and they got them in water. Then he scrambled around in the attic until he found his tree stand. Willie grumbled about how it wasn't worth having and in about two hours Luke finally had a fresh green tree in his living room. He talked Willie into staying to help him with the lights.

"Willie, why have you taken so long to get with me." Luke started, changing the subject. "I've been calling about your court case. Judge Jones tried to set that case for trial at docket call and may still give me a hard time about it. The DA says you need to be in prison."

"Boss, you know I was only protecting myself. That sorry nigger I cut's trying to ruin me. There's witnesses that can tell you that."

Willie's face fell, the sparkle leaving his black features. Luke felt Willie was telling him the truth, but wasn't sure he could get Gafford to see that. Willie was a hard working man with a family and a solid business. He did lawn care, landscape remodeling and any other job on the outside you might need. He did work for a lot of Hampton's upper crust and they all trusted him. But the man he had his scrape with must be raising Cain with the DA. They finished the lights and Willie got his stuff together to leave. Luke offered to pay for his help but Willie would have none of it.

"No, no, no! You'se doing 'nough for me. I goin' wind up owin' you a whole lot more than you'll owe me. You jest hold on to your money."

"Alright, Willie, but pay attention to what I'm telling you. Keep in touch with me. If I call your house you get back with me right away, you hear. And be working on that list of witnesses you say can help me with your case. This is serious, you understand?"

Luke hoped he was getting through to the man. A lot of Luke's clients from the black community seemed to think that if they ignored them, charges would just go away. Luke wanted to make sure Willie was not one of those.

"Yes sir, I got ya. I'm gonna be right here whenever you call me." Willie crawled inside his truck and drove away.

Inside, Luke admired the tree. It was pretty with only the lights. Maybe he could get Miss Advertising Executive over later tonight for a little trim-the-tree party. Five o'clock. He went out back to bring in some wood for a fire later on and then hurried to the shower. He was starting to look forward to the evening.

After the shower he stepped into the closet, pulling out a double breasted sport coat with some grey slacks. The coat was dark navy, almost black, with handsome gold buttons. He pulled out a white shirt to go with it and a red tie.

Christy called at six saying she was in town and would be ready by eight. Shortly before eight he left his house. The top was still down on his car and he started to put it up, when he remembered she also had a convertible. The air was cool but they would not be driving far. He climbed in and turned the heater on full blast. The night was cool and crisp under a clear sky and the ride was comfortable.

His date answered the door and he immediately saw she had taken his advice. She was wearing a silver sequined dress that fit like a second skin. And it was short. She had on shiny hose that matched the sparkle of her dress and metallic silver high heels. Her blonde hair was pulled back with sequined combs and there was some sort of shiny silver glitter in her hair. Luke's mouth was agape. She had looked good this morning in her running clothes, but this was unbelievable.

"Did I pick the right thing?" she asked coyly, knowing from the look on his face.

"I'd say you did just fine. Better than fine." Luke winced at his masterful choice of words.

"Do we need to go on now, or can you come in for a minute? I'd like you to meet my cousin." She stepped back away from the door so Luke could enter.

Christy introduced her cousin, Shelly Cox, a waif of a girl who was a nurse at Hampton Memorial. The conversation floated aimlessly for a while, until Luke said they should be going. When they got to the car, Christy laughed out loud.

"The top down, in December?" she asked comically.

"Well, it's not that cold out and with the heater on it's quite comfortable. Nice, actually. I can put it up if it's a problem."

"No, no, it's okay. As long as we don't go racing down the interstate. I don't want to lose this hairdo, you know."

"We won't be going anywhere near the interstate and we can drive as slowly as you like."

They did drive slowly. Luke was being a tour guide, giving her the run down on Hampton's populace, the good, the bad and the ugly. They arrived at the Lambert's shortly after eight and there was already a crowd.

"Wow, this does look like a lovely party," Christy exclaimed, looking at all the cars parked along the street. "And look at the decorations. I can't wait to see the inside of the house."

There were tiny white lights on all the small trees in front of the house. In the larger oaks, there were larger lights, giving the house a misty, surreal glow. All the shrubbery along the walk and the front beds had small white lights woven into them. The front door had a huge wreath of fresh cedar as wide as the door with fresh fruits adorning it. There were frosted apples, oranges, satsumas, grapes, pears, and a pineapple all arranged beautifully in the cedar hanging on the dark-stained, glossy wooden door. Garland from the same fresh cedar as the wreath and with the same tiny white lights draped the door down to two white poinsettia trees in moss covered clay pots on either side. Real candles in sets of three were in each window on both levels of the front of the house.

They were greeted at the front door by Mrs. Wilson Lambert. Luke introduced Christy. He had only met Rita a few times himself and had never noticed that she was as beautiful as she looked that night. She was wearing a straight black tunic dress with elegant black beading and sequins around the V-neck, along the shoulders, at the end of the sleeves, and along the bottom hem. The length was just below the knee with a slit that rose up her shapely leg covered in black stockings. She had on simple black heels that made her legs look stunning.

Inside, the decorations were even more lavish than the outside. In the living room was a shiny black grand piano with a man in a tuxedo playing Christmas music. The tree touched the 10 foot ceiling and was covered with the same little white lights as outside. Lavish ornaments all in varying designs of white hung expertly from every limb of the massive cedar.

In the dining room the table had a centerpiece of white calla lilies and different types of greenery. White ornaments were in the centerpiece and strewn around the food. A feast of meats, cheeses and fruits covered the table. A large butler's pantry next to the dining room had been converted to the bar where two black men in white jackets mixed cocktails for the guests.

Christy and Luke made their way with only a few stops from the front door and joined the crowd waiting for their drinks. Luke knew almost everyone there and the conversation had gone little deeper than his introducing Christy and her getting complimented on her good looks. Luke got them both a glass of wine and they moved on. In the kitchen there was too much activity for guests to stand and they were pushed on to the breakfast room. More food covered the table and the counter from the kitchen. Desserts too numerous to choose from were everywhere.

Luke grabbed a small piece of chocolate fudge, his weakness, as they continued to move through the house. The party spilled out onto the back porch and the patio beyond. There were people standing around in the yard and around the pool where a group of white candles floated. And every tree in the back yard was lit with the small white lights.

"Luke, this is absolutely beautiful. Thank you for asking me."

"Hey, my pleasure," he said as he put his arm around her waist and gave a gentle hug. "I'm certainly enjoying being here with the prettiest girl in the place."

"Thank you," was her simple reply.

The evening proceeded with them moving from group to group continually admiring the magnificent decorations until they finally came to a circle with Rita Lambert.

"Mrs. Lambert, I have to say, your house is beautiful," Christy began. "The decorations are more elegant than anything I have ever seen. Did you do them yourself?"

"Me and a wonderful group of ladies here tonight that helped out. Yes, we did it all," she said as if it were nothing.

"It's all so beautiful. Luke here thinks you had a theme. Do you? He said you were making the statement: 'White Christmas.'"

"Well, yes, Luke, that was the idea. I was wondering if anyone would pick up on it. We never get snow here and so I thought I'd give the old expression a new meaning. How clever of you, Luke. I'm impressed." She had known of Luke for a long time but had never really known him. She looked at him tonight as if for the first time.

Luke was visibly embarrassed. It had been so obvious to him he thought every one knew it and that his date, the advertising executive, would surely have noticed.

"I just noticed that every where I looked there was white. I didn't think I was being clever," Luke explained, trying to downplay whatever it was that made everyone start looking at him. Rita Lambert continued talking about the decorations and what she had done here and there with her theme. He had little interest in her decorating scheme, but suddenly saw in her a beauty he had never noticed until now. As she stood before him going on about the preparations for the party, he started realizing something else about her. As Luke scrutinized Rita Lambert, one of the servants interrupted.

"Excuse me, Mrs. Lambert, Arlita needs you in the kitchen."

"You folks will have to excuse me," she explained turning from the group, but before she left she looked directly at Luke. "Thank you, Mr. Daniels, for noticing about the decorations.

I appreciate that." She left the group and started toward the kitchen.

Luke didn't know why he suddenly felt awkward. The rest of their small group just stood there with no one offering to pick up the conversation.

From across the room, Luther Lambert had his eye on his daughter-in-law as she left the group with Luke Daniels. He saw Luke's eyes follow Rita as she went into the house.

"Who's that girl with Daniels?" he asked to no one in particular. He was standing with Judge Jones, James Germany and several other lawyers.

"I don't know, but let's hope she fares better than the last girl he went out with," Germany laughed at his own humor.

The party had not been without an ample amount of talk about Luke. As he moved around the gathering, whispers arose about the last night of Susan Weeks. For the past few weeks conversations around the town had been filled with other matters. But with the congregation of lawyers all in one spot tonight the spark of rumors had rekindled upon Luke's appearance with a beautiful woman. As the night wore on and the alcohol flowed the spurious accounts of that fateful night became even more exaggerated.

Not one of them even remotely resembled what really happened, but that did not deter the telling. They surpassed colored embellishment and moved into the ludicrous. Some of the more reasoned of the group began to notice the bizarre twist they were taking and became annoyed with the fervor with which some of the intoxicated lawyers were relishing the act, like a bunch of sharks in a feeding frenzy.

James Germany was the most vociferous. He was well into inebriation which had helped him forget that he and Lambert had been at odds since his departure from the firm. Tonight, in the group denigration of Luke Daniels they had once again become fast friends.

"There's no telling what happened to poor Susan," Germany said, the use of her first name implying his close personal relationship to her. He had taken on the role of her most revered suitor now that Luke took the butt of his attacks. "You know, I heard this is not the first time his violent temper has gotten him in trouble."

Judge Jones stood there saying nothing, knowing he should remove himself from any talk of a criminal investigation and at the same time frozen to the spot in hopes of hearing some new juicy tidbit of the story. He would not join in to this hearsay, but his ears were as tuned as a fine instrument. As Germany realized he had an audience, he became even more animated.

"They're saying now that there might be another woman involved. That he was trying to break it off with this other girl and when she found out he was seeing Susan she followed them around and she's the one who actually killed her."

"From what I hear, all the evidence points to Daniels." Luther Lambert joined the smear. "The girl's bedroom door was kicked in and the shoe print was a jogging shoe. I mean, I'm not one to point fingers, but they've already identified Daniels as being there that night." They all knew Luke was a runner. The implication was clear. "If the evidence places him there and his shoe kicked the door in it's not very likely that someone else was wearing his shoes." Lambert had no idea that the shoe print was Luke's. Gafford had only told him the door had been kicked in. His investigator had picked up from some of his detective friends that it was a running shoe. The pieces fit together nicely, though, in taking aim at Daniels.

"They're even saying now there might have been drugs involved," Germany jumped back in, reclaiming his spot in the grandstanding.

"Did they find drugs?" Judge Jones heard himself asking uncontrollably. He was fighting to stay out of the conversation and losing the battle.

"They're not letting out everything they know." Germany covered himself in the cloak of investigative secrecy, as if he were privy to certain confidential information. "There's no telling what they found out there in that house. I heard it was a wreck. Her roommate won't even stay there anymore; it was in such a mess. You know that was Bud Holt's daughter?" Everyone already knew the roommate was Jennifer Holt, lending credibility to the rest of Germany's fabrications.

"I'm afraid our boy Daniels may have bit off more than he can chew this time, folks. Ever since that deposition where he attacked Wilson, I've had my doubts about him." Luther paused long enough to let his words soak in. "Yeah, I knew then that there was something troublesome there. Why, if I hadn't come in he's liable to have jumped on Wilson. He grabbed his shirt and tore it with witnesses right there. Miss Margy was the court reporter. Ask her about it."

And with those few words Lambert planted a seed of uncertainty in the mind of the Circuit Judge that would ultimately hear the case of the murderer of Susan Weeks. Lambert didn't know for sure if it would be Daniels, but he had a strong suspicion that it might be.

By ten thirty some of the guests had already started leaving. The more abstemious said their good-byes to the Lamberts and thanked them on their way out for opening their house for the auxiliary party. To another faction of the Hampton Bar this signaled the beginning of the real party and the liquor flowed liberally. The gala got louder and the talk more raucous.

James Germany was drunk and getting more so by the glass. With each drink he assailed Luke's character with more hostility. He took pleasure in his calumny of a fellow member of the bar mainly because of the audience it gathered for him. Everyone wanted to hear more. As the party thinned and Germany grew louder his voice carried over the house so that all could hear. He was on a roll like a hawker at a cheap carnival. He set aside any learning he ever had of the caveat that all men are innocent until proven guilty and proceeded to convict Luke of the murder of Susan Weeks in the minds of those surrounding him.

Christy took note of the crowds gathering around Germany as she made a trip to the ladies' room. She didn't catch any name at first, only the truculent tone being spewed upon Germany's listeners. On the return trip, she happened to catch Luke's name and slowed her pace at a nearby food table to catch what was being said.   It didn't take long for her to be shocked. She quickly learned that a young bank employee had been killed and that the group she was listening to thought Luke had something to do with it. Her head turned slightly to hear better and her ears were pricked to their limit. A hand touched her waist causing a yelp to escape her lips.

"Hi, there, good looking."

"Luke, you startled me."

"Are you always startled when someone calls you good-looking?" he asked with a grin. "Should I say something less flattering? Maybe we should just talk business." Luke's face revealed the humor in his words and Christy laughed nervously. The conversation at the other end of the table remained constant and Luke could not avoid hearing them.

"Have you tried the shrimp? It's delicious," she said loudly, hoping to keep his attention away from the others.

"I haven't eaten much all night. I know the lady who catered this and she always does a great job. I think I'll get a plate and perhaps we can share it." He moved around her toward the end of the table where the plates were.

Germany did not see Luke approaching.   Lost in the booze and his theatrics, he was oblivious to Luke's slow movement down the room. Luke had never liked Germany and was now paying little attention to anything he had to say. Except for the fact that Germany was so loud, Luke might have been spared. He froze when he heard the phrase 'that poor girl,' knowing they were referring to Susan Weeks.

Across the room, Rita Lambert stood talking with Billy Gafford and his wife. When she happened to notice Christy standing by herself, the consummate hostess disengaged herself from the Gaffords and moved over to speak with Christy, who stood immovably by the shrimp remoulade.   Unaware of what was transpiring at the other end of the table, she engaged her guest politely.

"Christy, I'm so glad you were able to come. How long have you known Luke?"

"Oh, I'm sorry, Mrs. Lambert, what did you ask?" Christy turned to face Rita but kept glancing back over her shoulder.

"I asked how long you've known Luke." Until now managing the party had occupied her fully and she was relaxing for the first time that evening. She prided herself on being a good judge of other's feelings and quickly noted that Christy's attention was drawn toward Luke whom Rita saw down the table.

"Oh, we only met today. We were at a race where a mutual friend introduced us and he invited me to join him tonight. I've had a wonderful time, too. Your house is absolutely beautiful. The decorations are all so very lovely."

Luke still stood motionless taking in Germany's tirade. Anger raged up inside him that he tried fiercely to control. Germany was an idiot, he told himself, and everyone knew it. He glanced over in the direction of the group and one of the wives saw him looking in their direction. She nudged her husband who then noticed Luke and suddenly looked like a snared animal. He tried to smile at Luke which only made his expression more miserable. Someone else caught his face and then realized Luke was hearing every word that spewed from James Germany.

Luke knew that he should just turn around and leave the little bastard alone. That no one paid any attention to him any way. But something wouldn't let him. The weeks of tension he had endured seemed to well up inside of him at this moment, set off by the drunken rantings of a foolish weasel of a lawyer. All of Luke's thoughts were displayed in the expression on his face watched by those around Germany.

When Germany finally realized that he had lost their attention, he silenced himself and looked around to find what else could possibly have drawn them. In short order his eyes met Luke's.

"Well, if it isn't the devil himself," he chided with slurred words.

"And what exactly do you mean by that?" Luke was barely controlling his rage.

"Oh, I don't know. Why don't you tell us? Straighten us all out on what happened that last night you had with Susan Weeks?"

Luke set the plate down he was holding and turned to face Germany head on, moving a step in his direction.

"And what concern should that be of yours, Mr. Germany? I'm not accustomed to having to answer to you about what I do."

"No, but you're going to have to answer to someone about Susan Weeks. The poor girl didn't deserve to be violated the way you…"

Before he could finish his sentence Luke lunged forward and grabbed him by his lapel. Luke's swift action bumped the table toppling the candelabra with hot wax sailing.

Rita Lambert was the first to react. She leaped to the scuffle and pushed herself between the two.

"Stop it. Stop it right now," she shrieked. Along with the rest of the room she had watched the interchange in numbed silence and only tumbling candles shook her loose.

Luke stepped back at once, realizing the scene he had made. He glanced around at the horror stricken faces before speaking.

"Rita, I apologize. Mr. Germany over stepped his bounds. But apparently so have I and I am sincerely sorry." He reached over to set the candelabra upright and moved to retrieve the candles.

Germany was as white as a ghost. Luke was several inches taller than he and in much better shape. Germany spent a lot of time boozing it up and none on physical fitness. He slowly realized that, but for Rita Lambert, he could have just gotten his ass kicked. Rita gave him a look that was almost as bad as the one he had seen in Daniel's face. He stood there speechless for the first time that evening.

Rita didn't know what to do next. Luke had moved down and rejoined Christy and they were headed out of the room toward the front foyer, brushing by Gafford in their exit. Rita barked a quick order to one of the servers to get the room straight and then she followed after Luke and Christy. They were already out the front door when she caught up with them.

"Luke, I don't know what to say. I'm sorry."

"You? Why should you be sorry because I made a fool out of myself? I can't believe I let that little worm get to me, and the rest of your guests. They got quite a show, didn't they? I can't apologize enough." Luke looked about as hang-dog as a man could, she thought.

"Oh, the hell with them," she said frankly. "I'm more concerned with Christy. I'm sorry you had to see Hampton's finest in action. Luke's been under considerable pressure lately. I hope you won't judge him by this first encounter." She looked back at Luke sensitively.

With her last remark, Luke looked more directly at her face and into her eyes. He knew that the whole city had to be talking about him but no one he knew as casually as Rita Lambert made any comments to him. In her face he saw a compassion he had never noticed before; didn't believe was possible in any one connected with this family. The Lamberts were a thick-skinned bunch. But Rita suddenly appeared differently to him. What was it? Knowing? Understanding? Something passed between them. An identification. A recognition of something kindred. Something.

Luke noticed for the first time that Christy was shivering. The night had chilled considerably and her bare shoulders were cold. He took his coat and held it for her to put on. They parted from Rita and headed down the street to where he had parked the Cadillac with the top still down. He cranked it up and they sat in silence while the top covered them. Unsure what to say, they drove in silence.

CHAPTER SEVEN

Christmas passed and the holidays faded as Hampton moved into the New Year. January in south Mississippi was a month of gray days blended with cold and rain when folks stayed inside nursing cabin fever. Luke followed suit. Work gave him plenty to do. His practice was rolling despite the events of the fall and he allowed himself to be consumed by it, spending long hours at the office. There was little else that held his interest these days. He had not had a date since the fiasco at the Christmas Party with Christy. Their parting that night had been cordial enough with the promise to get together again soon but since then he had not been so inclined. There had been no event that he needed a date for and so he had not pursued the situation, preferring instead to immerse himself at work, to stick with what he knew.

That had proven beneficial. Several cases were moving forward in a timely fashion that he believed would soon be at trial stage. One of his strongest cases was for Karen Ainsworth, a nurse anesthetist who made good money in her profession. Unfortunately, she did not fare as well in choosing men. A longstanding boyfriend, Frankie Johnson, had experienced unsettled employment and a reputation for partying too much. He also had a bout with drugs and was busted for marijuana a few years before he met Karen. The boyfriend and she were together on a Sunday afternoon outing at a local lake when her car was stolen. Karen followed the usual procedures in making a claim against her insurance carrier who had been dragging their feet in paying. Their slowness turned into delaying tactics that angered Karen which brought her to Luke.

After their initial contact and Luke's demand letter got no response, suit was filed. Through discovery Luke learned that there was no reason the claim had not been paid and that, in fact, the company acknowledged in an interoffice memo it should have been paid long ago. The memo from one of the adjusters had been inadvertently left in the claims file.

Trial in the matter was set in February. Three weeks away and things were starting to click. Luke had the defense just where he wanted them. Through some key depositions he had the insurance company representatives conceding there was no reason they had not paid. That there was no reason Karen Ainsworth did not have her money for the car. Unfortunately, in depositions of his client and her friend, information surfaced that the boyfriend had a car stolen at a lake on a Sunday afternoon, much the same as Karen's. The defense also discovered that the boyfriend had been involved in drugs and was busted, spending a year in jail for something more than just a small amount of marijuana. The defendants had done their homework. Despite the fact that this had little connection to Karen, it created a cloud that could affect a jury's mindset toward a verdict that would punish the insurance company for its disregard of the rights of its insured. Luke scheduled Karen and her boyfriend to come into his office to discuss these details and other matters concerning the approaching trial.

When Karen arrived for the appointment alone, Luke was irritated but then decided to make good of the opportunity. After all, Karen was his client, not the bozo she was living with. Luke stepped out to the foyer and asked Karen back to his office. She was an attractive girl, really a woman at twenty eight. Well educated. Good income. So why did she hang around the other character, Luke wondered.

"Come on, Karen, have a seat," Luke offered as they entered his office. "Could I get you something to drink?"

"Some coffee would be nice. I was at the hospital until after midnight last night. It's still kind of early for me."

"We really needed to talk. Our trial is in three weeks. And you know what happened in that deposition. The defense is going to do everything it can to paint Frankie as the bad guy in this situation and then tie you to him to legitimize their failure to pay. Things will probably get pretty ugly. Did you know he spent a year in prison?

"Yes," was faintly released from Karen as she sat there with her head down. Luke examined her closely as he knew a jury would. They sat in silence for a few moments, Luke trying to pick up on some sign she might release. There was fatigue on her face but little else. Embarrassment, maybe, that she was involved with someone that held much lower standards than she held for herself. Luke continued to examine the face and her body movements. She was not a great beauty but took care of herself. She presented well, had a good education, promising career. Luke asked himself again, why was she involved with Frankie Johnson, a loser that couldn't hold a regular job and messed with drugs that could ruin her career.

"Luke, do you think we shouldn't go to trial?" Karen looked him squarely in the eyes, checking him out as he had done her.

"I didn't say that. I just said it could get rough. I want to make sure you're prepared for that. The defense will do everything they can to make it appear that you're the convicted felon, that you're the druggie, that you somehow had something to do with your car being stolen."

"But I'm not. And I didn't have anything to do with stealing my own car. I paid that damn insurance premium every time it was due and now I want to be paid for my car." Karen sat up in her seat and faced Luke squarely. She could make a good witness with just a little coaching.

"Karen, they have offered to pay you the fair market value of the car, plus interest from the date of the theft. I could pick up the phone now and tell them we would accept that amount and put an end to this. The decision is yours."

"I don't know," Karen slumped back into her chair. "Tell me what to do, Luke."

It was a statement Luke dreaded to hear but heard all too often. Clients wanted him to make a decision that they should make. Yes, he was the lawyer with knowledge of this case along with many others; but when the end result was not positive, clients blamed the lawyer for the loss.

"Karen, it's a good case. I think you'll make a good witness and we really have a shot at some punitive damages. But it's always a gamble with a jury. It's impossible to know what might influence them one way or the other. You know what we're up against with Frankie's past and what you have to deal with. You make the call and I'll run with your decision. But it's your call."

"I want to say go for it. Luke, these people took my money and then ignored me until I hired you. That's not right. They should be punished. I want to go for it."

"Then we do it. There's a pretrial conference set with Judge Jones next Monday, a week before trial, and after that we're ready to go. If you think of anything we need to talk about before then, give me a call and I'll keep you posted if there are any developments on this end."

Karen excused herself and left Luke alone in his office. He sat down behind his desk and tried to concentrate on Karen's case. He was glad she made the decision to go forward. Luke considered the case a good one that should give them a favorable verdict. And he could use the boost. He had had enough negatives in his life of late. It was time to get back on track with some good things.

Luke turned to the file and began dictating instructions for Liz. Subpoenas had to be issued. His trial brief had to be finished. He wanted everything ready when they had their pre-trial meeting with Judge Jones.

Judge Jones was going in late that morning. His first conference at eight o'clock canceled late last week and so he was sitting leisurely over his second cup of coffee with his wife at the old wooden table in the kitchen. Their house was built in 1910 and Mary Margaret had worked diligently at recreating the period authenticity with concealed modern conveniences. The oven was a reproduction of a turn of the century wooden stove complete with electronic settings and a microwave. The refrigerator had a paneled front that matched the other stained-oak cabinets. The classic ceiling fan finished off the room with an old world feel.

The smell of fresh baked muffins made you think you had stepped into the past. Mary Margaret Miller Jones enjoyed these mornings with her husband. It gave her a chance to pick his brain for tidbits of gossip that he collected the day before.

"Would you care for another muffin, dear?"

The Judge's waistline only fleetingly came to mind as he responded "Sure."

Mrs. Jones was known throughout town for her muffins. She had a full collection of muffin recipes which she made constantly and delivered around town to whatever friend was ailing. Like a Florence Nightingale she took her muffins to cheer up anyone that might be under the weather. The ailment needn't be anything major. The muffins were just an introduction to visit and brighten the day of her designee. Whether it was a physical malady, mental, emotional or just the doldrums, Mrs. Jones showed up with her muffins. They would laugh and talk and when she left the person would always feel better. And, Mrs. Jones' muffins invariably got the credit.

It was also therapeutic for the Judge's wife. She rarely left the stop without feeling good about having brightened the day for the poor soul. And, she rarely left without having acquired the latest Hampton gossip.

Mrs. Jones put down a big dollop of butter alongside the muffin on the Judge's plate. He immediately began to smear the soft butter on the inside of the steamy hot muffin.

"These are a new carrot muffin," she began. "I copied the recipe out of a magazine I saw over at Eloise Lambert's house. These are what they call heart-healthy. The carrots are good for you."

"Humpf" Judge Jones mumbled as he spread another chunk of butter on the other half.

"Eloise tells me that there may be some indictment soon on that bank girl's murder. She says she's been hearing that it may be drug related." She paused, waiting to see if the Judge had any comment to throw out. When he didn't respond she continued. "According to Eloise, a lot of people think that Daniels boy has been involved in drugs. You know, it's common knowledge he was with her that night. I just can't imagine something like that happening right here in Hampton. She was so beautiful. Have you seen her pictures in the paper? They say she did modeling, too. Just such a shame. I can hardly stand to think what that poor girl went through. The way she died and all."

Mrs. Jones picked at half of her muffin and put the other half on the Judge's plate. The Judge reached for the butter and started to spread. "I feel certain there will be an indictment soon," he began. "We just can't have something like that hanging over us here. What makes people think Luke's involved in drugs?" Judge Jones had heard something to that effect but did not think much of it.

"Well, you know the kind of clients he has. And that car of his was supposedly mixed up in some sort of drug deal down on the Coast. I hear that's how Mr. Daniels got it." Mrs. Jones did not know Luke well enough to be comfortable with his first name. From what she had been hearing around town, she didn't want to be on a first name basis with him.

Judge Jones knew Luke had some sort of flashy Cadillac now. He had heard it was some sort of deal with a client. He wondered if it was a fee in a drug case. Lawyers often took fees like that. When a piece of property was involved in an illegal activity, the state could have it forfeited. Crafty lawyers would often get it transferred to them as a fee in an attempt to make it exempt from seizure. The forfeiture statues for such cases were civil and had to be conducted separate from the criminal case. If title transferred before the prosecutor got the papers served on the civil side, then the lawyer could capture the property instead of the prosecutor. The Judge knew Luke was smart enough to pull this off.

"So that's how he wound up with that car, huh?"

"How's that?" Mrs. Jones wasn't sure what the Judge was talking about.

"That's how Luke got his new car?"

"I wouldn't know for sure, but that's what they say."

In these conversations between the Judge and his wife, the rules of gossip were not as stringent as the rules of evidence in his courtroom. And Judge Jones was not known for his mastery of the rules of evidence when he was in trial. Often his love of gossip carried over to the courtroom and he let witnesses talk about a variety of irrelevant subjects that should never be allowed in a trial. Whether it be hearsay or any other violation of the rules of admissibility, if the Judge wanted to hear it, he overruled any objection and let the witness drone on. It was one of the many issues the Supreme Court had repeatedly admonished but one the Judge considered to be within his judicial discretion.

Judge Jones now wondered just how involved Luke was with this client who had a Cadillac. He popped the last bit of muffin in his mouth and washed it down with a slurp of coffee.

"I'd better be getting to work. Enjoyed the breakfast, dear." He leaned down and kissed his wife's forehead. He looked around for his coat and headed out the door.

Driving downtown, Judge Jones stopped at a red light only a couple of blocks from the courthouse. Down the street he saw several cars he recognized outside Momma Doris'. Lawyers gathered around tables, picking apart some victim of their latest circulation of bogus stories, he surmised. He wished he had time to join them. Glancing at his watch, he knew there would be other lawyers assembled around the courtroom, awaiting his arrival. These, too, would be full of tales, so he hurried on through the light and down the street.

Judge Jones' office was in the Bedford County Courthouse, second floor, just across from the courtroom. As suspected, lawyers had already begun to congregate for the day's activities. He made his way through the gathering, shaking hands and slapping backs, always the politician. After all, they were all voters.

His secretary, Anna, met him at the door to his suite of offices where, inside, still more lawyers were milling about. He continued the glad handing, joking that they all only came up to get his donuts and flirt with his secretary. If Judge Jones was the best politician in the county, Anna was the second best. She had no intention of running for any post herself, but she intended that her boss remain an elected official. Job security. She worked the crowd as well as the Judge.

Shortly, she had him through the group and into his personal office and the door shut behind them. "Whew, what brought all this on? I was expecting a light day today."

"It's not all for you. They're out and about for the Weeks murder. Talk is that an indictment may be coming down soon." Anna had been listening to the lawyer's chatter for almost an hour before the Judge arrived. "The Grand Jury is upstairs."

The Grand Jury met on the third floor of the courthouse. It was in fact only an attic that had been converted to a meeting room, one large room with only one door; perfect for the secret proceedings of the Grand Jury. There was enough space outside the door for three chairs. Two were used by the bailiffs who could easily control who came up the stairs to the proceeding. The other was for a witness who may have to wait before going in to testify. It was sometimes used by the lawyer who came along while his client was inside. Witnesses called to testify before the Grand Jury had to go alone. Their lawyer could wait outside and they could come out and consult with him, but the testimony inside was for the prosecutor and his Grand Jury. The attic chamber only added to the secrecy surrounding the proceedings in Bedford County.

Indictments that were handed down literally came down from above. Judge Jones loved this aspect of the arrangement. So did District Attorney Billy Gafford. He loved the analogy of Moses coming down from the mountain with his charges written in stone. An indictment was no more than a formal charge. According to the law, the defendant was still innocent until proven guilty. But in Hampton, Bedford County, Mississippi, District Attorney Billy Gafford encouraged the concept that he, the Representative of the People of the State of Mississippi, came down with the law, with truth and a mighty sword. The showmanship served him well. It was hard to get a jury to try a criminal case that was not already aware that the indictment had come "from above."

He loved this part of his job, the Grand Jury phase. It was an easy part to love, since unlike the courtroom, there was no one to challenge him. These poor saps on the Grand Jury listened to everything he said with rapt attention and then did exactly as he said. No argument, no objection, no ifs, ands or buts. Just let Poppa Billy tell them about all these bad guys and let the good citizens vote to get them off the streets.

Crime in this area was the same as in so many other parts of the country now. Lots of drug cases. Gafford liked these because it was easy to get a lot of mileage out of them. "These drugs are destroying our young people," he would say. "We've got to get them cleaned up and off the street," he would go on. "They're a menace to all of us," he would repeat often. And he was right. Probably ninety-five percent of the cases he handled out of the District Attorney's office were drug related. Most of the burglaries and grand larcenies were to get money to buy drugs. The assaults usually took place in a wild night of drinking and drugs. Fights would break out and someone would get cut or shot.

From time-to-time there would be some young girl from the neighboring university abducted. It would wind up in Bedford County where she would be raped. The perpetrator was usually high on something and had no idea what he was doing. Often from a good family. It would be a tragedy for both families. But, Gafford's job was to be the lawyer for the People of the State and that meant in essence that he represented the victim. And so he would rant and rail about the rights of the victim as opposed to the rights of the accused and the public ate it up. These grand jurors really loved it. He would get wound up about the heinous nature of the crime and the poor victim and the nefarious perpetrator and the grand jury would be whipped into a frenzy ready to go out and lynch'em all. It had become so easy to Gafford. After fifteen years as a prosecutor, some of the cases he railroaded through for an indictment were comical.

His most recent assistant in the carrying out of the duties of the office was James Walter Clay, III. That was what he had on his business card. He liked to be called J. W. Most of the folks around Hampton knew him as Little Jimmy and that's what they called him. His dad had been in the construction business, as his dad had before him, and Little Jimmy came along when the family was doing well and became Jimmy the Third. Everyone called his dad J. W. and after his death in a construction accident while Little Jimmy was in college, Jimmy wanted the moniker to switch over to him. He introduced himself as J. W. Clay, but invariably everyone got around to calling him Little Jimmy. It was a misnomer since "Little Jimmy" had now grown to nearly six feet.

Little Jimmy was a fairly handsome sort, too. He was only twenty-nine, but his blonde hair was already showing signs of thinning on top. Despite that he carried himself well and was popular with the ladies. His job as a serious, rough-and-tough watch dog for the people helped him rise above the obsequious nickname. It also helped him promote the image that he was a stud.

"Good morning, Billy." It was Jimmy coming up the stairs to the grand jury room with a load of files. "Sorry I'm late. I've been over at the office for a while getting the files organized for this morning's presentation but I got mobbed downstairs. Did you see all the lawyers gathered up? It's almost as bad as docket call."

"They're all wanting to know what we have on the Weeks murder," Jimmy volunteered without a pause.

"I know, I know," Gafford came back. It made him anxious to even think about that case and where it was headed. "You didn't say anything, did you?"

"Of course not. You know I'd never do that." Jimmy feigned hurt feelings. What Billy and Jimmy both knew was that Jimmy liked playing up his secretive knowledge with the women and his macho buddies and on occasion let himself get carried away in conversation.

"So what all do we have this morning?" Gafford had done this bit with the Grand Jury so many times he rarely prepared. He just showed up and picked up files the secretary had put together for him. Wanda had been with him for so many years that he trusted her to keep him together. And now Jimmy had been there for almost four years and could handle most of the cases on his own. This morning's case list was like he had seen a thousand times before.

"Well, take them on in there and get started," he said to Jimmy. "I'm going downstairs for some coffee. I'll be back and join you shortly."

Nothing could make Jimmy happier. He often led the charge with Gafford in the room, but then it was hard to shake the feeling that he was the underling. Alone in the room, he was the authority, master in command. It gave him an indescribable thrill.

"Don't worry, boss. I can handle these. Piece of cake. All aboard!"

Jimmy put his hand up and pulled on an imaginary cord like he was the conductor of a train. It was a silly little joke between them implying the Grand Jurors were so simple and the cases even more simple that he'd get everybody on the train of which he was the conductor and railroad the whole process. At one time it was funny but after a couple hundred times it had lost its glitter; no longer entertaining, just meaningless and crazy. Like this whole job. Like his life. Gafford headed downstairs to find the coffee.

The crowd of lawyers milled around in the area at the foot of the stairs. Billy wished he had taken the stairs that led down to the Judge's chamber avoiding the crowd. He stepped on forward to the bottom of the stairs and every eye in the place caught his entrance. Conversations continued but the air was heavy with the unmistakable specter of grand jury. Billy tried to keep on his most lighthearted facade as he moved through the lawyers.

"Yes, yes, good to see you. Busy time. Gotta get going, let's get together soon," he heard himself saying as he quickly made his way through the group and stepped to the door into the Judge's ante room where there was coffee and refuge.

"Well, good morning, Mr. Gafford."

Standing by the coffee pot was Luther Lambert and Judge Jones. It was Luther with the greeting. And Luther that continued.

"How are things going up there?" Lambert's head made a motion indicating he was talking about the Grand Jury.

"Oh, you remember how it is, Luther. Same old bunk, same old faces," Gafford stopped almost in mid-sentence. He was afraid he may be giving away more than he cared to. Burnout was common in all professions but it was not a good idea to carry it on your sleeve when in politics. His state retirement faintly appeared in the distance. He quickly amended his demeanor and tried to appear jovial.

"It's good to see you, Luther," Gafford began sincerely. It was always good to see his old pal and mentor; the man who figured largely in the picture he had after retirement from this dreary job. "What are you up to this morning?"

"Oh, just a little coffee with the Judge. We had a conference scheduled this morning but it canceled so I wanted to get a time to reschedule. You know, never miss a chance to bend his ear." All three laughed heartily and all three knew that the joke was more truth than fiction. Luther would do more than bend his ear. He would make sure the Judge understood the case well.

Luther was a master at preparing attitudes, at helping someone see things in a certain light, helping them remember in just the right way. Judge Jones suddenly seemed uncomfortable and fidgety when Anna stuck her head in the door.

"Judge, you have a call on line 1. Can you take it now?"

Without even asking who it was, Judge Jones quickly responded that he would take it at his desk, excused himself and was gone.

Luther took the coffee pot and refilled his cup and Gafford's. Billy could see the edge of Lambert's Rolex sticking out from the white starched cuff of the tailored shirt. It was a fine piece and Billy wanted desperately to have one. But, not on the District Attorney's salary. That would have to come later. Perhaps when he was in private practice. Perhaps with Luther.

When Luther turned to face him after returning the pot, Billy also noticed the diamond tie pin. Nearly a carat, the dazzling stone radiated in its brazen gold setting. The suit was also top of the line. Billy guessed the suit cost $1,500.00 or more. Yet it did little for Luther's three hundred pound frame. The man was tall, six foot. But he was also obese. While the cut of the suit was superb and the fabric exceptional, the large man within stretched it at every seam. Though everything on the outside was the best money could buy, inside was still a worthless man consumed with consumption. His size betrayed much about his personality. But all Billy Gafford could see was a man he idolized. The trappings of wealth spoke clearly to Billy about his abilities, about his mastery of his profession, about Luther's attainment of a level that every one else craved, including Billy.

"So how's it going, Billy? That job keeping you on the go?" Luther began with his most benevolent tone.

"You bet, Luther. You remember how it was. Fighting crime day in and day out. Just trying to keep Hampton a safe place to live." There was a time when Billy actually believed that, but not in a long while. Now he just held on for that retirement and a good job prospect afterwards.

"Yes, I know what you mean. It's a shame we have to live in this, the way people are doing. And I know how it takes its toll on you dealing with it, Billy. It hadn't been that long ago, you know, that I was in your shoes. I remember well how the constant dealing with the criminal element begins to wear on you."

Luther's words were intoxicating to the District Attorney and he knew it. It was a lonely job and no one else could understand. But Luther had been there and done that and now he knew how to stroke the right chords. He knew which song would lure his prey closer. Not too fast. Not too slow. The master began his composition.

"That boy you got in the office now, Clay, is it? He helping you like he ought to, Billy?"

"Oh, yeah, he is. In fact, he's up there in the Grand Jury right now, presenting cases. Just some standard stuff. I can't let him tackle the serious cases."

"I understand. Best to keep your hand in those. But it's good you let him get the experience. Hadn't he helped you in a few trials?"

"Yes, and he's a big help, too. Still needs to get a little seasoning. You know, learn the tricks of the trade. Of course, he doesn't have the teacher I had."

"Billy, now you know I didn't teach you much of anything. You were just a quick study with a lot of ability."

What Billy knew was that Luther Lambert had an ego the size of a Buick and it constantly needed fueling. The best way to stay in good with Lambert was to let him know that you knew how great he was. Billy could recall working with the man when he was assistant DA, just how fragile the ego was. No matter what was done in that office and whose work product something was, Luther unmistakably took credit for it. In order to stay in his good graces, you had to devotedly keep him on a pedestal. And right now, Billy Gafford wanted to be in Luther Lambert's good graces.

"You know, it seems to me that boy may be some kin to Wilson's wife. She was a Clay."

Luther knew perfectly well that Rita and Jimmy Clay, the assistant District Attorney, were first cousins. Jimmy was a good bit younger than Rita, Luther seemed to recall. Jimmy's father and Rita's were brothers whom Luther knew, along with about everybody else in the county. But Luther had found that a little properly feigned ignorance served him well from time to time.

"Too bad he didn't get any of her looks. That Rita is a beautiful girl, even if she is my son's wife."

"You said it, Luther. Ol' Wilson did alright for himself." Billy checked before getting too enthusiastic in his praise of Luther's daughter-in-law. Like many other men, Billy had admired the beautiful Rita Clay Lambert from afar. He and many others had also wondered how the dimwitted Wilson Lambert had managed to snare such a fox. Everyone's conclusion was always the same: money. And, poppa had lots of it, so some of Wilson's lesser qualities probably didn't seem so bad when viewed through a veil of green.

"She is a beauty," Lambert continued. "That Weeks girl was a beauty, too. What a shame. I didn't know her, of course, but the pictures of her in the paper were incredible. And the way everybody talks of her, now, you'd think she was a goddess."

"Yes, yes, I know it," Billy nodded in agreement. "Everybody did think highly of her."

"People are really talking about her murder, Billy. I sure hope ya'll are getting close to nailing her killer. Will there be an indictment this time?"

The activities of the Grand Jury were totally secret and Billy was forbidden by law from discussing any cases, as was anyone in the room, the Grand Jurors themselves and everyone connected with the District Attorney's office: assistants, secretaries right on down the chain to law enforcement and other witnesses. Continually during the proceedings all those involved were admonished concerning the law on the confidential nature of the proceedings. Yet with so many people involved from time to time things did leak out.

Billy never worried about talking with Luther. Luther had been the prosecutor and Billy knew he could trust him. Yet, here in this setting where anybody could walk in and misinterpret things, Billy was apprehensive about such discussions.

"Maybe we should talk some other time, Luther." Billy made an almost involuntary glance over his shoulder.

"Oh, Billy, I don't want to pry. I'm just concerned about you, that's all. You know how vicious the public can be. There's so much talk out there about the murder and when it will be solved. It seems that every conversation I hear has something about Luke Daniels in it. I just assumed ya'll were building a case against him."

Billy knew that information flowed to Lambert from many different sources and this was not the first conversation they had about the murder where Daniels' name came up. Perhaps Luther was trying to tell him something. He might have picked up something on the streets that could be useful. They should talk later, though. Not here.

The door opened unexpectedly and Anna peered in from the Judge's chamber. Billy felt like a deer caught in headlights. He wondered if Anna noticed.

"Luther, you have a call from your office in here. You can take it at my desk." Anna's tone was nothing but business. If she noticed Billy's discomfort she didn't let on.

Billy was glad for the break and quickly regained his prosecutorial role. "Luther, can you come by my office? I'm headed back there now." Billy made sure Anna observed enough of his demeanor to understand that this was the serious work of the District Attorney.

Luther suppressed a smile and nodded subserviently to Billy. The fish had taken the bait. Now it was just a matter of making sure the hook was in.

"Billy, as soon as I get off the phone I have to drop some papers off at the Board of Supervisor's office and then I'll be right over."

"Right. Anna, get a note up to Jimmy for me. Tell him I'll be in my office if he needs me."

Despite the fact that Anna didn't like Billy giving her orders as if she worked for him, she responded affirmatively and took the note down on her pad.

Billy then turned in the other direction and escaped down the back stairs of the courthouse and across the street to his office.

Wanda Walker was on the phone and painting her nails when Billy walked in. She had expected him to be in grand jury all morning and was surprised at his return. She quickly got off the phone and followed him back to his office. He appeared distracted. What could have happened with the grand jury?

"What's up, Billy?"

"See if you can get Dick Limox on the phone. I need to talk to him right away."

"Sure thing." She returned to her desk without questioning him and dialed the direct number to the Hampton PD Detective Division. Limox answered the call.

"Hi, Dick. This is Wanda. Billy needs to talk to you. Can you hold?"

"Sure," he said as the phone went on hold.

"Dick, Billy Gafford. I need to get with you on the Susan Weeks murder. I'd like to be brought up to date on the file. See where we are. Are there any new developments?"

There were none. Not to speak of. Reports were in from the state crime lab that had not been delivered to the District Attorney but there was nothing new. The only thing Dick had were the reports of gossip around Hampton. He squirmed a little in his seat wishing he had something better to give the DA rather than rumors and gossip.

"Do you understand we've got to get moving on that case?" Gafford quizzed him. "The public's not going to let us pussy foot around. Why don't you come up here to my office and let's go over the file together. Make sure I have everything you have. Is anyone else working on the case with you?"

There was not at this point but Dick did not want to say that. He had been hoping to put the whole thing together himself and get all the glory but lately he had been thinking that he needed to pull in someone else to help share the blame of not having one solid piece of evidence that would nail the murderer. "Yeah, Tom Feder," Limox lied. "But he's off today." Safe enough. Limox would get Feder involved when he came in tomorrow and Gafford would never know.

"Well, come up here to my office right after lunch and bring that file." Gafford said it as more of an order than a request and Limox got the message. Nowhere was the pecking order more established than in the police department with all its macho militaristic regimentation. And, the District Attorney was the chief pecker.

"I'll get the file together and be right up, boss." Limox was in hopes that there might still be some glory left for him to grab in this case.

When Gafford put down the phone he looked around to see Luther Lambert standing in the door. He wondered how long Lambert had been there and how much of the conversation he picked up. Since this had once been Lambert's office the man felt comfortable in strolling around as if it were still his domain. In many ways it was. Gafford was so in awe of him there was very Little Lambert would want out of this office that was not his for the asking.

Lambert moved into the room closing the door behind him and taking a seat on the sofa without any word from Gafford. "It's good that you've got little Jimmy over there with the grand jury so you can concentrate on the more serious matters," Luther began without hesitation. "I know the Judge is certainly concerned about this Weeks murder."

Gafford wondered if Lambert and Jones had talked after he left. He felt overshadowed by these two personalities as if they held some dominion over him. And, of course, they did. There was a line between what was wielded by the two powers and what was self-imposed. That line had become obscured over time until now only the obeisance remained.

"Billy, I would hate to see this thing get you and the Judge in a crack. You know the election is just this summer. Right now neither of you has an opponent but when is that qualifying deadline? March isn't it. This could be a thorn in your side. There's been some talk on the street about Singletary running."

Chris Singletary had a small private practice. Billy had heard some talk himself that Singletary might run for DA but then there was always talk he was going to run for something.

Lambert continued.

"And you know yourself there's a few lawyers out there who would like to see Judge Jones get beat. Every lawsuit has a winner and a loser and those losers always want to blame the Judge. They like to talk about how he favored the other side."

Billy did, indeed, know about the talk of Judge Jones' favoritism. It was more than just talk. Jones was a politician, first and foremost and then a Judge. In every situation before him he judged the politics first and let that govern his rulings from the bench. The side most likely to help him stay in office was the side that got the favorable rulings. And, so much was in the Judge's discretion.

Gafford was immune from any disfavor from the bench because as prosecutor he and the Judge were both on the side of law and order. Teamwork made them prevail and teamwork could keep them both elected. Now the coach sat here in front of him setting up plays.

There was silence for a moment as Lambert let his words sink in. He watched Gafford closely. Best not to move too swiftly for the boy.

"You need a strong case right now to put you in a solid position before the election. If the Weeks murder is still hanging over your head... Well, I don't have to tell you what that could do. But you don't want to hand an opponent something to attack you on."

Gafford took in all that Lambert was saying. He wished they could talk about his stepping down from the Office of District Attorney; stepping down from a job which had become boring and mundane. He would like to discuss his going into practice in Lambert's firm. His eye again caught Lambert's Rolex. The suit. He thought about the fine automobile Lambert drove. He wanted to think about his getting into the big fees. But Lambert didn't seem to have any of that on his mind. The game plan now was to keep him on the right re-election track.

"I guess you know about that little ruckus Daniels had with the reporter at his office. Sure sounds like the acts of a man who has something to hide. Why else would he be so short fused?"

Lambert moved through his delivery deftly. His powers of persuasion were honed to such a fine level that it was like shooting fish in a barrel. In front of countless juries the silver-tongued devil had delivered his version of the facts in such a favorable way that disagreement was almost inconceivable.

Lambert had become so accustomed to having his way be the only way that anything else was unthinkable. It was a practiced assurance that grew into a foreboding presence permeating the air around him. But it was subtle. Oh, so subtle that the hapless victim rarely knew how languidly he was being drawn into the maneuver.

Gafford had heard about the run in between Daniels and the Hampton News reporter. At the time he had dismissed it as just another tale being thrown around. Perhaps, now, he should rethink his assessment. He and Daniels enjoyed a good working relationship. He respected Daniels' professionalism and had told him so on occasion. Through the years he had prosecuted individuals he knew but never anyone he was as closely associated with as Daniels. Hell, he liked Luke.

"It's a shame to think of anyone like young Daniels being involved in something like this, but you just never know. People will fool you." Lambert's statement came out almost as if he had read Gafford's mind. He could tell from Gafford's expression that the seeds he had sown were beginning to sprout.

"I know it's a tough job, Billy. I'm just glad the people of Hampton have someone like you who'll do the right thing. I know we can count on you to pursue this thing conscientiously. And you know you can count on me to be behind you one hundred percent."

Lambert stood up with his file. Gafford rose instinctively and the two of them moved out of the office and down to the reception area. Stepping off the elevator was Dick Limox. Lambert greeted him warmly with a big smile. He knew Limox was the main detective on the Weeks murder that would now go in to discuss the case with Gafford. He also knew that the witless Jerry Mason had already primed Limox on Luke Daniels.

"Let me get out of here," Luther started off. "I know you guys must have important business to work on, Grand Jury and all. I'll see you later. Wanda, you take care."

Lambert stepped inside the elevator and the door closed behind him. Inside he grinned with Machiavellian guile at his own unscrupulous cunning. Throughout his career Lambert sought to acquire and maintain political power without regard to any ethical consideration. The only rules that governed Lambert's actions were those that led to his success, no matter what the cost.

Lambert exited the building and started off down the street to his office with a quickness of step energized by his latest accomplishment. He couldn't be entirely certain of what would transpire back in the DA's office but he was smug in his assumption that he had set some wheels in motion. Now with only a little greasing a cycle of events would begin to slowly evolve into a passage of condemnation. For Luther Lambert it was simply another exhibition of his power. Let all stand up and take notice.

Luther turned the corner and half-way down the block saw Luke Daniels coming out of his office. In order to avoid any contact he quickly crossed the street before Luke could see him duck into another attorney's office and avoid the encounter.

Luke watched Lambert cross the street and recalled his last experience with the Lambert clan in a deposition with the younger Wilson. Wilson's acidic disposition had been at full steam on that particular day. Every question Luke asked had met with a caustic, contemptuous remark from Wilson. Luke's client had reached a near state of tears after two hours of the harassment when one of Wilson's portentous comments was one too many.

Wilson rose slightly in his chair when impulsively Luke reached across the table and lifted Wilson up by his shirt to bring them nose-to-nose. Luke's chair toppled over and the court reporter's machine was toppled in the process. The deposition was in the Lamberts' office where Luther happened by the door at that moment. He looked in to see his son in the clutches of Luke. The episode ended as quickly as it began, the deposition ended and the parties went their way. But the story was told over and over in the downtown gossip with a multitude of variations. Most knew the acerbic Wilson, often having wanted to do the same thing themselves, but refraining out of trepidation over raising the ire of the elder Luther.

When Luther had walked into the deposition he had expressed shock and dismay over the behavior of the two boys, as he referred to them. Luke, however, seemed to catch a glimpse in Luther that he, at times, had also wanted to squelch the sour and surly disposition of his only son. Nevertheless, in this setting, blood was thicker than water and, in his re-telling, Luther easily recalled the hot-tempered nature of Luke and his finding of Luke's fist in his son's face, along with his threatening demeanor.

Luke wondered now if Luther still carried a grudge over the incident. He had since apologized to Wilson and his father for his behavior with only another curt retort from Wilson. Luther had graciously accepted the apology with the response to think nothing of it. All in a day's work was his attitude. But Luke was almost positive Luther had seen him down the street and had deliberately moved across the way to avoid contact. Luke shrugged it off as being of little consequence to him. He had other fish to fry this morning. Judge Jones was in his office and Luke wanted to personally confirm the pretrial conference in the Ainsworth case.

Several lawyers remained scattered around the courthouse as Luke walked down the corridor and up the stairs to Judge Jones' office. Luke felt imaginary eyes following him up the stairs and a chill went through him to the bone when he reached the second floor and moved to the door to the Judge's office. This is crazy, Luke thought. Paranoia struck at his heart. His hand touched the door knob and it immediately jerked away from him, swinging open and he was face-to-face with James Germany. They had not seen each other since the incident at the Christmas party. They did not speak now. Luke had thought about apologizing to Germany but had not been able to bring himself to the task. Germany's eyes flicked with malice at the sight of Luke. Behind Germany Luke could see Anna and the Judge and some other lawyers. Something about their look made Luke think his name had been in the conversation.

Germany quickly stepped back from the door pulling it wide open giving Luke plenty of room to pass. There was a bit of drama to his action from which Luke tried to grasp some intent. Most lawyers loved theatrics, inside the courtroom and out. Germany was such a weak sister in most situations that he put on his best shows when there was no adversary. Luke realized Germany had just put on a show for this audience and there was little question who the performance ridiculed. Germany's step back and broad sweep open of the door gave wide berth to Luke to come in, a statement in itself.

The others in the room were speechless, looking like a bunch of scared rabbits. Judge Jones quickly turned back to his office without so much as a word. The other two lawyers buried their noses in the files they held. The ring of the telephone quickly saved Anna from facing Luke. Germany gave him another disgusted look and brushed past him without saying a word.

The door closed behind Luke and he stood there motionless. The two lawyers, Hanford Rogers and Winston Payne, peered intently at some file as if they were suddenly dealing with the most important matter of their careers. Luke stood alone without a word. The whole scene took on a surreal nature to him. Anna chattered away on the phone with her words sounding distant and foreign to Luke. The two lawyers seemed remote, oblivious to Luke's presence, as if there were some great chasm between them.

Luke wondered if he spoke whether anyone would hear him. He wanted to scream, 'Hey, doesn't anyone see me? What's going on here?' He watched Anna pick up a pen and start to write some message from her phone conversation. He couldn't make out the words. Like he had slipped into another dimension, Luke felt removed from his surroundings. Were these people really ignoring him? Watch it, old boy, that paranoia's going to grab you. Dread. What was he dreading? A queasiness started in his mouth and settled down to his stomach. This is crazy, he thought, what is going on?

Anna finished on the phone, hung up and put the final touch on the note she had taken. At that, she looked up at Luke with a smile.

"I'm sorry, Luke. It's been a little crazy around here this morning. People have been in and out of this office until I don't know whether I'm coming or going. Typical Monday morning. Do you have an appointment with Judge Jones?" Strictly business now.

"Ah, no. But I was hoping to confirm our conference next week. Do you think he has a minute?"

"I couldn't even tell you, Luke. We've had so much going on. Let me check his schedule. What time is it, anyway?" All eyes in the room went to the clock on the wall. "Eleven o'clock. I know we had things scheduled all morning. Have a seat and let me get with him."

Anna moved from behind her desk and to the door to Judge Jones' office. Hanford and Winston shuffled some files together and left out the door with only a slight nod to Luke. He stood there alone, wondering what had just happened.

Luke didn't want to be paranoid but what had happened? He didn't know Hanford Rogers and Winston Payne that well but they were almost rude. Could their files have been that important? What was going on before Luke stepped through the door? Germany, that prick. He was probably giving another of his exhibitions like at the Christmas party. Luke felt betrayed. He wished for the opportunity to confront Germany: to shut him up and stop this ridiculous gossip about him and Susan. But what could he do? People were going to talk. He would just have to endure.

Anna appeared at the door between the two offices and motioned for him to come on back. "The Judge has another meeting but you can have him for a moment or two," she said with a smile, all hint of the earlier distance gone.

Judge Jones was behind his desk with several files spread out before him. They exchanged pleasantries with the Judge reminding Luke of what a hectic day he had. He dug around on his desk and pulled out his calendar.

"Now what case are you worried about?"

"Ainsworth vs. Standard Mutual, Judge. We have a pretrial conference set for next Monday and the trial is scheduled for the following Monday. I'm ready to get this one to the courthouse."

"Any chance of settlement?" the Judge asked without pulling himself away from the work in front of him.

"Doubtful, your honor."

"Well, you're set to go. Pretrial conference next Monday and first up for trial the Monday after that. I'll see you then." Judge Jones' attention went back to the file before him, essentially dismissing Luke with his last comment.

Luke had hoped for a better reception, possibly even a question or two about the case from the Judge so he could set some preconceptions in the Justice's mind. But he was being asked to leave. Jones looked up at him.

"Is there anything else, Luke?" Jones asked with a can't you see I'm busy tone.

"Ah, no, Judge. That's all. Thanks for your time."

Anna still stood by the Judge's desk as Luke got up and headed for the door.

"Thanks again, Judge. See you next week."

Neither Anna nor Jones said a word as Luke walked out. In the front office he found two more lawyers had come in for conferences. One was Tyler Thompson, counsel opposite him in the Ainsworth case. They greeted one another.

"I just confirmed with the Judge our pretrial conference for next Monday, Tyler."

"I've got it on my calendar, Luke. I'll be ready. I hope you are, too." Tyler said with a challenge in his voice.

Luke hated defense lawyers. Without a response, he opened the door and left the suite of offices. He had two weeks until trial. He would be ready. He wanted to stick it to those insurance bastards and Tyler Thompson, too. A good punitive damage verdict would clear that smirk off his smart mouth. But could he get that? The Judge had wide discretion in what got to the jury. And it sure seemed to Luke that something had gotten to the Judge. What? Rumors. Luke knew how Jones was. He listened to every bit of gossip that came along and then pretended to be fair and impartial. Could Luke get a fair deal with Jones at this point in his life? Jones was up for re-election. How did that play into Luke's situation? But what else could he do? The trial was in two weeks. He headed back to his office to start getting ready.

CHAPTER EIGHT

The Magnolia Bar and Grill began serving lunch the week before. Prior to that it was only a night time spot, with the doors opening at five o'clock and dinner served until ten. Upstairs the bar was open until much later. But lunch was a new thing for the restaurant and there was a thriving crowd that filled the tables each day since the new opening time. The lunches were some of the same delicious meals served at night, except in smaller portions with smaller prices.

The customers were a mixture of businessmen in for a quick bite before back to work and the relaxed dining for those ladies whose husbands provided the living while they spent their days in pursuit of the best shopping bargains, the best civic responsibilities and the best lunches.

Today, Mrs. Wendell Garmon Jones, III, Mrs. Billy Wayne Gafford and Mrs. Luther Lambert attended a meeting of the Bedford County Bar Auxiliary. The meeting, held at the home of Mrs. Tyler Thompson, ended at eleven and as the ladies were leaving, Eloise Lambert suggested to her dear friend, Mary Margaret Jones that they continue their visit over at the Magnolia for lunch. Rhonda Gafford overhead them and joined in.

"I haven't been there for lunch, yet. Is it good?"

"Honey, neither one of us has made it over there, yet, either," was the response from Eloise Lambert. "That's why we were talking about going over. You know it's got to be good. Their night time menu is the best thing in south Mississippi. I'm wondering if they've got those little crawfish appetizers on the lunch menu. I can make a meal off those. Come on Rhonda, you can join us."

"That sounds like fun. You're headed over right now?"

"As soon as we can get to the car. Mary Margaret, you're ready aren't you?"

"Well, yes, I suppose. The Judge won't be home for lunch today. Busy schedule was forcing them to eat at the office. But I don't have a thing. You want to meet over there?"

"No, let's ride together," Eloise Lambert suggested.

"I'll have to take my car." It was Rhonda. "I need to get over to the school right after lunch."

"Thank goodness I don't have to do that run to the school thing. Mary Margaret, you come ride with me, then, and, Rhonda, we'll meet you over there."

Arriving by eleven thirty, the Magnolia was only beginning to get its lunch crowd. The three ladies were immediately taken to a table and menus laid out in front of them.

"This all looks delicious. And they do have that wonderful Crawfish appetizer. Lord, it's as much as some of the lunches."

"I know it. I don't know how they're going to be successful with this new lunch opening if their prices are so exorbitant."

Rhonda Gafford had to suppress a smirk as she listened to the two older ladies go on about the prices. Between the two of them they could buy the whole town; yet, they were complaining about the price of an appetizer as if it would cause them to have to miss their next meal. She was the one who had to worry. Billy's salary as DA was solid but nothing compared to the two husbands of these women. Luther Lambert was the wealthiest lawyer in the town and Judge Jones had family money that went back for generations; old bank money from his great grandfather.

Rhonda was hoping one of them would pick up her tab for the meal, but it sounded more like she would have to buy their lunch. "I'm ordering it, anyway," Eloise Lambert announced. "It's just too delicious to pass up, since I'm here."

The waiter arrived and offered wine which Eloise and Mary Margaret accepted without hesitation. Rhonda begged off on the wine reminding them that she had to pick up her children. The waiter disappeared for only a second when he set down glasses and the carafe of California blush they had settled on.

"Are you ready to order?" he inquired.

Eloise started off first sending for the crawfish appetizer, a salad and the grilled salmon. Mary Margaret also ordered the crawfish with a salad and the coq du jour, chicken florentine with buttered fettuccine. Rhonda ordered a hamburger and a coke.

The conversation roamed around from topic to topic for awhile. Each of them had picked up enough gossip at the Bar Auxiliary meeting earlier to keep the buzz going. The murder of Susan Weeks was again on everyone's mind and inevitably they came to the topic of Luke Daniels.

"You know, they're saying the house where she was killed was a wreck. Furniture pushed around, a door kicked in..." Eloise let her voice trail off. She loved being the one in the know, especially with these two political insiders who always seemed to get information first.

Not to be outdone, Mary Margaret Jones jumped in with her two cents worth. She knew that the Judge's position called for him to be unbiased and neutral. But disinterest in a juicy story was not a trait to be applied to Judge Jones or his wife. She was constantly picking him for information that she knew he was not supposed to know in the first place. And he could not hold it in any more than she could. It was always good to have a cover like the Bar Auxiliary for where her information came from. Right now she was about to burst.

"They're saying that he raped her."

"Who? Luke Daniels?" Rhonda blustered.

"Well, yes, dear. Where have you been?" Eloise scolded. He's admitted to several people that he was with her that night. A lot of people think that it was just a casual encounter, but that when it got down to the nitty gritty, she said no and he wouldn't accept that. He's kind of a hot head, you know."

"Oh, really. What makes you say that?" They both looked around at Rhonda. Sometimes she could sound as dumb as a stump. Sometimes Eloise wondered just how much she should say in front of her. But Luther had not given her any particular caution on what he had said to her about Daniels. She just assumed he got his information from Rhonda's husband. He was the DA and he and Luther did work together at one time. Eloise knew how much in awe of Luther Gafford was. And for the first time she realized that his wife, Rhonda, was just as much in awe of her.

Eloise couldn't help but smile. How flattering. She had never before had the sensation of someone being in awe of her. She looked closely at Rhonda's dismal and uninteresting face. Eloise had been a great beauty and the years had been kind, leaving her with a striking appearance at her age. It was hard to imagine what the years would do to the face of Rhonda Gafford. A kindness came over Eloise for Rhonda.

"Well, Rhonda, I'll tell you. Enough people know that it's no great secret. Luke was at my husband's firm taking a deposition with Wilson. Wilson and Luke got into a disagreement as lawyers will and Luke grabbed Wilson around the throat and, I guess, would have strangled him if someone hadn't stepped in. You know, Wilson is such a gentleman that he would never do something like that. I mean, lawyers get into disputes all the time. It's the nature of their job. But to resort to physical violence, well, it just goes to show you what kind of man Luke Daniels is.

"Yes, I had heard about that," Mary Margaret chimed in. "The Judge was really upset that a member of the Bar and officer of his court would resort to such violent behavior. He considered a public reprimand for Luke. The only reason he didn't is because Luther asked him not to. Luther said to the Judge that it could reflect badly on the Bar. And the Judge has always thought so highly of Luther."

Yes, Eloise thought, the Judge's opinion has grown proportionately with her husband's bank account. Judge Jones came from a long line of Judges. A distinguished Hampton family, big in local society as was the wife he married, unlike her husband's family who had moved into town from way out in the county years ago. Yes, there was a time when this family of Joneses looked down on the Lamberts. But the size of the Lambert bank account could do great things for a reelection campaign that loomed in the distance for the Judge. Eloise Lambert just smiled at Mary Margaret Jones and exclaimed, "How nice of you to say so." She then turned to Rhonda. "You're the one that should be in the know on this thing. Your husband's the District Attorney. Tell us, Rhonda. Is he going to indict Luke Daniels or not?"

Rhonda was appalled at the forwardness of the question. It scared her a little to think of these two people hearing her reveal what they all knew was confidential information from a secret proceeding. And, Billy was always so squeamish with talk about such matters. Yet, at this moment, she wished she had some inside scoop that would impress her lunch companions.

"You ladies know I can't say anything like that," she tried so desperately to sound appropriately discreet, like she knew so much more than she actually knew, when she didn't really know a damn thing. But she did dearly want to be in the know and having these two ladies look to her for insider information was like a drug. There weren't too many things in her life that made her feel important. But being able to one up the Circuit Judge's wife as well as Luther Lambert's could certainly do it.

"Oh, come on, Rhonda. You can tell us. We understand confidentiality." Mary Margaret Jones was beside herself with curiosity and her usual control over the reins of her busybody streak was almost totally lost at the moment.

"But what if someone overheard us?" Rhonda didn't know how much longer she could keep the cover over her total lack of any information on this subject. She knew one thing, though. She would get some information out of Billy tonight. For now all she could do was continue to be vague with just a hint of something held back.

"Well, the Grand Jury is in session right now and it's certainly no secret that the Weeks murder is the number one thing on their agenda." Rhonda had no idea if that made any sense at all but hoped it would be just enough.

"Oh, come on, Rhonda, don't tease us." Eloise Lambert couldn't tell if this was a game or if Rhonda really knew what was going on in the Grand Jury. She wondered if Gafford really did have Daniels before the Grand Jury for the murder of Susan Weeks. Before she could prod any further several other ladies from the Auxiliary came into the restaurant and were seated at the table next to them. Mary Margaret began a conversation with them just as the food arrived. From then on talk centered on the food and particularly the crawfish appetizer Eloise had. She was too involved in describing how you ate the shell and all.

After the hamburger, Rhonda excused herself while the others called for another glass of wine. She pulled away from the group with mixed feelings. Part of her was uncomfortable with the questions and the attempts to glean secrets of the District Attorney's office. Another part wanted to linger leisurely with these ladies of wealth and social standing, sipping wine in the afternoon and discussing the status of the community. She didn't have the money they had, but she did have something else. She had a husband that was District Attorney for Bedford County and she was beginning to see how valuable a position that was. Her precious little Billy. Tonight would be a special night for her darling husband.

Billy Gafford would need a good night tonight. His day was filled with the stress of the job and the stress of an unsolved murder case. He didn't relish the meeting with Limox because he knew the pressure was mounting for him to do something. He just wanted to do the right thing.

Limox stepped off the elevator and walked up to Wanda's desk with a big grin. "Hey, babe," he always wanted to flirt with Wanda and Wanda always thought he was full of baloney. He tried to act so suave, like he was such a ladies' man. But the years had not been kind to Limox. He was not quite forty and looked over fifty. He carried at least thirty extra pounds that he didn't need. He was always talking about working out, but he never looked pumped up, just puffed up. His hair was a wiry mix of dull brown and gray. And his face carried the scars of a battle with acne that he had lost.

Wanda was polite. It was her job. She recognized the name on the file under his arm and knew why he was there. After buzzing Billy she guided Limox back to the DA's office and shut the door. That poor girl. What she must have gone through! And poor Luke. It sure seemed to Wanda that the powers to be were out to get him. She couldn't help overhearing Billy's conversation with Luther Lambert this morning while she was doing her filing. He was pushing Billy to indict Luke. But what was his interest in this case, she wondered. She had watched him stroke Billy for years and then exploit their friendship for Luther's own personal gain.

Wanda picked up a lot more around there than most anybody realized. She'd never seen anything to suggest her boss would do something illegal. If she had, she would not be there. But still, there was a lot of buttering up as of late. Oh, well, her boss was a politician. He had to be to keep his job. And she wanted to keep hers.

In his office, Billy and Limox scoured the Susan Weeks files for more than two hours looking at various bits of evidence.

There were no witnesses. But there was lots of evidence. There were fingerprints on the wine glasses found in the living room. These same fingerprints were in the bedroom, on the headboard, on the dresser, on the nightstand. And, on the front door. The bedroom door had been kicked in and on it was the perfect print of a shoe, a running shoe.

"It's the same kind of shoe Luke Daniels wears," Limox offered. He didn't explain that he and his buddy, Jerry Mason, had checked that out some time ago. "And the fingerprints are his, too."

"How do you…" Gafford stopped in mid-sentence. He was almost afraid to ask how Mason had gotten hold of a fingerprint sample of Daniels.

"Daniels worked for a while in law school as a bartender. His prints were still on file with the State Alcohol Beverage Control Board. I just called 'em up and asked for a copy. Police business. That's all I said. Pretty routine. Of course, it's known all over town that he was with her that night. Not too far of a jump to see his fingerprints at her place. Kicking in her door is another story."

"So you think he killed her?"

"Yep, I do." He and Jerry Mason had kicked this around pretty good. They had come up with their own version of what happened and he wanted to impress Gafford with his superior skills of police work and analysis. He started his story off with a touch of drama that he thought the prosecutor would appreciate.

"He got her back over to her place, they had a bite to eat. You know, the leftover sandwiches from Robby's were on the table. They had a bottle of wine. On the couch things got a little hot and heavy. He'd had too much to drink. We have witnesses that saw them drinking earlier at The Magnolia. When she said no, he decided to change her mind. There was a ruckus in the living room; she tried to make him leave; another squabble in the foyer, where the statue got turned over; she tried to escape down the hall to her room. But the door wasn't strong enough. Especially for the legs of a runner like Daniels. All that running gives him enough strength in his legs to easily kick in the bedroom door. And you saw that bedroom. There was definitely a struggle in there. The bed was completely torn apart. He raped her. Who knows what all happened in that bedroom? She tried to escape again; he can't risk her reporting him, so he bangs her head on the floor and she's out. Maybe he didn't mean to kill her, but she's dead just the same. And Luke Daniels is the one who did it."

"And what about the sperm? Do you have a match on that, too?" Gafford asked with revulsion for everything he had heard.

"As a matter of fact, I do know the blood type's A positive. Same as Daniels."

Gafford raised an eyebrow but before he could say anything, Limox continued.

"He gives blood on a regular basis. It's not that hard to get his blood type. I haven't done anything wrong there."

"What you mean is that you haven't done anything you could get caught at."

"Whatever." Limox was getting a bit put out with Gafford's attitude. He almost seemed to be defending Daniels. What was the deal here?

"Look, if you don't want to prosecute, that's your business. But the facts all point to Daniels."

"I just want to be sure, okay. I don't want to go pointing fingers at someone for murder, unless I'm damn sure. Especially another lawyer."

Why? Limox thought. They're all a bunch of sleazebags.' But for now, he just let Gafford ponder.

After a few moments of silence, Gafford stood up.

"Alright," he said, "I'll get back to you in a couple of days. For now, let's keep this just between us. Don't talk to anyone else about the file. Who's that other fellow working with you?"

"Feder, but he's off today. He won't even know about our meeting. I'll just keep the file at my desk and leave him out of it." Pretty easy, Limox thought, since he's not really even involved in the case. At first, Limox had wanted all this glory for himself and then he wasn't so sure. But now he felt like an indictment was coming soon and he would be in the driver's seat. He couldn't wait to tell Jerry. He picked up his file and left.

As he was leaving the building, he bumped into Jimmy Clay coming back to the office. Jimmy was such a youngster to be in this job. He was twenty-nine years old and looked nineteen. Jimmy's thin blonde hair and thin body always made him appear younger than he was.

He tried to be such a hard line prosecutor, but from the police side that Limox viewed things from, it just didn't fit. After a few words of greeting, Clay's inquisitive eye caught the name on the file Limox was carrying.

"So, what's the scoop? We fixin' to indict that slime ball, Daniels?" Jimmy loved being blunt.

"Hey, keep your voice down. I've just come from a meeting with your boss. You want to get me in trouble? He told me not to talk with anyone about this." Limox's eyes shifted around the area in an effort to make sure no one overheard them. They were the only two around on the steps to the District Attorney's office.

"Hey, great, maybe we're about to start moving against Daniels. Look, I'm not trying to start anything that's not already brewing. You and I both know he killed her, and so does the rest of this town. You've heard the talk."

"Hey, talk to your boss. It's not me you have to convince."

"What are you saying? You don't think Gafford's with us on this?" Jimmy loved being on the inside with the cops.

"He says he just wants to be sure."

"Hell, I'm sure. The guy raped this beautiful girl and then killed her. The evidence is clear. Just because he's got a law degree shouldn't keep him from behind bars."

"Well, just don't let on to your boss that you talked to me about the case. He just told me not to talk to a soul."

"Hey, no problem. But you might want to cover up the name on the file for the next person you run up on. See ya," and Clay was off with a silly grin.

Upstairs, Clay went straight to Gafford's office. The DA was surprised to see him away from the Grand Jury and glanced up at the clock to check the time.

"What are you doing here? Who's with the Grand Jury?"

"Hello, to you, too. I'm just back for a moment to check my messages because the jurors are taking a short afternoon break. I've gotten through about ten cases, total, today. We all decided a cup of coffee and a stretch was in order. I saw Limox on my way in. We ready to present the Weeks case?"

"What did he say to you?" Gafford sounded exasperated.

"He didn't say anything. But I saw the name on the file he was carrying. Are you ready to go against Daniels?"

"Jimmy, I just want to be sure. It seems like everybody is sure but me."

"Well, I'm sure. I've talked to some of the investigators on the case and some of the people who saw Daniels and Weeks together the night she was killed. And that shoe print is the clincher."

"How did you know about that?" Gafford quizzed.

"Oh, I don't know, one of the detectives told me I think. Everybody knows Daniels is a runner. And the grid pattern on the bottom of the shoe matches the ones Daniels wears. It's his shoe. I mean, who else would want to kill this beautiful creature?"

"But that's just it! Why would he? What's his motive?"

"Sex. Drugs. You know, cocaine makes people do some weird things. Look at some of the stuff we've seen up here. People get all wired out on coke and go nuts, doing crazy things. I say things got a little out of hand that night and when she wouldn't let him pop her, he popped her. Did you see the bruises on that body?"

Jimmy picked up the file from Gafford's desk and pulled out the pictures.

"It's pretty obvious she went through quite a time with this guy. There's bruises and bite marks all over her."

"I'd say he got a little carried away, wouldn't you. And the coroner's report says she had extreme vaginal abrasions. Hell, this loony probably had sex with her after she was dead. We've waited long enough. There's no other explanation. Don't you think something else would have surfaced by now?"

Jimmy was right. He couldn't wait any longer. Hell, it seemed that everybody knew what had to be done but him. Luther made it pretty clear for him that morning. If this case hung out there much longer it would give an opponent in the District Attorney race plenty to attack him on. He was not too crazy about his job right now, but it was a job that paid him decently. One more term and he'd have a retirement and maybe Luther would be ready for him to come in there.

But what about Luke Daniels? They had talked about this some time ago and Luke had said he would come in and explain his side of the story. The way things were shaping up, that may not be such a good idea. He felt he should at least call Daniels and say something to him. What would he say? Luke, did you kill the girl? He kept coming back to the fact that, in this one, he just didn't know what to do.

"I'm headed back over to the Grand Jury. We shouldn't be there too much longer. Another couple of cases and I'm dismissing them for the day. Hey, if you want me to present at that Weeks case, I will. I know the son-of-a-bitch is guilty."

"Just finish up today and we'll get back to this later."

Jimmy walked out of the office with a tingle. Billy had not said no to his offer to present the Weeks case. He hadn't said yes but he hadn't said no. God, how he would love to offer that one up to the jurors. He'd have them worked into hysterics with the pictures of the poor girl's body. They'd be ready to go out and lynch Luke Daniels. Jimmy grinned at himself. He couldn't help but put his hand up like the conductor and make the sound of a train whistle as he rode down the elevator.

The rest of the day didn't get any better for Billy and when the clock hit five, he fled out of the office. Jimmy had made it back to his office and all he got was a wave from Gafford as he sprinted by his door. He was out the front door and in his car before anyone could way-lay him. He longed for the comfort of his home; the unconditional acceptance of his children. Oh, how he hoped Rhonda was not in one of her moods.

When he opened the front door of his house, the children were all seated around the kitchen counter eating their supper.

"Hey, what about me? Ya'll aren't waiting on your dear old dad?"

The surprised look on their faces was real since they rarely saw him before six. The two younger children quickly tumbled down out of the barstools and attacked their dad.

"Daddy, daddy, you're home. We're eating early 'cause we gonna get to stay at mawmaw's and pawpaw's tonight. Mawmaw's gonna take us to school tomorrow."

Justin was eleven years old and in the sixth grade; Alicia was ten and in the fifth. The two younger kids loved to stay over with Rhonda's parents. They only lived a few blocks away and while they didn't stay over there much on a school night, it did happen occasionally.

They were both all over their dad hugging and kissing him with him soaking up the attention. Glenna, their sixteen year old, was much too mature and cool to make a fuss, but she did get up from her seat and go over to plant a kiss on his cheek.

"I'm out of here, too. Got a term paper due soon and a bunch of us are going over to the university library. Sorry. You and Mom are stuck here all alone tonight," she finished with a wink. Billy managed to reach over to the smaller kids and give his eldest daughter a big hug.

"So what kind of paper are you working on?"

"English lit. I'm really just looking for a topic tonight. We have to have our subject matter and a statement of intent turned in by Friday. I'm thinking of doing mine on the Gothic novel. You know, Mary Shelly and all that. Maybe even focus on women writers. What do you think?"

"Sounds fine to me. I'm sure you'll do a good job." Gafford moved to a chair at the counter and got both the kids to finish their supper.

"So why are you two going to Mawmaw's?"

"She's taking us to the mall and to get ice cream. It's a treat because we helped her this weekend in the yard. Mom asked if we could spend the night and she said sure."

Rhonda came over to Billy and put her arm around him. The light touch was just what he needed and he turned to her and gave her a full body embrace, both pleased with the absence of the hostility that floated through their relationship. Billy's unsettled attitude toward his position and the accompanying stress often followed him home. The daily grind of dealing with a teenager and two smaller kids often left her crabby. There was little left in the way of tenderness for each other. This was a rare moment that came with perfect timing for Billy. Rhonda could feel his need as their bodies touched. Through their clothes the yearning tugged. Perfect timing for her as well. She was ready to have him need her. Want her. Because she wanted something, too.

Their embrace lasted only a moment but communicated their desire. Billy stroked her cheek as he looked into her eyes. She kissed him lightly and hugged again before moving away to tend the children.

"Justin, drink your milk."

The children were captivated with the lack of harsh words that usually went back and forth between their parents. Glenna loaded her plate into the dishwasher and went back to her room. Justin slurped down the last bit of milk and jumped down from the stool.

"I'm going to get my clothes for tomorrow. Come on, Alicia."

The kids disappeared and immediately Rhonda's mother was knocking at the back door.

"Hi, come in, mom. They just finished eating. They'll be out with their clothes in a minute."

"Hello, Mawmaw," Billy exclaimed. She hated him calling her that but he did it anyway and gave her a light kiss on the cheek. The stress he brought home was fading, being assuaged by the touch of a loving family; even his mother-in-law.

The kids romped out with their bag and filled the room with the excitement of children headed to grandmother's house. Rhonda checked their packing for the right items.

"Did you get your things for school? Justin, here's your back pack. Alicia, where's yours?"

"I got it, mom."

"You're all set, then. Let dad help you get the stuff in Mawmaw's car."

Billy grabbed up bags and stepped out the door to the carport with the children, leaving Rhonda and her mother alone.

"Thanks, mother. I know they'll enjoy this outing. We've been so busy around here. I haven't had a chance to do anything special with them."

"Don't worry, we'll have fun. You know how much your dad and I enjoy their company. And I'll get them to school just fine. You relax tonight and enjoy. You look a little stressed. Everything okay?"

"Oh, yes, fine. As soon as Billy and I get supper, I'm going in here to put my feet up and watch a movie and get to bed early. Thanks, again."

They moved out to Mrs. Johnson's car and she got in.

"Okay, gang, we all ready?"

With the two little ones bouncing in the back seat, she backed out the drive with Rhonda and Billy waving.

"It's all yours, folks," Glenna came out of the house. "I'm off to pick up Lindy and then to the library." Her old Mustang was parked off the driveway. The door creaked as she got in and slammed it shut. Slow to crank, the old car sputtered and spat and then fired off. She eased out of the driveway as Rhonda and Billy stood in the same spot waving goodbye.

Glenna was such a pretty girl. She also had the best of grades. Billy wished he could reward his daughter with a nicer car. He kept hoping to put enough away to surprise her at graduation. But with his election coming this year, all extra cash would have to go toward the campaign. Public office was getting more-and-more expensive. And this was not even one that he really wanted. Rhonda felt the cloud move back over his spirit.

"Hey, come on, now. The kids are gone. All of them. Let's don't get back in a funk. I've got a great supper for us. You hungry?" She hugged him again and tried to feel that need she got earlier in the kitchen. It was there. She didn't say anything for a few moments; just stood there in the driveway with her arms around him.

"We'd better take this inside. The neighbors are going to start talking. Just wouldn't be right for the District Attorney to be seen in a public display of affection."

Rhonda spoke lightly with a little tease in her voice. She rubbed her leg against his provocatively. She laughed and skitted away from him playfully. He chased after her and they slipped back into the kitchen where she pretended to busy herself at the stove. He came up behind her and put his arms around her waist.

"I love you," he whispered in her ear. His lips remained at her neck and she could feel his breath on her skin. His arms rose up to her body to just below her breasts and again he squeezed. Not so hard, but firmly he held his body close to hers, his cheek touching hers from behind. They stood there embraced, drawing emotion from each other, filling the void.

The touching of their bodies produced a flicker of desire that both of them had let fade for a long time. Their continual bickering doused any sparks that might now and then arise, usually before that spark could get anything going. The job, the kids, the usual. But tonight Rhonda was determined to kindle this little spark. She may be approaching forty and have a few extra pounds but she could still love this man. And tonight was the night.

Billy couldn't have imagined what was going on in Rhonda's head. He was so needy tonight that hugging would have sufficed. And he was too needy to allow anything to get in the way of the touch he so desperately craved. Rhonda whispered she loved him and all he could think of was more, more.

Rhonda wanted more, too. She wanted more than just a quick moment of passion that left him spent and her wanting. She intended for this evening to take a while. She held him close for a leisurely minute and then with a final tightening of her resolve gave him a squeeze and pulled away.

"Let's not rush things. The kids are gone and we've got all night. Besides, I'm hungry. How 'bout you?"

"Ah, yeah. Something smells good. What you got cooking?" Billy's answer was almost groggy.

"Your favorite. Lasagna. It should be just about done. I've got a salad already fixed in the fridge. I need to heat up the garlic bread and we'll be all set. There's a bottle of wine in there chillin'. Tell me what you think. It's an Australian wine someone was talking about today at the Bar Auxiliary."

Billy pulled open the refrigerator door and got out the bread and wine.

"Pretty fancy. Wine during the week. A Monday night even. What does this say?" Holding the bottle at arm's length, he read "Rosemont Chardonnay, Australia." Billy knew little about wines and was sure Rhonda didn't know much more.

"Does this go with lasagna?" he asked. Billy loved Rhonda's lasagna but didn't remember ever having wine with it before. In fact, he could not remember the last time they had a bottle of wine in the house. He couldn't help but wonder what good fortune had smiled down on him this evening when his day had been so lousy.

"Mr. Fred at the store said it would be fine." Rhonda was slathering garlic and butter on the loaf of bread.

"Mr. Fred?"

"You know, at the liquor store."

"Since when did you and the man at the liquor store get to be on a first name basis?" Billy didn't mean for it to sound like cross-examination.

She looked up at him with a bit of irritation.

"Since I graduated from high school with his daughter, that's since when." She turned back to her buttering and bit her lip. There was not going to be a fight tonight. There was not going to be a fight tonight. Her mind raced for words that would keep the tone where she wanted it.

"Why don't you open that and we can have a glass while I'm finishing up. Don't you want to go change?" She licked some butter off her finger and paused.

"Uummm, that garlic is strong." She looked up at him with her fingertip still in her mouth, allowing her lips to smack temptingly. "Is it too much?" She touched a buttery finger to his lips. "Here, let's have a wine glass," she reached high up in the cabinet, letting her breast graze against him in the process.

"We can eat in about five minutes. Why don't you go change into something more comfortable and I'll have it on the table when you get back."

Billy dutifully ambled off to their bedroom and came back shortly in a sweatshirt and jeans. Not the most attractive outfit, Rhonda thought, but at least he was comfortable. He certainly took her at her word. She wasn't dressed up but had on her most flattering blouse; low cut to show off her chest. And, a pair of black stretch pants.

The color didn't completely conceal the weight but it helped. She wished it wasn't there. She wanted to do something about it. It just never seemed to happen. After Glenna was born, there were five pounds that wouldn't go away. With Justin there was ten more and then with Alicia there was more than ten. Three kids and thirty pounds. Even though she didn't dwell on her size, the sensitivity to it was always there. Except when she ate. And, tonight, she certainly was not going to worry about it. Not with Billy primed and ready. There were other things to worry about besides the perfect body. She'd worry about that another time.

When she fixed their plates with squares of lasagna and buttered zucchini, she started to move into the dining room but left them on the kitchen bar instead. It was more familiar. And cozy. The extra warmth from the kitchen created a feeling of shelter from the damp, cold February night.

She tossed salad into bowls on the counter, ladling Thousand Island dressing, his favorite.

She pushed the steaming hot bread over nearby and placed the bottle of wine where they could reach it, then set out napkins and silverware.

"I believe we're ready."

"Looks great, hon," Billy said lovingly. As he was changing, he, too, determined to keep the mood amorous. Billy needed love tonight and he was going to take in all he could. "This sure is a great treat. What a lucky man I am."

Rhonda giggled girlishly and accepted the compliment by kissing him lightly on the cheek and snuggling her nose against him. She pulled her chair close so their legs could touch as they ate. They sipped wine and ate and Rhonda listened earnestly about what a rough day he had. Her sympathetic eyes conveyed the understanding she knew he needed. She asked all the right questions and paused at all the right spots for him to unload the pressures of the day and the harrowing strain of prosecutorial responsibilities. The struggle of dealing with law enforcement types who thought everybody was guilty. Defense lawyers who never had a guilty client. The Grand Jury was in session now and that just added to the weight he bore. No one could imagine the onus of being the District Attorney. Billy looked over at Rhonda whose eyes glistened appropriately.

"I guess I sound like a malcontent. Here you fixed me this wonderful meal and all I've done is gripe. This was just an especially bad day, though. A lot of bad ones sort of ganged up on me. Tough decisions."

"Oh, Billy." She eased off the edge of her chair so that she was right next to him. She let her arms circle his neck and laid her head on his shoulder. She was glad for this time of his opening up. He rarely did. Oh, she knew he was not happy in his job but she would not let him confide in her because she couldn't handle it for all her own problems. It was good for him tonight to unwind and unload. Must be the wine, she thought. And she was glad for it.

"Here, you finish this off." She poured the last bit of the chardonnay into his glass. "I've got another treat for you."

"What? It's not my birthday, is it? I know we just had Christmas."

"No, no. Just a little something I picked up today while I was out." She went to a styrofoam box that was setting on the kitchen counter and got out two plates. When she turned around he saw two luscious pieces of chocolate cheesecake with fresh raspberries on top.

"Wow, did you make this?"

"No, I wish I could take credit. I picked it up today at the Magnolia Bar and Grill. Everybody raves about it, though. Here."

She got a bite on the fork and held it up to his mouth. He closed his mouth around it and his eyes rolled back as he moaned. She reached up and kissed him, lightly. She didn't go back to her chair but straddled his leg instead. When he swallowed the first bite she got him another, twisting around to the plate. Her chest rubbed against his as she dropped the second bite into his mouth. This time she kissed him again, allowing her lips to linger on his.

The cheesecake was melting on his lips and she got the faint flavor of chocolate on hers. She got a bite for herself and intentionally allowed it to smear on her lip. She kissed him again with her mouth open.

Billy was taken aback. He was not accustomed to his wife being so erotic. He didn't even remember her being this way before they had kids. He knew he liked it, though, and whatever the reason he was for it all. He looked down at her hunched up against him. He could see down her blouse. The girl had always had nice tits, he thought. And he wanted one of them right now. His hand came up and cupped it from underneath, massaging the nipple. It was already hard. She wanted him, and he wanted her to have him, in the worst kind of way.

Rhonda tried to give him another piece, but he pushed the cheesecake away. With one hand still on her breast he brought the other up her back. His lips found hers again and he kissed hard. The heavily sensuous flavor of the chocolate still lingered on their tongues fusing with the passion of the kiss.

Rhonda could feel his leg against her. She could feel a firmness growing between them. They stood up and embraced, hanging almost suspended in a lost moment of long-neglected hunger. Their lips withdrew and Rhonda leaned against his chest as they both panted for breath.

She smiled again as she looked up at him.

"Come with me," she whispered as she pulled away and held up her hand to him. Before he could take it, she jerked it back and then made a motion with her index finger, again beckoning him to follow her. She giggled and ran to their bedroom with Billy following right behind her.

Billy awoke the next morning with a headache. He was not accustomed to drinking and the bottle of wine had left its effects. He could hear Rhonda bustling about in the kitchen. He lay still for a moment thinking over the events of last night. How wonderful she had been to him. What a night after what a day. Lying in bed with her had been great, talking about his problems, about the exasperating dilemmas he found himself embroiled in with his godawful job. He knew she didn't like to hear him talk about how bad it was but last night she was all ears. How refreshing for him to have his wife listen and understand. He felt like he could make it through another day. Rhonda might not be the prettiest girl in town or the brightest, but she sure made him feel like a man last night.

Rhonda appeared at the door with a cup of coffee.

"Better get up if you're going to make it to work today."

They sat on the edge of the bed together.

"So, do you think you'll get that indictment today?" Rhonda asked directly.

He had almost forgotten how much they talked about last night. She had shared all the gossip from the Bar Auxiliary and he had let flow what was coming in to him. Little of either had much to do with the facts. When he didn't answer, she continued.

"Honey, you know I'm behind you in whatever decision you make. But with the elec-

THE BOOK OF LUKE

tion coming up you can't leave yourself open. That snake Chris Singletary's wife was at the Auxiliary yesterday. She kept talking about 'that poor Weeks girl' and how nothing was being done about it. Like he could." Rhonda stood up and went to the dresser where she started brushing her hair.

Billy looked at her again. Gosh, she had gotten big. He fought to stay in shape, running when he could. His job kept him from any regular exercise program but he still managed to hold himself in check better than Rhonda. She must have put on fifty pounds, he thought. He decided not to look at her. He got up and went in to take a shower.

Rhonda came in and hugged him from behind, letting her hands play against his chest.

"I know my man's going to do what he's got to do. You won't let those people push you around, will you, Billy?"

"Yeah, yeah, I got to get my shower."

"How much longer is the Grand Jury in session?" she asked without letting go of him.

"Why do you want to know that?" He looked at her in the mirror.

"Oh, no particular reason. I was just wondering how much longer my poor baby was going to be having to deal with this awful stuff, that's all. You know I love you and care about you." Rhonda continued to let her hands caress his body. "So how much longer? When do you think you'll have to make a decision?"

"We'll probably finish up next week sometime." Her questioning was making him a little nervous and she could feel it.

"Good, we'll have us another special night after that."

Billy stepped in the shower and Rhonda went back to the kitchen. She could hear the water running in the shower from the kitchen. She picked up the phone and dialed.

"Hello, Eloise. Good morning. I hope I'm not calling too early. Yes, thank you. Listen I had such a good time yesterday at the Magnolia. We simply must get together again. Next time my treat. Well, no, my day is fairly open today. Say, have you been to that new coffee shop across from the mall. . . Shopping would be perfect..."

They chatted on with Rhonda in perfect contentment. She was meeting Eloise Lambert for coffee and then going shopping. What a day this would be. And this time Rhonda could talk with some authority.

When Gafford arrived at work shortly before nine o'clock, Jimmy Clay was already there putting together their day's files for the Grand Jury. Billy grabbed some coffee and joined him in the conference room where he had files all spread out.

"You look refreshed today," Jimmy started off. "Must have been a good night for you. What'd you do?"

"Nothing really. Just stayed around the house with the wife. How 'bout you?" Billy thought he might have blushed just a little.

"I worked out over at the 'Y' and then watched the tube. Real exciting for a single guy.

Not much going on to go out for. Must be the time of year. And everywhere I go now it seems like people want to talk about Susan Weeks. What we're doing and all. I sure get tired of putting them off."

"No question about it, though. Everyone thinks Daniels did it. And the worst thing is some of them are starting to look at me like we're going to let him get away. They think we don't want to stick it to him. Like we're afraid of him or something."

This was definitely Jimmy's macho side taking the brunt of the criticism from some of his buddies. It wasn't as bad as he was making it out. Much of what he took off the streets he brought on himself. In lawyer circles the subject stayed alive because lawyers were such excellent gossips, they loved to be on the attack. Several went right for the jugular last night.

"Chris Singletary's name keeps coming up more and more. They say he's considering a run. Most everyone I talk to thinks he's banking on your being vulnerable on the Weeks murder."

Jimmy had his macho side and he knew that Billy had his, too. It really went with the territory. You couldn't be a great and powerful prosecutor and not have a little John Wayne in you. The trouble in these parts was that there was generally way too much John to keep reason in perspective.

"Oh, is that so, is it?" Jimmy touched a nerve in Billy with that last one. "Well, we'll just have to see about that. I haven't been at this job for over eleven years without learning a little something about vulnerability, myself." Billy might be fed up with this job but he was not about to let some upstart like Singletary snatch it out from under him. He would leave the Office of District Attorney when he decided it was time to leave.

"Come on, let's get this stuff together. We need to get over to the Grand Jury room." Gafford's mind was working on what he could do quickly. He needed some good exposure on the TV. He thumbed through the files. Several drug cases that would look good on the evening news. He could be there when they served the indictments on a crack house.

"Should I get the Daniels file?" Jimmy asked anxiously.

"What? Oh. No. Not right now. I'll handle that in due time." Gafford was riled by Jimmy's information, but not enough to act rashly. He still needed some time on Daniels.

"Put these in the box and let's go."

Jimmy's ego was bruised somewhat by the slight from his boss. Yes, he was the boss and, yes, Jimmy was the assistant DA, but he still hated the idea of being the kid toting the briefcase. Jimmy decided to exercise some muscle himself. He called down to the Sheriff's office and requested a deputy to help him with delivering the materials to the Courthouse. The pecking order did not stop with James Clay, Esquire.

CHAPTER NINE

Mrs. Gafford was positively tickled with herself. Pulling up to Novelty House, she was ecstatic over the possibilities for the day. As she walked by Rhonda admired Eloise's new Roadmaster, she remembered the talk about it at lunch yesterday. It was a Christmas present from Luther. How nice. She squeezed past it and went in the front door.

Novelty House was an old Victorian home located in Hampton's Historic District that had been turned into a gift shop by a local doctor's wife. The shop was unique in south Mississippi and folks came from Jackson and the Coast to wander the rooms and survey the rare and distinctive gifts.

There were antiques of all sorts, furniture and other items. There were exceptional linens, hand embroidered, one-of-a-kind items. Every room held an assortment of books for both children and adults. The recently added array of fresh coffees brought a new group of customers to the establishment. Tables throughout the old house let you sit and sip coffee or browse the many wares and today Rhonda Gafford was meeting Eloise Lambert there.

Eloise was still examining all the different flavors of coffee, having just arrived herself. "Rhonda, good to see you again. You're looking radiant today. That's a good color for you."

Rhonda was wearing black again and was almost offended by the statement. But, instead, she smiled and took the compliment at face value.

"Thank you, Eloise. Wow, doesn't it smell great in here. I could enjoy this just taking in the aroma of it all."

After settling on a flavor, Eloise insisted on paying and they milled around the shop. After a time, Eloise protested about the heels she was wearing and they found a table.

"Let's sit for a spell. We'll be walking enough when we get to the mall. Oh, look, there's Betty Lubritz, the owner. Do you know her, Rhonda? Hey, Betty. Come over and join us."

Betty Lubritz reached their table and Eloise introduced Rhonda. The conversation came around to Rhonda and what she did. Betty knew of her husband and, in fact, had read about him recently in the paper.

"My sister lives in the same neighborhood as the parents of the girl that was murdered. Susan Weeks. I'm sure you two know all about it."

"Oh, yes. Terrible tragedy. It's hard to believe it could happen here in our little town. But Rhonda's husband is a tough man and he'll have the murderer behind bars soon." Eloise stared straight at Rhonda with a look of validation. Betty was looking at her, too, as if waiting for some response.

"You're right about that, Eloise," Rhonda heard herself say. "Why, just last night Billy and I were talking and he…" she paused mostly for effect, the moment she had been waiting for.

"Yes? Yes?" They said in unison from the edge of their seat.

"Well, I really can't say. You know Billy confides in me because I'm his wife, but it wouldn't be right for me to say things that he shares with me in private. But you can rest assured they know who the murderer is and they're watching him closely, waiting for just the right moment when their case is secure. Billy never likes to act hastily."

Rhonda stopped and sat back. Her mind went back to last night and him rolling off her. He did some things too hastily, she thought, without any regard for her feelings. But she got what she wanted from him. And that was the looks on the faces of the two women sitting in front of her. They were hanging on her every word.

Betty was the first one to speak, not being impeded by the possibility of a breach of confidentiality that is usually spread over from a lawyer to his wife.

"I've been hearing about that Daniels lawyer. That he's the one. I wouldn't know him if he walked in the door, but some of my customers do. They say he's a good looking man. Most of them say they don't believe the rumors even though they're discussed everywhere. Is he the one, Rhonda?" Rhonda didn't speak, but her silence said volumes. Eloise jumped in for her.

"They always say, 'Where there's smoke, there's fire.' I know the man's a hot head. Betty, you know he attacked my Wilson, don't you. Right in a deposition. The man has no class at all."

"He destroyed the poor girl's house. His fingerprints were everywhere," Rhonda reported with a flourish. Of course, this fact had been in the newspaper, but her telling now gave it another feature of authenticity, like it had just come from a special crime report.

"What on earth do you think happened?" Betty wondered aloud, shaking her head.

"They're saying drugs," Eloise put in. "That's what I've been hearing.

"No!" Betty sounded shocked, as if she had never heard the word before. "Did I mention my sister knows the girl's parents? Well, anyway, she says they are just salt of the earth. I understand the girl did some modeling in New Orleans. Do you think that was the drug connection? Her poor parents are just devastated. She was an only child. And such an achiever. Beautiful. Educated. My sister says her mother won't even come out of the house now. It's a shame, a real shame. I hope they stick it to this guy. Do you think he'll get the gas chamber?"

"If I know my husband, that's what he'll want. Bill Gafford is a tough man that won't stop until he gets the maximum for this monster." Rhonda was pleased to be able to defend her husband. A lot of folks came into this shop and Betty talked to most of them. She could be a real help in reelecting Billy. This was a good seed to plant.

"We'll certainly be behind him one hundred percent. I hope they fry Daniels for this. That poor girl."

Betty excused herself with having to get back to work. When Eloise and Rhonda started toward the door, Rhonda noticed that several others in the room had overheard their conversation. She felt good about boosting her husband's position. For years now she had been busy raising children that were only now getting to the point that she could have some freedom. Yes, she liked this. And she liked the attention from Eloise.

On Tuesday afternoon, Billy Gafford and Jimmy Clay finished up their session with the Grand Jury early. In two days they had amassed a group of indictments that would further the cause of justice in Bedford County and the cause of keeping William Porter Gafford in the Office of District Attorney.

Jimmy liked this cause, too, since it guaranteed him a job. He sometimes liked to speculate about his job possibilities here in Hampton. There were several firms where he wouldn't mind working. His cousin was married to Wilson Lambert. That would be his pick. Small but very successful. That Luther Lambert was notorious for being the deal maker. The Lamberts were always very friendly to him. They might be interested in a young, up-and-coming attorney in their firm. Two attorneys had left the firm just when Jimmy arrived here from law school. Another, James Germany, had left the Lambert firm a couple of years after Jimmy started at the DA's office. There were some rumors then of a rift but all that quieted down shortly after the split.

But Jimmy shouldn't have to worry about a job. Billy should be on smooth sailing back into office. As long as that pesky Singletary stayed out of things. And as long as Billy didn't let this Weeks murder get out of hand. They had to do something about it.

Jimmy liked watching Billy operate with the indictments they had already. The publicity around drug cases got eaten up by the public and Jimmy had never seen anybody rant and rave about it better than Billy.

Billy sat down at his desk and dialed the number of the Hampton News. "Mr. William Rogers, please. This is the District Attorney," Billy said with his most official tone. Billy maintained a good relationship with all the media. It was the perfect symbiotic relationship, nobody's harmed and they both benefit. Billy would spend a few minutes with William and then do the same thing with the local TV station.

"Billy, good to hear from you," William Rogers came on with a welcome voice. "How are things over your way?" William rarely received a personal call from the District Attorney unless it was something good.

"Tough, William, tough. Fighting crime in the streets day in and day out." Billy started out on a light note. He wanted to set the tone for his call as being purely out of an interest in helping his good friend William report the news. Of course, it wouldn't hurt if William decided to throw in something good about the valiant efforts of the noble prosecutor who keeps our district safe.

"Seems like someone told me there was a Grand Jury in session. What we got coming out of there?"

"That's just what I was calling you about, my man. In the past two days we've presented cases to the Grand Jury that should put a major dent in the drug traffic in this area. We've got indictments on several substantial dealers in the area and some of them should make quite a stir in the community. Ought to make for some pretty interesting reading. Thought you might like to get in on the serving of the indictments. Should be able to get some good pictures for the front page."

"Yes, indeed. That would be real nice. Any hint as to who might be the most desirable for that shot?" From Billy's tone William surmised that the intended victim for these busts was going to be someone prominent.

"Now, William, you know I'd be violating the law, myself, if I let out anything about the Grand Jury proceedings. You know all that is secret." Billy loved making the show, placing them in the position of confederates. "I'll tell you what I can do, though," he said with a lowered voice. "You have your photographer meet me over at the Metro Narcotics office tonight at midnight. I'm going to be in on serving the indictments. He can ride in the car with me, get the pictures he wants and then you'll have'em for tomorrow's edition. Sound good enough?"

It sounded good to Billy. Let him have the photographer for a while, buddy him up a little and snap a few good shots of the old DA in action. Who knows when they could use them!

"Send me someone you trust though, you hear. I don't want someone that's going to jump to conclusions about this thing and run his mouth," Billy continued. They changed photographers at the paper about as often as they changed ink in the presses.

"I got you, Billy. And I've got just the person for you. There's this kid working for us part-time. Writes a hell of a story, too. And he's good with a camera. Jeff Woodall's his name. I'll get him in here and talk to him right. He'll be just fine. He knows he's got a future in the newspaper business and is eager to learn. This little bit of excitement will fit him to a tee. What time did you say, midnight? Great. He'll be there."

"Good deal, William. I'll look forward to meeting him." Billy laid down the phone and without blinking an eye, dialed the TV station, ready to do the whole scenario over again.

"Hello, could I speak with Mr. Brown, please. This is the District Attorney." His query was direct and declarative. Norman Brown was the station manager. He and Billy were in college together. A long standing relationship that Billy hoped to continue.

"Billy, Good to hear from you…"

Another gambit was set in the game of politics in Hampton.

Eleven o'clock Tuesday night found Billy in his office. He had gone home early for supper and spent some time with the kids. Rhonda was back to her regular old self of bitching about everything. Why did he have to be out in the middle of the night? Why couldn't they serve the indictments without him? The only soft spot in her tone was when she asked about the Weeks case. A much different attitude than he had found just the night before. Women. Billy guessed he would never understand them. He could explain to Rhonda a thousand times about the importance of his being out in the field tonight and she would never understand.

Everything was set. The Chief of Detectives had pulled in some extras from the Hampton PD. Danny Hallowell and Limox would be there to help with serving the warrants. They had advised Gafford to wear a bullet proof vest. Things could get tricky tonight.

The indictments would be served on the drug case defendants in the dark of night. Most of these cases came from undercover work done by the Metro Narcotics Task Force, a cooperative unit made up of officers from several of the surrounding cities and counties. For these undercover operations they borrowed officers from similar units on the Coast and from Jackson so as to have faces that the local drug community did not recognize. They worked themselves into the trust of the dealers over a period of time, made several buys of whatever substance was going around and then this information was presented to the Grand Jury who returned indictment for the dealers.

This particular operation had several officers from the Gulfport Police Department. Billy liked working cases with them because they were all professionals. Their Chief of Police demanded high standards from his officers and you could rely on their cases being top notch. All their evidence would be good and solid, put together in an orderly fashion. No worry about tainted evidence that would be thrown out in court, forcing dismissal and embarrassing the DA.

Both newspaper and TV reporters were meeting him at the Metro unit office at midnight. He would take them around in his car, let them get a few shots of the dope dealers being dragged from their houses and then he would be interviewed about the depth of the operation and the impact it would have on the drug trade. The truth was it would do little to disrupt the drug trade. Billy understood that tomorrow there would be some other hoodlum out there selling the dope that users wanted. He worried about that only a little. Job security, he often mused to himself. In a job he didn't really want. What a laugh, he thought. Well, he did want it. At least for another four years. At least for him to find the right spot to work into after leaving the prosecutor's office.

Close to midnight, Billy went to the mirror to inspect himself one more time. He had on a fresh shirt and tie. Rhonda didn't understand that, either. All she saw was another shirt to iron. He looked in the mirror. The freshly ironed shirt had a few wrinkles around the collar but still looked good. The tie was perfectly straight. He pulled on the camouflage jacket over the fresh shirt to give him the look of the undercover team. He practiced a few serious looks for the camera. His 'we're cleaning up this town' look that he tried to catch from several different angles in the mirror.

"Okay, pardner. Let's go round up the bad guys."

When he arrived at the Metro headquarters, the news people were already there. They took shots of him getting out of his car, of him and the Metro director shaking hands and some shots of them looking over case files. Another showed them peering at a map.

They soon headed off to make the arrests. Billy had Jeff Woodall, the newspaper man, with him and the TV crew followed behind in their van. Billy chatted with Woodall about the cases, about the work of the officers and the role of the prosecutor.

After a while the reporter stopped writing and they began to discuss a wide range of subjects from Jeff's school courses and the direction of his career to Billy's career and other cases in his office. It was inevitable that they came to the subject of Susan Weeks. Jeff filled in the prosecutor about his visit with Luke Daniels.

"Yeah, that's one hot-headed fellow. He just grabbed me for no reason. I was trying to talk with him about Miss Weeks and he slammed me against the wall. And the look in his eyes… Well, I'm not ashamed to admit it scared me. He looked like he could have killed me just for asking a question."

"And you had never met him before this? I mean, you and Daniels didn't have any ongoing feud that could have sparked this?"

Billy knew about the ruckus between Luke and James Germany at the Christmas party. Germany's temperament was enough to make you want to smack him. Billy had wanted to punch the guy a few times himself. He could be such a jerk. But Jeff Woodall was a mild-mannered kid. How could anybody want to rough him up?

"No, sir. I'd never met him before. I was just by his office trying to get a story and he attacked me. I'm learning to expect that in some situations with this job. But this guy had no call to attack me. Unless, of course, he didn't want me asking him questions about Susan Weeks. I guess that was his reason."

They rode in silence for a few moments before arriving at a house where an arrest was to be made. They had a search warrant. The officers went to the door and knocked. The accused was in the living room and the arrest went without incident. One patrol car took him back to jail and they moved on to another house.

The entourage made its way to the next location where the house was lit up and a party going on. They nabbed two of their indictees and arrested several others on drug charges. All in a night's work, Gafford explained to the reporter. They moved on to another hit on their list.

The next house had only a light in the living room where you could hear the sounds of the TV playing. The officers were pumped from the excitement of the last bust. They got out and stood some distance away as the officers banged away on the front door.

"Open up, it's the police."

The TV people were right behind them as they busted into the house. A woman had opened the door and the officers pushed her to the floor and handcuffed her. She started screaming.

"Don't hurt my baby. Don't hurt my baby."

Billy suddenly could hear a child crying and they rushed up to the door. Two children had gotten out of bed and stood in the hallway, terrified. One was sobbing uncontrollably. The TV cameras were getting it all. Woodall snapped a few pictures while Billy tried to get with the officer in charge to find out what was going on. When no one else was found in the house, they got the woman up and learned that the indictee was not there. He had been her boyfriend but they had broken up weeks ago and as far as she knew he had moved back to Jackson with his parents. The children would not let the officers touch them without wailing even louder.

Billy quickly got everybody out of the house and had the officer take the handcuffs off the mother. He gave her a few moments to console the children before trying to talk to her. What a mess. And with pictures. He had to think fast to get this back on track. He had the officers talk to the news people about the dealing of drugs from this house, with the children present. Oh, yeah, she knew. She put her children at risk. No, they were not the defendant's children. No, they did not have a warrant for her at this time.

Billy sat down with the woman to try to defuse the situation. He got her to admit that she knew he was into drugs, but she denied that she knew he was dealing. She told them they had split up over his drug use and some of the friends that came around.

Billy scared the poor woman with stories of how she could be indicted and lose her kids if she didn't cooperate with them. She was to say nothing about this to anyone. Understand? The terrified mother of the two small children could not answer, but shook her head in an affirmative response. The two children, a boy and a girl, were huddled on the couch, next to her.

"How old are you, son?" Billy tried with his most paternal tone.

The little boy held up three fingers. The little girl couldn't have been more than two. Jeez, what a job, Billy thought. He spoke again to the mother.

"Remember, if we don't get your full cooperation, I'll have the welfare department over here to get these children." Billy could see the terror in the mother's eyes. And the hate. Oh, well, he couldn't be loved by everybody.

They left her there with the children, still sobbing quietly. Billy quickly crossed the yard and got in his car where Woodall waited.

"I think that's enough for one night, don't you, my boy?" Billy cranked up the car and turned on the heater. He had just a bit of a chill.

On the way back, they discussed how the woman was involved in the drug traffic but how Billy hated to separate a mother from her children. If she and the guy were really split he might let her slide. You know, you have to use a little humanity in this job, he explained to Woodall. The young reporter seemed to comprehend completely and responded with admiration for Billy Gafford.

Back at the office, Billy quickly had a similar conversation with the TV people. They had to appreciate the delicacy of a situation like this. Billy had a job to do, but he didn't want to hurt some poor innocent little children. They understood and would not do anything to jeopardize the continuing investigation. Billy was relieved when they all drove away. He got back into his car and headed home.

Those bastards. The Metro should have known this guy was not there any more. Almost messed up his good publicity shots. But thanks to his quick thinking he turned the bad scene into even better coverage than he could imagine. The media got to see him being not only the tough prosecutor but also the kind, compassionate father-figure with a heart for children and family. He couldn't wait to see tomorrow's news.

On Wednesday morning Jimmy Clay arrived at work a little late, knowing his boss would be slow to rise today after being up all night with the Metro serving indictments. Usually in by eight, Jimmy strolled off the elevator at nine fifteen. There was no rush today. The Grand Jury was excused for the day to catch up on personal matters after all the hard work they had done. And tomorrow they would be doing a few visits to schools as part of their report. Jimmy was a little surprised to find the foreman of the Grand Jury, Sam Martin, sitting in the lobby.

Sam retired from the state's employ nine years ago at age fifty after serving twenty-five years with the Sheriff's department. After retirement he turned a part time interest into a full time business and now had a successful operation installing security systems, also known as burglar alarms. Sam was a no bull kind of guy, law and order all the way. He was the perfect choice for foreman of the jury, strongly prosecution oriented. Jimmy and Billy could always count on him seeing things their way and helping them with any unruly sort that might pop up. Once he accepted the role of foreman, he took the job seriously and dared anyone to challenge his authority.

"Good morning, Sam," Jimmy started off. "Good to see you. What brings you in here today?"

"Oh, I wanted to talk with you and Billy about a few things, if you've got the time."

"Sure thing, Sam. Come on back. We'll get some coffee. I doubt Billy's in. Did you see the news this morning?"

Both the TV and the newspaper carried top stories this morning about the drug arrests made during the night. Neither carried anything about the house where the woman and children had been terrified.

"Wanda, have you heard from Billy today?"

"No, but he said yesterday not to expect him too early. He looked pretty tired last night. Probably still asleep. I've got some coffee ready. Should I get you some?"

"Would you, please? Sam, come on back to my office. Tell me what's on your mind."

"I guess you recognized some of those names you saw on the news this morning since you helped make it possible to get them off the street. You folks are doing a good job with this Grand Jury." The small talk continued until Wanda appeared with their coffee. Sam thanked her profusely and she finally excused herself shutting the door behind her. Sam went right to the point.

"We're taking a lot of heat because we haven't done anything about this Weeks murder."

Jimmy was taken aback at the statement.

"We?" he asked. "Who is we?"

"The Grand Jury. We are charged with investigating matters relating to the public safety and here we let this Weeks murder stagnate. It's beginning to smell and it reflects badly on us."

Jimmy was flabbergasted, not knowing what to say or how to respond. He was somewhat amused but could tell from the foreman's face that he was dead serious. He knew he had to handle the situation delicately. Before he could respond, Martin continued.

"We've been talking about this some and everyone agrees that I should go over the evidence and report back to them." His lips set firmly as he finished his statement.

Despite his usual swagger, Jimmy realized he was in way over his head. He was always wanting to grab the reins and run with things. Now all he could think of was "Billy, Help!"

"Well, get the file. Let's look at it." Sam carried just a little exasperation in his voice.

"I, ah, well," Jimmy stammered around, trying to come up with a suitable response. His discomfort was not concealed.

Sam, on the other hand, was quite comfortable. He had been in the District Attorney's office many times working on cases as a deputy sheriff. In his twenty-five years he had worked with several DA's and even more assistants. He knew the in's and out's of this office as well as Jimmy, probably better. Hell, he was in charge of the trusties that moved all the files over to this new location twenty years ago.

Before that he worked with Lambert when he was DA, with Raybern and then Gafford before retiring. He was already working cases before Gafford even thought about law school. And now he was foreman of the Grand Jury and he was not about to let his jury get bad-mouthed. The firm set of his jaw let Jimmy know he meant business.

"Let me see what I can do," Jimmy said as he rose from his desk and exited the room. Think, boy, think. What can you do here? He'd get Billy on the phone, that's what he'd do. This was his problem, not Jimmy's.

He went straight to Billy's office and buzzed Wanda.

"Have you heard from Billy, yet?"

"No, I haven't. Is everything alright?"

"Just hunky dory," Jimmy responded as he switched lines and dialed Billy. Busy, busy, busy, the buzz on the line reported. Damn. He slammed down the phone and fell into Billy's chair, only to see Sam standing in the door to the office.

"Did you find it?" Sam had been in this office many times and was comfortable here, too.

"No. No, I didn't. It's not in the filing cabinet and so I was trying to call Billy. He's probably got it with him, but I can't reach him now. His line's busy at home."

Sam moved on into the office and stood in front of the desk. Both their eyes fell on the file at the same time.

"Well, here it is right here. I'll bet Billy was planning on giving it to us today if we had met. Let's see what we got here, Jimmy."

Jimmy was as white as a sheet. He was in his boss's office, sitting in his boss's chair, looking at a file with the foreman of the Grand Jury without his boss's permission. He didn't like this position.

"Maybe we should wait on Billy," was his unconvincing rebuttal.

"Nonsense. He knows I've got a job to do, just like he does. He'll probably be glad we went ahead and got this together. Let's see, umh, uh." The sounds emitted from Sam's thick jowls as he thumbed through the pages of the file with the trained eye of an old investigator.

Jimmy sat silently, immobile, not knowing what to do.

"Looks to me like our boy, Daniels, is in a heap of trouble."

Jimmy shook his head in agreement. He, for one, was ready to indict Daniels. They certainly had enough evidence. But Billy had said wait. And he didn't like the idea of going against his boss. Mainly because he liked his job. He needed that paycheck. It wasn't as if he gave the file to Martin. The man just barged in and took it. And he was thirty years Jimmy's senior; he did it with such authority. How was he going to explain this to Billy?

"So what about tomorrow?"

"Huh?" Jimmy didn't know what he meant.

"Why don't we present this case tomorrow?"

"What?" Are you crazy, he wanted to add. "Sam, you know that's a call only the District Attorney can make."

"Well, you're the District Attorney," Sam pumped. "And I'm foreman of the Grand Jury."

"Assistant District Attorney," Jimmy reminded him. "And it's a position I'd like to keep. I'm sorry, Sam, you'll have to take this one up with Billy." Feeling a resolve with his last statement he reached over and picked up the file marked "WEEKS." "Tell you what. I'll leave it right here on Billy's desk. You can come back and talk to him this afternoon if you like. Maybe he'll let you present it."

Sam made a face but relented.

"You leave him a message that I want to talk to him."

"Let's go out and get Wanda to do that. She'll be sure he gets it." Jimmy was relieved to get him out of Billy's office and back to the lobby.

"Wanda, could you take a message for Billy. Tell him Mr. Martin wants to see him as soon as possible. They have an urgent matter to discuss. Anything else?"

"Certainly. Billy called saying he had a meeting outside the office and would get back with me after lunch."

Jimmy grimaced over not having gotten to talk to Billy, but, at the same time, was relieved that he would have some time to come up with a story on how he had let someone in Billy's office go over a confidential file. As if reading his mind, Martin responded.

"Don't worry, Jimmy. I understand the confidential nature of this. And so do my jurors. You don't have to worry about us. Get with Billy and have him call me."

Billy had more important things to deal with now. The exposure on TV and the paper had brought him some great attention. He was on the phone all morning. Rogers was arranging a noon meeting on Thursday with Rotary Club. Norman Brown had good news for him, too. Jim DeWeese had been in his office earlier and commented on the piece. They needed to get together and talk.

"DeWeese's agency handles the Bedford General account. They've got a presentation to do on their work in the area of drug and alcohol abuse. One of their speakers came down with the flu. DeWeese can work you in the program. It'd be a natural. Can you do it? It's this Friday and Saturday on the Coast."

"Yeah, I can do it." Bedford General employed about twenty-five hundred people and that didn't include the doctors. A good place to make some points, have people saying nice things about him.

"Why don't you stop by his office? He said he'd be there the rest of the day. I'll give him a call and let him know you're coming. What time?"

Billy looked at his watch. It was half past ten. He had thoughts of a little lunch with Rhonda. She was somewhere in the house.

"How 'bout one thirty?"

"Sounds good. If he's got a conflict I'll get him to call you back personally."

Rhonda was in the laundry room in front of the washing machine, her hair tied up and a scowl on her plump cheeks. One look told him the lunch he had in mind would not be today.

"How about some lunch, honey," Billy tried.

"There's some leftover soup in the refrigerator. I've got work to do. Just because you stayed out half the night and slept all day doesn't mean the rest of us can." Rhonda quickly bit her lip. This was an opportunity she was bungling.

As Billy slunk back down the hall to get a shower, Rhonda called after him.

"I could fix you a hot sandwich to go with it. The soup's good. Vegetable. Some I got at the farmer's market." She saw the news this morning, too. But there was nothing about Daniels. Maybe that was coming up.

When Billy got out of the shower, Rhonda had laid out a freshly ironed shirt for him. She was still in their closet and they chatted about his meeting. She picked out a tie to go with his blue suit. And then she told him all about meeting Betty Lubritz and her sister knowing the Weeks family and everything. Everything that pointed to Luke Daniels.

Billy arrived at DeWeese's office promptly at one thirty. DeWeese had just returned from lunch with Lambert who filled him in on the status of Mr. William Porter Gafford. After an instruction to the receptionist to hold all calls, DeWeese took Gafford back to his main office.

No sooner had they sat down than the phone rang. DeWeese snatched it up.

"I'm sorry, sir, but he said it was urgent."

"Who is it?"

"He wouldn't say, just that it was urgent." She knew the voice but pretended not to. DeWeese punched the flashing red button. He knew it was Lambert.

"I'm on my car phone headed to the coast."

As if it was a big deal to have a car phone, DeWeese thought, you big dolt.

"I wanted to remind you that it would probably be best to keep our business relationship strictly confidential, capeche? Especially with our little friend there in your office. Any problem?"

"No, no problem at all. Sounds good to me." God, how he hated that bastard. How did he ever get into this mess? Capeche! Well, the godfather had spoken. DeWeese hung up the phone.

"Now. I'm sorry, Mr. Gafford. Let's talk about your re-election."

Billy arrived at his office elated over his meeting with DeWeese, feeling like he would be a shoe-in. He grabbed his messages from Wanda and went straight to his office. Jimmy heard him come in and stuck his head in the door but Billy was already on the phone.

"Not now, Jimmy, I've got to catch up on these." He spoke over the phone and made a motion toward a stack of messages.

Jimmy slumped. He wanted to get to him before Sam Martin did and explain what happened. Or at least try to. Exactly how he was going to do that was still questionable in his mind.

Back in his office, Jimmy tried to formulate some idea of an explanation to Billy. He took a few phone calls and thumbed through some files. Nothing seemed very clear cut. With still no plan he ambled back down to Billy's office. He wasn't there. Jimmy made tracks to the front lobby just as Billy was stepping onto the elevator.

"Hey, I really need to talk to you."

"It'll have to wait, Jimmy. I'm meeting some people at five. I'm not sure how much I'll be in here tomorrow, either. And I'm out of town Friday and Saturday. I'm sure whatever it is will wait. Hell, and if it won't just handle it. Do something, Jimmy, even if it's wrong."

And with that last statement, the elevator door shut.

"Damn! I hate it when he does me this way." Jimmy's foot stomped. He turned back to Wanda, sitting at her desk with a grin.

"I know, I know, Jimmy. I haven't been able to get with him today, either. He just flung messages on my desk and said, "get back with them." Now what is that supposed to mean?"

"I guess it means we do the best we can, huh, Wanda?" He walked over behind her desk and began to massage her shoulders. "We just do the best we can."

She soaked up the touch from his gentle rubbing on the tense muscles of her neck and shoulders.

"Yep, we just do the job we got to do," he spoke as he continued kneading her absently.

On Thursday morning Billy stopped in for a haircut on his way to work. Fred opened up early and Billy could usually slip in on his way to work, get a trim and catch up on the latest word in local prattle.

The barbershop was small. Just Fred and his buddy, Cliff, standing behind the old barber chairs, cutting one head after another while the customers sat around waiting their turn, chewing the fat on subjects from cattle prices to hunting dogs to politics. Billy knew he could always count on getting news he could use.

As Billy pulled up, he could see Luther Lambert sitting in the number one chair. He spied Billy from his perch and waved vigorously. His was the random luck of a man with a mission.

"Billy, good to see you, again. You looked good on TV yesterday. What do you think, boys? Is our man, the DA, looking good for the camera?"

Fred and Billy and one other customer were the only ones in the shop at that early hour. But Luther was always one for the theatrical. They all nodded in agreement and congratulated Billy profusely.

"Glad you're getting that exposure. Great stuff for an election year. You made any moves in that direction?"

"As a matter of fact, I have, Luther. I met with DeWeese Advertising yesterday about my campaign.

"Is that right. I hear he's good."

"He's got some great ideas. Already got me a speaking engagement with some choice exposure that should keep me ginning in the right direction."

"Great. Great. Let me know whatever I can do. You know I want to help you. Say, has anything else come up about that Daniels boy?" Luther lowered his voice but you could still hear his heavy tone in the street outside. "I'm hearing more and more that he has a bad drug problem. That he's out of hand with it."

"Oh, yeah? That's interesting. I didn't know that."

"Oh, yes. It's true. They're saying he just won't let anybody help him. It's sad."

Luther paused to let the two-edged sword sink deep. He had a motive for this, and a backup plan just in case the Daniels thing didn't stick. He just wanted the Weeks deal over with as soon as possible, and didn't care who might have committed the crime or went to the gas chamber for it. With the election over and the Susan Weeks issues gone, he could continue with his power brokering safely with his own crew still in place.

"Well, let me know about the campaign. I'm ready to help. I'll come up with a little money for you, too." And to the rest of the shop, "Now, you boys know this here is our man. It's Gafford all the way."

"Thanks, Luther."

Luther paid from a roll of cash out of his pocket with a generous tip for Fred. The haircut was still only six dollars.

"Well, fellows, I'm off to try to make a living. Good luck with the campaign and I wish you the best in trying to deal with that Daniels boy. I know it's a tough one for you." Luther popped out the door and the rest of them watched as he piled his hulking frame behind the wheel of the new Cadillac and drove away.

Luther was grinning as he drove off. He was thrilled with his own performance. This little barbershop would hum for days with the story he just laid out, slowly taking on the semblance of truth, cloaked in the authenticity of word-of-mouth. And Billy Gafford was at the heart of it in a most effectual way. He was the District Attorney.

Billy left the barbershop swimming in a morass of strife and despondency. Competing interests. It was what plagued him constantly about this job and why he would like to escape. After Luther left the barbershop, a dark cloud settled in surrounding Billy in a thickening swell of gloom. Anxiety and dread trapped him in the small shop. A couple of new customers came in while the scent of Luke Daniels' blood lingered in the conversation and all eyes fixed on Billy as if to say 'What are you going to do about it.' They were all looking to the District Attorney to prosecute the killer and they were all certain it was Daniels. So why didn't Billy do something?

Billy wondered himself. There was clearly enough evidence for him to take to the Grand Jury. They were the official body charged with bringing the indictment. So why? He knew it was because somewhere deep inside he could not believe Luke Daniels murdered Susan Weeks. He didn't know why, but it was a strong inner apprehension that pressed against him whenever he considered the evidence. There was nothing concrete for him to base this feeling on. No tangible facts to go on. Hell, all the evidence pointed to Daniels. But the feeling was there, subtle and still in the recesses of his mind. He had to shake it off.

The barbershop episode put Billy in a miserable state. Instead of going straight to the office he drove, letting his mind wander. He had to do something. He didn't need this damn murder thing hanging over his head while he contended with re-election. And Luther was right. The exposure from nabbing the killer of Susan Weeks would be sensational. The free publicity would be stuff money couldn't buy. Hoping for some inspiration he found himself in Willow Oaks near Susan Weeks' house, the scene of the crime. Jennifer Holt was still with her parents, leaving the house vacant.

As Billy turned down Birch Street toward the house he could see it peering at him through the thicket of bare trees and underbrush. The winter landscape left the surrounding grounds thinned out enough to see the house through a screen of gray. Billy pulled into the driveway and stopped. The front door still had police tape across it which identified a crime scene. He could see down the side to the end bedroom where the murder occurred. He turned off the car and sat for a while taking in the sight, letting his mind go. He had to do something. He had to do something. What should he do?

Billy arrived at the office several hours into the morning. As soon as he walked in Wanda gave him a weary look and started off.

"Where have you been? This place is a zoo this morning. The Grand Jury is out making their rounds today and getting people hacked off at every stop. They were at the junior high school before eight o'clock, telling the principal how to do his job. He wants you to call him back and, in his words, "tell him what the hell is going on." They're scheduled to meet with the County Superintendent of Education at eleven and word's already gotten to him about them. He's called, too. I sent Jimmy over to try to intercept and run interference on 'em for a while. Here. Here's your other messages."

Wanda handed him a stack of calls that he started thumbing through. From that moment on the day was a whirlwind for Billy. There was one crisis after another keeping him occupied until suddenly it was five o'clock. Wanda came back to his office and plopped into one of his chairs.

"Whew. Another day like this one and I'm having a nervous breakdown. I deserve it. I worked for it and I'll take it if I want." Wanda laughed at her own joke and continued.

"I'm leaving. How 'bout you?"

"Is everybody gone? Where's Jimmy?"

"That little afternoon jaunt you sent him on with the Grand Jury. He's still not back. I talked with him a little while ago and he's probably just going to head on home when they finish up. They were way down in the south part of the county."

"What were they doing down there?"

"Looking at some work one of the Supervisors did. One of the jurors had the idea there were some misspent funds or something."

"These guys are driving me crazy. The last thing I need is the Grand Jury going around taking things into their own hands and pissing people off, like one of the Supervisors. I'll be blamed."

"I'm sure Jimmy will set 'em straight. Look, I'm out of here. You going?"

"No, I've got a few more things to do. I'll be gone tomorrow, you know?"

"Seems like I vaguely remember you throwing that at me some time over these last two days," Wanda said with a grin. "Yes, I've got it on my calendar. You're covered."

"Okay. I'll see you Monday. You guys try to keep this place between the ditches tomorrow while I'm gone. We don't need another day like today."

"We'll do our best. See you Monday."

When Wanda left, Billy started through the remaining messages and cleared out the ones that needed tending before he left.

As he rearranged and shuffled papers on his desk, he was about to get everything in order when he came to a file. The Weeks murder file. In the silence of the empty office behind the desk of the District Attorney, Billy could not escape the fact that he had to do something. His earlier drive and the viewing of the scene rendered little relief. He sat for only a moment before he picked up the phone. As it rang, he almost hoped it wouldn't be answered.

"Hello, this is Luke Daniels."

"Luke, this is Billy. Billy Gafford."

"Oh, hi, Billy. I just about didn't answer the phone. All the secretaries are gone and I'm the only one here. How're you doing?"

"Oh, fine, fine. And you?"

"Good, can't complain. Working hard. Staying busy. Things are going okay." There was tension across the line. The voices of the two lawyers were forced as they spoke the perfunctory openings.

"So, what can I do for you, Billy? I somehow gather you didn't call to inquire about my health." The strained air annoyed Luke, moving him to get to the point.

"Listen, Luke, I'm getting a lot of pressure to do something about this Weeks murder." Billy paused in mid-thought, as if he wanted Luke to say something.

"Yes?" He knew the moment he heard Billy's voice, the call had something to do with Susan's murder.

"Well, damn it, Luke, everybody in town knows you were the last one with her. That y'all were together the night she died." Billy was hoping that Luke would immediately say that he had proof positive he didn't kill her.

Luke said nothing. The gravity of this call was slowly permeating his perception, leaving him muddled. Luke was a good lawyer, accustomed to thinking fast on his feet in perplexing situations. This was different. The feeling of isolation was overwhelming. He felt stranded in a storm, with nothing to help him stay afloat.

"Billy, I've never denied being with her that night. I told you way back when this first happened that there were two sides to every story and that whenever you were ready I'd be glad to sit down and go over everything that I knew about Susan Weeks. I'm still ready to do that whenever you say. I have nothing to hide."

Billy let out a sigh of relief. Anything from Luke was better than nothing. He wanted to hear Luke's version before he went to the Grand Jury. What Billy didn't know was that the foreman of the Grand Jury had already poisoned the minds of everyone on that panel. Billy had not heard from Jimmy how the foreman had come to him demanding to see the Weeks file. They didn't understand proof, they just wanted blood.

"Well, sure, Luke. I remember. Listen, when do you want to get together?"

"How 'bout tomorrow morning?" Luke was ready right now, for that matter. The sooner the better for him. He was ready to put this behind him.

"No, I can't tomorrow. I've got to be out of town on a speaking deal. You know, this election coming up this year."

"Yeah," was all Luke could utter.

"How about Monday?"

"That's fine with me, Billy. But listen, with all the rumors that have been going around, I feel like I should bring counsel with me."

"A lawyer? Sure, no problem. Nine o'clock Monday okay with you?" Billy was glad to have something happening.

"Yes, that's just fine."

"Well, alright, then. Ah, see you then, Luke."

"Sure, Billy, see you then." Luke heard the click from the other end before he put down his receiver. He held it in his hand next to his head, immobile and still. The dial tone clicked back through the line and the buzz blocked out all other sound in the already silent office. There was calmness in the tone. Luke slowly laid down the receiver and sat in the stillness without thought; without feeling; without anything. He sat for a long, long while.

Slowly he began to have an idea that maybe he could finally get the rumors stopped. He knew all along that what he heard was bad and he was sure he only heard a little of what was being said about him. Well, on Monday he would get it all behind him. That was a good feeling. He looked down at the file before him and had no ability to focus. That's enough for today, he thought. He'd get through tomorrow and the weekend and then on Monday there could be some closure. Really. When he explained everything to Billy, they would then be able to deal with the rumors and get on to finding out what really happened to Susan.

Luke awoke on Friday morning from a sound sleep, the best he'd had in a while. He showered quickly, got dressed, grabbed himself a bagel and headed to his office. He had a hearing this morning before a Parole officer that needed some more preparation.

At his office he went over his research on the case, equipping himself for the nine o'clock argument. When Liz arrived, they talked briefly about the day's projects before getting to their desks. Shortly before nine, Luke put his file together and left the office walking the short distance to the courthouse.

The hearing was held in one of the many anterooms of the county courthouse. An informal proceeding, the hearing officer listened to testimony from any witnesses and then made a decision, usually against the parolee. It didn't take much to get parole revoked and the offender sent back to jail. Luke wouldn't normally even take such a case, but this kid's parents had come to him for several other matters. Only as a favor had he agreed to stand in for their son accused of being out past curfew and in a bar in violation of his parole. He didn't like taking cases that were not winnable, yet here he was.

His primary task this morning was demonstrating that the main witness against the kid, a deputy sheriff, carried excessive hostility toward his client. This kid was nineteen, young and dumb. It shouldn't be a crime but Deputy Rayford Howard thought all boys that age were young punks with criminal intent.

When the short exchange was over, Luke was optimistic. His cross-examination of the deputy showed him to be highly prejudiced against the young offender. His responses revealed attitudes and opinions that were intolerant and pre-conceived with little bearing on the facts. At the conclusion, the hearing officer took all the testimony under advisement and retired to review his notes, promising to give a decision before five o'clock. The deputy left in a huff, glaring at Luke.

Leaving the courthouse, Luke felt ill at ease. He didn't like the way the deputy's cross-examination concluded. But, hey, he had a job to do just like the deputy did. Lawyering. What a way to make a living, Luke thought, as he moved across the courthouse parking lot.

In the same Courthouse on the third floor, Jimmy Clay was getting run over by the Grand Jury that he thought he had under control. Sam, the foreman, had taken control and Little Jimmy didn't know how to stop him short of wrestling him down. He wanted to talk about the Weeks murder and it appeared that everyone else in the room did also. Before Jimmy could protest that they didn't have that file before them, the foreman pulled it out and laid it on the table. Jimmy was shocked upon learning that Sam had walked into the office this morning while Wanda was just opening the door and then picked it up off Billy's desk. Jimmy felt his own death was imminent.

Sam seemed unconcerned with Jimmy's protests, as did the other Grand Jurors when the pictures got passed around. They gawked at the sordid semblances of death and then the foreman went straight through the evidence like a trained professional. His days as an investigator for the sheriff's office had him do this many times before. And his conversation with Luther Lambert last night convinced him it was the right thing to do, what with Billy being so busy with re-election and all. Before Jimmy could get his file back together, they were voting on what to do. There was only one choice. They were not convicting Luke Daniels. They were only charging him with the crime. The vote was for a true bill, without any dissenters. Sam already had the form to sign off. Luke Daniels was indicted for the murder of Susan Weeks. What was Jimmy going to do now?

Luke had another file with him that he wanted to check on before he went back to his office. As he tramped over to the Sheriff's Department, the wind picked up, setting a chill in the air that sent a shudder under Luke's thin jacket. The February sky was gray and damp with bare tree limbs quaking in the gusting wind. Luke quickened his step to the front door of the Hampton County Sheriff's Department.

At the front desk he stood briefly trying to shake off the cold while he looked for someone to help him. He caught the eye of the Sheriff's main secretary and called her name as he had done many times before. They had known each other for years and Luke knew he could always call on her for a kindness.

She looked up and acknowledged him. As she walked in Luke's direction, her face held a sternness he was unaccustomed to seeing. Before he could ask anything, she spoke to him bluntly.

"Luke, the sheriff needs to see you. He's in his office."

"Can you come on back?" she held open the locked door that led back to the offices.

"Sure," was his response. His mind jumped around on several subjects trying to come up with some notion of what the sheriff needed to see him about. Perhaps he was angry about the skirmish Luke had earlier with his deputy. When he stepped into the private office Sheriff Walter Jenkins, Jr. stood up and said hello. His next statement took Luke by surprise.

"Luke, I've got those papers for you," Walter said without looking directly at Luke.

"What papers?" was the only thing Luke could say.

The Sheriff looked straight at him, studying his face.

"You don't know?" the sheriff was more surprised than Luke. "No, I don't, Walter. What is it?" Luke's curiosity piqued. "What are you talking about?"

"You really don't know?" He picked up some papers and handed them to Luke.

As he read the word indictment and saw his name he also heard the sheriff. Susan Weeks. Murder.

"You're under arrest for the murder of Susan Weeks."

The statement stunned him, sending his brain reeling in a whirl of thoughts and para-noia. Fear billowed about him like a dark cloud from an explosion. What the hell was going on here? Billy just told him last night they would get together Monday and talk through this thing. Rage boiled up through him as he looked at the paper in his hand. The sheer insan-ity of the situation infuriated him as a sick feeling settled in the pit of his stomach. His mind raced, unable to concentrate on any one thing. Panic snapped at the edges of his reason, taunting him with the desire to run. He glanced back to the door where two large deputies stood with arms crossed. Of course he couldn't run. He laughed inwardly at the thought of the two deputies outside. Surely they didn't think he would run.

Okay, he had handled situations like this for many clients. He would handle this, too.

The sheriff was still droning on about the right to remain silent, any thing you say… blah, blah, blah.

"Sheriff, you can stop all that. I know the routine. There must be some mistake. I didn't kill anybody. Gafford knows that. I just talked to him yesterday."

The sheriff seemed surprised at his statement, but he had heard so many excuses from so many criminals before, he rarely let himself be surprised. He continued with his by-the-book style.

"Don't say anything to me, Luke. I'm just doing my job. You know I'm going to have to book you. Fingerprints, the works."

Sheriff Jenkins moved spontaneously to the door and pushed it shut with the deputies standing outside in the hallway. He hesitated for a moment as if looking for the right words.

"Look, Luke, I hate this. You have always dealt with me and my office in a professional manner and, hell, I like you. But this is out of my hands. Why don't we just go ahead and get the paperwork done, let you make bond, and then you can get to work on it."

"Make bond?" Luke had not thought about that part. "Surely you can release me on my own recognizance. It's not like I'm going anywhere. As a lawyer, I'm an officer of this court."

Sheriff Jenkins hung his head somewhat.

"I'm sorry, Luke. I can't. The word from upstairs is that you'll make bond just like any other criminal. It's five hundred thousand."

"Bond is already set?" So much was racing at Luke he could not take it all in. They had already set bond meant they knew this was coming. Word from upstairs had to mean the District Attorney's office. So why had Gafford called him last night? If there was an indictment, why had he wasted his time? And bond set! Five hundred thousand was outrageous. It was not that extraordinary for a typical murder case but even that was usually set once the suspect was in custody. And this case was in no way typical. Luke Daniels, Attorney-at-Law, was not a murderer. The whole thing was preposterous. What was Gafford doing?

"Come on, Luke. Let's go."

With that, Sheriff Jenkins opened the door to his office and gave a nod to the two deputies. They reached to take Luke by the arm which he quickly jerked away. Tension swiftly filled the air and the four of them stood there, no one knowing what to say.

"Look guys, I know the way. You don't have to be so hostile." Luke was totally incapable of concealing the animosity he was feeling. His tone was bitter and mean.

"It's okay, men. Mr. Daniels knows this procedure. Just take him across the hall and the people in the jail will handle it from there."

Sheriff Jenkins' voice was serious, leaving no room for misunderstanding. He wanted this one handled right by the book. They led Luke down the hallway, the deputies on either side of him, front and back. The shock of the situation was slowly seeping into Luke. He could feel the blood pumping in his brain, like the pounding of a distant drum. Boom, boom, boom.

When they stepped out into the wide open central hallway of the public building, other people looked up at them. Several faces Luke recognized, but he was unable to speak to them. A small voice came to him faintly. Okay, boy, get a grip, get a grip. You can deal with this. Don't let go; don't let go.

They crossed the hallway in what seemed an eternity and entered the door that went to the jail. Inside there was a double glass sliding door. One of the deputies gave a wave to the control room which you could see through the doors. The first door slid open and they stepped into the entrance. Immediately, the first one closed behind them, briefly locking them in a glass enclosure. Luke had been through these doors many times before. Had given the same wave to the control room operator who had then let him in. This time a sudden terror grappled at him, causing his throat to tighten to where he couldn't breathe.

Time stood still for Luke in the few seconds before the second door opened and they continued into the jail. Before him were familiar faces that he saw regularly. Guys he talked to while he waited for a client to be brought around. Luke tried desperately to summon up his old cordial self. He knew he was innocent, but he also knew all these people were looking at an accused murderer.

Luke followed the two deputies up to the window of the control room where all processing began. There were several deputies there that Luke knew well. Ricky Barnes was a student at University of Southern Mississippi in Criminal Justice who worked part time as a deputy. Luke was always encouraging him in his studies. Rosie Hinson, another deputy, sold make-up on the side. They said hello. Yes, they knew why he was here. Their faces were cheerless, unable to express real feelings over the predicament of their friend, Luke.

The phone rang, breaking into the surreal silence that hung in the air. Ricky answered it, spoke a few words, and then turned to Luke with a puzzled look.

"It's for you," he said. And then back to the phone, "I beg your pardon, no. I don't know. Who is this? What? You'll have to check with the sheriff about that." He hung up the phone.

"That was the paper. They wanted to know if the indictment had been served on Luke Daniels, yet." Ricky was flustered. He was not a lawyer and not a full-fledged officer of the law. But he knew enough to know that Grand Jury indictments were supposed to be kept secret. It was obvious to everyone that they had known about the indictment well before it was served.

"Boy, those guys are good, aren't they? Now I wonder how they knew about this and I didn't?"

Luke tried to chuckle, but it came out more like a whimper. Darkness crept in on him. He felt close to the edge of sanity, teetering on the brink and struggling hard to maintain control.

He was being locked up like a common criminal. All of his learning, all of his education, all of his smarts couldn't stop the system from functioning right on through the process. And they put him through it. The fingerprinting, the mug shot, the works. Right down to the orange jumpsuit. This was despite the fact that his phone call got help on the way and he would make bond soon. The wheels of justice in the Office of the Sheriff of Hampton County, Mississippi, continued to grind. Each time he started to protest, the words of the sheriff rang in his ears, "I'm sorry, Luke, but you are to be treated like any other criminal."

Strong currents circulated around the process that carried Luke along. He could feel them pushing against him, pounding away at his strength, each one battering him a little more.

When the booking process was over, there was nothing left for the deputies to do. They had aligned themselves in two groups, those that relished seeing the lawyer in the weakened condition and those that pitied Luke's predicament. Some were cordial, some drooled with joy. Luke grew oblivious to most of it. When there was no more paperwork to be done, they led him down the hallway to the first floor cell. Without speaking a word, the deputy motioned Luke into the small concrete room. It was only a small holding cell they explained but since he was probably going to make bond shortly, he could sit there until then. The light was out. The floor, also concrete, was filthy, issuing a stench that lingered from past events. Barely inside, the door was slammed shut behind Luke and he heard the heavy click of metal against metal as the door locked him in. Before his eyes adjusted to the absence of light, he was enclosed in darkness, alone. The sounds outside were muffled and distant. Luke put his hand to the cold, rough wall, feeling his way down to the bench. He dropped into the corner and sat without emotion. Earlier, he was scared. He was mad. He felt betrayed. Now he was drained. Luke sat silently and stared into the darkness.

CHAPTER TEN

Spring comes early in Bedford County, Mississippi. Despite the forecast of Puxatawney Phil on February 2, winter starts to withdraw its cold hand to make way for the sun to shine warm upon the expectant ground. Heated sap rises in the multitude of trees and shrubs in the landscape of south Mississippi making them alive and watchful for nature's call. Witnesses to this transformation are the buds of trees swelled to bursting from the change in temperatures. Night time mercury may still drop low and gusty blasts of frosty air occur from time to time. But the days warm up and the season looks to change long before the vernal equinox. One day bare twigs fill the skies and the next shades of green are hovering over you like messengers of good news. Winter is behind and summer fun is on the way.

Young people and even those that aren't so young herald the change with the casting off of winter's clothes and donning of summer attire. Shorts show up with the slightest hint of warm weather and legs white from the absence of sun pop out around the towns. They may shiver and shake and rush around but the shorts remain, a testament to their Southern heritage of limited winters and abundant summer weather.

By the time March rolled around the whole population was ready for a spring break. The winter doldrums were fading rapidly and everyone was enjoying the pleasant days of south Mississippi springtime.

In Hampton the season could not be more beautiful. Everywhere you looked was color. The streets were painted with the rich hues of nature at her best. Azaleas exploded in every color of the palette with choruses of white dogwood singing the praises of creation. Twigs adorned with green in every hue danced about, bathed in the gentle warmth of spring.

The office of Luke Daniels took little notice of the changes going on outdoors. All attention focused on the matter at hand. A month had passed since the sheriff handed Luke a piece of paper that brought an explosion to his life like a hurled grenade. Shrapnel went everywhere causing damage that was not readily apparent.

Trust was suddenly completely gone from his life. Everywhere Luke went and everything he tried to do was affected by the blast. Aftershocks continued to jolt Luke making it increasingly difficult for him to do anything but hold on. His practice suffered. Lawyers on the other side of his cases found creative ways to delay, hoping that the wait would benefit them in someway. Some were sympathetic. But most anticipated a time when the axe would fall and there would be one less lawyer to deal with in town.

Clients divided into two basic groups. Those who feared him and those who believed he was unjustly accused. Both groups worried about their own cases and how well Luke could function as their attorney. A steady stream of clients filled his office to discuss their respective files. Many of them sympathized with his plight, but mostly they wanted to know how it was going to affect them. As he talked with them he could see the suspicion in their eyes. No matter how desperately he tried to reassure them that this was all a big mistake and that he would have it cleared up shortly, their apprehension remained.

To every client, their case was the biggest thing that had ever happened in their lives and they could not be comfortable with a lawyer under indictment himself. One-by-one they slowly picked up their files leaving Luke with fewer and fewer cases to work on. In many, he hardly had the energy to fight to hold on to them. His strength was being consumed by the effort it took to hold himself together under the pressure of the indictment.

His main concern was not his practice, but, whose client he would be. He had made an initial appearance by himself before Judge Jones. The Judge conducted himself sternly with Luke and admonished him to refrain from taking this lightly and find himself an attorney. A month later Luke had still not done so. Not for lack of trying, but Luke's ability to concentrate failed him in the aftermath of the indictment. And his judgment was bombarded with so many things at once that he could not unravel the intricate issues assaulting him. He needed someone to think for him. He needed a lawyer. In this quandary he found himself going around in circles with a decision eluding him more and more.

What further eluded him was a defense, a defense against a crime he hadn't committed. Who killed Susan Weeks? Was he the only one left in the world with that question? There was at least one person out there that knew the answer. The murderer. Who the hell was he, or she?

Finding someone that he would feel confident as an attorney with was a difficult process for Luke. Prior to the death of Susan Weeks Luke had what he considered several close personal friendships with other lawyers. The shadow of the murder estranged him. Whether from their indifference or Luke's preoccupation with his situation there was now a separation between them. Isolated from those associations, Luke found himself not knowing where to turn. He also found that assuming some of them were still his friends was error.

John McWheter, a long time associate, was ten years Luke's senior. When Luke first started practicing on his own in Hampton, John was a mentor to him, offering advice, helping him with cases and even sending him a client or two. McWheter was a successful attorney, managing partner in his firm of Eure, Thompson and McWheter. He was well respected in the bar and would be the perfect choice to help get this mess cleared up so he could get on with his life.

Luke had spoken with John on several occasions since Susan's death with John expressing a supportive view. They had never actually talked about Susan, but it was clear to Luke that John knew of the rumors and ignored them. Luke called him up to set an appointment and the secretary came on the line to tell him John was out of town. She was pleasant and informed Luke that John would be in the office tomorrow.

She could tell Luke was distressed over the information.

"I'm sorry, but I doubt I'll talk with him today. If it's an emergency, I could try to locate him."

"Oh, no. No emergency," Luke answered and then mumbled, "It's just my life."

"I beg your pardon?" The secretary couldn't understand him.

"It's nothing. Just tell him I called. If he could get back with me soon, I'd appreciate it. Thank you."

The secretary took down the message and wrote another bit of information. "Sounds disturbed," on the message pad.

When McWheter arrived at his office early the next morning, he decided to try Luke who answered immediately.

"Luke, I was hoping to catch you this early. How are you, son?"

"I've been better. No doubt you know what's going on with me?"

"Oh, yes, I read the papers. How are you doing?"

"I'm holding on, I guess. Listen, that's why I called you yesterday, I need some advice. Can we get together sometime and talk?"

"Sure thing. Whenever is fine with me. What would be good for you?"

"How 'bout this morning?"

"Well, let's see. I was out of town yesterday. But I believe I can squeeze it in. Could you come on over now?"

"I'll be right there."

The Law Offices of Eure, Thompson and McWheter were only a block away from Luke's office. He let himself out his back door and scurried down the street at a fast pace. The brisk morning air filled Luke's lungs as he banged on their back door. It opened immediately and John invited him in.

"That was quick. I was hoping you'd come to the back door. No one's up front. Come on up to my office. It's a little warmer in there. No heat on last night. I believe the air conditioning was on when we left yesterday. Crazy weather, isn't it?"

John walked ahead leading the way to the office Luke had been in several times before. Usually, it was when they had co-defendants or similar cases they discussed for their mutual benefit. Luke always felt John appreciated his thoughts and that they shared a mutual respect, even though John had ten years of experience on Luke. They arrived in the office and John motioned to a chair for Luke while he took a seat behind his desk. Without wasting time on small talk, Luke began.

"John, I need a lawyer."

"So, you do, Luke. So, you do." John's hand went to the side of his face and he stared off into the distance as silence hung awkwardly in the air.

Luke didn't know what to say next. Should he wait for John to respond? Was it clear that Luke wanted John to be his lawyer? Did he need to say it more succinctly? There was no question John knew of the charge. The papers carried it front page all the way to Jackson. It was the lead story on the TV news two nights in a row. And every lawyer in a hundred mile radius had talked about it in one form or another. Luke didn't know what else to say at this point. He waited for some response from John who sat rubbing his chin with a far away look in his eyes.

The quiet lasted for so long that for a moment Luke thought John had forgotten he was in the room.

"So? John? What do you think?"

"Huh?"

"Can you represent me?"

"Gosh, Luke, this puts me in a real dilemma. You know I want to help you. But I've really gotten away from doing criminal work. You know this partnership of ours has grown so that I'm locked down with work that we already have. Just about all I do any more is insurance defense. These companies like that personal touch and that means me here talking to them when they want to talk. I've pretty much had to divest myself of any other practice so I can do what I have. You understand how that is, don't you? I'm just not doing any more criminal work."

John looked straight across the desk at Luke. Luke looked back at him feeling a bit addled. He knew John did criminal work. Or, did at one time. They had worked on criminal cases together, less than a year ago, in fact. Luke tried to grasp what John had just told him.

"John, I, ah, I don't know what to say. I sure need your help. Couldn't you take just one more? I need someone who knows I'm innocent." Luke's words came out sluggishly with much effort.

"I'd like to help you, Luke. You know I would. Hell, we've been friends for a long time. But, you see, I've made a commitment to the other members of this firm and our overhead's so high now that I've got to think of that. I mean, you wouldn't want me to go against that, would you?"

"But I can pay you. I'm not wanting you to do this without pay."

"It's not a question of money. The issue is that there are only so many hours in the day. If I take on anything else, I'm liable to crack. That's why I've limited my work to what I have now. I'm really sorry, Luke, but it wouldn't be fair to you or my other clients. If there's anything else I can do, you know I will. I'm with you on this one. You just call me if there's any thing else."

Luke realized that John had stood and was waiting for him to do the same. He was actually ushering Luke out. McWheter moved around the desk sticking his hand out to shake with Luke and as he did patted him on the back. Luke stood also and before he knew it was whisked down the hallway and John was telling him goodbye out the back door.

When the door shut behind him, Luke started toward his office in a daze. What just happened back there? Was he being paranoid or did he just get brushed off. What's the real reason McWheter turned him down? Surely, John was being honest with him. I mean, there was no reason to lie. Luke picked up the pace back to his office as he admonished himself. Careful, fellow, don't get berserko now. The man is busy. You already knew that. He's just narrowing down his practice. A lot of lawyers do that. Especially ones that have been at it as long as John. You'll just have to find someone else, that's all.

Back in his office, he buzzed Jenny for any messages.

"The phone was ringing off the hook when I got here this morning. This person called you twice." She handed him the messages.

Luke smiled when he saw the double caller was Jane Archer. He and Jane had been friends since undergraduate. She had then shown up in Law School where their friendship continued. They had bolstered each other through the grueling insanity of the study of law and a good friendship remained.

Since the indictment he had not talked with Jane. She practiced on the Gulf Coast and they still saw each other once in a while. He immediately dialed her number but his heart fell when her secretary told him she had gone in to a deposition and could not be disturbed.

"Well, okay, just tell her I called. This is Luke Daniels. My number is…"

"Oh, Mr. Daniels, I'm sorry. I didn't know who you were. Mrs. Archer left word that she was not to be disturbed except for you. Hold on a minute."

"Well, Daniels, what did you do? Bore the poor girl to death?"

Luke laughed out loud at the sound of Jane's voice. Only she could make light of his situation and get him to look at things with humor. Of course, this was no laughing matter but you couldn't cry all the time.

"Well, you would certainly know about that, wouldn't you?"

"Okay, okay, enough. How are you, Luke, really?"

"Really? I'm terrible. How'd you find out?"

"I was at the courthouse down here. Standing around gabbing with a bunch of lawyers. You know that routine. Anyway, one of them has a case with a lawyer in Hampton who told him about it. I guess you know the gossip. Hey, I can't talk anymore now. I've got this deposition going on with a court reporter and two other lawyers sittin' in my conference room. I've got to be in Jackson on Tuesday. Why don't I swing by Hampton on my way back home in the evening? We could have dinner or something.

"That sounds great. I could use a good visit."

"And why haven't you already called me, you jerk! You think you don't need your friends anymore?"

"Jane, I…" he couldn't even answer. Boy, did he need a friend. "Let's talk Tuesday."

"Okay, Luke. I'll call you when I finish up in Jackson. Later."

The phone went dead in Luke's hand and he tried to hold that spark in her voice. He couldn't wait 'til her visit. He needed the comfort of an old friend.

Tuesday, Luke started watching for Jane before noon. Knowing it would be much later when she arrived in Hampton he kept his eye on the clock all day until she finally called at four o'clock. Her day in the capital city was grueling, she was beat, would arrive around six.

Jane Archer pulled up to his house promptly at six. Always a stickler for being punctual, even her private life kept to a schedule that revolved around the clock. It was one of the things Luke liked about Jane. When she said she was going to be somewhere at a specific time, she was there doing what she said. Unfortunately, she demanded the same from people around her which played hell with her private life. While Luke thought it was an asset, her ex-husband and ex-secretary thought it a liability.

Jane got out of the car looking good. Jane was a short little thing with a page boy haircut on dark brown locks pushed to one side that always looked stylish on her. It danced around her shoulders giving her a lively spirited appearance that was further accentuated by the sparkle in her dark eyes.

They had first gotten to know each other when he coached her sorority flag football team. He was dating one of the other players at the time and he and Jane became friends without any romantic overtones. She was a good lawyer, smart as a whip. Aggressive. He watched her now with one bare leg out of the car as she reached back for her purse and sweater. As she shut the door behind her he saw the short black skirt and admired the matching sleeveless sweater that clung to her buxom upper torso.

Tough as nails and sweet as lemons, he remembered from an old song. He bounded down the steps to meet her for a big hug midway in the yard.

"Jane, you don't know how good it is to see you. I would say you're a sight for sore eyes if you wouldn't harass me about being a redneck from Hampton, Mississippi."

The sincerity in his voice made her skip her usual sarcastic raillery. She looked at his forlorn expression and gave him another hug.

"Let's get inside. People in this town are talking about you enough. Next thing you know they'll be saying you were having sex in your front yard."

Inside, they settled in the kitchen with Jane standing to stretch her legs after the drive from Jackson. She kicked off the black heels and stood in her stocking feet as Luke began to go through the tangled web of events that led to his current status.

"So what evidence do they have? Do you have any discovery?"

"Jane, I don't have anything. I don't even have a lawyer."

"Well, that's the first order of business. I wish I could represent you but I don't do enough criminal work to take on a case like this. Of course, you know I'll help you in any way I can."

The statement touched Luke at his core. He had heard that statement before and would hear it many times again but he knew that this old friend meant it as faithfully and as sincerely as she had ever meant anything.

"Okay, let's just say I'm your counsel to assist you in finding the right lawyer. Have you thought of anyone?"

"I talked with John McWheter last week, but his civil practice is so full he's not taking any other cases. No more criminal work, he said."

"Well, who else is here that you'd want to use?"

"That's just it, Jane. You know what terrible gossips lawyers are. There's been so much talk about me around here that every lawyer I see gives me this look of reproach as if I'm already guilty and have to prove myself innocent."

"You know that's really the way it is, Luke. We lawyers pretend and preach that the constitution guarantees that a defendant is innocent until proven guilty, but in reality we know that's not the case. You get tried in the media, you get tried in the gossip of the local yokels and then you're found guilty in their rumored tales because they love to conclude the worst about somebody. And in a small town especially, all this has a cumulative effect."

Luke's saddened and doleful expression told Jane she was not accomplishing her goal of cheering him up.

"What we've got to do is find you the right lawyer," Jane said with an upbeat tone. "Enough of this bellyaching. Let's get to work. Who else is there in Hampton that you would consider?"

"There's Jack Raybern. He's good, used to be the District Attorney. But I have some misgivings about his political connections. What I think is best would be a cross between Jack and Martin Douglas. You know him, don't you? From Collins?"

"He ran for governor a while back. Very clean, white-hat sort of fellow." Jane knew him.

"Exactly. And Jack Raybern is the master at creating a smoke screen in criminal cases. I've watched him in court and he can always find a goat to hang the case on other than his defendant. Sort of like they did in the O.J. trial. If I could find a cross between Martin Douglas and Jack Raybern, I would be home free."

"I know this guy down on the Coast that may be just the person. Nick Chestillo. He retired with the DEA and then went to law school. He's practiced less than we have but from what I hear he's excellent in criminal matters. He was involved in a lot of trial work as a drug enforcement officer with the feds. He's good at cross-examination. You want me to check him out for you?"

"Janie, at this point, I'm open to anything. I really don't trust even my own judgment anymore. This whole thing's got me so stressed out that I don't know what I'm doing."

Jane thought that without his telling. She had known him since college and she'd never seen him like this. Luke was an extremely competent lawyer who could think on his feet and had the brains to back it up. But now, his whole persona was apprehension and distrust. She wished there was something she could do to reassure him.

"How's your running?" She knew that was a source of comfort.

"Psh, not too great. There's a rumor going around that the killer wore the same running shoes I do. You know what an uproar that's brought about. Everybody in this town knows I'm a runner. That takes the joy out of running for me. I feel like every time I put on my shoes, I'm giving them something to talk about."

Jane winced. She wanted to leave him on an up note but was having a hard time.

"Luke, I'll call Chestillo first thing tomorrow and let you know what he says. I know he can help us. And besides, he's got this great investigator working with him. Guy named Cody Raybern. Good looking guy. You've got to have an investigator. Maybe I'll get to work with him. I hear he's single now. I'd be tickled pink to do a little investigating with him." She winked at Luke and gave him a smile, anything to try and lighten his mood.

"Let me get on home. I may try to call Nick tonight. Or maybe I should just call his investigator. You know I hear he's fluent in several languages. Do you think he may know Italian?" She grinned at him as they walked outside to her car. She kissed him on the cheek and gave a quick hug before jumping in her car and taking off.

Luke felt despondent as she drove away. Having to go talk to his lawyer gave him a funny feeling. He knew what it meant to be a lawyer and now he would find out what it meant to be a client. He felt good knowing he would have someone representing his interests. He certainly wasn't capable in his current state He laughed inwardly because he had given that speech to so many others. You have to have someone do the cool-headed, detached thinking for you during a time like this. Luke certainly understood the meaning of those words now. He could not be cool-headed or detached. There was so much emotion tied up in this situation that he felt a little demented, like all the wires in his brain weren't connecting quite like they should. But with Jane's help he would get it on track. Her energy had buoyed him up better than anything for quite some time. Her leaving drained away some of the new found strength she had aroused and he drooped in her absence. Dragging himself back inside, he plopped down on the couch, fully clothed and fell asleep.

When the phone woke him, it was not yet six a.m.

"Hey, you're not asleep, are you? Better get up. We've got things to do." Jane spoke merrily into the phone. "I just hung up from Nick Chestillo. He can see us this afternoon at 3 o'clock. Can you make it?"

"Sure. Anything you say. You're my lawyer that's picking a lawyer."

"Boy, I wish all my clients followed my instructions that well. Look, I gotta run. Literally, I got to run. Did I tell you I've taken up jogging? I meet some girls in my neighborhood at six a.m. and we do three or four miles. Why don't you do the same? It would be good for you. The hell with what all those people up there are saying. You need the exercise. Get your blood pumping. See you at three, right. Bye."

Jane talked so fast and enthusiastically that he was now wide awake. Why not take a run this morning? Probably, no one would see him at this hour. He quickly got into his shoes and shorts and took off.

He took off down his same old path. Since moving into this house he followed a five mile course devoutly by the old school, across Green Street and down the avenue lined with old historic homes. He loved this run. The March morning was crisp with the freshness of springtime. The old architecture and the beautiful yards now in full bloom made him think of the New Orleans Crescent City Classic winding through the Garden District. Maybe he could talk Jane into meeting him over there for that run at the end of the month.

The idea of meeting Chestillo held mixed emotions for him. He hated the idea of having to rehash everything again, but he welcomed being able to engage someone who was not exposed to the slander going on in Hampton. Getting an attorney of record would also begin to move this thing to a conclusion. And, an investigator would be the first chance to find out who had really killed Susan.

He picked up his pace as the run cleansed his lungs. He began to let go of a lot of tension and stress, feeling lighter in the process. His pace picked up even more until he was in a swift run, his lungs pumping hard to keep up with the urgency of his muscles.

As he made a turn he noticed lights on in several houses. He also noticed Judge Jones' house as he came up the street. Their kitchen light was on. He wondered if the Judge was up. He wondered about the Judge. The indictment put Luke's case in Judge Jones' court. He would have to recuse himself, surely. Luke had too much of a personal relationship with the Judge for him to sit as a jurist, ruling impartially.

Of course, he might be biased in Luke's favor. Jones knew what kind of person he was. He knew Luke was not a murderer. Luke reflected on the Judge's position as he strode past, surveying the house as he did. Where would Judge Jones be on this thing? The man had as much political savvy as anyone Luke had ever known. He would undoubtedly consider many things in coming to a decision. Luke's mind raced along as his feet moved him past the house.

Inside the kitchen window, Mrs. Jones saw the runner outside staring at her house. She had heard stories of burglars wearing jogging clothes. She wanted to get a good look at the man in case their house got hit. She moved into the dining room where there was no light. As she peeked through the organdy sheers hanging under the silk brocade drapes, she gasped when she recognized the face. It was Luke Daniels, staring at her house. She jerked back quickly so he would not know she had seen him. A chill ran through her. He had been staring at their house with such a fierceness that it scared her. What was he doing out there scrutinizing them so? Why, it was hardly light out. Running around in the darkness like that. What was wrong with him?

She scampered back to the kitchen where the Judge had just sat down to the table. He looked up at her in surprise.

"What's the matter with you? You look like you've seen a ghost."

"Well, not quite. But I wonder."

"Huh?" The Judge had a muffin on his plate, spreading butter.

"I just saw Luke Daniels outside our house looking mighty suspicious."

"What do you mean?"

"Well, I first saw him right out this window. He was out there in the street staring up this way. And then he moved on to the side of the house. I went to the dining room window and he was still staring up this way, like he was checking out our house for some reason. That boy is strange. What do you suppose is wrong with him? That poor girl. And now he's out here at our house in the middle of the night."

"Honey, it's not the middle of the night. It's six thirty."

"It's not even light out, yet. I don't like men staring up at our house like that in the dark. Any man. And especially one accused of murder. You're going to have to do something about him."

"I'll speak to Luke," was the Judge's reply. But after thinking about it, Judge Jones realized he couldn't speak to Luke. That would not be appropriate since he was under indictment in the Judge's court. This thing was a mess. What was Luke doing out there, anyway? He would speak to Gafford about it.

The day moved quickly for Luke and at one o'clock he left the office headed to the coast. He was meeting Jane at her office before driving over together to Chestillo's. The drive down was mostly pleasant for Luke. It was a beautiful day and a great time of year for this part of the country. He tried to focus on the beauty of the scenery and succeeded except for an occasional attack of anxiety. He shook it off and focused on the positive. This was going to be the beginning of turning this nightmare off and for that he was ready to get started.

When he arrived at Jane's office, she joined him immediately. "You look a little better today than you did last night. Ready to get over to Nick's?"

"Let's go."

The Law Office of Nicholas J. Chestillo was near the Federal building in Biloxi, Mississippi. When they arrived Jane walked straight to the receptionist and announced them.

"Nick is expecting us. We have a three o'clock appointment."

"Yes, Ms. Archer. If you'll have a seat I'll let him know you're here." She left her post only briefly before returning to them.

"Mr. Chestillo will be right with you. He asked if you wouldn't mind waiting for him in our conference room. Would you follow me, please?"

They followed her down the hall to a room with a large mahogany table surrounded by high back leather chairs. The table looked like one with some history to it. There were gouges and scrapes on what had once been a beautiful piece of furniture.

Luke admired the workmanship as he studied the style. There were big round legs that supported a massive top with a vibrant burgundy tone like a fine wine. Luke commented on the elegance of the piece as they took a seat.

"Yeah, there's some story that goes along with it. It was in another attorney's office before Nick got it. The old man retired and sold off all his office furnishings. Nick had admired this piece for years so the old lawyer held it for him. I think the lawyer's wife found this in an antique place in France. And there's something about it once being in a casino in Monte

Carlo or one of those places. Maybe Nick can tell us."

"Tell you what?"

They both looked up immediately to the voice and found Nick Chestillo standing in the doorway.

"What can I tell you?" he asked again.

"Oh, Nick, hi. This is Luke Daniels. I was telling him about your table."

Nick and Luke shook hands before Nick took a seat. His shirt was open at the neck with the tie pulled down. He had wavy black hair with no gray. His face was weathered and tan like men everywhere that lived on a coast. Yes, he owned a boat and never had as much time as he wanted to spend on it but he tried to get out there as much as possible. He appeared a healthy man in good shape. Luke tried to pinpoint his age with some difficulty. Had Jane mentioned that? She had said that he retired from some federal employment and then went to law school. Had practiced less than they had. Luke guessed late forties.

As they talked casually around the table, Nick also took his measure of Luke. Twenty years of dealing with the criminal mind from the law enforcement side had given him a good basis for criminal law. Thirty years of gauging behavior and assessing culpability made his a discerning eye. He rarely made the call at first impression, preferring to decide later after cautious reflection. He prided himself on weighing many elements in a determination, including his own gut. Right now his task was to absorb.

Jane sat back during the pleasant conversation and laughed underneath. She regarded the show going on before her with amusement. The two men were like a couple of old dogs sizing one another up. She knew them both to be good lawyers and couldn't help but be entertained by their maleness. As she watched the malarkey, from behind her eyes she thought of Dian Fossey and her life in Africa. Girl, you didn't have to go to Rwanda to see a bunch of apes. Wounds from her divorce still hurt enough to make her cynical about men. It didn't take her long to have enough of the sport from these two. She sat up in her chair and opened the file she brought with her.

"Nick, I know you're a busy man and I've still got some work to do today so why don't we get down to it. I told you on the phone this morning about the charge. Here's a copy of the indictment. No surprises there, really. Murder, plain and simple."

"I've known Luke for a long time and he's a good guy. Certainly not capable of murder." She glanced Luke's way and stared directly into his eyes. There was a closeness between them like kinship. Despite not seeing each other that often when they did get together the bond remained. She believed Luke did not kill anyone. The look was to reassure herself.

A short silence settled on them before Nick started his interrogation. His questions came fast and furious, sounding accusatory. Luke narrated the events as he knew them, again trying to be as direct and candid as possible. The session lasted for three hours. At its conclusion Luke was exhausted.

"Alright, Luke, I'll take your case." Nick made the statement with some finality.

The pronouncement took Luke by surprise. It had not occurred to him that after going through the entire deal Chestillo might say no. He didn't realize there was an appraisal going on for his fitness as a prospective client. He had taken Jane's recommendation of the lawyer as rock solid. He had assumed Chestillo would readily accept the case. Luke suddenly became aware of something he had never fully grasped in the practice of law. How the client felt. A rush of feelings filled him with disturbing angst. He began to feel removed from the situation. Cut off. They were the lawyers now and he was the client. The accused. He needed defending. No longer the advocate, the role he knew so well, he was now the one charged with a crime. Murder. He looked back at Jane and Chestillo as though a great distance had come between them. He felt removed from them now that they had taken the different roles.

The two lawyers were talking between themselves as though Luke was not there. Their review of the situation was going back and forth between them, leaving Luke the onlooker. He knew exactly what they were saying, what they were talking about but was unable to get into the conversation. He felt isolated and alone even though he could reach out and touch them both.

"I'll give the District Attorney a call. What's his name? Gafford?" Chestillo questioned. "I want to talk with him on the phone. I'd like to send my investigator up there to pick up the stuff and then have him snoop around a little. See what he can pick up on the street and see what he can gather about other suspects."

"Yeah, sure, Nick. That sounds great." Luke was trying very hard to get into the action. He was having a tough time thinking straight with himself being the one on the line.

"Cody Raybern is the investigator I use. Does all my work. He and I served in DEA together so I know he does good, thorough work. He knows how to ferret out any deadly undercurrents. We'll get to work on it right away. What about a preliminary hearing? Have you given any thought to waiving it?"

"Ah, no, not really." Luke tried hard to make himself function lawyerly. "What do you think, Nick?"

"Well, I usually don't waive them. Gives me a chance to check out their evidence and get a better feel for it. Maybe we'll put that off for a while until I deal with Gafford some. Let's stay in touch over these next few days and see what develops."

There was a moment of silence and Nick continued.

"Okay, I've got both your numbers here in the file and Jane's. Is there anything else?" Chestillo stood with the folder in one hand and stuck out the other to Luke.

They shook hands and moved to the front of the building.

"Look, if you think of anything I should know, jot it down somewhere. I know it's hard to think of everything while we sit here talking. Just keep a list of your thoughts and we'll work on them when we get together. Remember, you're the lawyer here, too." Chestillo slapped Luke on the back and kissed Jane goodbye before turning back to his office. Jane and Luke got into her car without saying much. They were silent the whole trip until she pulled up to her office.

"Well, what do you think?" Jane started off.

Luke didn't know what came over him but he desperately fought off tears, embarrassed and humiliated that Jane would see him be this emotional. He stared out the passenger window for a long time before responding.

"I guess I think I never thought I'd be in this position. Coming from the office of my lawyer, who is going to defend me for murder." The words caught in Luke's throat and again he was afraid the tears were going to expose his emotional state.

They sat in silence for a while. Jane had known this man for a long time. Their friendship was one of mutual respect and admiration. They shared a camaraderie that she had with no other person, something she cherished. They had comforted each other on many occasions over many things. For the first time ever she was at a loss as to what she might say or do that would lend some solace to his beleaguered spirit. Their usual manner was to trade gibes and banter back and forth. Right now she couldn't do that. She had no words that sounded right. All she could do was reach out her hand and touch his arm. He placed his other hand on top of hers and they sat quietly.

Luke slowly regained his composure. He patted her hand and finally looked around at her face. She, too, looked as if tears were nearby.

"I'm sorry, Luke," was all she could muster.

"I know. It's alright. I'm going to get through this. Somehow. I have to. After all, I haven't done anything wrong. You do believe that don't you, Jane?"

"Yes."

He reached across the console and gave her a hug. Jane put her arm around him and hugged him back.

"Yes, Luke. I believe you. I know you could never do something like this. It's not going to be an easy time. You know that, don't you?"

"Yeah." He gave her one final squeeze before pulling away. "I'm not going to let them get the best of me, though. I'm tough. I can handle their crap. I didn't kill anyone, Jane. So there's no way they can prove I did."

"Look, I'm going to head on back to Hampton. I got cases I need to be working on. Trying to minimize the fallout from this thing's a full time job."

"Okay, Luke. You call me if there's anything. Anything. You hear me?"

"I hear you. Trust me, you'll be the first."

As he shut the car door behind him, Luke turned and stuck his head down to the window.

"Thanks, Jane. So when are you going to get to meet the investigator? Maybe the two of you could come up to Hampton and do some investigating together! Maybe I'll call

Chestillo and insist on that." He gave her a quick smile and turned back to his car, as she shouted back to him.

"Now there's a good thought. Make yourself useful."

The trip to Hampton went quickly. He had been lost in thought since pulling out of Jane's parking lot and remembered little of the journey home. Getting an investigator on the case was a good idea. Most of Luke's criminal cases didn't merit investigating. The majority of them were guilty defendants and the biggest part of his job was working out a punishment that fit the crime. Find out what the prosecutor could prove and then negotiate a plea. Most criminal defendants couldn't afford an investigator and they didn't want to go to trial. If this guy was any good, maybe he could help Luke find out who really killed Susan. Luke was too busy trying to keep himself from drowning in this flood of vicious gossip and perverted accusations. He felt like the turbulent flood had carried him into a raging river with the merciless current trying to pull him down to his death. But he wasn't going down. The fight to stay alive in the swirling undertow left little energy to devote to finding the real killer.

He thought that would happen when he met with his good friend Billy Gafford. The lying bastard! Setting him up to come talk and then indicting him before they got together. Why did he do that? It made no sense. Nothing made any sense about any of this. That's why he needed a lawyer, and an investigator. And Jane. Sweet Jane, he thought, and recalled the old song as he drove along back to Hampton.

He noticed the gas gauge on his car signaled the need for a quick stop. There was a station ahead where he could fill up. He pulled in to an open pump and got out to operate the self-service. The car across from him left and another pulled up straight away. A woman got out and started to operate the pump.

Luke paid her little mind as he continued with his own situation. It was around seven and light was fading rapidly from the early evening sky. The outside lights were not on yet making it difficult to see anything clearly. The woman was having some trouble getting the pump started when the voice box came on from inside.

"Restart the pump, please."

Luke could barely see the top of the woman's head across the top of the pump and could hear her frustrated reaction.

"Please restart the pump," said the voice box again.

"I'm trying to restart the goddamn pump," was her muffled response under her breath as she slammed the nozzle back into the pump, switching levers and pushing buttons.

Luke snickered at her predicament. He finished filling his car and put the nozzle back.

"Here, maybe I can help," he offered.

"Thanks," came a hesitant reply as the woman looked up at him.

It was Rita Lambert.

"Oh, hi," she offered before quickly lowering her head, diverting her eyes away from

Luke. "This damn thing won't work for me."

Luke's first reaction was that here was another one who didn't want to have anything to do with him. But before she turned away he thought he caught something in her eye, in her tone that revealed more than she intended to have him see. Her eyes looked a little puffy. Had she been crying? Luke examined her more closely. She was a beautiful woman, really. Nice legs. She was wearing shorts. A few pounds overweight, maybe, but still fine for, what was she? Thirty-five, maybe?

"Here. Let me give it a try." Luke fiddled with the switch, putting the nozzle in and out a few times before it clicked on. He placed the hose in her car, put the switch on for automatic fill up and stepped back.

"Maybe that will do it." He looked around at her with a big smile, his normal expression. Rita thanked him with hesitation in her voice. He looked directly at her now and noticed her face. Her auburn hair fell across one side almost obscuring one eye. Her skin was already looking tanned, giving good color to her. She was wearing a long cotton sweater with a V-neck that revealed a superb chest and a cute rear end. The shorts barely stuck out below the sweater.

"I must look a mess," she offered. "I was driving with the window down and my hair was going every which way. I think I got some dust in my eyes, too." Her hand went nervously to one side of her face fidgeting with her hair.

"I think you look pretty good." Luke said without thinking. "Look, I'm not deaf and dumb. I know people are talking about me all over. If I'm making you uncomfortable, I'm sorry. I'll go on."

"No, no, that's not it at all. I don't pay any attention to that stuff. I guess I'm just a little on edge, that's all."

"Are you okay?" Luke looked at her again more closely. Her eyes were more than just dusty. One of them looked swollen. The hair had covered it up before but he could now see some puffiness in it. "Is something wrong?"

"Just a disagreement with my husband." She immediately wished she had not said even that much. She wanted to say a lot more. She would like to tell the world what a son of a bitch Wilson Hughes Lambert was. But this was not the time.

"Well, I can understand that," Luke said lightly. "I'm sure you've heard all about my disagreements with Wilson."

"Oh, yes. Your name's been taken in vain in my presence before," she said with a laugh. The smile touched at the corners of her mouth.

"Hey, that looks much better. A good-looking woman like you should smile all the time. It makes your eyes sparkle." He looked directly into the little spark that was barely visible. It gleamed a little brighter with his words. Luke couldn't help thinking what exquisite eyes she had, even with a little puffiness. There was no make-up on her face and, yet, she glowed.

"You might want to be a little more careful driving with the windows down. This one's looking a little swollen." He reached up and brushed back her hair.

Her hand went up instantly to her face, brushing his hand away in the process. He knew. Her hand rested on his as it moved back from her face. They looked at each other without expression.

How could a man hit this beautiful woman, Luke thought. Simple enough if you're not a man but a worm called Wilson Lambert. Luke looked at her face and then into her eyes recognizing fright. What was she afraid of? Did Wilson do this on a regular basis? The badass Lambert beats up on his wife. What a jerk he was.

Rita felt a comfort issuing from Luke. She started to plead with him not to say anything, but then realized there was no need. Luke would not expose her secret. It would remain a confidence between the two of them.

"Thanks, Luke." She squeezed his hand, turned to the gas pump that had finished and then scurried inside to pay.

The lights of the station were struggling to come on. They sputtered and blinked while Luke watched Rita run across the lanes into the station with her wallet in her hand. He stood there until she came out the door. She came around the pump with a smile as if nothing had happened.

"Thanks, again, for your help." She went straight to her car, got in and drove away.

Luke wasn't sure what just happened. He knew one thing. That was quite a woman old Wilson was beating up on. He should be mighty careful. Luke had the feeling that if she ever turned on him there would be hell to pay.

CHAPTER ELEVEN

The pretrial conference in Ainsworth vs. Standard Mutual did not go forward as planned on the Monday after Luke's indictment. Judge Jones' had approved a rescheduling based on a conflict with counsel opposite. Tyler Thompson conveniently had himself in federal court that day and Anna had called Luke's office to inform him of the postponement. It was just as well. Luke was in no shape to make a court appearance. But he was determined to hold on to the case and not let his current status affect his client's well-being. This was a good case and Karen Ainsworth had stuck with him. He appreciated her loyalty and wanted desperately to succeed in this case.

After days of constant pressure he finally got a resetting, but not without a down side. Tyler Thompson had filed a motion for summary judgment. Despite the fact that the time for filing all motions had passed, Judge Jones agreed to hear it at the newly scheduled pretrial conference.

Straight out of a form book, the motion claimed there was no conduct on the part of the defendant that would allow for punitive damages. Luke focused on notes in the claims file where the adjuster and his supervisor had discussed the issue of holding off paying the claim in hopes they could frustrate the claimant enough to drop the claim. There was even a note about her boyfriend's past which they were trying to use against Karen. Their statements were the smoking gun he needed to get to the jury. Twelve of Karen's peers would be offended by the company's blatant disregard of her rights and would be ready to punish the company monetarily. That's what Luke wanted.

Tyler Thompson had a different idea. He delayed as long as he could in hopes Luke's criminal situation would allow him to get out of a bad deal. The company knew they were caught and he had settlement authority for a hefty sum. But then Luke got indicted and everything changed. He wanted to argue a motion for summary judgment and have any punitive aspects kicked out by the Judge. The fact that his firm and several members individually were poised to make substantial donations to Judge Jones' reelection bid would not hurt. He didn't think Luke would be in much position to be making political contributions. Despite the recent success of the young whip, Tyler doubted that with his attorney's fees and a floundering practice there would be much left for donations. The scavenger moved in to pick off the wounded.

Luke sat in the foyer with Anna waiting for the hearing, his first court appearance since the indictment. He knew he would not be able to keep this up long but hoped to get this case to trial before he had to quit. Tyler arrived with a baby lawyer in tow, brought along only to hand him papers and imply to the Judge the importance they put on the case.

"Good morning, Tyler. Jay, how are you doing? Tyler's not working you too hard, is he?" Anna stood up from behind her desk. She made it a point to know all the new lawyers' names. "If this is everybody, I'll let the Judge know you're here."

She disappeared into the other office, leaving the three lawyers standing in silence. Luke had nothing he wanted to say to Tyler. Thankfully, Anna returned shortly and announced that the Judge was ready for them. They entered the office and took seats in front of the Judge's desk. Without any of the usual formalities, Judge Jones began.

I have the court file here before me and have gone over all the information. I've read the depositions and examined the responses in other discovery. It's all very straightforward. Tyler, I have your motion here. Let's begin with that."

Luke felt an uneasiness all of a sudden. The procedure was standard run of the mill, but something else was afoot. Tyler started his argument on the motion for summary judgment with practiced assurance. Jones listened intently, his gaze fixed on the defense attorney. And, he didn't look at Luke.

Luke tried to shake off the paranoia and focus on the argument. He would have the opportunity to respond when Thompson finished. He knew what the argument contained and was ready to get the Judge refocused on the acts that led to this action being filed. If Karen Ainsworth had been treated fairly, this lawsuit would not even exist. Judge Jones had to hear this matter because two goons at the insurance company conspired to deprive Karen of her money and they should be punished for that.

Tyler finished his whining and Jones looked over at Luke without saying a word. Luke began his argument with how Karen never wanted anything but to be treated fairly, pointing out the parts of the deposition where he had quizzed the two agents about their conduct and the fact that they had no reasonable explanation. The only conclusion that could be drawn was their total disregard for the rights of the insured. Luke finished on that note and waited.

"Mr. Thompson, do you have any rebuttal?" Jones asked formally.

Tyler sputtered out a few words about the inappropriate nature of punitive damages and then concluded. They all sat silently waiting for Jones to pronounce his decision.

"Gentlemen, I will take this matter under advisement. I know you are both anxious for a decision and we need a trial setting. I will have you an answer as soon as possible. Thank you."

Luke was amazed that Jones did not deny the motion immediately. It was clearly frivolous. He even wanted to ask for sanctions against Thompson for bringing the motion in such a blatant case of bad faith. But he was not allowed to say anything else. Anna entered the room and ushered them out. Thompson and his assistant left quickly. Luke headed back to his office with an uneasy feeling about the whole matter. He knew there was no way Jones could legitimately rule favorably on Thompson's motion. The case was just too strong. Back at his desk he organized his file and decided to put it together in preparation for the trial.

Shortly before five o'clock a fax came into his office from Judge Jones, a one page ruling granting summary judgment, the punitive damages claim struck from the case. They could proceed on the loss of the vehicle itself but the company would not be subject to any punitive measures.

Judge Jones gutted Luke's case. The strongest bad faith case he had ever had was just cut out from under him. Reeling from the Judge's decision, Luke sat at his desk and reflected on the finding. In one fell swoop Jones reduced a half million dollar case to a twenty thousand dollar case. There was no reason for it. He would have to appeal. Except that in bad faith cases, the Judge's decision was almost always final. An appeal would be a futile exercise. A trial would be ridiculous. They had offered to pay the actual damages.

Luke went over in his mind what had happened here. There was no good answer. Something other than the facts of the case had governed this decision. For several hours Luke sat at his desk going over and over and over the circumstances surrounding the Ainsworth case. There was a lot for him to think about. Something persuaded Jones in this case. But it was not in the file labeled Ainsworth vs. Standard Mutual.

At the same time in Biloxi, Nick Chestillo was sitting down with Cody Raybern. Cody served the government alongside Nick for many years with the DEA. In his early years with the Agency, Cody attended a myriad of survival trainings and went undercover in Mexico, Columbia and other places he still wasn't supposed to mention. His swarthy good looks and ability in several languages gave him the perfect combination to carry out the drama of an international theater with the drug lords. At one point, DEA had him on assignment to CIA who was working in conjunction with a United Nations group that Cody never even knew who the director was. They paid him well, though, and the money always went directly to his savings account, so it didn't matter who was the boss. When he finally got a stateside assignment, one of his co-workers was Nick Chestillo.

After retirement Chestillo went to law school and Cody did a term consulting with DEA administration in Washington where he was again paid handsomely. He now worked as a private investigator up and down the Gulf Coast. With an office in Biloxi, he handled much of the investigation out of Nick's office. Nick handled his divorce a couple of years ago from his second wife. He was forty-one years old and wasn't expecting divorce, hadn't seen it coming. The failure of his second marriage got to Cody a little and Nick had been as much counselor as attorney-at-law. Their old friendship had grown strong again. Shortly after the meeting with Luke, Nick called Cody to get him to find out what he could about this lawyer's troubles up in Hampton. They were now huddled in Nick's office.

"It's a bum deal, Nick. I talked to a good sampling of people from other lawyers to law enforcement to general folks. There's no direct evidence on him. It's all circumstantial. No eye witness, no murder weapon, no nothing to say he did it."

"But there's plenty of circumstantial. He was seen with the victim the night of her death. His fingerprints were all over the house: kitchen, dining room, living room. And the bedroom was the scene of the crime. And, get this. The bedroom door was kicked in leaving a shoe print. The same type and size running shoe that your boy wears. And, he's known all over town to be a runner. I'd say they got the goods on him."

"You think he did it?"

"That part I'm not sure about. Public opinion is a little wacky on this one. A good number of people don't think he did it despite the evidence. One thing's for sure. The DA's out for blood. It's an election year. For the Judge, too. So justice may go out the window. You know how these small towns can be."

"What is your gut reaction? It's usually right on target."

"My gut? The one thing that bothers me is motive. Why'd the guy go out and murder some gorgeous – and that part is unanimous, she was a looker – some gorgeous gal he hardly knew. Some implied it was drug related, that the boy's got a cocaine problem. One source told me the assistant District Attorney is spreading that one around. Maybe trying to create some bad karma for the dude. My source thought he was just trying to cover up his own dallying. At any rate, I suppose it's possible. They get hopped up on cocaine, have a night of wild sex and the girl gets double boinked. Who knows? Hey, that's you lawyers' job to figure out."

"Thanks a lot. I'll tell you, my first reaction was the guy didn't do it. Jane Archer brought him over here. She's known him for years. Says there's no way. She doesn't quibble over his bedding the girl. But she's with his story the whole way."

"Did you see or hear of any evidence of drug abuse," Nick continued after a pause.

"If he's a user, he's conceals it well. None of the usual signs. No big debts or mortgages. Car paid for. Good health. He's a runner, for chrissake. And most people think he's a helluva nice guy. You just can't get this murder rap to fit."

"Okay, then. We'll just see what happens. I may need you to do some follow-up as things develop. We probably need to start looking at who did kill the girl. Anything come up on that?"

"Well, in addition to the job at the bank, she did some modeling. A lot of it through an agency called DeWeese Advertising. When I tried to talk with the owner, Jim DeWeese, he refused. Said he was too busy. Looks like he could be a coke head. He and the girl spent a lot of time together, it seems. Trips to New Orleans, but it appears to be a pretty respectable business."

"Why don't you follow up on that a little. See what you can find out about DeWeese. Maybe he could be the goat we need to create reasonable doubt. You know it only takes one juror."

"Yeah, I gotcha. So what's the deal with Daniels and Jane?" Ever since his divorce, Cody had wanted to get to know her better, but it hadn't happened.

"Been friends with Luke since before law school. She assured me it had never been anything romantic. Just good friends. So you still got your eye on her? Why don't you let me fix you up?"

"We'll see." Cody didn't want to appear too needy.

The Daniels discussion ended and the two old friends picked up another topic. Nick pulled a couple of beers from the mini-bar fridge across the room and tossed one to Nick. It was time to unwind. They both enjoyed this part of their job best. They could relax and commiserate about what a tough job it was to make a living, despite the fact that neither of them would have it any other way.

On Thursday morning, Billy Gafford grabbed a file from his desk and headed straight for Judge Wendell Jones' office. He had sat long enough on the Weeks murder and now was the time for action. Daniels was indicted, thanks to that lunatic foreman of the Grand Jury. Billy had been out of town and they had done it over Jimmy's protests. Billy wondered just how loud Jimmy had objected. Billy knew Jimmy wanted this to happen, but Billy had wanted to wait. He was furious when he returned to find they had acted without him. Luther Lambert had called him that Sunday morning to congratulate him on the fine job he was doing and Billy was dumbfounded, forcing him to act like he planned it that way. Luther praised the Grand Jury foreman unusually, Billy thought. But of course, they had worked together when Luther had been DA. It was only natural for them to still be friends.

Anyway, it was out of Billy's hands now. Going back on the actions of the Grand Jury after Luke had been served with the indictment and taken to jail would be preposterous. Billy would be the laughing stock of the whole county. All he could do now was go forward. There was no question about the political edge this case could give him, as long as he got a conviction. He would have liked to have done things a little differently but here he was. Daniels had been indicted for almost three weeks now and there had not been a search of any of his property. He should have ordered that long ago, certainly before the indictment. That would be his normal procedure. But his procrastination had not allowed it to happen as it should. This morning Billy had a search warrant that he wanted the Judge to sign that covered Luke's house, office and car. It was not yet eight o'clock but the Judge was expecting him.

Billy went up the back steps of the historic old courthouse and let himself in through the large double doors of beautifully refinished hardwood. The building was over a hundred years old and had been restored in a massive renovation that cost the county a fortune. Most of the lawyers in Hampton had been in favor of the project and had contributed in various ways to fund-raising efforts. His shoes clicked on the handsome marbled tile floor that had once been concealed by cheap floor covering before the remodeling. The walls held a wainscoting of brown marble, different from the floor but no less remarkable in quality.

Above that the stucco walls were painted a rich cream that complimented the varying shades of brown of the marble below. He quickly made his way up the quietly luxurious car-pet runner on the hardwood stairs to the Judge's office.

"Good morning, Judge Jones," Gafford started off mannerly. He wanted desperately to keep this activity matter-of-fact. All in a day's work. But Jones knew what was being asked of him this morning was a sensitive issue that could have repercussions.

"Let me see what you've got there." Jones snatched the file out of Gafford's hand, quickly pulling out the proposed warrant. He began studying it intensely. His eyes ran down the first page and onto the second.

"Where's the memorandum I asked for?"

"What?" Billy pretended he didn't remember the Judge asking for anything.

"I told you I wanted a memorandum of law on these points. Asking me to issue a search warrant for his house and car is one thing. But you want me to let you search a lawyer's office. What about the confidentiality of his clients? You know the papers will get this and I'll look like I've violated his inner sanctum."

"Judge, the man's a murderer. He killed one of his clients and I intend to get to the bottom of it. How can I do that if you won't let me search his office?"

"How do you know she was a client?"

"A confidential informant." Billy didn't have a good answer for that one so he threw in the old law enforcement catchall. The identity didn't have to be revealed except in extreme circumstances which would never cover this one. Billy's source was general police department gossip but Limox had assured him the information was reliable. It was as sure as Billy could be when dealing with that bonehead.

"Billy, you'd better have your act together on this one. I swear, if you get me in trouble on this you can forget ever getting a break in my courtroom again. Isn't there some way we could limit what you have access to in his office?"

"Judge, I don't know what she was seeing him about. How can I tell you what it is without looking. That's what I want the warrant for, to look for something that would give me a motive."

"From what I hear, the man's a sex maniac. Isn't that motive enough? Didn't he beat her up pretty badly right in her own bedroom?" Without even realizing it, Judge Jones slipped into the talk of the streets. His wife had filled him in on the female view of the story.

"Judge, it was awful. The poor girl was a mess. We'll have the pictures at trial, but you can take my word for it. The guy went crazy, probably drugs. But I want to make sure there's not something in his office that would give us some clues to the story."

"Alright, alright. I'll sign it, but I still want that memorandum in the file to cover my ass. And yours." Sometimes Jones had to watch out for the Office of District Attorney as well as himself. Gafford would go off thinking he could do anything because he was the prosecutor and run slipshod over the law. Jones' legal mind might not be the most acute but his political savvy was unparalleled. Gafford could go down playing this thing loose, but Judge Wendell

Garmon Jones, III, would not go down with him. He scribbled his name on the warrant and then dismissed the prosecutor without another comment.

Gafford wasted no time in getting the ball rolling. He called Limox right away and ordered him up to his office. By the time he arrived, Gafford had the paperwork done and the warrant was ready to be served.

"I've already had someone check. Daniels is in his office this morning. Me, you and Jimmy will do the search there. You can get some of your other goons to work on his house and the car. How much time do you need?"

"One phone call. They'll need to come by here and get copies of the warrant, of course. Have you made enough?"

"Yes, here's one for you to take to his office, another for the group at the house and the third one for the car. It's all together. I want to talk with Jimmy before we go down there. And let's take a couple of officers with us to his office. They can stand out in the lobby while we do the search. Get on it right away and let me know as soon as you're ready."

Gafford buzzed Jimmy Clay as Limox moved out of his office and down the hall to the conference room to get on the phone. Jimmy joined Gafford and together they started going over the steps for doing a clean sweep of the law office of Luke Daniels.

Luke arrived in his office at his typical time, well before eight o'clock. At eight sharp he called the clerk's office to get Nicholas J. Chestillo entered as counsel of record. Donna, one of the deputy clerks that Luke often dealt with, advised him that they would need an entry of appearance document. She would go ahead and put Chestillo down in the docket book this morning. They agreed that Luke would have Chestillo fax them an entry right away.

Luke hung up the phone and dialed Chestillo's office. His secretary knew exactly what they needed and suggested she could go ahead and fax it up. She had already put together a file and the entry of appearance was a standard procedure for them. She took down the clerk's fax number and sent it while Luke was still on the phone. When they finished, Luke called Donna to let her know the fax should be there, which she found and put in the file. Luke thanked her and breathed a sigh of relief. Having someone else officially on the case eased his distress a little.

It was good to have someone to think for him. Not that he wasn't thinking a great deal, he just wasn't sure how rational he was being.

"They say misery loves company," Luke said aloud.

"What," Liz stuck her head in Luke's office. "Oh, god, now he's talking to himself."

"I didn't know you were here," Luke offered to his secretary.

"Hey, that's worse. I'm the only other one here so that means you really were talking to yourself."

"Give me a break. It's too early for your baloney. Come in my office and let's get some instructions for the day."

Liz came in and plopped down in the chair across from him.

"I've hired a lawyer," was his abrupt statement. Liz said nothing but waited for him to continue. She knew this was hard. The only thing she could think to do was sit and be a good listener. She had assured him over and over that he had her support. She knew this man and would stick by him through whatever.

Luke continued, slowly going over all the details. Jane's recommendation of Chestillo. His background. Liz knew Jane from her stops at the office and from Luke's comments about the strength of their friendship. She was glad for her counsel to Luke. The lawyer sounded like a good choice. She listened intently as Luke went on.

At the courthouse, Donna was filing away some leftovers from yesterday's forms when Luke called. She had the fax in her hand when she went back to her chore. When anything came in to be filed it was first stamped filed and the date and time entered on the document. That way, if there was any question about the order of filing, the time stamp kept it specific. Normally, once the time stamp was on the document they were placed in a box for entering in the docket book and filing away in the official court file. Every case had its own file. This morning that was the job she was doing. Filing away the documents left over from yesterday. When she went back to the job with Luke's fax in her hand she took it as her next document and straight away entered it in the docket book. She had already entered the lawyer's name as counsel of record for Luke at the top of the page. She next put the original in the official court file labeled State of Mississippi vs. Luke Daniels. This was the normal course of her job. After that one, she picked up the next document and went on with her duty of entering it in the docket book and then into the court file. One after another. It was a boring job that everybody in the office hated. But Inez Tanner, the Circuit Clerk, was adamant about this task being done consistently. They tried to get them all in the books before leaving each day. If not, then first thing in the morning this job was done before any other. And that's what Donna was taking care of today. Her mind wandered as she performed the rote task.

In her distraction she did not see Billy Gafford come in shortly after eight o'clock. He went in to Mrs. Tanner's office and shut the door behind him. He didn't stay long. In only a few minutes, the door swung open and he rushed out in a hurry. Mrs. Tanner had the documents he left for filing in her hand when the phone rang. It was the President of the Board of Supervisors, technically, her boss. She sat back down in her chair and talked, laying the search warrant she held in her hand down on the desk.

They talked for a while before she was able to get off the phone and take up where she left off. Picking up the warrant she went out to the counter where she stamped the time and date on the document. Donna had finished the filing from yesterday when Mrs. Tanner laid the paper in the empty box to be filed as soon as the next deputy clerk got around to it.

In Gafford's office he and Jimmy finished up their discussion of search and seizure as Limox returned to the office to say his team was on its way. They'd be there in ten minutes.

"And Daniels is still in his office. We shouldn't have any problem."

Limox had Jerry Mason keeping a look out for that action. Jerry had a little friend who was chums with the receptionist for Luke and Tommy Chipman. He had her calling to chat and finding out about Luke's plans. As far as they could tell, he would be in the office all morning. Billy did not inquire as to how Limox knew of Luke's activities. He wanted this to go smoothly himself and anything that would help was all the better.

"Jimmy, you got the warrant? Okay, let's go. Dick, we'll meet your people down on the street and have them drive us around to Luke's office."

They left the office with an intensity fueled by the thrill of the hunt. They were about to attack a lawyer in his inner sanctum. The fire of some basic primal instinct burned them onward to their quarry. What started out as a responsibility of office was turning into something else, more sinister, tainted with the sin of selfish indulgence and gratification. The group of men appointed as sentinels of the rules of order of society charged forth on the prowl for blood. They were a company of greedy, self-centered egotists bent on pursuing a prize to hold up to their gods of vanity and pride. Justice took a lesser standing to the attainment of the goal of a successful hunt. That end would now justify the means.

On the street, two more detectives pulled up as they left the building. They all piled into the car with instructions to head straight to Daniel's office, a short two blocks away.

Across the street at the sheriff's office Betty Jowell, a featured writer with the Hampton News, saw the car leave out after loading up the District Attorney and his assistant. She recognized the unmarked car by its telltale double antennae. A deputy standing alongside her had witnessed the gathering.

"I wonder what's going on there," she asked. Betty was not a reporter but working at the paper developed her natural curiosity. It was the same thing her mother had called nosiness.

"I heard they were going down to Luke Daniels' office to serve a search warrant. You know he got indicted for the murder of that bank girl."

Betty did know that and was off to her car before the deputy even finished his sentence. She'd had her car phone for almost a year in hopes of calling in a hot scoop to her cohorts at the paper but had never gotten the chance. She was so excited she couldn't even remember the number. Thank goodness for speed dialing, she thought, as she hit star seven for the main number at the paper.

"Ludie, this is Betty. Put me through to Mr. Rogers. Hurry, it's an emergency."

The conspicuous unmarked car of the Hampton Police Department pulled up to Luke's office at nine thirty-five. They double parked and all five occupants got out and paraded into Luke's office. There was no one in the lobby of the building but the receptionist, Jenny. The five big men filled up the entryway putting Gafford right at Jenny's desk. Jenny knew who he was even before he announced himself.

"My name is Billy Gafford and we have to see Mr. Daniels. Could you tell him to come out front, please."

Jenny was flustered by the commotion and pushed the wrong button, sending her message to Liz's desk. Liz quickly appeared out front to see what all the commotion was.

"Where's Luke, Liz?" Jenny asked trembling.

"He's in his office. Why?" She recognized the crew immediately.

"Mr. Gafford needs to see him. I just buzzed him."

"No, you buzzed me. Just hold on. I'll get him."

Liz turned and stepped back through the door to the foyer. Before it shut behind her Gafford grabbed it and followed behind her. He was at her heels before she could even speak to Luke. He brushed past her and stood in front of Luke.

"Mr. Daniels, we have a warrant to search the premises. You are to permit this search and assist us in whatever way we request." Gafford dropped the warrant in front of Luke.

"What the…" Luke grabbed up the paper and quickly read over it. "Now just a minute, Billy. You can't come in here and start going through my files. This is an outrage. These are confidential records. The bar forbids this sort of thing and you know it."

Outside his office, Jimmy Clay and Dick Limox were already snooping around, looking at files laying on top of the cabinets in clear view. Liz was standing helplessly outside the door to Luke's office as he and Gafford raised their voices higher and higher.

"You know damn well you can't come in here and start this crap. How the hell did you get Judge Jones to sign this piece of garbage?" Luke was furious, unable to stay behind his desk, moving out into the hall.

"Hey, you two keep your noses out of my stuff." Luke noticed Limox poking around in some open files. He moved over to the cabinet and grabbed the files up out of Limox's face.

"Gafford, call off these goons or I'll… I have to protect the privacy and confidentiality of my clients."

"Is that a threat?" Jimmy Clay tried to bow up to Luke.

"Yeah, and who are you calling a goon?" Limox got nose to nose with Luke.

"Get out of my face, you stupid…"

Luke dropped the file and pushed Limox back off him. Limox caught the side of a table with his leg and fell back, catching himself on one knee. Clay grabbed Luke by the arm and Luke swung around and clipped him in the side of the head. The two detectives quickly stepped in and wrestled Luke up against the wall. Limox regained his stance and was ready to belt Luke when Gafford stepped up.

"That's enough. That's enough I said." Gafford did not want this kind of scene.

As he spoke the foyer door opened letting Jeff Woodall pass through who snapped several shots with his camera before Billy had control of the situation.

"Who the hell got him here? Boy, Gafford, this is some piece of work you've done here." Luke tried to shake himself loose from the hold of the detectives. "Tell these guys to let me go." Luke's voice had reached the shouting stage.

"Now everybody just calm down. Luke, can you control yourself?"

"Me? I'm not the one out of control. If these bastards touch one more thing in this office I'm gonna show you out of control."

"Now, just a minute. We've got a valid search warrant and we intend to execute it. If you've got a problem with that you can take it up with the Judge."

"You damn right I got a problem with it and you can bet I'm going to take it up with the Judge. I want my lawyer here. When he gets a hold of this you guys are going to be dead meat."

"You don't have a lawyer of record. I talked with John McWheter yesterday and he told me he was not taking your case."

"Who said anything about McWheter? How did you know I even talked with him? He's not taking the case, but I hired Nick Chestillo yesterday."

"Well, we don't have any record of that. I checked with the Circuit Clerk's office this morning and they have no record of you having an attorney."

"Yeah, you can't delay our investigation with these tactics, Daniels. We intend to pursue this case vigorously and put you behind bars." Jimmy Clay jumped in belligerently.

"Oh, shut up, Jimmy." Luke wanted to belt Clay in the mouth.

Jimmy Clay moved toward Luke.

"Oh, yeah, you're tough now. I got two clowns holding me back. Let's go outside and I'll whip your little ass."

"Jimmy, Jimmy, back up here." Billy grabbed him by the arm and pulled him back away from Luke.

"Now tell these two oafs to let me go." Luke's anger was getting more provoked by the minute.

"You just better watch it, mister. I'll have you charged with assault on an officer of the law." Limox sneered in Luke's face. "I don't appreciate your interfering with the duties of a police officer."

"Don't threaten me, Limox. I got witnesses that you started this whole mess." Luke looked around and realized that Liz had disappeared. There was no one there to witness what happened but the three detectives, the two District Attorneys and Jeff Woodall. Luke could imagine what he was over there scribbling on his pad. An awareness of the situation came over him, leaving him with a sense of foreboding. He realized that in the telling, this little incident would have him be the bad guy. Some of the fight drained out of him, leaving him weak.

"You guys can let him go," Gafford said, sensing the change in Luke's mood. "Who is Nick Chestillo?"

"An attorney in Biloxi. I met with him yesterday and we faxed his appearance to the clerk this morning." Luke wanted to fight back with his attorney but found himself lacking the energy. He struggled to hold his own in this contest.

"There are no exigent circumstances here, Gafford, and you know it. This girl died months ago and I've been right here practicing law. I have the right to protect the confidentiality of my clients and to have an attorney present during the search. You go forward now and we'll be fighting about this forever."

Luke could tell he was getting to Gafford. The District Attorney's expertise in these areas was limited to what he picked up in conferences in between social events. He was used to getting away with what he wanted to because the Judge supported his every action in an effort to maintain the law and order image popular with the voters. They were quite a team.

"I demand a hearing on the validity of this warrant before Judge Jones with my attorney present. You know, Gafford, once I make that demand and draw the warrant into question, then if you proceed the warrant could be voided and then you'd be in trouble."

Luke was flying by the seat of his pants now, but he had Gafford going.

"I want to get Judge Jones on the phone right now," hoping the move would work with Gafford.

It worked. Gafford agreed and they called the Judge with both of them over the phone. Luke did his best to keep his cool and soon they were talking with Judge Jones.

Jones was afraid when he signed the warrant that something would go awry. He should have known not to trust that dunce, Gafford. The argument bounced back and forth with Luke harping on the confidentiality of his clients and the violation of their trust, with Gafford clamoring about the needs of the state to search out the evidence. He crowed loudest about the possibility of some piece of evidence being jeopardized. Luke laughed out loud, pointing out the time frame that had elapsed. Judge Jones thought Gafford's argument a bit ridiculous. Still, he couldn't refuse the warrant and at the same time didn't want to offend any client of Luke's that might be strong politically. He finally agreed to a hearing on the merits.

"Alright, we'll set the hearing for first thing in the morning. Luke, you'd better have your lawyer there. No exceptions. If he's not, I'll find him in contempt. In the meantime, you can't touch anything in that office. I'm putting a uniformed officer in there to keep an eye on everything and you are to stay away until after the hearing."

Luke protested loudly but the Judge would not budge. He even chastised Luke severely for arguing with him about it.

"You stay away from that office and I mean it. There will be an officer there from now until we finish the hearing tomorrow. That's final." Judge Jones hung up the phone, leaving a buzz on the line.

Gafford gave instructions to Limox to get someone over there in uniform right away. They withdrew outside to the car and made the arrangements over the police radio. Gafford hovered over Luke while he gave instructions to Liz.

"Okay, Luke, you're out of here, too," when he thought they'd had enough time.

"Don't rush me, Billy. This is really too much and you know it." Luke gave Gafford a contemptuous glare. "I'll be out in a minute."

As Gafford stepped into the foyer, Luke felt so drained he could hardly stand up.

"I'll be at home, Liz. Call me there if you need anything."

Luke stumbled into the foyer where Gafford was still moseying around. They went out the front door together without a word. Luke gruffly brushed by the detectives standing on the sidewalk in front of his office. Jeff Woodall had their attention with his pad out still writing furiously. Luke strode mulishly to the parking lot and pulled away with tires screeching. It was not the smartest exit for him to make but at this point he was in no mood to care.

Tommy Chipman arrived at work late on this Thursday morning. He had been at a loan closing at the bank since eight. He had no idea what had transpired in his office. After parking his car he came in through the front door with a bright hello to Jenny. The wind had blown around his hair, bleached out by the sun from the many hours on the golf course. He brushed it down as he entered the building. He was the first person in the office since the commotion and his entrance startled the receptionist.

"Oh, good morning, Tommy. No, no. No messages." Jenny was not known for volunteering information. Her job was to answer the phone and take down messages. She never offered up anything else without being asked.

Tommy thought her reaction a little strange but kept on walking, opening the door to the hallway where he found a uniformed officer sitting in one of the office chairs reading a magazine. He said hello surmising that this was Luke's client since Jenny had said nothing to him. He went down the hall to his suite of offices where he found Liz talking with his secretary.

"Good morning, ladies," Tommy entered cheerfully. He had a round of golf planned for the afternoon and knew this was going to be a good day. Their solemn faces spoke for them that perhaps this morning was not so good. "What's going on?"

"Well, you saw that officer up front, I guess?" Liz didn't know where to start.

"Yes, what's he doing here. I thought he was somebody here for Luke."

"Well, he is, sort of."

Liz despised being forced to explain events she'd rather not have been through. Slowly, deliberately, she poured out what had happened that morning.

Tommy's first reaction was shock. He couldn't believe this had happened right here in Hampton. How could Gafford pull a stunt like that? His bank people were supporters of Gafford and his law and order stance. Still, this was ridiculous. And right here in this office. His office. The air suddenly changed for Tommy. He was breathing in and out with a slight change in heart rate taking place. This was his office, too. They told him about the reporter being here. No doubt the TV station would have a spot on the six o'clock news which would probably be a shot of where the action took place. The front door of this office. His office. God, what would the bank think?

Their name was not out there, but his was. And their ties to him were well known. His father-in-law would be furious, not so much at Tommy but at all the calls he was probably going to get because his son-in-law shared space with an accused murderer.

"Where is Luke now? I need to talk to him." He had needed to have a conversation with Luke for a long time but put it off for one reason or another. They were both busy, their schedules conflicted, the time was just not right. Hell, he was flat out avoiding it. Robert Fowler was always asking him about the situation and their friendship had become strained because of Tommy's evasive responses on the topic. And, if the current president, Wildmon, got picked for the new job in Jackson, Robert would be the new president of the bank. Tommy didn't want to be at odds with him. His in-laws certainly wouldn't appreciate that. Damn Luke.

"Liz, see if you can get him on the phone. I want to talk with him." He stomped into his office and shut the door.

Liz tried Luke's number from the phone in front of her but only got a recording. She left a message for him to call Tommy and then got out of the room and back to her desk. Luke did not call back the rest of the day.

Luke talked to Nick Chestillo, and to Jane. He went straight to his house and called Chestillo's office. He was in a deposition and could not be reached was the secretary's explanation. Luke countered that he had to be reached, explaining what transpired that morning and the hearing tomorrow. Luke hung up from the secretary and called Jane. She got on the phone immediately and said little as he related the episode.

"And what am I going to do about Chestillo. The Judge was adamant about the hearing tomorrow. It's got to be a go because the police are sitting down there in my office."

Jane put Luke on hold while she called Chestillo's office. "He's here in town, Luke," she offered when she came back on the line. "They're gonna get a message to him to call me immediately." Jane could feel the despair in Luke's voice as they talked on about the situation. She knew he was trying very hard to keep the whole matter professional. He could work on a brief of the topic this afternoon. He had his lap top at home so he could type it himself and have it ready for Chestillo first thing in the morning. They made a list of things he should touch on in the brief and what else he could be doing to prepare.

"Luke, hold on, Chestillo's on the other line."

She left the line and Luke listened to the silence with his mind racing about the conversation she was having with Nick. After what seemed like a long time, Jane was back on the line.

"Okay, Luke, here's the deal. Nick can't make it tomorrow, but I can," she threw in quickly before Luke could feel abandoned. After suggesting Chestillo she didn't want his prior commitment to affect Luke's case. "He's going to associate me for this hearing. I'll come up in the morning and argue that the time frame is unreasonable. That he only took the case a day before the hearing was set. That notice is insufficient and that fairness dictates that the hearing be rescheduled."

"But what about that guard dog at my office? We can't leave him there until we get to a hearing on the merits." Luke could feel the trepidation creeping into the edge of his senses.

"I'll argue the unreasonableness. It amounts to an unfair limitation on your freedom, a form of restriction of your liberty. Hey, you're an innocent man. The Judge can't do that."

"I don't know, Jane. You don't know Judge Jones. Or, Bedford County. This town likes to project the image of being progressive and the picture of the New South but in reality it's as good ole boy as they come. Jones is going to stick his finger to the wind and make a decision from that."

"He's got to stay within the law, Luke. But tomorrow we won't argue the merits. We'll argue the fact that Nick is your lawyer and he had a prior federal court appearance and couldn't be there. The Judge will see reason. You go ahead and prepare that brief on the law of searching an attorney's office and I'll be preparing my argument on continuing the matter. All we'll be asking for is until sometime next week, Luke. The rules all say you get at least five days. You know that."

"Yes, I know that, Jane. But there's more to it than what the law says. These guys are all political mavens. They'll play to the media. You weren't there this morning. It was insane."

"What else do you want me to do, Luke?" Jane knew the declaration sounded harsh, but she didn't know what else there was to do. She couldn't make Nick appear at the hearing. She acknowledged her lack of experience in criminal cases, but wanted to do what she could for Luke.

"You're right. You're right. That's all we can do. If Nick can't be there, then he can't." Luke didn't want to offend Jane. She was a dear friend that he needed right now. "I'll do research today and we'll sock it to 'em tomorrow. After all, we've got two good brains here. We'll be fine."

The phone call ended flatly. Jane would be at his house before eight and they would go to the courthouse together. After hanging up, Luke walked out his back door and stood in the yard. Above him was a beautiful azure blue with the sun rising toward its peak in the spring sky. Luke soaked up the sun's rays for a while, letting the warmth penetrate his body. Not a day he wanted to spend in the library but he had no choice. The sun's position indicated it must be getting on close to noon. Looking around Luke realized his back yard needed a good cleaning. He thought about Willie and his case. There was a lot to do that was getting harder to tackle with the stuck feeling that bogged him down. He needed to be unstuck and get to work.

He started back into the house to get his laptop and go to the library. At the back door he turned again to consider what work he needed in the yard. Over his shoulder in the distant western sky he could see a little cloud no bigger than a man's hand peeking over the neighbor's trees, a blemish on the perfection.

The next morning Jane knocked at Luke's front door at seven thirty. She'd been up since five. Wasting little time on pleasantries, she pulled out a folder and they started in on the case. Shortly, they packed it all up and headed to the courthouse.

When they arrived at the Judge's office before Gafford, Anna greeted them cordially. Yes, the Judge is here, in his office. The small talk ground on Luke until Gafford and Jimmy Clay walked in.

Everyone was cordial. Handshakes were passed around with Luke introducing Jane. How nice to see you. Without warning, Judge Jones entered the room from his office and announced that the hearing would be in the main courtroom where his court reporter was setting up. Perhaps everyone would be more comfortable there since it was almost nine. He intended to start promptly this morning. He had delayed two other hearings for this matter so they couldn't dally.

The room cleared, with Judge Jones holding the door open while all filed out into the foyer and then to the courtroom. The court reporter was at her desk in front of the bench. She chatted with them briefly. Judge Jones broke into the room with robes flowing, taking up his judicial post and banging the gavel.

"This court will come to order. Case is State vs. Luke Daniels. This hearing time was set by me. What says the state? Gafford, are you ready?"

"We are, Your Honor." Gafford spoke solemnly with all the weight of his task of protecting the people.

"Counsel, we've not been introduced. I presume you are here on behalf of the defendant. What might your name be?" Judge Jones' curt remarks were directed at Jane. Without hesitation she stood and squared herself toward the bench.

"Judge, My name is Jane Archer. I'm appearing here today for the defendant on behalf of his counsel of record, Mr. Nicholas J. Chestillo. Mr. Chestillo had a prior engagement in federal court in Biloxi this morning. He only had notice of this hearing yesterday at noon and could not get release from his appearance there.

"Mrs. Archer, I am well aware of the time frame. I set this hearing. Everybody else had the same amount of time."

"In light of that, Your Honor, we have a motion to file at this time. May I approach the bench?" Jane stepped from behind the table and moved to the Judge handing him a copy of the motion asking that the hearing be postponed until Luke's counsel could appear. She then handed a copy to Gafford who was already on his feet to protest.

"Your Honor, I haven't seen this before now but we're here ready to proceed on a highly sensitive matter. Enough time has passed on this already."

"That's not our fault, Your Honor. Mr. Gafford could have filed this motion and set a hearing on it as the Rules of Procedure require, but instead he has chosen to try to get in through the back door." Jane's eyes flickered as she plunged into the argument.

"Just a minute, young lady, I don't appreciate your tone. We have dealt with this matter professionally, waiting until our information was complete. Now that we have an indictment we have to move forward." Gafford was having some difficulty coming up with a good excuse why he hadn't moved before now. Both lawyers stood in front of Jones with Clay hovering a few feet behind.

Jones listened to the banter back and forth for a few minutes without comment. He still didn't have a memorandum of law on the issue of the search warrant for the law office. And, he was now getting the distinct impression from Gafford's pained looks that he didn't have one and wasn't ready for this hearing. He was huffing and puffing about the rights of the people; sure signs of his all-too-familiar cry of 'Judge, get me out of this.'

"Mrs. Archer, why wasn't this filed yesterday?" Jones fired off bluntly.

"Well, Judge, the hearing was only set yesterday. As soon as we found out we started preparing." Jane stammered out an answer, stunned by the Judge's position. How much faster could she have done it?

"Nobody called me. Does this… what's his name," Jones pulled up his glasses and looked down at the paper, "Nicholas J. Chestillo think he's too busy to call up a Judge in little ol' Hampton, Mississippi."

"No, your honor, it's not like that at all." Jane was trying hard to retain her composure.

"I should hope not. This is an important matter. I don't care how long he's had something set in federal court in Biloxi or where ever the hell he is, for that matter. A young girl has been murdered here and the Grand Jury indicted your client. You'd best be taking this seriously. Your motion for time is denied and we'll proceed with the hearing on the search warrant."

"But, Your Honor, I," Jane tried to start again but was cut off.

"No, buts. You hear me, young lady. You got five minutes to get it together. And just be glad I'm not finding your partner in contempt of court. I believe I told Mr. Daniels yesterday that if he wasn't ready with his lawyer this morning that I'd do that." He glared down from the bench at Luke.

"This court will stand in recess for five minutes." Jones pounded the gavel, bounded off the bench and was gone.

Jane turned to Luke stunned. She didn't know what to say. The Judge had run over her roughshod without any consideration of the law. Luke tried hard to keep his face from revealing his inner thoughts. He knew exactly what Judge Jones was doing. He was keeping himself and his DA out of trouble. But there was no time to worry about it now. The Judge would be back in less than five minutes and things would be rolling again. He and Jane just looked at each other. Luke was the first to speak.

"Ok. I've got my brief ready. I don't know that it's best for me to argue it. I made a short outline that I think you can follow. I've also got copies of the cases. That always gets Jones excited. I can hand them to you in order as you go through the argument.

Jane had still not said anything. She was fuming, having already gone from shock, to dismay and now into anger. That was good. Get her fighting spirit up.

"Let's pretend that we're arguing our moot court case in law school. This'll be fun." Luke tried desperately to appear calm and collected without giving away the dizzying effect this was having on him. This was his life, for God's sake and the Judge had treated his counsel like a dog. He feared the bad treatment was not over. Jane started skimming over the papers Luke handed her.

"Billy, you've got a call. It's here in my office." Anna called to the District Attorney from the door to the courtroom. Gafford and Clay stopped their whispered murmurings for Gafford to leave and take his call.

Inside the door to Anna's office Gafford found Judge Jones in a rage.

"Where's my memo on that search warrant?" Jones barked out.

"I've got the cases in my file." Gafford returned lamely. Actually, all he had was the handout from the last prosecutor's conference on search and seizure. But he knew he could wing it with the Judge and get by.

"I don't like this, Gafford. We're skating on thin ice here. The voters will be reading about this in the papers. I can't let them get the upper hand. You better have us covered." Jones knew when he said it that he couldn't count on Gafford to have the savvy needed here.

"Look, Judge, we have the best interests of the public on our side. There's been a murder and the Grand Jury has indicted Daniels. We have the right to pursue the case in the interest of justice. That means searching the office. He can't hide behind any cloak of confidentiality. That veil was cast off when he committed murder. If we're going to get a conviction on this we have to have the evidence."

Jones stared back at Gafford and his smug expression. The DA's large frame gave a ring of certainty to his words. It was Gafford's strong suit. Jones had often seen the trait lull a jury into credulity. He was a master at knowing just enough law to make him dangerous. Jones had to make sure this one did not turn on such precarious elements.

"Get back out there and let's get this show on the road."

Gafford pranced back into the courtroom and, shortly after, the Judge entered from his side chamber. Luke and Jane still had their heads down into the case law when Jones banged his gavel, calling the room to order.

"Let's go, Mrs. Archer. You need to get your head out of that book and stand up here like…" Jones hesitated. He was going to say like a man, but then thought better of it. Jones had never been too fond of women lawyers, his disdain often showing up in his rulings from the bench.

Jane had been in this position before. She bristled at the thought of what she knew was "stand up here like a man." She rose out of her seat and stared directly at Jones, hoping he would make some reference to her gender. It would be a good start on attacking any ruling he made as prejudicial.

"Stand up here like you have some respect for this Court, young lady. Your impudence will not be tolerated." Jones twisted the situation to his advantage, implying insolence on her part.

"I'm ready to proceed, Your Honor. I apologize to the Court for any misunderstanding about my intentions. I am only trying to represent my client on short notice." Jane took an unassuming tone in hopes of easing the tension. Having the Judge angry would not do Luke any good.

Luke sat silently at the table. Unable to vent the rage he felt, he just sat, trying to keep his head from hanging too low. The hatchet job on Jane disturbed him. Jones was putting Jane through the grinder and that was not doing Luke any good. He wanted to stand up to her defense but could not. He was the defendant, completely powerless to do anything but sit and listen.

He was furious with Chestillo. Jones would not try these tactics on him. Or at least if he did, Chestillo would be able to withstand it better than Jane. She was not a criminal lawyer and he knew that. She had no experience in these matters. While she was a seasoned lawyer with superior trial skills she had little in the way of preparation for the court of Judge Wendell Garmon Jones, the Third. He looked over at Gafford and his self-righteousness, strutting around his table.

The argument began. The double team from Judge and prosecutor was too much. Jane tried valiantly to defend her position for Luke, but she was in an unfamiliar and treacherous arena. The case law she presented was sound and her logic and application solid. She did an excellent job.

Gafford's law was weak, patchy. His presentation was pocked full of platitudes and clichés with little application to the case. Throughout the production Jimmy Clay handed Gafford copies of cases which were then laid before Jones with superfluous gestures. Gafford was adept at the dog and pony show of criminal prosecutor. The full performance lasted less than an hour. At the conclusion, Jones sat silently at the bench, looking meditative, as if absorbed in the weighty affair of judicial performance. After a few moments of feigned reflection he spoke.

"I need a few moments to go over my notes and these cases you have presented me. If you will remain seated, I'll review this in my chamber and give you an answer momentarily."

The gavel banged and Judge Jones left through the side door. Silence hung in the room. Gafford and Clay mumbled to one another lightly. Jane and Luke sat quietly, neither of them knowing what to say first. Jane had been double-teamed. She felt drained and could only shuffle papers, trying to put her file back together. Luke sat without movement. He knew Jane had done her best and that he should tell her so, but he found no energy for compliments. The seconds ground into minutes. Only after Jane shuffled and reshuffled until her file was completely arranged did she stop and stare straight ahead. She turned and looked at Luke with sadness in her eyes, tears at the brink.

Before she could form words, the side door opened. Jones entered stepping straight away to his chair. He pounded the gavel needlessly to the silent courtroom.

"This is a case of some magnitude. I've looked over all these cases and am compelled to a decision. On the one hand we have the demand to honor the confidentiality of the clients of a member of the bar. On the other hand, we have a murder and the needs of the state to pursue evidence. The loss of human life must be the overriding and prevailing interest. In reaching this decision I am not incognizant of those clients who have put their trust in this lawyer who is now a defendant." Jones paused long enough to give a disdainful stare in Luke's direction.

"Therefore, I am going to limit the scope of the search somewhat. Mr. Gafford, you may conduct your search. Mr. Daniels, you may have your attorney present at the time of the search. He, or she…" Jones paused again with a look toward Jane, "may not interfere with the investigation of the Office of District Attorney."

No one said anything as Jones continued.

"Mr. Gafford, you are a member of the bar with awareness of the confidential nature of this proceeding. Therefore, anything you find in this search must be held with the strictest precautions. Anything you wish to identify as evidence to be used at the trial of this matter must be delivered to this court to be held until trial. Any matter that may come to your knowledge as a result of this search that is unrelated to this case must be treated as confidential and you are bound by your oath as an attorney not to reveal anything you may learn. Do you understand me? You are to look for things related to the death of Susan Weeks and nothing more."

"But Judge, if I find something related to another crime, I'll have to act on it. It is my duty of office," Gafford whined.

Jones wanted to reach down and bop him one.

"Gafford, if you find evidence of a crime, any crime, this one or anything else, you bring it to this court, first, and a decision will be made at that time. Do I make myself clear?"

Gafford had an expression as if he wanted to say more but quickly amended it with an affirmative nod.

"Judge, what about the policeman down there? When is the search to be? I know Mr. Chestillo can't be here before Monday." Jane tried hard to think through all the possibilities that needed to be answered.

"What about tomorrow? Do you think Mr. Chestillo will have a conflict in federal court on Saturday?" Jones' voice declared his disdain. And it riled Jane. He was being ridiculous in his criticism of Luke's legal counsel. She had never heard any Judge be so reproachful of a lawyer's conflicting schedule. There was a lot she wanted to say in response to his chiding, but she decided this was not the place. She did her best to respond with delicacy.

"One of us will be, Your Honor. I feel certain that Mr. Chestillo, himself, will want to be present for such a serious matter." She could not help the contemptuous inflection.

"So be it." Jones pounded the gavel again. "You people need to clear the courtroom. I've taken up enough of my schedule with this. There are other cases behind you."

"One more thing, Your Honor." Jane spoke up stubbornly. "We still have a man, an officer... a policemen standing guard at Mr. Daniels office. Do you really think that's necessary? Mr. Daniels is an officer of this court by virtue of his standing in the Bar. The presence of this watchdog implies a judgment. Is this Court insinuating something other than his complete innocence until proven guilty?"

Jones glared down at Jane as if he could strike her. He seethed at her suggestion but settled quickly and looked over at Luke.

"Mr. Daniels, you are still an officer of this court until proven guilty. May I have your word that you will not enter your office until the time set for tomorrow's meeting with the DA and your attorney?"

"But, Judge," Gafford was on his feet.

"Shut up, Gafford. Luke, swear it or else I'm leaving the officer there." Jones knew that Chipman was also in that office and knew he nor his primary client, the Bank, liked the idea of a uniformed cop keeping vigil. And Jones didn't like the idea of irritating the bank.

"Do you swear it, Luke?"

"Yes, Your Honor. I will not go to the office until we have the search."

"All right. Next case." Jones banged the gavel.

Luke looked down at his watch. Fifty-nine minutes had elapsed since the Judge first banged his gavel to start the proceeding. Now Jones was pushing them out of the way. As Luke grabbed his file to leave, he turned to see four other lawyers had entered the courtroom for the next hearing. Their stares quickly dissolved as Luke scrutinized them. He didn't know how long they had been in the courtroom but evidently it was long enough to stimulate speculation. Luke felt exposed, naked, as if he needed to cover himself. He wanted to crawl under the table. But there was no place to really hide. He had to move forward.

Jane could sense his uneasiness. She too felt a panicky tension, as if she were breathing in fear from the air. Gafford and Clay had already moved down the aisle and were glad-handing the lawyers, drawing their attention away from Luke and Jane where their eyes had been fixed. Jane watched as nervous glances were cast their way. The four lawyers huddled around the prosecutors listening to their jabber.

Luke felt glued to the floor. His feet would not move from the spot behind the counsel table. He knew exactly what Gafford was doing. He had already begun to try his case against Luke with the power of suggestion and innuendo. Although they spoke in hushed whispers at the back of the room, Luke could feel the barbs cutting through him. Gafford was crowing about his fresh victory before Judge Jones; about his attack on the murderer, Luke Daniels.

Luke's bitterness toward the DA swelled. That bastard! How could he smile and fake friendship to Luke and then turn around and castigate him? Luke stared back at them with loathing. Finally, Jane pushed on him and he almost fell over the chairs.

"Come on Luke. Let's get out of here."

They quickly descended the stairs and made it outside without a word. In Jane's car, she pulled it into gear before realizing she didn't have a clue where they were headed. They couldn't go to Luke's office. She didn't think his house was where they needed to be right now.

"How 'bout Shoney's?" she asked. "I could use some nourishment after that fiasco. Boy, that Jones is a creep. I'd love to bring him up before the Judicial Performance Committee. He had his nerve, treating me like that. Male chauvinist bastard. I've never seen a Judge act so hostile."

Jane glanced at Luke as she steered the car away from the courthouse and out to Shoney's. He sat in silence and watched the scenery flick by the window as they drove.

When they arrived, Luke didn't want to get out of the car. But he didn't have the strength to argue with Jane when she popped right out ready to go inside. He felt drained. His world unfolded in slow motion. It took a lot of effort to get to the front door. They took a seat and Jane immediately went to the buffet. Luke fixed his coffee and sipped for a few moments in solitude. The restaurant was filled with people but Luke was oblivious. He stared straight ahead across several tables and out the window on the other side of the room. Outside the sun was gleaming down on the shrubbery, glistening off the verdant shades of new growth. The leafy textures were pleasing to Luke's eyes as he sat in a moment of peaceful oblivion. The movement of a body in his periphery caused him to refocus his gaze. He realized his fixed expression across the room must have appeared that he was staring. He blinked and cleared his head, moving his eyes away. But then he looked back. The body that disturbed his vision glanced his way again. He looked back at her, suddenly realizing it was Rita Lambert, who probably thought he had been staring at her.

Luke attempted to convey apology. He didn't want her going back telling anyone that this accused murderer was staring at her in public. Their eyes met for a brief moment of naked honesty. Luke was embarrassed and didn't know why. There was a fleeting connection between them, as if in this crowded restaurant, they shared a moment of intimacy. They both caught a glimpse of bareness in the other that was not intended.

Luke felt a comfort in her glance like some chord being stroked in him of knowing. He had the feeling that she was looking deep into him seeing everything about him, his hurt, his pain, his innocence. And, he was seeing into her also, her misery and heartache. That's why she was here. She came to this crowded restaurant to be alone. To sip coffee and sit unnoticed. Exactly what Luke was doing.

"Are you okay?" Jane sat down on her side of the booth with a plate filled with food. "You look like you're off in never never land. Look, Luke, I'm sorry about this morning…"

Luke's vision was interrupted. When he looked back at Rita she stared straight ahead, a silhouette outlined against the glass with sunlight streaming around her.

"Luke, hello. Are you in there? Have you heard anything I've said. Aren't you hungry?"

"Yeah, I need to get a plate." Maybe the food would help. Maybe he could say something to Rita. Apologize for staring at her. She must think he's a lunatic. Where was he there for a moment? His situation must be stressing him out more than he realized. But he could have sworn she was there, too. He picked up a plate at the buffet, but then glanced around to where Rita was sitting. The seat was empty. He moved around the line of people and suddenly she spoke to him.

"Hello, Luke. Good to see you, again." She moved by him in the crowd of folks.

They didn't touch physically. But Luke could not speak any apology. They exchanged something that wouldn't let him speak, communicating more than words. There was a quickening in the space between them that melded more than flesh and blood.

"Thanks for helping me the other night," the sound of her voice came to Luke but her words did not register.

"Oh, you mean with the gas. Hey, sure. It was nothing."

The texture of her voice was like fine, beautiful silk fluttering toward him with a narcotic effect. It stirred through the air and then into his head with a gentle, hypnotic softness. His eyes reflected the peace he felt in her voice. His candid and unassuming demeanor enthralled her. So different from the pompous family where she found herself inescapably chained. Several steps from each other, they exchanged an understanding, a knowing of the predicaments in which they found themselves.

Afraid to linger too long, afraid that someone might notice the void in her, Rita spoke again faintly, "Well, I must be off to my errands before this day gets away from me. No more solitude," she said with a nervous laugh. "See you around, Luke." Again, the pause in her bearing, the chink in her constantly guarded armor.

Luke wanted to touch her. He wanted to reach out and embrace her, hold her to him. Clutch at her and feel an easing of the pain that enveloped him. It was almost as if he knew her touch would be healing. The sensation startled him. But, yes, he thought he could be healing to her, as well. Hell, what could he do for her now in his current predicament? He watched her lower her gaze from him and turn away, walk down the aisle and out the front door.

Luke looked around the room for a sign that anyone else had witnessed what happened. What had happened? He didn't have a clue. What happened took place in no more than a few seconds and to the casual observer was nothing but a chance passing in the buffet line at

Shoney's. Luke looked down at the empty plate in his hand.

"Are you in line, mister?"

A short, fat woman in a brightly colored Hawaiian shirt was peering up at Luke from cat-eye glasses. Sunglasses stuck out from the top of a badly dyed red mop of curly hair.

"Ah, yes, I just wanted to get a biscuit." Luke moved forward in the line and grabbed the biscuit. The food on the line might as well have been plastic for all the appeal it had to Luke. He put on a couple of pieces of fruit and then wandered over to his table.

"Your coffee's probably cold," Jane said as she took the pot and refilled his cup. "What'd you get? No wonder you stay so slim eating like that."

"I just don't have much of an appetite this morning." Luke played with the biscuit and sipped on the coffee. His mind wandered back to Rita Lambert. Of all people. She was married to one of the wealthiest lawyers in town. Or at least his father was. Wilson was by association. Wilson was also one of the biggest jerks. Luke was not alone in that presumption. He wondered if Rita thought so, too. Something was definitely bothering her. There was trouble in those eyes. That's what connected them. A common thread of torment and misery woven into their lives. Luke's was just more public than hers. It was hard to imagine anything being as bad as being accused of murder. But into every life… He looked over at Jane who was trying to focus on her breakfast. Her usual spunk subdued by the morning's hearing, she was reserved and quiet. Neither of them knew quite what to say to one another at this point so they ate in the absence of conversation, save an occasional remark about the food.

After several cups of coffee and contemplation, Luke began.

"I suppose we need to get to a phone and talk with Chestillo about this. I sure wish he could have been here this morning."

"Luke, I'm sorry. I…"

"Hey, I don't want to hear those words again. You have absolutely nothing to be sorry about. It's not your fault that Jones is an SOB. I just wish we hadn't given him any fuel for his fire. He was being totally ridiculous. But he's still the Judge. Why don't we go back to my house and give Nick a call. Surely he'll be in his office by lunch time. You probably need to check in with your office, too. I might call Liz and see what's happening at the practice I used to have."

Luke stood up, giving Jane a wry grin. Jane stood, too, putting an arm around Luke's waist and giving him a squeeze as they walked off.

At Luke's house they put in the call to Chestillo and Jane handled several matters that had cropped up at her office. A check had finally arrived from a settlement on a case and she was all smiles and ready to buy lunch which Luke declined. Shortly, the time reached noon and Chestillo called. They talked at length about the hearing and about tomorrow's search of Luke's office.

Luke assured them both there was nothing to find because Susan had never been at the office. Once again he went through the story of how he met her at the Magnolia and they wound up at her house. He felt a little loathsome giving the story once more to Jane and he didn't know why.

At the conclusion of their discussion, Chestillo announced that unfortunately he did have a conflict. He had agreed to some depositions in lower Alabama for tomorrow morning and then he and his wife were heading to Florida.

"Luke, do you think it absolutely necessary that I be there. I mean, after all, you say there's nothing there for them to find."

Something about the phrasing of Chestillo's comment irked Luke. He said there was nothing for them to find because there was nothing for them to find. Yet, he had the imperceptible sensation that the lawyer might not be fully convinced of that. Jane was watching him closely from her position on the other line. Gawd. Lawyers.

"That's right, Nick. There is nothing there. So tomorrow's little exercise is going to be an exercise in futility for old William Porter Gafford. My main concern is their desire to snoop around in matters pertaining to other clients. Judge Jones assured us that they were not to do that. But still."

"Yeah, I know. Of course, I don't know what I could do to stop that even if I could be there."

"Don't worry about it. I believe I can raise enough hell tomorrow to stop anything they may try to pull. I've got Judge Jones' number."

Luke knew they were not going to find anything in his office but he was also learning something else about the attorney-client relationship. The client wanted the attorney there no matter what. Luke didn't want anything going on without his lawyer present and now his lawyer had missed one important skirmish and was going to miss another. Uneasiness crept into Luke over his relationship with Chestillo.

"Well, okay, then. If you think it will be alright. I'll call you first thing Monday morning and we'll go over our next step. Jane, what about you? You going to stay up there for tomorrow?"

"I think I just might. I may get into this criminal law thing. Besides, I made money not even being in my office today. I think I'll stay up here and take this man out on the town tonight." She gave Luke a wink.

Luke returned a half-hearted smile. Right now he hardly had the energy to hold the telephone, let alone go out on the town. What he really wanted was to lie down and go to sleep and wake up with this whole horrible mess over. They finished the conversation and as Luke hung up he flopped back on his sofa.

"How about a nap?" he spoke to Jane as she came back from the kitchen.

"Why, Mr. Daniels, you fresh thing. Is that an indecent proposal for your bedroom?" Jane feigned shock.

Luke chuckled. Right now he didn't think he had the energy to get himself up off the couch let alone anything else. Jane moved to a recliner where they remained in silence while Luke flipped the TV channels with the remote.

Saturday morning arrived. Despite Luke's protestations Jane demanded to stay over. She assured him that the lack of any clothes for the next day only gave her an excuse to go shopping and spend some of the money that had arrived at her office in her absence. She also insisted on taking him out to dinner and the evening turned out to be as pleasant as possible considering the looming activities of the next morning.

They arrived at the office around seven thirty to find a patrolman sitting across the street in his car. Before eight, Gafford, Clay and Limox arrived. Liz showed up also at eight. Luke had requested her presence late yesterday with the assertion that no one knew the set up of that office better than she did, including Luke.

"Let's set a few ground rules, shall we?" Jane started off with Gafford.

"The ground rules are that we're going to search the premises for evidence." Gafford spoke up in his tough guy mode.

Luckily, Jane let his abruptness go unchallenged. She was in a much more agreeable mood this morning and Luke was glad for it.

"Luke and I discussed his office set up last night and can direct you if you have a plan for conducting the search." A trace of sarcasm leaked into the sentence, slanted at what Jane perceived as Gafford's total lack of any organizational skills. "Liz, here, can answer any questions probably better than anyone else. Liz, do you have any specific information on how best to assist these gentlemen?" Unbeknownst to Liz, Luke and Jane had talked about Gafford's scattered approach to order. They agreed that with the right placed words and with Liz involved, they could direct the search themselves. Jane had a good start and let Liz continue.

"The files over here are all closed and have been since before Susan Weeks'…" Liz hesitated. Before Susan's… death? Murder?

"Where is her file? Luke has told us she was a client."

"She never had a file set up. Or at least I never set one up. Luke made the appointment with her but she never made it to the office."

"Did she ever have a file or was it destroyed? Luke, what were you seeing her about anyway?"

"Hold on there, Mr. Gafford. I may not be the expert criminal lawyer but I watched enough Matlock to know Luke doesn't have to answer any questions here. This is a search for evidence, not a free deposition. Liz told you there was no file set up so what are you looking for?"

Gafford didn't have an answer for that one. He didn't know what he was expecting to find. He just knew that a search had to be conducted.

"We'll start in Luke's office. Jimmy, you and Dick go in there and scrutinize every inch. I'll stay out here and go through these filing cabinets with Liz. Luke, you can stay out here and watch if you want. I'm not going to give you anything to report me to the bar about but I am going to look through these cabinets.

The tedium that followed put Luke on edge. He knew there was nothing to find but yet he had to stand by and watch his professional accouterments violated. The sanctity of this hallowed turf crumbled as he stood by helpless, unable to come to the rescue of something he had worked years to build. Watching a stranger touch his files hurt him like an assault on a child. He wanted to fight back. He was a lawyer, damnit; he was supposed to fight back. Yet, he knew that a fight would only further damage the situation. And so he stood by and watched in pain.

The minutes drug on to hours. After a while another detective showed up to help Limox. Luke knew it was only an inherent curiosity and desire to snoop. He joined Limox with Clay switching out to assist Gafford. Luke prayed that this would soon end.

"Hey, Gafford, take a look at this." Limox called from Luke's office.

Gafford found the two officers with the furniture turned upside down and moved about. After several minutes he returned to the area where Luke, Jane and Liz waited.

"They found a strand of long black hair Limox thinks is Weeks'. We'll send it down for testing."

"Oh, is that all." Luke looked at Jane and let out a sigh of relief. He knew that was a safe find. Susan had not been in his office and so the hair could not be hers.

"Okay, Gafford, what else do you want here?" Jane echoed the exasperation everyone was feeling. "Don't you think this has gone on long enough? Luke's told you she wasn't here. What else do you need to do?"

The boredom of the search had worn Gafford down also. He wanted to argue with Jane but didn't. He was tired of this and wanted to go himself. He was hungry, too, and it was approaching lunch time on a Saturday. Daniels had probably scoured the place for evidence anyway. They certainly wouldn't find any fingerprints after this late date. He knew the hair was a long shot. He didn't really think Luke was lying to him about her not being here. He walked through the rooms again scanning the objects hoping for a sign. He bumped into Limox down on his knees in one area.

"What do you think, Limox? Anything else we need to do? We've checked through all the files for anything that might be related to Weeks. And I looked through the appointment books for a month before the day she was killed. Nothing. You got any other ideas?"

"The secretary looks scared to me. Like she's hidin' something. Or knows something she's not tellin'. Maybe we ought to stay on her." Limox tried so hard to sound important.

"Maybe so. But we can't do that right now. I meant with the search."

"No, he's got this place cleaned up pretty good. We're not going to find anything here. We should have done this right after the murder."

"Well, we didn't."

"Hey, we got the hair, though. And my guess is the lab will identify it as one from Susan Weeks." It didn't matter what Daniels said. Limox knew exactly where this hair came from.

Gafford walked back out to where the others waited. He gave Liz a long, studied look, trying to determine if Limox might be right. He could tell it made her uncomfortable. What was she hiding? He'd have to stay on her.

Stretching back and puffing out his chest, Gafford sized up the room one more time.

"Well, I guess our work here is done, Jimmy. Luke, you can have your office back. We've made some notes of things that after investigation we may have to come back. So, don't think you can go destroying evidence."

What the hell was he talking about? Destroying evidence? He was so glad this was over with that he wanted to shout.

"I tried to tell you this was a waste of time, Gafford. Susan Weeks was never here in my office and I certainly didn't kill her. I've told you that all along." He was able to muster enough drive to add a dash of contempt to his words.

"Luke, don't. Just let them leave. You don't have to say anything." Jane rushed to his side.

Gafford noticed again that Liz sat in her chair with quiet apprehension, looking very much the scared rabbit. Why was she so easily upset by all this? Limox may be on to something with her. Gafford made a mental note to check her out.

Soon they had all their notes and other paraphernalia of the search together and made their way out the front door. It was twelve noon.

"Whew. Thank gawd that's over." Jane turned the key locking the front door and came back to Luke and Liz. Neither of them had said a word to each other.

"Anybody hungry?" Jane surveyed the two of them with a big grin.

There were no smiles on Liz or her boss. Luke watched Liz's unsettled countenance as she fidgeted with things on her desk and around the computer. She made no comment about the situation. Her eyes did not turn up. Luke had known Liz long enough to recognize a mood. He thought this the best opportunity to talk freely.

"Liz, are you alright?"

"No, I'm not alright. I don't like this. I'd rather not be put in this position. I want to help you, Luke. But Gafford and the police running around here unnerves me. They're so intimidating." The words burst out of her almost without control. She didn't realize fully what a nervous wreck the morning had made of her. "I felt like a criminal myself."

"What do you want me to do about it?" Luke made the direct request in hopes of meeting whatever need had been disturbed with Liz.

"I don't know. I'm just going home and trying to relax. All this stuff is giving me the willies. I'll have a case of nerves before it's over."

Liz picked up her purse and wandered toward the back door, mumbling the entire way. They could still hear her talking to herself when the door slammed shut behind her.

"What a light weight," was Jane's first comment. "Is she always this high strung?"

"Hey, cut her some slack. She's been under a lot up here. You know, people are constantly asking her things about me. And I'm sure she doesn't tell me the half of it. She'll be alright. Come on. Let's go eat."

When Jane left Hampton, she was still appalled at the actions of the last two days. She was a little miffed at Chestillo. She knew it wasn't his fault, but Luke was her friend and he needed help. She decided she would call the investigator herself and talk with him about the situation. She had his cell phone in the file.

After his wife left him and the divorce was final, Cody Raybern sold his large house and moved to a modest three bedroom in the picturesque town of Bay St. Louis. The seat of Hancock County, Mississippi, the little seaside village now contained the Casino Magic. Cody decided to take up residence there because of the close proximity to New Orleans and easy access to the city's international airport. With a short drive of about forty-five minutes he could get just about anywhere in the world. Despite the advent of the casino, the city maintained its quaint character with a diverse community of people, local shops, some good restaurants and a laid back way of life.

He chose a particular house because of its pier on the bay which gave him the perfect spot to tie up his sailboat. Sailing had become a passion for him. One of his undercover operations years ago required him to become a sailor who could smuggle. When the covert assignment ended, he was so hooked on sailing that he had to have his own boat.

DEA had paid for him to become an expert in the field and his first small boat was almost a chore to operate. After maneuvering the large crafts used in the sting, the one he could afford was too small. He began the process of trading up and now had his pride and joy.

The C & C Landfall 41 was about ten years old when he bought her five years ago at a government auction of vehicles seized by the DEA. The price he paid was a steal, but it took one helluva chunk out of his savings, and it needed some work. A ten year old boat is not necessarily an old tub, but this one needed repair.

Cody now had her in excellent condition, running as well as she ever had. The Landfall 41 was a sloop rig which meant a single-masted yacht with a headsail and a mainsail. The interior had two berths, fore and aft, with double beds in each, and a main salon with full galley comprised of a small refrigerator, stove and double sinks. Cody completely remodeled the inside by himself, masterfully refinishing the fine teak wood and replacing it piece-by-piece.

Today was Saturday and after taking care of a few chores, he headed to his boat with no plans for the rest of the day except to be on the water. Fixings for lunch and dinner were already on board and he was ready to set sail when his cell phone rang. He didn't recognize the number and decided not to answer, not wanting anything to interfere with his afternoon sail. Cody could sail for hours not caring where the wind took him. Often he would get out in the Gulf and head east toward Gulfport and Biloxi. Sometimes he just went due South straight out into the gulf, letting the wind direct his course. The only thing that mattered was being away and alone.

The alone part was an interesting component of his sailing. Gliding through the water alone took him away from work, from his past, from a lot of things that he didn't have any need to look back on. After two divorces and a few years of dating, he had grown accustomed to being alone. After a life so much in the public eye, he enjoyed his privacy. But there was a difference between aloneness and loneliness. He still enjoyed the company of the opposite sex and the boat was a great setting to take a date. The boat would easily entertain four couples but was also just right for one. His dating life had been sporadic since his divorce. He met lots of women, had gone out with quite a few, but nothing had stuck. Right now he was spending a lot of time on his own.

His cell phone rang again and the caller ID reflected the same number that he had declined to answer before. On impulse, he picked it up and said hello.

"Cody, this is Jane Archer. Can you hear me?"

"Yes, Jane. I'm out on my boat and the wind is whipping up pretty good, but I can hear you. What are you up to?"

"I'm on my way back home from Hampton. I was wondering if we might get together. I've been with Luke Daniels and there are some things about his case I'd like to discuss."

Cody's analytical brain quickly assessed the situation. He had a nice leisurely afternoon on the water planned and he didn't want to discuss work. He wouldn't mind having a woman along on the trip. But he didn't want to discuss another man that held her interest. However, Nick assured him that the interest was purely platonic. He had wanted the opportunity to get to know Jane better in any event.

"I'm taking my sailboat out in a little while. In fact, I'm out here checking it right now, getting ready to leave. I guess you could come along." Cody avoided any display of eagerness.

"I could be in the Bay in fifteen minutes," referring to his city the way the locals did. "If you've got a place to change, I'd be ready to roll." Jane remembered the new outfits she bought on her shopping spree in Hampton.

"Great. The boat is here at my house." Cody supplied her with directions and, after giving the boat one more going over, headed back to his house to wait for Jane and spruce up a little.

Jane arrived and quickly changed into shorts and a T-shirt. Despite living on the coast for many years now, she had spent little time on a sail boat and looked forward to the adventure. She also looked forward to having someone to talk to about Luke. They sailed out and then headed south into the gulf.

Jane held off going straight to business, trying to be sociable and appreciate the ride cutting though the waves with the wind blowing through her dark hair. She rambled through her purse to find sunglasses to protect her eyes from hair and sun.

The March wind was blowing strong, punching up the sails and carrying them through the water at a brisk pace. The sun came down warm and she guessed the temperature must be getting close to eighty degrees. She thought that this was a good opportunity to start working on a tan. Her dark complexion rarely faded too much, but the sun tanned her olive skin to an even deeper glow.

She watched Cody as he stood behind the wheel, maneuvering the boat alone, keeping the nose to the wind. His hair whipped back from his face that was already deep toned, the look of a man who spent a lot of time behind the wheel. She noticed a bit of gray flecked around each temple and wondered his age. She figured he must be about the same age as Nick. What was that? Forty, maybe. He looked good for forty, she thought. Despite the bit of gray, he looked young and very handsome. His chin and cheeks carried a thick stubble that had been left unshaved since the past morning. His shirt opened down a few buttons and the wind pushed it back revealing a good-looking chest covered with the right amount of hair. His legs were tan and lean. She could see a bit of untanned skin around the rim of the boat shoes on his feet.

As she looked, he kicked them off. Her sandals were already sitting beside her, legs propped up for maximum exposure to the sun which was beaming down warmly. She decided to strip down to the new bathing suit she had on underneath. The recent addition of running to her fitness regimen toned her to about the best shape of her life. Since hitting thirty, she had paid more attention to her body, particularly since she was single and lived in an area where opportunities for wearing bathing suits abounded. She must have at least twenty, adding another two or three to her wardrobe each year. She liked the way this new one looked.

Cody liked the way it looked, too. He had only seen Jane in business suits, lawyer-looking stuff and never realized what a great body she had. She had her face straight into the breeze and her brown eyes closed behind the stylish sunglasses. So, how did we get here? What do I say next? He was starting to get a little hungry and offered to fix lunch.

"I ate with Luke in Hampton before we left, but I'd be glad to fix you something. What have you got in there?"

Cody pointed in the direction of the cabin. The interior finish was a dark rich teak that Cody polished and oiled religiously giving a lustrous warm feeling and air to the space down below. She found the food in the fridge and came back up shortly with a turkey sandwich and fruit salad. He took the food, sat down behind the wheel and put his foot up on it to guide. He seemed to know exactly what to do. She disappeared again and came back with two bottles of water.

"So how is your friend, Luke?" he asked innocuously. "You said you wanted to talk about him. How is the case?" He kept his eye steady on the wheel and the sea ahead.

"Terrible. I've been up there for two days filling in for Nick. The DA and the Judge are real jackasses. Thought they could run over me. The Judge is a sexist pig. I'd like to report him to the judicial performance committee." Jane filled Cody in on the events of the past couple of days: the hearing on Friday and her being double-teamed by the Judge and DA, and then the search this morning.

"It was awful, Cody. As a lawyer, I can't imagine that happening to me. The idea of someone searching my office, it sounds so un-American."

Cody spent most of his adult life working with prosecutors and Judges. His arena was the federal level where those positions were appointed, not elected. But occasionally there was overlap between the two jurisdictions and he was acquainted with a few stories of overzealous prosecutors whose dedication went more to re-election than justice.

"So, what do we need to do?" This was Nick's case, but he asked Cody to investigate and, at this point, he didn't mind aligning himself with Jane.

"You tell me, Cody. Criminal work is not my primary field. I just want to help Luke. We've been friends for many years. He doesn't deserve what they're doing to him. If he was guilty, I'd approach this differently. He would still be my friend, but I understand the law and he would have to pay his debt to society. But he's not. I know he slept with the girl. But he didn't kill her. And he's not on drugs. I don't care what they say. Mine and Luke's relationship has been very close over the years. It was nothing romantic, never sexual, but still almost intimate. So I know him like family. He didn't do what they're saying."

Cody wondered what it would be like to have a friend as loyal as Jane. He'd never met a woman quite like her. Strong. Independent. Smart. Attractive. Yes, very attractive. He had known many attractive women, but never with all the other qualities. Her sincerity made him want to help Luke and he didn't even know the guy. He had already talked to a couple of contacts in Hampton and picked up on the claims of drug abuse which led nowhere. There wasn't much else in the way of motive. "You know, Jane, I've seen drugs make a man do crazy things," speaking lightly, he watched for her reaction.

"You may have, Cody, but that's not the case here. I'm telling you, I would bet my life on it. There's another reason why this girl was murdered. It may be drugs, but it wasn't Luke Daniels."

Jane sat straight up after her last statement. "What if the girl was doing drugs and that's what she came to see Luke about. Or, had another very serious problem which is why she went to Luke to begin with. Luke has said over and over that he left and that they never discussed about her case.

Someone must have come in after him. And, that someone might have been part of the problem to begin with. But nobody's given a tinker's dam about what Luke said. Maybe drugs have something to do with this murder, but it's not Luke. There's no motive, at least as far as Luke's concerned."

"Maybe not, but from what I picked up so far, she ran a fairly steady course. The girl stayed busy all the time. Not much of a party type. She had the bank job, was working on her PhD and filled up the rest of her time with modeling."

"But you always hear about drugs being around models, especially in the fashion industry. That's where we should be looking. Why hasn't anyone looked in that direction?"

It was a good question, Cody thought. As a former officer of the law and now a private investigator, he thought he knew why. They had all the evidence they needed for a conviction pointing toward Luke. Why waste your time looking elsewhere. All that does is muddy the water. And it was an election year. That had to play into it in this small town, Cody thought.

"Jane, we're not talking New York. The fashion industry you're talking about is a girl doing some local spots and a few in New Orleans. Seems like they said she did some in Florida, too, but most of the folks up there think the girl could do no wrong. Very straight arrow."

"But if she's making trips to New Orleans all the time, she can't be a saint. That may not be New York, but it ain't Mayberry, either. And you're an investigator, there could be a past. Many people move out of larger cities and into smaller towns because there's something that goes wrong in larger cities. That something could be a serious matter. Has anyone really looked into her background?"

"From what I understand, most of the stuff she did lately was with DeWeese Advertising. What if I check that out and see what I can find? Maybe I can pick up something there. Like Nick said, if we can plant a seed, all we need is one juror that doesn't accept the DA's version."

Jane smiled a little and thought about Luke, his life hanging in the balance hoping one person would believe in his innocence. She believed. And, she wouldn't stop believing. Suddenly, the air was not as warm as earlier and she picked up her shirt and pulled it on. Cody was back at the wheel watching the area ahead.

"We'd better start on back. Looks like some clouds over in the west. I don't want to have to outrun them." His intense eyes darted from the horizon to the direction of his house.

The wind was still strong, pushing the exquisite boat along. Cody started to make the turn and the fine vessel keeled over to one side, making a perfect arch in the water. Jane held on as they turned back against the wind and started the return to Cody's house. Salt water sprayed her face, dampening her shirt.

The ride exhilarated her. Not far from the shore, she could see the houses that dotted the coast. White caps flecked the gulf waters, making the deck toss her to and fro. So this is getting your sea legs she thought. She could do some of this. Maybe if she and Cody stayed in touch working on Luke's case, she could come out again. It was definitely an experience that she felt she would enjoy repeating.

CHAPTER TWELVE

Monday morning was a sluggish time for Luke. He could hardly muster the energy to pull himself out of bed. The clock on the bedside table beeped softly while he stared at it without moving. Finally, slowly, laboriously, Luke's hand reached the button and stopped the unrelenting signal that a new week was underway.

From the bedroom window Luke could see signs of the new day. The sun streaked bits of light onto the deep burgundy walls of the room. The heat had not moved in yet, but you could already tell it would be here before long. The dark walnut blades of the brass ceiling fan turned round lazily as Luke lay in his bed. He finally pushed himself up and moved to the kitchen where he put on coffee and gazed out the window while the machine percolated. When enough was in the pot he poured the hot black liquid into a cup and gulped down half of it.

The acidic brew gurgled down into his system and pushed the caffeine through his veins. He gulped another mouthful and then staggered back to the shower. Everything was operating in slow motion. After a while he was out of the shower and working on getting dressed. He filled his mug with another cup of coffee in the kitchen where he sat at the counter and resumed his gazing out the window.

Luke had to do something about his situation. This matter of Chestillo's absence bothered him. Would this pattern of the DA and the Judge running over his lawyer continue? If so, then he was doomed. Luke knew he was in no shape to represent himself, but what good was Chestillo doing him? After a period of reflection on his next step, he was out the door heading to the office.

The lethargic morning put him at the office after everyone else. Tommy was in and Luke welcomed the opportunity to talk with him. They had only seen each other in passing and Luke realized that Tommy deserved some of his time, and an explanation. They were friends and Luke wanted to confide in someone he could trust, but lately the mere thought of having to go through the whole scenario one more time left him feeling drained. So he had shied away. This morning was as good a time as any.

"Good morning, good morning, good morning." Luke mustered up energy and put on a smile. "How's the world of high finance these days?"

"Fine, Luke. Just fine." Tommy needed to visit with Luke; had needed to for some time. His procrastination shackled the need for so long that their relationship was now in jeopardy.

But where could he start?

For a while the conversation dawdled around the fine spring weather, old acquaintances they had seen recently and other ramblings. When the conversation reached plans for summer, a lull fell in their dialogue.

The silence that followed was uncomfortable, neither knowing where to pick up. Tommy felt compassion for his old friend and, at the same time, anger over the impact Luke's predicament had on the entire office situation. There was no denying the ripple effect on everyone connected with the office. Luke was well aware of it; helpless to do anything about it. He was on a roller coaster ride that took all his energy just to hold on. There was nothing else left. Luke wished he could prevent the fallout from hurting Tommy, Liz and the rest of the crew. There was no time or energy. Yet, as he sat in the still of the morning with Tommy, the magnitude of the crisis started settling in. The cloud hovering over him shadowed the lives of so many of his friends and associates. Friends. Luke was learning the true meaning of the word.

"I guess it's kinda hard for you to make plans for the summer at this point," Tommy uttered a soft stroke at the subject. "Do you know what's going to happen next?"

"No. After Friday and Saturday, I was so drained I haven't thought much ahead."

"You know, Luke, this whole thing puts me in a terrible position. I represent the bank where Susan worked and here I am in the same office with her accused murderer."

"Tommy, you know damn good and well that I didn't kill her."

"Yeah, I know that. But you've got to know how this looks to the bank. I'm catching a lot of flak that, until now, I've shrugged off. The bank's officers are constantly looking at me with questions. I don't have any answers for them. I don't know what to say anymore. I've given them the runaround until they're beginning to doubt me."

"What do you mean?"

"Look, Luke, even my father-in-law's getting on my case. He keeps telling me that the bank's interests must come first, that I have to consider my relationship with them above all else. And now that Robert Fowler is in line to be president, I have to be careful. You know what a stickler he is for appearances."

"Oh, yeah, I know quite well. That's why he fools around on his wife with young girls in the bank."

Fowler's penchant for approaching attractive young girls in the bank used to be the source of much joking between Tommy and Luke. Fowler's marriage was more a merger of money. Since law school days, J. Robert Fowler had managed to keep chasing young skirts without getting caught.

"That's not the point and you know it, Luke. You're hurting me by association."

The statement came out hard and strong. Tommy hated to sound so self-interested, but he had to at this point. He couldn't do anything to help Luke.

Luke's head hung low even as he fought to hold it up. What little energy he had that morning was now gone.

"Okay, Tommy. So what do you want me to do?" Luke's words came out slow and deliberate. He wished he could rail at Tommy, at somebody, but there was no point.

"Luke, this is hard for me, but I don't see any other alternative. I think the only thing left here is for us to sever our professional relationship."

"What do you mean?" Luke eyed Tommy from a withdrawn posture.

"I'm moving out, Luke. The bank has a piece of property I'm going to buy. They've made me a great deal. Friday's my last day here. I'll be completely out over the weekend. I know we have a lease with this building, but your situation has made this location untenable for me."

Damn, Tommy felt like such a heel. When he made these decisions in the cool reserved atmosphere of the bank with Fowler, they were logical and reasonable. Here in front of Luke he felt like a rat deserting a sinking ship. They had known each other for a long time and he really didn't believe Luke was capable of murder. There had to be some legitimate explanation for the whole mess, but at this point he had to consider his and the bank's best interests. Everyone had pointed that out to him.

"I guess you've got to do what you've got to do, Tommy. I wish we could have talked about this. I mean, I don't know what I could say or do to change things right now. I'm trying to understand."

"Do you know what you're going to do, Luke?" A sense of compassion was sweeping over Tommy. He wanted to be Luke's friend but there was no easy way for him to do so. He was caught on a line between his long-standing friendship with Luke and his income producing relationship with the bank. Tommy was not much of a church-goer but he suddenly had a strong mental picture of Judas running off with a satchel filled with thirty pieces of silver.

"I'm sorry, Tommy. You know I didn't ask for this. I would do anything to make it go away, but I'm here and there's no running away from it, nothing short of acknowledging guilt. And I can't do that when I'm not guilty."

Luke stood and extended his hand to Tommy looking him straight in the eye as he spoke those last words. They had known each other since college. How long was that? Fifteen, eighteen years of a friendship that held strong mutual respect. Now a multitude of unspoken thoughts raced through their minds. There was no way to articulate them now.

Luke did the only thing he could in the situation by sticking his hand out. The gesture made Tommy feel worse than he already did. Between his father-in-law and Fowler he had been convinced that the best course of action was to get away from Luke. That regardless of the outcome of the situation with Luke, it could not be good for the bank or Tommy. Now, in Luke's presence, that didn't seem right. There was no way to know exactly what would come of all this, but one thing was certain: Luke Daniels was a decent man. He deserved better than what was being thrust upon him. Tommy wished there was some way he could help him, but there wasn't. The wheels of justice in Bedford County were turning, and turn they would until an outcome was accomplished. Those wheels could run completely over a man, and they might run over Luke. There was nothing Tommy could do about that. Nothing but get out of the way.

"Good luck, Luke," was all he could say as he grabbed the hand extended to him with a farewell grasp. And then he let go.

Later that day, Luke sat in his office trying to make sense of where he was. He had to slow down and take stock. A mishmash of events swirled through his head in chaos, the discord leaving him scatterbrained and dizzy. His strength slowly trickled away from him as he sat at his desk, listless. There was no noise to disturb him. The phone didn't ring. Liz was still at her desk. An occasional sound from her area alerted him that she was out there doing something.

Luke tried to look at files on his desk but couldn't get his eyes to focus. The names on labels looked foreign to him. This would be a good time to return some phone calls, he thought, but the message sheets held names that he couldn't put together with any specific information. Sitting there was totally useless, yet he didn't know what else to do. What next? What should he do now?

Luke desperately needed answers. He needed someone to confide in. Someone he could depend on. He thought about calling Jane, but pulled back his hand as he touched the phone. He trusted Jane, but somehow that was not what he needed right now. The absence of Nick Chestillo in the two events that transpired with the District Attorney left his confidence in that relationship shaken. Not that Chestillo had done anything wrong. The incidents had been wholly the concoction of a little home-cooking, with a recipe from his dear old friends the Judge and the District Attorney. Luke laughed at the thought of it. His dear old friends. Just a short while ago he would have said that with conviction. He respected Judge Jones. He considered Gafford a friend. Now they were his adversaries. Luke wondered if they really thought he was guilty or was it something else?

Again, the whirl in his brain gave him vertigo. He stood up, holding on to the desk in the process. Maybe if he got out of this office for a while. A little sunshine. He stepped from behind his desk and made his way out to the hall.

"Liz, I need to go up to the bank," he lied. "Shouldn't be gone long. Hold down the fort until I get back." He delivered a weak smile with his sentence.

"Sure." Liz's response went back to him with hardly a glance in his direction.

In the foyer, Luke passed on his lie to Jenny. She had little to say in response, continuing to read without looking up. The front room was empty, no one waiting to see a lawyer. Luke figured Tommy had already advised his clients about his move. There was no one scheduled to come in for Luke. He opened the front door and headed himself into the fresh air.

Jenny looked up from her book as the door closed. She could see Liz through the blinds that hung in front of the secretarial area. Marking her place, she left her desk.

"You want a cup of coffee?" Jenny spoke to Liz from the hallway.

"Yeah, that would be good." There was stuff she could be doing, but nothing seemed too pressing.

"Pam, how 'bout you. Want some coffee?" Jenny stuck her head around the door to Tommy's area. "Is Tommy in there?" she mouthed with her head nodding toward his office.

"No, he left. I don't have time for a break but I'll take one anyway."

The three of them gathered around the coffee pot and Jenny filled their cups.

"Gawd, I wish I had a cigarette," Pam started off. "This moving business has me a nervous wreck. There's so much to do. Tommy thinks I should just be able to pick up and set down in a new location. Men!"

"It's a good thing I don't smoke." Liz said flatly.

The other two looked at her and burst out laughing. Liz looked at them like they were crazy. "What's the matter with you two? What's so funny?"

"Oh, you are, Liz. Luke's deal has got to be driving you crazy and you just keep right on going as calm as ever."

"Maybe on the surface. Underneath, I'm a frantic duck. So, when are you guys out of here?"

"This week is it. We'll work over the weekend and then try to get set up for business in the new location next week. What about you? What are you going to do here?"

Liz and Jenny looked at each other. Jenny had been thinking about it. She got half her salary from Tommy and had thought about how Luke was going to pay the whole thing.

"Do you think Luke's going to want me to stay out front, Liz?"

"Honey, I can't answer for him right now. I don't think he knows which end is up. My guess is yes, but don't quote me on that."

"What about you?"

Jenny and Pam looked at Liz with apprehension. They could both see the strain. Her quick wit and sassy demeanor were muted, reflecting some of the stress of her boss.

"What do you mean?"

"Are you going to stay with Luke?"

The question took Liz by surprise. Half the surprise was that she had not considered it before. She was angry at him for being in this situation, but she knew it was really not his fault. She resented having to deal with all the consequences, but she couldn't abandon him at this point. She was frustrated that there was nothing she could do to help him, knowing that if the situation were reversed that he would be rushing to her rescue. She chided herself often for leaving the night he had the appointment with Susan Weeks. If she'd stayed around, perhaps he would not be involved in this mess. What a mess!

But would she leave him?

"Of course not," she said out loud.

"You're quitting Luke?" they both spoke together.

"Of course not," she looked at them as if they were crazy. "I couldn't leave him now. Luke is… well, whatever they're saying about him now is not the man I know. He's certainly not a murderer and he didn't kill Susan Weeks. I don't know what happened but I know Luke could never have done what they're saying."

Liz's voice quivered as she formed the words. She hadn't confronted the situation as strongly as she just had. She had heard the rumors; many had asked her about things and she had encountered the prosecutor face-to-face. Still she had never thought of Luke and murder coupled together.

"It just doesn't fit," she spoke aloud again.

"Huh?" a comeback in unison.

"I know that man. I've worked with him for enough years. You know how they say, 'you think you know somebody?' Well, I do know him and I'm not going to run out on him now."

Liz spoke the words as much to herself as to the other two. The question had been forming in her for some time but she had not let it surface. Faced with the inquiry from her two working buddies, she came up with the only answer she knew she could live with. She would stay on as long as Luke wanted her. And as soon as he got back she would tell him so.

Up the street Luke kept a brisk pace. The fresh sunshine beaming down on him poured energy into his sluggish system. His listless idling began to accelerate as he pushed himself along the sidewalk. Breathe in, breathe out, he paced himself as he often did in running. He breezed past the bank, drawing in the refreshing oxygen of the brilliant spring morning.

After several blocks he felt some energy coming back. The stimulating walk reminded him of the runs he had been missing and their importance to his disposition. Running didn't just keep his body in shape, it kept his mind operating smoothly. Problems presented themselves with more clarity and keys to resolution came much better in a brain pumped full of oxygen. He would not allow anything to get in the way of that exercise from now on.

He rounded the corner by the drug store as Hays Kennedy was coming out, almost bumping into him.

"Good morning, Mr. Kennedy." Luke summoned a sociable face as he encountered the fellow lawyer. He waited for a reaction.

"Where're you headed in such a hurry, Luke?"

"Just down the street to the bank, Hays. How 'bout you?"

"Same place. A little out of town getaway to the coast this weekend left me flat busted. I need some pocket change."

With Hays' welcoming recognition, Luke slowed his pace and the two men walked down the street together. Hays Kennedy was about the same height as Luke, but a much heavier man. He'd been a wrestler in college and still carried the weight. He was in pretty good shape for a man of forty-five. His barreled chest made his foulard tie stand out from the black sport coat he wore. His light brown hair had receded enough to frame a big forehead. The overall picture exposed an aggressive style that was not afraid of the courtroom. From what Luke knew of Hays, he inclined toward the acerbic, not always a bad trait in a lawyer.

"Luke, you seem to have everything stirred up lately. You're the talk of every circle I approach. How come you get to have all this free publicity?"

Luke laughed out loud at the question. Lawyers were notorious for taking the position that it didn't matter what people were saying about you as long as they were saying something. Luke had not thought of his current status in that light. Hays' attempt at humor got the best of Luke.

"Hays, anytime you want to share any of this limelight, I'll gladly move over."

"Well, you know I'm not afraid of the spotlight. I got plenty of that in Jackson. You have to toughen up and go on, focusing on your objective."

The comment struck a chord with Luke. He did have to stand true during this attack on his character and integrity. He looked the lawyer over as he considered the last statement.

Hays was about fifteen years Luke's senior who had worked in the United States Attorney's office before returning to private practice in Hampton. Hays' practice focused mainly on the lucrative area of environmental law. He did little criminal work to the best of Luke's knowledge. Hays continued to inquire about Luke's status.

"Is it true, what I was just hearing in the drug store about them searching your office?"

When Luke did not answer immediately, Hays went on.

"That's pretty low down, especially after all this time. You know what's happening there, Luke. The coppers have sat on their butts and don't have their ducks in a row on this case and now Gafford's worried about his hide come election time. Judge Jones, too, would be my guess."

"You're probably right, but that doesn't change the fact that it's me they're trying to use in their little political gambit."

"What's your lawyer saying about all this?"

"That's a good question," was his response.

Luke hesitated for a moment but then began to pour out the misgiving he had, telling Kennedy the recent events: about Gafford's search warrant and the hearing; about Jones' antics in the courtroom and then Gafford's ludicrous mishandling of the law.

"I despise such maltreatment, Luke. Those two can make you want to commit murder. On them."

"Hays, I didn't kill anyone. I can assure you of that. The thing is, I'm beginning to wonder if I can prove that with everyone being against me. They're going to have me tried and found guilty long before we get to the trial. I don't know if an outsider can fully understand what they're capable of."

"Luke, why don't you come by my office. I'd like to talk with you more about the case."

"How about over lunch?" Luke was on a roll and eager to continue.

"I'm already booked, and the rest of my day is pretty full. Why don't you come over around five?"

"I'll be there, Hays. You can bet on it."

They shook hands and Luke breathed a sigh of relief. He wasn't sure why, but a small amount of calm settled over him as he bid farewell to Hays and struck off back to his office, forgetting about any plans to go to the bank.

Liz watched him walk through the front door and was grateful for what she immediately recognized as a change in mood and spirit. He left less than an hour ago and was back now minus the frown. She followed him up to his office.

"What'dya do, rob the bank?"

"Huh?"

"You left out of here a little while ago looking like you didn't have a friend in the world and now you're back… well, I don't want to get too carried away. I wouldn't say you're smiling, but you definitely look better. What happened?"

"The sunshine warmed me up. Got my blood to pumping. I'm ready for the day now."

"Well, good. Me, too." Liz paused for only a moment. "Listen, Luke, I'm going to stay."

"What?" Her statement caught Luke off guard. "I didn't know you were leaving."

"Well, I wasn't. I mean, I'm not now. Oh, shoot, Luke. I don't know what I'm saying. I just mean that I'm going to stick with you through this trial and all. I mean, if there is one. I hope you can get all this to go away without a trial, but if you can't, I'm with you. No matter what. I don't care what people are saying."

Silence. A calm settled in the room while both of them sat without moving. Luke knew how hard this was for Liz. He watched her Saturday face-to-face with Gafford and knew that she was frightened. Anxious.

Liz had never asked him point blank about Susan Weeks. He never tried to explain much because he never thought he had anything to explain. Now explanation seemed pointless. He looked at Liz and her imperturbable quality of fixed loyalty. She was in his corner no matter what.

"It doesn't matter to me that Tommy and Pam are leaving," she was saying. "They have nothing to do with us. Jenny, I can't speak for her. If she stays, you'll have to pay her full salary."

"Why don't you ask her to come in."

Liz stepped out of the room and came back with Jenny. Jenny looked scared, not knowing why she was being asked back to Luke's office.

"Jenny, you know Tommy and Pam are leaving this Friday. Liz has just informed me she is not leaving. You know the situation I'm in. My practice has been good but with all that's happening, who knows? I'd like you to stay with us. If you choose not to, I'll understand." Luke stopped and waited for a reaction.

Jenny sat there without expression. She looked at Liz, and recalled her words of support earlier. Her stand on Luke's behalf impressed Jenny. In the midst of all the rigmarole about Luke, Liz had made her choice based on her first hand knowledge of the man. So much of

Jenny wanted to run away from the situation, but a bigger part of her admired Liz for staying and she wanted to stay, too.

"I'll stay, Luke," she heard herself saying. "I don't have another job and don't want to look for one. I guess you're just stuck with me." She tried to laugh.

Luke laughed with her, and so did Liz. It was the first laugh out in the office in quite a while. It wasn't much, and was a little bit nervous, but Luke was so delighted in their decisions that he stood up and hugged them both.

"I appreciate this more than you two will ever know. I don't know if this is the right time, but I believe I can swing a small raise for you. Both of you, and on top of your full salary Jenny. We had a good year last year and while things aren't that good right now, I know that pretty soon we'll be back on the right track and this office will flourish. It has to with great folks like you working with me."

They beamed at each other and after another hug and some tears the two women went back to work. Luke settled into his chair and, for the first time in days, began to make some sense out of the tangle on his desk.

In no time the afternoon was over and the clock pointed to five. Luke was ready to leave right behind Liz and Jenny. They locked the door and headed to their cars. Luke never mentioned that he had another appointment. He was looking forward to talking with Hays Kennedy again.

He arrived at Hays' office as his own secretaries were leaving the building. Yes, Mr. Kennedy was expecting him and he could go right in. He walked on when Hays motioned him to take a seat while he finished the phone conversation.

"Good to see you again, Luke." Getting right to the point, he added, "There's some folks mighty hacked off about that search at your office. You told me she was never at your office or your house, either. Right."

"Yes, Hays. And I tried to tell Gafford that. I don't have anything to hide about any of this."

"I'm sure you don't, Luke, but why wasn't your lawyer at the hearing before Jones? They won that round, you know."

"He already had something in federal court in Biloxi and Jones wouldn't delay the hearing. It was stupid, really."

"It may be stupid, but do you think it wise to be letting Gafford get the jump on you like this."

"What do you mean?"

"What I mean is that there's more to winning a lawsuit than what happens at trial. Public opinion can infiltrate so pervasively that it will seep into the jury no matter how hard you try to keep it out. Gafford's trying you in that venue already. Do you think your lawyer understands that?"

"I don't know."

"Luke, to put it bluntly, this is no time to flounder. Don't you realize your life is on the line?"

Luke swallowed slowly trying to hold down the knot that formed in his stomach. His jaw tightened into a clench and his teeth gritted together. He felt a wave pass over him. Fear. Dread. Terror. As a lawyer, he was usually able to think of his circumstance in terms of hearings and arguments and justice. Hays' comment caught him a little off guard. It was a definite reality check.

"This is not a game, Luke. You need somebody up here fighting for you. Is this guy Chestillo capable of doing that? How did you get hooked up with him?"

"I, ah… " Hello, Luke, old boy, get back in the game here. Get a grip. The spinning nausea came on Luke again. He wanted to be sick, and he needed to get a grip.

"I have a friend on the coast, an old friend from school that knows him. She thought he would be the right choice. I met him and we talked. He took the case." Luke recalled his first meeting with Chestillo. It seemed like ages ago and it was only last week.

"Are you comfortable with him now after you've seen what's happened with the dog and pony show they're putting you through here?"

"I don't know, Hays. Everything has happened so fast. No, I guess I do know. I didn't like it that he wasn't here. But it wasn't his fault. He had a commitment in federal court. Jones was just unreasonable."

"Do you think that's going to change? This is an election year for him and Gafford. This is a high profile case. They're going to be playing to the media every chance they get. Law and order, you know their game. You'd better have you somebody that can stay in there and pitch with them."

"Like who?"

"Well, I've been here long enough to know the tricks of the trade in their arena. You're probably familiar with some of the skirmishes I've had with the big dogs."

Luke was. Hays represented a school teacher in a case that became a big political battle against the school board and the City of Hampton. Judge Jones should have recused himself but didn't, as he was likely to do when it didn't suit his needs. Kennedy caught him in a crossfire with the defendants that could have spelt conflict of interest for the Judge and disaster for the defendants. The case quickly settled after that for an undisclosed sum.

Hays was not afraid to defy the powers that be. Several other cases of his had been high profile where he had to stand toe-to-toe with some strong personalities and not be intimidated. Luke had not thought of using Hays before. Now he seemed a clear choice. He was right here in town. He knew the players, a very important element that Chestillo lacked. Nick may be a good lawyer but without first hand knowledge of the local terrain even the best could be hornswoggled.

"I'd like you to consider taking the case." Luke still talked about his dilemma in the abstract.

"Luke, I've not done that much criminal work but I believe I could do the job you need here."

"Does that mean you'll take it?"

"Well, I don't make a habit of stealing cases from other lawyers, but if you discharge this guy on the coast then I'll take it."

"Consider it done."

"Okay. You get whatever file he has and we'll sit down again."

"He doesn't have anything. I'm telling you he only talked with me last week. We haven't even talked on the phone. I'll get with him right away and explain the situation. I'm sure there won't be a problem."

At DeWeese Advertising that night, Jim sat alone at his desk with a bottle of scotch. The few small ice cubes from the little fridge in his bar were gone and now the plain brown liquid filled the glass without interference from ice or water. He sipped as he had been doing for quite a while. Shortly after the stroke of five he had needed a little cocktail to relax the tensions of the day and loosen his creativity for tonight's shoot.

The session tonight was wedding pictures. Not exactly his favorite subject in front of the camera but this one was different. The couple met here at DeWeese Advertising. The bride-to-be was a beautiful young girl that Jim used in some of his advertising campaigns and the groom was a football player that did modeling for a local department store client. Both were college students graduating this May. Sometime last summer they had been here at the same time and attraction sparked. Now they were getting married in June, just a couple of months away.

Tonight's pictures were a combination wedding present from Jim and an opportunity for him to put together a wedding portfolio of a different nature. The couple started off in the traditional gown of white and the tux with tails. DeWeese and the girl had gone out and cut lots of greenery for backdrops. The dogwoods were out and they looked good in pictures. He had also brought in some traditional flowers that she would be using: white roses, some calla lilies and white tulips. Together they had put together a set that rivaled a soap opera wedding. After two rolls of film on each of them and a couple together, they started a few non-traditional poses.

Her white veil was the first thing that came off. Then his tie was loosened and the white starched shirt undone to expose the tanned muscular chest underneath. He undressed his future bride adroitly for the camera, letting Jim take shot after shot of the two bodies brushing together. Their youthful ardor played well to the skilled eye of the photographer, ignoring his presence as they continued stripping off the wedding garb. Her wedding dress made a billowy layer of white as the two young frames continued.

The eye of the camera followed the long white stockings down her leg as the boy sensuously removed the garter, pausing gently in tiers of pure, undefiled silk and innocence. Jim was breathless as he felt his own body respond to the raw sensuality of the youth before him. Their energy built gradually and fervently as the couple continued on in their consummation of the marriage that would not take place for several more months. When the crescendo came to a spectacular and frantic end the two co-eds lay back in bliss on the wedding finery strewn around them.

Jim, too, was spent. His bottle of scotch was over half empty now. The performance was intoxicating and the liquor pushed him even farther. He sat behind his desk now deep in thought. The show was over and he sat there alone, drunk and sad. He wanted to do more than just watch. He wanted some love in his own life. His mind drifted to the last time he had known any tenderness. Sheer tenderness without any sexual elements. He recalled a beautiful raven-haired girl who danced around in front of his camera with such grace and style. Who touched him with more affection and love than all the sexual trysts he had ever encountered.

Oh, the trips back to New Orleans occupied him. They were a numbing distraction. The bars, the late nights and the drugs. Plenty of women. And men. But nothing would ever affect him, nothing would ever grip him like the gentlest touch from Susan Weeks. Then, in one night it was over. The pictures in the papers were hideous and the shock of it all still too hard to bear.

A rattle at the back door shook him back to reality. He popped out of his chair and raced through the big open shooting area to get to the noise.

"DeWeese, open this door. It's me."

Lambert. Damn. The last person in the world DeWeese wanted to see right now. He thought momentarily about pretending to be gone, but knew Luther could see his car outside so he took out his key and opened the steel door to let Lambert through.

"And how are you, tonight, partner," Lambert started as he came through the door. "You got any more of what's made you so drunk?"

DeWeese's appearance betrayed the amount of the bottle inside him. He didn't like Lambert seeing him like this. Hell, it was almost ten o'clock. This was his time. The man didn't own him.

"All the ice is gone, and most of the scotch." DeWeese tried to dissuade Lambert from the drink that might make him linger. "I was trying to lock up and get out of here. I've been working all evening and I'm tired."

"Yes, I saw your subjects leaving. Good looking couple. Who are they?" Lambert found his way back to the desk and noticed the near empty bottle of scotch. Without waiting for Jim's help he poured himself a slug in a coffee mug.

Through the fog, DeWeese realized that Lambert must have been outside spying on him. The two kids had been gone for thirty minutes. He shivered spontaneously. The man gave him the creeps. He didn't know why he was in business with such a criminal, other than the money. Lambert always reminded him of the money. Well, it didn't make up for the loneliness, and it would never make up for Susan.

"I was at the office today and on my desk was the note payment on this building and all the equipment. Thought I'd come by and pay my respects to my investment."

"That money was there in plenty of time," DeWeese said defensively.

"Well, yes, yes," Lambert eased himself into the chair behind the desk. "Actually, it was two days late but I think they give you a seven day grace period."

"Whatever. I've been busy. In fact, this has been a long day and I'm beat. I was just about to clear out of here. It's after ten o'clock."

DeWeese made a motion toward leaving but Lambert sat complacently. He sipped on the scotch and continued. A car alarm sounded outside the building, but quickly shut off.

"Sit down. Looks like you were right in the middle of a drink. No need to rush out. I just got here. Why are you so nervous?"

DeWeese had no interest in hanging out with Lambert or having a drink with him. The note was paid. The studio was doing well. DeWeese Advertising was a success. Thanks to the hard work and talent of Jim DeWeese. Not Luther Lambert, the low-life bastard.

"You should be proud. This place is doing well. You're getting to be quite the celebrity around Hampton, what with your California ties and all. Take any good pictures lately?" Lambert burst out with his loud, coarse laugh and slapped his knee.

DeWeese cringed at the crude, uncouth ogre and his attempt at humor. Hidden in the remarks were also the ties that bound them. DeWeese reached for the bottle of scotch and poured himself another good dose.

"So who were those good-looking kids anyway? Are you taking their picture?" Again Lambert roared and slapped his leg.

DeWeese's eyes went to the camera on his desk and then darted away.

"Yes, they're getting married. I'm doing their wedding portfolio."

He tried to respond nonchalantly but was afraid Lambert may have seen something in his eyes when he glanced at his camera. The last thing he wanted was to get embroiled in another fiasco like Lambert cooked up with Susan.

"Just some kids from over at the college that want to have a nice wedding album. She was in some ads I did for Dillard's and wanted me doing her pictures. I did a few tonight for her to have as samples. Of course, the real thing can't be done until the wedding. But she already had her dress and wanted to see how it looked. He dressed up in a tux. It was nothing, really."

"Well, I sure hate how our last deal got all messed up. That poor Weeks girl could have made you famous all over again. Too bad about her. I guess they're going to nail her killer, though. Looks like Luke Daniels. Seemed like a good kid. But I hear he got himself messed up with a bad cocaine problem. You know, that can mess a person up bad."

Again, DeWeese cringed. What was Lambert saying to him? He wondered how much Lambert knew about his time in Los Angeles, and in New Orleans. Any mention of cocaine in his presence always brought back a flood of memories of the nightmares in LA. He had been clean now for over seven years. Well, almost. Occasionally, in New Orleans, he would indulge. And, sometimes at the studio, like Halloween weekend. He dabbled alone or with friends, but nothing like the constant binges and blackouts in California. There was no way Lambert knew about New Orleans. Or could he?

Lambert had a way of knowing a lot about people. In some instances he did it just by watching his subject. People would tell you a lot if you sat back quietly and let them. They may not use words but there were many other ways to communicate. Lambert prided himself on heeding those ways to know all he could. And, of course, there were other techniques.

"Well, I see you're not very sociable tonight. I guess I'll take it on to the house. See my wife." He gave DeWeese a little grin. "You take care, now, you hear. You look like you do need to get on and get your rest. I know how it feels. But, while you're over here working, if you discover anybody that might want to do business with us, you let me know. Understood, partner?" the last bit uttered with all seriousness.

"Sure, Luther, you know I will. Partner." DeWeese tried to place as much sincerity into his response as his disposition would allow.

Lambert stood up and shook hands with DeWeese, pulling him up to go out the door in the process. But before he stood up he felt under the edge of the desk for the little bit of metal. It was there right where Mason told him it would be. And it was working, too. As was the one in the main studio. A tiny transmitter that allowed Lambert to hear all that went on in the studio. Just like he heard everything earlier in the photo session. The clicking of the camera. And, the moaning and groaning and the screams that went with it. The camera wasn't the only thing that recorded the activities of the two lovers.

Lambert had his copy of the transmission, also. The one DeWeese lied to him about. He wondered about that. He didn't like being in business with someone who lied to him. He'd have to think about that and just what to do. For now, he shook DeWeese's hand and went on home.

He didn't know everything that had gone on between Susan Weeks and DeWeese, but he knew a lot. He knew enough. And any hint of Luther's involvement was diminished from the outset. Luther's name was not on the note at the bank. He had only put in a good word for DeWeese with his dear friend Ken Wildmon. And now he was leaving for Jackson. Robert Fowler wouldn't be any problem. Luther could handle him. His love for money overruled every other concern. Yep, Luther didn't have a thing to worry about, but DeWeese had better keep up his end of the bargain in the deal. Lambert wanted more out of this than just the note being paid, and he knew more about DeWeese than he could ever imagine.

Outside the building, Luther got in his Cadillac at the same time DeWeese loaded into his sporty Lexus. They pulled away in opposite directions. About a block away, DeWeese noticed the time on the Guaranty National clock. Eleven o'clock p.m. He couldn't remember if he had put the alarm system on at the studio, but didn't want to go back for fear of running into Lambert again. He needed to be free of that man. Maybe he would have a heart attack, the big slob. DeWeese thought of how easy that would be. The scotch had his brain so sodden he couldn't think straight and could hardly drive. He could think about one thing, though. He wished old Luther was dead. His morbid thoughts continued as he careened his way home.

Back at the studio, another set of eyes had watched the two exit the building and drive away. Cody Raybern wanted to help Luke. He had never met the man, but he liked the way Jane talked about him. Must be a heck of a guy. Cody had now made several trips to Hampton and was taking a liking to his assignment which was getting more interesting with every trip. He had learned that DeWeese Advertising was owned by a man that thought he used to be a big shot in LA. He had learned about some of the places he hung out were in New Orleans. And he had learned that the boy was a player. Or thought he was. Tonight, as he was about to leave town, he made one more swing by the studio. And there were the two kids leaving. They must be in love because he thought he recognized that healthy glow about them. Then he witnessed another interesting occurrence. Luther Lambert drove up.

Cody knew Luther from years ago when Cody had been involved in an operation on the Mississippi Gulf Coast. Luther represented one of the defendants that had been under investigation. Cody had monitored the progress of the smugglers for weeks, knew right where the stuff was headed. When they felt like the operation was compromised, they moved in and arrested several parties. One of their officers died in the bust. He left the main group to pursue a lead that turned up nothing, but it cost him his life. One of those defendants hired Luther Lambert to represent him.

Now Cody was seeing him again. Isn't that a coincidence, Cody thought to himself. He watched Luther bang on the door like he owned the place and saw DeWeese let him in. Cody was pretty sure no one else was in the building so he called on some of his old skills to find out what was going on inside, not a difficult task for someone with his training. He quickly had himself rigged up to hear every word that was said. It was so easy that he did it at the same time he let himself into Luther's car to see what he could find. Interesting little tape in the crude eavesdropping setup, eons behind the equipment Cody used.

Wouldn't Nick and Jane be interested in this stuff? And, Susan Weeks had been involved. He couldn't wait to see the looks on their faces. What had these two boys been up to?

Before he left, he thought it wouldn't hurt to snoop around inside. These guys couldn't have anything sophisticated enough to slow him down. Probably just some puny alarm system put in by some local yokel. When Cody let himself in he found that DeWeese had not even remembered to turn it on, but he didn't find much else. A few pictures in a file marked Susan Weeks. Definitely a looker, Cody thought. But nothing illegal. He found an interesting little listening device under the desk in DeWeese's office and a couple in a few other strategic places which, he thought, accounted for the tape in Luther's car. He left them alone. Since he had taken the tape in Luther's car, he thought that would upset things enough.

What he didn't find were the pictures and tapes of Susan that DeWeese had in his safety deposit box at Guaranty National. No one knew those existed except DeWeese, and when Luther realized the tape in his little recorder was missing, he blamed Jerry Mason's idiocy for not loading the cassette. He never dreamt someone could have gotten into his car and taken it.

Cody was on his way back to the coast, eager to let Jane know about his find. Not much in the way of solid evidence, but a good start to take some of the attention off Luke.

CHAPTER THIRTEEN

Hays Kennedy never liked Billy Gafford. There were not many opportunities for confrontation between them because Hays didn't represent many criminals in the district. He handled a few minor infractions for his civil clients, mostly family members whom Hays was asked to help out by one of his serious clients. He recalled his last venture into that realm. Robby Clark's mother had a sexual discrimination case against the power company. When she was passed over for promotion several times she got angry. When they hired a younger male as her boss in a job that she knew well and had done for several years she hired a lawyer. That was Hays Kennedy.

In the course of her representation nineteen year old Robby was home from college one weekend, got pulled over for speeding and in the process was arrested for possession of marijuana. Momma was devastated and came to Hays for help.

Billy Gafford was tough on drug cases. He exploded before the news media with all the typical lock-em-up rhetoric and the public loved it; as long as it wasn't their teenager. Billy didn't give a damn about kids getting high but he sure loved the cameras carrying his picture into the homes of Hampton and Bedford County. That's why he was tough on drugs.

He was tough on Hays Kennedy when he came before the court with little Robby Clark. Hays wanted to impress momma with his ability to get a slap on the hand for her baby and Billy wanted to send a message that these little dope-smokin' punks would not get light treatment in his district. The two were at odds immediately. The two lawyers resorted to name-calling and ridicule before Judge Jones stepped in to placate the raging tempers.

That was their last professional encounter. Now Hays was dialing the DA's number to inform him that he would be representing Luke Daniels. He and Luke had gone over the whole scenario several times with Hays learning that the prosecutor was making a case solely on circumstantial evidence. Hays also talked to Nick Chestillo out of professional courtesy. That had gone well. Nick was nice enough about it. No, he really had nothing in his file. Yes, he had missed a hearing. No problem for Hays to take over. Let him know if he could help. That was it.

Now Hays waited for Gafford to come on the line so he could inform the prosecutor of new counsel. Hays waited with an impudent smirk, eager to advise the DA of his involvement in the case. Like a gladiator ready to do battle, Hays looked forward to the fight with Gafford. As he saw the situation, it was a no-lose proposition for him. If the verdict was not guilty Hays' reputation would escalate far-and-wide. People would talk about his skill in maneuvering the accused to freedom. The news media would want to talk with him. There may even be a book in it.

On the other hand, if Daniels was found guilty, there would be the appeal and the opportunity for publicity. The news media would still want to talk with him. And, there could even be a better book in that. Yes, this was a good case for Hays. He was ready for the fight.

"Hello, Hays. What's up?" Gafford was pleasant enough despite his loathing of Kennedy.

"Billy, how ya doing? Just checking in. I need to get with you on discovery in the Daniels case."

"What?" with a decidedly different tone.

"I'm going to represent Luke Daniels. Chestillo is out and my secretary is headed over to file my entry of appearance. You'll get your copy. So, I need to find out what your case is based on. Do I need to file a formal motion or can we consider this phone call an official request?"

"Ah, that's fine. You can have all the information we've got for discovery. So, when did this happen? What got you in the case?" The answer had to be money, Billy thought.

"Luke came to me earlier in the week and we talked a couple of times. Then he talked again with this guy on the Coast and, after that, signed up with me. You sound surprised."

Billy was surprised. Chestillo was a crackerjack criminal attorney. Billy didn't understand the switch. Hays was just a cracker. In his opinion, Hays was a cantankerous and abrasive bastard that alienated himself in all cases. Billy knew Judge Jones detested his haughty and discourteous nature. This ought to be easy, Billy thought, like shooting fish in a barrel. Hays would get the Judge hacked off and the jury irritated putting Billy in a position for smooth sailing.

"Well, that's good, Hays. Glad to be dealing with a local lawyer that understands how we do things up here. So when's your client ready to enter his guilty plea? Whaddya say, twenty years on manslaughter?"

"Very funny, Gafford. Seriously, I need to get the disc..."

"I was serious. You wait around and that offer's withdrawn. You know he's going to fry. We got the goods on him."

"Well, whatever. Give me those goods and we'll talk then. C'mon, Gafford, I've hardly talked with my client," Kennedy lied.

"Alright. Why don't you come up here and pick it up? We can talk some as you look over the material. Let me answer any questions you may have."

"How about two o'clock this afternoon."

"That'll work. See you then."

Billy put down the phone with a smile, picking it up again to buzz Wanda.

"Get the Daniels file and come in here, please."

When Wanda laid the file before him, Gafford started through it with Wanda looking on.

"Hays Kennedy will be over here at two o'clock to pick up discovery in this case. He's representing Luke now," Billy could hardly contain himself.

"Are you kidding?" Wanda couldn't believe it. She liked Luke and was surprised at such a choice. "Has he lost his mind? Kennedy doesn't do any criminal work, does he?"

"Oh, occasionally. You know, we have a thing or two. Not much. And Judge Jones can't stand him. It's great, isn't it?"

"Not if you're Luke Daniels." Despite her job, Wanda didn't want to see Luke go down. She would rather her boss lose this one. She just didn't believe Luke was guilty, but she kept her opinion to herself. This job was important to her.

"We're not going to give him all of our work product. He's not entitled to everything. Here, give him the shoe print match. The one we took from his house on the search and the picture from the smashed in door. That'll shake'em up. And the semen samples. And the fingerprints. If that doesn't dominate the jury... Whew, Daniels is going down."

Gafford could only think about the headlines he could make in this trial. There would be no plea bargain. The trial would be too sweet for his campaign. Of course, a plea could be used to his advantage, also. Save the taxpayers money because of his strength of office and investigation. Gafford could see the headlines already. Oh, what a gift!

Wanda left the office headed to the copy machine. She wished there was some way she could ease the situation Luke was in, but there wasn't. She was bound by the confidentiality of her position. That didn't mean she had to like it. Or the joy her boss took in his attack. Still, if Luke didn't kill the girl... somehow, Wanda just couldn't accept it.

When Kennedy arrived, the discovery package was ready. Gafford courteously delivered him to the conference room where he could look over the information in the prosecutor's presence, giving Billy the opportunity to observe any reaction to the evidence against Daniels. The effect of the bulk of papers was cumulative and often helped the DA begin his best work in arranging a guilty plea. Gafford liked that outcome, less work preparing for trial. Just herd them into the courtroom and have Judge Jones assign guilt and dispense a sentence. Trials were simply too damn much work for Billy.

Except, of course, in an election year. The coverage of a trial of this magnitude would secure better exposure than he had money to buy. He settled into the driver's seat as Kennedy perused the documents. All he had to do was sit back and cruise toward re-election.

Hays Kennedy remembered his feelings about Gafford. Their artificial courtesy belied the deep-set apprehension that played in this game of cat-and-mouse. The Office of District Attorney carried with it an air of credibility that William P. Gafford was merely upholding the law on behalf of the people. Here in his presence, Hays could experience the authority of the office. Gafford had a job to do and was going to do it.

"There's a copy of everything in my file for you. You know, it's in our best interest to let you know where we're coming from so this matter may be resolved in the most appropriate way. I know you've got a tough job, Hays. Luke was a friend of mine, too. But the facts in front of you don't lie. I mean, who would have ever thought the man was guilty of rape."

"Rape? He's not charged with rape."

"No, no, of course not. But from the evidence you can see the violence that girl endured. Just look at the coroner's report."

The coroner's report was intense. Murder scenes were rarely pretty and the coroner reported all the gory detail with emphasis on the carnage. They knew that at some point they could be called on to testify so they made their case early from the scene of the crime.

"I'll tell you what it looks like." Billy waited for the words to sink into his target.

"What's that?" Kennedy was hoping to pick up some insight into the prosecutor's perspective, as he often did with defense attorneys in civil cases.

"Drugs. Had to be. You can see from the report of the autopsy the intensity, the brutality of the attack. You know, cocaine can make a man go wild." Gafford watched the words sink into Luke's lawyer.

"And, what makes you think there were drugs involved? Is there some evidence of drugs in this file? The girl's autopsy?"

"No, but Daniels is a known drug user. Really a dealer. We've got tapes of him making drug deals."

"You've got what? Let me see them. I want to hear what they say."

Gafford could see clearly that this last part had taken Hays by surprise. Billy was on thin ice and he knew it. Daniels was not on trial for drugs.

"He's not on trial for drugs. He's on trial for murder. And we have a strong case. His semen is in the girl and on the bed. His fingerprints are all over her house. How much plainer does it have to be? The guy killed her. He's not on trial for drugs. But if he takes the stand with that lame-brain story of his I'll use the drug tapes to impeach him."

"I want to hear the tapes."

"Is Daniels going to testify?"

"I can't answer that right now."

"Well, I don't know what I'll use in rebuttal, either. How can I know that until trial? You know rebuttal evidence is not discoverable."

Hays wasn't really sure. Not in a criminal trial. He had a lot of work to do, that was for sure. And he needed to talk with Luke about this drug stuff, too. Sitting here any longer was a waste of time. He had a copy of the file. He could go over it with Daniels later. Hays stood up to leave.

"If you have anything that exonerates your client, you know you are bound to turn it over to me, as well." Billy could tell he had agitated Kennedy. He decided to keep the heat on as they moved toward the exit.

"I'm telling you, if your client takes the witness stand, we'll burn him with his drug dealings. Of course, he doesn't have to but... well, you just let me know."

Kennedy mumbled out a departing word as the elevator shut behind him. This thing was taking on a whole different character. His analysis that Luke would walk had been shaken by Gafford's spiel. He was furious at Luke for not telling him about the drugs. How dare he try to hoodwink his own lawyer. How could he adequately represent him if they were not totally honest with one another. When Hays got to his office, the first thing he would do was get Luke in there face to face.

"I'm telling you there are no drugs, dammit. What kind of complete fool do you take me for? Do you think I would lie to my own lawyer. Hell, I'm a lawyer, too. I know the importance of telling you everything."

Luke stood in front of Hays' desk with his voice raised to a shout. He was churning inside with anger at that prick, Gafford, for telling such a lie. He was furious at Hays for falling for such an obvious attempt to blur the real facts.

"Look, Luke. I'm your lawyer. You can tell me the truth. I'm not here to pass judgment and you must understand that I've got to know all the facets of your life if I'm going to adequately represent you. Don't leave me hanging out to dry on something like this. Those tapes could make us look pretty bad at trial.

"I'm telling you there are no tapes because I've not made any drug deals."

Luke screamed the words at Kennedy as if shouting loudly would make him believe that Luke was telling the truth. Hays watched Luke's features reflect the intensity of the words. He thought about Gafford's words that cocaine could make a man go crazy.

"Are you still using cocaine, Luke."

"Goddammit, Hays, have you not heard anything I've said!" Luke pounded his fist down on the desk, hitting several things and knocking them flying.

"Look, Luke, you don't have to get violent about it. I'm on your side." Hays watched Luke cautiously.

"I'm not getting violent. Hell, I feel like I'm being accused of beating my wife. Are you still beating your wife? No. Oh, when did you quit." Luke knew the display in front of Hays was not in his best interest but, damn, he shouldn't have to defend himself to his own lawyer.

"Let's move on, we can come back to this another time. There's plenty of stuff here in black-and-white that we need to get clear on."

Luke was ready to move on, but he didn't care to come back to this subject another time. He expected Hays to believe him the first time. He was not in the habit of lying about anything he did and he didn't appreciate having to restate his position to his own lawyer.

Hays handed him a copy of the coroner's report and they read over it together. Hays had his secretary make an additional copy of everything for Luke. They continued through the documents with Luke explaining his account of the facts as they related to the findings at the scene of the crime. For three hours they pored over documents and details and explanations until Luke was exhausted. Finally, they were both too tired to continue. They shook hands and took to their own cars to leave. Hays stood by his vehicle as Luke cranked up and drove away. His brain sifted through the different components of the case that had been piled on him today. Nothing stuck. There was too much and his brain was too tired. He had to let it all go until another time.

Judge Jones was a politician. He had to be elected to the position of Circuit Court Judge every four years. He was now looking to be elected to his third. He spent a good bit of time during his four years working toward reelection. His judicial performance was tempered with a finely tuned sense of the political winds. This time would be no exception. He polished his relationships with those that could help him politically and financially. Jones and his wife were from old established families of Bedford County that had left them a wealth of heritage and capital. Their families lived comfortable lives and acquired property which had passed on down to Wendel and Mary Margaret. Between the two of them their portfolios of stocks and bonds, real estate, gold, and other commodities made them fairly strong financially.

Jones didn't like spending his own money on politics, however. He preferred the contributions of his many benefactors: the supporters he courted and groomed during his time in office in order to call on their backing at election time.

That time was nigh. Monday was the filing deadline for all candidates. There had been talk of an opponent but it stayed quiet. Most lawyers didn't want to enter a race against a sitting judge that could later be hearing their cases if he won the race. While the law of electing judges was designed to make them representative of the people, it invariably had the opposite effect. It was difficult to get anyone of any caliber to run against a sitting judge because of the politics. If they didn't win, their practice would suffer.

No one understood this better than Wendell Garmon Jones, III. In his first run for the judgeship, he had defeated an incumbent that had alienated one too many lawyers. When the disgruntled members of the bar rallied behind Jones, he narrowly defeated his opponent. In his second race the crafty Jones had gone uncontested. Now up for his third term he had eight years of politicking under his belt to pull all the right endorsements.

Unfortunately for the Judge, all lawsuits are adversarial. Every time there's a winner, there is also a loser. In Jones' masterful efforts to keep his mystic finger guiding him to winners with clout he also made some enemies in the losers. It was inevitable and those losers were a thorn in his side. He often liked to bluster about how the losers were just that, but this was not always the case. Some of those Jones categorized as losers kept on keeping on and gained in strength. Enough strength to support another candidate, and they remembered the drubbing they got from Jones some time back. So did Jones.

There had been some talk about another candidate in the judges' race. Jones had done his best to ferret it out and squelch it; to pull in his support early with various and sundry methods. If he could just get past Monday, things would be alright. The right words in the right place could work to discourage any potential candidates over this weekend and get him smooth sailing into another four year term.

This state of affairs brought him to a meeting that Friday afternoon in the office of Luther Lambert. Luther considered himself a political guru who carried some weight in the minds of many who sought office in Hampton and Bedford County. His expertise in the field of political discernment came in large part from his money. It was easy to predict the outcome of an election when one side had an abundance of funds over the other. Having the best campaign manager, the best commercials, the slickest ads, the most workers, all lent heavily to which way an election went. These things took money. And, Luther had money. Lots of it.

A few years the junior, Jones had always been a bit leery of Lambert. They were friends and had been for many years, particularly during the eight years of Jones' judgeship. Their wives were fast friends, spending many hours together working for countless local organizations and in trips to Jackson, New Orleans and Florida. Eloise Lambert had the time and money to spare and Mary Margaret Jones loved the little extras that being a judge's wife brought.

Jones telephoned his wife from Luther's office to tell her of his late meeting. Don't worry about supper. We'll go out later. Some place special, he declared. Some place with lots of voters to glad hand, he thought.

Luther stepped into his conference room where Jones was finishing up on the phone. "Wendell, how good to have you down here," Luther extended his hand to the Judge.

"Always good to see you, Luther."

The pair shook hands and took seats at the conference table. Behind Luther was Janet Hammond, his long time office manager. Judge Jones greeted her warmly. They had known each other for many years, Jones being only a few years older than Janet.

"Janet, why don't you get us something to drink. We've got coffee or cokes. Or maybe something a little stronger. How 'bout a little bourbon and coke?"

"Make it bourbon and water and you've got a taker. After all, it's after five on Friday night. I guess one drink won't hurt the old judge's reputation too much."

"Certainly not here. Janet, I'll have the same."

Janet left the two discussing the weather and returned shortly with their drinks. The rest of the office was empty except for young Wilson who popped his head into the conference room on his way out. He and the Judge shook hands. Wilson hung around with small talk acting as if he might stay until his father gave him a look that indicated that this was to be a private meeting. With his feelings hurt and looking very pitiful he slinked on to the back door and headed out to parts unknown.

Luther wondered just where his son might be going. He knew the boy was probably not going home. There was a distinct air emitting from that household that Luther didn't like. He procrastinated over talking with Wilson about it, afraid of what he would learn. Right now his attention needed to be on a different matter. He moved his eyes back to Jones who had been watching him.

"Children, what do you do?" Lambert laughed heartily.

"Yeah, I know what you mean. That boy of mine is a doozy. We're just about to survive his high school years. You know he's a senior now. Playing baseball is his strong suit. His grades are decent but baseball is the love of his life. Thank goodness he'll be graduated before this election gets underway."

Jones wanted to get the conversation around to what Luther knew about this election. He knew Luther wanted to keep him in the judgeship, and that interest kept Luther attentive to the developments of other candidates.

"What are you hearing on this election, Luther?"

"Well, Judge, you know, it's hard to be in a position such as yours without making some enemies in the process. There are some lawyers that feel aggrieved. I've been hearing that some of them are trying to get together a candidate." Luther watched his words sink into the Judge.

"They're trying to keep it pretty quiet. I think they'd like to run in there Monday and get their man qualified at the last minute. You know, keep them out of your displeasure 'till the last minute."

"Who do you think it's going to be?" Jones' distress crept into his voice. He had hoped for smooth sailing into another four year term without the necessity of campaigning, of the kowtowing and bootlicking the contest would take. Now he was learning from Lambert that the race was on.

"My information is that Nelson's going to run. You know those boys down the street have been talking to several different lawyers trying to find someone they could support against you. I heard they talked to Jack Raybern and he turned them down."

The boys down the street were a group of plaintiff's lawyers that were at odds with Judge Jones. They felt he was too Republican for their blood and that his rulings against them were unfounded and based on getting the support of the big defense firms with all the money. His leanings were not without costs. Jones' decisions were based on who could give him the most support, but now the other side was rallying. They were pressing another candidate into the race. Jones was rankled. Just wait 'till the bastards showed their face in his courtroom again.

"Of course, I don't think you have anything to worry about. I don't see how Nelson could be a viable candidate against you. My guess is Jack wouldn't run because he knows you can't be beat."

Never hurt to blow a little smoke the Judge's way. Build him up a little, Lambert thought. Best to keep him worried. That way he could be more use to Luther's interests.

"Still, you never can tell about an election. You know how fickle the public can be. You'll have to run a strong campaign but you know I'll help you any way I can, Judge."

The sparkle in Lambert's eye told Jones a lot. He could count on Luther for some financial muscle. His own and the others he could pull in. He could also count on Luther's connections to keep him informed. That network was better than the best marketing research.

"What you need, Judge, is some good exposure. Some cases that would get a lot of publicity with you being real judicial. Flowing robes and all that. Get people talking about you and they'll overlook the opponent. Have you got anything like that coming up?"

"There's a medical malpractice case against Bedford General coming up that should get to trial before the election. The plaintiffs are from Jasper County. You know, that's way out of my district. And their lawyer's not from around here, either. All the support in that case should be behind the local employer. The news media will run with it big time if I give them the leeway. I'll be able to look judicial in that one."

"What about criminal matters. You know this law and order thing's big right now. The public wants a judge that's tough on crime."

"Well, I've always had that image. There's plenty of criminal cases that I can pull in."

"Any big ones?"

"Well, there's the Daniels case."

"Oh, yeah, I'd forgotten about that. That's a scary one, isn't it. I've been hearing what he did to that poor girl. It's just a shame, and him trying to still practice law. Well, I guess it's true what they say about drugs. It's ruining our country."

"What do you mean?"

"Well, here Daniels was an up-and-coming attorney with a bright future and then he let himself get mixed up in drugs. Now a girl is dead because of it. It's just awful. People on cocaine can do scary things. Sometimes they have blackouts and never even remember; or don't want to remember. You see someone like that and it scares you. You know, how close it is. Why, I don't know what I'd do if my Wilson got himself caught up in that kind of life. I don't have to tell you, what with your son going off to college next year."

"Well, I just tell you, Judge. I, for one, am damn glad that we here in Hampton have a Judge like you that won't stand for such malarkey. You send 'em a strong message."

Somehow, Jones felt like he had missed something in the conversation. They were talking about the election and the next thing they were off on drugs. Jones didn't quite make the connection. Except that his strong stand against drugs would be good for his reelection, and that Luther was implying that drugs were somehow involved in the Weeks case. That much he did understand."

"So, who's going to be running your campaign?"

"I'll probably do the bulk of it. It's hard to find someone you can really trust."

"I've got an idea. Why don't you talk to Jim DeWeese? That agency of his is doing some bang up business, I understand. He had some experience in California. I'll bet he could put you together a hell of a campaign."

"I guess the main thing is to see who gets into the race on Monday. Don't you think that will affect our strategy?"

"Indeed. Why don't I do some checking over the weekend and maybe we can squelch this thing before Monday. Perhaps there won't even be a race," Luther responded to the Judge again with the twinkle in his eye.

"That would be great. A lot less stress on the judiciary." Jones chuckled heartily and finished off his drink.

"Here, let's get you another one of those. Come on back here to the kitchen and we'll catch the news. See if there's any great breaking story for Hampton. I want to see what the fishing's like for the weekend."

In the back room of the office of Luther Lambert the bottle of bourbon came out for a second drink and the news appeared on the television. The Judge and his host settled down around the TV and talked about the good looking news anchor. About fishing and families and the politics finally faded away for a while.

Saturday morning found Luther back at his office early making a call to Jerry Mason. The ringing at the other end of the line shook Jerry out of a deep sleep. Doris was snuggled next to him with arms and legs entwined. She moaned and groaned as he picked up the receiver and gave a barely audible hello.

"Oh, hi, boss. Yeah, I'm up."

Damn, that must be Lambert, she thought. Who else would Jerry be calling boss? And who else would be calling them at, what. She looked over at the clock. Shit, seven o'clock on a Saturday morning. Despite the fact that her husband was a private detective and subject to odd hours, she hated to lose him on a Saturday morning. Again.

Doris could feel a fight brewing deep inside her. She was all too aware that the majority of her husband's business came out of the law office of Luther T. Lambert. But that didn't mean she had to like his being jerked out of her bed. It was raining outside and she wanted to stay in bed with her man. She could tell from the tone of the phone conversation that this would not be the day.

Jerry hung up the phone and rolled back over in bed, trying to snuggle back to Doris. The reception was less than he had hoped for.

"You've got to go this morning, don't you?" Doris asked sullenly.

"Not right this minute. I've got a little time." Jerry tried to snuggle closer.

Doris knew exactly what that meant. Long enough for him but not for her. She wanted the whole morning. She could feel herself bristle at his touch. She didn't even want his touch now. She wiggled away from him.

"Fine, be that way." Jerry responded with hurt feelings. He turned back to his side of the bed and sat up.

"Why did you even answer the phone, anyway?" Doris was getting madder by the moment.

"Look, Doris, you like to eat, don't you? You like for me to make the house payment, don't you? Then I have to work. That's all there is to it." Jerry leaned back in the bed and kissed Doris on the arm.

"Look, baby, I don't want to have to get out in this weather either, but the man needs me. I need him to keep needing me. This is probably a little something, but my dependability keeps getting me the big somethings. You know that."

Doris could do nothing but let out the cold shoulder, brushing back Jerry's attempt at a tender kiss. She was mad now, and not even really sure why, other than she wanted something this morning and now she couldn't get it because of Luther Lambert. She stood up and grabbed her robe.

"I'll go put some coffee on," she said curtly.

"Don't bother," Jerry called to her as she huffed out of the bedroom.

Jerry stepped into the bathroom to splash cold water on his face before going in the closet to get dressed. He scrambled around trying to find something to put on in the cramped space. There were shoes all over the floor. Several pieces of clothing had fallen off hangers and were on the floor, as well. His agitated state with Doris only added to the confusion he felt in the cluttered mess found in the closet. He flung several shirts out the door and onto the floor of the bedroom before finding a suitable one. The jeans he finally came across were not ironed so he threw them out on the bed also. He settled for a pair of khakis and then started the task of shoes.

By this time he was furious, bordering on having a temper tantrum. He hurled several pair of shoes out the door of the closet. He wanted a pair of boots but they were not there. Damn Doris. Why couldn't she keep this house in better order, since he had to work all the time. He didn't want the rain ruining any of his good shoes so he settled on a pair of tennis shoes, sat on the bed to put them on and then bounded out to the kitchen.

Doris had settled some from her anger but Jerry was in a frenzy now. She had him a cup of coffee that he tried to refuse, but then, thinking better of it, took the cup with a quick thanks before leaving out the door. No goodbye, no word, no nothing.

Doris stood in the kitchen with tears streaming down her cheeks. She watched Jerry back out of the driveway and then disappear down the street. Raindrops spattered against the window and then rolled down in big beads like the ones that continued down her face. Wandering around the house, Doris didn't know what to do with herself now. She was miserable. The tears slowed until she reached the bedroom and then they broke again.

The room was a mess. Clothes were everywhere. Sobs worked through her body now and she eased herself down on the bed for support. After a time of staring around the room, the tears stopped. She picked up a shirt and folded it neatly. And then another. Straightening the room got her busy and took her mind off her emotions. Jerry did have a lot of clothes. As she did. And shoes. Good lord, just look at the shoes he had thrown around. This closet had needed some order for a while and now was as good a time as any, she thought. She pulled out some more shoes and tried to organize the ones that were there. There were boots and loafers and tennis shoes. Dress shoes and work shoes.

She decided to do her own side first. When she finished that, she started on Jerry's. There were too many shoes in the closet. She needed Jerry to pick out the ones he didn't wear anymore and let her have a garage sale. There were several pairs of tennis shoes she hadn't seen him wear in ages. She held up a pair of running shoes from the back of the closet that looked almost new. She hadn't seen him running, except when Luther Lambert called. Jerry was always talking about getting into shape, going to the gym. Doris brushed them off good and put them in the line with the others so maybe he would remember he had them and wear them some more. When she finished with the shoes, she lined up the shirts and then the pants. She saw that the jeans needed ironing. That probably made Jerry mad earlier.

She took herself back to the kitchen where she got out the ironing board, fixed herself another cup of coffee and turned on the TV. Having the room cleaned up and all his clothes put up neat would be a good project for the morning. Maybe Jerry would be home before long and they could pick up in a better place than where they left off.

Jerry was at Luther's office. This project wouldn't take long, according to Luther.

"I need your help on a little something. You know this election thing is coming up this summer."

"Yeah, looks like it could heat up, too. Our buddy Gafford and the Judge could both have opponents."

"Yes, that is of some concern. Jones was by here last night trying to tie me up. I'm going to have to support Jones. We got too many things ridin' in his court between now and August."

"So what about this other fella that's running? Nelson."

"Well, that's just it. He hasn't qualified yet but he probably will Monday. Jones has made some enemies in his eight years on the bench. His rulings are sometimes, how shall I say, a little obvious. He's made some lawyers mad, and they have families. So do the criminal defendants."

"One thing about old Wendell Garmon, he's tough on crime."

"That's what he wants people to think. He's tough on crime because his political barometer tells him that's what people want to hear. On the other hand those criminal defendants have families, sometimes big families with lots of voting age relatives and friends who all think their boy should get a break."

"So, you think Nelson might have a shot?"

"I don't know," Lambert spoke the words slowly and drawn out. "But lawyers have to watch that sort of thing. I sure don't want to get caught with all my eggs in one basket."

"So what are you thinking?"

"I've got this little project for you. I need you to go over to Nelson's camp and poke around a little. Let's see what their thinking is."

"I thought you said he wasn't even decided about running yet."

"I said he hadn't qualified yet. The deadline's Monday, but I have a feeling he's going to do it. I want you to take this envelope over there. Don't give it to anybody but Nelson."

Jerry took the envelope. He wanted to ask what was in it but before he did Lambert continued.

"It's some money. They'll know where it's from. It should loosen up their tongues, too. See what they have to say. This way, regardless of the outcome of the election, we'll be clear. I don't want him to get the idea we won't work with him."

Mason folded the envelope and put it in his pocket. It didn't fold easily. It had to be hundred dollar bills and a bunch of them. Maybe a couple of thousand. Pretty hefty donation to a candidate that wasn't even registered to run yet but Jerry didn't get paid to ask too many questions. Or give too many answers, other than the ones he knew Lambert wanted to hear.

And Lambert knew what he was doing. Most of the time. Jerry would make the delivery and then do a nice clean report about Nelson and his supporters and their intentions toward the race for Circuit Judge. For that he would get paid.

"Oh, and one other thing. There's a couple of kids doing some work for DeWeese Advertising. You've seen 'em. I think they're students out at the college or something. See what their story is. The girl's a real looker. The boy's a football type. Real muscular. Check them out for me."

"Sure thing, boss." Jerry Mason had learned to take Lambert's suggestions without too many questions, either. The reasons would usually flow in later. For now all he had to do was take the money and see Nelson, then maybe he could get back to Doris.

Rita Lambert was up early herself this Saturday morning. She had Arlita scheduled to come to her house that day for some spring cleaning. There was a lot of extra cleaning that needed to be done and Saturday was the best time. Wilson was out of town at a seminar and the kids spent the night away. Arlita showed up at eight ready to get started, bringing along her eldest daughter to help out with the chores.

"Okay, let's begin at the top and work our way down. We'll go from the back of the house forward. I've pulled out a bunch of clothes from my closet and Wilson's that I want to clear out. Take them to Good Will or something. Arlita, maybe some of them you can use. Let's move them all up to the kitchen table and you can go through them."

They worked at a good clip for three solid hours before Rita declared lunch time. Her helpers said they would work on through lunch, but the lady of the house would not hear of it.

"I want the refrigerator cleaned out, also. There's some good leftovers in there that we need to see about. Come on."

In a matter of minutes Rita had a feast laid out. Arlita's eldest, Roseanne, was fourteen years old, a growing girl with a healthy appetite. She was almost the same size as her mother. They all pulled up bar stools to the counter and grazed over the spread that spilled out of the fridge.

"Lordy, Miss Rita, there's no way we can eat all of this. You put out too much."

"I want the refrigerator cleaned. We can't do it with all this stuff in there. What we don't eat I'm going to throw out and then go to the grocery store."

The three girls ate their lunch and talked freely. Rita was having a good time. She could-n't help but notice Roseanne eyeing the pile of clothes that accumulated on the kitchen table.

"Roseanne, I'll bet there's some things in here that would fit you. I'm not as young as I used to be, but I still like to buy young clothes. Then when I get then home I feel silly wear-ing them. Let's take a look and see what's in here."

Rita ignited a gleam in Roseanne's eye. She was eager to dig into the pile of clothes. Arlita got into the act also and before long they were having a ball. They started trying things on with Rita feigning offense that the things never looked as good on her as they did on Roseanne and her mother. The two were thrilled with their new finds and Rita was thrilled for them. She would much rather see them off her hands and their enjoying them. The shar-ing gave everyone a closeness that lingered into the afternoon. Finally, the two older women tackled the kitchen while Roseanne was sent upstairs with clean sheets for the beds.

"Arlita, that's a good girl you've got there."

"I suppose you're right. She does me well. She makes good grades in school. I worry about her, though, so many tough decisions for kids these days. And, without a man in the house, it's tough on me."

"I thought you had a man around. What happened to Willie?"

"Willie Terrel? Oh, he's still around. But he's not their daddy and we're not married. 'Course, he's been more of a daddy to them than their own. That sorry no count don't help atall. Last time they even seen or heard from him was when he breezed through here from Atlanta."

"Do you think you and Willie will ever get married?"

"I don't know. He's got a little trouble to work out."

"What is it?"

"Oh, he was out one Saturday night. Not with me, mind you. If he had he wouldn't a got into this mess. Anyway, him and another dude got into a squabble and Willie cut the boy pretty bad. He says it was self-defense but they got him charged with aggravated assault, just the same. According to his lawyer, he could get up to twenty years. He was in a little trou-ble back when he was a kid and they use that with this one. I don't know about all that stuff."

"Maybe, I could help, Arlita. I'd talk to Wilson for him and see what he could do, if you want. Who's his lawyer now?"

"Mr. Luke Daniels. And, no, I wouldn't want you talking for him on my account. Besides, Willie thinks the world of Mr. Luke. He wouldn't trade lawyers for anything. He does some work for Mr. Luke, too. And, Willie ain't got no money to pay another lawyer."

Rita felt herself smart at the mention of Luke's name. She could almost see his face, the way he looked at Shoney's. God, he was a handsome man.

"That Luke's a handsome man," she heard herself saying without thought. The look she got back from Arlita was of surprise. Quickly adding, "He's a good lawyer, too. I know him through different functions with the bar." Rita's words fumbled out of her mouth.

Arlita was not as educated as her employer here or some of the other high-falutin' folks for whom she worked. She struggled to take one course each semester at the community college. But she was not a fool, either. She knew the look she had just witnessed on Rita Lambert. She saw a spark. Ms. Rita better watch herself or there'd be trouble. That family she was married into was not one you'd want to cross.

Rita tried to quickly pass off the flush she felt by thinking of the work at-hand.

"I'm glad to have this oven cleaned, though. The whole kitchen is starting to shine."

Rita moved around the room with sounds of exhaustion. Arlita continued to finish the oven and gather up the cleaning supplies while watching Rita out of the corner of her eye. She knew Rita Lambert was not happily married. Working so closely with her as they cleaned the house let Arlita see things. She'd worked in some other houses through the years where the man paid too much attention to his work and left his wife out in the cold. And, where the woman was too busy to give any attention to her man. Arlita knew the look. Rita never said anything outright, but there were a lot of things that a woman could just tell.

This was not a happy house. It was beautiful with lots of money to make things right, but Rita Lambert was miserable. There was a void in her life that needed filling. And that only spelled one thing. Trouble.

Arlita considered the difference in their situations. Arlita had five kids, no husband and no money. Rita had two kids, a successful husband and lots of money. 'Course, all this didn't appear as pretty a picture when viewed in the light of having to live with Wilson Lambert. Anytime Arlita came into contact with him she felt uncomfortable. Occasionally, when she was cleaning the office, he would be around. He was sometimes still at home when she arrived to help Ms. Rita. He was always arrogant, always condescending. Rude. Despite the fact that he was a fairly handsome man, his gruff personality and haughty nature made him unbearable. Arlita hated to be around him for five minutes. She couldn't imagine how anyone could live with him. She saw him on several occasions treat Rita with such disrespect and contempt that it made Arlita wonder how there could be any love between them. The look of hate she often observed in Rita revealed her inner heart.

Arlita thought about the fine house they lived in; about all the beautiful furnishings that she helped keep clean and neat. It was so different from the small three bedroom house she lived in with her five children. Yet, Arlita was basically happy and Rita was the miserable one. This was a strange world. Arlita shook her head and kept on cleaning.

Rita scurried around the kitchen busying herself with wiping here and there. The flush had left her face but Luke Daniels was still on her mind. She recalled the tenderness in his voice when she saw him at the gas station. She winced at the memory of a sore eye from a tussle with Wilson.

Wilson. The bastard. His inattention was a relief. Their relationship had never been strong. Now it was so cold that she felt nothing. Not hate. Just indifference. Inside, she longed to be touched, to be held, to be loved, but not by Wilson. The control she watched his father exert made her almost pity him. Almost, but not quite. Not quite because she had to endure it with him. What she wouldn't do to be able to escape. To run. If it weren't for the children, she would be gone. Maturity, influenced by the agony of a life in the Lambert clan, had taught her that as a young girl she should not have given a damn about those awful pictures. She could have chalked it up to youthful ignorance and gone on. Her parents would have gotten over it. There would have been pain, but not so much that they wouldn't all have survived and gone on with healthy lives. Not nearly as much pain as a life as a Lambert.

Now she couldn't leave because of the children. She knew without a shadow of a doubt that Luther Lambert would immediately tell her children what a slut their mother was. She would never be able to convince them otherwise. Those pictures would suddenly reappear in any divorce action. What lawyer could she ever get to represent her in this town anyway? The nightmare of leaving Wilson would be much worse than the nightmare of living with him. She would stay. Miserable as she was, she would stay.

She stood by her kitchen window staring out into the beautiful backyard, manicured so perfectly; at the pool with the exquisite patio furniture around it; at the gazing ball in the flower bed blooming abundantly with spring flowers, touched lightly by drops of water from the light afternoon shower sent out by their irrigation system. As she looked at all the beauty surrounding her in the room with the maid and her daughter working to make everything shine, a tear formed in her eye and trickled down the cheek of the former beauty queen from Ole Miss.

Arlita watched from behind. She was careful not to stare. That went with the territory. She just observed. She felt certain that Ms. Rita had forgotten she was even in the room. She noticed the woman's slumped shoulders and could have sworn there were tears in her eyes. Arlita's heart went out to her despite the obvious contrast in their worlds.

Right at this moment, Rita Lambert stood at the window detached from her surroundings like a woman who had nothing. Her frame slumped under the weight of the extra poundage that crept onto her after the second child, a beautiful woman with no reason to make her care about her appearance. A load of sadness dumped on her spirit hiding the beauty within.

That was the kindred spirit that she shared with Luke Daniels. From their few brief encounters, she had come to realize that he didn't deserve what had been dumped on him. She wished she could help him. But she couldn't even help herself.

Arlita didn't have time to put on any extra weight. Even after five babies her body was back in almost the same shape as before she had the children. Running to take care of them, running between two jobs, all her running left little time to be fat. She was proud of herself for looking so good at thirty-two. If she could just hold out a little longer, she'd have a college degree and her babies would be big enough to take care of themselves. Roseanne would finish high school about the same time as Arlita finished her degree work, and then her life would be different. With hard work she would make it.

CHAPTER FOURTEEN

Luke woke Sunday morning to the sound of a lawn mower outside. He cursed the neighbors for their early bird ways before realizing that the mower was in his yard. He twisted around in bed to see that the clock said eight. Not that early, he guessed, for someone who wanted to enjoy the day. He would have liked to have avoided the day altogether, but now, what the heck was Willie doing over here this early and on a Sunday morning no less? His brain awoke enough to start to understand the situation and realized it didn't make any sense for Willie to be over here that early. If it was Willie. Luke scrambled up out of bed to look out a window. Yep, it was Willie, alright, riding along on his big green machine, smiling from ear-to-ear. He waved grandly when he saw Luke's face in the window.

He must be drunk, Luke thought. Why else would he be over here so early on a Sunday morning? Damnit, haven't I got enough problems without a drunken client showing up in my yard on Sunday morning. Luke grabbed some shorts from the dresser and stumbled to the front door bare-footed. Outside on the porch he motioned for Willie to come over. Without alighting from the mower, Willie turned the big machine toward the porch and pulled right up to the shrubbery before killing the engine, allowing the Sunday morning silence to settle back down.

"Willie, what the hell is wrong with you? Have you lost your mind? Don't you know it's Sunday? Most people think this is their day off."

"Well, boss man, I just had to get over here to see you and I thought, as long as I was comin' this way, I might as well bring my stuff along and take care of your yard."

"What do you mean you had to see me?"

"Well, you's my lawyer, ain't you?"

"Well, yeah, but that usually applies during normal business hours. Why did you have to see me this morning? You haven't landed yourself in some other trouble, have you?"

"Oh, no. Nothing at all. In fact, I just got out of trouble."

"What do you mean?"

"Mr. Jones died last night."

"Who?"

"Roselle Jones. You know, that nigger that jumped on me and I had to cut 'im."

"Yeah? What happened?"

"Him and one of his buddies was out last night with two gals. They's headed to the coast. His buddy was driving when him and the girl in the front got into a fight. Roselle was in the back seat makin' out with his woman. Anyway, they swerved off the road and hit a bridge. The car flipped out over the bridge and killed the three of them. The only one lived was the girl Roselle was with. The rest of them died. Roselle was thrown from the car and decapitated. Cut his head right off, they tell me. Serves him right, the sorry bastard. He wun't no good, anyway."

"Who told you all this?"

"The girl that lived, she stayed next door to my auntee. They was all up with her last night. Then my auntee called me first thing this morning. Don't this make me out of trouble?"

"Well, maybe." Luke tried to think like a lawyer. "They probably don't have a case if they don't have a witness; don't have a victim. I'll have to talk to the DA's office."

At the mention of the DA, Luke's manner changed. He was glad for Willie, but reminded of his own situation. Hell, the way Gafford had been acting, he'd probably try to prosecute Willie without any witness. Anything to go after Luke seemed to be his current modus operandi.

"We'll see, Willie. We'll just see. I'll talk to them tomorrow and get back to you. Better yet, why don't you come by my office late tomorrow afternoon."

"Sounds good to me. For right now, I'll just keep gettin' ya' yard all cleaned up pretty."

Willie touched the starter on the big riding mower and took off around the house in a roar of engine and blade. The yard was starting to look good already, Luke thought. He breathed in the fresh aroma of newly cut grass with a smile, a childhood memory coming to him, cutting yards around the neighborhood. He looked around noticing some of the shrubbery should have been trimmed already. Luke had been too occupied with other things, but the calendar was about to flip over to May and it would be too hot to get much growth if they waited any longer.

Willie was going to get to work on that, too. Maybe a little work in the yard would be just the ticket for clearing Luke's head. When Willie finished cutting the grass, they worked together for several hours and Luke began to relish the grooming of his home. The exhausting labor enervated Luke and sweat poured from every part of his body. He hadn't had a work-out like this in weeks. Willie had fertilizer they put out in all the right spots and by the end of the day there was a huge pile of leaves and limbs and debris at the back of his lot.

Luke's house looked great, and he felt good even though he was a little sore in spots. It was good to feel alive. He hadn't felt that way in quite some time. This was a good start, Luke thought. It was time to get some other parts of his life straightened out, too.

Willie finished up with his big blower cleaning off the porch and all the walkways. Light speckled through the two big oak trees onto the freshly cut lawn and played on the leaves of the artfully trimmed bushes around his house. The entire place shined beautifully. Luke thanked Willie again and reminded him to contact his office the next day.

Afterwards, Luke sat on his front porch and allowed himself to bask in the beauty of the landscape. Willie was a good man. Luke was glad things were going to work out for him. He wished it would be the same for himself, but it wasn't. A car wreck was not going to fix his situation. What would? Finding out who killed Susan would help. But Luke could get no one interested in that subject because they all thought that he did it. Or so it seemed. Only Luke knew for sure. He did not kill Susan. And for the first time he began to seriously wonder that if he didn't, who did?

The Office of District Attorney of Bedford County shared a parking lot with the County Courthouse. William Porter Gafford had a reserved space along with several other high ranking officials of the county, such as the Chancery Clerk, the Circuit Clerk and Judge Wendel Garmon Jones, III. Arriving at almost the same time that morning put them walking through the parking lot together.

"Morning, Judge. How ya doing today?"

"Hello, Billy. I'm fine. And you?"

"Yeah, fine. Just fine. Lots of work and little pay. You know how it is. Trying to keep myself working on this campaign. You don't have an opponent, do you?"

"Not yet. Today's the filing deadline. We'll see. If Brian Nelson gets in the race, that'll change things. Cost me a bunch of damn money's what it'll change."

The Judge's humor was less than pleasant. Billy already had an opponent that was giving him grief. Suit him just fine if the Judge had one. Billy was about to be in a race. The Judge might as well be in one. Maybe a challenge would put the two incumbents into a better frame of helping each other.

Billy was never sure where he was with Jones. The Judge helped him out a lot but he always acted as if it was such a chore. Billy couldn't help which cases came his way, or the way the defense lawyers advised their clients. He did the best he could with what he had, and he didn't have Judge Jones' money. There was nothing wrong with Wendell Jones having to work just as hard as Billy.

"Well, Judge, I'm hoping you don't have an opponent. Sure puts a lot of extra work on you. I know, I'm already having to scurry around with Chris Singletary. He's running around putting his mouth in gear before his mind comes up with anything worth saying. He'll be singing a different tune when this race is over and I'm back in the District Attorney's seat for another four years."

Billy's words carried an air of vindictiveness that Jones detested. There were a lot of things about Gafford that Jones detested. Unfortunately, there were probably more things about Singletary that rubbed the Judge the wrong way. In choosing between two evils, Jones felt like he'd rather have Gafford's incompetence than Singletary's pompousness. At least Gafford followed Jones' directions. After their years of working together he could get Gafford to do just about anything he wanted with the right words and selective instruction.

Singletary was another story. He was impossible to work with on anything, and always had a generally sour disposition. Worse than Gafford. Gafford would whine and sulk and act like a child, but Jones could get him to behave. The choice was not gratifying but it was clear. Jones needed to do what he could to see Gafford get reelected.

What about Brian Nelson? The possibility of his own opponent was still an issue. If he could just make it 'till five o'clock. He wondered if Gafford knew anything.

"Have you heard anything about Nelson getting into my race?" He popped the question to Gafford.

"Brian Nelson?" Gafford answered quizzically.

"Yes, yes." Gawd, Jones thought, Gafford could be such a dimwit at times. "Of course, Brian Nelson. Surely you've heard some of the talk about him getting into my race."

Gafford had heard the talk. He and Jimmy discussed it late last week. Gafford didn't care for Nelson. He was a short, stubby man with a lackluster practice standing on the edge of the legal community looking in. Billy didn't understand how anyone thought people would actually vote for Brian. He was simply the only candidate those who were opposed to Wendell Jones could get to run. He didn't have much of a practice that could be hurt by Jones as the victor in the campaign. There would be no contest between him and the sitting judge. Billy's race was where the challenge was.

"Well, I've heard a little talk. Do you think the man's crazy enough to try to run against you, Judge? I never give Nelson credit for being too smart, but I thought he had enough sense to know better than to get in a race against you."

"They're keeping it pretty quiet. All I know is that those boys over on First Street want somebody in the race against me. They may be able to talk Nelson into it. I don't know. I hope they know what they're doing. That's all I've got to say."

Billy Gafford knew exactly what he was saying. He was glad for the law and order motives that bound him to the Judge. He didn't want to be on the bad side of Wendell Garmon Jones.

"Is there anything I can do to help, Judge?" Billy thought this a perfect opportunity to get in some brown nosing. "Maybe we can help each other. I would sure be obliged to have your help. You know that, Judge. Probably nobody in this county understands the voters like you do. If you've got any ideas on what we need to do, then I'm ready to hear them."

"Well, I was thinking, do we have any fairly big cases on the criminal docket that we could get some publicity out of today. I'm clear most of the day. If we could get some plea set for early afternoon, then we could have the news media here and get on TV and in the paper. You know they'll be reporting the candidates on qualifying day. Let's get the jump on them and get our mention along with a strong send 'em to jail statement. The public loves that crap."

"I hear you. And, I think I've got just the case. Let me get to my office and check on a few things. I'll call you as soon as I can."

The thrill of being in cahoots with the Judge against their opposition excited Billy. Likewise, despite his grumbling about the money, Jones himself thrived on the energy of campaigning. Getting the drop on his adversary, stealing the thunder, Jones was like a kid in a candy shop. All the more delectable was the victory when accomplished with blow after successful blow. He'd show Nelson how it was done, and his friends on First Street better watch out.

Billy walked into his office with more glee than Wanda had seen in a while. She didn't know what brought about this adjustment in his attitude but she was glad for it. His somberness was wearing on her.

"Get John McWheter on the phone. And I need all those files on those drug busts we had a while back. You know the ones where the TV camera followed us around." He swooshed past her desk and on to his office.

Wanda went to her feet immediately and followed in behind him to the file room. She grabbed a box of files and was in the office with Billy by the time he got in his chair.

"Which ones you need, Mr. District Attorney?" Wanda liked her job. Most of the time.

"I need John McWheter on the phone."

"Hold on, I've got his number right here." She pulled one of the files from the box and opened it to get his number from the inside. As she dialed the number on Billy's phone he pulled the box of files to him and set it behind his desk, within reach but out of view of anyone else.

"Mr. McWheter, can you hold for the District Attorney? Thank you." She hit the hold button and extended the phone toward Billy.

"All yours, Mr. Gafford. As you requested, Mr. John McWheter is on line one, sir."

"Alright, Wanda, you can go back to your post now. I can handle it from here." He was happy to have her be so accommodating but just as soon she not be privy to his conversation with McWheter.

"John, glad I caught you this morning."

They rambled on for a few moments about the wife and kids: baseball, golf, summer activities and such while Billy made sure Wanda had time to meander back to her desk before getting down to the crux of his call.

"Listen, I've got some things we need to work on. I have a couple of files on your clients. You know those drug cases we made a month or so ago? You and I had discussed some potential plea arrangements. Are you still interested?"

"Well, I'm always interested in trying to arrive at what's in the best interest of my client."

"I understand you've got the discovery. You can see the predicament your client finds himself in. Two of them, really. If we go to trial they're sure to be found guilty and Jones will give them thirty years. Second offenses and all."

"Just which ones are we talking about here. I need to pull my files on them."

"I'm looking at Ponce. James Lewis Ponce. And Devotie. Leslie Earl Devotie."

"Just a minute."

Billy could hear McWheter calling out the names to his secretary before he came back on the line.

"Billy, you there?"

"Yeah, what you got."

"I'll have the files in just a minute. I know who you're talking about now, though. What did you have in mind?"

"This is not a regular plea day in court, but Judge Jones is on the bench. We had another case settle and he asked me if there were any other matters we could clear up today."

"Yes, I've got my files now."

"Well, then you can see that both these fellows have several charges pending. Both have multiple sale counts and both are repeat offenders. I believe getting these guys off the street will put a damper on the drug trade," Billy lied. He didn't believe there was any real way to inhibit the flow of drugs, but he liked to make it sound good. "If they'll plead today, I'll let it go off on the possession charge. They get the maximum on the possession, but that's three years versus a possible twenty. What'dya say?"

"I think that's more than generous. What happens to the sale charges?"

"I'll pass those to the file. They'll be dead as long as these two don't come back here and get into any more trouble. I'm sure they'll have learned their lesson by that time."

Billy spoke with tongue in cheek. These types never learned their lesson and he knew that as soon as they were back on the street they'd be back in trouble again. But right now he needed some bodies in front of a camera getting the maximum.

His diaphanous efforts were not lost on McWheter, but at this point John was not eager to delve into the District Attorney's reasons. He thought it best to make whatever contribution he could to the cause.

"Billy, I'll do my best to get them there. You know the main problem will be finding them. Can you give me an hour?"

"You do what you can, John, and let me know. I'll be waiting on your call."

The hour went fast for McWheter. He put two people on tracking down the clients who were found with surprising ease. Convincing them was also a simple task. They might not understand the ins-and-outs of varying degrees of criminal culpability and the manifold statutes they were charged under, but they could see plainly that three was less than twenty. John was back on the phone to Billy inside the hour.

"Billy, we can be there at one-thirty."

"That should be perfect. We'll see you then. I'll have the plea agreements ready."

Luke Daniels spent the better part of his Monday morning checking out the information he got from Willie Terrel on the wreck. Everything seemed to be just as his client told him. There was a wreck, car hit a bridge and three people were dead. One of them was Roselle Jones, the injured party in the fight with Willie. Luke felt certain that this would put an end to the charges against Willie, but didn't want to say much to the client until he had checked everything himself.

That check included talking with the District Attorney about the situation. Shortly after lunch he placed the call to Gafford's office. Wanda took the call with a pleasant greeting and informed him that Billy was in the courtroom with Jones taking some pleas. Luke wanted to catch the two of them and get an agreement that the charges against Willie could be dismissed. He took up the file and started out toward the courthouse after a brief word to Liz.

In the courtroom, there were a few folks gathered up as always when the Judge was on the bench. A trial had been scheduled for today that settled earlier. Jurors were notified, but some brought themselves on anyway. Lawyers floated in and out of the courthouse and around the main chamber regularly. Luke immediately recognized his friend, John McWheter.

He and Gafford had their heads together over some papers at counsel table. Jones was off the bench in his robe, talking with the court reporter. No one seemed to be in any hurry, although everyone was busy. As Luke observed the activity, a noise at the rear took everyone's attention.

Television cameras were being set up outside the courtroom. The evening news anchor came through the door, greeting people along the way. He made his way directly to Jones who had already started making his way to the forefront of the assembly to get the newsman's attention. The Judge welcomed him warmly and began to introduce people that Luke was certain already knew each other. In the process Luke recognized Woodall, the reporter from the Hampton News.

The drama continued to unfold. Two men sat at the counsel table opposite the District Attorneys. No doubt they were criminal defendants. McWheter moved across to their table and sat down, speaking in hushed tones to the two who looked scared and uneasy with all the activity.

Luke wanted to talk with Gafford about Willie Terrell but could not get his attention. Judge Jones seated the newsman and reporter on the front row behind Gafford and returned to the bench. Luke decided to take a seat in the back and take in what was happening. A couple of other lawyers that appeared in the courtroom waved but none made their way over to him. They took seats behind the reporters.

"Hear ye, hear ye, the Circuit Court of Bedford County is now in session, the Honorable Judge Wendell Garmon Jones, III, presiding." The deputy sang out the opening.

"This court is now in session," Jones bellowed with a banging of the gavel.

"Mr. District Attorney, you have some matters for me?"

"Your Honor, we do have pleas in two criminal matters. May Mr. McWheter and I approach the bench?"

The two lawyers talked with Jones for a short while at the bench and then backed away. Gafford then spoke with thespian intonation.

"State of Mississippi versus Leslie Earl Devotie and State of Mississippi versus James Lewis Ponce. Mr. Clerk, would you hand those files to the Judge?"

The Circuit Clerk stood up and laid two files in front of Jones, who began to pore over them immediately. After a few moments he turned his attention back to his audience.

"Alright, Mr. Gafford. What says the State? These two individuals are present in the courtroom today? The files show they are represented by the Honorable John McWheter."

"Yes, Your Honor. And my clients are here with me." McWheter spoke with all respect as an officer of the court.

"Bring them around, then. Let them face the bench."

Luke watched the proceeding from his perch in the back of the room. Here was McWheter representing two criminal defendants when only a short while ago had told Luke he wasn't handling any more criminal matters. Luke felt an awkwardness when John looked out and their eyes met across the courtroom. McWheter quickly looked away, putting himself back into the action at-hand.

The matter was handled quickly. The two defendants were ready to enter a plea of guilty to the charge of possession of crack cocaine. The District Attorney did not have a recommendation as to sentencing. These were both second offenders, each having finished their first sentences on probation only a couple of years ago. Now they were back again.

Judge Jones spoke to them sternly, lecturing the two on the menace to society that drugs were, ruining the lives of so many young people and, particularly, Bedford County and the City of Hampton. The nearby university community got mentioned and the lives of the young people. Luke wondered about the production Jones was making. He was known for grandstanding from the bench, but today's speech was more politicking than usual, shot straight at the media.

McWheter stood by silently as his two clients endured the harangue of Judge Jones. After a lengthy oratory, Jones stopped and looked down at the two accused drug abusers from his perch. "And how do you plead, James Lewis Ponce, to this charge of possession of a controlled substance, crack cocaine?"

Ponce squirmed uneasily, turning to his lawyer for a few words consultation before uttering his plea.

"Guilty," he said, barely more than a whisper.

Jones turned to the next man.

"You, Leslie Earl Devotie." Jones' voice boomed through the room. "You are also charged with possession of a controlled substance, to wit: crack cocaine. How do you plead?"

Leslie Earl was as white as a sheet. He stood slumped over slightly without looking directly at the Judge. His voice came out weak and without substance.

"Guilty."

"Guilty, indeed."

Jones paused for effect before proceeding.

"I have some questions to ask of you two before I accept that plea and pass sentence. Are you pleading guilty because you are guilty and solely for that reason? Has anyone promised you anything in return for your plea?"

Jones' voice went on with the standard set of questions to qualify these defendants for their plea. He ran through the series of questions with such speed that it was doubtful either of the two boys knew what they were answering, both nodding at the appropriate times. McWheter occasionally urged them to respond verbally and not with just a nod.

"James Lewis Ponce, I hereby sentence you to the maximum time under the statute. Three years in the custody of the Department of Corrections. In addition to that sentence I hereby order that you attend drug rehabilitation before your release."

"Leslie Earl Devotie, I sentence you to the maximum under the statute. Three years. Also, you are required to attend drug counseling during your stay at the penitentiary."

"You, boys, better listen to me good. These drugs are messing up your lives and the lives of your family. Do yourself a favor and get yourself straight, so that when you come out of prison, you can make a productive life for yourself without drugs. Do you hear me?"

"Yessir," both nodded. "Thank you, sir," DeVotie added as they were led away by the sheriff's deputy.

The reporters on the front row were writing furiously. As soon as Jones struck the gavel they were up on their feet, getting a statement from the Judge.

"Why only three years? Well, son, I'd have liked to have given them more, but that's all the statute allows. More time might save their lives, but until the legislature sees fit to give me more leeway in these matters, I have to follow the law."

The TV camera had peeked in the back door and the newsman pulled Jones aside to get the best shot possible, over no objection from the Judge.

McWheter shook hands with Gafford before picking up his file to leave. On the way out Luke put himself in McWheter's path in hopes of speaking to him. But McWheter doglegged his steps and put himself down another aisle that avoided Luke. Oh, well, Luke laid it aside. He would talk to him another time. Luke needed to catch Gafford before he got away on this Terrell case, so he moved to the front quickly.

"Billy, hi, ah, you got a minute."

"What is it, Luke? Gafford's tone remained dead serious.

Luke quickly laid out what he had learned of the situation with his client and the death of the accusing witness. When Luke finished, Gafford said nothing. Luke waited for a response.

"So, what do you say?" Luke tried to be jovial.

"I'm not in a position to say anything at this point, Mr. Daniels. I will look in to the matter. I'll have my investigator check out your story."

"My story?" Luke felt his blood heat up. Story. Did Gafford think he was lying to him?

"I was hoping we could resolve this today while Judge Jones was on the bench."

"Mr. Daniels, I'm not sure what you're trying to pull but I'm not doing anything on your word at this point. The best I can tell you is that I'll investigate your account of what has happened and get back to you. Do you intend to continue representing Mr. Terrell?"

"Well, of course. And why wouldn't I?" As soon as Luke said it he wished he could pull back his statement. He knew he left himself open in front of all the bystanders. One of them was Jeff Woodall, Luke noticed, writing furiously on his little pad. Luke began to feel very exposed.

"It's just that, well… " Gafford paused briefly, before continuing condescendingly. "Why don't you have your lawyer give me a call?"

Luke was frozen in his tracks. He wanted to put his fist through Gafford's mouth, the source of those repulsive words, but he was immobile. Paralyzed while the courtroom staff stood by gaping at him. Gafford was smirking at Luke. Woodall was writing. Luke could find no words to respond. Finally, Gafford picked up his files and walked away and the rest of the group standing around began to shuffle off. Luke caught sight of Jones still talking with the evening newsman. Despite being involved in their own conversation, they both caught the interchange between Luke and the District Attorney. Luke made himself breathe. In. And out. Slowly, he walked down the aisle of the courtroom and down the stairs. Outside, he continued to breathe and walk. All the way back to his office.

The evening news carried the story of Jones and Gafford being tough on crime. As tough as the law would allow. They got much better press than the short blurb announcing the candidacy of Brian Nelson. Luther Lambert watched it from the TV in his conference room along with son, Wilson, and investigator, Jerry. And Janet. She stayed as long as Luther stayed to answer the phone. To mix drinks. To kowtow to Luther's instant whims.

He liked being doted on and treated with veneration, as if his every word and act was of divine inspiration. After years of catering to his every whim, Janet had her reverence down to a science. And, Jerry fell into the game well. Poor Wilson wanted his father's love and approval so badly that he fell in, also. He vacillated between fawning and trying to be a clone of the elder lawyer. Both left him feeling empty and appearing stupid. Wilson was an unhappy man living in the shadow of something he would never achieve.

The news animated the group as they watched their elected public officials primp and preen for the camera. Judge Jones tried to be disappointed in the limitations he was given and Gafford tried to be bulldog prosecutor. They were off the streets, which was the important thing both men cited. The cameras ate it up and the newsman ran with the line, moving on to the hard job of keeping criminals off the street with laws that favored the defendant. When the station went to commercial, Luther was ready for talk.

They laughed and joked about the Judge and District Attorney playing to the camera. It was great entertainment watching the elected officials prostitute themselves for the vote.

"But don't you know they're proud of themselves," Luther laughed. "Why, I bet Gafford's at home trying to boss his wife around, right now, feeling powerful and all." Luther laughed out loud.

Janet and Jerry laughed, too. Wilson laughed the loudest.

"Janet, see if you can get Gafford on the phone. I want to talk with him." Luther picked up his hulking frame and moved off to the bathroom while Janet worked the phone.

"He's on line one, Mr. Lambert," she said as she heard the bathroom door.

Luther took the call in his office, away from the rest of the group, talking with Gafford in private, using all of his best lines to make Gafford feel important. While in the other room, they still laughed at Luther Lambert's ability to manipulate. To dominate. To orchestrate the lives of people in Hampton. They laughed at how funny it was. And they laughed to see it happen to someone besides themselves for a little while.

Gafford waited on the phone for Hays Kennedy to come on the line. He didn't like to wait and he didn't like what he was waiting for. But there was no getting around it. They had to get to the matter of Luke Daniels.

"Hello, Billy. How are you this morning?" Hays wondered about the call.

"Fine, thank you. Hays, you have the discovery in Daniels case. Isn't that correct?" Billy wasted no time in getting right to the point.

"Yes, I do." Silence. He wasn't sure where Gafford was going next.

"I've got to do something on this case. I'm giving you one more chance. Get your client to talk with me about pleading guilty and let's see if we can't get the Judge to go along with a life sentence."

"Billy, my client continues to tell me he didn't kill anyone and frankly, I have to stand with him on this." Hays could bluff superbly in civil cases. He hoped it worked the same in criminal matters.

"Hays, have you looked at the file materials we turned over to you? This was a brutal murder. I'm going to crucify this guy in court. He was hopped up on drugs, you know that, making him crazy. The poor girl suffered through a rape from a madman before he struck the fatal blow. Do you have any idea what that's going to do to a jury? They won't be able to get to the death penalty fast enough. Is that what you want?"

Images flashed through Hays' mind like an old movie. Bits and pieces of scenes from the photos he saw of the murder. The girl's nude body laying in a pool of blood. The room a wreck. He didn't know what to say to the District Attorney.

"You'd better talk to your client, Hays. The boy's going down. If he doesn't want to go all the way to six feet under he'd better come to his senses."

Another long pause filled the line between the two adversaries. Billy knew that his words were striking right where he wanted them to. He waited a few more moments for them to sink in before continuing.

"Look, Hays, I've always liked Luke myself. He was a good lawyer. But the drugs have made him into something else. You and I can't help that. He did it to himself. Maybe if he'll go ahead and plead, the life sentence will get him off the drugs and who knows? Maybe he could be paroled. Maybe he would turn his life around. I've never thought of Luke as a killer, but the man that wasted poor Susan Weeks was a cocaine-crazed killer. You and I have a job to do. Now, I don't really want to see him get the death penalty, but if I'm forced to go to trial I won't have any choice. The ball's in your court, Hays. You can help save his life. What's it gonna be?"

"I'll talk to him."

"Well, do it soon. You know we're on the docket for trial next month. I'm not going to allow any continuance. Neither is Judge Jones. We're catching flak for letting a murderer walk the streets. Suppose he goes on one of his binges again and another victim bites the dust. That one will be on you, Hays."

When he got no response, Billy hung up the phone without saying anything else. He liked leaving Kennedy with that monkey on his back. Let him think his client might kill again. Do him good. Or, at least, it might do Billy some good. He laughed to himself.

He thought about his conversation with Luther Lambert. Wish ol' Luther could have heard him on the phone with Kennedy. He was masterful. Played that sucker just right. Had him eating out of his hand. He whistled himself right out the front door and off to lunch. Wouldn't hurt to go do a little politicking down at Momma Doris'. Shake a few hands, talk about his upcoming trial. Everybody needed to know how compassionate he was trying to be with the unfortunate Luke Daniels.

Luke sat in the waiting room at Hays Kennedy's office trying to be patient. The call came down to his office from Hays' secretary saying it was urgent that they get together right away. Luke left his office and arrived there at five 'till three. It was now five after and he was waiting. Luke didn't wait well, especially when he was waiting on the lawyer who was defending him for murder. Every time Luke thought of those words he tried to pinch himself to wake up. This had to be a dream. He was not a murderer and the idea that he was in this predicament, having to defend himself against such a charge, was madness. He thought about the night that brought all this on him. About the first time he saw Susan.

Oh, Susan. So wrapped up in his own thoughts and problems, so much weighing him down and hurting within, he couldn't bear the pain of thinking of Susan. He rarely even let himself think her name. When he did, her face came to him and after seeing her face he almost felt her touch on his arm, ever so slight. Her laughter filled his ears and the rest of the world was gone for an immeasurable space in time. Susan, what happened to you that night? It was as if he begged to know, but froze at the point of any consideration.

It was all such a blur. Sometimes, she even seemed like a dream. Too good to be true. He only knew her for a few hours, but in that time they touched an inner yearning that made them both feel whole. Complete. Like it was meant to be. Luke thought about how he had often laughed at people who talked about finding their soul mate. Was Susan his soul mate? Was she a perfect match for him? Or was it all a dream? He reached this point often whenever he allowed himself to even think of her. She was only a dream. That her sheer perfection was only an illusion. Oh, but it felt so real. Now it was hard to know what was real and what was an illusion. For her there was no past, no present and no future. Just what had happened between them that night.

"Luke. Luke." Hays spoke the name a little louder as he examined his client sitting on the green leather couch in the waiting room of the law office. Luke's eyes looked a little glazy. His face had a tired, drained appearance. Overall, he was disheveled and slovenly. From the way he slumped on the couch and his shoes that needed polish, he looked totally unkempt. Luke's eyes slowly turned to Kennedy.

"Oh, Hays, I'm sorry. I guess I was off in another world. The secretary said you wanted to see me. So here I am. What's shakin'?"

"Come on back to my office, Luke. We need to talk."

Luke pulled himself up out of the depths of the plush leather sofa and stood before Hays.

They walked quietly back to Hays' office, neither making the effort at small talk. Hays settled into the chair behind the desk and Luke fell into one of the straight arm chairs in front. Stillness settled into the room when neither of them spoke. Each took in the other without comment.

Hays' thoughts played on the seeds planted by the District Attorney. He wondered how to broach the subject tactfully with Luke. He wanted to phrase his terms in just the right way to elicit the most honest and straightforward responses. If the DA's charge was in line, then his client was lying to him. He hated that and didn't feel he could adequately represent a man that would deceive him. Perhaps Luke was deceiving himself. Perhaps the drugs had so blurred his senses that even he didn't know what the truth was. So how could he be truthful with his lawyer?

Luke sat in silence for lack of energy to do anything more. His earlier thoughts of Susan, as always, brought him to a dead end. He had no energy to think anymore, but this time he wished he knew what had happened to her. He'd like to have the murderer right here and punish him with his bare hands. So much hope was destroyed in that act, the loss of Susan.

For her. For him. For a life for the two of them. Now in front of his attorney, what was there left for him? He felt despondent. What good was it to even be here sitting with this lawyer?

There was not much fight left in Luke. He was losing all his practice. The money had slowed to a trickle. Thank goodness he had saved his recent earnings and invested them well. He had money to live on but he didn't have much of a life. What he was doing didn't seem much like living. He got up in the morning and went through the motions. He arrived at his office, shuffled papers for a few hours, went home, and later, he went to bed. There was little else. Little joy. Little more than existence. Now there was defending himself for a crime he didn't commit. For that, he hardly had any fight left.

"Luke, tell me again, exactly what happened that night. Let's go over it one more time."

Luke stared back at Hays as if he was crazy. They'd gone over that so many times. How on earth could Hays even ask him again? Luke wanted to protest, but then he couldn't. It was easier to just go on and mumble out the tale that began to end his life. He laughed to himself. The beginning of the end.

Hays saw the subtle, hidden snicker. He didn't know where it came from but he didn't like it. It appeared to him to portend a lie. He wanted to urge Luke to be as candid as possible, but only listened. He listened intently for a flaw in the telling. Some inaccuracy from a previous rendering. A variant. Anything that would let him get to the truth.

Luke began again. He had recounted the story so many times that the words came out of his mouth without the need for any mental effort, which was a good thing since he had almost no mental energy. Luke's mind took a break while the words fell out of his mouth.

When the words stopped, Luke brought himself around to look straight at Hays. During his talking, Luke thought of why Hays had him retell. Why did he want to hear it one more time? Did his lawyer need to be convinced? Did he believe Luke?

"I got a call from Gafford this morning." Hays started out with a bland move. Just the facts.

"Well, what did my good friend William Porter Gafford have to say? Did he apologize and say all is forgiven?" Luke couldn't help his snide comment.

"No, he didn't. He said he liked you and that he didn't want to see this happen, but he had no choice. He wants me to convince you to take the plea and accept a life sentence. Get yourself straight and be paroled in a few years. I think he could be convinced to reduce the charge to manslaughter."

"And I'm supposed to be glad for that?"

"Look, Luke, I'm on your side, but you never know what a jury is going to do. Right now you're looking at the death penalty. Is that what you want? Those are mighty high stakes you're playing with."

"Of course it's not what I want. I don't want to be here at all. This whole thing is preposterous. I didn't kill Susan. Do you hear me, Hays? I did not kill Susan Weeks." Luke's voice had risen to a roar. He was a big man and his voice could boom out with fervor, often exposing him when there was nowhere to direct his anger.

"Okay, Luke, calm down. What do you think's going to happen to a jury when you have one of these outbursts? It's getting to where every time we get together, you wind up shouting at me. You're going up in front of a jury that's going to decide whether you live or die. What will they think when you explode like that?"

Silence fell between them again. Luke pushed himself back in the chair sullenly. His mood swings were frightening even him.

"Gafford says we go to trial next term. That's barely over a month away, Luke. Are you ready for that?"

"I can't plead guilty, Hays. I can't stand up there and say I did something I didn't do. I can't. Do you realize that there's someone out there that did do this? Do I let a real murderer go free?"

"Then are you prepared to die for something you didn't do?"

Luke didn't think he could be any lower than he already was. Until now. Hays' words caused Luke to feel the world was going to open and he would be swallowed up. He looked back at Hays who began to seem far away as if Luke were being drawn into a tunnel. Blackness was settling in around him. His hands clutched the sides of the chair he sat in. He felt that if he let go he would be sucked into the depths of the earth. No release. No escape. No hope. The blackness was so real he could almost reach out and touch it.

"Luke, I have to ask you this. Sit up here and listen to me."

Luke tried to focus on Hays and bring himself back to reality. This was no time to be losing it.

"Take a look at these. I don't think you've seen them." Hays had their file out and pulled the pictures of the crime scene. Before Luke could say anything, Hays had them spread out on his desk.

There was Susan. There was her room. The living room. The kitchen table. The busted door with the footprint. Luke recognized the print. He saw it often when he was running. It was the same print his shoes made. His eyes went back to the pictures of the bedroom. The last time he saw that room he was… Luke swallowed hard and looked away.

"Luke, do you think it possible you killed Weeks and don't know it? Maybe you've blocked it out of your mind so that in your thinking you didn't do it. That it was another person acting out inside of you. Drugs can make a man do crazy things. Were there any drugs used that night? Think about it, Luke. Don't answer me now. I just want you to think about it. We need to be sure. The stakes are too high to approach it any other way."

"Go home now. Get some rest. Have you been sleeping well? You look a sight, Luke. You certainly don't want to go to trial looking like you do right now. Go on. Sleep on it and call me back."

Luke could say nothing. No words came to him. He doubted he could have uttered them if they had. His mouth was dry and parched. He felt dazed. Confused. What was Hays saying to him?

"Our trial date is the Tuesday after docket call. That's the tenth of next month. You say the word, Luke. It's your call, you know that. You're a lawyer, too. You take the plea or we go to trial. It's up to you."

Luke didn't have anything to say. He mumbled something to Hays and left his office. He got to his car and cranked up. He didn't know where to go. He pulled the car in gear and just drove.

CHAPTER FIFTEEN

Luther Lambert sat in his living room with the sun shining through the sheers behind heavy brocade drapes. Light struck the crystal lamp base sitting on the table sending beams of color about the room. The sun was already strong making for a hot sultry day.

In the cool of the eastward facing living room Luther felt protected from the heat building outside. He enjoyed his coffee as he went through the selection of Sunday papers. The Clarion Ledger carried little to interest him that morning. The Times Picayune was a thick pad of a paper with all sorts of stories that Luther passed over without attention. His real interest was the front page of the Hampton News.

"TRIAL DATE SET IN WEEKS MURDER" was at the top of the page. Luther had read the article when he first picked up the papers that morning but went back to it now to savor the details. The story had all the particulars about the murder and the meticulous detail work of the Hampton Police Department. Several quotes lauded the investigators' efforts, describing how they had painstakingly gone through all the evidence in an effort to find the killer. Immediately after, the article mentioned that the Grand Jury indicted Luke Daniels and trial was set in two weeks. Jurors would report on Monday for jury selection and the trial would begin on Tuesday.

Luther read the parts of the article about the victim over again. Without accusing Daniels, the article mentioned the police suspicion that drugs were involved due to the evidence of violence found at the scene. Gafford hinted that the proof could establish a case of capital murder, the underlying crime being rape.

Luther was beside himself. He could hardly sit still as he read the article over and over. This was better than even he had imagined. Jones and Gafford had done an excellent job with the press. This article even carried the story of Daniels' little incident with the reporter, Jeff Woodall, in a subtle way.

Woodall was quoted as saying all he did was try to ask the man a few questions about what happened between him and Susan when the man attacked him violently and threw him out of his office. The little sonofabitch probably deserved it, Luther thought, but it sure looked good on paper. Ha, hah, Luther heard himself laugh out loud.

But the biggest reward of all was seeing that playing up the drugs had provided the motive that pinned Luke to the wall. Luther didn't care whether Luke was innocent or guilty; all he cared about was getting someone behind bars for the crime. He knew that the drugs opened the door to a murderer no matter who it was. Just as well it was Luke.

Eloise Lambert appeared at the door of the front room, instantly noticing the smile on Luther's face, a rarity with the gruff lawyer.

"Well, you're in a good mood. What's got you all smiles today?" She so seldom saw her husband in anything but a huff, complaining about all the work he had on him that the smile caught her off guard.

"What's the matter? Can't a man be happy in his own home?" His usual brusque tone returned. He was so accustomed to speaking to his wife harshly that his manner fell without thinking. He didn't intend unkindness and tried quickly to amend.

"Why don't you get some coffee and come join me for a moment?"

"Wilson and Rita are coming early for lunch today. They're supposed to be here at eleven. The kids, too. Don't you remember? I need to be getting ready."

"Oh, you're always beautiful. Grab a cup of coffee and we'll sit for fifteen minutes. We never get a chance anymore. What do you say?"

"Alright. I'll get my cup."

Luther stretched and stacked up all the papers with the Hampton News on top. As he held them in his lap, he scanned through the story one more time. The smile returned. Yes, Luke Daniels was going down. Luther had heard about the plea bargain talks, but he felt the Judge and the DA were smart enough to know that a trial would do more for their image, win, lose or draw. Especially, since he planted those seeds at every opportunity. He smiled again to himself.

Eloise returned with her coffee and brightened up at the sight of her husband sitting in the morning sun with a smile on his face. She slid a Louis XIV arm chair across the plush Persian rug to position herself next to him. She smiled and settled into the seat with pleasure at having a few moments of the man's attention. He gave it to so many others, but seldom to her.

"Looks like we're finally going to get the case of that poor Weeks girl concluded. That wild man, Daniels, won't be walking the streets like some cocky punk for much longer." Luther crowed for his wife.

"I am so glad. Did I ever tell you about Mary Margaret Jones seeing him outside their house in the middle of the night? Just staring at them. It scared her so. I can't believe they've taken this long to get him."

"Well, dear, justice must prevail. You know that. You wouldn't want them to get the wrong man, now, would you? They've got to be sure, especially in a case like this one. Gafford had to be certain before he went out trying to indict a member of the bar. And, we never really know what the defense has lined up. They often have a suspect of their own. Gafford has to make certain that this is an open-and-shut situation."

"Well I know, and I'm glad we have someone as thorough and as dedicated to doing the right thing as he is. Still, I'm just glad we're going to get that murderer off the streets."

"Yes, me, too, dear. Me, too."

They sat in silence for a few moments before Eloise excused herself to the bedroom to get dressed for their Sunday dinner company. Luther got up also and set the stack of papers on the kitchen counter before heading back to the bathroom.

The Wilson Lamberts arrived in a flurry shortly after eleven o'clock. Eloise was just walking up to the kitchen when she heard them at the back door.

"Come in, come in." She grabbed her Little Will, the nine year old Wilson Hughes Lambert, Jr., and gave him a hug.

"Cut it out, Grandma. You know I'm too big for that stuff."

"Oh, you're never too big for me to get a hug," Eloise chided him as she grabbed her granddaughter next.

"Elise, you're getting prettier every day." The grandmother took a second hug from the youngest before leading them back to the kitchen. The children fled to the den where they fought over the TV control.

"Wilson, your father should be out any minute. We've been lazy this morning."

"Maybe you have. I'm never lazy. I just had less strenuous things to do today." Luther strolled through the kitchen in his golfing attire, prepared to bolt out the door as soon as he could hurry them through lunch.

"How's my favorite daughter-in-law?" Luther made a big show of giving Rita a kiss on the cheek. Without skipping a beat, he moved right on to another topic.

"You folks seen the paper this morning? Looks like we're finally going to get the chance to throw that sorry Daniels away for good." He handed the front page to Wilson.

"Yeah, I saw it. The bastard. I'm glad he's finally going to get his. You remember how wild he got that day in our office. He's a madman. I hope they lock him up for good. Hell, I hope he gets the gas chamber."

"Not much chance," Luther spoke with authority.

"Why do you say that?" Wilson came back to his dad.

"Gafford's just crowing about it being a capital crime, rape and all. I'll bet when it's all said and done, it'll come down to just a simple murder. Daniels didn't rape her. Probably didn't intend to kill her. Just let himself get crazy on drugs. She may have tried to get him to leave her alone and wham-o. She get's a lick upside the head that's too much. He runs off. There's no capital crime in that."

"But if Gafford goes with simple murder, he can't run around town spoutin' off about going for the gas chamber. That makes a much better story, especially in an election year. When it's over he can only bluster about how these damn laws keep his hands tied and how he's going to work to get them changed when he's re-elected."

The two men settled around the table across the bar while Rita assisted Eloise in the kitchen. Sunday dinner was a feast. Out of the oven came a roast with potatoes and carrots. On the stove were the butter beans, corn, rice and gravy. The rolls were ready to go in the oven.

"We'll eat as soon as the bread's done," Eloise said.

"I don't know how you do this," Rita complimented her mother-in-law. "A full meal pulled out here like it's no effort."

"Well, it's not, dear. I just put a few things in a pot out of the freezer."

"Is it twelve o'clock, yet?" Luther called from his perch at the table. "I think it's time for me to have a beer. Eloise, hand me one out of the fridge. Wilson, you want one?"

"Sure."

Anything to be more like his father, Rita thought.

When the oven beeped, the freshly baked rolls came out piping hot. Everything else was on the table and they all sat down to eat. Luther and Wilson continued their lawyerly bashing of Luke Daniels until Rita could stand it no longer.

"Can we please change the subject?" she said with some authority.

Luther and Wilson stared back at her with surprise, unaccustomed to her speaking up so strongly.

"What's the matter with you?" Wilson spoke to her with his usual lack of tenderness.

"There is nothing the matter with me," she returned a disdainful look to her husband.

"Surely you don't think the man's not guilty?"

"It has nothing to do with Luke. We have little ears here," she said with a motion toward her children. "Don't we have some more appropriate mealtime conversation we could engage in?"

"Sure." Wilson's indifferent response left the table silent for a few moments, the air thick between him and his wife. After a while, Luther broke the silence.

"Well, you don't, do you?" his comment was directed straight at Rita.

She wanted to avoid him but everyone at the table looked straight at her. The children's eyes were fixed on her as well.

"Have you two finished eating? Look at those plates. I want that meat eaten. Those little growing bodies need the protein. Eloise, you need some more ice for your tea. Here, I'll get some for all of us." She stood up from the table completing ignoring Luther.

Wilson was oblivious to her lack of response. He watched her go into the kitchen and retrieve the ice. She moved around the table filling up the glasses with Eloise following after with the pitcher of tea.

"Luther, you haven't touched your tea." She reached over and shook the can of beer. "You want another one of those? Wilson, how about you?"

They both knew she disapproved of drinking, although Luther did not know it was his son's violent rages when he drank that set her against it. Wilson declined her offer.

"I'll just finish my tea, thank you. I need to get to the golf course, anyway. I don't want to miss my tee time." Luther wolfed downed the last couple of bites on his plate and then stood up, excusing himself.

"Great meal, dear. I'll see you tonight."

Wilson moved himself to the den and the TV while the children went outside. Rita sat at the table and continued to sip the fresh glass of iced tea.

"Please, Eloise. Sit down. Just because everyone else has to rush off doesn't mean we have to ruin our meal. Sit. We'll clean up the mess in a minute. This tea is delicious. I want to enjoy it."

Rita breathed deeply and thought about Luke Daniels. She had read the article earlier and wished there was something she could do to help him. Now that she heard her husband and his father get so heated up over Luke she wished she could help him even more. Anything those two favored had to be something she needed to look the other way on. And her senses told her Luke was not the culprit. All the wrong people thought he was. All the more reason for Rita to believe in his innocence.

Luke Daniels sat at home on Sunday crashed on the couch flipping the channels with his remote watching images flash before him on the screen. The paper was spread out on the coffee table in front of him. Since seeing the headlines, his spirit had taken a nose dive, leaving him spiraling down into despair. The day was hot outside. When he walked out earlier to get the paper he could tell this was going to be a scorcher. All the more reason to stay inside. Alone. Unshaven, undressed, uncaring.

He was glad for the solitude. He didn't want to talk to anyone. He wanted to be alone. He had a lot of thinking to do. A lot. His trial date was looming, two weeks away, and in his head were the words of his lawyer.

"Death penalty. Is that what you want? Plea bargain. Blocked it out of your mind. You killed Susan? Think it over, Luke."

Words and phrases swam together in his head making him dizzy, unsteady. Since leaving Hays' office, Luke had been unstable. Almost irrational. Nothing made sense to him. He tried to think of his case as a lawyer, but he couldn't. Trying to look at it logically didn't work. His brain couldn't focus. His thought processes fell apart on him and he found himself off in madness. Then the paranoia set in. Was he really insane? Was there a possibility that he killed Susan? What happened that night? He remembered leaving. He remembered being in his car driving away from her house. He knew he wanted to go back. But he didn't. Did he? And, he didn't use drugs.

Convulsions attacked him at this point. He became physically ill, tearing to the john to empty out his insides. When the heaving finally stopped he pulled himself back to the couch in the living room and plopped down exhausted, so tired he wanted to die. His body collapsed but his brain didn't. When was the last time he had eaten?

His mind raced along with thoughts and images and visions of Susan. The pictures on

Hays' desk came back to him. Her immaculate beauty spoiled there on the floor. A pool of blood encircling her head like a halo of death. Again, the sickness came to him. His body spent, again the spasm wrecked what remained of him. Somehow, he made it back into the bathroom, falling to the floor as the heaves took over. When the spell passed, he couldn't move. The smell of the small room smothered him, making breathing nearly impossible. He managed to crawl out into the bedroom and get himself up on the bed where he could feel the cool blowing of the air conditioner against his face. He lay there numb. Even his brain stopped working. No thought.

A little painful, harsh relief. His eyes were open but unfocused; fixed on nothing. He lay on the bed unmoved, like a nonliving object. All feeling was gone. Even the bed beneath him had no sensation, as if he were floating. Removed. His ears ceased picking up any sounds. All contact with the real world was receding. And, he didn't care. He couldn't. The release from it all felt wonderful. Lightheaded, he floated away into another state of consciousness. Letting go. Letting go of it all. Until he was completely gone.

His body lay on the bed without movement, his breathing so weak it was barely noticeable. He didn't make a sound. The ceiling fan turned quietly in the space above him. In the living room the soft muffled noise of the television continued to drone. In the kitchen the pot of coffee was hot, growing stale, sending out the fetor of a distasteful brew. Outside the sun bore down on the day without regard for the ruin in the house.

On Monday morning Liz arrived at the office at her regular time, but there wasn't much to do. She wondered what Luke would have lined up for today, if anything. She shuffled a lot of papers, talked a lot on the phone, often with other legal secretaries whose employers had taken over Luke's former client's cases.

Liz sat down at her desk, thinking she would organize until Luke arrived and then see what he had on the agenda. A phone call or two took up some time. That was good.

Jenny had been gone for about a month now. Sheer boredom had pressed her into finding other employment. When Wilson Lambert's secretary left and put him in the hunt for a replacement, Jenny jumped at the chance to get into a full-fledged legal secretary's job. Or so she said.

Liz surmised that part of it was an escape from not only the boredom but the oppressive cloud which now hung over the law office of Luke Daniels. Rumors outside that office reached epidemic proportion. She and Luke laughed about how utterly ludicrous some of them had gotten. One of the best was how Luke was involved in a Columbian drug cartel and had lost favor when he bedded one of the leader's women. Ironically, that one had come to Luke from Hays Kennedy, who felt compelled to share all that he picked up about Luke.

Another was how Luke would probably commit suicide rather than have some of the things he was involved in come out. She knew that Luke's strength of character would never allow him to even consider suicide. Okay, he was a little spacey lately, but that didn't change the man she knew. Of course, she never thought he would come into the office looking the way he had lately, but he was under a lot of pressure. A lot of pressure.

Liz turned herself around and adjusted her radio to another station. Something more peppy. Luke would be coming in here any minute. She needed to shake herself and get to work. There were some files that should be boxed up. She would just work on that until Luke arrived.

At noon, the boxes were tied up neatly and her desk was clean. The morning had actually zipped by pretty fast after she got herself busy. By now she was hungry, but where was Luke? She tried him at home again for the third time. He was obviously not there. It really wasn't like him not to call. Where was he?

No answer again. Well, she was hungry. She would leave to get something to eat. She'd just have to see him after lunch when he got in. She locked the front door and headed up the street with the intention of going to Momma Doris' when she found herself at her car instead. There was a new little place that she heard had great sandwiches for lunch. Today would be a good day to try it. She might even be able to sit outside and soak up the sun. Today was not as hot as yesterday. It would be bearable.

Thames & Company was not very crowded. She got in and ordered the shrimp salad sandwich and found a place on their deck where she could feel the breeze. She spoke to several acquaintances but ate alone. Finishing quickly she didn't want to go straight back to the office. In her car she drove around some, taking a turn into a residential neighborhood admiring the summer flowers brought out by the warm sun. At a stop sign she lingered, taking in the beauty of a mandevilla twining around the porch rail of the house across the street.

Above the stop sign she noticed the name of the street. It was Luke's street. She was only a couple of blocks from his house. She could not stop herself from turning in his direction. She knew he wasn't there but she thought she would take a look.

She approached along the side of his corner lot and made the turn into the street in front of his house. There was his car. That was odd. Maybe he had just come in. Maybe he was here for lunch.

She pulled in the driveway behind his car. She couldn't see any lights but got out of her car anyway and went to the porch. Knocking and listening, she could hear something. The TV. She peaked in the porch window and could barely make out the flashing of the screen on his big television through the sheer curtains and the slats of the blinds. She went back to the door and knocked again.

"Luke," she called out to him. "Luke!" She called louder and banged louder again. Still no answer. What was he doing? Was he in the shower? She went back to the car and honked her horn a couple of times. Nothing from inside Luke's house showed life, but she did see a face behind the drapes of the house across the street. Some little old lady wondering what all the commotion was about, Liz thought. She went back to the porch and banged again.

Could he have gone off with someone else? If so, why didn't he call her. Maybe he didn't have a chance. Several of the rumors flashed in her mind with disquieting glimmers. She tried her best to peer in the living room window. She went to the back door, banging and calling his name some more. She hoped she didn't sound as panicked as she was feeling. For some reason she was becoming very alarmed. There was a key to Luke's house at the office. Damn, why didn't she bring it with her?

"Because you didn't know you were coming here, silly," she spoke the words out loud, chiding herself.

She looked under both mats checking for a key. Nothing. Back in the front she spied his car again and went to it immediately trying the front door. It was unlocked, again not like Luke. He always locked his car and took his keys. Maybe there was something in the glove box. But before she got there she noticed the ignition. His keys hung there from the steering column with a house key, his office key, and his locker key at the gym. His gold key ring with his initials was engraved on the tag. Those were Luke's keys that she had seen a thousand times before. She grabbed them immediately and started for the house without thinking.

As she slipped the door key into the lock and it turned easily she realized the door was not even locked. She just hadn't tried it. What a dummy, she thought, and then she thought about what she was going to find inside. Sickness came over her. Maybe she should stop. Should she call the police? Maybe so, but she couldn't stop now. The door was open. She was standing in the living room.

"L-u-u-k-e?" her voice called his name with a stutter. The room was a mess with newspapers all over the table. The TV noise was the only thing she heard. In the dining room stale dishes sat on the table. A vile odor filled the air. She moved past the dining room and into the kitchen, unable to stop her investigation.

The coffee pot held a black syrupy goo with a burnt rancid smell. She flipped the switch off and put the overheated pot into the sink.

"Luke?" she called again.

She thought she heard something from another part of the house and froze. What the hell was she thinking coming in here like this? Was she out of her mind? Was there some henchman from a Columbian drug lord hiding in the other room waiting for her to approach?

"Luke, it's me, Liz." Great. Let'em know my name before they kill me. She walked on through the kitchen, the breakfast room. There on the table was the portable phone. She picked it up. They've probably cut the lines. She clicked it on and held it to her face. The dial tone buzzed loudly. She stood at the door looking down the hallway, fear gripping her. She thought of calling 911.

Instead, she continued her steps down the hall to what she knew was Luke's bedroom. At the door she saw him. She gasped immediately, calling his name aloud again as her fingers touched the numbers 911.

Luke's body lay sprawled across his bed. On his stomach, his legs stretched across the bed, she couldn't see his face until his head raised up as if to ask, what are you doing here.

"This is 911. What is your emergency?" The voice was a clear and comforting sound. The operator on the other end was looking at her screen, making a record that the call came in from the residence of Luke Daniels, 621 Carnathan Street.

"Luke, are you alright?"

For a moment, Luke didn't know where he was. He was weak. He recognized Liz. Where was he? He looked around the room, groggy. This was his room. He pulled himself up in the bed. What was Liz doing here?

"This is 911. Are you alright? Is there an emergency?"

They both heard the voice come across the phone as they stared at the portable Liz held in her hand. She had forgotten she had even dialed the number.

"Yes, yes operator. I mean… this is 911, right. No, there is no emergency. I just thought there was. I mean, everything's fine now." Her voice came out in bursts, as she gasped for air after having held her breath for so long. She must have been holding it the whole time she was in the house.

The 911 operator was at the police station, trained to pick up on any nuance that might indicate distress. This woman was obviously in distress. The words she was speaking and the sound of her voice did not match.

Liz assured her everything was fine and hung up the phone. The police department employee recognized the name Luke Daniels, almost a household word in the town now with the trial looming. She didn't want anything coming down on her later so she radioed for a police car to go check out the situation just in case.

Luke didn't know what was going on. Why was Liz here in his bedroom on a Sunday morning? He sat up and pulled the sheets up to him, still flustered from the rude awakening.

"Liz, what are you doing here? Couldn't it wait until tomorrow, whatever it is? Why didn't you call me?"

"I did call you. Several times. When I drove by and saw your car I got worried."

"Since when have you started checking up on me on a Sunday morning?"

"Sunday morning? You moron, it's Monday afternoon. Have you gotten so bad you don't even know what day it is?"

Luke scratched his head and stared back at Liz as if she were the crazy one.

"Monday? Are you sure?"

"Yes, I'm sure. I was at the office this morning. I went to work along with the rest of the world. You're the one here in lah-lah land, don't even know what day it is. Did you get drunk last night?"

"No. I, ah… " Luke's voice trailed off. What did he do? The last thing he remembered was being on the couch with the Sunday paper. Oh, yeah. He got sick.

"Liz, I was sick."

"I'll say. What was it? Something you ate?"

"I got sick yesterday morning. I was throwing up. I must have passed out."

"Yesterday morning? You've been asleep since yesterday morning?"

"I don't remember exactly. I must have been. I was on the couch, reading the paper, watching some TV. I got sick and went to the bathroom. Several times. I guess I fell into bed here. I don't remember much else. Except dreaming. I was dreaming about…" Luke's voice trailed off again and his eyes faded out of focus.

Liz watched his face. He badly needed to shave. And the crib head gave his hair a funny shape. He needed to get in the shower. The whole room stank. She sat there on the side of the bed watching his face as he pondered his dream. What in the world was going on in that man's head? This trial business must be about to push him over the edge.

"I know what I have to do, Liz." He said it strongly and with such resolve that she felt the strength coming into him as they sat there in his bedroom.

"Yeah, so do I. You've got to get your butt out of this bed and down to the office. I'm not running that show by myself, you know." She tried to be light, not sure if he had taken hold of reality or if he was still off in some dream.

"No, seriously, Liz. I don't have to wonder anymore."

"What?" Despite the resolute aspect of his face, his words were not connecting with Liz.

"I don't have to wonder about what to do. Since my last session with Hays I've been driving myself crazy over his counsel. I didn't really get into it with you before, but they're pressing him to get me to plead guilty."

"Who is?" Liz's heart broke over the pain she saw in the man she admired so much.

"The DA. He's telling Hays they're going to crucify me if I don't plead. Ever since leaving Hays' office the other day I've been playing it over and over in my head."

Luke stopped again. His eyes seemed to be going over a list, as if one more time he was checking to make sure he had everything in order. He finally focused back on Liz sitting on the end of his bed.

"Liz, I can't stand up there in the courtroom and lie. I am a lawyer, trained to seek the truth. I would have to lie to enter a plea. I can't do it. I can't stand up there and say I did something that I know I didn't do. The words wouldn't come out of my mouth. There is no choice for me. I have to go the only way I can."

Liz looked at him, not knowing what to say. His appearance had completely changed for her. She had always admired the man, respected him. He had somehow moved into another realm for her. A higher plane, if that were possible. He was facing death, yet even in that moment he could only do the right thing. She could see plainly that there was no other choice for him and felt in awe of his amazing bravery. The strength she felt in his presence overwhelmed her. She didn't know what to say.

Luke stood up and put on his robe.

"So who's running the office now? Are you just taking the afternoon off, or what?"

There was humor in his voice that made her smile. How did he do it, she wondered? What kept him from going insane? She didn't know what was in that dream he talked about, but she wished she had some of it.

"Luke, you're the strongest man I know." The words came out of her without any thought, just simple expression.

He put his hands out on her shoulders.

"Thanks, Liz. I realize this decision of mine has a direct bearing on you. In two weeks, all hell is going to break loose. You'll be subjected to all sorts of assaults and criticisms. If you want to leave now, I'll understand. You can go if you want."

"Are you trying to get rid of me? Listen, I'm not leaving. Do I look like some rat that's going to desert a sinking ship? You can forget it. I'm going back to the office. And you'd better hurry your ass up and get down there, too. Laying up here in the bed half the day. The very idea. We've got work to do. Get it in gear, buddy."

She'd stood up and made it the door of the bedroom. There was really nothing else to say. She was right, there was work to do. Liz turned on her heels and left. When he heard the front door close behind her, he took a deep breath and stretched. In the reflection of the dresser mirror he caught a glimpse of himself. What a sight! He was ready for a good hot shower and shave before striking out for the rest of the day. Maybe even a haircut with shoe shine before arriving back at work.

He paused only briefly with his reflection. The eyes stared back at him. His decision was not without some apprehension. There was fear. The road that lay ahead of him was fraught with dangers. He knew they were out to get him. He wasn't sure why exactly, but he knew he would survive. One step at a time.

Before Liz could back out of the drive way her path was stopped by the police car pulling in behind her. What the hell does he want, she thought? She could see him pulling himself out of the patrol car. She stood up from her seat and stood by the car with the door open.

"What is it?" she queried him first.

"Ma'am we had a 911 call from this address. A call came in for me to check it out."

"Oh, yes, I made that call. No, everything is fine. I just misunderstood the situation here, that's all."

"What situation is that, ma'am?"

"My boss lives here. I just came by to check on him, that's all."

"Are you sure? He didn't try to hurt you did he?"

"Of course not, what on earth would make you think that?"

"Well, this is Luke Daniels. You are aware he is charged with murder, aren't you, ma'am?"

"Yes, of course, I know that. I'm his secretary."

"And what were you doing here at his house?"

The tone of the officer's question offended Liz. She knew she didn't need to make a fuss but his approach bothered her, whatever it was he was insinuating.

"Look, I told you I was the one that made the call but it was in error. I told the operator that took the call that there was no emergency. Now what is the problem?"

"Whenever we get an emergency call from the residence of a man accused of murder, especially when the caller is the same MO as his victim, we tend to take notice of it."

"Well, I was the caller and I'm telling you there was no emergency. Period. Now may I please leave?" Liz was starting to get upset.

"Why are you getting so upset, ma'am?"

"Because I need to get back to work and you won't let me." Liz's voice became louder.

"Is Mr. Daniels at home? This is his car, here?" The officer made a motion toward Luke's Cadillac.

"Yes, it is. And he's at home, and he's fine. And this is my car, and now I need to get in it and get back to my office to prepare for his arrival. May I do that, please?"

"Fine, that's fine. If you would, just give me your name for my report?"

"Your report? Why are you making a report?"

"Just routine, ma'am. Routine paperwork."

Liz gave the officer her name, home number and office number and even had to show him her driver's license. By the time he let her go and she got in her car, she could hardly contain herself. Tears streamed down her face. She looked out the car window at Luke's house realizing he was oblivious to this little incident. She was glad. He didn't need anything more to upset him right now. She knew from the officer's attitude that he already had Luke convicted. She wondered how many others had already done the same thing. When it came down to the trial, how much of that bias and supposition would settle into the courtroom and work against him?

She knew he was innocent but she had her doubts whether he could prove it or not. She hated it for him but this was a town where rumor and innuendo flourished. The power of suggestion could be so all pervasive that the truth could get buried in a bank of allusions. Luke would be guilty until proven innocent. Tears continued down her face as she backed the car out of the driveway and drove away. Across the street the officer watched and recorded her tears in his report.

CHAPTER SIXTEEN

O n Friday before the start of the trial, Luke was at Hays' office to go over the jury list provided by the Circuit Clerk. The prospective juror names were pulled from the voter registration rolls which were often outdated with much of the information obsolete. One hundred names were on the list along with addresses and phone numbers. Of course, it was illegal to attempt to make any contact with any possible juror and so the phone numbers came as surplusage. Often, lawyers would call the numbers just to see if the person was still alive and, thereby, clean up the list.

The study of the list was a significant portion of the trial preparation. Luke and Hays went over the list together, pooling their collective knowledge of the local community in an effort to familiarize themselves with the people who would be called to make up the jury of Luke's peers. After a couple of hours with the list, they had the hundred names whittled down to about seventy-five that were still living in the district to the best of their knowledge.

Luke took the list that remained and left Hays' office. The trial would start Tuesday after jury selection Monday. Luke would not plead guilty. Hays had accepted Luke's report of the same with indifference. There was no more protracted discussion on the subject. Luke made his pronouncement and Hays said alright, moving right on into the things they still had to do in preparation for trial.

This would not be a lengthy trial, Hays explained. There weren't many witnesses. Luke had no alibi witness: no one or nothing to corroborate where he was at the time Susan Weeks was murdered. But the DA had no eye witnesses. No one who could put him at the scene of the crime at the time it occurred; only a medical examiner's rough time-of-death projections.

Hays had a way of presenting things that made Luke feel stupid. His lawyer's voice did not carry an air of confidence over the situation. Luke perceived in Hays the notion that the smart thing to do would be to plead guilty and try to work on the least amount of time possible. That was not an option for Luke and so they no longer discussed it.

Monday, they would meet in the courtroom to pick a jury and then on Tuesday the day would begin that would determine Luke's fate. He was ready. Regardless of any other person's thoughts, he had resolved this matter in his own mind. He could not plead guilty. He would place his fate in the hands of twelve people of Bedford County. Please, God, let them be just.

Luke looked down at the list in his hands. He had until Monday to learn all he could about these seventy-five people. There was no time to waste.

At his office, he made several copies of the list before pulling Liz back to the break room to start going over the names. Some she recognized. There were several retired school teachers, several from out in the county and some she scratched off as having moved away.

They worked on the list the rest of the day. After going over it together, they separated, taking to the phones to contact others for help. Lawyers did this all the time. It came with the job to know what you were looking at with the twelve in the box. There were no other lawyers that Luke could call on this, however. There were lawyers in the town who sympathized with him but none who wanted to step out and actually help. Their words of encouragement came to Luke, but he understood that they would defend him very little. No one wanted to take a stand. They had their own problems to deal with and if another lawyer went down, then, hey, that's one less in the food chain.

He thought of the friends he had in the community that could help. Who did he trust? No one. As time rolled by since the indictment, his interaction with other lawyers had dwindled to almost nil. He didn't visit with any socially anymore. Since his split with Tommy Chipman there had not been another lawyer in his office. For anything. Business or personal. He'd not thought of that one so plainly before. Phone conversations had been the extent of his contact with any member of the bar outside of Hays Kennedy. Jane still called him regularly but they'd only talked on the phone.

Jane realized that he had already suffered so much defeat that he was no longer thinking like a lawyer, but as the accused. It hurt her to understand his pre-occupation with his own condition, but understood the mixed emotions that run rampant in people from all walks off life accused of crimes, especially one's that they did not commit. It can wreak havoc.

The light on Luke's phone indicated Liz was at her desk calling people continually. Luke couldn't think of anybody he wanted to call. He settled down into the blue leather of the high-backed chair he'd bought only a few months ago, a time when his life looked bright instead of the shades that now loomed before him. Where would the next week take him? Could he survive the onslaught that this trial would bring? Would he be able to weather the chaos and upheaval of this storm? Even if found not guilty, his life would never be the same. Regardless of the outcome he was forever altered. He sat up suddenly in his chair as if someone or something had addressed him.

"Luke!" the buzzer on his phone had sounded.

"Yes? What is it?"

"Willie Terrell is on the phone. Do you want to talk to him? I told him you were busy, but he said he had something to tell you."

"Probably that he's got another lawyer. Yeah, I'll talk to him." Luke punched the flashing light on his phone and picked up the receiver.

"Hey, Willie. What's up?"

"Boss man, how you doing today?"

"I'm alright, Willie. A little busy. What d'ya need?"

"My cousin, Freddie Johnson, you remember him?"

"Not really."

"His wife had a wreck a couple of years back. I tried to get 'em to use you as their lawyer but they got somebody else."

"Yeah, seems like I do remember." Luke didn't see why he needed to know this now.

"Yeah, some guy named Germany or something. Anyway, they got screwed. Wished they'd used you. Well, my cousin's got jury duty next week."

Damn, that's it, Luke thought. He's on the jury list. Luke scrambled around to his list and ran down the names. Yeah, there it is.

"Isn't that you, boss man. I mean, I don't want to pry into your business, but I read the papers. Reckon he's going to be on your jury?"

"Yeah, Willie. He's on the list. Listen, I need somebody to help me with this list. Go over the names and all. Help me learn as much about the people as possible. Could you come down here and help me? Go over it with me? See if there's anybody you know that you could give us information on?"

"Sure, boss. Be glad to. When you want me?"

"Right now, if you can."

"I'm on my way."

Luke lifted his head upward and with his eyes toward the ceiling, uttered a soft but clearly audible silent prayer, 'Thank you!'

Willie arrived shortly and the three of them gathered around the break room table and started over the names together. In a short time, Luke realized that Willie knew more about the goings on in Hampton than most lawyers. He was a wealth of information about both the black and white communities. Luke was amazed at how much the man picked up just by being out cutting grass.

By the end of the day they had something on nearly all of the prospective jurors on the list. The three of them plus Hays had come up with information that many law firms paid great sums of money for professionals to do. There would be more work on Monday when they actually looked at the people in person but for now they had a good start. Liz agreed to come in tomorrow to organize all the data and type it up under each name. Willie was taking a list with him and working on more material over the weekend. He would call Luke Sunday night if he had anything else.

The preliminary work was done. Jury instructions were roughed out. A trial brief was already at Hays' office. His three character witnesses were ready. Luke would testify as first witness for the defense. That was his case. Hopefully, the prosecutors' circumstantial case would fail and this would all be over next week.

There was no direct evidence. No eye witness. No murder weapon. By Luke's own admission, he was there. His honesty and sincerity would withstand their insinuation and the jury would not be able to conclude his guilt beyond a reasonable doubt. How could they? He hadn't done it. Luke was eager for the process to begin. The end was in sight.

Billy Gafford had his jury list, too. He also had the advantage of the entire law enforcement community and all its resources to help him in his preparation. Limox had a copy of the list getting all the information that he could. As an officer of the law, he felt it his duty to make sure those on the list knew he had done his job to keep this community safe and they, the jurors, needed to do theirs and find this criminal guilty. Nothing wrong with that at all, he felt. Just his job.

Billy had a copy of the list made for Jimmy, Wanda, and their investigator. The sheriff had a copy. Several of his deputies were going over that one. With all the law enforcement in the district going over the list, pumping information back to the District Attorney, there wouldn't be a soul show up Monday that didn't know in advance that Luke Daniels was guilty. Or so they thought.

Wanda had the standard jury instructions for a murder trial printed out with State of Mississippi vs Luke Daniels printed at the top. Their trial brief was the same one they used in numerous other murder cases. The weak spots had been fleshed out in several other trials with Judge Jones' approval.

The preparation was not that great for William Porter Gafford. He had done this before. He would do it again. With the Judge's help, they'd put another criminal behind bars.

The only difference this time was that it wasn't the typical defendant. Much more high profile, and the election loomed. This could be the biggest case of the year, possibly his career. A win would easily carry him into the election riding high. Not a time for mistakes. He might get so much good press off this that he could position himself for another office. Possibly statewide.

Billy had toyed with the idea before of seeking another office. If he won this case and then was re-elected to another four year term as District Attorney, he could be in a position for something bigger. Attorney General, perhaps. Maybe Congress. Yep, a lot riding on this one.

He was ready. The right jury on Monday and he would be sittin' pretty. He didn't see how he could lose, really. He knew the kind of jury that usually turned up in Bedford County; had picked countless jurors in his tenure as prosecutor. Hell, everybody connected with the case knew Daniels was guilty, from the courthouse personnel to law enforcement. Even his lawyer buddies didn't understand why the man turned down the plea bargain. Well, most of them. It was like a stroke of luck for Billy that there wasn't a plea. This way, he got all of the exposure of the trial. It was win-win for him. He was ready.

The Bedford County Courthouse filled up on Monday morning for a poll of prospective jurors. A total of sixty-three people showed up and took seats in the courtroom waiting to be told what to do. They came in response to a notice sent out by the Office of the Circuit Clerk. The letter said nothing about any specific trial. Just that they were commanded to personally appear before the Circuit Court of Bedford County to serve as a juror in said court at a term thereof. Most of them had the writ in their hands when they showed up.

The writing also stated that a failure to report could constitute contempt of court, punishable by a fine or imprisonment or both. Some people ignored that part and didn't show. If they knew about the proceedings of this court they knew that Judge Wendell Garmon Jones was the person who would apportion any punishment and nearing the election that was unlikely to happen.

There were few no-shows that day. Most had read the paper yesterday morning and were well aware that the trial they would be asked to render a verdict on was designated State of Mississippi vs. Luke Daniels. The lawyer accused of killing that girl. Sunday's paper recapped all the conjecture associated with the death together with pictures of the beautiful Susan Weeks. Several sections carried different parts of a story. Even the fashion section had an article on her modeling career with statements from some of the New Orleans agencies and stores that used her work. The collective conclusion was of great loss.

If anyone arrived that morning not knowing the trial agenda they soon learned. Luke was at the defense table with Hays Kennedy. Gafford and Little Jimmy were on the other side. Judge Jones had not yet made his entrance. The court reporter set up her equipment and then left. The bailiff milled about answering whatever question might come his way, shouldering importance that he got to carry on this day alone. Many of the jury pool knew him and gabbed freely, asking inappropriate questions about the trial, adding their views on guilt. No one had yet been instructed not to discuss the matter.

As murmuring rumbled around the room, eyes invariably settled on Luke. He tried desperately to appear calm and professional, just another lawyer at the table, but the surveillance of the crowd disturbed him, making him uneasy. Whenever he saw two heads together in whispers, invariably one of them turned to him. Apprehension crept onto their faces that coupled with the normal distrust of lawyers to form a preconceived image of the role they were about to play.

First, we kill all the lawyers. The line came to Luke from out of the commotion of restrained whispers that he tried to avoid hearing. He and Hays had their list of the poll out in front of them. Luke tried to concentrate on making sure Hays had all the information at his fingertips when the questioning started.

Judge Jones entered the room at twelve past nine. Instead of entering through his usual door from chambers, he came through the double doors at the back of the courtroom walking down the center aisle of the room, robes flowing. His gait was slow, magnanimous. He took his time, shaking hands and waving like a contestant in a beauty pageant. The District Attorney recognized the Judge's maneuver for what it was and went out to greet him, shaking hands with the Judge halfway down the aisle before grabbing another hand, then another.

The processional made its way to the front of the courtroom where Jones entered the bar through the passage held open by Gafford. Hays stood and extended his hand to Jones, as did Luke. Jones just waived and moved quickly to the bench.

"All rise," the bailiff bellowed his commencement call as the Judge reached the bench.

"Ladies and Gentlemen of Bedford County, thank you for being here this morning. Your attendance today is a responsibility of the citizenship that you enjoy in this great land of ours."

The voice droned on with the audience mesmerized by Judge Jones' effective oratory. He was good, there was no doubt about it. Of course, most of the people in this captive group didn't realize that he gave this exact speech, almost verbatim to every jury panel that came before him. By the time he finished with the group they were so eager to get on the jury that they fought for position on the front row, as if that would put them closer to doing their duty for God and country.

The members of the local bar had heard the discourse so many times that they could just about repeat it in unison with the Judge. Luke watched the faces of the assembly with concern. Out of this group of people would come the twelve that would decide his fate. Several looked familiar. No one he knew well. They stole furtive glances at him from their positions in the reception of the Judge's address. Luke tried to be placid and composed, reflecting the image of dignity in this crude and unbecoming position in which he found himself. Time slipped by.

At the prosecution table there were smiles all around. Just another day at the office for them. Gafford nodded at all the right places in Jones' talk. Little Jimmy was picking up the nuances of the persona, watching Gafford's courtroom demeanor closely. He gave the clear impression that he and the Judge were a team, working together to keep this land of ours free from criminals like the one that was sitting over there. His sideways glance at Luke came with a look of disdain for his kind.

Luke wanted to go over and punch him. Just a short while ago, he was Luke's friend. Let's do everything we can to help poor Luke. Well, I don't need any help from you, Gafford. Luke could feel the betrayal. Gafford was going for blood and Luke had better be ready.

"And, as is the case and custom of this court and others in this great land of ours, the prosecution will go forward first. They have the duty of proving their case and, thus, will lead off with the voir dire. Now, voir dire is a Latin term which means to seek the truth. You people may have watched a lot of Perry Mason or other lawyers on TV, but in my court you must recognize that I don't allow a lot of shifty lawyerin'. Our goal is to seek the truth. To arrive at the truth through the help of you people called here today."

"Now, if we can proceed. The case we are called to try on this day is entitled State of Mississippi vs. Luke Daniels. Mr. Daniels is charged with murder."

"What says the prosecution? Are you ready to proceed, Mr. Gafford?"

"The State of Mississippi stands ready to proceed, your honor."

"And what about the defense. Mr. Kennedy, are you ready?"

Hays stood and answered with a "Yessir!" to the Judge.

"Very well. Mr. Gafford, you may begin."

Gafford took to the podium where the microphone would pick up his voice. His navy blue suit would not button in the front around his large pot of a belly and his tie hung askew. His appearance in general was just unpolished enough to say to the jury that he was one of them. Two older men in the crowd had on ties, without jackets, but for the most part this was blue collar citizenry. His initial delivery echoed the sentiments delivered by the Judge, aligning himself with justice, truth and the American way in the minds of the jurors.

The clock moved on into the eleven o'clock hour. Not once did he ever mention Luke Daniels by name. He referred to the defendant and the barbaric crime. The life of a young girl cut down in her prime. So young. So beautiful. Such a waste.

"But we cannot decide a case on emotion. I want each and every one of you to promise me that you will reach a verdict based on the facts and the evidence. Can you do that?"

They all nodded yes eagerly. Gafford loved it. He always liked to get the jurors saying yes to him early on. It made it easier for them to keep saying yes. He nodded with them.

"And when I give you the facts to prove that the defendant is guilty, will you vote yes to find him guilty?" Gafford's nodding continued as the audience renewed their head work in affirmation.

"Thank you, ladies and gentlemen. That's all I ask of you." Gafford took to his seat with a look of pride in the good, fine, upstanding jurors that fate had handed him. He knew they were all going to do the right thing and vote to convict, regardless of which twelve went in the jury box. This was starting off just dandy for Billy.

Judge Jones made note of the hour and asked the panel how many were ready for lunch. Well over half raised their hands with grins on their faces. Luke wanted to get Hays up to do their portion before lunch, but Jones ignored them.

"Very well. We're going to break for lunch a little early. That way we can get back and start up right at one. I know you would all like to beat the lunch crowd and get in before twelve. We'll reconvene at one o'clock p.m."

The gavel struck the block with a solid ring and Jones stood, still making eye contact with as many of the voters as he could, smiling broadly. I'm your friend, I'm the one you need to vote for, his message was clear.

Before one o'clock most everyone was back and Jones took to the bench after spending the last twenty minutes among the crowd, smiling, back-slapping. Before the "all rise" got out of the bailiff's mouth, the Judge banged the gavel to begin the afternoon events.

"Mr. Kennedy, you may proceed." Jones announced coolly.

Hays took to the podium with his file filled with a mass of loose sheets of paper. He opened them up, peering down out of his glasses before speaking. He finally looked up and addressed the jury.

"Judge Jones has already informed you that we call this section of getting to the trial voir dire, which means to seek the truth. We are here to arrive at the truth, and no other purpose. Do you all agree with me on that?"

The response was generally assenting but lackluster. Many appeared to have already answered on that issue and were not wasting any more energy in reply. Hays moved on.

"Now, you all know that the prosecution must prove that a crime was committed." There was no response at this point.

Luke felt they were all wondering about Hays. Of course, a crime was committed or why would we be here?

"Do you already have any opinion concerning the guilt or innocence of my client because he has been charged with a crime? That crime is murder. Can you answer me on that?"

Luke followed the utterance around the room as it sank in, going from face-to-face hoping for some glimpse into the mind of a juror that was already against him. How many thought he was guilty at this point? Would it be possible to pull together a fair and impartial jury of his peers?

"Do you believe where there's smoke there's fire?"

Luke pushed himself to maintain a level of composure as more and more eyes moved to him. He tried to meet their inspection of him straight on.

"Is there anyone here who feels that he must have done something wrong or he would not have been charged with a crime?"

Luke felt control slipping. More and more eyes fixed on him as Hays continued with his statements. Luke had been keeping himself in the role of attorney, but as the faces peered at him directly he started feeling like the hunted. Like the criminal they were talking about. For years, he had stood in this room in the role of attorney talking about presumed innocence, that the defendant needed to be proven guilty. Suddenly he realized what a lie it was. In this seat you were guilty unless you could prove you were innocent.

"Now, you must accept the concept that indictment is merely a means of bringing a case to trial. Then, would you agree that indictment is not proof and is not evidence to be considered in reaching your verdict?"

There was no movement in the group. Not a sound was uttered. And, so, Hays continued.

"You realize that neither I nor Mr. Daniels was present at the grand jury proceeding."

Of course not. Why would they let some criminal up there with the high and sovereign work of the grand jury? Luke felt his throat tighten and wondered how much of the fear he felt right now showed on his face. Be a lawyer, be a lawyer, he kept telling himself. You're the professional. You've not done anything wrong.

"And do you understand that Luke Daniels does not have to present any evidence, does not have to testify? And that I don't have to cross-examine any witness, because there is no burden on us to prove anything?"

Luke thought he had never heard anything so preposterous in his life. He was a lawyer and he knew what Hays was saying was the law. But from where he sat right at this moment, in the defendant's chair, it sounded totally ridiculous. Almost laughable. The jurors had to be laughing at him for even saying such things. Luke tried to look back at the faces which all seemed to be looking at him now. They all looked at this criminal the District Attorney had to pull up here for them to pass judgment on.

"Can you accept that the entire burden of proof rests with the prosecution and never shifts to my client?"

Oh, Hays please sit down, Luke thought. Everything that came out of his mouth sounded asinine to Luke, as if with every sentence he was bringing the panel of prospective jurors closer to the idea that Luke must be guilty. Luke continued to scan the group, while Hays went on. The words became weak to him, distant, unrecognizable as he watched the faces that were taking in the maxims from his lawyer. Those faces became blank, expressionless as Hays went on and then, finally, concluded. He sat down beside Luke and began to go through the lists of names where he had made notations while he stood at the podium. Hayes knew that he had made his point, but Luke, self-involved, couldn't quite get past the implied onus of guilt.

Judge Jones took over the show again, telling the panel that they would be excused for a few moments while he met with the attorneys in an effort to pick the jury. On the stroke of the gavel, the group filed out amid whispers and muted cacophony.

"Okay, Luke what did you think?" Hays whispered to Luke at the table.

"Huh?" Luke mumbled back to Hays.

"The Judge will be calling us back to chambers soon to make our selections for the jury. Did you make any decisions about the people you saw? Any sympathetic looks? Automatic strikes? Come on, Luke. We haven't got much time. You know I'm counting on your help in this."

Luke pulled out the notes he'd gathered together over the weekend and started the process of elimination, hoping for a stroke of genius as they picked the twelve. Hays quickly took in the few comments Luke had from his personal observations and struck some names from the list. But he made sure Hays knew they wanted Freddie Johnson on there.

"Gentlemen, if you will join me in my chamber, we'll get this process started." Jones' order came tersely. Without waiting for any response, he disappeared through the door behind the bench with Gafford and Clay trotting dutifully along immediately.

"Come on, Luke. Let's get this over with."

In his chambers, Judge Jones sat in his chair behind the desk, high and proud, even haughty. From that perch Jones looked down into the eyes of his subjects. The desk was of the same dark veneer that rose majestically before the Judge in the courtroom. There were two wing chairs in front of the desk with a lavish brocade cover where two lawyers could sit and almost hide their faces from one another. Gafford took one and Jimmy pulled up an arm chair beside him. Hays took the other chair leaving Luke standing amidst the group like a kid called to the principal's office. He felt oafish standing there, but there was no place for him to put himself. No place to run and hide.

"Luke, pull that stool up and use it."

Judge Jones motioned to a step stool over by the bookcase. Luke grabbed the stool and tried to position it like a lawyer next to Hays. A table placed by Hays' chair kept him from getting too close and so Luke wound up awkwardly facing Hays, Gafford, Clay and Jones. The short stool put his knees up in his face and his body wrenched forward awkwardly.

"Okay, Gafford, what do you have on this. Any challenges for cause."

"We have none, Your Honor."

Luke caught a devious glance that carried some hint of cunning from the District Attorney, a flash behind his eyes that denoted more than he meant to show. Before Luke could center on Gafford's breach, Jones jumped in drawing attention his way.

"Alright, then, Mr. Kennedy, what do you have?"

Hays shuffled his papers, dropping several to the floor. Luke hastened to pick them up and get Hays' answer. Hays stuck them out to Luke and mumbled something as his finger pointed to a name on the list.

Why was Hays mumbling to him? He was the lawyer. Speak to the Judge. Luke looked down at the name. Berle Springer. White male. Retired. The name meant nothing to him. Why was Hays concerned with it? He looked at Hays without response.

"Judge, prospective juror number nine failed to indicate that he was willing to follow the law if he disagreed with it. You know he must follow the law regardless of what his own opinion is. I ask that he be struck for cause."

"Well, just because he didn't answer your question doesn't mean he won't follow the law. I'm not going to strike him. Anything else?"

"Yes sir, prospective juror number 20 said he was a neighbor of the District Attorney's."

"But he said that wouldn't influence his decision, Judge." Gafford chirped up without waiting for a response.

"Gafford's right. If I struck everybody that knew one of us or was a neighbor or whatever, we'd never get a jury. I'll allow him. Anybody else?"

"Yes sir. Juror number 23 said he was some kin to Jimmy Clay."

"Well, same reason again. I can't let that keep us from getting a jury. I'll allow him."

Three strikes, you're out, Luke thought. Hays got no where with Jones. Damn. What was happening here? Luke watched the others in the room shuffle papers and appear pensive, absorbed in the solemn business of deciding on the twelve, but something about the process bothered Luke. There was some connection between Billy and the Judge. A confederacy of mutual concern over their common plights in the political arena. Luke wanted to stand up and expose them. Make them stop this charade of justice, but what would he say? To what one tangible thing could he point. He would be thought even more of a lunatic than they considered him now. No, that would not help him.

Hays was oblivious to it all. He sat in his chair locked in the realm of the voir dire, not realizing there were other elements at work here. Luke wanted to tell him to wake up.

"Alright, the first name on the list then is Adrian McCarthy. Mr. DA, what do you say?" Jones wanted to move things along. Perhaps they could get this done in time to get some good shots on the evening news.

Adrian McCarthy was a white male, fifty-nine years old, owner of a local shoe store. Very Republican. It didn't take Billy Gafford long.

"We accept."

"Mr. Kennedy?" Jones didn't waste any time.

"We accept."

Luke looked at Hays warily. He wouldn't have accepted Mr. Adrian McCarthy. Too tight laced, Luke thought. He also thought it was clear from his notes that he would prefer not to have him. He was hoping that Mr. Adrian McCarthy was too tied up with his business to come in today, but he appeared and Luke would have struck him.

Gafford struck the next, a black woman. Prosecutors didn't like having blacks on criminal juries. Not likely to convict anybody, they said.

Gafford accepted number three, a white female, homemaker. She looked very much like juror number one, very prosecution oriented. Let's lock up all the criminals.

Hays was fumbling with his papers. Jones rapped his pencil repeatedly on the desk in wait. Finally, Hays accepted. Again, Luke was astonished.

"Hays, are you sure?" Luke tried to whisper to his lawyer in the close quarters.

"Yeah," Hays whispered back. He held up his folder and spoke behind it in a tone that surely carried to the others. "You're a good looking guy. She'll probably think you're cute. Try to wink at her."

Luke thought of winking at one of the decision makers over the fate of his life. His mind went blank at the very idea.

I can't wink at a juror. That's ridiculous, isn't it. He tried to mull over the idea, but his brain wouldn't work on it. It just didn't compute. He sat back on his stool with his legs up to his chest and wrapped his arms around them, feeling lost.

The jury selection went on. Luke did not speak again and let Hays finish the job. Jones pushed the process and finished it in short order. In less than an hour they had twelve names and two alternates. Judge Jones stood and ordered the others back to counsel tables to which they dutifully returned.

"All rise." The bailiff's cry went out again as Judge Jones took the bench. Those milling around in the audience took their seats as the Judge handed the list of names to the Circuit Clerk to call forward to the jury box.

Inez Tanner, the Circuit Clerk was here herself today. Rarely did she attend trials, usually sending one of her deputy clerks up to fulfill her duties while she attended to more pressing matters in the main office. Not this time, a politician herself she was present and taking care of business in this trial. She called out the names slowly and deliberately.

Adrian McCarthy came forward when his name was called. Apparently Adrian was not worried about his shoe business today when he could sit on the jury for one of the biggest trials of the year, maybe biggest ever in Hampton. They might get a shot of him on TV. He was fifty-nine and a successful business man with a no bull attitude. His hair was gone and his face was aged, but his mind was sharp. In his thirty years in business in this town, he had dealt with shoplifters and other types of thieves. His store had even been burglarized. He knew what to do with criminals. They were ruining this country and had to be dealt with seriously.

Mrs. Louden Stevens, Peggy, the homemaker, came up when her name was called. She was a fifty-five year old white lady who had worked hard all her life. She and Mr. Stevens had a boy in college and a boy in high school. She hoped neither of them was ever in any trouble like this Luke Daniels. She'd been to the beauty parlor to get her hair done early this morning because she didn't want to be all frumpy looking if they caught her on TV.

Next came Freida Mixon, sixty-one and white, a grandmother from the rural part of Bedford County. Gray-haired and with a face that was sunburned from taking care of her vegetable garden, not really looking like she wanted to be there. Rather be at home watching her stories, but they called her name so she came up to take her seat. Her garden needed tending. There were tomatoes that were ripening every day. The squash was putting on blooms. She just liked to be there and watch it grow. Maybe this would be over with quickly. She didn't let on when they asked all those questions, but she had seen the news about what happened to that girl. Just awful.

Mrs. Wallace Batson, sixty-five year old white female, also a retired grandmother who had taught school for thirty years. She was stern-faced and stood upright to five feet ten inches. Three years ago she left the school and was glad to be able to serve in this capacity. She took her seat next to Mrs. Mixon, eager to do her civic duty. She was a stalwart member of the Becker Street Baptist Church.

James Hutchinson, thirty-one, white male, was assistant manager of Beemon's Groceries, a local supermarket. He bounced up to the jury box with a spring in his step and a broad grin on a plumb round face, beaming proudly as he looked toward the District Attorney's table. The face turned sinister as he moved his gaze around in Luke's direction. James thought he had seen it all in the grocery business. He knew how crime was affecting this country. Mr. Beemon, the owner of the line of grocery stores where he worked didn't like him being away from the store, but he understood that this service was necessary to keep our land safe.

Philip Dunbar was a thirty-eight year old white male nurse, working four days a week in a hospital in New Orleans. He traveled back and forth from his primary residence in the southern part of Bedford County. He was originally from New Orleans before moving his family to the rural countryside of Mississippi ten years ago to get them away from the bad influence of the big city. He had seen a lot in the emergency room in New Orleans. Not much could phase him. He just wanted to do the right thing.

Joe Lee Pigott was an electrician with a local contractor. He was white and forty years old, a stout man with a sour disposition whose wife and children feared him. His salt and pepper hair was combed straight back and he loved country music.

Next came Freddie Johnson, forty-two year old black male who had numerous laborer skills having worked as a brick mason, a welder, a roofer and a carpenter. He was Willie Terrell's cousin and he didn't say anything, but he and Willie had talked about this case. Freddie was a little nervous that something might come out about Willie. Willie sure thought a lot of this lawyer that was on trial for murder.

Roanda Richardson was a twenty-nine year old black female who worked at Guaranty National as a teller. She was a pretty young woman with milk chocolate skin. She was single and the mother of two small children whom she struggled to support. The bank teller's salary wasn't much but it kept her off welfare. She hated to have to miss her income for jury duty, but she didn't want to get herself in trouble by not showing up. Roanda was an honest, hard-working pious young woman who made sure that her children were always in church. She took her role as a juror as seriously as she did her job as a bank teller, dealing with other peoples' money. Here she would be dealing with someone else's life and she would be as cautious and exacting in this role as she was at the bank.

Janet Mosby was a twenty-eight year old homemaker, mother of three whose husband worked as a driver for the local beer distributor. Her three children had come in three years and her weight reflected what that did to a woman. Her mother kept the children for her this week, so the break of jury duty was a nice relief from being stuck at home with the kids. This would be much more entertaining than daytime television. She was looking forward to the break.

Kareem Townsend was a used car salesman. He was a black male, thirty, with over two years of courses toward his college degree. He was still taking a course or two at the University but didn't attend full time. He was a good salesman and the only black man in sales at the dealership. He did well for himself, despite some of his friends' quips about him acting white.

Rozelle Thompson was sixty-nine years old. He was black, the retired janitor from the high school. His hair was mostly gone and he walked with a stoop. He lived on his social security check with his wife of fifty-four years in a small house in the poorest section of Hampton. He had seven children and they all had college degrees.

There were two alternates, Elizabeth Hartley and Joel Duncan, who would sit and hear all the testimony and then be dismissed unless, for some reason, one of the regular jurors could not finish out their service. Both looked resigned to the fact that they would have to spend the next days of their lives caught up in the courtroom of Bedford County.

Twelve people filled the jury box that faced Luke. He looked at them solemnly, trying to face them without fear and with courage. There was no reason for him to be craven. He tried to assess the twelve's perception of him. Did they see him as the innocent man he was? Or did they all hold the general public's preconceived notion of lawyers in general? Beads of sweat formed on his upper lip and his breathing was being restricted by the knot forming in his stomach. His usual portion of intestinal fortitude was in jeopardy of being consumed by the carnivorous stranglehold of anxiety. Breathe, Luke, breathe.

For several moments the jury and Luke took each other in. They gawked at him as if he were a hog going to the slaughter block. Luke's eyes were fixed on them, also. Everyone in the room was aware of the exchange. Gafford sat in his chair praying that the jurors were getting their disapproval of the defendant in order already. Without hearing a word they could form ideas that would survive any testimony presented. Despite all the court's admonition about how they were not to begin their deliberation until all the evidence had been heard, most of them would have their minds made up long before the testimony finished. And many would make a decision in these few minutes.

Judge Jones let the situation simmer for a few moments. He watched from his perch behind the bench as the twelve men and women and two alternates sized up the job they were about to embark upon. He had no idea how Luke felt. He tried to read the man's face but found a blank there without any feeling, with no emotion registering. How could the man face the prospects before him so unruffled? So cool. Perhaps he really was the cold-blooded killer.

"Alright, ladies and gentlemen of the jury, now that we have you twelve selected I have some instructions for you. Some rules we have to follow here in this court. I may have asked you already, but how many of you have served on a jury before."

Judge Jones looked out at the group of men and women. No one said anything.

"Well, then, that's good. You can all learn this together."

Jones started the process of going through the preliminary instructions to the jury. More definite instructions on the law would come later at the conclusion of the trial, but for now, he carefully led them through the business that they were about and what was expected of them. With warmth and humor he had them eating out of his hand by the time it all finished.

"Alright, then, that's about it. We've gone a little over today. My court reporter's pointing out to me that it's a little past five. I'll try to do better the rest of the time. You are all ready for your work tomorrow. If there's nothing else, we stand in recess until tomorrow at morning at nine o'clock."

The gavel struck with its sound of dismissal and the room began to clear. Luke stood with Hays, as did Billy and Jimmy, while the jurors filed out of the box and down the aisles of the courtroom. Luke's jaw clenched and released as he watched each one of the twelve depart to their respective lives, watching closely for some glimpse of insight, some wisdom on what it would take to convince these people that he was not a murderer. He hadn't killed anyone. The only death he was responsible for was the hope of knowing love like that of Susan Weeks. With her name floating into his head he fought back tears. He wished he could lay his head down on this very table in front of him and cry. His shoulders drooped and as he saw the last man go out the back door he sunk back to his chair and sighed intensely, letting the air escape from his lungs where it had been held captive while the jury exited.

CHAPTER SEVENTEEN

Tuesday's front page headlines pronounced, "JURY PICKED IN DANIEL'S TRIAL. TESTIMONY STARTS TODAY." Under pictures of Luke and Susan side by side, the articles portrayed Susan as an angel and Luke as the devil.

TV news gave its version. Film clips of Luke leaving the courthouse and the bank where Susan worked filled the screen while the reporter talked of the Honorable Judge Jones and his masterful command in the courtroom. Money couldn't buy this type of coverage and Jones showed up ready to fill the shoes of the learned master portrayed by the media.

Unfortunately, Judge Jones' view of that role was not fairness and justice but showmanship demonstrating that he was tough on crime. Just what the voters wanted. And he had twelve voters sitting in front of him when he took the bench for the trial of Luke Daniels.

"All Rise" came the call as Jones entered the courtroom and stepped up behind the bench. He continued to stand as he welcomed the jurors. He inquired of their health and a good night's sleep in preparation for the job they had to do today.

They had not been sequestered over the request of Luke and his counsel. All the jurors had assured the Judge that they would not watch any news and would not listen to anyone or discuss the case in any way until he instructed them to begin their deliberation. No one wanted to be locked up for the duration of the trial and the Judge didn't want to have to make them. So they all went home with Jones' admonition that they were good honest folk that he could count on to be fair and impartial in their handling of the grave matter before them. They loved him for it.

"Please be seated," Jones continued as he pulled up his seat. "Mr. Gafford, are you ready to proceed?"

"We are, your honor."

"And you, Mr. Kennedy?"

"Yes sir, Judge." Hays stood and answered confidently.

"Alright, then. Mr. Gafford, if you wish to make an opening statement, then you may proceed."

"Ladies and gentlemen of the jury, you have been called here today to render a decision on the facts you are about to hear. A young girl has been murdered, brutally, in the prime of her life. She was twenty-six years old, well-educated, with a great job, and her whole future before her. Until she met Luke Daniels. Her life changed that night and now that life is no more. We come before you with the evidence necessary to find this murderer guilty."

Gafford started in on just what that evidence was, quickly going through the state's proof. He ran down each witness and the role that person played in the prosecution. He never mentioned drugs, he never mentioned rape. Not specifically, but his words left so much unspoken that every juror's mind would have to be wondering what caused a man to do this?

"No one else was there that fateful night. Wouldn't it be great if we had an eye witness to tell us exactly what happened and make our job easier? Unfortunately, the only person that knows exactly what happened is Luke Daniels, and he is the one that brought about this nightmare for Susan Weeks. When you have heard all the evidence, there will be no doubt in your mind that he is the one, and we will then ask you to find him guilty."

Gafford sat down at his table with a solemn face, knowing that every juror was starting to form an opinion. Even though the Judge would continually remind them that they couldn't do that until all the evidence was presented, the game started now.

Jones watched the jurors. He didn't want to hurry through this part, allowing the jurors to cogitate. He had already told them that what lawyers said was not evidence and that they should only consider testimony presented by competent witnesses, but he knew how it worked. These were human beings whose senses were already feeding information to a brain that was adjusting perception. Now, he had to give Hays a shot.

"Mr. Kennedy, do you have anything to say?" asking almost disdainfully.

Hays stood up and brought his prepared speech to the podium. He knew all about juror bias. In this day of rampant crime and nonstop reporting, trying to keep at least some of the members of the jury open-minded was a formidable task. Some of them looked like they were ready to convict right now. Hays needed just one to block a conviction. He kept reminding himself of that fact as he looked over the panel.

"Ladies and gentlemen, I am proud to be here representing this man because I know he did not do what they are trying to convince you he did. Luke Daniels has been a friend and colleague for many years. I've known him professionally. I've seen him in the courtroom doing exactly what I'm doing now and I know what kind of man he is."

The words caught Luke off guard. They had not discussed the opening statement and Luke had no idea what Hays was going to say. From the discord that had plagued their relationship, Luke was uncertain about how Hays would present him, but Hays was a consummate professional. He was doing what lawyers do. He was putting all personal feelings aside and representing his client.

Hays was taking the high road and he was determined to carry Luke with him. This jury had to feel that Hays believed in Luke's innocence, whether that was the truth or not.

"Luke Daniels only came into contact with this woman because he was trying to do his job. He is a lawyer and she came to him for legal advice. He is also a man and she was a woman. A very beautiful woman, there is no doubt about that. You will get to hear even

Luke testify about that himself. You will hear him say how from the moment he met her, something happened between them that changed his life. A life that he wanted to share with Susan. Unfortunately, there was something going on in her life that she needed to straighten out first. Luke never learned what that was, and now that she's gone we may never know, but Luke is not her killer.

In hindsight, he wished he had made different decisions in this situation. He wishes he had stayed at his office and handled this matter like he had done so many other times in his years as a lawyer. He wishes he had not allowed emotions to get in the way and cloud his judgment. He wishes he had not left her at all that night, because he knows in his heart that if he had not, she would be alive today. So, you see, ladies and gentlemen, Luke does feel some responsibility for what happened to this young woman that night. Not because he killed her, but because some different choices might have brought about a different outcome.

There is no question that he was with her that night. We have never denied that. Yes, they did go to bed together. Don't let sex interfere with the real facts and cloud your judgment. You have all taken an oath that the state must prove this case to you beyond a reasonable doubt. That doubt should remain in your mind throughout this trial because the state cannot give you one good reason why this man would have killed this woman. There is simply no motive. When you hear Luke Daniels tell you what happened that night, then you will know that he is a good and honorable man that could never have done this. The prosecution has taken the easy road with a collection of evidence that does nothing more than tell you these two were together that night. Luke has never denied that. While the state spends all their time trying to convict an innocent man, the real murderer is loose. When you find this man not guilty, perhaps they will then get on to finding out who really did this. Thank you."

Luke was amazed. For the first time in a long time, he saw a glimmer of hope. Everything Hays said was exactly right. Luke knew they had wasted their time on him when the real killer was out there somewhere. If only Jane and Cody could come up with something that would help take the focus off Luke for just a little. Cody had the subpoena for DeWeese. Luke still wasn't sure what good that was going to do them. Hays had talked to him and all he did was praise Susan and curse Luke. That didn't sound too much like help from Luke's chair.

He looked at the jury. There was no way all of them would be convinced by Gafford. This was going to be tough but he was going to get through it. One step at a time.

"Mr. Gafford, you may call your first witness." Jones didn't waste any time before moving things forward. Hays had done a superb job and he didn't want the jurors dwelling on his comments too long.

"The State calls Jennifer Holt."

Gafford had it figured that this was his best first witness. He always presented his case in as close to chronological order as possible. Jennifer was the first to see the dead girl. They were roommates and so he hoped to get off on a personal note attaching some intimacy to the deceased with the jury.

After being sworn, Jennifer answered some preliminary questions about her residence, employment and marital status before getting to specifics.

"How did you come to be acquainted with Susan."

"We both worked at the bank." Jennifer went on to discuss how they had become friends and then roommates. After some lengthy discussion of their close personal relationship, Gafford moved to the weekend of the murder.

"Yes, I was out of town, visiting friends in Gulfport. Susan was supposed to go with me but she backed out at the last minute."

Jennifer continued with where she was on the Coast, how long she was gone and when she returned. She stopped when she got to the part about coming into her house.

"I know this is hard for you, Jennifer, but I need you to help me here. What did you do when you got back to the house?"

Jennifer went on about going inside and how cold it was. She went to turn on some heat but started seeing things around the house and how strange she started to feel. She described seeing crumbs on the dining table, wine glasses in the living room. Her testimony said clearly that two people had been there in a social setting. She said she knew something was wrong because Susan was always so neat. She would never have left crumbs on the table or used glasses out.

Gafford continued, with his questions leading her along. And what did you do in the living room? And what did you do in the foyer? She told about noticing the overturned lion and becoming frightened. And did you go down the hall? Yes. And did you go to the bedroom? Yes. And did you go on in?

The tension in the room was extreme. Every juror was on the edge of the seat, eyes and ears tuned in to Jennifer Holt. Gafford was leading the witness but Kennedy made no effort to raise an objection. Luke tried to talk to him but Hays shushed him. Hays was also mesmerized by the girl's account of coming to the scene of the crime.

Jennifer's hands came up and she buried her face, sobbing.

"It was horrible. The room was a wreck. Everything all torn up. There was blood. Susan was…" The voice broke off into sobs while the DA moved to the witness stand and paternally stroked Jennifer's back comfortingly. It was highly irregular for a lawyer to make physical contact with a witness but here Gafford played the role of paternal protector to the hilt.

After a while, the sobs settled and Jennifer looked out at the jury. She told of running out of the house and down the driveway. How she was hit by a car and the police came and finally she stopped. Gafford thanked her for bearing with him through this difficult process and allowed the bailiff to give her some water.

"Now, Ms. Holt, do you know the defendant?

"Yes, I do." Her tone changed dramatically, signifying her antagonism toward him.

She talked about how long they had known each other. How they had gone out on occasion. No, she had not ever seen him and Susan together, but she knew they had been together that night.

She had no first hand knowledge of this and so was not a proper witness to testify about it. Yet, again Hays made no effort to object. Luke again whispered to him about it, but Hays shook his head and turned back to the witness.

Luke and Jennifer had been friends. He didn't understand how she could be displaying such venom for him now. She had no reason to lie, and she wasn't really lying, but everything she said about Luke was contemptuous and scornful. Her eyes, her face, her words, all came together to present an odious image of the man accused of murder. She pointed her finger at Luke when asked to identify him and spoke with disgust.

"That's Luke Daniels."

The words hung in the air accusingly, as if she had identified the murderer. Several jurors squirmed in their seats, their minds making one inference after another. Some had their arms crossed as they looked Luke over scornfully. Luke fought to hold his head up but felt the weight of the accusations bearing down on him. He had originally thought Jennifer would be a good witness for them to start with because they knew each other and she liked him, but the pervasive slurs and insinuations of the last several months had distorted Jennifer's view of Luke. She had not lied in any way, but her truth was far from complimentary. With only a few words she had pitched Luke behind a dark shadow of fate. He felt clouds of doom forming around him and couldn't even look at the jurors.

Hays questioned Jennifer about Susan's activities. Who was she dating? There was no one. Had Susan ever mentioned anything about Luke to her? No, she had not. Did she know any reason Luke Daniels would have to harm Susan? She had to say no, there was nothing. Did she know of anyone that might want to harm Susan? What did she know of Susan's modeling?

"The only thing I know is that it made her a nice sum of money for what, to me, seemed like just having fun. She would get to go off and play dress-up and come back with a big fat check."

The jurors all got a chuckle from that. Hays touched again on how Susan never mentioned anything that might be bothering her.

"She never said anything to me and I never saw anything in her that seemed to be upsetting. She never talked to me about anything she might need a lawyer for. Everything in her life seemed to be going great. She was busy. Between the marketing job at the bank, the modeling work and taking courses on her doctorate, she was on the go all the time, but nothing seemed to be bothering her. Frankly, I was always amazed at how she seemed to balance everything so well. If there was something wrong in her life, something she needed legal advice on, she never shared it with me"

Jennifer's tone seemed to be setting the stage that Luke's version was a lie. Hays established with Jennifer that she could not say who killed Susan and knew nothing about what happened with Luke. He reiterated that point before sitting down. The DA did not have any redirect for Jennifer and the Judge dismissed her while moving quickly to get the DA to call his next witness.

"We call Detective Dick Limox."

Limox appeared from the witness room and strutted to the stand. In the audience he noticed his friend, Jerry Mason, whom he gave a little wink, appearing a little cocky, but friendly and easy-going. The clerk swore him in before Gafford began his questioning. They went through the name, employment and other background information before getting to his role in the trial.

"Sgt. Limox, how did you come to be involved in this matter?"

"I was in my car and got the call over the radio when I immediately drove to the scene of the crime. Being the only detective there, I took the lead and immediately began my investigation into the murder."

"Was this your first murder investigation?" Gafford prompted his witness.

"Heck, no. I've been on the force for over ten years. Seen all kinds of things. I've been a detective for six. I've investigated numerous murders."

Yeah, most of the middle of the night drunken brawls was Luke's assessment, but the jurors were enthralled with the witness and the captivating field of police detective work. They had front row seats to a crime scene investigation. Limox relished the limelight. His responses became slow and deliberate, setting out how he had followed all the rules of law in his expert inspection and analysis of the evidence. He wanted them all to know what an excellent job he had done and Gafford allowed him to flaunt it. He had done his job and now he needed these fine people to do theirs and convict this murderer.

Luke felt indignation at the detective's tone. He and Limox knew each other. They had worked on cases together. Luke had represented clients whom Limox had arrested. Drug busts. Burglaries. Assaults. Their working relationship was always amiable and good-natured, but now it was a different story. Limox appeared certain Luke did it. What was it that convinced him? Luke knew quite a bit about Limox and some of his investigatory tactics. Luke discovered on more than one occasion Limox's stretching evidence to meet his needs, and he was certain that Limox had planted drugs on one of his clients.

"And what other evidence did you observe?"

"Well, there was a shoe print on the door where it had been kicked in. The facing was busted off inside the bedroom.

"Have you had this evidence analyzed."

"Yes, we have. My follow up report had the results of my testing. The shoe was a running shoe, a Nike size ten and a half."

"And have you recovered the shoe that made that mark."

"Well, not exactly."

"What do you mean, not exactly?"

"During our execution of a search warrant at the home of the defendant, we recovered a pair of Nike running shoes, size ten and a half."

Gafford paused, allowing the weight of the evidence to sink in. The door was kicked in by a Nike running shoe just like the one found at the home of the defendant. He knew there was not an exact identification, but he wanted the jury to have time to think about it being the same shoe.

"Could you explain to us your identification?"

"Well, it's definitely the same kind of shoe…"

"Objection, your honor, the witness has not established that it was the same shoe."

"I believe he said it was the same kind of shoe, Mr. Kennedy. Not the same shoe. Continue, Detective." Jones' attention stayed on Limox with irritation at Kennedy's interruption.

"Yes sir, Your Honor. The shoe print on the door was made when the door was kicked in. The force of the shoe against the door and the paint and all made an exact identification impossible. All we know for sure is that the shoe we found at the defendant's house is the same kind of shoe that kicked in the door where the victim was murdered."

Silence. Gafford paused over the papers at his desk without looking at anything in particular. He wanted to smile but knew he couldn't let the jury see him express any cheer when they were talking about death. But glee was what he felt over his prowess in the strikes he was getting at his prey. When he turned back to the witness he caught the same look in the Judge's eye. They were racking up the points together.

His direct examination of the witness continued. Whose fingerprints were on the table? Luke Daniels. Whose fingerprints were on the wine glasses? Luke Daniels. Whose fingerprints were in the bedroom? Luke Daniels. Over and over again they put Luke in the house but nothing more.

"Sgt. Limox, what did you find to be the cause of death of the Susan Weeks?"

"Objection, your honor, this witness is not qualified to testify to…"

"If he did in the course of his investigation, I'll allow it." Jones' ruling was a quick message to Gafford to ask the question a different way.

"Sergeant, in the course of your investigation, what did you find was the cause of death?"

"She suffered a subdural hematoma from several severe blows to her head."

"Several?"

"Yessir. From the condition of the room and the condition of the victim's body, we concluded that there was a struggle with quite a bit of physical effort expended. There were bruises on her legs and back. We found teeth marks consistent with the dental patterns of the defendant."

The hushed intake of quick breaths from the jury made a faintly discernible stir like the rushing of light wind that left the courtroom screaming in silence. No one made a sound. Luke sat dumbfounded. He knew how those bite marks got there. He remembered his teeth against her flesh, the taste of her skin in his mouth. He wanted to cry out loud. The pain of remembering was tearing him up inside, but all he could do was sit motionless. Without words. He could feel the eyes of the jury on him again, peering into his very spirit. He didn't care. Maybe they would see inside and know the truth. That it was life, not death, that he celebrated with Susan.

"The abrasions around her vagina were indicative of intercourse consistent with the theory of rape."

"That's enough. We object, Your Honor. This witness doesn't know what he's talking about and has no basis to be giving this kind of testimony. We ask that the testimony be stricken from the record."

It was Luke standing up making the objection, screaming it loudly, much more loudly than necessary for the Judge to hear. Jones started banging his gavel. Gafford moved forward and started shouting that Mr. Daniels was out of order. Bang, bang, bang, the gavel beat against the wood as the bailiff slipped his hand to his revolver.

Hays was pulling on Luke, trying to get him to sit down. He stood beside Luke and pushed him in the chair, before speaking to the Judge.

"Your Honor, this witness is testifying about matters which he is not qualified to present. We ask that testimony outside the scope of his position be struck from the record and the jury advised to disregard it."

"Mr. Kennedy, who's the lawyer here? You are counsel of record, Mr. Daniels is not. Now, if he's going to get so involved that he can't control himself, we'll have to dismiss you and let him be the lawyer." Jones knew who the better criminal attorney was.

"I understand, Your Honor," Hays responded meekly.

"Mr. Daniels, do you understand?"

Jones glared down at Luke who sat there without response. He had no words at all. Nothing came out.

"Mr. Daniels," Jones barked out the name, "do you understand?"

The Judge's nostrils flared and his complexion reddened under the thin red hair on top of his head. He was unaccustomed to getting no response from a subject and Luke's failure to reply unnerved Jones. His irritation was apparent to the entire courtroom. Before he could say or do anything else, Kennedy jumped in.

"Your Honor, we do understand. I believe I can speak for my client as well as myself that you will not have any more of this. In light of the circumstances, I would like to request a five minute recess."

Jones continued his scowl down at Luke, never raising his eyes to Hays as he spoke the request. No one in the courtroom made a sound while the Judge's breathing came over his microphone distinctly. Finally, the Judge sat back, picked up the gavel and before striking it, made his announcement.

"Granted. This court will stand in recess for five, no make that ten, minutes."

The gavel banged the wood hard, sending a sharp clap through the room. Jones immediately swept from the bench and through the door leading to his chambers with his robe waving behind him. The door slammed behind with a solid thud and the courtroom was left in silence. No one moved.

Gafford shuffled papers briefly before announcing that he was going out to make a call. Dick Limox stood up at the witness stand and stretched, amused by the whole affair. He stepped down from the stand and walked over to the prosecutor's table with a big grin to Jimmy. The bailiff disappeared, then returned quickly from the Judge's chamber going straight to the defendant's table.

"The Judge wants to see you," he announced to Hays.

"Just me?"

"That's what he said." The bailiff stumbled off without more.

Hays looked down at Luke who still sat mute at the table. They had not spoken since the outburst. Luke had not moved.

"Well, I wonder what this is about? Gee, Luke, nothing like helping out your lawyer. See if you can think of another way to help your case."

The sarcasm dripped from his lips, Hays was furious with Luke. He was also furious with himself. He felt like he was getting run over and he didn't like it. There was something else afoot here, but he couldn't quite put his finger on it. He stared down at Luke who still had not spoken. Was Luke hiding something from him? What was going on here that Hays couldn't identify?

"Well, guess I'd better not keep the Judge waiting. I'll just go on back and take the ass-chewing you earned us."

Hays disappeared through the door to the Judge's small back office. Luke watched him withdraw into the secluded room where he had gone many times before in civil cases and criminal matters. Heated discussions, near fights, shouting all occurred behind that closed door. And when the lawyers returned to the courtroom their appearance typically belied the goings on outside the presence of the jury. Luke stared at the door, without movement. His mind was flipping around like a top on a bumpy floor. He couldn't believe his own outburst.

He felt the discomfort of the jury just a few feet away from him. Jones was so mad he forgot to dismiss them. They were still sitting in the box. Some of them had stood up. Others were squirming in their chairs, not knowing what to do. Luke didn't know what to do, either. Apparently, Jones had lost it, as well, since he popped out of the courtroom without removing the jury.

The whole situation was crazy. His being here was crazy. His blurting out the objection was also crazy. The total absurdity of the circumstances made Luke want to laugh. He felt the tension loosen on him and his body relaxed. He looked around to meet the gaze of several of the jurors. He wanted to say I'm sorry to them. Sorry that they had to be here. He was certainly sorry he had to be here.

The black girl on the front row continued the fixed look she had on Luke. What was her name? Richardson. Luke thought he could detect a slight bit of compassion in her. Some understanding. Freddie Johnson, Willie's cousin, watched him, too. Freddie didn't like the way they were picking on Luke. He wanted to tell Luke not to worry, but he didn't want to be caught up in any trap. It was becoming obvious to Freddie that Luke was being bamboozled. What was that they had said about drugs? Willie hadn't said anything about that. Freddie didn't want a murderer to get off, but he did want to help his cousin. He would just have to listen closely to everything. Meanwhile, Hays returned to the table and sat down beside Luke.

"So, what's up?" Luke asked solemnly.

"You're not, that's for sure. If you get up again or have another outburst of any sort, the Judge is going to find you in contempt. Maybe even put you in handcuffs."

Before Luke could respond, Jones returned to the bench without the usual 'all rise', leaving the bailiff in a tizzy and Limox scrambling to get back to the witness chair.

"Ladies and gentlemen of the jury, I apologize for the interruption. I know the hour is getting on toward noon and you all must be hungry. The attorneys have assured me that they can finish up this witness before lunch and we'll break then. So, if you'll bear with me we will go ahead and get back to business. Mr. Gafford, proceed."

Gafford felt he had accomplished everything he could with this witness. Daniels was not charged with rape and so he couldn't go into any details on that subject. He only wanted to touch on the brutality of the murder and the attack in a way that he knew would survive the Supreme Court's scrutiny. The jury certainly heard the word rape. That's all that mattered.

Limox answered a few more questions from Gafford with an all-in-a-day's work manner, sounding like the consummate professional. He was the hard working detective who had done his job. Gafford finished quickly and tendered the witness to Kennedy for cross-examination.

Hays wanted to be extremely careful with this witness. He knew that most of the jurors were impressed with his position as a law enforcement officer. A detective at that. Law and order. They needed his protection or there would be anarchy. Limox had a job to do and he had done it. That's why they were here. His investigation of the murder got Luke Daniels charged with the crime. This is how it worked. Hays knew he had to be cautious.

He started off his questions slowly, without rocking the boat that carried the jury's preconceived idea that Limox was just doing his job. He wanted to get them to understand that an unsolved murder didn't set well on his record. That Limox had other reasons besides the truth. He knew Luke would acknowledge being at the house that night so decided to go with what they were already in agreement on.

"Detective, you know that Luke Daniels was at Ms. Weeks' house that night, don't you?"

"No question about it. We have his fingerprints everywhere."

"Yes, yes, you do. And you said she was… the cause of death was a subdural hematoma?"

"That's right. The subdural hematoma was caused by several intense blows to the head."

"And what caused the blows. You don't have the instrumentality of death, do you?" Hays was proud of himself in his efforts to get the detective to admit they did not have a murder weapon.

"No sir, we don't." Limox paused only briefly. "But by our calculations and the results from the state crime lab the weapon could have been a man's hand, especially one crazed from the use of drugs."

"Your Honor, I object to the witness being unresponsive and ask that the last remark be stricken."

"Well, he has a right to explain his answer. And you did ask the question. I'll allow it."

Hays recoiled from the Judge's ruling and the blow Limox just gave him. The hands of a man crazed with drugs. Damn. Why did he ask that question?

"And did you find any evidence of drug use in the house that night?"

"No, sir, we did not."

"And what about with the defendant?" Hays knew he would have to answer that he did not.

"Well, we never tested the defendant because of his status as a lawyer and all, we didn't pursue him as a suspect until we had all our evidence back from the state crime lab. Mr. Gafford wanted to be absolutely sure we had the right man before making the charge."

Bam! Another blow. Luke was ready for Hays to sit down and get this witness out of there. His responses were cutting Luke to shreds. Every answer he gave tied Luke more to the scene, made the prosecution look good and the defense look bad. Shut up, Hays, and sit down. Luke thought about times before when he had watched lawyers do their clients more harm than good. But he had never been the client. Now he felt the depth of each cut by the witness. He could sense it sinking into the jury. Yes, I was there, but I left, he wanted to plead with them.

"But you can't say that Luke was there when Susan was murdered, can you, Detective Limox?" Hays must have read Luke's mind. Can you be sure that someone else didn't come into the house after Luke left? A formal acknowledgment that Luke was there. No, he couldn't be sure. There was no evidence to indicate that anyone else had been there. But Limox had to admit that just because Luke was there earlier didn't mean that he was there when the murder took place. Hays looked directly at the jury as he walked back to the defense table. He put his hand on Luke's shoulder for a moment, merely for effect in allowing the moment to settle in and around the jury box. He took his seat, arranged some papers for just a moment and then told the Judge he had no other questions of the witness.

Gafford stood up and announced to the court that he didn't have anything further at this time. He didn't really think Hays had done too much to help Luke. He would, however, like to reserve this witness for recall in rebuttal. Yes, the Judge noted it before dismissing the witness. He then dismissed the jury for lunch, which would be provided by the County. They could eat in the jury room. They had good hot plate lunches from Momma Doris'. They all knew it well and were eager to get to it. They left quickly and the courtroom cleared of all spectators, and soon completely emptied except for Luke and Hays Kennedy sitting alone.

"Luke, I don't know what to say. We talked about how you had to control those outbursts. About how the jury would perceive you. I think we did as well as could be expected with Limox but you didn't help yourself with that explosion."

They were both well aware of their positions. Hays was the lawyer, Luke was the defendant. The accused. Hays was not on trial here. Luke was. Their individual positions were clearly defined. Luke's life was on the line. For Hays it was just another case. For Luke it was everything.

"Luke, if you don't want to follow my direction, if I can't be in command, then there's no way I can continue as your lawyer. If you want to represent yourself, then just say so and I'll announce to the court that I am withdrawing."

"Is that what Jones said to you?"

Luke thought about what transpired in the Judge's chamber. The Judge and his lawyer alone. What did they talk about? What did Jones say to Hays? What did Hays say to Jones? Fear crept over him. He had become suspicious of everything. Was he now suspicious of his own lawyer? Should he be?

"You tell me, Luke? It's your call. Do you want to go on or not?" Hays sounded aloof, detached from the whole situation, as if he could wash his hands of the whole situation right now and never look back. Luke understood it. He'd been there with clients before. If they didn't want to listen to him, then he didn't feel like he could continue to represent them.

And why should he? The client was paying him for a service. It was like going to a doctor who prescribed a course of treatment that the patient failed to follow. Why waste your time?

"Okay, Hays. You're the lawyer. I'm sorry. It won't happen again. I realize I'm not objective, that I can't be objective. It's just that they're lies. All of it. I didn't kill Susan Weeks and they're making it sound like I did. Even I'm starting to doubt myself. I can imagine what the jury must be thinking."

Hays stared at Luke without saying anything. Luke looked back at him through anguished eyes. They were quiet. Still. Eventually, Hays shifted and cleared his throat as he started putting some of the file in his case.

"Alright, Luke. Look, I've got to go over their next witness. I don't think we have anything more to discuss. I'm going back to my office to prepare for the afternoon. I'll see you back at one thirty. Okay?"

He stood and waited for Luke to do the same. Luke stood and pushed his chair up and held on to the back of it.

"Well, if there's nothing further, I'll see you back after lunch."

Hays darted off from the table with the files under his arm escaping out the back door of the courtroom. Luke pushed himself away from the chair and headed back to his own office where he could hide behind his desk until the afternoon.

The trial resumed promptly at one thirty with the sound of Jones' gavel commencing the proceedings. Their next witness was another detective, Dunagin, who did the crime scene detail work. He had the qualifications to present all the technicalities of the investigation. His job at the police force was to come in to a crime scene and collect all the physical evidence and preserve everything to regurgitate at trial. He was organized, methodical, thorough, and he did a good job that day.

Often his work consisted of gory details of murder, rape and other abhorrent crimes. He presented his research and analysis with detached professionalism. His dispassionate documentation of the events surrounding the death of Susan Weeks were so scientific that one could almost forget the atrocity he described.

Not Luke. He listened intently as the detective talked again of finding the fingerprints. The shoe print. The blood type. The semen samples. This part of the trial was technical and academic. Here's where they sent me. Here's what I found. You decide.

Luke's thoughts finally wandered from the testimony and from the courtroom, this space he had found himself in. For a while the drone of the witness's voice grew far away. His ears were hearing but his brain took little note. He watched the prosecutor as if on a screen where he could change the channel. Jimmy directed questions to the detective: very mundane, routine, go-down-the list. Hardly worth Luke's attention. He was hardly there.

From outside himself he felt another presence. Someone watching him. His eyes moved around to Hays who was intently writing something on his pad. At the bench, Judge Jones focused on the witness. From the prosecutor's table, Gafford's attention stayed on his assistant and the witness. In the jury, there it was. The girl in the front row was looking at him again. Her name was Roanda Richardson. Her eyes were on Luke. He gave her a slight nod, barely discernible and turned his eyes down to what Hays was writing. But he could tell she continued looking at him. It was a long time before she looked away.

They finished with the detective. Hays' cross-examination touched only on the lack of anything specific to say who killed the victim. No, there was nothing. Only the evidence he presented. There was nothing that positively identified the murderer.

The representative from the state crime lab was much the same. Technical details of death, all in black and white. Numbers and figures and percentages of this and that. Some of the jurors dozed while Jimmy Clay again pored through the tedium. It was hard to make this part engaging so Gafford saved himself for the more stimulating testimony.

By late afternoon everyone in the courtroom was drained. The jurors were dozing off and the lawyers looked harried. Judge Jones had heard all he wanted of the perfunctory details and it was clear the jury needed a break. What the detective and the state crime lab man didn't cover, the coroner certainly included with ample minutia. Cause of death, facts and figures, estimates of time frame, everything they could possibly want or need to know about the death of the deceased was finalized in the afternoon of the first day of trial testimony.

When the coroner finished pronouncing the girl dead, Judge Jones decided that it was time for a break.

Every effort from the prosecutors all day had been to connect Susan Weeks and Luke Daniels, preparing them to say who else could it have been. They were glad to wrap it up before five. They could leave the jurors to sleep on it when all they had in their minds was a dead girl and a lawyer. Susan Weeks and Luke Daniels. The names repeated over and over again all day long. They had a poor girl struck down as she moved toward the zenith of her life. They had a lawyer, one who bedded the girl on the night of her death. Was it rape? What was it? It probably didn't matter. The public loved to hate lawyers and Gafford knew it. He would ride it for all it was worth. He would ride it until Daniels went down and the wave carried him to another term as District Attorney.

Gafford stood with a smile on his face as the Judge dismissed the jurors and they filed out of the courtroom. Some of them had been asleep half the afternoon but it didn't matter. There were a couple that would lead the others to the right choice. How could anybody not reach the conclusion that Daniels was guilty? Gafford's smile got even bigger when all the jurors were gone. He and Jimmy gathered up their materials and left the courtroom.

At his office he would prepare for another day of assaults on his opponent. He should probably start preparing for his press conference after Daniels was found guilty. It needed to be just right to sail him on into an election victory. Yes, there was plenty to do he thought as he bounced back to his office, whistling.

There was no whistling at the defendant's table. Luke felt like he couldn't be more miserable if he had been beaten for eight hours. He ached. Thank goodness there were no reporters to hound him. They had torn out of the courtroom before the final gavel struck, racing back to their desks to conjure up tales of morbidity. They would have their work cut out for them today, as boring as some of this stuff was, Luke thought. They would write something designed to make a good story and it didn't take Einstein to figure out who they would crucify.

Hays was methodically arranging his files, returning forms and documents to their rightful position in the volumes that had become Luke's life. Everything in its place. Nice and neat. By the time he finished, the courtroom was empty and they sat alone again. Quiet for a moment, Hays asked him if he had any thoughts to share before they parted. Thoughts, Luke laughed softly.

"Well, hell, Hays, I guess you mean things that would help the situation. No, I suppose not. You're the lawyer. What do you think?"

"I don't know, Luke. They've hammered us pretty good today. Let's see what happens tomorrow. Remember, though, this was your decision to go forward with this trial. You know we don't have much to rebut their allegations. Are you ready to take the stand?"

"I guess I don't have any options. Sure, I'm ready. I can tell them what really happened."

"What really happened? Do you know what really happened, Luke?" When Luke did not answer, he continued, "I thought you left."

The statement stung Luke like a venomous barb, catching in the vulnerable recesses of his scarred psyche. He did leave. He didn't know what happened to Susan, but he didn't do it. Whatever happened, he didn't do it. Did Hays really believe that? Luke could see the skepticism in his lawyer's eyes. Here he was in a fight for his life and even his lawyer didn't believe him. What hope did he have?

"Hays, I have been over and over that with you. I've set out clearly what happened between me and Susan a dozen times or more. I've spoken it to you and I've written it down. You've asked me questions and I have answered as candidly and sincerely as I know how. I have hidden nothing from you. If you don't believe me then what are you doing here?"

Was it the money? Luke had paid him a handsome sum and would probably wind up paying more if there was an appeal. Was it the exposure? Hays' name was certainly getting enough air play. Every news medium within a hundred miles was carrying the story of the murdering lawyer and Hays' name was being thrown in enough to be a household word. How much more would all of this exposure bring to Hays? Luke knew he was not the only one thinking of that.

Hays had all his folders and files in order returned to his case ready to leave. There were two big square satchels filled to capacity. He had one in each hand. Luke had another of his own. Hays was standing, ready to walk out.

"We don't need to be fighting between ourselves, Luke. C'mon. Let's get out of here. I've got their list of witnesses for tomorrow. Let's go back to my office, go over their statements and prepare for our cross-examination. You know, two heads are better than one."

Luke didn't know what else to do so he stood and followed Hays out of the building and down to his car. They each drove alone to Hays' office and went inside to begin the process of preparing for the next day.

CHAPTER EIGHTEEN

The next day came quickly. Even though the night dragged on with only fitful, restless sleep, the morning arrived and return to the courtroom appeared in a blink. Newsmen already filled the halls when Luke opened the front door. He steeled himself for their onslaught, knowing that their vituperative queries had little to do with him and much to do with making a job for themselves. He read the papers. There were minimal facts and ample sensationalism to capture their readers' imaginations. Luke wondered for a moment who the person really was that they were writing about.

He tried to move through them without a response but his path was blocked. There was Jeff Woodall, his body positioned squarely in front of the courtroom door.

"Mr. Daniels, can you tell me now when was the last time you saw Susan Weeks alive? I asked you that question once before but received no answer, only your violent ejection from your office. Do you have an answer now?"

Woodall spoke with a contemptuous arrogance, taunting Luke. Luke wanted to smack him again, but knew that's what Woodall wanted. Cameras were aimed at them, clicking away. Luke's face could not hide his animosity, but he controlled himself.

"You answer for your behavior, Mr. Woodall, and I'll answer for mine. There are two sides to every story. I'm sure you'll get to hear mine when I testify. Until then, I have nothing to say."

Luke reached behind the reporter and pulled the door open, pushing Woodall aside in the process. Hays was at the defense table unloading files from his briefcase. He and Luke had talked earlier and were ready for the first and probably last round of the prosecutor's case. The case had a conspicuous lack of witnesses to testify.

"The way I see it, the ones they've given us on this list will go pretty quickly. We'll do little in the way of cross-examination and let them go. You're our big canon. This whole case is going to turn on whether or not you alone can convince the jury."

Hays finished his statement taking Luke in. He wondered if his client would be up to the testimony and the grilling by the prosecutor. Most certainly it would be Gafford himself. He'd never let Clay handle that one and steal the limelight. Hays hoped like hell Luke would control his temper. If Gafford did something to pique the rage that lurked under the surface of this client, then the case was sunk. But Hays doubted they would get through the prosecution witnesses today.

"How you sleeping, Luke?" Hays inquired of his companion at the defense table. "You look like hell. What'd you get last night? Two hours tops?"

"About that." Luke grinned a little. He was glad for the absence of friction between them this morning. His system didn't need it.

Gafford and Jimmy Clay arrived at their table. The bailiff directed jurors back to their resting place as things started to take shape. The Judge announced his presence, asking the bailiff to inquire if everyone was ready. When the two sides indicated they were, the Judge signaled the bailiff to bring in the jury.

"Welcome back, ladies and gentlemen. We again thank you for your efforts in returning for another day of trial. I know each of you have lives that need tending but we have a system of justice that requires your participation. We could not have the greatest country in the world without good citizens like you doing your part to see that our structure of government operates competently and effectively. Just like you have a responsibility to vote for your candidate, your presence here insures that justice, fairness and truth are maintained in our lives. I thank you."

"Mr. District Attorney, we concluded with the witness you had up yesterday. Who do you have next?" Jones finished his speech and peered down over his spectacles at Gafford with a feigned reverence over his own magniloquence.

Gafford stood and faced the Judge, then paused. He turned back to Clay as if they had something of utmost importance to discuss.

"Judge, one moment please, if you would indulge me."

He turned back to the table where he and Clay put their heads together again. From across the room Luke and Hays watched the two of them curiously. What could be going on? Gafford moved around the table again and he and Clay scrutinized a file, making marks as they went down some sort of list. At last he raised up, shaking his head with an affirmative motion to Clay who cut his eyes over to the defense table with a sneaky grin.

"Your Honor," Gafford began again from behind the prosecution table, "the state rests."

What? The statement took Luke by surprise. They had gone over a list of about seven more witnesses that Gafford told then would be presented today. Now they were saying that they had finished their case. A murder trial with only one day of witnesses? Hays was flabbergasted.

Gafford knew that he had just dropped a bomb, catching his adversary off guard. He fought back the smile of seeing Luke Daniels and Hays Kennedy squirm. This was brilliant. The idea came to him last night in a conversation with his old friend Luther Lambert. Gafford often talked with Luther during trial to get his sage advice over particular issues. Gafford remembered watching Lambert maneuver in and out of trials when he first came to Hampton. He still called him up to get some of that knowledge. So last night when Luther called to congratulate him on his first day of testimony, he took advantage of the opportunity to pick the old master's brain. He was glad he did. They were all squirming.

Judge Jones took it all in stride. He learned earlier this morning of Gafford's strategy. How the hell Gafford had come up with that on his own was a mystery but it was clever. It just might be the trick, with the Judge's help. Keep his case in chief short and sweet and then do his major damage in the rebuttal where Daniels wouldn't be able to refute. Unless the Judge let him. We would have to see, Jones thought, but for now it was time to keep going.

"Very well. Mr. Kennedy?" Jones turned his attention, "What do you have at this time?"

"Ah, Judge, ah, Your Honor..." Hays stood to his feet just a short distance from the jurors looking like he didn't have a clue what to do next.

Hays didn't know what to do or say. He had some motions in a file somewhere that he planned to file at the conclusion of the state's case but that should be tomorrow sometime. He wasn't ready for this. Damn that Gafford. What the hell was he trying to pull? Hays was getting angry and it was showing. They were making him look like a fool in front of the jury, like he didn't know what he was doing and he didn't like that. Gafford told him yesterday that they would have a full day of witnesses, probably more. And now he was saying he was done. Sonofabitch. What was he going to do? He had to regroup quickly.

"Ah, Your Honor, may we approach the bench?"

"Yes," came the Judge's colorless response.

Hays stepped from behind his table, giving Gafford the eye as he did. Gafford refused to look his way, keeping his head straight toward the bench. They arrived in front of Jones together.

"Judge, Mr. Gafford told me yesterday that he had seven or eight more witnesses to put on and that he would not finish up until tomorrow or the next day. Of course, I planned my case around that. I relied on his representations." Hays' voice went high and sharp, revealing the anger and irritation seething underneath.

"His misrepresentation is highly unprofessional and unethical. He knew I was relying on his statements to prepare my case."

"Now, just a minute. I don't like your insinuations, Kennedy." Gafford moved up tighter to the bench, gritting his teeth at his opponent. "I never told you I was definitely calling all those people. I said they were on my witness list."

"That's a goddamn lie and you know it, Gafford." Hays was furious with the last statement.

"Oh, now you're calling me a liar, are you? You've got a lot of nerve, you miserable..."

The two touched shoulders right before the Judge as tempers flared and Jones thought for a moment they were going to come to blows.

"Gentlemen, I'll have none of that. Back off, both of you. This is my courtroom and I'll make the rulings without you two getting into any sort of fracas. The very idea. This is a court of law. Now, act like professionals or I'll find you both in contempt."

Hays and Gafford stood immobile, shoulder to shoulder, neither ready to concede first. Hays had never been in this situation before and was amazed at his own lack of control. He was certainly not accustomed to having a fellow member of the bar look him in the eye and lie as Gafford had done. He wanted to say more but with Jones berating them through clenched teeth, he exhaled and moved his focus back in the Judge's direction.

"Your Honor, in light of this misunderstanding, I'd like to request a continuance until tomorrow morning."

"We can't do that, Your Honor. This trial needs to move forward. It's not my fault if Mr. Kennedy is not prepared. It's not my job to present my case in his best interest. Last night, we looked at the situation we were in and decided the jury had enough information for a guilty verdict. Therefore, there is no need for us to continue to burden the jury with surplus. They know who the killer is."

With his last statement, Gafford couldn't help but give a little sneer in Hays' direction. Hays was ready to go after him again. His eyes warned of the eruption that was just below the surface. Jones could see it clearly from his elevated post. He had to do something quickly. The gavel began to pound.

"This court will be in recess for ten minutes. Gentlemen, I'll see you in my chamber."

Jones swished off the bench with Gafford and Kennedy right behind him. Luke sat alone at the table wondering what was being said behind the closed doors.

The jurors were confused. They arrived ready for the trial to continue and then witnessed a clash between two lawyers that nearly came to blows. And they said so. James Hutchinson and Joe Lee Pigott were the first to start the talk. Pigott leaned down from his seat in the second row to whisper to Hutchinson followed by muffled laughter from those around them. Then they all started to mumble softly.

Luke observed the faces and tried to pick up on what they were saying but it stopped quickly as everyone strained to listen. There were loud voices coming from behind the door to the Judge's chamber. Shouting. It wasn't clear what was being said but it was being stated with a lot of force. Just as quickly, it settled.

Everyone sat in silence waiting for the next outburst. Jimmy nervously rapped his pencil on the files at the prosecutor's table. The bailiff looked awkward and uncomfortable. He was closest to the door that separated them from the clash of the lawyers. He pretended not to be trying to listen.

They waited. Snickers and snorts of laughter came from several lawyers who had wandered into the courtroom. Each had his own version of what was going on and what would be the outcome. They all loved the drama that was being played out before them. Yes, this was something the likes of which Hampton had never seen before. The spectators were all ready to let the show go on.

They didn't have to wait long. The two attorneys returned and Jones was on the bench immediately.

"Ladies and gentlemen of the jury, at this time in the trial we have some matters that must be resolved of an administrative nature, purely housekeeping. I'm not going to confine you to the jury room, but I am going to ask that you don't leave the building. This court will stand in recess for one hour."

The gavel banged the dismissal. Jurors stood and huffed around. Several of the guys snickered again.

"Awh, you mean we're not going to get to see the fight?" came from one of the guys and they all laughed as they filed out of the box and made their way out of the room.

"What's going on, Hays?" Luke was anxious to hear what transpired.

"I've got ten minutes to get my file together to make my motion for a directed verdict. After that, we begin our case. In other words, you're up Luke."

Luke swallowed hard. He was up. Was he? Was he ready for this? Could he do it?

"What happened? Where's their other witnesses?"

"Apparently, Gafford thinks he has enough already for a conviction. He told the Judge that after careful consideration last night, they had decided to rest. Lying bastard. He told me yesterday they would use up all of today. He knew I wouldn't be ready. But we have to be. After we do the motion for a directed verdict, which I'm sure Jones will deny, we start our case in chief. And that's you, Luke." Hays finished up solemnly.

"Are you ready for this, Luke?"

"I guess I have to be, huh?"

"Yeah, I guess you do."

Hays finished pulling several files from the case and sat down. He focused on the motion that was already written out. He had a supporting brief, which Luke wrote, and copies of the case law to hand the Judge. Three different folders. There was the copy to the Judge, copy to Gafford and little Jimmy, with one for Luke to follow with Hays' copy. Everything was in order. Jones returned to the bench briefly and called everyone up to him.

"I have the court reporter setting up in my office if you will join me there, we'll get this going."

The procedure took only a short while. Hays presented his motion orally after handing out the copies, along with the brief and case law. Gafford responded with his argument that the state had made their case against Daniels and even requested a directed verdict in his favor, which was not going to happen. Hays tried to rebut some of the prosecutor's erroneous interpretation of the law and facts but Jones waved him off, denying the motion summarily.

"Gentlemen, be ready to begin at ten fifteen sharp. Is that understood?"

Everyone nodded in agreement and Jones dismissed them. Hays steered Luke out of the room and back to their table. He grabbed up a file and pulled Luke along. They headed to a witness room where they could sit alone for a few minutes and regroup. Luke's opportunity to tell what really happened was about to begin.

The trial reconvened at ten fifteen. When everyone was in their seat, Judge Jones announced to Hays that he could call his first witness. It was no surprise.

"Your Honor, the defense calls Luke Daniels."

There was not a sound as Luke stood, moved from behind the table and took the stand. Before he could sit, the clerk stepped in front of him and spoke.

"Do you solemnly swear that the testimony you are about to give is the truth, the whole truth and nothing but the truth?"

"I do." Luke said as he looked directly at the jury.

"You may be seated."

Luke calmly sat down, adjusted the microphone and looked Hays squarely in the eyes. His heart beat loudly in his own ears, the blood coursing through him faster and faster. He could feel each pump, feel the surge moving through his veins, through his arms and legs. Each pulse brought him closer and closer to his fate. He forced himself to breathe.

"State your name, please," the questions began.

"Luke Daniels."

He answered clearly, plainly. Cool, calm and collected. There was little outside that indicated the fear, the terror that gripped him. He was on the witness stand. What had built for months was now upon him. He had his shot at setting the record straight. Let's go; let's go.

The initial inquiry was routine. Uneventful. He graduated from high school, went to college. Honors. Part time jobs. Law school. Distinguished career. Law journal. The answers came smoothly. Much easier than he had thought.

Yes, after law school he went to work with Harris and Wells. That lasted five years before striking out on his own. The years of struggle. The marriage. The divorce. First failure. No, he didn't really maintain contact with his ex-wife. They'd been divorced for several years now and he only bumped in to her occasionally.

"The nature of my practice? Well, let's see. How would I classify that? Of course, in a small town, you do just about anything. But I'd say mostly personal injury. A plaintiff's practice. Domestic work. Property cases. A general practice for this area, I guess."

"Luke, tell me how you came to be acquainted with Susan Weeks?"

The question, what he knew had been coming, was finally here. Subtly, she blended right in with his practice. Yes, he was acquainted with her.

"She called my office one morning for an appointment. I'm usually in the office early, before everyone else. It was a Friday. She called just about eight o'clock. No one else was in yet when I took the call."

"And did you set up an appointment?"

"Yes, yes I did. She was going to be tied up for most of the day at some bank function out of town, but she would be back before five o'clock. She asked if she could come in then. I said yes."

"Your Honor, we object to what the deceased said on the basis of hearsay."

"Sustained. Mr. Daniels, you know the rules of evidence. You can testify about what you did or said but not someone else."

Hays looked exasperated at the pettiness of Gafford's objection, but Jones did not give him a chance to respond.

"Proceed."

"Well, she was supposed to be at my office before five o'clock. But she didn't make it."

"She never came to your office?"

"No. She called just moments after my secretary left. The receptionist was already gone. I was still at the office about to leave myself. It was Friday afternoon and I was tired and ready to get out of there, but then she called from her car saying she was running late."

"Objection. Hearsay." This time it was Jimmy Clay and even Jones looked annoyed.

"Go on," was all Jones said.

"Anyway, it was going to be well after five thirty before she could get to my office and I really didn't want to wait around. I tried to convince her to come in Monday but she urged me to see her that day. She suggested we meet somewhere for coffee. We agreed on the Magnolia Bar and Grill."

"And did you meet her there?"

"Yes."

"How long were you there?"

"Oh, maybe an hour. We arrived probably close to six o'clock, then left around seven. Maybe a little after. I don't remember exactly. I wasn't watching the time closely."

"We were going to get something to eat. When we realized that every place would be crowded on a Friday night, she suggested we go to her house so we could talk. We went by Robby's for some po-boys and then drove to her house. I guess we were there around eight o'clock."

"You arrived at her house around eight with the food?"

"Yes. We came in and spread the sandwiches out on the table to eat."

"And did you leave after eating?"

"No, I didn't."

"What did you do?"

"Well, we moved in to the living room and listened to music for a while. She put on some CD's and we just sat and talked."

"Was this a business discussion?"

"Not really."

"What do you mean?"

"We never really got around to business. I mean, we didn't plan it, but one thing led to another and we wound up in the bedroom."

"Did you have sex with Miss Weeks?"

"Yes."

"Did you spend the night with her."

"No. I left."

The words stuck in his throat. He'd been over this time after time and thought he had come to grips with it, but here in front of these people, strangers, exposing the cold facts made him feel loathsome. Repulsed at himself. He tried to look at the jury but all he could think about was the absurdity of getting up and leaving her. If only he'd stayed, we wouldn't be here. He felt as if it was all his fault.

"What time was that?" Hays knew they were in a hole at this point and that they'd have to dig out of to survive. He was trying to keep the flow moving and not let the jury settle in on Luke's leaving the scene of the crime in the middle of the night. It was bad, but it would be even worse if this all came out on Gafford's cross.

"Just before midnight. I remember the clock in my car said 12:17." He didn't mean to sound so nonchalant about it.

"Where did you go then?"

"Home."

"Did you see anyone else that night?"

"No."

"Did you have any other contact with Susan Weeks?"

"I tried to call her the next day. Several times. But I never got an answer."

"When did you first learn that Ms. Weeks was dead?"

"Monday morning when I got to my office."

The questioning went on and on. They went over Luke's office procedure. He explained how it was against his policy to see any client outside the office and he only made an exception here because she insisted. He took great pains in explaining how he never intended what happened. He was not that kind of man.

The trial took a lunch break and then Luke was back on the stand. He went until mid-afternoon when he and Hays had covered everything they could possibly do to rehabilitate his wretched situation and then they stopped. Hays finally told the court that he had nothing further."

"I tender the witness to the prosecution, Your Honor."

"Alright, we'll take a ten minute recess before we proceed with the state's cross-examination."

Jones dismissed the jury who exited while everyone stood. As they filed out of the box most had their heads down solemnly. Luke's testimony had been intense. His candid explanation came across as genuine and sincere. Several jurors looked his way as they passed. He looked them in the eyes hoping they could see in him the truth he had tried to convey. He wished he could do more as they moved on by him. But there was nothing else for now. Now, he just had to wait until the District Attorney took his turn.

Hays sat down after the Judge dismissed the jury. Luke floated down beside him. They didn't talk. They had no words for this time as they waited for the DA.

Gafford was at his table with Clay going over his list of questions. They were the same basic questions he used in other murder trials with the addition of those specific to these particular facts. He'd never had a lawyer on trial before. He wanted to leave no room for error. Jones had helped him thus far but his own re-election weighed in the balance. He wanted no mistakes.

When the recess ended, the jury returned and Luke took the stand. Gafford moved to the podium and laid out his folder of questions. He took his time, looking over the evidence table of exhibits that all pointed to Luke. The wine glasses were there. Luke's running shoes, size ten and a half. Samples of his fingerprints. Gafford pushed several pieces around before returning to the podium.

"Mr. Daniels, did I understand you correctly, the first time you ever heard of Susan Weeks was the day she was murdered?"

"The first time I ever knew of her was when she called my office. I don't know anything about her murder."

"That's right, she called you for an appointment. Do you have any record of that appointment?"

"No, I don't," Luke said after a pause. "When I took the call that morning none of the secretaries were around. I was at my desk and didn't make any notation. I knew my calendar was open after four and that I would be at the office."

"So you made an appointment for her to come to your office. Did she ever come to your office?"

"No, she did not. As I testified earlier, she called after the time for the appointment and asked if I would meet her."

"Oh, that's right. It was her idea that you meet. At the Magnolia Bar. I believe you said for coffee. Did you get some coffee when you arrived at the Magnolia?"

"Ah, no. We didn't."

"No, you didn't, did you? What did you have?"

"We had a glass of wine."

"Oh, you did. Not coffee. And who's idea was that?"

"Well, it was Susan's, actually. She was very apologetic for being late and thankful for my agreeing to meet her and she suggested a glass of wine."

"So is that all you had?"

"I believe so, yes."

"Isn't it true that you had several glasses of wine?"

"I don't believe so. I really don't remember exactly."

"So you couldn't deny it if someone saw you there and remembered that you had several drinks."

"Well, I, ah… we weren't there that long."

Gafford went through the time they left, the time they were at Robby's, the time they arrived at her house. His questions were rapid fire at times, hardly giving Luke time to answer before spilling out with another. The jurors followed the story again intently. Their eyes were riveted to the action as Gafford fired the questions at Luke, who fired back answers.

Luke's energy pumped up as he became embroiled in the contest. Ordinarily he considered himself an able match for Gafford's limited talents, but the events that brought them to this trial had cast his lot with a disadvantage. Gafford had the upper hand. He was the State with a powerful case, and all the power of office to support him. Luke stood alone and fought. In this part of the battle, Hays seemed far away.

"So you went to her house. I believe you told us that was her idea, too."

"Yes, it was. She thought we might be able to talk uninterrupted there."

"Yes, and did you talk? Let's see, you took food there. And she got out a bottle of wine, you said. More drinking?"

"Well, yes."

"Is this the bottle of wine that Ms. Weeks got out?"

Gafford grabbed the bottle from the table of exhibits that Detective Dunagin recovered from the house. It was State's exhibit number seven. He waived it around in front of Luke's face.

"I guess so. I didn't really pay that much attention to it at the time." Luke tried not to sound insolent, but that night he didn't pay much attention to anything but Susan.

"It's the only bottle of wine we found at the victim's house. And you said you did have more wine. You don't deny that this is the bottle."

"No."

"And you saw the wine glasses. I guess you don't remember those either, do you."

Luke fought back the anger he felt toward Gafford. This was ridiculous. He was a grown man. A practicing attorney. Gafford knew him. He had to know Luke didn't do this. How could this be happening to him? This whole charade was out of control, like some loose canon rolling down a hill spewing destruction everywhere. He wanted to stand up and scream he didn't kill her.

"Now what else did you do that night?"

"As I testified earlier, we listened to some music."

"What kind of music? Who was it?"

When he asked the question, suddenly Luke could hear the music playing in his head. As if a piece of it came across time, he heard those sounds again. He remembered Sade's silky voice as they sat on the couch and then Billie Holliday as they walked down the hall together.

"Answer the question, please, if you know."

"A female vocalist called Sade and the other was Billie Holliday."

"And what else did you do while sitting there drinking and listening to music?"

"Well, nothing really. We just talked."

"Were you talking while the music was playing?"

"Yes."

"What else were you doing?"

Luke recalled the touch of Susan's hand under his shirt, brushing lightly against his skin. The smell of her hair came to his nostrils. He felt a little light-headed. The collar on his shirt was suddenly very tight. He tugged at his tie a little. He felt hot, frustrated. How could anybody dare say that he had killed Susan? This whole process was a bogus farce of justice. Luke reached for the glass sitting on the ledge and sipped the cool water, easing the parched sensation on his lips.

Gafford saw the subtle change in his manner. He hoped the jury did. He'd love to crack Daniels on the witness stand. Boy, what the papers would do with that!

"What else were the two of you doing that night, Mr. Daniels. What were you doing? What kind of drugs did you take that night?"

Hays was on his feet immediately, but before he could protest, Luke's answer burst out.

"I wasn't taking any drugs that night, Gafford, and you know it."

Hays shouted at Luke to be quiet and rushed up to Gafford standing before the Judge. Jones sustained the objection with a stern look toward Gafford.

"Stick to the facts, Mr. Gafford."

Fine with Gafford. He got what he wanted. He turned around and caught the eyes of Adrian McCarthy, the foreman of the grand jury who had caught the gist of it all.

"So you weren't taking drugs that night, Mr. Daniels. What did you do after you listened to music? How long did you listen to, who was it, Shoddy?"

"Sade. I don't recall exactly. We sat there for a while and then went, she… we went back to her bedroom."

Luke knew he sounded confused and didn't understand why. It was just that being here in this chair made it hard to recall quickly. And Gafford kept jumping on him. What was Hays doing over there? Couldn't he find an objection to distract Gafford?

"You went back to her bedroom?"

"Yes, that's what I said," Luke growled lowly.

"I beg your pardon? You went back to her bedroom and had sex with her, isn't that correct."

"Yes."

Gafford turned slightly to observe the jurors. The three older women were not liking this at all. They had Daniels pegged as a louse for sure. And from the looks on their faces it wasn't far for them to conclude that he did the poor girl in.

"Did you have sex with her against her will?"

"No."

"Are you sure, Mr. Daniels? Because you heard the reports from the state crime lab medical examiner that their findings were consistent with rape."

"No, that's not true. She wanted it, too. I mean, we both did."

Every nerve in Luke stood on end. He looked at the jurors who studied him intently. His eyes flicked about from one to the other. The white men had sneers. Sorry bastard, they must be thinking. The white women had horror in their eyes, as if he were the most lowlife creature they had ever observed. The black men were expressionless. Luke couldn't imagine what they were thinking. Roanda Richardson, the black female bank teller, took in his every gesture.

Luke exhaled the breath that was caught in his chest, not realizing that the movement made him look contrived, less than genuine. His mind was too busy with other things to notice the inappropriate signal. He tried to control his discomfort. His anxiety. He tried to hold on.

Gafford loved it. He recognized the floundering pauses in Luke's voice. It was distinct and noticeable to him and everyone else in the courtroom, particularly the jury who sat straight in front of the witness chair. He was close to the edge. If Gafford could push just a little more, Luke would crack. He was sure of it. Hit him hard at this weak moment.

"Isn't it true, Mr. Daniels, that the poor girl said no. And when she did, you insisted. That she tried to get you to leave but you wouldn't. That you forced yourself on her. That she escaped to the bedroom but you pursued her. Kicked in the door and then raped her."

"No, that's not true. That's not true at all. I made love to her. Passionately. Lovingly. She never tried to resist. She drew me to her…"

Hays was on his feet shouting an objection, trying to raise his voice above them, hoping the jury would be distracted enough to miss what was happening. Jones banged his gavel, louder and louder, calling for order in the courtroom.

Luke's face burned with the rage boiling inside him. He didn't kill Susan and he couldn't stand hearing someone say he did one more time. He wanted to strangle Gafford. Wanted to put his hands around his throat and make him shut up. His breathing was now deep and furious, pumping his chest in and out.

Gafford backed off, standing right in front of the jury so that Luke's gaze on him would be centered to the box of twelve people who would vote to convict this maniac. Luke didn't crack enough to admit the murder, but he came so close that it probably didn't matter. They could all see the killer in him without his confession.

"I want order in this court. Mr. Kennedy, your objection is noted. Mr. Gafford, you are not to assault the witness with a string of accusations. One question at a time. Now, let's keep this in line. This is my courtroom and another outburst like that and I'll have the deputy taking you out of here."

"Mr. Daniels, do you hear that? You've already been warned once. Don't force me to have you physically restrained."

"But, Judge, he…"

"Don't Judge me nothing. I said to control yourself. Do you understand?" Jones cut Luke off. "One more time and I'll have you locked up. I will not tolerate your misconduct in this trial. Now, answer me. Do you understand?"

Luke wanted to spit in the Judge's face. He knew every eye in the place was on him and that Jones had just castigated him into a submissive position. Anything else from him would be insolence and only hurt him further. Trying to maintain as much dignity as he could under the circumstances, he answered slowly.

"Yes, Your Honor."

"Very well."

"Judge I'd like to request a ten minute recess for us to regroup."

"Denied. We're going to finish this trial. Everyone is going to control themselves or I'll do it for them. Mr. Gafford, continue."

Gafford had not moved from his position next to the jury. He pondered his next move, taking a moment to clear his throat and give the jury time to grasp everything that had happened. Allow them to take one more step toward guilty. It was the only logical conclusion. He may not have an eyewitness to the crime, but the jury could certainly witness the unbalanced man in front of them. Surely, they could see he was capable of murder.

He wanted to leave that hanging in their minds as long as possible. He walked back over to the prosecution table where Jimmy sat quietly. He rearranged some papers, opened several files, as if he were looking for some pivotal piece of evidence. "Judge, if you would indulge me for one moment, please."

Gafford leaned over to talk with Clay, pointing to some things on his file. He sat down briefly and explained to Jimmy how he would like to end this day on Daniels' wild note. Let the jury sleep on it. He felt like they were well on their way to a guilty verdict and letting this soak in could just do the trick. After shuffling papers some more and rearranging files, he stood and asked the Judge if he could approach the bench.

"Very well."

Jones' comment was strictly business, ready to hear Gafford's weighty comments on his position. Kennedy approached with him and Gafford started his pitch.

"Judge, I've looked over the rest of my cross-examination and there's quite a bit more I have to cover. There's no way I can finish today. It's almost four-thirty and I've got at least two hours, maybe more. If it pleases the court, I'd like to suggest we break for today and resume this cross in the morning. Hays, you don't have any objection to that, do you?"

Hays did not. He was as ready to get out of that room as anybody. He didn't care whose idea it was and didn't think far enough ahead to consider what last image of Luke the jury would take with them.

"Well, if you two are in agreement, I'm not going to force your hand."

Jones knew exactly what was happening and was astonished at Gafford's faculties in calling for the break. He usually had to do that sort of thing for the lame brain. Guess he must be learning something after all these years. The two lawyers took their seats, leaving Jones to dismiss the proceeding for the day. The jurors appeared relieved. The tension of the day had drained them as well. This was not the normal tempo in their daily lives and all were ready for a break.

Luke stepped down from the stand before Jones' excused the jury. At the table he was numb and unfeeling. The full day under the gun, the constant harangue from the DA, had depleted all his energy. There was little for him to discuss with Hays and hardly any strength for it. They departed the courthouse together and then went their separate ways. He thought about food as he pulled from the parking lot. He'd barely eaten anything all day. But his mind settled on nothing. He just wanted this over.

CHAPTER NINETEEN

The next day of trial started with the same players. Luke took the stand ready to survive the onslaught no matter what Gafford pulled. He'd gone home fatigued and fell into bed early, sleeping like a dead man until the alarm jarred him alive that morning. Now he was poised for his final joust with Gafford.

"Mr. Daniels, at what point did Ms. Weeks come to your office?"

"I told you yesterday, she never came to my office. She was late and I agreed to meet her at the Magnolia."

"You're absolutely sure she never came to your office. Never set foot there at all. Perhaps she's been there before this occasion and you don't remember."

"Mr. Gafford, Susan Weeks was not the kind of girl you'd ever forget once you met her." Luke was indignant at Gafford's comments. Just how stupid did they think he was, not remember that she was in his office. What was he doing with that?

"Mr. Daniels, you never did get around to telling us what was the compelling reason, the urgent matter that Ms. Weeks had to see you about. What was it that was so important that you agreed to meet with her away from your office?"

"I don't know. We never had a chance to discuss it."

There it was. The question that Luke and Hays agonized over the appropriate response. Hays found it incomprehensible that someone called him up for counsel on an urgent matter and they never got around to discussing what it was. Then again, Hays never met Susan Weeks. Hell, it even surprised Luke. That's why he couldn't answer the question without bewilderment on his own part.

"I beg your pardon, Mr. Daniels. What did you say?"

Gafford heard the response but wanted to reinforce its absurdity for the jury's benefit. How could he not know what she called him about? How could he have failed to address something that even he had told the jury was of such considerable importance to the client? Perhaps there was no urgent matter and it was just another lie used for cover. The logic seemed simple to Gafford. Daniels was lying about that and about a lot of other things.

"Well, after we got together that night, we started talking about other things, personal matters, and never had a chance to discuss business. It was as if she really didn't want to talk about it, so we just skirted the issue."

"Skirted the issue? What do you mean by that? Did she tell you what was on her mind or not?"

"Well, we talked about her job and her schooling. She was in a doctoral program. I thought it had something to do with her job, but I don't remember why. She seemed sensitive about some areas there, that's all."

"She seemed sensitive." Gafford repeated the comment with ridicule. "But you don't remember exactly. So you can't tell us why you were having an after hours meeting with a client who had a pressing matter that required legal advice. I guess you were just so charming that she was swept off her feet and forgot all her troubles."

"Objection, Your Honor. Mr. Gafford is mocking the witness. I ask that you strike the question and instruct him to keep his cross-examination to appropriate matters." Kennedy was still steamed over Gafford's lying to him yesterday about his witnesses.

"Mr. Gafford, just ask your questions directly and leave the sarcasm out of it." Jones' deadpan admonition hardly delivered any punch. He didn't even look up from his writing.

Gafford began a new series of questions with one intent: to make Luke look bad in the eyes of the jury. He asked him about the car he drove. A Cadillac separated him from the relatively blue-collar make-up of his jury. He asked about his clothes, where he shopped, his last vacation; things that were totally irrelevant to the matter at-hand and introduced solely for the purpose of drawing a line between the defendant and his jury. Jones allowed it all, over sporadic objections from Hays. The District Attorney continued to batter and chip away at any affinity the twelve might have for Luke. The separation would make it easier for them to reach their conclusion of guilt.

Gafford managed to keep a succession of questions going until almost noon. His queries seemed illogical at times but over objection from Hays he assured the Judge that their relevance would materialize as the remainder of the trial unfolded.

When he finally tendered the witness to Hays, the Judge was anxious for Hays to continue. Jones urged him to begin and keep the trial moving. Even though Hays would have liked to have waited until after lunch so that the break could have given him time to regroup, he went forward. There was little he wanted to do on his redirect. His plan was to let Luke have the chance to speak freely about the encounter with Susan. He wanted to finish up with Luke's appeal to the jury of his innocence; that his relationship with Susan was a serious one. He had instructed Luke to look the jurors straight in the eye one by one as he took his last shot. He hoped he remembered.

"Luke, tell us again. We know you only met Susan Weeks the one time, but explain what your relationship was in that brief meeting."

"I know it sounds crazy, but I fell in love with her at first sight. When I originally saw her in the Magnolia and we took a table together, I remember thinking how beautiful she was. But as we sat there, I came to see so much more than just physical appearance. There was a quality that glowed from inside her, radiating with a splendor that transcended anything I had ever known. There is no way I can put into words what happened to us that night. To me. But we touched something in each other. Some hidden spot that both of us were shielding until that night. I fell in love with Susan Weeks."

Luke stared straight at the jurors, slowing moving his gaze from one to the other. The sound of his voice was genuine and stable. Some of the jury watched him with sympathy and understanding. The two young females, one black, one white, were near tears. The older women looked distressed and troubled. Few of the men returned much expression.

Hays didn't know what else to say. He looked at each of the jurors, trying desperately to get some feel for their reaction to Luke's story. His plaintive rendition of the events left them all moved. Even the men who showed little emotion listened intently to Luke, hanging on every word. Hays could only think of one thing to finish off.

"Luke, did you kill Susan Weeks?"

"No, I did not. I left her that night sleeping so sweetly." Tears welled up in Luke's eyes. "I left, but my heart stayed with her. I wish I hadn't left and maybe we wouldn't be here. But I could never have harmed her in any way. I loved her."

Hays remained at the podium, staring at his papers while the whole room waited in silence. Luke's last words hung in the air leaving everyone still. Even Judge Jones sat pensively in the huge leather chair behind the bench.

"Your Honor, we don't have anything further." Hays walked quietly back to his seat.

"Alright, Mr. Daniels, you're dismissed. You may retake your seat." Jones' voice carried a sensitivity that had not been present before. He cleared his throat before continuing.

"We're now very close to the noon hour. This court will stand adjourned until one thirty."

The gavel struck with a clap that echoed through the hushed courtroom. Jurors were escorted from their seats and Jones disappeared into his office.

Luke ambled to his seat and dropped in his chair. He didn't look at the jurors as they left or anyone else. He sat without feeling, without emotion. He was numb to everything around him. Hays made a couple of comments while he arranged the table but nothing registered with Luke. Finally, he turned his gaze to his lawyer who stared directly at him.

"Come on, Luke. Lunch is at my place. I'm buying. The secretary's gonna have it there for us when we arrive. Let's go."

When they arrived at Hays' office, Jane Archer greeted them at the door and Cody Raybern was right behind her. Luke's eyes brightened at the sight of Jane. Without thought they hugged each other. She was there to be his first character witness that afternoon.

The bad news was that there would be no serving the subpoena on DeWeese. He was out of town on business and his office would not tell Cody where. There was no time for any detective work to find out. His parents were in Florida, the neighbors had filled him in on that, but no one knew where Jim DeWeese had gone. He thought it a little odd that his secretary would not tell him where DeWeese was. All she would say was out of town on business, like she was told to say, nothing more.

Cody got the idea that she didn't know where he was exactly herself. Something about the way she said it, which made the whole thing a little suspicious.

Hays still didn't see what good DeWeese could do Luke and told them so as he ate. From his conversation with the man, all DeWeese could do was make Susan look good and Luke look bad, and he thought that had already been done. He didn't see anything suspicious about the man being out of town. He had a business to run. He would have thought it suspicious if he had known that when the subpoena was issued from the clerk's office, Sam Martin was in there picking up subpoena's to serve for some other lawyers, a little business he did on the side. Sam had been the foreman of the grand jury that indicted Luke and so, had followed the case closely. Now that they were at trial he wondered why they were getting a subpoena this late. He inquired of his old friend, Luther Lambert, just why they would want that DeWeese boy in on this. Luther said he didn't know and hung up the phone, quickly dialing DeWeese. With a few short sentences he had DeWeese packing.

When the group returned to the courthouse after lunch, Jane joined them at the counsel table while others drifted around the room. Yes, she was ready for her testimony. Yes, she would tell these people about Luke's character.

"You are a character, you know," she said with a grin.

Luke laughed softly. His energy was slowly building after the day and a half grilling on the witness stand.

"I hope you don't waste as much time up there as I did." He tried to return her humor.

She would be the first witness of the afternoon followed by Judge Sutton and Liz, Luke's secretary. These three would talk about the character of the man on trial and how he could never be capable of murder. It was not in him. When they called her name, Jane stood up and took the oath.

Jane took the stand with her usual aplomb. Her connection to Luke over the years supplied ample knowledge to impart the character and temperament of the person of Luke Daniels. She was ready.

Hays spent some time on their relationship. Nothing romantic; strictly professional over the years. Almost like family, she talked of their mutual support during the trying times of law school, of her counsel during his divorce and his devotion to always doing the right thing. She spoke about his habit of continually thinking of the best interest of others, even when it worked against him. The testimony was short. Hays finished and turned the witness back to the court for cross-examination by the prosecutor.

Gafford started off his questions smoothly, without assaulting the fellow member of the bar. Had she ever met Susan Weeks? Was she aware of the intensity of Luke's feelings? Had she ever seen him in a fight with anyone?

"No, Luke is not the fighting kind. He can be aggressive without being hostile."

Jane was thinking in terms of his abilities as a lawyer realizing as soon as she said it that it sounded different than she meant. Luke was aggressive. A good lawyer had to be. That didn't mean he was capable of murder.

"Ms. Archer, how often would you say you see Luke?"

"Well, regularly. As regular as we can with busy schedules and living in different cities."

"What does that mean? Do you see him every week? Every month?"

"No, not every month."

"Okay, in the past year, how many times have you seen him?"

"I, ah, couldn't say, really. We talk on the phone occasionally."

"Have you seen him ten times in the past year? That wouldn't be quite as much as once a month."

"No, not ten times."

"Eight times? Six times?" When Jane didn't answer, Gafford continued, "Did you see him five times? I'm talking here about the year before the murder of Susan Weeks."

"No, I'd say maybe three times." Jane wanted to say more but couldn't.

"So, you've seen him maybe three times in the year before the murder. That wouldn't be enough to know if there had been a change in his lifestyle, now, would it, Ms. Archer?"

"I don't think his lifestyle has changed in several years, except for the better. He's become more successful in recent years."

"Yes, he has. And you haven't really had the opportunity to see him much during that time, have you?"

"I don't know the intimate details. I didn't know he had slept with this girl, if that's what you're asking. But I knew him in law school and before. Luke always had women interested in him. And from what I hear, Luke Daniels was not the only man Susan Weeks had ever known." Jane was trying her best to insert something, anything that would divert a little attention away from Luke.

"But you don't know the details of his life now, do you?"

"I'm not sure what you mean by details. I know Luke Daniels, and I know he didn't kill anyone." Jane pushed the statement into her answer, trying to be assertive.

"Well, now, Miss Archer you're an attorney and you know that this trial is not over. Tell me, if the facts prove otherwise, would you change your opinion?"

Gafford stepped back after delivering the treacherous question. There was no way for her to give an answer that would help Luke. If she said yes, then she hurt Luke's position. If she said no, then she was being irrational and would also hurt the defense. Gafford withheld any expression waiting for her answer. Jane looked straight at the jury, ignoring Gafford altogether as she responded.

"I'd have to really question those facts. There would be something else wrong because

Luke Daniels didn't do it. I'd want to know who else this woman might have slept with and what all went on with her modeling career. I've looked around and have found that there were other situations."

"Nothing further, Your Honor." Gafford picked up his papers from the podium and took his seat. He'd hoped to catch this witness but her response was sound. His wily quizzing had failed to achieve its calculated reaction. He was alright, though. She didn't break the sequence that was leading the jury to a guilty verdict.

Hays decided to give Jane the chance to elaborate on some of Gafford's questions on redirect.

"Ms. Archer, did you know Susan Weeks before her death?"

"No, I did not, but I've since learned she was into a lot of different things. I know she worked in a bank that kept her hopping from branch to branch." Jane wanted to pump in as much of the information she could that Cody had given her. "I know she was in a graduate program, that she worked as a model in some real skimpy outfits, half naked." Jane gave the jury a knowing nod of the head.

"Your Honor, we object to her slandering the deceased like this." Gafford jumped up.

"I'll allow it, but let's be brief." Jones couldn't see how this was hurting anything.

There wasn't anything else to say. She knew it was weak, but at least it was something to deflect a few of the assaults on Luke. She was sure at least some of the jurors had taken note. If only they could have gotten DeWeese up there.

Jane stepped down and Hays immediately called his next witness. Judge David Sutton from the next district over. He respected Luke and his professionalism and was eager to support him now. Several years older than Luke, he always credited Luke's father with encouraging him to go to law school.

On the stand, he said so.

"I wouldn't be here now if it weren't for that man's father," he said pointing at Luke. When that boy was just a child and I was in college wanting to quit and join the navy, his father prodded me on, telling me to finish my education. I know the influence he had on me and I know the kind of boy he raised. That boy didn't grow up to be a murderer."

"Thank you, Judge Sutton. No further questions. Your witness, counselor." Hays turned to Gafford with a flourish, as if to say, 'see if you can top that one.'

Gafford started off slowly with the Judge, asking about his day-to-day knowledge of the accused. They saw each other sometimes socially, but he kept up with his career and his reputation in the community. He knew Luke to be a good man. What Sutton didn't say was that he knew Gafford and Jones, also. And there wasn't much about them that he liked. He knew they double-teamed their cases and played politics like a game of monopoly without requisite justice. You get this, I'll get that. You scratch my back, I'll scratch yours. Sutton answered Gafford's questions directly, without putting any effort into covering up his contempt for him.

Gafford spent some time with the witness, knowing the jury would respect the fact that an equal to Judge Jones had come here on Luke's behalf. Gafford declined to do any risky cross-examination, too afraid of what a real judge might do to him. Sutton stepped down and Judge Jones instructed Hays to call his next witness.

"The Defense calls Liz White."

The bailiff brought Luke's secretary from the witness room and she took the stand. She was the last witness for Luke and Hays thought he was saving the best for last. She didn't have much in the way of actual facts, but would serve as another character witness. She would say good things about Luke.

She stated her name as Elizabeth Sims White. She was divorced over a year ago. She'd worked for Luke for six, no, almost seven years now. They spent a lot of time together. No, there was never anything romantic between them. Her divorce came because her husband was the one who found romance outside the marriage.

The remark drew a chuckle from the jury and across the room, helping Liz relax a little. She was extremely nervous, afraid that she would say something that would hurt her boss. She didn't want to do that. She only wanted to help.

When Hays finished with her, she let out a long, deep sigh. That wasn't so bad. She could handle this.

Gafford started his questions hard. He remembered the day in Luke's office with Liz. She was afraid of something. If he could chip away at her enough, she would crack, he was sure of it.

"Have you ever seen him act angry and upset?"

"Sure, lots of times. He's a lawyer."

Another chuckle from the jurors. They liked Liz. But Gafford stayed on her.

"How does he show his anger? How do you know when he's mad?"

"Just like anybody else. You can see it in him."

"What do you mean by that. Describe to us, please, how you can tell when Luke Daniels is mad."

"His eyes flare up. His face gives it away all over. He turns red and puffs up. He looks like he could…" Liz paused.

"Like he could what, Ms White?"

"Well, like…" Liz paused again, afraid that she had misspoken. Afraid that she was telling them something she didn't want to say. "Like anybody looks when they get mad. I don't know how to be more specific. He just looks mad, that's all."

Liz looked frightened and everyone could see it.

"Have you ever seen him look that way, Ms. White?"

"Yes." Liz didn't want to say any more.

"Have you ever seen him get violent with anyone?"

Immediately, Liz saw in her mind the scene of Luke physically throwing the reporter out the front door of their office. Up until that day she would have never thought him capable of that. She was still shocked at his actions. The picture in her mind formed on her face without any words coming out. She couldn't answer the question no. She did see him get violent with the reporter.

"Yes, I have," she answered slowly, quickly adding after "but only when he was provoked."

"So what you're telling us is that Mr. Daniels is capable of violence when provoked. Are you aware of what that would be? Of what things could provoke him?"

"Yes. I mean, no. I mean, I don't know everything about him but…"

"No, that's right, Ms. White, you don't know everything about him, do you? Nor, apparently, does everyone else. I have no further questions of this witness, Your Honor."

"Mr. Kennedy, any redirect?"

Hays stood and mumbled out some questions trying to recover from the disastrous blows she'd delivered unwittingly. His feeble attempts helped very little. Liz's testimony had gone from strongly supporting Luke to laying fuel on the fire that burned toward guilt.

Liz looked over at Luke with tears in her eyes. She tried to remain composed but she was so afraid of hurting his chances at acquittal. She knew her words were detrimental, but she couldn't lie. Damn it, why did they ask her such things? Luke returned her gaze with compassion.

"Your Honor, we have no other witnesses. At this time the Defense rests."

Luke looked up at him wondering where he picked up the false bravado. Luke felt anything but assured at the moment. Hays stepped from behind the table as he and Gafford approached the bench. Luke watched them exchange messages before the Judge. They talked outside of Luke's hearing as he witnessed it from afar, wondering what they were saying, what part of his life they were disposing of now.

This day was done. The time was five o'clock. Jones noted the hour from the bench and declared that they would have to resume the next day. He gave some announcements to the jury about the status of the trial. They were finished with the State and the defense's case in chief. The State would now have rebuttal, but before they got to that there were some motions and other procedural matters that needed to be done and, therefore, he would allow the jury to be released until the morning. They circulated out and down the hall with Luke standing at the table alone. Not one of them looked in his direction.

Things had been going so well, and then suddenly it all seemed so bad so quickly. Now they were done. At least his chance was done. There seemed to be so much else that needed to be said, but what? The jury was gone now and Luke sank back down as Hays formally proclaimed the motions that Jones would surely overrule. Luke tried to be optimistic, but it was becoming harder and harder.

The prosecution's first witness in rebuttal was Leon Harris, senior partner at Harris and Wells, his old employer. That didn't make any sense to Luke. What on earth could he have to add to this case? He had nothing to do with the situation. Gafford took him through a series of frivolous questions that Luke considered a complete waste of time. What was the point?

"Now, Mr. Harris, when you terminated Mr. Daniels from your firm, what were your reasons?"

Luke quickly grabbed Hays' arm and started talking into his ear.

"He didn't terminate me. I left there on my own. What are they doing?" Luke was fuming.

"Calm down, Luke. We'll get to cross-examine him."

Luke didn't calm down. He got madder and madder. Harris went on about how Luke's violent temper made him out of place in their operation. His lack of control didn't fit in with their goals. Outright lies were all Luke could think.

"Mr. Harris, you are familiar with Mr. Daniels' reputation in this community?"

"Yes, I am."

"And what is that reputation?"

"It's bad."

"Thank you, sir. Nothing further, Your Honor."

Hays got up for cross-examination with questions Luke scribbled out for him to contradict the notion that Luke was fired. Harris answered them all with his calm demeanor. Each one held enough truth to give them a ring of sincerity, but each one contained enough false information to create suspicion about the character of Luke Daniels.

When Hays finished, the District Attorney called his next rebuttal witness. This time it was Luther Lambert. Over vehement objection from Hays, which Jones overruled, he was allowed to testify about his knowledge of Luke's violent temperament.

"Yes sir," he responded respectfully to the prosecutor's questions. "He was at my office for a deposition in the conference room with my son. I was in my own office working when I heard a commotion. I quickly went down the hall and found Daniels making threats to Wilson with clenched fists. I really believe if I had not come in Mr. Daniels would have physically assaulted him. Over nothing."

Luther's tone was one of shock and dismay over Luke's uncivilized behavior. With limited words, he painted a picture of a barbaric attack by a crazed man.

"Yes sir, I don't know what would have made him be that way. He looked dazed. There was a wild look in his eyes that even scared me."

Hays again objected, but Jones merely waved him off and instructed the witness to continue. The testimony was completely out of line, making Luke out to be a monster with reports that had nothing to do with the issues at hand.

Hays' cross made things even worse. He accomplished nothing with the lawyer and even gave him the opportunity to get in a couple of extraneous digs at Luke. Hays finally shut up and sat down.

Gafford recalled Dick Limox next and started the same tirade over Luke's character. Yes, he knew Daniels. Yes, he knew his reputation for telling the truth. It was bad.

Luke was outraged. The Judge was allowing Gafford to parade witnesses in front of the jury that had no relevance to the trial. Their sole cumulative effect was to crucify Luke as they hammered in to the jury what a bad person he was. They left the elements of the trial and were creating an aura of wicked and evil around Luke, pushing him further behind a dark veil of depravity.

"Now, Detective Limox, are you aware that the defendant has testified that Ms. Weeks never came to his office?"

"No, sir, I was not aware of that," Limox lied. He wasn't supposed to know what had been testified about, but Gafford had coached him well. They were on the same side, after all. They had to work together.

"Do you have anything that would indicate otherwise?"

"Yes, sir, I do."

Luke sat to the edge of his chair. What the hell were they trying to pull? He punched Hays in hopes of getting an objection. This is outrageous, he told him. She was never in my office.

"We found a hair sample in Mr. Daniels' private office that matched that taken from the deceased."

"That is a lie," Luke stood to his feet.

Hays was standing, also, making his objection. He created such a scene that Luke's eruption was hardly noticed.

"Your Honor, this is highly improper. Gafford knows this is outside the scope of rebuttal. There was nothing about this in our case in chief. Gafford is out of line and I ask that we be heard on this outside the presence of the jury."

Hays was steaming, moving toward the bench without waiting for the Judge's invite. He glared over at Gafford as he continued to object in front of the Judge.

"Your Honor, we have nothing about this in discovery. Whatever Gafford is trying to do here should not be allowed. He has violated the canons of ethics by failing to respond properly to my requests for information."

"Now just a minute, Kennedy. Who do you think you're calling unethical?"

Gafford came toward Hays like he was going to slug him. Hays didn't back down, puffing up as he reiterated his objection to be heard outside the presence of the jury.

"If you'll settle down just a minute, I'll respond to the objection." Jones banged his gavel, trying to inject himself between the two lawyers. "Both of you approach the bench."

When they were close enough to hear him without shouting, he spoke to them through clenched teeth.

"What are you two doing? This is intolerable."

"Judge, he has no right to be going into this. He has not given me any advance notice. He has not listed finding any hair in his reports. It is certainly not appropriate in rebuttal."

"Your Honor, I didn't know about this until this morning. When Daniels testified that the girl never came to his office, this came out. The detectives told me about it when they read it in the newspaper. If she never came to his office how did the hair get there? It's perfectly proper in rebuttal, and ethical!" Gafford glared over at Hays.

"Mr. Kennedy, what do you have to say? How did the hair get there? Sounds to me like they've caught your client in a lie. I'm going to allow it."

"But, Judge…"

"No buts. You'll have your shot at cross. If you care to go there. I'd say you and your client are on dangerous ground.

Gafford continued with Limox finishing up what he started about finding the hair in Luke's private office when they executed the search warrant. Luke couldn't believe what he was hearing. He knew Susan was never in his office. But here they were telling it like the truth. Oh, yes, she was there. Daniels just lied about it. Like he's lied about everything else. The man's a natural born liar. Don't believe anything he says. Even Hays looked at him suspiciously.

Cross-examination was a complete waste of time. If anything, it only drew more attention to the fact that Luke said she was never there and the good, fine police officers said they found a hair from her head there. Even after all that time elapsed between the death and the search, some of her hair was still found in Luke's office.

Jerry Mason was the next witness. Yes, he knew Luke Daniels. In his work as a private investigator, he got to know a good number of the lawyers in and around Hampton. Yes, he had done some work for Daniels. And, yes, he was familiar with Daniels' reputation in the community. What was that reputation?

"It's bad." He looked down at Luke with disgust.

Cross-examination was ineffective to accomplish anything for Luke. Gafford called two more witnesses who continued with their innuendo and fraudulent suggestion. Janet Tidwell, Luther's long time secretary, talked about the attack on poor Wilson in his own office. She gave the impression of speaking for the entire community of legal secretaries.

Another secretary from the bank where Susan worked testified to the same thing. Yes, his character was bad. Oh, yes, he was prone to violence. No foundation for how she knew these things, but Judge Jones delighted in hearing the soap opera renderings of the days of Luke Daniels. He wasn't about to slow down the show. This courtroom had not seen a performance like this in years and he didn't want the audience disappointed.

One spectator was not entertained. Rita Lambert thought her husband was going to be a witness and she wanted to be there for his account. Until now, she had only followed the trial from the news. She read the articles in the paper that recapped each witness. The writer's depiction of the testimony made everything sensational.

As she read his account of Luke's story, her heart grew heavy, thinking of the compassion she perceived in their few brief encounters. The testimony of the other witnesses for Luke sounded credible. Jane Archer testified that she had known Luke since undergraduate school and that he was a man of character. She had stated that he was not capable of such a gruesome act. They quoted her as saying that if the evidence proved otherwise, she would have to question that evidence.

Rita certainly would question anything in which the Lambert's were involved. Luther's interest in this case seemed more than just a passing whim. She was all too familiar with his appetite for manipulation. The article went on with the testimony of Judge David Sutton. She was familiar with that name because he was being considered for a position on the Federal bench. A good one to have as a witness, Rita thought. The other witness for Luke was his secretary. The article didn't say much about her testimony other than she knew nothing about a client named Susan Weeks.

Rita didn't know why she felt so drawn to Luke. Maybe it was because he needed someone and she had not felt needed in such a long time. She kept having an inexplicable urge to help him. The recurring response to her query was that whenever her husband and his father were in favor of something she knew by experience that she should run the other way, and their position was clear on this subject. They both let it be known what a bad guy Luke Daniels was.

She'd heard them talk about the savage attack on Wilson. She knew her husband and what he was capable of inciting. She was well aware of his less than gentle nature. She rubbed her cheek, thinking of the time she encountered Luke at the gas station after one of Wilson's outbursts. She knew that anything Luke may have done to Wilson was provoked. She wished he'd done more. She'd love to see Wilson with a black eye. She'd love to see him get a little dose of his own medicine. She wished she knew how to give it to him herself.

Watching Luke subjected to the continual indignities and humiliation from the witnesses saddened her. She grew angry listening to Luther spout off about Luke. He's certainly one to talk, she thought. She identified with the helplessness he must be feeling. She watched his face, the pain repressed only slightly below the surface. Her heart went out to him as she sat in the courtroom filled with people who all seemed ready to tear him apart. Ready to attack and devour in a ruthless frenzy.

Luke listened to it all in shock. He didn't know where they were getting all this nonsense. He listened to person after person get on the stand and talk about what a bad person he was. He felt isolated and alone. It was as if he were being held up for public ridicule, the facts no longer germane. Anyone and everyone who cared to come by and belittle him could take their shot. People whom even he considered honest and trustworthy were standing before him and the world proclaiming his villainy and wickedness.

Luke heard them revile him as such a horrible creature that he didn't see any reason for the poor schmuck to live himself. His every weakness, his every flaw was being brandished about the room like a chant from a carnival hawker. 'Yes sir, ladies and gentlemen this here is by far the worst human being ever allowed to walk on the face of the earth. Step right up and cast your vote for the guilty conviction that the fiendish brute deserves.' Each witness reveled in presenting more scurrilous abuse than the one before. Gafford had his people on a roll.

His next witness was Jenny Hester, the former receptionist at Luke's office, now working as Wilson Lambert's secretary. What on earth was she going to testify about was Luke's initial reaction? Maybe she could help him.

She didn't. Gafford politely delivered his questions that slowly got around to her witnessing the attack, as he posed it, on Jeff Woodall. She described it in much more detail than Luke ever remembered Jenny possessing before. In his office she was always quiet with little to say. Very few comments. Now she was masterful with the particulars of the event as if she had been trained. Her testimony made Luke look like an ogre. Like a monster that could devour anything in his path.

"Now, Ms. Hester, you've told us that you are familiar with Mr. Daniels."

"Yes," she had a frightened look about her.

"And you are familiar with his reputation in the community?"

"Well, yes, even more so now that I work away from his office."

"And what is that reputation?"

"Oh, it's bad. Very bad. Why, if I had known what people thought of him when I was there, I'd have left in a minute. Now that I'm away I can look back and see just how bad he was."

"Thank you, Ms. Hester. Your Honor, I have nothing further of this witness."

Jenny Hester stepped down from the stand while Gafford conferred with Jimmy Clay at the prosecutor's table. After several minutes he stood erect and cleared his throat.

"Your Honor, the State would now rest."

A rumble of whispered voices began. Judge Jones banged his gavel, demanding silence. Luke urged Hays to call for surrebuttal. Something that would give him the chance to refute the damning testimony they had heard all day.

Jones called the lawyers to the bench where heated words were exchanged between Gafford and Hays. The Judge's voice sounded above their clamoring which suddenly ceased. Before they could get back to their seats, Jones started talking.

"Ladies and gentlemen of the jury, testimony in this matter is now concluded. I have to caution you, though, that it is not yet time for you to start your deliberation. We will take a short break before coming back and I will have some instructions for you. I will instruct you on the law as it applies to this case. It will be your duty to apply that law to the facts of the case as you find them and make a decision. Until that time I ask that you bear with us a while longer before you are asked to retire and deliberate. We will stand adjourned for fifteen minutes."

The inquisition was over. No more testimony. No more lies. After the Judge read the instructions the two lawyers would be allowed to make closing statements. They would argue their case one final time before the jury took it behind closed doors.

When the break was over Jones started the process of reading the jury instructions.

Through argument before the Judge, the prosecutors wound up with nineteen approved and the defense with fourteen. A total of thirty-three paragraphs that read like a case book from law school on the issue of murder. When Jones finished, the jury knew as much about the elements required to be proved in a murder case as most any lawyer. They would be allowed to take them into the jury room to look over and use in making a decision. The only thing left was closing arguments.

The State went first. Gafford got the first shot on the premise that the State had the burden of proof. The defendant was innocent until proven guilty. The Defense then got their turn. When finished, the prosecutors would have one more shot. In theory, they had as long as they needed. In practice, Jones didn't allow any long-winded nonsense.

It was Friday afternoon. Jones wanted to get things finished as soon as possible. He didn't want this dragging on, he told the lawyers. They had one hour each and then twenty minutes for Gafford's rebuttal. Let's get to it, he goaded them on.

Gafford started off slowly and methodically recapping the evidence. He began with Jennifer Holt's testimony about finding the body. He flashed the pictures of the murder scene in front of the jurors. This is what she saw.

He then walked through who took the pictures, the detective work. With quiet, almost sad intent, he carefully laid out the findings of the state crime lab. The fingerprints, the hair samples. The semen.

"Yes, Mr. Daniels told us he had sex with her. They were smitten with each other, I believe he said. Or something like that. Then tell me," Gafford paused for effect. "Why did he have to kick the door in?"

The quiet that followed haunted the vast space in the huge courtroom, filling it up and lingering with no place to go, making all uncomfortable. Luke could feel the question echoing around in his head. But I didn't, he wanted to say. I didn't do it. He wanted to cry.

After Gafford finally sat down, the Judge instructed Hays that he had one hour. Hays picked up the prepared version of his closing statement and moved to the podium. He nodded respectfully to the Judge and turned to the jury. His words did not start out immediately, but instead he took them all in, gazing back at their fixed expressions.

This was the hard part of the lawyers' life. Some liked it. Hays usually did, but now he looked over at Luke and realized that the man's life was in his hands. The lump in his throat reminded him of the gravity of the position. For the whole week he had been caught up in staying in the fray, keeping himself head-to-head, toe-to-toe with Gafford. Now it was just him in front of the jury who waited for his last words. He tried to push the lump aside so the words could get out.

"Ladies and gentlemen, a man's life rests in your hands right now. You are charged with an awesome responsibility. The one thing we know for absolute certainty is that a young woman is dead. The District Attorney has paraded an ample number of witnesses before you to establish that one fact, but there is not one bit of evidence that says for sure that she died at the hands of Luke Daniels. When we go back over everything you've heard, all we know for sure is that Susan Weeks and Luke Daniels were together that night. We know that they were in bed together…"

The lump reasserted itself with his last sentence forcing Hays to pause and clear his throat. He swallowed hard, hoping his vocal cords would relax and allow him to continue. The jurors were hardly breathing, his tension transferring on to them. They all sat motionless, waiting for his next utterance.

Hays continued going over the undisputed evidence of the case. Luke was there. Luke had sex with her. And then he left. He couldn't talk about Susan's legal problem because that had never been revealed. But it was clear she had called Luke because his secretary knew he had the appointment with her. She never came to the office, despite the hair found there. It didn't make sense that Luke would lie about that.

He went on about all the uncertainties in the case. Reasonable doubt. There was plenty of reasonable doubt and the prosecutor had to prove his case to them beyond a reasonable doubt. If there was doubt in their mind, they had to vote not guilty.

He talked at length about the idea of innocence until proven guilty. Then he moved on to what it took to prove the man guilty. He relaxed and as he did, so did the jurors. Some were still mesmerized by his comments, listening intently as he talked about the need to weigh every bit of evidence.

James Hutchinson didn't think he needed this lecture about how the law worked. He knew the law. He'd listened to everything that had been presented in testimony. And he'd listened to a few other things, too. He knew they couldn't tell it all here in the courtroom. But there was more to this case than they were letting on. He'd read between the lines and figured out that there was some kind of drug involvement that they hadn't been allowed to bring out about the defendant. His friend, Jerry Mason, had pretty much said so.

As his mind wandered, he turned to Daniels. Lawyers. Hell, they couldn't be trusted. James knew all lawyers were liars. You couldn't believe what they told you half the time. Daniels had to be lying about the girl. Look at him, smug bastard. Driving around town in his Cadillac. Yeah, well, the gigs up, mister. I'm not falling for some cock and bull story. I know what really happened.

"The District Attorney has presented nothing to identify who killed this woman," Hays continued. "Everything you heard from the prosecution is all circumstantial. There is nothing, not one shred of evidence, that gives my client a motive for killing Susan Weeks."

Hays wondered where he was with the jurors. The older white women had a wall up that he couldn't seem to get around. The blacks were listening, at least, especially the young black girl who sat on the front row. Hays thought she was probably his strongest ally, but how strong was she?

The three younger white men appeared to dismiss everything Hays said. He kept trying to make contact with them mentally, but they would not acknowledge anything he said or did. The youngest was cocky, rebuffing any effort by Hays to get his attention. He moved on to another as he continued with his time rapidly slipping away.

"And so, in closing, I ask you to consider the lack of any direct evidence against this man. You may not agree with his actions that night, but please don't let that convince you he is guilty. Luke Daniels may have had an error in judgment. He may have violated his own standards of conduct. You heard him say that; that he wishes he'd done things differently. We all have those epiphanies in our lives about things we really wish we'd done much differently, but that doesn't make us guilty of a crime. It doesn't make Luke Daniels guilty. So I ask you, when you retire to consider this case, do the right thing. Do the only thing that, in good conscience, you can. Find this man not guilty."

Hays nodded solemnly and, with a quiet thank-you, sat down. There was not a sound in the room. But Jones didn't waste any time in getting the next step moving.

"Mr. Gafford, you have twenty minutes."

Gafford was on his feet quickly, ready to break the spell Hays conjured. Yeah, it was a good effort, Hays, my boy, but the man's going down. Gafford pranced to the podium.

"Ladies and gentlemen, enough has been said, so I won't bore you with more tedium. In just a word, I'd like to re-iterate the facts. The man killed the girl. It's as simple as that. We all listened to that baloney about love and whatever. Great story, wasn't it?" Gafford paused only for a breath.

"But, you know, where I come from it's not love when you kick the door down. It's not love when you won't take no for an answer. This is violence, pure and simple. You ladies on the jury, you need to send a message. You men, how can you let this go unchecked? Find him guilty. Because he is."

Gafford gave them all one last firm look. He was convinced and they needed to be also. With a conclusive thank-you from a determined expression he took his seat without taking his eyes off them. He was law and order and they needed to be, too. They were on his team to keep this community decent and upstanding.

"Alright, ladies and gentlemen, you've heard me say over and over again that this case was not yet before you for deliberation and that you should withhold any discussion until such time as it was. Well, now it is. You are now to reach a decision."

"Bailiff, will you escort the jurors to their room, seeing to any needs they may have."

They filed out, one by one. No one looked at Luke and he didn't look at them. He tried to hold his gaze straight ahead, without emotion. It took all his effort as they passed before him.

When the last one cleared and the door shut behind them, Jones pounded the gavel announcing that court would stand adjourned until the jury reached a verdict. He instructed the parties to be within reach for return upon that decision. Then he left the bench. It was four o'clock on Friday afternoon.

As the courtroom cleared, a few lawyers who had watched the closing arguments came over and made comments of well-wishing to Luke. He thanked them absently without moving from his seat. The prosecution table cleared quickly as they moved back to their office and soon he and Hays sat alone in the big room.

Jerry Mason hurried back to Luther Lambert's office to fill him in on the closing statements that he'd just heard. He scurried down the front steps of the courthouse making his way quickly to be the first with the report. He figured several people would be calling Luther to give him their rendition but Jerry wanted to be first.

CHAPTER TWENTY

Inside the jury room, the twelve milled around, exchanging chitchat softly, putting off the inevitable as long as possible. The room was simply a table with twelve chairs. There was a table in the corner with a coffee pot. The chairs were comfortable, but most hoped they didn't have to find out just how comfortable. They didn't want to spend a long time in them. There were two windows on one wall that looked out onto the grassy area behind the court-house. The windows had old-fashioned blinds and some nondescript beige curtains. One by one they found a spot around the table, segregating by sex and color.

Adrian McCarthy was the ordained foreman for the group, taking his seat at the head of the table. James Hutchinson wanted the position, but the group leaned toward the maturity of the shoe storeowner. James took the spot at his side as assistant foreman, eager to help out in any way. Both were ready to get a guilty decision to take back to the Judge. It was obvious to them that it was the right solution.

Next to James sat Joe Lee Pigott, the electrician and then the nurse from New Orleans, Philip Dunbar. Peggy Stevens was next and then Freida Mixon, with Mrs. Batson, the retired teacher, on the end. She'd managed a classroom of tenth graders for thirty years so it was nat-ural for her to take a spot at one end of the table.

To her right was the young Janet Mosby, mother of two daughters. She'd had Mrs. Batson in the tenth grade and still thought the world of her. She wasn't quite sure what to make of this whole mess but she knew Mrs. Batson understood. She made up her mind to listen to whatever Mrs. Batson had to say and then do the same thing herself.

Roanda was in the next seat. Janet was the only white person on the jury that had been nice to her. Roanda had not said a word about her ideas that Luke was innocent. No one had asked her.

Kareem Townsend was next to Roanda. He came to the bank often where she was a teller. He made good money as a car salesman and saved quite a bit at Roanda's bank. Freddie Johnson was next and then Rozelle Thompson. Rozelle had retired from the school about the same time as Mrs. Batson. She was always so nice to him. He thought a lot of that white lady. He had his own mind about how to vote here, but he was interested in how she saw the situation.

The twelve of them sat around the table and talked about the lawyers and the witnesses freely. They laughed about the lawyers getting into a huff with one another.

"I'd like to see 'em go at it real serious one time," chuckled Joe Lee. "I'd bet ol' Gafford could whup Kennedy."

Several snickered at the thought. Adrian wished he had a gavel like the Judge.

"Alright, I guess we'd better try to get down to business. Does anyone have any questions about what we've got to do here? Anything you want to discuss?" There was silence around the room for a minute, until Joe Lee spoke up.

"I just don't understand why he did it. I mean, I've seen some people get crazy on drugs. We've had some guys at work get on cocaine, but I still can't imagine him killing a client. There's was no proof he had ever done drugs in the first place." Joe Lee had seen some craziness, alright. He had dabbled in the stuff himself, but he didn't understand it making you want to kill somebody for nothing.

"I'm thinking he didn't mean to do it, but in some crazed drug state, he lost his temper and wham-o. She was dead." James had a cousin who went crazy on drugs and they had to have him committed because he was dangerous. "I think the man did it and he's guilty."

"So do I," piped in Adrian. As foreman, he wanted to stay in charge. Adrian was sure the Judge and the District Attorney knew Daniels did it. Probably knew much more than they could let get to the jury and so he wanted to give them the right verdict. The Judge's wife was one of his best customers. "I've got some paper here to pass out. Or can we just do it by a raised hand?"

"Let's do the first one by paper," offered Mrs. Batson from the opposite end of the table." She'd worked with groups of kids enough to know that was the best way to see what everyone would say.

"Does anybody have any questions?" Adrian tried to be in charge.

No one said a word at first. They sat solemnly around the table until James popped in a quip.

"Wonder who his clients will switch to when we send him to jail?" He snickered, drawing a grin from a couple of others.

The sheets of paper were quartered and passed around the room. A box of pencils followed the paper around until each one had what they needed to vote.

"Okay, let's write out our vote and see what we get," Adrian instructed the group.

Even though the vote was secret, several of the jurors made no secret of what they were putting down, writing their answer in plain view for all to see. Mrs. Batson knew the ladies on either side of her wanted to see her decision so she let them. Janet Mosby wrote the same thing on her paper. Rozelle Thompson knew what it was all the way down on his end of the table. He sat still without writing for a long time. He could see clearly what Adrian put down, also. Kareem Thompson sat across from Joe Lee Pigott and saw his vote. The confidence with which he wrote out his view bothered Kareem. Maybe he was right.

When everyone finished, they passed the pencil box back around to collect the ballots. Adrian took the box and started through them. Guilty. Guilty. Guilty. Guilty. Guilty. Five in a row came back guilty. The sixth piece was blank.

"This one's blank," Adrian reported, turning the paper over in his hands. "Who did that? Didn't you understand what to do?" He looked directly at Roanda as if she was the one.

"It wasn't me," she quickly responded, as if his accusatory tone had insulted her. She wasn't stupid.

"Just go on and see what else we have." Mrs. Batson volunteered.

"Not guilty," he called out from the next ballot, disgustedly. Everyone knew Adrian's position.

"Guilty. Not Guilty." Again, the disdain for what he considered their lack of good sense. "Didn't you people listen out there?" He tried to belittle their reasoning.

"Not Guilty. Not Guilty. Guilty. Alright, what have we got here? That's one, two, three, four, five, six, seven for guilty, four not guilty, and one who doesn't know. Now what do we do?"

"It's obvious to me the man is guilty." Hutchinson started off first. "How can you not see that? He may not have meant to but he did. I believe he was hopped up on drugs. I mean, kicking the door in. What more do you want?"

"Yeah, I like a little as much as the next guy, but you can't let it make you that crazy." Joe Lee laughed heartily at his joke looking across the table at Kareem and Freddie who laughed only a little.

Mrs. Batson didn't find their humor amusing. She knew he was guilty and didn't find anything about the situation to be a laughing matter. She gave Joe Lee the eye that had settled many a rowdy teenager before and he knew he'd better be quiet.

Philip Dunbar had the pictures of the murder scene before him. He'd not seen anything like this since he left New Orleans. There you were always getting this kind of stuff on the evening news. His work at Touro Hospital gave him all he wanted to see in a lifetime. He looked at the hair falling around the face that all had described as beautiful. Something about this disturbed him but he wasn't sure what. He wasn't certain about Daniels' guilt like the others seemed to be, but he didn't have any other explanation either. He sat passively while those that did seem certain crowed.

"There's four people in here that don't think he's guilty. Would you like to tell us why you don't think he is?"

Adrian thought he knew who it was but wanted them to identify themselves so the rest of the crew could work on them straight up. No one said anything as the eyes in the room looked around, taking in their fellow members of the jury. Adrian thought he would try another tact.

"Mr. Hutchinson, do you have any questions?"

"Nope. I know he's guilty. I've known it since the beginning of the trial." James didn't know he set himself up in violation of the charge to the jury. He wasn't supposed to have an opinion of guilt or innocence until the end of the testimony.

"Mr. Pigott, do you have anything?"

"No sir. I'm kinda like James. The man's guilty. What else could it be?" He looked around the room to see if anyone would offer a response to his question. As far as he was concerned there was no other answer and it was Friday and he wanted this over with so he could go home.

"Mr. Dunbar, what about you?"

"I don't have anything to add." He still wasn't sure, but he didn't have anything to add. His ballot had been the blank one before. He wrote nothing on it because he didn't know what he thought. The blank said he was undecided. If Daniels didn't do it, who did? He had doubt, but still, was it reasonable doubt.

Peggy Stevens didn't have anything to offer, nor did Freida Mixon. When he got to Mrs. Batson she felt compelled to add something. The educator in her had to take the leadership role.

"The Judge told us that it had to be beyond a reasonable doubt. I just can't come up with a reasonable explanation why the man's not guilty. He had to have done it. Sweet young thing like that. He's admitted to being with her that night and with…," she paused, not sure what words to use. "Well, you know, having sex with her and all. Something's just not right about this story. Why did he kick the door in? Sounds like something else got involved there. I know they never said it outright because the judge wouldn't let them, but it was drugs. I've seen kids in the school go crazy when they get on that stuff, wild and all."

She stopped and looked around the room. Philip Dunbar heard what she said about drugs making a man crazy. In the emergency room he once saw a man who was hopped up on cocaine grab a woman and slit her throat. He was standing so close that part of the blood got on him. His eyes locked in with Mrs. Batson. Yes, she was right. Drugs could make a man do crazy things. It didn't have to make any sense. She looked back at him knowing that he was agreeing with her, no longer undecided. Part of her feelings on the case came from outside the testimony. She hadn't told anyone that she lived next door to Jerry Mason's parents. They knew a lot about this case that hadn't come out in testimony.

"I don't like the idea of having to convict the man, either, but I don't see how we have any choice. It ain't our fault he's guilty." She finished up with a firm set of the jaw and hard looks at those she thought were not in the camp. She didn't know what to think about the blank ballot.

Janet Mosby stated she agreed with Mrs. Batson. Roanda told them she didn't have anything to say. But that was not the truth. She didn't see it the same way all the others did but she knew she'd never be able to convince them. Maybe she was wrong. Somehow, she didn't really think so, but what could she do. The people at the bank would think she was crazy for going against all these other good people.

"Kareen, how 'bout you?"

"Well, I guess he's guilty. Why else would we be here?" He wasn't sure but he was going to go with the majority. He wanted to be agreeable.

"Freddie, what do you think? Anything to add?" Adrian assumed he voted guilty.

"Nothing, Mr. McCarthy." Freddie had nothing to say. He had voted not guilty and he wasn't changing it. He realized that a lot of the evidence pointed toward Mr. Daniels, but his cousin Willie said he didn't do it. He would take his cousin's word on it before he would take the word of the clowns he had seen out there on the witness stand. They wasn't there no more than Willie was. They didn't know what really happened. Freddie knew how the law could run over somebody.

"Rozelle?" Adrian knew him from his years at school.

"Sir?"

"Do you have anything you'd like to say? Do you have any questions? Or are you ready to vote guilty?"

"Oh, yessir. I'm ready."

"All right, then. Let's do this again and maybe we can get home."

They passed out the papers and everyone wrote down their vote. When they were gathered up and counted, there were ten guilty, one not guilty and another blank one. Looking around trying to decide who it was, the jurors' faces were dour. Most everyone had made their decision known. Only a few said nothing, keeping their opinions to themselves. A strange element suddenly seemed loose in the room. The more vocal group took a condescending posture, expressing disdain for those who had not voted guilty. Philip Dunbar had voted guilty, but he wasn't all too sure. The possibility of drugs had swayed him, despite the fact that there was no testimony that Luke Daniels ever used drugs.

Freida Mixon didn't say much about her vote. She voted guilty, but she didn't feel that strongly about trying to convince others. That was not her way. They could decide for themselves. All she could think about was that poor girl. She voted guilty because somebody had to pay for what happened to that poor girl. It was just awful.

Kareem Townsend didn't think much about it. He didn't want to say much. He just wanted this to be over with so he could get back to work. This was a slow time of the year and there wasn't much in sales. Every moment he was away, someone else was getting what few sales there were. This was costing him a lot of money. He wanted to be back at his job. It looked like the police had done theirs or why else would we be here. Let's just vote and get it over with. He wasn't comfortable saying that to anyone. He would just be quiet and hope to be finished soon.

Freddie Johnson wondered who the other not guilty vote was. He wasn't about to ask because he wasn't sure they knew that he was one of them. He couldn't say much because he didn't want to say anything about his cousin, Willie. He didn't want to get himself in trouble. He wasn't about to let that happen, cousin or not.

Adrian McCarthy thought he knew who kept them from a unanimous verdict. He was ready for this to be over. They didn't need to drag it out. The man was guilty and they had to convince the two unbelievers.

In the courtroom Luke sat alone at the defendant's table. His mind was no longer racing. The adrenaline that had pumped through his veins for days ebbed to a trickle. He felt the spigot close up tight and his body grind to a standstill. And so he sat in the chair without energy to move. No one came by to bother him, no one appeared to take note of his presence.

Hays wandered off after talking with Luke briefly. He'd given him the speech about how the jury would act. If they came back quickly that was bad for the defendant. If they took a long time then the defense was in good shape. Luke knew the story well and hardly registered the words. Hays wandered off leaving Luke at the table alone.

Luke was glad for the solitude. His brain worked in slow motion, bits and pieces of the trial coming back to him. Practically on automatic pilot his lawyer brain rehashed the battle that brought him to this point. Over and over he heard the words of former so-called friends saying bad things about him. How did Luke get so bad so quickly? He'd listened to people he hardly knew talk about him with spiteful intent as if they knew him better than he knew himself.

What did the jury think? That was the question. How could they form a reasonable opinion based on the perversion of the facts that had been paraded in front of them? Did Luke have any chance of them reaching the right decision?

Pictures of the trial continued to filter through his head like clips on a news story, playing over the testimony of the week. He saw Liz on the stand looking like a scared animal. He knew she wanted to help, but the desire only made her appear to cover up, something less than truthful. Jane's statement was excellent. I'd have to question that evidence. If only they'd do that.

Luke wondered why so many people were set on putting him down. How did they come to get on the witness stand to say what a bad person he was? When did he get so bad? It seemed like such a short while ago that his life was moving forward brilliantly. And then Susan. And then bang. The explosion rocked his entire world. He wanted to help her so much. Wanted to fix whatever was wrong in her life and then include her in his. But it didn't turn out that way. She was gone and his life was in shambles. What would he do when this was over?

Emptiness filled the foyer at the top of the stairs at the entrance to the courtroom. Reporters had scurried off to telephones and the coffee shop across the street. Several spectators from the trial drifted over for coffee and conversation that centered on their theory of the jury's verdict. Everyone had an opinion. It was the only subject at every table.

Rita Lambert had her own thoughts about the case, but she kept them to herself as she listened to her friends. She sipped her Brazilian Hazelnut Supreme and took in the banter around her. A man's life hung in the balance across the street and here it was being kicked around like just another social event. The little shop with its bare old brick walls and heart pine floor was brewing more than coffee today. Everyone in the place had an opinion about what the jury would do.

Rita wished it was Wilson on trial. She'd love to see his impudent little ass on the line like Luke, his every transgression held up for inspection. She could tell them a thing or two.

Her eye was fine now. Now. And it would be fine. She had her mind made up that he wouldn't do that to her ever again. Whatever demon prompted his rage, the fury would have to find another target. She would not be the victim again.

Watching Luke Daniels being crucified disgusted her. She didn't know what her father-in-law was up to but she was certain that his appearance at the trial was more than a desire to serve the truth. She knew him too well. He had something to gain by it all. She wasn't sure what, but she knew he never did anything for nothing.

Their coffee was finished. The other ladies announced their departure and all stood up to leave. Outside the others went on to their car. Rita looked up at the courthouse across the street and wondered what the jury was doing. On impulse she walked across and up the steps. Inside she went up the stairs finding the vacant foyer. The thick carpet softened her steps as she went to the door to the courtroom and looked through the windows. She could see Luke sitting alone at the table, his fate being decided just a short distance away in the jury room. Even though he sat upright in the chair at the defendant's table, he looked almost lifeless, abandoned and all alone.

No one else was in the courtroom. She wanted to go in and comfort him. She wished she had some words of encouragement to offer like he did her at the gas station. His sweet words came back to her, the compliments. Then at Shoney's where she saw him with his friend, Jane Archer, whose picture had been in the paper with the article about her testimony. His look then was so tender and dear. The kindness of his smile. The imperceptible affinity they shared tugged at her heart.

She wanted to go in and speak to him now. To return the kind word, the smile, and the comfort she had gotten from him. He probably didn't even know how significant their brief encounters had been to her, but she knew. She wanted to give back to him, but what on earth could she possibly say or do that would change anything for him?

"Pretty miserable creature, isn't he?"

"OOohhhh," she let out a scream.

Jerry Mason came up behind her speaking the words softly only inches from her ear. He'd come up the steps quietly admiring Rita's backside and sidled up to her carnally, trying to rub against her in the process. His face almost touched her hair as he spoke the words, taking her by surprise.

"Mr. Mason, please, you scared me. What are you doing creeping around here in the courthouse?" She wondered how much he had observed.

"I could ask the same about you. I was up here as a witness, just came back to see how long it was going to take to fry'im. What are you doing?"

"I was across the street at the coffee shop and just walked over to see if the jury had come back. Everybody over there was talking about it. I heard my father-in-law testify earlier. He did a good job." She tried to cover her fluster.

Yeah, yeah, Jerry thought, you don't have to remind me who your goddamn paw-in-law is. She was always uppity, he thought. Like she was better than anyone else. Jerry thought he knew just what she needed to get that out of her. He wondered what she was really doing up here.

"Yeah, I was just down at his office. He's interested in the outcome, too. The whole town is. Get this murdering bastard off the street. You ladies will all be safer."

Jerry's very presence made Rita uncomfortable. She never liked him. Always something lecherous about his bearing, making her feel wary and apprehensive, like she should be on her guard. He was around a lot, always peeping over their shoulder, gathering up anything he could run tattle back to Luther. She backed away from the door, leaving him peering through the small glass opening.

"I've got to be going to pick up the kids. I'm sure I'll hear about the outcome."

She scampered to the stairs and went down. Jerry said goodbye as his eyes followed the sexy sway of her hips moving down the steps. What was she doing up here, he mused with a grin on his face. He was well acquainted with her lack of affection for her father-in-law. She hadn't been up here to spur him on. Probably just natural curiosity like everybody else. Still, Daniels did have a way of attracting the favor of pretty women. Jerry hoped that didn't happen in the jury box. Nah, couldn't. That was already taken care of. Just had to wait for them to come back with the guilty verdict.

In the jury room, everyone was standing and stretching and moving about. Exasperation seeped out from several of the group who thought it ridiculous that they still did not have a unanimous verdict. Several knew it was just a matter of time. Adrian postponed another vote until after they had stretched and resettled. He tried to rap his pen on the table like a gavel to get everyone to pay attention.

"Our not guilty voters need to tell us what we don't know. We've got ten people who think the man's guilty, but two disagree. Maybe you two need to tell the rest of us what we missed."

The sarcasm dripped from his last sentence. Several people squirmed but no one said a word. The big group was ready to jump on whoever it was, making it more difficult for the nonconformist to come forward. Joe Lee Pigott and James Hutchinson stood over by the windows, both with a chew of tobacco. The building was all no smoking, but Kareem Townsend had opened a window, then lit up and Janet Mosby had joined him. They were all chatting, but the not guilty folk had yet to identify themselves.

Adrian rapped his pencil on the table again, asking everyone to take a seat so they could get back to business. James Hutchinson drummed his fingers on the arm of his chair, looking as though it was incomprehensible to him that anyone could consider voting not guilty. Mrs. Batson eyed each juror long and hard. Philip Dunbar fidgeted with the papers in front of him. Kareem Townsend tapped his foot, ready to get out of here. After a long while with no one saying anything, the foreman spoke up.

"If no one wants to talk about this any more, then I think we need to take another vote. Let's see if there's any change."

Hutchinson tore each of three regular sheets of paper into four parts like he had done two other times now. When he had twelve, the pieces were handed out again. Everybody had a pencil they put to the paper and then raised up and folded it in half. For some reason, no one made a big show of how they were voting.

The outspoken guilty jurors simply put down their vote and folded the paper. The basket went around collecting the papers. They were handed back to Adrian who this time had a plan.

"I guess all I need to look for is not guilty," he said, flipping through the papers. Guilty, guilty, guilty, he mumbled, going through every piece calling out guilty as he refolded the piece and went to the next. After twelve times, he looked up at the group without any doubt in his mind about what he was doing. He was going to flush out the oddball by ignoring their vote and calling it guilty. Again, two people wrote not guilty on the paper but Adrian McCarthy ignored the NOT part and read only the word guilty. He surveyed the group waiting for the dissenters to respond. Nothing came.

Freddie Johnson was one of those that voted not guilty. He didn't know what to do. He looked around the room at all the satisfied faces. He started to speak, but didn't. What was Mr. McCarthy doing? Did he think no one would say anything? Freddie kept trying to decide what he should do. They couldn't just run over him like this. He thought about his cousin Willie. If he said anything and made a spectacle of himself, they might figure out that Willie had talked to him about Mr. Daniels. Freddie didn't know the law but he was afraid there was something wrong with that. But there was something wrong with this, too. He looked at McCarthy. McCarthy felt him looking and their eyes met, neither of them sure what the other was going to do.

McCarthy knew he was on dangerous ground. What was he going to say if someone spoke up? The others would support him, he was sure of it. He was only trying to get the dissenters to stand up for their position so the group could discuss it. After only a moment, McCarthy looked away and busied himself with the papers in front of him.

Roanda Richardson was the other dissenter. She had voted not guilty but was afraid to say anything. If she spoke up and she was the only one that blocked the verdict, her people at the bank would never let it go. It was the bank where Susan worked. How could she have let the murderer get away? Everyone would know that she was the only one. She didn't know that Freddie had voted not guilty, also. And, he didn't know about her vote. They both stayed quiet and the vote stayed the way Adrian McCarthy called it. Finally, Hutchinson spoke out.

"Alright, that means we're done," he clapped his hands together. He'd watched the pieces of paper closely and knew what Adrian was doing. This needed to be over. It scared him a little to think what might happen if this got out. But no one would know. And if they did, probably all that would happen was that the murderer would get a new trial. So what. "What do we do now?"

"I believe one of our instructions was a form of verdict that we need to follow," Mrs. Batson advised. She had the folder of instructions in front of her going through them.

"Here it is." She pulled it from the pile and started reading. "We, the jury, find the Defendant, Luke Daniels, guilty. If you'll give me a piece of paper, I'll write it out."

She wrote out the verdict on the paper James handed to her and then passed it to McCarthy. "See if that looks right to you."

"Yep, that's what we need."

McCarthy signed his name to it nervously, not sure now about what he had done. One more time he looked around the table to see if anyone wanted to speak up. No one said a word. No one tried to stop him and he went back to the paper and put foreman under his name. The condemning mentality swept around the table, making it futile to oppose. It was useless to resist. McCarthy was a little shaken by what he had done, but he knew it was the right thing. Daniels was guilty and it wouldn't be right to put that murderer out on the streets and put the taxpayers to another trial. Let him work on his appeal from jail. Adrian had done the right thing. He didn't think about how he had violated the process. That he had committed a crime against an innocent man. Adrian just convinced himself he had done the right thing for law and order.

Outside the jury room, the bailiff sat with his chair leaning back against the wall, in a near doze. His eyelids were heavy as he sat and waited. The knock on the door jolted him awake making him nearly tip over in his chair. He jumped to his feet and opened the door a crack.

"Yes, what is it?"

"We're ready."

"What?" He looked at his watch and couldn't believe the time. "Alright, I'll go tell the Judge and be right back."

Judge Jones was in his office on the phone when the bailiff appeared at his door. He was contemplating leaving for a while to have dinner with his wife who was on the line with him.

"They're ready," came the word from the bailiff.

"Oh, honey, I've got to go. The jury's got a verdict. Huh? Oh, no, of course, I don't know what it is. The bailiff just informed me. Let me go and I'll call you as soon as we get through."

Jones hung up the phone and started barking orders to Anna and the bailiff to start rounding everybody up. Call the DA's office. Find Hays Kennedy. The jury's ready to come back. The Judge was in a dither about the news, dashing about to grab his robe and get back to the bench.

"My robe's in the other office behind the courtroom. I'll go get it and be in there. You two hurry. What are you standing around for? Let's get moving."

Anna rolled her eyes since she was already on the phone to the DA's office. Billy answered the phone on the first ring. She admonished him to hurry back to the courtroom before hanging up and dialing the clerk's office. She gave them the news and then dialed the coffee shop across the street. Next she decided to try Hays' office in case he was back there. She wondered where Luke was.

Luke was still in the courtroom all alone. He'd thought about getting up and moving about several times but had never mustered the energy to accomplish the task. All was silent in the great chamber while the commotion went on outside his presence. The back door cracked and the Judge peeped his head in, quickly closing it before he thought Luke saw him.

Jones checked in his private office behind the courtroom for his robe. It hung patiently behind the door, waiting for Jones to don the judicial fabric. On impulse, he shut the door and moved down the hall to the jury's room. He could hear them moving about, muffled sounds of repressed voices. He wanted to know what their verdict was. He knew he was supposed to wait but his curiosity was overriding his better judgment. He decided he could stick his head in with some bit of legal admonition and maybe get a clue.

His head went in the door before he could have a second thought. They all looked shocked to see him. Most were still sitting. A few were standing by the coffee pot. The foreman spoke first.

"Judge we have a decision."

Jones looked him directly in the eye. He felt like he knew what Adrian McCarthy's opinion of the case would be and his pleasure at having a decision must mean it went his way. Jones breathed deeply and looked around the room. Not all the faces had the air of content that the foreman displayed. Some would not look at him and some looked downright miserable. Jones decided he needed to get out of there quickly.

"I just wanted you good folks to know we were getting everyone back together as quickly as possible. They scattered a bit while you were deliberating but we should be ready to bring you out momentarily. We appreciate your patience with us just a little bit longer."

He shut the door behind him and turned around in the hall face to face with the bailiff.

"Everybody's in there, Judge. We're waiting on you."

"Good, good. Let's go then. I'll get straight to the bench and you can go ahead and bring them out."

Jones had hardly sat down when the first juror started through the back door of the courtroom. Not one sound emitted from those already present while the twelve filed into the box.

They seated themselves slowly. Jones didn't waste any time.

"Mr. Foreman, it's my understanding that you have reached a verdict." Jones articulated each word distinctly.

"We have, Your Honor." Adrian McCarthy stood as he responded to the Judge.

"Mr. Daniels, would you stand, please. Madam Clerk, would you please hand me the verdict."

Luke stood up from his seat, his feet seemingly unconnected to the floor. His hands rested on the table before him lightly. His eyes fixed on the jurors. None of them looked at him. They all kept their eyes riveted on the Judge, as if he were about to impart some great wisdom. Luke felt suspended in time; everything slowing down, like the world was about to come to a stop. His eyes glanced over to the clerk.

Inez Tanner stood from her seat and went to the jury box, taking the folded piece of paper from the foreman. Without looking at the inside, she handed it up to the Judge who opened it and read the contents without expression.

Each movement seemed to take eons. Jones' face was without expression. What did the paper say? Guilty. Not guilty. Luke thought the earth would stand still before the decision was announced. Jones folded the paper again as every eye in the place fixed on it. Time and space merged into another dimension for Luke, warping into a thickness of existence. Luke's eyes stayed on the piece of paper as it lingered in the air, hovering suspended at the bench before the Judge. Finally the article of paper drifted over to the hand of the clerk.

"Madam Clerk, you may publish the verdict."

Mrs. Tanner opened the piece of paper like she had done in so many other cases. She cleared her throat for the reading out loud, for the declaration to be made for all to hear.

"We, the jury, find the defendant guilty."

Luke heard the words reverberate through his head, guilty, guilty, guilty. He couldn't move, he couldn't think, he couldn't breathe. Guilty, guilty, guilty. Like standing on the edge of a canyon, the words echoed back to him over and over again. His entire body was immobile, turned to stone from the black magic of the term. Guilty, guilty, guilty, the words repeated inside him, settling down into the pit of his stomach. Guilty. The words shrouded out any glimmer of light left in Luke's existence. From a distance, down a long tunnel of darkness he could barely make out the Judge, sitting high above him in this crisis of soul and spirit.

The room outside of Luke buzzed with murmuring. Everybody talked at once. The clerk talked to the court reporter about the verdict she had read. Several jurors blabbed to each other. Hutchinson smirked as he and Joe Lee eyed Luke suspiciously. Adrian McCarthy had a firm set to his jaw, thinking that he had done the right thing. Mrs. Batson whispered to the ladies near her.

Everyone in the audience was talking. Reporters rushed to the bar to try to get some remark from Luke. Jones banged the gavel until the striking sound could be heard above the din of confusion. The reporters continued to shout at Luke above the Judge's banging.

Luke didn't hear any of it. Not one muscle had moved since he heard the word guilty.

Hays was standing beside him speaking curtly to the reporters, slapping them away like bats from hell. Luke was oblivious. Jones banged and banged on the gavel.

Finally, Jones' roar could be heard above the cacophony of voices clanging around the room. He continued to shout and squawk, banging all the while until the dissonance settled to a low rumble.

"Order in this courtroom," he shouted one final time. "Bailiff, send for more deputies. I'll not have my court turned into a barroom making a mockery of justice. You'll have to control yourselves or I'll have you removed."

Luke continued to stand, unable to do anything else. He stood alone. Hays was there but not in Luke's place. As the room settled his lone erect presence became the focal point for the stares of the multitude. When they could no longer prattle, their eyes moved to Luke and their communication became nonverbal. Heads wagged and eyebrows raised over smirks. Got what he deserved. Poor girl. Lawyers. Thought he could get away with murder.

With the room quiet Judge Jones moved swiftly to keep control and finish the proceeding. The jury had returned his guilty verdict. Gafford had done his job. Now it was up to him to put the finishing touches on the case. Jones knew the cameras were turning in the hallway through the blinds over the windows in the courtroom door. He wanted to make this good. Yessir, money couldn't buy this kind of good exposure.

"Will the defendant come forward, please?" Jones ordered. He had this moment rehearsed. He knew what he was going to do. A quick glance to Gafford. Yes, they were in agreement on this one.

Hays Kennedy stood up, still in shock over the verdict. Beside Luke, still standing, he pushed him forward. Luke had still not made a sound. Not one word. He stumbled forward in front of Hays, stopping only a few feet from the bench.

"Luke Daniels, you have been found guilty by a jury of your peers. Do you have anything to say before sentencing?"

Luke uttered not a sound. Hays began to speak out about the nature of the crime, Luke's position in the community. A pre-sentencing investigation should be conducted. The words sounded foreign to Luke. He knew them but they registered little with him.

"I'm ready to proceed with sentencing." The Judge ignored Hays' remarks and kept things moving.

"Luke Daniels, in light of your conviction for the murder of Susan Weeks, I hereby sentence you to life in prison without parole. You are hereby remanded to the custody of the sheriff to await transport to the state penitentiary..."

"Your Honor, we request that Mr. Daniels be allowed to remain on his same bond pending an appeal. I can assure you we will be filing the same immediately."

"Denied. He is hereby remanded to the custody of the sheriff. Sheriff, you are ordered to take the prisoner."

Luke was numb. He looked at Sheriff Jenkins as he came toward him. He knew these people. They were his friends. He looked up at the bench connecting with the Judge eye to eye. What are you doing, Judge? Surely, you must know I didn't kill anyone. Jones felt the look. Despite his own denial, Jones saw an innocence in Luke, which he quickly shook off. In the brief contact of their eyes Jones suffered a quick chill down his spine. Something was wrong here. But, hey, I didn't do anything. The jury found him guilty.

"Luke, don't worry, I'll have you out of there in no time." Hays kept muttering at his side. "I'll get the appeal expedited. I'll go to the Supreme Court and ask for supersedeas on your case."

Luke felt something on his arm and looked down. The sheriff had put handcuffs on one wrist and was pulling his other arm around to finish the job.

Gee, Wally, you know me, Luke thought. You don't have to do this, as he was jerked around by the sleeve and pushed toward the back door of the courtroom. Reporters jammed into the bar area, snapping pictures of Luke, asking him all sorts of senseless questions.

What happened, Daniels? Was it rape? Do you have a statement now? Why'd you kill her, Luke? The last one took him by surprise, cutting to the bone. He stopped quickly, jerking back from the sheriff, looking directly into the eyes of the newsman.

I didn't kill her was his thought, but he said nothing. He just looked at the man who thought he killed the only person he ever loved. As the sheriff pulled him out of the courtroom, darkness settled around Luke making him blind with despair.

CHAPTER TWENTY-ONE

At home in her kitchen preparing supper for her children Rita Lambert looked up at the small TV by the microwave when the broadcast came through. The regular program was interrupted for this special announcement. Luke Daniels, local attorney, has been found guilty of the murder of Susan Weeks.

Rita stopped dead in her tracks. There on the screen was the courtroom with Luke being hauled away in handcuffs. His face was blank and his head hung low.

When he glanced around the camera caught his eye as he was being led away by the sheriff. The announcer droned on about the jury verdict of guilty and the Judge's sentence of life in prison, leaving many to wonder why he didn't get the death penalty. The camera switched back to the reporter and then to shots of the murder scene and pictures of Susan Weeks.

Next came the interview with District Attorney Billy Gafford. He said he was pleased with the verdict and then tried to quickly amend his statement to something more seemly.

"Of course, I'm not happy about the murder but it's good to be able to punish the guilty. This was a difficult case because of my association with the defendant through the local bar, but the people of this district gave me a job to do and I will never shirk that responsibility."

Rita grew sick watching the spectacle. Gafford played to the camera and the audience of voters behind it. The reporters, grasping for anything that they could make into news, let him strut on about the exacting demands of being the prosecutor. Rita wished they'd show another shot of Luke.

She didn't know why she felt such a strong urge to help this man. Over these last several months, their paths kept crossing so unexpectedly. Today, when she watched him in the courtroom sitting all alone, she just wanted to do something to help him. Now he had been found guilty of murder. Now he was convicted. Life in prison. He looked so vulnerable and defenseless as they led him from the courtroom. Perhaps that was it. He needed someone, and so did she.

She felt helpless, trapped in this sick marriage to a man she didn't love allowing his father to control both of them. God, she hated Wilson. And Luther. She didn't know which she hated more. Luther for being the domineering tyrant, Wilson for subjecting the whole family to his father's domination, or herself for staying in it.

She loved her children though, and would do anything to keep them from harm's way. She would never break away from the Lambert clan because breaking away would mean separation from her children as well. Luther would see to that. She would never be able to get any reasonable custody settlement with Luther's tight relationships with the Judges in the county. It was a hopeless situation for her. She was stuck with little she could do about it. It made her want to cry.

Instead, she pulled the casserole from the oven to let it cool. She put rolls in behind it and started to set the table for her and the kids. Wilson was not there. He rarely was very much these days. He was at the office. Or somewhere. She really didn't care where he was anymore, as long as he wasn't here bothering her.

"Will. Elise. C'mon. Supper's ready. Let's eat." She called out to the children.

She laid out the napkins as they gathered around the table and then sat in her own seat. They laughed together for a few moments. Can we watch a movie, please?

"We'll see. We'll see." She took them each by the hand and then bowed her head to give thanks for their food.

The District Attorney was elated with his victory and the extended play he got on the news. When they finally left Little Jimmy Clay had their papers all neatly packed away and they were ready to scurry back to the office. Billy bounced along two feet off the ground as they carried their materials back.

Wanda met them when they got off the elevator all filled with congratulations. Yes, there had been several calls of praise for a job well done. Billy took the stack of notes from her, heading straight back to his desk. Clay followed close on his heels. He didn't want to miss out on any of the basking. Shortly after they sat down Luther Lambert was on the phone.

"Mind if I come over? I just want to shake the hand of the man who put that murderer behind bars."

"Come on, come on. I'll be right here." Gafford couldn't help himself. He knew the case was his ticket to re-election.

Dick Limox appeared at the door. Behind him was Jerry Mason. He'd made his call to Luther from the courthouse as soon as the verdict was announced. He already knew Luther was coming over to the DA's office.

Luther arrived moments later. The five men filled up the office of the District Attorney like a pack of wild dogs. Wanda stood by Billy's desk, joining in the congratulations.

"This call's for a toast. Wanda, do you think you could scare us up some ice somewhere. I know Billy's got to have a bottle of bourbon hidden away."

Luther gave Wanda his sweetheart smile as he dispensed the order. Wanda stood up from her perch.

"Luther, now you know I don't have any alcohol up here."

"Billy, please." Wanda drug out the word. "You don't think you can fool this group of old hats, do you?"

She walked straight over to the two-drawer filing cabinet sitting next to the bookcases that lined one wall of the office. She bent over into one of the drawers and pulled out a bottle of Jim Beam. It was empty.

"See, I told you I didn't have any alcohol up here. I drank it all." Gafford snickered impishly.

"Okay, okay, just hold on. I'll be right back," Limox said over the burst of coarse laughter. "Wanda, you just take care of getting the ice.

Those remaining started going over parts of the trial, blowing smoke about how particularly brilliant Gafford had been at this point or that. Mason knew the game well and followed Luther's lead. Jimmy Clay tried to inject himself into the discussion as much as possible, moving his chair so he could lean on the desk of the District Attorney.

When the phone rang, Billy answered to find Judge Jones on the other line. Luther urged him to get the Judge to come on over. Jones, never one to miss out on any post-game show, advised he'd be right over. Dick Limox returned with the bottle they needed and they were still getting the top opened when Jones appeared.

Bourbon and water filled the cups that were passed around. Wanda excused herself saying she had plans for the evening, leaving the room full of macho bluster and nonsense. Billy ate it all up. They were here because of him, to pay homage for his great victory. He leaned back in his chair and sipped the mellow bourbon.

Wanda got herself out of there quickly. She was glad for the win, glad that her boss would keep his job. Glad that she could keep her job, but she wasn't glad it was at Luke Daniels' expense. She couldn't for the life of her get a fix on his situation. Why did he kill the girl? Why? She didn't buy the drug story, and she didn't buy the rape. Luke Daniels didn't have to rape anybody. That was not him. Why, why, she thought, as she rode down the elevator. She didn't have an answer as she made her way to her car.

She looked across the street at the jail and thought of Luke being there. Something was just not right. Luke did not belong in jail. She saw a lot of criminals in this job. Saw names and faces and lots of bull. Her sense of discernment had sharpened over time and she felt she could spot the criminal every time. Luke Daniels was not one of them

Across the street in the jail, Luke was locked up like a criminal. He was now convicted as a murderer and that changed his status drastically. In the jail he was chained to the chair while they processed his papers. He was a prisoner held by the sheriff in the custody of the Department of Corrections to be transferred to the State Penitentiary at Parchman as soon as possible.

People in the jail, workers he'd known for years merely nodded. No communication, just the nod, eyes quickly diverted to something else. The sheriff dumped him off without a word. Just doing his job was the attitude. Luke wanted to tell him he was the same person he always was, but nothing came out. It all seemed useless.

After a while they loosened the handcuffs from Luke and moved him to a cell. It was dark, the light bulb was gone. There was a concrete bench formed from the same pouring as the floor. Luke sat erect, unsure what would come next.

He didn't feel badly. He didn't feel in danger. He didn't feel anything. His feelings started shutting down when he heard the word guilty some time earlier in the courtroom. How long ago was that - twenty minutes? An hour? A lifetime? He had no idea about time anymore. All he could do was slowly breathe in and breathe out. There was a slight ache in his chest near where his heart beat slowly, letting him know he was still alive. He was glad for that. He'd hate to be dead.

A little smile moved across his lips. He thought he could just about lay down on this cold concrete and die. Let go, and be gone. What was he going to do? Life in prison. That sounded close to death. Right now he couldn't say which would be better. Or which would be worse.

The District Attorney's office was fully alive. The bottle of bourbon was empty and the stories were flying. Luther Lambert had pulled out his pack of tobacco and stuck a big chew in his mouth, pushing it to one side, talking all the time. He loved the spotlight and his cud-chewing take was all part of the act.

Billy watched him push the big chaw of tobacco into his mouth, pieces falling on the massive gut that stuck out from his torso. He talked with his mouth full spewing bits and pieces of the shredded leaves about the room. Judge Jones moved back to avoid getting spat upon. He'd much rather be home with his wife's good home-cooked meal but Luther enjoyed the audience so much that the Judge couldn't get himself extricated from the group without drawing attention to his departure.

Luther laughed the hardest as his story wound down, slapping his leg for effect. Judge Jones saw his opportunity to excuse himself and stood for an exit.

"Mary Margaret expected me two hours ago. I'm sure I'll be in the doghouse now."

"Yes, yes, I've got to get going myself. We don't want to keep our illustrious District Attorney from his appointed rounds. Let me congratulate you one more time."

Luther stuck his hand out to Billy who stood with the rest of them. Jerry Mason hopped up right behind Luther, ready to follow him parrot-like in every movement. He planned to follow Luther closely this evening.

Limox pushed the chair he'd been sitting astride back to its place in the conference room and the group made its way to the elevator, each moving in his own inebriated fashion. Luther was a large man and it took a lot to get him soused, but he'd had a couple at his office before he left. Outside it appeared he wasn't ready to quit.

"C'mon, Jerry. Let's me and you take it back to my place and we'll have one more for the road."

Luther got behind the wheel of his car and unlocked the passenger door for Jerry to get in. "I'd say that went pretty well, wouldn't you?" Luther gave Jerry a little wink.

"Oh, yeah." Jerry wasn't sure what he meant but he knew to agree with him. They swerved their way the two blocks back to Luther's office and pulled up to the back door in Luther's private parking area. Luther fumbled to find the door key.

"Come on, we'll have one more to celebrate our own good fortune," Luther called out.

He finally got the door open and they sashayed into the building.

Inside, Arlita had come to clean.

"Damn, I reckon I can pay a light bill. Every light in this place must be on."

Every light in the building was on. Arlita cleaned this office five days out of the week. The office was not officially open on Saturdays so usually she waited until Sunday night or sometimes even early Monday morning to get the job done. She was here this Friday because she was spending the weekend at her sister's on the coast and didn't want this chore hanging over her head. If she was late Sunday she wouldn't have to worry about it. She was leaving early Saturday morning. So, tonight she waited until she was sure they were all gone from the office before going to clean.

The office was a mess and it looked like it was going to take her a while. She emptied all the trash cans first, and then the ashtrays. She straightened as best she could. She knew never to touch anything on anyone's desk.

In the front reception she put all the magazines in place and realigned the furniture. She finished the vacuuming, saving the dusting for last. She had just put up the vacuum cleaner when she heard the back door open.

It scared her at first. Who was in here with her? The downtown area was usually deserted this time of night and she often fought off the fear of someone coming in on her alone. The voice she recognized froze her in her tracks. She clutched the dust rag in her hand as she held her breath. Her first instinct was to hide. Maybe they wouldn't know she was here and whoever it was would get what they came for and go on. She slipped into the closet near the conference room where she had just put the vacuum cleaner and pulled the door almost closed. It pressed against her large breasts and wouldn't go any further unless she moved the mops and brooms in the closet and she didn't want to make any noise.

Mr. Luther scared her. Even though she worked for him here at the office and in his home, being around him made her uneasy. He stared at her sometimes in a disturbing way. She always tried to keep her distance from him and, in the years she'd worked there, only rarely made contact. She could hear him now in the kitchen with someone else.

"I don't have to go digging to find any bourbon. I've got some right here. How 'bout another drink, my boy?"

Without waiting for a response, Luther had two glasses sitting on the counter filling them with ice from the refrigerator. He sloshed a good portion of the rich brown liquid over the crackling ice and handed the glass to Jerry.

"I believe this will be a little better than that rot gut stuff we had up at Gafford's."

Luther took a long swig from his. "Yes sir, Mr. George Dickel at twelve years old serves up a mighty tasty drink."

Luther took a seat at the table and Jerry followed suit. They talked briefly about the bourbon, what made it so good. Luther seemed to be the bourbon expert. Jerry couldn't care less, but he did enjoy its effect. The whiskey in his glass and the conviction of Daniels was combining in an intoxicating way, leaving him feeling freer than he had in many months. Jerry didn't drink much. Doris didn't like him when he was drinking, and she had a way of coaxing him to as she said. As did Luther. Jerry did what Doris wanted at home and what Luther wanted at work. He didn't think about it much but sometimes he yearned to stand up and do what he wanted.

Jerry was smashed. His tongue was loose and he felt invincible, like nobody could tell him what to do. Luther was fairly loaded himself. They were both loud, talking in voices controlled by the alcohol rather than the need to communicate. They sat at the table only a few feet from each other but their voices carried throughout the entire building.

"So what do you think will happen to old Daniels now?"

"That pretty boy will probably find him some sweet black man to take care of him at the penitentiary." Luther howled with laughter.

"I'm glad to have this thing behind us. The trial and all." Jerry breathed a sigh of relief, watching Luther closely. They had never really talked directly about what happened that night. Luther didn't want to talk about it now. The conviction of Luke Daniels put an end to it as far as he was concerned, but something in Jerry couldn't let it alone. He wasn't quite as cold and calculating as Luther. Not yet.

"I don't think she would have ever done what we wanted her to, anyway, Luther. Susan Weeks had a mind of her own." Jerry thought out loud.

"Well, we'll never know, will we? We don't need to worry about it now. There'll be another. As soon as all this dies down, I'll get DeWeese on it again. Those little girls love to get their picture took." Luther grinned lasciviously, his mind off in the distance.

"But Susan was different from most girls. Those pictures you had of her. I don't think she would have given in to our threats. I think that's what she was seeing Daniels about that night."

"You sure been doin' a lot of thinking." Luther gulped down the last third of his drink and stood up to fix another. He poured himself one without offering to Jerry.

"We'll never know what she went to him for, will we? Since he killed her."

Jerry looked straight up at Luther who stared down at him with menace.

"I'd say he did us a favor, don't you think?"

Jerry couldn't figure out what Luther was doing. Did he really think Daniels killed her? Surely he knew the truth. Had he deluded himself for so long that even he didn't know what was truth and what was fiction?

Jerry felt uneasy. He'd gone to her house that night to assure her cooperation. At Luther's direction. Had Luther forgotten that? Jerry wanted to forget what happened, but he didn't necessarily want Luther to forget. Not until he had compensated Jerry properly. Luther did have a way of forgetting these things. He'd instruct Jerry to do something, give him vague, rambling suggestions about what should be done and then allow Jerry to figure out the rest. Often, it kinda scared Jerry. If anything ever came of it, Luther would be free and clear. Jerry would be the one hung out to dry.

But Luther wouldn't do that to him. He needed Jerry too much. Jerry took care of too much for him. The alcohol in his head made his judgment a little blurred. He stared back at Luther who stared back at him. Jerry shook off the shudder that settled over him and got up to mix another drink. His head was already spinning but another drink seemed like just what he needed.

Luther proceeded about DeWeese, "You know I told the boy just to leave town. They were about to subpoena him. Probably already investigated his association with her through the years. He always wanted that girl... and had still been strung out on cocaine. Did it in New Orleans. And sometimes around here."

"Luther, you know she was going to tell him everything. The pictures, the threats, the coercion, the demands.

"Why, I never threatened that girl in any way."

"Come off it, Luther. This is me you're talking to. I was there, remember."

Jerry's tone made Luther furious. He'd like to shut him up right now.

"You never threatened her, eh? What about those pictures you got from DeWeese? She knew what you wanted."

"I merely suggested that I would make my business partner destroy the pictures if she would help me out on a little matter. I didn't force her to pose in the nude."

"Yes, but you knew and she knew that if those pictures got out her career in the banking business would be over."

"I never wanted that to happen."

"What did you want to happen, Luther?"

"She was free to choose her own path. You said yourself that she had a mind of her own." Luther needed another drink. The conversation was sobering him up. He brought the bottle to the table and poured another, not bothering with the ice.

"Bob Fowler is a pompous ass, who looks down his nose at everybody. I just wanted her to help me keep him in his place, that's all. It could have benefited her and me. You know, they just made him president over there. If she had cooperated, we could have both been sitting pretty with the new bank president. All she had to do was let us get some pictures. But no, she had to act so prim and proper. Like she was a virgin or something. You saw those pictures. Nothing virginal about the bitch. She shouldn't have acted so high and mighty about it."

Luther was full blown drunk now. So was Jerry. Neither of them could hardly stand.

"The whore deserved what she got. She didn't have to act like I was such an ogre. She was certainly no saint." Luther's words came out more for himself than Jerry. "If she'd just listened to us, Jerry. She didn't have to die."

"Why didn't she listen to you, Jerry?"

Luther's words caught Jerry off guard. It was the first time Luther had ever acknowledged anything about Jerry making contact with Susan.

"I don't know, Luther. When I followed her to the Magnolia Bar and saw her leave with Daniels, I freaked. I thought she was telling him everything. It surprised me when they went back to her house. You were right, the little whore. You should have heard them in that bedroom, like a couple of animals. Then he left. I knew she was in there alone. I thought it would be the perfect opportunity to get her attention. If she knew that I had pictures of her and Daniels…"

"Did you?" Luther salivated.

"No, but she didn't know that. I watched them on the couch. She was all over him. And then they went back to the bedroom. When he left, I just decided to go in and have that little talk with her. Rough her up a bit, like you suggested. Make her see things our way."

"But she was tough. When I showed up at the door planning to slip in she met me there, thinking it was him coming back. I grabbed her but she fought me like a tiger, scratching and kicking. She nearly knocked me unconscious. That's when I got pissed. The bitch got away from me and locked herself in the bedroom."

"The shoe print? How did that happen anyway?" Luther was intrigued.

"I saw Daniels at the mall a few weeks before buying new running shoes. While they were eating dinner, I raced out to the mall and bought me a pair the same size."

"So he wasn't even wearing running shoes!"

"No, but everybody knows he's a runner. It'd be the perfect cover. I didn't expect to have to kick the door down, but, hey, you can never be too careful in my line of work. I wore gloves. I didn't do detective work for all those years for nothing, you know. I figured if anything happened it would be easier to cover up with only Luke Daniels' shoe prints around."

"So what did she say to you when you finally got her down."

"I never got a word with her. She kept fighting and screaming. I tried to hold her down until she settled…"

Jerry's voice drifted off disquietly as his mind replayed the events of that night. Through the drunken, murky gloom that descended over them Luther could barely hold on to the words. He gazed across the table at Mason, slouched down in the chair looking as doltish as Lambert always thought he was.

"You stupid bastard. You didn't have to kill her," the words came out of Lambert's mouth before he knew it, the alcohol breaking down his resistance and control of thought and action.

"Why didn't you just leave her alone?"

"Hey, you're the one who sent me over there." The words came out of Jerry harshly, a belligerent tension creeping over his body.

"I didn't tell you to kill her," Lambert shot back at him.

"I didn't mean to…"

"I'm sure you didn't, but it doesn't help us that she's dead. And you're the one who really did it!"

"She can't talk."

"You stupid idiot. I know she can't talk, but she can't do a damn thing for us six feet under. We had that girl right where we wanted her. She was in the bank. We could have had Fowler eating out of our hand. And you had to go and spoil it for us."

Luther's tongue lashed out with the condemnation, making Jerry cringe. Jerry always liked being in Luther's good graces and now it seemed a chasm was forming between them. Jerry knew full well Luther wanted him to tend to the girl, but now he was acting as if Jerry had not done his bidding.

"I only went there to do what you wanted me to." Jerry shot back.

"Yea, and because of that I knew you had to be protected at all costs. With guilt riding on Luke Daniels and DeWeeese. Now where does it go? The alcohol had both of them in a truculent temper. Jerry had always felt guided by Luther. Now he only felt distance. Luther wanted to reach over and bop Jerry on the head just for being the simpleton he was. Luther wished the fool would just get out of his sight. Idiots all around him. He couldn't accomplish what he really wanted to half the time because he had to rely on dimwits like Mason. Even in his practice he had to put up with the childish nonsense of Wilson. When was that boy going to grow up?

He was lucky Gafford had enough sense to get a conviction on Daniels. And now that he had, he'd probably have to listen to him boast and brag about it forever, never realizing that he wouldn't even have had a case if Luther hadn't planted the seeds in his manure for brains head. What a loser.

And the Judge. He'd probably be down here with his hand out for something now that he sent Daniels up the country, like he'd done it all for Luther.

"I'm sick of all of you." Luther blared out loud.

Jerry looked at him like he was crazy. Well, I'm sick of you, too, you rotten, wicked, malicious old… Jerry held his tongue but inside wished he could see Luther dead. The thought crept through his brain and across his face.

"You think I give a damn what you thought or did." Luther's words lashed out at Mason. "Why don't you get your ass out of here and go see if you can do something right for a change."

Luther tried to stand, staggering around from his chair, grabbing on to the counter. Jerry stood up, too, looking every bit as drunk as Luther. He wanted to smack the old man. He'd love to pound him in the face, knocking him to his knees. His hand balled up into a fist.

But he held back. He held his drink in his hand, gripping it rigidly. He was shaking all over. He'd never felt this much rage in his life. He should never let himself get this drunk. He saw the glass leave his hand and go sailing across the small room, smashing into bits against the counter.

"Get out of here. You hear me! Get out of here right now!" Luther screamed the words.

Jerry turned, barely able to stand up, and staggered out the back door, letting it slam behind him. Luther continued to hold on to the counter, so drunk he could barely maintain his grip on the edge. He eased himself back over to the chair and slipped his hulk down into the seat. His chin rested against his chest, his breathing fast and deep. He didn't know what just happened in there but something in it scared him.

Luther didn't scare easily. His mind wouldn't think clearly enough to sort anything out right now. He'd worry about it later. For now he just sat, listening to the sound of his own deep breathing, in and out. In and out. Either Jerry or DeWeese might have been a link to him. Only Daniels was clean and out of his path. Daniels had to be the one from the beginning, and the system, without any other information, had no choice but to convict him. Who the hell else cared?

From her hidden spot away from the commotion, Arlita hardly allowed herself to breathe. She'd heard almost every word, frozen in her spot unable to move. Tears barely held back in her eyes, she regretted ever coming in here tonight. Why did she have to do this tonight? She should have waited until Monday morning. She should have planned to come back early enough Sunday to do it. Why didn't she wait 'til then? She wouldn't have been stuck there tonight hearing things she never should have heard.

The door slammed shut the first time. Then she thought she heard it slam shut again. Finally, maybe they were gone. She waited for a long while listening, but heard nothing. When she was able to convince herself it was all right, she opened the door slightly and listened some more. Nothing.

She pushed the door all the way open and stepped out in the hall. Inhaling deeply, she wondered how long she had been holding her breath. She stood still there in the hall trying to figure out what she needed to do. She needed to get out of there. But first, she needed to make sure she was all done. What else did she have, she wondered, pushing her mind back to what seemed like hours ago? She'd finished vacuuming because she was putting up the vacuum cleaner when they came in. That was still in the closet. Trash was emptied and bathrooms were clean. All she had left was dusting.

That could wait, she told herself. She eased back to the front of the office and turned off the lights, coming toward the back flipping light switches as she went down the hall from room to room. Everything looked the same, but it felt completely different to Arlita. Everything in the office felt evil to her now. She hated being there. She wanted to get away as quickly as she could. She flipped the switch in the conference room, leaving only the light in the back room where the argument had taken place. She could see pieces of the broken glass glistening in the light. That had to be cleaned up, she thought, turning back to her hiding place for a broom and dustpan. Her only thought was to get the glass up and get out of there.

The broom knocked against the door as she came into the kitchen and saw Luther still sitting in the chair. He roused up from the noise, sitting up straight as she stepped through the door.

"Arlita, when did you get here?" he asked, lifting up from his groggy drowsing.

"Oh, Mr. Luther, I'm just doing my cleaning." She stood paralyzed only two feet from the big man.

Luther looked up at her through blurry eyes and an alcohol soaked brain. His mind had drifted off into an anodyne bliss from the overindulgence and he now sat still, unsure about the time and event in front of him. His eyes focused more clearly and he saw the broom in Arlita's hand.

"Yeah, well, go ahead, don't let me stop you," he blubbered out.

Arlita quickly got herself down and swept the pieces of glass into the pan, trying to get it done as swiftly as possible. Behind her Luther stared down at the silky brown skin of her neck under the short haircut. His eyes drifted on down her slim back to the round buttocks as she squatted at the floor over the glass. She stood up with his eyes following her hips and her tight pants. Jeans that had a familiar look to him. Her shirt was tight, too.

She turned around and Luther's head was eye level with Arlita's beautiful round breasts. Luther aroused even more as she stood there with the broom and dustpan in her hand. He reached behind him and pulled the wastebasket around.

"Here, you can dump it in here." He held the can in front of him.

Arlita's heart pumped fast while she fought to remain cool on the outside. She took one step toward him and leaned over to dump the glass in the basket. Her lean made the tight shirt pull even more across her breasts. Luther's eyes looked straight down into the shirt, feeling the urge to put his face into her, the chocolate brown skin making him lick his lips.

Arlita pulled herself back quickly to avoid his carnal leer. She stepped around the wastebasket moving swiftly to return the broom to its closet and get out of there.

Luther sat in the chair with his mind racing along with rapacious thoughts of dark skin. The parts of her breast he saw only made him want to see more. He pushed himself up in the chair and stood, turning around to the door. It was the only way out for her. She had to come back this way.

Arlita put the broom up. Her heart was beating so hard in her chest she could hardly think. She wanted to race out the front door and avoid even seeing Mr. Luther again but she couldn't. She had to go back by him and out the door as fast as she could, before he had time to think that she had heard them. Her heart beat louder and louder. As she turned around to bolt through the kitchen, there he was.

"You all through now, Arlita?"

"Yessir, I'm going on now."

"Did you get this done," pointing toward the conference room. "I don't want any mess left in here. The trash was pretty full earlier."

"Yessir. I did that first thing. If you find anything else you need done, you jest let me know." She looked for some way to squeeze by him.

"Well, let's see if this is done right. That table top looks kinda smudged. I want it cleaned. You see that mess."

Arlita had not cleaned the top of the conference room table because when she went through it looked fine. She didn't know how he could be seeing anything now with the lights out. The only light left in the place was coming from the kitchen behind Luther. The only way out. His huge frame was outlined in the light leaving his face in a sinister shadow, eyes glaring from darkness.

"Are you sure, Mr. Luther?"

"Yes, look right there."

He slowly advanced on Arlita, forcing her through the door of the conference room. She tried to look at the table without taking her eyes off of him. Fear pumped inside of her with every beat of her heart that she was sure had to burst any second. She could smell the alcohol on Lambert, his foul breath coming closer and closer to her. She kept inching away trying to appear calm, even though she was terrified. This man that she never liked had her here alone. This man that only moments earlier she had learned was capable of murder. The evil she saw in his eyes made her believe he was capable of anything. She wanted out of here. She wanted to bolt for the door and run. Run. But instead she froze in terror of what he might do. Did he realize that she had heard everything? Did he comprehend that she was there when they fought? She was so afraid.

Luther's mind was elsewhere. His eyes looked at the prize he wanted and would not be denied. He wanted his lips on that perfect brown bosom. He wanted his hands around that small taut waist. He wanted her.

Lambert had her against the head chair at the conference table. Arlita struggled to get away but felt powerless against him. She was so petrified that her limbs felt stiff and weak. She was totally helpless. Luther pushed himself on her. They fell back on the table with his hands groping at her body, grabbing and tearing at her clothes. Buttons popped from her shirt and his face fell into her chest, biting into her skin until it hurt. The full weight of his massive body pushed against her making it impossible to fight. His hands continued to grope her body, pushing at her pants, tugging and yanking.

She felt his own pants slide down his legs. Tears welled up in her eyes as she bit her lip, hoping it would soon be over. He pushed himself higher up on her, pressing against her chest until she thought she couldn't breathe. Tears rolled down her cheeks, but no cry came out with them. Only the wet trails down her face.

Luther was oblivious to her anguish, to everything but his own lustful desire. His craving for sexual gratification fueled his attack, propelled by the alcohol's loosening of his faculties and his covetous penchant to control everything within his grasp. And right now, this black woman was in his clutches. He tried to push himself up on her more and more. He wanted dominance. He wanted her to know that he was the master and she was the slave. He wanted her to feel his power over her, but he couldn't.

His efforts failed him. The attempt was futile, his impotence spoiling the ravage he desperately wanted. His hulking frame lay on top of Arlita like dead weight. He lay there. He didn't move for a while. Arlita was too scared to think about what must be going on. She grew more afraid as he pressed against her. Disgusted, Luther rolled off to the side and pushed himself back into the chair. Arlita pulled her torn shirt to her body sobbing. The tears that fell in silence before now came out with retching. She pulled herself from the table and stumbled against the wall. She looked over at Luther who sat in the chair staring straight ahead, as if he were hardly aware she was in the room.

Arlita eased down the side of the wall and out the conference room door. She moved into the kitchen and out the back door. She heard the door click behind her and she ran. She ran down the street as fast as she could go. She didn't stop running for blocks. It was late now and no one was really out on the streets. After a while she slowed down to catch her breath and walked for a while. She straightened her shirt as best she could. The buttons were popped off and it was ripped in several places. She held it to her and walked all the way home.

When she reached her house she slipped in the back door and went to the bathroom. Her oldest daughter, Roseanne, had the car and should have been home by now. The two younger kids were on the couch in front of the TV. She got a bath quickly, dressed herself and then threw some clothes in a bag. As soon as everything was ready for the trip to her sister's, she went to the couch and hugged the children. She held them close to her and told them she loved them. They hugged her back and she started to feel a little better.

When Roseanne got home with the car they were ready to go. She loaded them all up and they drove away with Arlita behind the wheel. She was okay. Everything was okay. Except for one thing. She couldn't stop crying.

CHAPTER TWENTY-TWO

The weekend passed all too quickly for Arlita. Sunday evening arrived too soon. When the time came for them to head back home she made the decision to stay another night. They could get up early and make the hour drive back in time for school. That was fine with the kids. They were having a great time with their cousins and another night sounded good to them.

The alarm rang at five o'clock the next morning, the time Arlita had set for them to get going back to Hampton. They dressed and had breakfast and climbed in the car. Arlita hugged her sister. She never told her what happened Friday night. She never could make herself talk about it. All she did was cry quite often.

"I don't know what's wrong with you, girl, but you've got to snap out of this funk. I don't care what you say, I know it's got to be something to do with a man. You need to dump that sorry Willie Terrell and get on with yo' life. He ain't gonna be nothing but trouble."

Arlita tried to rebuff her but only came up with more tears. It wasn't Willie, she tried to say. It's just a bad time, that's all. She crawled in the driver's seat and cranked up, fighting the tears back as she looked up at her sister.

"When you coming up to see us?" she tried to lighten up.

"Soon. Real soon. I'm coming up there to whip that Willie's ass for messing with my sister."

"Oh, go on." A slight smile crept across her face as they hugged through the window. Arlita pulled back and they took off to Hampton.

The drive went smoothly and they arrived home at seven o'clock. The kids were not yet dressed for school so she shooed them inside and pulled out clothes for the day. Within thirty minutes they were ready and headed back out the door to the car. She could deliver each of them to school before going to work herself.

When the last one was out of the car and walking into school, Arlita found herself alone for the first time since Friday night. Her head rested down on the steering wheel as a big sigh expelled from her body. It was Monday now. She had to get herself together and get to work. She had to work. She had to have the money. She hadn't talked to a soul about what happened Friday night. She couldn't. She had to put it behind her and get on with things. There wasn't time in her life to dwell on what happened. There was only time to work and take care of her family. The rest would have to take care of itself.

If only there was someone she could talk to. She felt like she was going to explode. Deep inside there was a pain that wouldn't go away. It kept gnawing at her, keeping her close to tears. There was a constant struggle going on inside of her to hold them at bay.

In addition to her feelings over her own assault, ever present in her thoughts was the fact that at the jail sat a man convicted of a crime he didn't commit. Arlita was well aware of what happened to Luke Daniels. She followed the happenings in his life closely because of Willie.

Willie. She thought of trying to get him to help but what could he do. He was just another nigger with a felony charge pending against him. His case had never been dismissed even though the victim was dead. She knew that sorry Roosevelt Jones deserved what he got from Willie. Anyway, what good would it do to tell Willie? What could he do?

From behind her a car horn honked, making her realize she was still blocking traffic at the school. The car was in gear but her foot was on the brake, her head oblivious to where she was. She pulled away from the school and drove. She needed to get to work. She was supposed to be at Mrs. Eloise's this morning.

The thought made her shudder. What if Mr. Luther was still there? What would he do? What was he thinking? What if he put it together that she heard them talking? She wanted to run. But she didn't have anywhere to run to. The tears started up again as she drove on.

At the jail Luke sat in the same dank cell he had been in since Friday night. For three days his brain played over and over the events that brought him here. There were gaps in the logic of the sequence. How did he get here? He was at the trial, he saw and heard everything that happened. But the outcome… His brain reached blanks where no answer would materialize. He always came back to the same question. How did this happen? How could he be in jail? How could he be convicted of murder? And, who killed Susan?

Murder. The thought put him into convulsions of nausea, physically pushing him to the edge of sanity, and beyond. He wondered if he was totally insane. There was nothing in him that had any awareness of murdering Susan Weeks. The pictures of the scene from the police flashed in his mind, mingling with his memories. Her beautiful face, her soft skin, her sweet kiss, the bed. And then the picture of her nude body laying beside the bed, cold and still, the matted hair covering her face. His eyes watered, then tears streamed down his face, again. For so many times this weekend he went through the same thing. His memory betrayed him, playing one scene against the other, confusing his thoughts of reality. The dark cell contributed to the turmoil he felt, leaving him unable to distinguish which part he experienced and which part he only saw in pictures. The confusion made him crazy, the tears made it worse, the torment making his body shake from one end to the other. He felt like he would explode if he didn't get some relief. The tears turned to sobs that racked his weak frame. The sobs turned to a crying groan that began deep in his lungs and slowly came out without any restraint, reaching a screaming point from the agony he felt inside.

Three days stuck in the darkness was getting to him. The fetters of his situation weighed on him, body, soul and spirit. They were going to put in a new light bulb but they were out of them. They could get some Monday. Luke didn't complain. He didn't care. He didn't eat. He sat with his mind playing over the misery, the grief, and the sorrow of what had happened.

Outside the cell, two deputies heard Luke scream out. His cell was separate from the rest of the prisoners, only a short distance from their control room. The sheriff had come in, too, just in time to hear the disturbed sound escape from the cell. He knew it was Luke, and he knew he wanted him out of there, out of his jail as soon as possible. If something should happen… He didn't know what, but he'd talked to the District Attorney about it. And to Luther. They both thought he was wise to get rid of the prisoner.

"I just talked to the people at Parchman," Sheriff Jenkins announced. "They have an opening for him now. We're taking him up there tonight. We'll leave here at six o'clock."

The two deputies looked at each other. Amazing. They knew, as did everyone else in the state, about over-crowding at the prison. It took weeks, months generally, for them to find a space for a new prisoner. This one had taken only a few days.

"Have the transport van ready right away. I want this to be as quiet as possible. No one is to know. Is that clear? No one. I'm not telling the driver until he's ready to go. You two keep it to yourselves."

Jenkins barked out the last statement, sending them a clear message that he meant business. The clearest point to them was that he wanted Luke Daniels out of there, although they weren't sure why. When the sheriff left, they mumbled between themselves with theories.

"It's because that girl worked at the bank. Money. Those money people don't want him getting any special treatment."

"The Sheriff wants everybody to see how tough he is. He don't want nobody saying he's soft on a criminal, especially a lawyer."

"This lawyer ought to have him a bunch of clients come tomorrow. When he gets to Parchman, there'll be plenty of criminals for him to take their cases. I don't guess he'll be getting much pay, but he'll have plenty of clients."

Inside the cell, Luke's struggle continued. The weakness he felt invaded his body, making it difficult to sit up. He let his body crumple over on the hard concrete bench. A deep, long sigh emitted from his lungs. His whole body felt so very tired. He wished he could sleep, but that eluded him. In the darkness, he could hardly tell when his eyes were open or closed. His eyes saw the same thing, staring into darkness, while pictures of Susan haunted him.

Luther had been at his office since early that morning. He'd already been on the phone with the sheriff. Walter confirmed their previous conversation that the prisoner would be heading out to the state penitentiary today.

That was some assurance. He hadn't talked to Mason all weekend long and was somewhat concerned about the boy. Jerry was fairly solid; he usually did what he was told quite well, but sometimes he was lacking in smarts when left to his own devices. He was a much better tool when he followed Luther's instructions.

Luther had never found him to be lacking in discretion. That was one of his good points. He kept his mouth shut. Quiet. Still, something bothered Luther. He wasn't altogether sure about this situation. Maybe it was going to be all right. Maybe his uneasiness was fueled more by the hangover he nursed all weekend than anything else. He had only this morning started to feel okay.

Saturday, he thought he was going to die. Not as young as you once were, old man, he told himself. The alcohol of the night before left him in more of a fog than he was accustomed. Reading the paper Saturday hurt. He managed himself through the day with a couple of Bloody Marys. The old 'hair of the dog' trick. Sunday was another day of recovery. Today he was much better, almost good as new. Maybe a little golf later in the day when it cooled off.

It was worth it, though. Daniels was being shipped off in a short while. That would put that problem to rest. With the boy in prison it didn't matter much about Mason. He'd be quiet. There was no reason to talk. The District Attorney got his conviction and the case was closed. Judge Jones sentenced him and now the sheriff was getting him out of town. Even Deweese would be unsuspecting. He was glad it hadn't been DeWeese.

Just what I needed, Luther thought. With this deal out of my way we can get on to something that will be more fruitful. Damn, Mason. This one could have been most productive if he hadn't jumped the gun and done the girl in.

The uneasy feeling came back. He vaguely recalled their talk Friday night. Whew, too much alcohol made it blurry. Mason told him it was an accident. He didn't mean to kill her. Damn, the boy could be a little thick at times. Didn't mean to kill her. What a line. Uummm. There was the headache again. Luther pulled out a bottle of painkillers from the drawer, throwing down a couple. He let out a deep sigh and leaned back in his chair to wait for the pills to ease the pain. He'd be all right. He just needed to relax.

Arlita had driven around for almost an hour. She didn't know where to go or what to do. She never called Mrs. Eloise to tell her she wasn't coming. Maybe that's what she should do. She stopped at a store and went in to use the pay phone. Even dialing the Lambert number made her nervous.

"Hello. Oh, good morning, Arlita."

Mrs. Eloise was as pleasant and gracious as ever. No, Mr. Lambert was already gone. He left early today.

"I'm about to leave, too, Arlita. I'm headed to New Orleans with some friends for the day. They just called on the spur of the moment and we're taking off. You'll have the house to yourself. I don't believe you'll find that much to do here today. Just the general cleaning."

Arlita never said anything about missing today. She didn't want to go to the Lambert house, but when she found out she wouldn't have to see Luther the idea seemed okay. She could go there and do her regular cleaning all alone without having to face anybody. Probably just what she needed. She didn't have any place else to hide.

"I'll leave your money on the counter like I always do. I've got to run. You just take it easy here. You sound a little sickly, Arlita. Are you well?"

"Oh, I'm fine, Mrs. Eloise. Moving a little slow for a Monday, that's all. You go ahead. I'll be on over in a little while and have things all cleaned up for you when you get back from your trip."

When Arlita hung up the phone she felt better. She had some direction. She drove around a bit longer to give Mrs. Lambert time to get gone and then went on to their house to start her cleaning. She pulled up to the big house and parked in the empty garage shutting the door down behind her.

When the creaking of the electric motor of the door stopped, she was all alone. She'd been here many times before when no one was home, but this time the house seemed spooky. She tried to shake it off, forcing herself out of the car and into the door to the kitchen. The house was quiet, not a sound of anything. Arlita stopped in the kitchen and listened.

Through the kitchen she could see over the counter and into the den. Clouds forming outside cast long shadows of darkness into the unlit room. Arlita had never been this uncomfortable here before. She tried to shake it off and go on.

"The best thing I can do is get me some lights on," she spoke out loud.

She went about the house turning on lights, working hard at putting her thoughts about Luther out of her mind. There was nothing she could do about that. Nothing. What she needed to do was get to work. Parts of the house hadn't been touched since her last visit. Mrs. Eloise kept the house mostly clean herself. She checked the bedrooms.

Nothing to do there. She wiped a little dust and headed back to the master bedroom. When she stepped through the door she saw a light on in the bathroom. Arlita froze in her tracks, unable to move. Her first instinct was to run. Run fast. As fast as she could to get herself out of there.

But she didn't hear anything. Was there someone in there? Or had Mrs. Eloise only left the light on? She made herself push the door open. When she saw there was no one in the bathroom the breath rushed out from her chest in a large sigh.

"Girl, you 'bout crazy today," she said aloud. "You better get to work and quit being crazy."

The house was empty. She finally convinced herself of that and got down to cleaning. She started in the bedroom, pulling off the sheets and taking them down to the washing machine. She moved slowly, still not her usual energetic self. She got the sheets going in the machine and then headed back to the bedroom and bath to finish up that end.

As she worked into the routine of her regular cleaning, Arlita relaxed and began to forget about her troubles. But she continued to think about Luke. She knew he didn't kill the girl. She knew who did. But what could she do about it? Here she was standing in the house of the man responsible for it.

He was as responsible as if he had pulled the trigger as far as Arlita was concerned. She knew who Jerry Mason was and knew he went around doing Luther's bidding. He tried to pretend like he was his own man, but those that knew him also knew that was a joke. She wondered if anyone else knew just how much he did for Lambert.

No matter how much she tried Arlita couldn't keep her mind off the things she heard Friday night. If she didn't do anything about it what might these two do? If they could get away with murder, then what else? She didn't understand why they had killed the girl. Something about trying to blackmail her.

Arlita started moving quickly now. She finished drying sheets and took them back to be put away. She would get the vacuuming done and then only the kitchen would be left. The big machine took care of the carpet in no time. She was hurrying herself now, ready to get this job done and get out of the house. She barely pushed the vacuum into the extra bedrooms after finishing the master bedroom. She was coming down the hall pushing it furiously ready to tackle the living room.

The vacuum made a loud noise. Arlita didn't hear anyone come into the house. She didn't hear the shoes against the kitchen floor approaching from the back. She was pushing the vacuum with a vengeance when the hand reached out and touched her on the shoulder.

"Aaahhhh," Arlita let out a scream as she turned, tripping over the cord and falling hard to the floor.

"Arlita, I didn't mean to startle you," Rita Lambert said as she flipped off the machine. "I am so sorry. Here, let me help you."

The cord was tangled around Arlita's legs and her face was full of panic. When she screamed it scared Rita so badly that she screamed, too, scaring Arlita even more. The tears that she'd fought back all day rushed out and down her face. Her breathing rushed in and out so fast that she couldn't speak and for a short moment, she fainted. The black woman's face turned pale as a ghost.

Rita Lambert quickly ran to the kitchen to get some water. She thought about calling 911. She didn't know what was wrong with Arlita. She returned quickly with the water and held up the maid's head, talking gently to her.

"Arlita, Arlita, here drink some water. Are you all right?"

The spell lasted no time and Arlita assured her she was all right. She felt weak, sipping on the water that Rita held to her lips. When she could sit up, Rita started to untangle the cord from her feet. She stood with Rita's help and moved over to the couch, sitting down heavily. She started to shiver.

"Arlita, are you cold? Please forgive me. I didn't mean to startle you. I wanted to let you know I was in the house. Where's my mother-in-law?"

"Mrs. Eloise went to New Orleans with some friends for the day. I talked to her this morning before I got here. I wasn't feeling too well and started not to come, but since she was going to be gone I came on. She told me there wasn't much to do."

"Well, you gave me a scare."

"What time is it?" Arlita wondered aloud.

"It's after one. I came by to pick up some things for the children. I didn't know Eloise was going to New Orleans."

"She said it wasn't planned. Some friends called and asked her to ride with them."

"Why don't I put this vacuum cleaner up? You've done enough with it, haven't you?"

Arlita didn't argue. She tried to stand as Rita came back into the room but fell back to the sofa.

"Arlita, are you sure you're alright? Here, let me help. Let's go into the kitchen and get you something cool to drink."

With her arm around Rita the two of them made it into the kitchen where Arlita slipped into one of the chairs at the counter, leaning heavily on her hands and elbows.

"How about some Coke?" Rita offered.

"Yes, please."

Arlita held on at the counter with barely enough strength to keep herself sitting upright. The scare she got when Rita touched her arm took all her energy. The days of fear and doubt, of apprehension and misgivings, took their toll. Holding it all inside had made it worse. The constant dread that she kept pushing back was eating her up, sapping her energy and strength.

"Here you go." Rita set the glass of soda on the counter. "Drink this down and see if you don't start to feel better."

Rita came around and touched Arlita on the arm.

"Gosh, you feel cold. Maybe I should have given you something warm."

Rita rubbed her on the back and sat down beside her.

"What's ailing you, girl? Do I need to get you home and tuck you into bed?"

Arlita thought about going home. The idea didn't appeal to her because going home didn't feel like a safe place anymore. She felt so unsettled and afraid. The struggle to hold it all back failed her now and the panic of her situation seeped to the surface.

"Arlita, what's wrong. You look like you've seen a ghost."

"I have," the black woman responded without thinking.

"Hey, it's just me. Rita Lambert. I'm no ghost."

Hearing the name Lambert gave Arlita a chill. She didn't think of Rita as a Lambert. Not like Luther. She was different from him and Wilson. The Lambert men had always scared her, and now with good reason. She'd never liked being around Wilson or Mr. Luther. She'd never known why, just something about them that bothered her. Luther Lambert was a man to be feared. He got Susan Weeks killed. And he could kill her, too.

"You're shivering again. I'm making that coffee. You need something hot. Have you had anything to eat today?"

Arlita thought about it and realized she hadn't. This morning when the children were eating she only had coffee. Now it was past lunchtime.

"I need to go," Arlita tried to stand up, but again, almost fell.

"Sit back down. You aren't able to go anywhere. This coffee will be ready in a minute."

Rita looked directly into Arlita's eyes. They were not tired and sickly looking. They were wild, filled with fear, and she was trembling. Rita went back and poured the water into the coffee maker and flipped the switch. She didn't know what was wrong with Arlita but something told her it wasn't a physical ailment. Something was going on in there. Something had her scared to death. Rita came back to her and put her arm around her. She had always felt close to this poor black woman. She worked hard to provide for her three children, struggling all the way. There was a bond between them in some regards. Rita struggled hard to provide for her children, too. It just wasn't a financial struggle.

She struggled to stay in a marriage where there were no feelings, just to keep her children. Staying provided a safe haven for them to grow in a nurturing environment. All of her affection went to her children. There was none for Wilson. She didn't really hate Wilson. She just felt nothing where he was concerned.

She did hate Luther. She hated him in so many different ways. She hated him for tying her to Wilson. She hated him for his extortion of her life over past transgressions. She hated his control over Wilson. For a long time she hated Wilson for letting his father control him. But at some point she realized she was hating Wilson for the same thing that she was doing. Letting Luther have control.

After that she didn't hate Wilson anymore. The hatred turned to something less passionate, something faded and weak, until finally she had no feelings at all. She lived with the man. She slept with him. They had sex. But she had no passion, no feeling, no emotion of any kind where Wilson was concerned. She took care of her children whom she loved desperately and lived without any other feelings. There was no anger anymore for Wilson. But neither was there any joy.

Rita often felt that most of her life was dead. She was alive with the children but outside of that there was nothing. She didn't get excited about much. She wondered if she would ever feel again. She wanted more in her life, but the deadness overwhelmed everything. Only occasionally did she think there might be hope. Right at this moment she felt very drawn to Arlita. The woman was afraid of something other than the little fright she got from Rita. She needed someone. Rita recognized the distress in her eyes. Whatever it was, Rita wanted to help.

The coffee finished brewing and Rita fixed them a cup. She came back to Arlita with the warm liquid.

"Now drink this and let's talk. You're going to have to tell me what's going on, Arlita. What is it that's bothering you? I hope you realize you can trust me."

Arlita looked at her sideways, their eyes meeting directly across from each other. Arlita did need somebody to trust. But it didn't need to be somebody named Lambert. They were right here in Luther Lambert's house.

"No, it's nothing, Mrs. Lambert. I just need some rest, that's all. Maybe I've been working too hard. This weekend wore me out being down at my sister's and all. If I could get this kitchen cleaned up for Mrs. Eloise then I could go on home and get some rest."

"Alright. If that's all it is, then I'll help you." Rita stood up and grabbed an apron hanging on the refrigerator. "Let's get to it," she said with a smile.

Arlita laughed lightly. Rita was truly trying to make her feel better. But it would take more than a few cheerful words to improve her situation. The gloom returned to her almost immediately. Still, if she got the kitchen cleaned she could get out of the Lambert house. With another long sip from the coffee she got up and the two of them tackled the cleaning of the kitchen.

"What do we need to do?"

Arlita looked in the oven. It was fine. The refrigerator was okay, too. There were a few dirty dishes in the sink. She loaded those in the dishwasher and instructed Rita to start wiping down counters. Arlita pulled a mop bucket from the storage room near the back door, filling it with warm water and a little cleaner mixed in. She set it down and put the mop in. It felt like a weight. She hardly had enough strength to lift it.

Rita watched her movements, sluggish and lethargic. This was the dynamo that cleaned at her house. Whatever was wrong had sapped all of her strength.

"Here, Arlita, let me help you."

Rita took the mop from her and finished the floor with a few brisk swipes. She dumped out the bucket in the sink in the utility room, rinsed out the mop and returned them to the closet. When she looked up, Arlita stood there watching, her eyes filled with tears.

"Arlita, what is it? I've never seen you like this. What has happened to you?"

Arlita burst out into full blown sobs. She coughed and wheezed, barely able to talk.

"It's nothing, Mrs. Lambert. I'm just not feeling well, that's all."

"You expect me to believe that? You're not yourself. For one thing you keep calling me Mrs. Lambert. You never call me that. I don't even like it. I hate being reminded that's my name."

Rita finished up the statement with a look of disgust. The disgust was short-lived and tears followed behind it that she tried to hold back. Arlita saw them, saw Rita try to suppress them. Rita didn't know why she felt so sad all of a sudden. When she realized Arlita was staring directly into her eyes and saw the sadness that shone back, the two of them peering through blurry eyes. Suddenly they both burst into laughter mixed with tears and Rita put out her arms to Arlita. Arlita returned the embrace and they stood there in silence with the tears binding them together.

"Listen, I've got some things at my house you could help me with. Wilson's gone off on some deposition or something. Won't be back until tomorrow. You need to just come on over to my house and we can visit while we work. And you can get paid for it."

"I don't know, Ms Rita. I need to be..."

"You need to be at my house with me. You don't need to be alone. Whatever it is that's bothering you, I think the two of us can handle it."

Rita saw the fear return. Her face, her eyes, her whole countenance signaled confusion and alarm. The look made Rita want to cry. Her heart went out to the meek, submissive servant girl that stood before her. Rita had such respect for her. She worked hard. She raised three children single-handedly. Through the years Rita had always wanted to do more for her than she had.

There was some envy there. Arlita did not have much in the way of material things. No fine house like Rita. No fancy car. But with all the trappings of wealth that Rita enjoyed, this simple black woman had something she didn't. Independence. Rita had all the things that money could buy, but she didn't have what Arlita had. She didn't have freedom. She was enslaved to a past transgression that her father-in-law held over her head like an axe that waited to fall. No matter how much money, how many beautiful things she gathered around her, it didn't block out the curse that overshadowed everything in her existence.

Arlita didn't feel very much like the champion today. All she could see was the darkness that loomed over her in the shadow of Luther Lambert. She didn't know what he was thinking. Or, how drunk he was that night. She just knew she was scared, and she needed to talk to someone. Rita Lambert had always been nice to her. As nice as anyone that Arlita had ever worked for. Always so supportive and encouraging. If only her name wasn't Lambert.

"Okay, I'll come help you," Arlita heard herself saying. That would get her out of this house, and she didn't know where else to go. Oh, dear Lord, please help me know what I need to do, she prayed.

Rita pushed the button on the garage door and walked Arlita over to her car. She went on to hers and waited for Arlita to crank up the old Ford and back out. Rita was almost embarrassed about her Jaguar. At one time it meant something to her, but now it was just another of those expensive toys that had lost their value.

They drove to Rita's house with the Jag following the Pinto. In the driveway Rita punched the button for the garage door to open and motioned for Arlita to pull on in. Wilson's car was not there so she parked in his space. They got out and went inside where Rita immediately put on some tea and got out some sandwich fixings for Arlita.

"I've got some homemade soup I picked up at the farmer's market, too. I think that'll be just the thing for you."

They fussed around for a while getting the soup, getting the tea and making a sandwich. Rita was determined to get some food in Arlita. She still looked a little pale and Rita was certain the food would get her to feeling better. They chatted lightly with Arlita's expression remaining somber. She wavered from nearing laughter to fighting tears. Finally, Rita could stand it no longer.

"Arlita, what is it? I've never seen you like this before. I don't know what's bothering you but you've got to talk about it. You're going to drive yourself crazy."

Arlita felt she was already crazy. She wanted to hide. She wanted to cry. She wanted to run. She wanted her brain to stop with all the 'what ifs,' and 'what abouts' and maybes and everything. She wanted to scream. She didn't know how much longer she was going to be able to take it. Maybe she could get her kids and move down to the coast with her sister. Or, somewhere else.

But where? She didn't have any money. If she went to her sister's, they couldn't stay for long. There wasn't enough room. Maybe New Orleans. But that place is expensive. What would she do for money? She could clean houses. It might take her a while. At least she would be away from this town. Away from Luther Lambert. She couldn't face him ever again. She couldn't go back to that office, but what would he do if she didn't? What if he found her in New Orleans? Would he try to have her killed like he did that other girl?

Her spinning head was too much. Rita watched her eyes flicker and dart back and forth, wondering what in the world was going on in that head. The fear that settled in her eyes scared even Rita. What on earth was troubling her? She looked so afraid. Rita reached out to touch her hand. As she did, Arlita drew it back with a jerk. And then their eyes met again.

Arlita burst into tears. She crumpled over on the counter and sobbed. Rita put her arm around her as she wept. Rita wept with her. She didn't know why. But the pain that brought this agony to Arlita touched something in Rita that moved her to tears also. For a long, long time they remained there in the same position. Arlita slumped over the counter crying and Rita leaning over her back, arms around the troubled woman offering what solace she could. After a while, Arlita sat up and looked at Rita.

"I can't tell you what he did." The statement came out flatly and with no emotion.

"What who did? Of course, you can tell me. Arlita, look at you. You're a wreck. You can't go on like this. Who has hurt you? Was it Willie?"

"No," Arlita said with some antagonism. "Why does everybody think it's Willie?"

"I'm sorry. I'm just trying to come up with something. Who else thought it was Willie?"

"My sister. I went, me and the kids, went down there this weekend. I didn't tell her what happened but she knew something was wrong. She asked if it was Willie. It's not."

"Arlita, a blind man could tell something's wrong. She's like me, probably. Just trying to get a handle on why you're so upset."

"I was raped." Arlita whispered out the words.

"What?"

Nothing but more tears came out of Arlita. Rita went on.

"What happened? Who did it? When did it happen? Have you been to the police?"

Arlita shook her head negatively.

"We have to go to the police. They'll catch the person."

Again, Arlita shook her head no vehemently.

"Arlita, do you want this person to do it again. What if he tries to get you again?"

With this line, Arlita broke down again. She collapsed on the counter weeping loudly.

"Okay, let's skip over this part about the police. Who was it? Can you tell me that much?"

No response.

"Arlita, you've got to trust someone. I promise you I'll help you through this. Tell me who it is?"

Arlita looked up at her through blurred eyes and hesitated. She wanted so badly to tell someone, but how could she tell Rita Lambert it was her kinfolk. But there was no one else to tell and Rita was right. If she didn't tell someone she was going to die. And what good would she be to her kids.

"It was Mr. Lambert."

Rita was too stunned to say anything but "Wilson?"

"No, no, Mr. Luther," Arlita spit out the words.

Rita was even more stunned. Luther Lambert raped Arlita. That son of a bitch. That lowlife bastard. The years of suppressed anger and hatred welled up inside of her and came near to explosion. She looked at poor Arlita huddled over the counter. Poor Arlita that wouldn't hurt a flea. That fat, evil, gluttonous bastard.

Oh, how she would love to kill him herself. For all he had done to her. For what he had done to Wilson. To countless others. And now to Arlita. Rita's eyes fixed in the distance. All the pain inside of her smoldered, never fully extinguished. Now fanned by this abuse of Arlita. How much better this world would be if that man were dead.

Arlita watched her face, looking for some hint about what she was thinking. She had been so afraid to tell, but now the hatred she saw in Rita's eyes gave her comfort. She hated him, too. For so long she had feared the man, fear mixed with awe. She was still afraid, but here looking into Rita's eyes her feelings turned to hate.

Rita turned her attention back to Arlita who looked more scared than ever. She put her arms around her again in an embrace.

"You'll be alright, Arlita. I won't let that bastard hurt you."

The words fell onto Arlita like a sedative, soothing the raw nerves that tormented her since Friday night. She breathed deeply, letting the air issue slowly from her lungs, carrying out a little of the burden. A little, but not all.

"There's more, Rita," she uttered the words with a grim resolve.

Rita pulled back from her, looking into the sad face with swollen eyes. She waited for Arlita to go on. Arlita's face dropped, her head and eyes cast down into her lap where her fingers fiddled with a piece of thread.

"He… he didn't really rape me… not completely. I guess it was more of an attack. He tried to rape me."

Tears filled her eyes again and dropped down onto her hands that trembled. Her teeth bit into her lip while her whole body drooped. The fatigue of carrying this weight was tiring. She could hardly get the words out. Days of tears had drained the life out of her slight frame. Rita didn't say anything, allowing the story to come on its own. With her head down, slowly, Arlita tried to continue.

"I went by to clean the office last Friday. I was supposed to go down to my sister's over the weekend and thought we'd probably be late getting back Sunday. I didn't want to have to worry about getting back and cleaning up the law office so I decided I'd do it on Friday night. You know, they're not there on Saturday. So, anyway, before I could leave, Mr. Luther was there in the kitchen and he started saying things to me and…"

Her voice trailed off again. Rita waited patiently without saying a word. She was standing close enough to have a comforting hand on Arlita's arm.

"Well, he started saying things to me and looking at me funny and I… well, I went back to put up the broom and when I came back he was standing in the hall. He was drunk, Rita. He was real drunk. I've seen him drinking before at parties and all but never like this. It was like he didn't know where he was. Anyway, he kinda cornered me in the hall and blocked the way. I tried to ease into the conference room but he moved right in behind me and then he touched me and I backed into the table…" sobs choked off the words.

"I didn't know what to do, Rita, I swear. I was so scared. He grabbed my blouse pulling it hard. So hard it ripped the buttons off. He pressed himself against me with his hands groping all around on me, in my pants. I thought he might kill me if I tried to resist. He was acting crazy."

"He jerked my pants down. He pulled my bra down, breaking the snaps off. But then… then… he couldn't do it. He wasn't ready… his, you know…"

Arlita didn't know exactly how she should explain this. How she should tell this part.

"He just couldn't do it."

The two women stared at each other. Rita's eyes were as big as saucers. The whole story was so incredulous.

"So, you mean he couldn't get it up?"

"Ummh." Arlita nodded affirmatively.

Rita couldn't help herself. She burst out laughing. Arlita thought she was crazy, but then she couldn't help it either. The two of them started laughing. They leaned together and laughed until they were sobbing on each other's shoulder. Tears streamed down both their cheeks, but they were healing tears, so much different than the ones that had afflicted Arlita for days.

"So what did he do then?" Rita asked her through the droplets of water that coursed down her face.

"He just kind of rolled over onto the table like a big old hawg."

Arlita did not intend it to be funny but Rita could not contain herself. The picture in her mind was so absurd. She howled out loud again with Arlita joining her. They laughed and laughed with tears and hollers renewing themselves each time they looked up at each other.

Finally, they settled down again. Arlita settled first. She remembered there was more to this than the funny picture of Luther Lambert. The other picture was not very funny at all and its seriousness took over very quickly when she stopped laughing for a moment. She had to tell the rest of it, too.

"There's still more, Rita."

"I hope you're going to tell me you rolled that big lard ass off on the floor and stomped on him. That's what he deserves."

"No, it was before that."

Rita pulled a tissue out to wipe her own eyes. She could tell this was very serious.

"When I first got there, no one was at the office. I went on with my cleaning and finished up with just about everything. I was headed to the back when I heard Mr. Luther come in. Him and Jerry Mason."

Mason, that scum bag, Rita thought. She never liked him, either, the creep.

"I was going to leave but, I was putting the vacuum cleaner up in the closet when I heard them. Mr. Luther always makes me so nervous, I never like being around him. So anyway, I stood there for a few minutes thinking they would leave, but they didn't. They got into a big argument."

Arlita was wide-eyed with fear again. The earlier look of something ominous and evil returned to her. Rita couldn't imagine what she was about to hear.

"I hid in the closet, pulling it to, but I could still hear them. They got into a big argument over something Mr. Luther had told Jerry to do. It was confusing at first."

She stopped, not sure whether she should go on or not. Really not sure if she could. The words stuck in her throat. Tears welled up again and burst down her face. All color drained from her again and the terror that filled her was so tangible Rita thought she could feel it coming from her skin. Rita got the shivers just sitting next to her.

"Arlita, what is it? It's okay. You can tell me. I promise you can trust me. You know you can

"They killed her, Rita. They killed that girl."

Arlita was barely able to utter the words. They stuck in her throat. Her tongue refused to form them properly.

"They killed who, Arlita? Who did they kill?"

"That girl Mr. Daniels was supposed to have killed. Jerry Mason went in there and killed her after Mr. Daniels left. He admitted it. And Luther was ready to pin it on DeWeese if he had to. That was all those drugs. But Mason did it. And it looked like from the conversation that Luther had wanted him to do it."

"Oh, my god, Arlita. Are you sure? How do you know?"

"That's what they was fighting about. Mr. Luther sent Jerry Mason over there to straighten her out or something. They had some pictures of her. Something like that and they was blackmailing her to do something and they was afraid she had told Mr. Daniels."

"Oh my god."

That was all Rita could say. When she heard the part about pictures and blackmail, she saw Luther's face. She saw herself, a young, innocent girl. A young, stupid girl, sitting in his office, the safe behind his desk open and that folder open in front of him. The pictures of her in California. The tape. It all came back to her in a rush.

Most of the time she kept it pushed back out of her memory as if it never happened, almost as if she just married Wilson because she wanted to. Not because his father blackmailed her.

She wanted to be sick. She wanted to throw up all this trash she had just heard and make it go away. She was pretty good at it. Most of the time. Now she looked at Arlita and realized she couldn't pretend it didn't happen. It did. That poor girl. Jerry Mason murdered Susan Weeks, and Luther was behind it all.

"Oh my god," the words came out of her again. "Poor Luke. Arlita, do you realize Luke Daniels is in jail convicted of that murder. We've go to do something."

Arlita couldn't say anything. She was stunned by the retelling of the story, hearing it again left her dazed, feeling lost and alone. But she wasn't alone. She scrutinized Rita and the look on her face. Hearing the story again made her weak all over, but it lifted the burden some having Rita here. She was slowly realizing that the woman hated her father-in-law. Why did she hate him so much?

"Arlita, I know you may find this hard to believe but that man did the same thing to me."

"He tried to rape you?"

"No, no, no. He tried to blackmail me. Actually, he did blackmail me. I sold my soul to that devil to protect something that I thought needed protecting, but now somehow it doesn't seem to matter. We can't stand by and let an innocent man go to prison. You and me. We're the only hope for Luke Daniels."

The two women stared at each other. Both of them were scared. Both of them were afraid of the man that should be in prison. If they didn't do the right thing, what might happen? Luther Lambert was capable of murder. If that were true, then he would do anything.

They didn't know what to do. Rita knew she couldn't go to the DA. Or the Judge. And not Hays. They'd have to get to someone outside of Hampton. Right now, she didn't have a clue who that might be.

Luke sat in his cell still oblivious to time or space or anything else. They finally got a light bulb in the ceiling fixture locked behind a mesh wire cage. He almost wished they hadn't. The light let his eyes see the horrible condition of the six-by-six concrete box where he'd been since Friday. The darkness made him crazy and now the light made him crazier.

He wondered what was going on out in the real world. He hadn't talked to another human being since Friday; the only contact with one was when they opened his cell door to deliver meals. Most of those had been picked up untouched. It wasn't that the food was bad, although it was; but, rather that they held no appeal to him. From the time he arrived at the jail and the metal door clanged shut behind him his appetite left. Along with a lot of other things. His body shut down. There was a toilet in the room that he hardly used. Water tasted like poison. The tea that came with the meals was like acid.

The only thing that seemed to be working in full force was his brain. And it worked at double overtime. His thinking would not stop. He longed for some release there, just let his mind stop for a little while. Rest eluded him. Hour after hour he sat in the darkness with the memories of the past that had put him here.

He tried to run in his mind. He envisioned himself outside going through some stretching exercises. He would start off, down his old route looking at the houses and landscape. It was a beautiful day, the sun shining down. He would soak up its rays like he used to do. His eyes took in the areas he ran through.

But even that worked against him. His mind began to see houses that became negative forces. There was the Judge's house and off he went on the ways Judge Jones handled this case, so decidedly against Luke. Jones had never shown any disdain for Luke. Suddenly at the trial it was as if he had decided Luke was guilty before the testimony even started. He set himself against Luke and never took another thought about it.

Luke pushed himself away from those thoughts and back into a run. Running helped for a while. He even stood and ran in place in the darkness. The physical exertion felt good. In his mind's eye he went back to the sunshine, but after a while another house would pass into his view. The District Attorney's house. That was not in Luke's normal run but it came into his head. Gafford, that low life. He was normally such a dunce Luke didn't know how he ever got a conviction on anything, but now he understood. Everyone helped him. The Judge, the police, his assistant. They all contributed to making him look good. The bad guys, really, were all on his side

Run, Luke, run. When his thoughts started getting weird he made himself get back to a run, standing up and going hard, lifting legs as high as he could. Faster, Luke, faster. There was not much air movement in the small cubicle so he could work up a sweat in no time. The lack of food in his system made him weak and that tired him out quickly. He pushed and pushed until he could go no more, falling back on the concrete slab gasping for air. He lay back flat on the bench making his mind go on in his imaginary run.

There was another house. Luther Lambert's. Luther got on the stand and testified about things that he knew were an absolute lie. Why? That little incident in his office with Wilson? Surely he knew what a jerk Wilson was. Everybody else did. Such a little wise ass. And he's the one that started it that day, popping off to Luke about what his client would and would not do. He knew the rules. Hell, half the lawyers in this town would love to smack Wilson up side the head. Luke hadn't done it then but he was certainly in the ranks of those that would like to. He probably should have. Then at least they'd have something to talk about.

Luther never looked Luke in the eye at the trial. He avoided him. He knew he was talking trash. Nothing he said had any relevance to the case. He just painted this bad picture around Luke so the jury could draw some erroneous conclusions. And they did. The jury came up with twelve ballots that said Luke was guilty. Guilty of murder. Tears didn't come this time. He'd had put out so many that now all that was left came were more pictures in his brain. Susan's house. He was running around her drive way. Running around and around. She was inside and he could hear her calling his name but he couldn't go in. He just kept running around-and-around in the driveway. He heard her calling his name over and over. "Luke! Luke!" He saw her face. Beautiful and smiling. "Luke! She called to him again. He could see her house as he ran. At the bedroom window there were shadows. He looked inside. And there she was. On the floor with her hair across her face. There was a man standing up at the bed, just a blank shadowy figure. Luke couldn't see a face, only an outline of a body, big and muscular. He couldn't make out any details, except for one thing. He could see the running shoes on his feet.

In the cell there was not a sound except for the heavy breathing from Luke's body. It was deep and solid with a harsh rough sound. It came out of him as his body lay back senseless, oblivious to his situation. It was the closest thing to sleep he had known in three days.

Rita Lambert had the phone book out going through the list of lawyers trying to find somebody that she thought she could trust. It was four o'clock. The children were home. She had them in the playroom watching TV, far away from her post in the kitchen so they couldn't hear anything she had to say.

Arlita was still there, pretending to clean for the children's benefit. Nothing out of the ordinary. She called her neighbor to get the children and let them play at her house. It was several blocks from her house. They should be safe there. Momma had to work. They would understand.

"Arlita, I've got a Jackson phone book here somewhere. We need to find it. I've gone through the entire list of attorneys here in Hampton and I don't see much help. I've pulled out two names, but let's look in Jackson first."

Scrambling around for the phone book, finally Arlita pulled it out of the closet in the study. It was a couple of years old, but it would do for their purposes. There was also a book for the Mississippi Gulf Coast.

"Surely in all of these names we can find one honest lawyer," Rita exclaimed. "There's got to be somebody that will help us."

Rita scanned the Jackson phone book while Arlita went through the coast directory. Arlita didn't have any idea what she was doing. She didn't know any lawyers and she didn't know anybody else that she thought could help. Maybe she should call her sister.

Rita's task was taking longer. There were tons of lawyers in the Jackson area and so far no name had jumped out and grabbed her. She felt desperate, consumed by the desire to expose her father-in-law. Working to help Arlita and Luke was only the mask that covered the real significance of her efforts. The true cause for her was her own freedom.

Listening to Arlita, the story she heard appalled her. She slowly realized that Luther had done the same thing over and over again. He had brought about the death of Susan Weeks. He had taken all the life away from Luke Daniels by getting him convicted of a crime he didn't commit. Just like he had taken her life. Rita stopped for a minute, staring off into the distance. Luther had stolen her life. He'd forced her into an existence that she hated with a man that she couldn't respect. Her life. She had no life.

Luther's hand extended into every area. There was no escape, from her husband to her house, including their cars. Even the rearing of her children was overshadowed by the sphere of his influence. He dictated every detail of their lives to Wilson who tried to mete out the same to Rita. It was the source of all their fights. Wilson would try to bellow out commands that she knew came directly from Luther. She resisted. She fought back. She might not be able to fight against Luther but she could against Wilson.

Now it would be different. She was going to expose Luther, and she would relish watching him twist and squirm. When this came out he wouldn't be able to touch her again. His might would be gone. Destroyed. He would be completely impotent, she thought with a smile as she continued going through the names.

When she found nothing in Jackson, she took the coast directory from Arlita and first went to the yellow pages under lawyers starting in the A's. Suddenly, one named jumped out at her. Jane Archer. She had testified for Luke. There was her office number and the clock was passing five. With a little luck, she would still be there.

Jane was still at her office catching up. She had been out so much lately with Luke's case that her work was behind. The office staff left a few minutes before and she was dictating instructions for tomorrow. After her testimony, she had gone to Luke's office to think. What was he going to do with all his files? She assured him after the verdict that she would help Liz get it settled. When the phone rang, she almost didn't answer. But Cody was coming over and she thought he might have dialed it instead of her cell phone.

"Hello, this is Jane Archer."

"Ms. Archer, this is Rita Lambert. I'm calling from Hampton and I need to speak to you about Luke Daniels. A horrible thing has happened."

At first, Jane couldn't imagine what might have happened. Had something happened to Luke? She knew he was in jail, awaiting transport to the state penitentiary. But that sometimes took weeks, months. And who was this person calling her?

"Hello, Ms. Archer are you there?"

"Yes, I'm sorry. I'm here. What is it?" Jane said, suddenly realizing who this person was. It had to be the wife of Wilson Lambert whose father had testified against Luke. Why was she calling here?

"Ms. Archer, I have information about who killed Susan Weeks."

The statement brought Jane straight up in her chair.

"I didn't know who else to call. I need to talk with you but I'm not comfortable talking over the phone."

"Is this a joke, Mrs. Lambert, because if it is, I don't find it very amusing."

"Ms. Archer, I know you must find this incredible, especially that it's me calling you. I'm sure you know who my father-in-law is."

"Yes, yes I do."

"Well, I don't know where to begin but we didn't know who else to call. And then I found your number in the phone book and I remembered that you testified for Luke so strongly at the trial."

"Who is we?" Jane asked warily.

"Oh, I'm sorry. My maid, Arlita Johnson. She, ah, overheard something at Luther Lambert's office that…" her voice trailed off. Rita didn't know this woman and didn't know how to say this. She assumed she could trust Jane. She testified for Luke. Surely, she would want to help him.

Jane looked up from the phone to see Cody standing there. She put her hand over the phone and mouthed that she was so glad he was there.

"Mrs. Lambert, someone has just come in. Could I put you on hold for just a second? Please don't hang up. I do want to talk with you. Please, I'll be right back…" She pushed the hold button and looked up at Cody.

"You're not going to believe this. This is Luther Lambert's son's wife on the phone. Says she has information about who killed Susan Weeks."

Cody's face froze. He didn't know if she was serious or not. She sure sounded serious. Jane quickly filled him in on her mysterious phone call. They quickly agreed that he should talk with her.

"Mrs. Lambert, my investigator, Cody Raybern, just came in. He is retired from the Drug Enforcement Agency. He operates a private detective agency here on the coast. I think he is more qualified to handle this than me. I trust him implicitly. You can say anything to him that you would to me. In fact, I'm going to stay on the line. Cody, can you pick up the phone on that desk?"

"Hello, Mrs. Lambert, this is Cody Raybern. Do you mind if we record this conversation?"

"Well, I don't know. Would it be possible to meet you somewhere? I know you are an hour away but…" Rita started thinking about her kids in the house. She didn't want them to know what their grandfather had done and she didn't want them to know what she was doing.

"Where would you like to meet?" Cody asked. He could hear Rita talking with someone. He turned to Jane and said there was someone there with her.

They finally agreed to meet at a catfish restaurant near Wiggins. She gathered up the kids and told them she had to run to help Arlita with some things and she might be late getting back. She arranged for them to stay over with some friends across town. They all loaded into her Jag and left Arlita's car hidden in the garage. When the kids were deposited, they headed off toward Wiggins.

The truck stop was barely a thirty minute drive. On the way, Arlita called her kids and told them not to go home, making up a lie that there might be a gas leak and that they couldn't go back until the plumbers checked it out.

When they arrived at The Catfish Shack it was almost seven o'clock and Jane and Cody were already there, glasses of tea sitting in front of them. Rita and Arlita slid in the booth across from them and they all looked at each other. Away from Hampton, Rita was a little more relaxed. She introduced herself and then Arlita.

"I know you think we're crazy but we didn't know what else to do. Arlita here works at my house, and at my mother-in-law's house and she also cleans the office for Luther and Wilson. Something happened at the office Friday night. She overheard a conversation between Luther and a guy named Jerry Mason."

Rita couldn't bring herself to call Mason a detective. "But really Arlita is the one who should be telling this. She's the one it happened to."

Arlita started her story. She started with going to the office Friday night and with Luther and Mason coming in drunk. She told them about hiding in the closet and what she overheard. She told them about coming out and finding Luther still there. About his trying to rape her. Then she was quiet. No more tears for Arlita. She was glad to tell her story. Neither Jane nor Cody said a word when she finished. They both sat there silent for several minutes. Cody's brain was working on what to do next. Who was the right person for him to call?

At seven o'clock sharp the door to Luke's cell clanged open and a gruff voice told him to step outside. His supper served at four thirty still sat untouched on the floor by the door. Luke pushed himself up from the seat enough to peer out the door. Two deputies stood there along with the chief jailer and another person Luke did not recognize.

"What do you want?" Luke asked.

"We want you to step outside," came the reply without any touch of humor in it.

Luke had no idea what was happening. He was a lawyer. He knew what his rights were.

He also knew there were four large men outside the door ready for him to follow their instructions. He decided this would not be the time to press the issue of his legal knowledge. With lethargic, deliberate effort he moved himself out the door of the cell to stand surrounded by the four men. One of them handed him a manila envelope which he took automatically.

"What is this?"

"It's yours. Go ahead and look in it. It's your stuff."

"Why are you giving it to me now?"

"Mr. Daniels, you're being transferred to the custody of the Mississippi Department of Corrections. We have a van ready to take you to the facility in Parchman, Mississippi."

The word Parchman stung Luke. Parchman was the State Penitentiary. The word was synonymous with the most wretched place you could be in the state. Luke had represented more than one poor felon whose acts had put him in a position that imprisonment was the only choice. That meant Parchman, and now Luke was going there.

He knew this would happen. When the Judge sentenced him to life it was automatically at the state penitentiary at Parchman, but his mind had not moved to this point yet. He hadn't looked forward. So far, all he had been able to do was replay the past. Now he stood out here ready to be hauled away.

"But I haven't talked to my lawyer. Does he know about this transfer?"

One of the deputies almost snickered. Luke didn't find it the least bit funny, but he did understand. The time for lawyers was past. When Judge Jones denied him bail pending appeal that meant he had to start serving his time. How could Jones do that to me? What has he got against me all of a sudden? Luke's mind started to race again. What could he do?

"I want to call my lawyer."

The chief jailer knew Luke well. He'd been with the sheriff's department for ten years, starting off as a deputy on patrol about the time Luke started practicing law. Luke had talked to him on numerous occasions. Even bought him a bottle of whiskey as a congratulatory present when he got the job as chief jailer. Now Mr. Chief Jailer Ray Pitts was all business.

They used to know each other fairly well. Ray was a runner. Or at least he used to be. Luke hadn't seen him at any races in a long time, and it showed. He had gained a considerable amount of weight. They were about the same age and height but now he had a huge gut that hung out over his belt. His hair receded back to about midway of his head, making him look much older.

He led Luke down a corridor to the back door. Through the bullet proof glass Luke could see the van that apparently would be their ride to the penitentiary. The four of them stood in a square with Luke in the middle, each of them watching him closely. He wondered what they must be thinking.

They each had a gun. They each looked ready to use it. Surely, they didn't think he would try to escape. Escape. Luke hadn't thought of it. But....

"Here, spread your legs."

Another jailer appeared with a sack full of chains which he dumped on the floor in front of Luke. From around the corner appeared another jailer with another prisoner. A woman. She already had her chains on, shuffling along clumsily behind the jailer.

"You've got to be kidding." Luke was incredulous. "Surely you're not going to make me wear those things."

Luke looked up at Ray shocked and dismayed at the idea of having to be put in chains. He looked over at the poor female prisoner. She looked like an animal with the chains hanging from her hands and tied to her feet. The deputy was already stooping at Luke's feet attaching the irons around his ankles.

"Ray, please. You know this isn't necessary. You don't have to put me in chains."

Luke's plaintive lament was a near whimper. He didn't mean for it to be. He didn't want to give them the satisfaction of knowing it bothered him. But chains. Luke swallowed hard letting a deep breath follow. He looked Ray squarely in the eyes as he held out his hands.

"I'm sorry, Luke, but it's the sheriff's direct orders. I can't give you any special treatment."

"Hey, it's okay. I don't expect any." Luke's jaw clenched tight after the words.

The deputy at his feet finished attaching the irons around the ankles and then slapped the cuffs around Luke's wrists. He pulled the chain up from the feet where it attached to the chain between Luke's ankles. When he got the length adjusted he locked it to the handcuffs, making it impossible for Luke to lift his hands any higher than his waist.

Luke didn't flinch. He stood strong and stared straight ahead. Ray Pitts had to move out of his gaze. Two deputies were behind him and the other was getting the keys to the van. He made a wave to the control room as he rounded the corner for them to open the back door.

The woman shuffled out first. Then Luke hobbled along, his feet only able to move about six inches at a time. At the side door to the van one of the deputies almost picked the girl up and threw her into the front seat. Luke tried to make the jump without any help. He hopped, trying to duck at the same time. His head hit the top of the van and his shins scrapped down the edge of the floor board. The pain doubled him over, but it was enough for him to catch on the side of the second seat. He quickly pulled his knees up to the edge of the floor, pushing himself up more on the seat and rolling on in to the van.

Somehow, he managed to twist himself around in the seat so that when his motion stopped he was facing forward, sitting upright. He never looked back to the side, keeping his eyes forward in the van, staring straight into the rear view mirror where he could see his reflection.

The driver climbed behind the wheel on the other side of the thick wire grid separating him from the prisoners. He motioned for the control room to raise the overhead door in front of him. With a clank and creak the heavy metal door began its upward motion, slowing making enough of an opening for the van to drive off into the night. When they pulled up to the street a flash on the right sidewalk made Luke twist around to look. Then another flash hit him squarely in the eyes, a burst from the reporter's camera trying to get a last shot for a final story on Luke Daniels.

Maybe not the final story, Luke thought. Maybe the appeal would give him another chance. Maybe he could work on his case at the penitentiary law library. Maybe something would come out that would help him. Anything. Somewhere the truth that would prove his innocence had to be found. He didn't know how he was going to do that from prison, but somehow he had to. He couldn't spend the rest of his life in prison.

As the van drove a light rain turned heavier with the passing miles. Darkness settled around them in the silence. The van radio didn't work and the driver had on earphones from his own radio. The rain beat against the window beside Luke with the drops running together and then hurrying down the glass at an angle. Like tears he thought, but his face was dry. There were no feelings left to let him cry.

The unmarked car pulled up to Jerry Mason's house at twelve thirty that night. Two men in plain clothes got out and went to the door. The third stayed in the driver's seat.

When Jerry came to the door, they flashed their highway patrol investigator's badge along with the announcement that they had a few questions for him. They had already taken a full statement from Arlita Johnson and one from Rita Lambert. They invited themselves in over Jerry's objection that fell on deaf ears.

In one of their pockets was a pen that contained a transmitter sending their conversation back to the car where it was being recorded. Chief Investigator George Price sat in the car making sure the tape ran smoothly getting everything down. He even had a second tape running. Just in case.

Jerry's initial response was that he wanted to see his lawyer. He wasn't saying anything. They assured him he was well within his rights. He could call his lawyer. Of course, they wouldn't recommend his calling Luther Lambert since he was not going to be much help in this case.

"You see, Mr. Mason, we have enough information to charge you with the murder of Susan Weeks. We know that Mr. Lambert was also involved in this matter. I guess it's up to you whether you take the full blame or whether you assist us in reaching the person we feel is actually responsible for the murder."

Jerry was getting agitated. He hadn't forgotten his conversation with Lambert Friday night. He particularly hadn't forgotten how Luther failed to remember it was his request that Jerry go out there. How he reacted when Jerry said it was all an accident.

Jerry knew then that when the chips were down, Luther was going to take care of himself. He'd let Jerry fry without a second thought. His eyes went back and forth between the two men. They were very business-like. Just like Jerry saw himself. He could've been in their shoes. He could've been an investigator for the department. He got an application once.

Then Luther urged him to go out on his own. To go private. He could make tons of money. Why, he'd get all the business there was in Hampton. It was another lie. He hadn't made that much. Just enough to get by. He paid the bills each month and there was nothing left. Nothing. The lawyers made all the money.

Luther, that sonofabitch. He made all the money while Jerry and Doris scrimped and saved, pinching every penny. Every once in a while Lambert threw him something. Some hint of the big money, some case that would hold a big bonus for him. It never came. Never. It was always Luther.

Doris was at his side now. She had no idea what was going on. Jerry never talked much about his work. Especially what he did for Luther Lambert. What could this be about?

"We have a search warrant, Jerry" the first man said to him flatly.

"Okay, look. I'll talk to you but not here. Can we go somewhere else?"

"Whatever you say Jerry, but we've got to do the search first. Unless you want to make it easy for us."

"Okay, okay. Just give me a minute to think."

He turned to Doris who sat next to him holding her breathe, not really understanding everything she heard. One thing was clear. Jerry was in a bunch of trouble.

"Honey, listen I can explain all of this later. Right now I'm going with them to try to straighten it out. I… ah… you just go back to bed. I think I can get it all worked out."

"Tell you what, let me get a bag in my room and we'll go," Jerry said to the men.

When he started toward the back of the house one of them followed quickly on his heels, leaving Doris alone with the other investigator.

"Is he going to be all right?" she asked lamely.

"We'll see, ma'am. We'll see."

Jerry returned with a bag and the officer behind him. In his hands the officer held just one pair of jogging shoes, which were not the same size as the other shoes that were in the closet.

Jerry hugged Doris in a long but despairing embrace. She was so confused that she didn't know what to do or say.

The two men stood by the door trying to give Jerry a few moments before the first one motioned that it was time. He separated himself from Doris and then followed the investigators out the door into the night. The awaiting car was completely dark. When they opened the back door for Jerry he and one of the two crawled into the back seat. The other went around to the front. When they were all in, the driver cranked up and put the car in gear. Before removing his foot from the brake he turned to the back seat.

"Thanks for coming, Jerry."

The voice stunned him. He couldn't see the face clearly in the dark but he knew that voice. He was completely surprised. Luther would be, too.

When the call came in to Luther's house in the middle of the night, he started not to answer.

Probably some damn wrong number he thought, but his hand went for it and he said hello.

Luther got all sorts of phone calls. People loved to call him and tell him all manner of things. Most of it was garbage, but occasionally he picked up some tidbit that was of some importance. Sometimes, it ended up being the difference between making and breaking a deal. It was these pieces that made it worth wading through the trash. Middle of the night calls were usually trash. Usually, but not always.

When he picked up the phone he didn't recognize the voice. The person on the other end acted like Luther knew him so he went along, just like old friends. The man talked like it was the middle of the day; like he had just called to chat. He went on and on about how sick he had been; had been in bed all day; now he couldn't sleep.

"I was up listening to my police scanner and I heard the darndest thing. I live just down the block from Jerry Mason's house. I can see his front door from my living room. I know he does a lot of work for you. It was so crazy."

"What is it, old man," Luther whispered to himself.

"I just couldn't figure out why an unmarked police car would be going up to Jerry Mason's house in the middle of the night."

Luther sat straight up in bed, his ears perked up to full awareness.

"I knew it had to be some kind of law enforcement, though, because it had those funny little antennas on the back. The weird thing was what I picked up on the scanner. They was asking him questions about that Weeks girl. I couldn't hear everything that was said 'cause my signal was jumping around. You see, I got one of those new kind of scanners that picks just some of it up. My brother down in Biloxi, his next door neighbor is a policeman and he gets this catalogue… Hello, hello?"

The phone clicked and went back to a dial tone. Luther had slammed down the phone so quickly that it rattled the whole table.

"What is it, dear?" his wife lifted up from her pillow.

"Oh, nothing. Nothing, the phone slipped out of my hand. Just go back to sleep. Wrong number, I guess. I'm going to get something to drink. You go back to sleep."

Luther whisked himself out of the bedroom and down toward the kitchen. He was wide awake. What were they doing at Jerry's house? Who was it? What was going on? He didn't like this, didn't like this at all.

He had to get to the office. And to the safe. He needed that stuff out of there. And some money. There was plenty there. He stood in the kitchen, drumming his fingers. He'd take his wife's car. Maybe they'd be watching for his.

He slipped back into the bedroom where the steady breathing told him Eloise was asleep. Shutting the door behind him in his closet, he turned the lights on and put on some clothes. He grabbed a few more outfits and stuffed them into a bag. Turning the light out he eased the door open and exited the closet slowly. Eloise slept soundly.

He crept silently into the garage. The door was down. He worried that its raising might wake her, but at this point, it didn't matter. Taking his wife's Buick, he hit the button on the opener and the grinding garage door lifted. As soon as the opening was big enough to get the car under he let it roll back out of the garage and press the button for the garage door to descend. Whirling around, he put the car in drive and started down the driveway. As he drove off, he looked back and didn't see a light anywhere in the house. All the better.

The time on the dash showed almost two o'clock. What the hell was going on with Mason? What an imbecile. Why hadn't he called Luther at home? Who was he talking to? The man had said he heard them ask about Weeks. Did he leave with them? Did he leave with the unmarked car? Did the man say that?

It didn't matter. What ever it was, it wasn't good. He had to get to the office and get the stuff out of that safe. Quickly. And then what? He thought he knew. He thought he knew just how to handle this situation. That damn Mason. What an idiot. Well, he may think he's being smart, but he may not be as smart as he thinks. Lambert pushed forward through the streets, running stop signs and red lights. It was after two when he pulled up to his office.

He went quickly to his desk and the safe behind it, flipping through the numbers. With the door swinging open he raked the contents into a satchel by his desk and was out the door in less than a minute. He was pretty sure no one saw him.

The downtown area was deserted, empty streets receiving him as he left out the back door of his building. He threw the satchel into the front seat beside him and screeched off in his wife's car. Most everyone in the town knew him and knew the black Cadillac he drove. He got the same thing every year, just another newer model. He somehow had it in his mind that no one would recognize him in his wife's Buick. He should have taken the pickup. Nobody ever saw him in that.

He was fine, he told himself. He was already on the road away from his house. Her car phone was there. He would get this mess handled. He didn't know what the hell Jerry Mason was up to but the little pissant better watch his step. He'd have to have a lot more than his little wimp ass to match wits with the skilled Luther Lambert.

What were they doing at Jerry's? And who was it? He needed to know. Damn, why didn't he pay more attention to what the caller told him. Plain car, plain clothes, did he say? Jerry left with them? Damnit to hell, what was going on? He needed to know. He picked up the car phone and dialed a number then just as quickly he laid it down. His anonymous caller picked up his tidbits from the air waves. Luther didn't want to be picked up. He was at the interstate with the truck stop right there. A telephone. He wheeled into the parking lot, pulling the car as close as possible to the phone. Stretching himself as far as possible, he barely tipped the phone off the holder and used a pencil to push the numbers. He didn't want to get out of the car.

"Hello," the voice on the other end was solemn.

Luther talked, quickly asking questions with rapid fire. One of the privileges that money bought was being able to procure information. They all loved to talk to the man with money. Anything to win his favor. In a very short while Luther learned it was worse than he thought.

For some reason he had never connected his conversation with Mason and the incident with that black bitch, Arlita. She had heard them. How the hell had she gotten anybody to listen to her? He finished the conversation quickly, trusting no one or nothing else at this point. This was bad. It was really bad.

He punched the numbers on the phone again, getting another sleepy hello on the other end. He talked briefly and quickly. There was no time for excess. He had to get going fast. He finished the call and threw the receiver back at its holder.

"Mr. Lambert?"

The sound froze him. Without breathing, he looked around slowly.

"I thought that was you. You're out awfully early."

Highway Patrolman Benny Taylor waved at him from his car.

"I was just pulling in to get me a cup of coffee. I thought I recognized you. Good to see you."

"Yes, you too Benny." Luther breathed a sigh of relief.

He fought the urge to squeal out of the parking lot, slowly putting the car in gear and easing back to the street. With guarded caution, he rolled down the street to the interstate entrance and took the ramp south toward New Orleans.

Benny Taylor's car pulled on up to the truck stop building and got out for his coffee. He watched Mr. Lambert drive down to the exit and get on the interstate. He was driving mighty slowly, Benny wondered if everything was alright. Sure is funny seeing him out here in the middle of the night. Of course working this midnight shift Benny was used to seeing people out that he didn't expect. Some of them were up to no good but some of them were just out. Like Mr. Lambert, Benny thought as he walked on inside to get his coffee. That should hold him the rest of the night. He looked at his watch. Just over three more hours before he got off at six. He could survive with one more cup of coffee.

Jerry Mason signed the statement that the officer typed up from their conversations over the past few hours. George Price was pleased. He had what he needed and a car was on the way to Luther Lambert's house to bring him down to the station. Wouldn't old Luther be surprised, Price thought. They went way back, way back indeed.

Price had found Lambert at the heart of several matters over the years. Somehow, when the information got turned over to the powers that be, Luther Lambert was always able to elude prosecution. He always managed to be just one step ahead. Enough to pull himself out of the fray and give the appearance of clean. George Price knew better. He knew what a thug Luther Lambert really was and the company he kept. This time he had him and there would be no mistakes. He couldn't wait for the man to be brought in before him.

"Captain Price, there's a call for you. You can get it at that desk." The officer pointed to a phone near George.

"Hello," he said into the receiver.

"Captain, we're here at Lambert's house, but he's not here."

"What?" George was incredulous.

"The only person here is his wife, Eloise. She doesn't know where he is." The officer's voice was meek, as if he didn't want to say the words he knew George Price didn't want to hear.

"Where is he?"

"We don't know. His wife says he was here just a short while ago. He got some phone call. Said it was a wrong number and his wife went back to sleep. When she woke, he was gone. His car is here, but hers is gone."

"Damn, damn. How long ago was the phone call?"

"She said about one thirty or two."

"Well, he can't have gotten far. Where are you now?"

"We're still at the house. Mrs. Lambert has been very nice."

"Well, get back here. I'm putting out a BOLO for Lambert. Get here as fast as you can."

The officers thanked Mrs. Lambert, apologizing for disturbing her in the middle of the night. She was so nice, they didn't want to leave her all upset. Outside in the car they quickly got out of the driveway and started back to the station. In only moments they heard the 'be on the look out' announcement or BOLO in police lingo.

Benny Taylor got back in his car just in time to hear it, too. He got his cup of coffee from inside and made his way back to the car, only chatting briefly with the girl at the counter. When he cranked up his patrol car, the first thing he heard was the BOLO. What in the world, he wondered. There was very little information in the announcement. Just be on the look out.

'Well, I just saw the man,' he said out loud. 'I better call and see what this is about,' he spoke to himself as he picked up the phone. 'This is crazy.'

When Benny's call finally got patched in to the station, they put it through to Captain Price. He listened to Benny tell him about the casual hello to Lambert. And he listened to the telling of how Luther drove off and entered the highway toward New Orleans. 'What luck' was all George could think as Taylor's voice came over the phone.

"What time was that?" George wanted to know.

"Well, I looked at my watch 'cause I was thinking about how much longer I had on my shift.' It was about a quarter till three."

George looked at his watch. Thirty minutes ago. Depending on his speed he could be almost to the Louisiana line. He thanked Benny profusely and then started barking out orders.

"Who else out of the department was on the highway toward New Orleans?" He was on the phone with headquarters in Jackson. "Get a hold of them and reemphasize the BOLO. We might want a road block."

George Price continued to roar out orders, determined to get Lambert in his custody before the man could do anything to offset the case they had against him. With Mason's statement and the testimony of the two women, Lambert was not going to slip out of this one.

There was no highway patrol office in Pearl River County. With budget restraints and other cuts they had only two men that covered the entire strip of interstate that cut through the county. One of them was out sick tonight, leaving one man available to them. George had Benny Taylor racing down the highway looking for the Buick but with a thirty minute head start it was unlikely he would catch up to him.

There was no guarantee he would stay on the highway. They had nothing to go on to make them think he was headed to Louisiana. Only a hunch. But since it was all they had at this point, George was going to act on it.

"The man's headed to New Orleans. I just know it." George spoke out loud.

He had Officer Keeton, their man in Pearl River County watching at the state line. Keeton had two patrol cars from the city of Picayune with him. Reinforcements from adjoining Hancock County Patrol were coming up to help out and should be at the Pearl River bridge any minute. Price had a helicopter on the way to patrol the area from the sky. He contacted the Louisiana Highway Patrol who would have a road block set up on the other side of the bridge stopping all cars there, looking for Luther Lambert. They came out of Slidell where they had ample manpower.

The helicopter pilot spotted the Buick at three forty, only a few miles from the bridge across the Pearl River. Even in the dark, he recognized the shape of the vehicle and saw it more clearly in the lights of the occasional eighteen-wheeler. Using the special binoculars his copilot locked in on the license plate assuring them of their target. They radioed their information in to headquarters who immediately transferred it to Captain Price.

They estimated his arrival at the bridge in about ten minutes. Highway construction had one lane of the interstate closed at the bridge which was under repair. All southbound traffic was routed across the median and then fed single-lane over the one bridge that usually handled two lanes of northbound traffic.

The pilot of the helicopter kept himself positioned away from the car toward a couple of big trucks hoping to avoid detection by the driver of the Buick. They wanted him to go straight on to the bridge where he would be apprehended. From the radio they learned that the Hancock County Highway patrolmen were at the bridge, too, and all vehicles were being stopped.

Luther had his car cruising down the highway at nearly a hundred miles an hour. He should hit that state line and cross the river into Louisiana in only a short while. He'd had to make one call on the car phone but they talked in terms that only the two of them could understand. No one in this area would recognize his voice and they certainly didn't use any names. This was going to work out okay. Luther was going to be alright, he grinned to himself.

The sound of the helicopter's whirling blades caught him unaware sending his blood pressure skyrocketing. Calm down, calm down, he told himself. There was a NASA station near here and it was not at all uncommon for a helicopter to be out. The sound faded into the distance letting him relax a little. Only a little. He could feel the tension in every part of his body. The pump, pump, pump from his heart ached in his chest.

Luther forced himself to relax. This was under control, he told himself. He had another car set up in Slidell. He'd switch vehicles and then... well, they'd see.

He came out of the curve and up ahead saw the trucks stopped in the highway. The blue lights were flashing everywhere. The trucks were moving through the line fairly quickly. The highway barrels started moving the traffic into a single lane where they had to cross over to the other bridge. There was nothing for Luther to do but keep moving ahead. Two trucks had already come in behind him. He moved slowly forward, making his way to the group of patrol cars, waiting anxiously in his seat.

Officer Keeton saw the gray Buick tucked in between the row of semis. Only one other automobile had come through since they started this operation. He also heard the helicopter set down in the field away from the highway. The pilot must know this is their man. Keeton waved the last truck in front of the Buick on through, making way for the car to pull up to him.

"What seems to be the trouble, officer?" came the driver.

"Could I see your license, please?"

"Certainly," pulling his wallet out.

"Mr. Lambert, could you step out of the car."

Luther Lambert had no intention of getting out. He looked around the officer and saw the other supporting men. The road was blocked.

"Was I doing something wrong?" Lambert put on his innocent best.

"Ah, no sir."

Keeton was really new at this and didn't know exactly what to say. He knew he was dealing with one of the craftiest lawyers around. The officers had talked about their quarry as they waited. Keeton knew his boss, George Price, wanted the man badly so he'd better not screw up.

"Well, then, what seems to be the problem?"

When the officer hesitated, Lambert continued. As he did he watched the truck that had been in front of him clear the top of the bridge and drop out of sight down the other side.

"Am I under arrest?"

Keeton thought so but he hadn't seen him do anything wrong. In the rush to get the man before he left the state, no paperwork got down to the roadblock. Maybe they had it in the chopper. The shrewd Lambert suspected that and pursued.

"Do you have a warrant for my arrest?"

This further confused Keeton. He didn't have a warrant or any other papers. He knew that they didn't go to all this trouble for nothing, but here they were and he didn't know what to do.

"Mr. Lambert, could you pull over here for just a moment, please."

Luther smiled. He knew he had the man confused. He knew in his own way he had muddled the issue for the officer. He looked again at the bridge as he took particular effort to appear calm and most obliging. Another officer walked up to Keeton, speaking a few words in his ear. While their attention was diverted from Lambert, he saw a chance. He stomped on the gas pedal of the Buick making its back tires spin before catching on the pavement. The back end slid to one side bumping into the officers, sending them tumbling to the ground.

The car tires finally caught traction and shot the car off up the highway and onto the bridge. The other officers had their guns pulled but no one seemed to know what to do until someone yelled out stop him. Shots rang out, but only a couple as the car continued up the single right hand lane of the bridge while other unsuspecting vehicles came down the other side. There was no way to get a shot at Lambert's vehicle without endangering those on the other side.

The car was slipping and sliding in the loose gravel that sprinkled the surface of the bridge, veering from one side of the lane to the other. It hit the center dividers once, twice then bounced off the other side. Just at the top the car went completely out of control and crashed into the outside railing of the bridge, knocking off the rail and going partly over. The car teetered briefly, almost at a stop. Then, with a last dip, dropped down to one side and went over toward the water below.

The stunned officers bolted out of their positions racing up the bridge. The car plunged nose first and went completely under before popping back up. The river was full from recent rain and moving swiftly, taking the car away from the bridge at a brisk pace. By the time they got to the top of the bridge they could see the hood of the car about to go under. There was no sign of anyone in the water. The brisk current moved so strongly that it would have been impossible to swim it.

The patrolmen stood on the bridge looking, but there was nothing to see. The car was gone. The river moved on briskly under the night sky. The glow from the officer's lights flicked around on the surface and along the banks hoping to catch some sign, but they never saw a thing.

Rita Lambert wiped the sleep from her eyes as she rounded the last turn into Parchman, Mississippi. She felt like she had enough coffee in her to float a battleship. This had been a long night. No sleep. After finally being connected with George Price things had moved pretty swiftly. His professionalism impressed her, as did his concern over an innocent man being in jail. He was very persuasive in getting Judge Jones' signature on an order for a new trial for Luke Daniels. That order held specific language releasing him from the custody of the Mississippi Department of Corrections. She insisted on hand-delivering the order all the way to the desk of the warden of the state penitentiary. He was to be advised of her coming by the time she got there.

Luke arrived at the prison in the middle of the night, unaware of anything else that had gone on. His treatment there was the same as any other prisoner. He was put into a holding cell to await the morning shift processing, which was done by personnel with regular eight to five jobs. He would wait until eight o'clock. Until then, he sat in a cell with a dozen other men of various convictions. At eight thirty, the cell door opened and a large black guard came to the door and called out Luke's name.

"Luke Daniels, come with me."

There was no explanation. Luke stood in the same clothing he had on for days now and walked: down one gray corridor, through barred gates, along another gray corridor, past electric doors, into an elevator, up one floor and out onto carpet.

The guard continued walking with Luke behind him. There were offices here with what looked like regular people in them. Luke had no idea what was happening. Finally, they stopped at a desk outside two wooden doors.

"This is the prisoner," the guard said without feeling.

The lady behind the desk stood and smiled at Luke.

"Mr. Daniels, would you come with me, please."

Luke was dumbfounded. What the heck was going on here? The guard made no motion toward him but, instead, turned to leave. The lady at the desk spoke again.

"Right this way, Mr. Daniels," as she held the door open with the sign marked WARDEN.

Inside the room was a man behind a desk, apparently the warden, all smiles and Rita Lambert. Luke blinked, thinking he had been out of it too long; he must be hallucinating. She looked like an angel.

"Mr. Daniels, I'm Gordon Fike, Warden of the facility. I believe you know Mrs. Lambert. She has just delivered an order for your release."

The shock on Luke's face must have been apparent. The warden continued with a limited explanation.

"I don't know all that brought this about, but I do know it's authentic. A new trial has been ordered in your case. You're free to go."

The words hit Luke so hard he almost fell down. His knees buckled, forcing him to hold on to one of the chairs. Rita came up from her seat and grabbed him, putting her arm around his waist.

"Do you need to sit down, Mr. Daniels?" the warden asked.

"No, no. I'll be alright. I can go? I can go right now?"

"Yes, you can." the warden answered.

"My car's outside, Luke." Rita spoke tenderly. "I'm taking you out of here."

"But, what… " his voice trailed off. He was overwhelmed. There was no voice left.

"You don't have to talk. I'll fill you in on the way."

The warden escorted them out of the building and right to Rita's car. Luke got in on the passenger's side and Rita took the driver's seat. She pulled the car around and got them out the main gate without either of them saying a word. After a few moments he managed to inquire.

"I don't understand. What happened?"

"Well, are you ready? Okay, then. Listen to this…"